R·SCOTT BAKKER

THE WHITE-LUCK WARRIOR

Book Two of
The Aspect-Emperor Series

www.orbitbooks.net

ORBIT

First published in Great Britain in 2011 by Orbit
This paperback edition published in 2012 by Orbit

Copyright © 2011 by R. Scott Bakker

Excerpt from *Echo City* by Tim Lebbon
Copyright © 2010 by Tim Lebbon

The moral right of the author has been asserted.

A CIP catalogue record for this book
is available from the British Library.

ISBN 978-1-84149-540-8

Typeset in Goudy by Palimpsest Book Production Limited, Falkirk, Stirlingshire

Printed and bound in Great Britain by CPI Group (UK) Ltd, Croydon, CR0 4YY

Papers used by Orbit are from well-managed forests
and other responsible sources.

MIX
Paper from
responsible sources
FSC FSC® C104740
www.fsc.org

Orbit
An imprint of
Little, Brown Book Group
100 Victoria Embankment
London EC4Y 0DY

An Hachette UK Company
www.hachette.co.uk

www.orbitbooks.net

To Roger Eichorn

The heavens, the sun, the whole of nature is a corpse. Nature is given over to the spiritual, and indeed to spiritual subjectivity; thus the course of nature is everywhere broken in upon by miracles.

—HEGEL, *LECTURES ON THE HISTORY OF PHILOSOPHY III*

Contents

Appendices

What Has Come Before . . .

Wars, as a rule, fall within the compass of history. They mark the pitch of competing powers, the end of some and the ascendency of others, the ebb and flow of dominance across the ages. But there is a war that Men have waged for so long they have forgotten the languages they first used to describe it. A war that makes mere skirmishes out of the destruction of tribes and nations.

There is no name for this war; Men cannot reference what transcends the short interval of their comprehension. It began when they were little more than savages roaming the wilds, in an age before script or bronze. An Ark, vast and golden, toppled from the void, scorching the horizon, throwing up a ring of mountains with the violence of its descent. And from it crawled the dread and monstrous Inchoroi, a race who had come to seal the World against the Heavens and so save the obscenities they called their souls.

The Nonmen held sway in those ancient days, a long-lived people that surpassed Men not only in beauty and intellect but in wrath and jealousy as well. With their Ishroi heroes and Quya mages, they fought titanic battles and stood vigilant during epochal truces. They endured the Inchoroi weapons of light. They survived the treachery of the Aporetics, who provided their foe with thousands of sorcery-killing Chorae. They overcame the horrors their enemy crafted to people his legions: the Sranc, the Bashrag, and, most fearsome of all, the Wracu. But their avarice at last betrayed them. After centuries of intermittent war, they made peace with the invaders in return for the gift of ageless immortality – a gift that was in fact a fell weapon, the Plague of Wombs.

In the end, the Nonmen hunted the Inchoroi to the brink of annihilation. Exhausted, culled of their strength, they retired to their underworld mansions to mourn the loss of their wives and daughters and the inevitable extinction of their glorious race. Their surviving mages sealed the Ark, which they had come to call Min-Uroikas, and hid it from the world with devious glamours. And from the eastern mountains, the first tribes of Men began claiming the lands the Nonmen had abandoned – Men who had never known the yoke of slavery. Of the surviving Ishroi Kings, some fought, only to be dragged under by the tide of numbers, while others simply left their great gates unguarded, bared their necks to the licentious fury of a lesser race.

And so human history was born, and perhaps the Nameless War would have ended with the fading of its principals. But the golden Ark still existed, and the lust for knowledge has ever been a cancer in the hearts of Men.

Centuries passed, and the mantle of human civilization crept along the great river basins of Eärwa and outward, bringing bronze where there had been flint, cloth where there had been skins, and writing where there had been recital. Great cities rose to teeming life. The wilds gave way to cultivated horizons.

Nowhere were Men more bold in their works, or more over-weening in their pride, than in the North, where commerce with the Nonmen had allowed them to outstrip their more swarthy cousins to the South. In the legendary city of Sauglish, those who could discern the joints of existence founded the first sorcerous Schools. As their learning and power waxed, a reckless few turned to the rumours they had heard whispered by their Nonman teachers – rumours of the great golden Ark. The wise were quick to see the peril, and the Schoolmen of Mangaecca, who coveted secrets above all others, were censured and finally outlawed.

But it was too late. Min-Uroikas was found – occupied.

The fools discovered and awakened the last two surviving Inchoroi, Aurax and Aurang, who had concealed themselves in the labyrinthine recesses of the Ark. And at their hoary knees the outlaw Schoolmen learned that damnation, the burden that all sorcerers bore, need not be inevitable. They learned that the world could be shut against the judgment of Heaven. So they forged a common purpose with the twin abominations, a Consult, and bent their cunning to the aborted designs of the Inchoroi.

They relearned the principles of the material, the Tekne. They mastered the manipulations of the flesh. And after generations of study and searching, after filling the pits of Min-Uroikas with innumerable corpses, they realized the most catastrophic of the Inchoroi's untold depravities: Mog-Pharau, the No-God.

They made themselves slaves to better destroy the world.

And so the Nameless War raged anew. What has come to be called the First Apocalypse destroyed the great Norsirai nations of the North, laying ruin to the greatest glories of Men. But for Seswatha, the Grandmaster of the Gnostic School of Sohonc, the entire world would have been lost. At his urging, Anasûrimbor Celmomas II, the High-King of the North's mightiest nation, Kûniüri, called on his tributaries and allies to join him in a Holy War against Min-Uroikas, which Men now called Golgotterath. But his Ordeal foundered, and the might of the Norsirai perished. Seswatha fled south to the Ketyai nations of the Three Seas, bearing the greatest of the legendary Inchoroi weapons, the Heron Spear. With Anaxophus, the High-King of Kyraneas, he met the No-God on the Plains of Mengedda and, by dint of valour and providence, overcame the dread Whirlwind.

The No-God was dead, but his slaves and his stronghold remained. Golgotterath had not fallen, and the Consult, blasted by ages of unnatural life, continued to plot their salvation.

The years passed, and the Men of the Three Seas forgot, as Men inevitably do, the horrors endured by their fathers. Empires rose and empires fell. The Latter Prophet, Inri Sejenus, reinterpreted the Tusk, the First Scripture, and within a few centuries, the faith of Inrithism, organized and administered by the Thousand Temples and its spiritual leader, the Shriah, came to dominate the entire Three Seas. The great Anagogic Schools arose in response to the Inrithi persecution of sorcery. Using Chorae, the Inrithi warred against them, attempting to purify the Three Seas.

Then Fane, the self-proclaimed Prophet of the so-called Solitary God, united the Kianene, the desert peoples of the Great Carathay, and declared war against the Tusk and the Thousand Temples. After centuries and several jihads, the Fanim and their eyeless sorcerer-priests, the Cishaurim, conquered nearly all the western Three Seas, including the holy city of Shimeh, the birthplace of Inri Sejenus. Only the moribund remnants of the Nansur Empire continued to resist them.

War and strife ruled the South. The two great faiths of Inrithism and Fanimry skirmished, though trade and pilgrimage were tolerated when commercially convenient. The great families and nations vied for military and mercantile dominance. The minor and major Schools squabbled and plotted. And the Thousand Temples pursued earthly ambitions under the leadership of corrupt and ineffectual Shriahs.

The First Apocalypse had become little more than legend. The Consult and the No-God had dwindled into myth, something old wives tell small children. After two thousand years, only the Schoolmen of the Mandate, who relived the Apocalypse each night through the eyes of Seswatha, could recall the horror of

Mog-Pharau. Though the mighty and the learned considered them fools, their possession of the Gnosis, the sorcery of the Ancient North, commanded respect and mortal envy. Driven by nightmares, they wandered the labyrinths of power, scouring the Three Seas for signs of their ancient and implacable foe – for the Consult.

And as always, they found nothing.

Some argued that the Consult, which had survived the armed might of empires, had finally succumbed to the toll of ages. Others thought that they had turned inward, seeking less arduous means to forestall their damnation. But since the Sranc had multiplied across the northern wilds, no expedition could be sent to Golgotterath to settle the matter. The Mandate alone knew of the Nameless War. They alone stood guard, but they suffocated in a pall of ignorance.

The Thousand Temples elected a new, enigmatic Shriah, a man called Maithanet, who demanded the Inrithi recapture the holy city of the Latter Prophet, Shimeh, from the Fanim. Word of his call spread across the Three Seas and beyond, and faithful from all the great Inrithi nations – Galeoth, Thunyerus, Ce Tydonn, Conriya, High Ainon, and their tributaries – travelled to the city of Momemn, the capital of the Nansurium, to swear their swords and their lives to Inri Sejenus. To become Men of the Tusk.

And so was born the First Holy War. Internal feuds plagued the campaign from the very beginning, for there was no shortage of those who would bend the Holy War to their selfish ends. Not until the Second Siege of Caraskand and the Circumfixion of one of their own would this fractiousness be overcome. Not until the Men of the Tusk found a *living* prophet to follow – a man who could see into the hearts of Men. A man like a god.

Anasûrimbor Kellhus.

Far to the north, in the very penumbra of Golgotterath, a group of ascetics called the Dûnyain had concealed themselves in Ishuäl, the secret redoubt of the Kûniüric High-Kings. For two thousand years they had pursued their sacred study, breeding for reflex and intellect, training in the ways of limb, thought, and face – all for the sake of reason, the Logos. In the effort to transform themselves into the perfect expression of the Logos, the Dûnyain had dedicated their entire existence to mastering the irrationalities of history, custom, and passion – all those things that determine human thought. In this way, they believed, they would eventually grasp what they called the Absolute, and so become true self-moving souls.

But their glorious isolation had been interrupted. After thirty years of exile, one of their number, Anasûrimbor Moënghus, reappeared in their dreams, demanding they send to him his son, Kellhus. Knowing only that Moënghus dwelt in a distant city called Shimeh, the Dûnyain dispatched Kellhus on an arduous journey through lands long abandoned by Men – sent him to kill his father.

But Moënghus knew the world in ways his cloistered brethren could not. He knew well the revelations that awaited his son, for they had been his revelations thirty years previous. He knew that Kellhus would discover sorcery, whose existence the forefathers of the Dûnyain had suppressed. He knew that given his son's abilities, Men would be little more than children to him, that Kellhus would see their thoughts in the nuances of their expression, and that with mere words he would be able to exact any devotion, any sacrifice. He knew, moreover, that eventually Kellhus would encounter the Consult, who hid behind faces that only Dûnyain eyes could see – that he would come to see what Men with their blinkered souls could not: the Nameless War.

For centuries the Consult had evaded their old foe, the School of Mandate, by creating doppelgangers, spies who could take on any face, any voice, without resorting to sorcery and its telltale Mark. By capturing and torturing these abominations, Moënghus learned that the Consult had not abandoned their ancient plot to shut the world against Heaven, that within a score of years they would be able to resurrect the No-God and bring about a second Apocalypse. For years he walked the innumerable paths of the Probability Trance, plotting future after future, searching for the thread of act and consequence that would save the world. For years he crafted his Thousandfold Thought.

Moënghus knew, and so prepared the way for Kellhus. He sent out his world-born son, Maithanet, to seize the Thousand Temples from within, so that he might craft the First Holy War, the weapon Kellhus would need to seize absolute power, and so unite the Three Seas against the doom that was their future. What he did not know, could not know, was that Kellhus would see *further* than he had, think beyond his Thousandfold Thought . . .

And go mad.

Little more than an impoverished wayfarer when he first joined the Holy War, Kellhus used his bearing, intellect, and insight to convince ever more Men of the Tusk that he was the Warrior-Prophet, come to save Mankind from the Second Apocalypse. He understood that Men, who embrace baseless beliefs the way drunkards imbibe wine, would render anything to him, so long as they believed he could save their souls. He also befriended the Schoolman the Mandate had dispatched to watch the Holy War, Drusas Achamian, knowing that the Gnosis, the sorcery of the Ancient North, would provide him with inestimable power. And he seduced Achamian's lover, Esmenet, knowing that her intellect made her the ideal vessel for his seed – for sons strong enough to bear the onerous burden of Dûnyain blood.

By the time the battle-hardened remnants of the campaign at last invested Holy Shimeh, he possessed the host body and soul.

The Men of the Tusk had become his Zaudunyani, his Tribe of Truth. While the Holy War assailed the city's walls, he confronted his father, Moënghus, mortally wounding him, explaining that only with his death could the Thousandfold Thought be realized. Days later Anasûrimbor Kellhus was acclaimed Aspect-Emperor, the first in a millennium, by none other than the Shriah of the Thousand Temples, his half-brother, Maithanet. Even the School of Mandate, who saw his coming as the fulfillment of their most hallowed prophecies, knelt and kissed his knee.

But he had made one mistake. He had allowed Cnaiür urs Skiötha, a Scylvendi chieftain who had accompanied him on his trek to the Three Seas, to learn too much of his true nature. Before his death, the barbarian revealed these truths to Drusas Achamian, who had harboured heartbreaking suspicions of his own.

Before the eyes of the entire Holy War, Achamian repudiated Kellhus, whom he had worshipped, Esmenet, whom he had loved, and the Mandate masters he had served. Then he fled into the wilderness, becoming the world's only sorcerer without a school. A Wizard.

Now, after twenty years of conversion and bloodshed, Anasûrimbor Kellhus plots the conclusion of his father's Thousandfold Thought. His New Empire spans the entirety of the Three Seas, from the legendary fortress of Auvangshei on the frontiers of Zeüm to the shrouded headwaters of the River Sayut, from the sweltering coasts of Kutnarmu to the wild rim of the Osthwai Mountains – all the lands that had once been Fanim or Inrithi. It was easily the equal of the old Ceneian Empire in terms of geographical extent and likely far greater when it came to population. A hundred mighty cities, and almost as many languages. A dozen proud nations. Two thousand years of mangled history.

And the Nameless War is nameless no longer. Men call it the Great Ordeal.

The Judging Eye

Achamian

For twenty years Drusas Achamian has kept a painstaking record of his Dreams of the First Apocalypse.

He lives as an exile, the world's only Wizard, on the savage northeastern frontier of the empire Anasûrimbor Kellhus has raised about his supposed divinity. The Sranc once besieged his half-ruined tower, but the scalpers have driven the inhuman creatures over the mountains, chasing the Holy Bounty. For years now Achamian has lived in peace, hunting his sleep for hints and rumours of Ishuäl, the hidden fastness of the Dûnyain. If he can find Ishuäl, he believes, he can answer the question that burns so bright in so many learned souls . . .

Who is the Aspect-Emperor?

This peace is shattered when Anasûrimbor Mimara, the daughter of his former wife, arrives demanding that he teach her sorcery. Her resemblance to her mother, Esmenet – who has become Empress of the Three Seas – returns the old Wizard to all the pains he sought to escape. He refuses her demand, bids her to leave time and again, but she defies him and takes up a vigil outside his tower.

Mimara, who has never forgiven her mother for selling her into childhood slavery, has fled the Imperial Court with no intention of returning. She is one of the Few. She possesses the ability to see the fabric of existence and so the power to learn sorcery – and this, she has decided, is the one thing that will lift her from the mire of shame and recrimination that is her life. She believes she has nothing else.

But she also possesses a different kind of sight, one both more precious and more significant: on rare occasions, she can see the *morality* of things, the goodness and the evil inherent to them. She has what the ancients called the Judging Eye.

Day and night she howls at the old Wizard in his tower, demanding that he teach her. The first time he comes down, he strikes her. The second time he tries to reason with her. He explains his lifelong quest to discover the truth of Anasûrimbor Kellhus – her stepfather. He seeks the location of Ishuäl because it is the Aspect-Emperor's birthplace, and the truth of a man, he insists, always lies in his origins. He tells her how his Dreams have slowly transformed, abandoning the epic atrocities of the First Apocalypse and focusing more and more upon the mundane details of Seswatha's ancient life. Because of this, he now knows *how* to find Ishuäl: he must recover a map that lies hidden in the ruins of ancient Sauglish, far to the north.

'You have become a prophet,' she tells him. 'A prophet of the past.'

And then, in yet one more attempt to win his tutelage, she seduces him.

Only in the shameful aftermath does she tell the old Wizard that he has dwelt upon his suspicions for too long. The Aspect-Emperor has already embarked on his quest to destroy the Consult and so save the world from a Second Apocalypse. The Great Ordeal marches.

Achamian abandons Mimara at his tower and strikes out for the nearest scalper outpost. Here he contracts a company called the Skin Eaters to join his quest, deceiving them with promises of the Coffers, the Holy Library's famed treasury. The Captain of the company, a Veteran of the First Holy War named Lord Kosoter, troubles him, as does Incariol, his mysterious Nonman companion, but time is short, and he can think of no one else who would accompany him on such a mad trek. He must somehow reach the

Library of Sauglish, and thence Ishuäl, before the Great Ordeal reaches the gates of Golgotterath. The scalper company departs shortly thereafter, planning to cross the Osthwai Mountains into the Sranc-infested North.

Mimara is not so easily dissuaded. She shadows the scalpers without appreciating the cunning of their forest craft. She is discovered, and Achamian is forced to save her, saying that she is his wilful daughter. Fearing that she will reveal his true purposes, he at last relents. He allows her to accompany him on his quest and agrees to teach her sorcery.

Shortly after, they learn that a spring blizzard has closed the passes through the Osthwai Mountains, perhaps delaying them for weeks – for too long. Only one path remains open to them: the accursed halls of Cil-Aujas.

They camp before the entrance to the derelict Nonman Mansion, plagued with apprehensions. Then, with the coming of dawn, they descend into the heart of the mountain. For days they wander the wrecked halls, led by Incariol and his ancient memories. Deep in the Mansion, Mimara finally confesses her sporadic ability to see the morality of things, and Achamian, obviously troubled, tells her that she possesses the Judging Eye. She presses him to tell her more, but the old Wizard refuses. Before she can berate him properly, the company discovers that it is not alone in the Mansion.

Sranc assail them with fury and countless numbers. Despite the sorcerous toll exacted by Incariol and Achamian, the company is overcome, and the survivors are forced to flee down into the bowels of Cil-Aujas. Achamian is knocked unconscious by a Sranc bearing a Chorae. Mimara kills the creature and pockets the thing. They flee through the mines that riddle the foundations of the mountain and find themselves on the scorched rim of a burning lake. The Sranc pour after them, a howling tide. They flee along a stair and would certainly perish were it not for Incariol and his sorcerous might. Their route sealed behind them, they find themselves in an ancient slave pit, huddling among the bones of a dead dragon. Only a handful survive.

While they recover themselves, Incariol dispenses Qirri, an ancient Nonman remedy. Mimara finds herself staring at her Chorae. It is an abomination in her sorcerous eyes, yet she persists gazing. The Judging Eye opens, and the thing is miraculously transformed. Suddenly she *sees* it for what it truly is: a white burning Tear of God. She turns to Somandutta, the scalper who has become her protector with the Wizard incapacitated. But he sees nothing . . .

Then she notices the stranger sitting in their midst.

Incariol recognizes the figure as the shade of Gin'yursis, the ancient Nonman King of Cil-Aujas. The wraith dons the Nonman as if he were clothing. While the company stands watching in dread, the Qirri finally revives the old Wizard. Recognizing their peril, he begins screaming at them to flee.

Again they race into the black, while something dark and nebulous pursues them. In desperation, Achamian brings the ceiling crashing down, sealing the company even deeper within the doomed Mansion.

They find themselves at the bottom of a vast well, what Achamian remembers as the Great Medial Screw from his ancient Dreams, a stair that plumbs the whole mountain. The sky is little more than a prick of light above them. The battered Skin Eaters rejoice. All they need do is climb . . .

But Gin'yursis rises from the deeps to claim them, dragging Hell itself as his mantle.

Mimara's Judging Eye opens. She raises high her brilliant Tear of God . . .

The Great Ordeal

Far to the north, young Varalt Sorweel finds himself staring down upon the boggling might of the Southron Believer-Kings. He is the only son of Varalt Harweel, the King of Sakarpus, who has resisted the Aspect-Emperor's demand to yield his ancient city and its famed Chorae Hoard. Standing with his father on the high curtain walls, the adolescent realizes that he and his people are doomed. Then, miraculously, a stork – a bird that is holy to the Sakarpi – appears on the battlements above his father. The two commune in the charged silence that follows, then King Harweel turns and commands that Sorweel be taken to safety. 'See that no harm comes to him!' he cries. 'He will be our final sword-stroke! Our vengeance!' Dragged away screaming, the young man watches sorcerous flames engulf the parapets and his father upon them. A desperate flight ensues, and it seems that the *Aspect-Emperor himself* pursues them through the chaotic streets.

The pursuit ends in the apparent safety of the citadel. Blasting through walls, Anasûrimbor Kellhus effortlessly kills his protectors. He approaches the adolescent Prince, but rather than seizing or striking him, he *embraces* him. Tells him that he is forgiven.

The city secure, the Great Ordeal prepares for the long march across the trackless wilds. Sorweel finds himself desolate for the loss of his father and the shame of his new circumstances. As the new King of Sakarpus, he is naught but a tool of the New Empire, a way for the Aspect-Emperor to legitimize his tyranny. Before the host departs, none other than Moënghus and Kayûtas, the eldest sons of Anasûrimbor Kellhus, visit him in his palace. They tell him he is to join the Ordeal as the symbol of his nation's commitment to their holy cause. The following day Sorweel finds himself part of the Scions, a horse company composed of princely hostages from across the rim of the New Empire. This is how he meets and befriends Zsoronga ut Nganka'kull, the Successor Prince of Zeüm.

A Mandate sorcerer named Eskeles is assigned to tutor him in Sheyic, the common tongue of the Three Seas, and through him the young King learns the reasons why so many worship the Aspect-Emperor so fervently. For the first time he begins to doubt his father . . . What if the Aspect-Emperor spoke true? What if the world *really was* about to end?

Why else would someone so cunning march so many Men to their doom?

Sorweel is also provided a slave named Porsparian to attend to his needs, a wizened old man who is anything but the submissive thrall he pretends to be. One night Sorweel watches him tear away the turf and mould the face of the Goddess Yatwer from the dirt. Before his eyes, mud bubbles up as spit from her earthen lips. The slave palms this mud and smears it across the incredulous King's cheeks.

The following morning Sorweel attends a Council of Potentates with Zsoronga and Eskeles. His dread waxes as he watches the Holy Aspect-Emperor move from lord to lord, declaring the truths they think hidden in their souls. He fears what will happen when he sees the hatred and treachery smouldering in his own. But when Anasûrimbor Kellhus comes to him, he *congratulates* Sorweel for grasping the truth and, before everyone assembled, declares him one of the Believer-Kings.

Esmenet

Far to the south in Momemn, the capital of the New Empire, Esmenet struggles to rule in her husband's absence. With Kellhus and the bulk of his armed might absent, the embers of insurrection have begun to ignite across the Three Seas. The Imperial Court regards her with condescension. Fanayal ab Kascamandri, the Padirajah of what had been the heathen Kianene Empire before the First Holy War, grows ever more bold on the fringes of the Great Carathay Desert. Psatma Nannaferi, the outlawed Mother-Supreme of the Cult of Yatwer, prophesies the coming of the White-Luck Warrior, the god-sent assassin who will murder the Aspect-Emperor and his progeny. Even the *Gods*, it seems, have turned against the Anasûrimbor Dynasty. Esmenet turns to her brother-in-law, Maithanet, the Shriah of the Thousand Temples, for his clarity of vision and strength, yet she wonders why her husband would leave the Mantle in *her* incapable hands, when his brother is Dûnyain like himself.

She also has the travails of her own family to contend with. All her eldest children have gone. Mimara has fled – to Achamian, she hopes and prays. Kayûtas, Serwa, and her stepson, Moënghus, ride with their father in the Great Ordeal. Theliopa remains with her as an adviser, but the girl is scarcely human, she is so narrow and analytical. The next youngest, the mad and murderous Inrilatas, Esmenet keeps imprisoned atop the Andiamine Heights. Only her very youngest, the twins Samarmas and Kelmomas, provide her with any comfort. She clings to them as if they were flotsam in a shipwreck, not realizing that Kelmomas, like his brother Inrilatas, has inherited too many of his father's gifts. The boy has already driven away Mimara with the cunning of his insinuations. Now he plots deeper ways to secure sole possession of his mother's heart.

He will tolerate no rivals.

In the city of Iothiah, meanwhile, the White-Luck Warrior reveals himself to Psatma Nannaferi, who summons all her High Priestesses to plot the destruction of the Anasûrimbor. None other than Yatwer, the monstrous Mother of Birth, moves against the Aspect-Emperor. As the Goddess most favoured by slaves and caste-menials, she commands tremendous temporal power. Unrest spreads among the servile poor.

Even as the first rumours of this sedition reach his mother in

Momemn, young Kelmomas continues his own devious insurrection. Where before he had driven Mimara away, now he engineers the death of his idiot twin, Samarmas, knowing that grief for his loss will make his mother even more desperate for his love.

Capsized by the death of Samarmas, bewildered by the possibility that the Hundred themselves now hunt her family, Esmenet turns to her brother-in-law, Maithanet. He reminds her that the Gods can see neither the No-God nor the coming Apocalypse and so perceive her husband as a threat instead of a saviour.

At his bidding, Esmenet summons Sharacinth, the officially sanctioned Matriarch of the Yatwerians, with the intention of setting the Cult against itself. When they fail to cow the woman, Kellhus himself arrives and breaks her will to resist with sheer force of presence. The blubbering Matriarch yields, promising to wrest her Cult from Psatma Nannaferi. The Aspect-Emperor returns to the Great Ordeal, dismaying his Empress with his indifference to their son's death.

Realizing that his mother turns to him the more circumstances turn against her, Kelmomas sets out that very night, using his Dûnyain blood to steal across the Imperial Precincts, and murders Sharacinth and her retinue.

Rumours of her assassination travel quickly, igniting the embers of sedition among the slaves and caste-menials. Riots erupt across the New Empire.

Esmenet does turn to Kelmomas for comfort. At night, she takes to embracing him in her bed while the smell of smoke and the sound of screams and shouts waft through windows. Intoxicated with success, the young Prince-Imperial begins plotting against his uncle, Maithanet, knowing that the man alone possesses the ability to see through his deception.

CHAPTER ONE

The Meorn Wilderness

Without rules, madness. Without discipline, death.
—NANSUR MILITARY MAXIM

**Spring, 20 New Imperial Year (4132 Year-of-the-Tusk),
the 'Long Side'**

Even when the Skin Eaters walked ways sheeted in sunlight, some
shadow of Cil-Aujas lingered in their eyes. The reflection of friends
lost. The glint of things not quite survived.

Not two days had passed since they had escaped the derelict
underworld mansion. There was madness in the deep, and the
scalpers wore it more as fact than trophy. Decimated by Sranc.
Pursued through serpentine deeps to the very brink of Hell. They
had been transformed, these men who had survived seasons of
hunting and harvesting inhuman scalps in pursuit of the Holy
Bounty. Their hearts, which had been heaped with scars, now
stood cracked open. They walked raw, whether trekking across
mountain ridges or filing through forest tunnels. And for all their

regret they were thankful. Gentle breezes carried the kiss of blessings. Shadows. Rain. Any sign of an open sky, no matter how
indirect, occasioned some small rejoice.

They walked with the wonder of those who could not fathom
their breath, their heartbeat. Who could not believe they still
lived.

Too few of them remained for the old scalper discipline to hold
– or so it seemed to the old Wizard. If any Rules of the Slog
remained, they would have to be discovered on the way.

The Captain still commanded them. If anything he seemed
more archaic, more inscrutable and cruel. His Ainoni garb, which
was tattered before, had been reduced to black-stained rags. His
shield, which he wore slung over his back, sported innumerable
dents and clefts. But his authority, like everything else, had been
transformed by their passage – not so much eroded as superimposed
over other possibilities. Events had sorted them.

Sarl was the primary example. Once the mouthpiece of the
Captain, he now skulked in the rear of their ragged line, his eyes
fixed on his drunken steps, his fingers picking at the scabbed
remnant of the wound on his cheek. Periodically he would cackle,
a sharp, glutinous sound that jarred the others from their marching
reveries. He spoke to no one, content to endlessly mutter to
himself – nonsense about seeing Hell mostly. Once or twice a day
he would begin barking about the Coffers. 'The Slog of Slogs!
Yes! Yes!' The few glances he spared his Captain were filled with
wounded terror.

If the decimated company yet possessed a second it was Galian.
The Nansur had emerged almost unscathed from Cil-Aujas – a
tribute to his luck and a boost to his prestige. Aside from soldiers,
no one understood the importance of luck quite so profoundly as
scalpers. Galian, along with Pokwas and Xonghis, had become a
nucleus of sorts, a kind of conspiracy of the sane within the greater

company. Strangely enough, they found their power in *keeping* their counsel. When the Captain described this or that course of action, the Skin Eaters' eyes inevitably turned to the Nansur Columnary. Almost without exception Galian would pause for the sake of words unspoken, then nod his head aye: he was never so foolish as to contradict the Captain.

And the Captain was never so foolish as to provoke his contradiction.

As always, Xonghis ranged ahead, continually trotting where everyone save Cleric trudged. Were it not for his hunting skills, the expedition would have almost certainly perished. Pokwas, his scalp gruesome with clotted blood, rarely ventured from Galian's side. Every dusk the three would find a place apart from the others, gnaw sorcery-cooked meat, and trade murmurs. Xonghis was always glancing about, fingers combing his slight Jekki beard, his almond eyes sorting his surroundings even as he spoke or listened to his comrades. He rarely laughed. Pokwas invariably ministered to his great tulwar, sometimes praying as he did so. Something in his voice continually seemed to swing about the possibility of outrage, like a drunk nursing grudges. His laughter typically boomed. Galian always seemed to be sitting between them, even though their little triangle possessed no centre. The former Columnary was forever scraping the stubble from his chin. He seemed to watch his scalper brothers to the exclusion of the world, his eyes as keen as an alarmed father's. His laughter was always silent.

For whatever reason, Soma and Sutadra found themselves on the outside of this impromptu cabal. The gaunt Kianene, Sutadra, remained silent and watchful the same as before, though an intensity had crept into his eyes that was almost audible. He looked like a man hanging on the words of his wife's murderer, waiting for a confession. Soma was perhaps the least changed, the one most inclined to speak and act in the old ways. And true to form, the Nilnameshi caste-noble seemed utterly oblivious to the distrust that this incited in his comrades.

Nothing should be the same after Cil-Aujas.

The surviving Galeoth formed another small faction, one that was at once more mutinous and more complacent. If they were more liable to bellyache or, worse yet, openly question the expedition, then they were also more inclined to shrink from the scalding chill of the Captain's gaze. For whatever reason, the underworld trial had exacted the heaviest toll from them. Wonard's injuries, which he took to hiding like a wounded dog, had become septic. He marched with the flat-eyed look of someone who simply carried himself from place to place without wit or comprehension. Hameron continually cried out in his sleep, and seemed to sob as much as breathe over the course of the day. Only Conger seemed to improve as the days wore on. Despite the endless trudging, his limp had all but vanished.

But no one had been more transformed in the collective eye than Cleric. Where before they had walked with an enigma, one rounded warm and smooth by long acquaintance, now they walked with a Nonman *Ishroi* . . . a Quya Mage.

Even for men so bitten, it was no small thing to walk with a legend. And for a Wizard steeped in the ancient ways, it was cause for more than a few sleepless watches . . .

With the Osthwai Mountains to the southwest, night fell with the finality of a hammer. Since this was skinny country, they marched 'on the dark,' as Sarl had put it, without fires or illumination of any sort. They became a company of shadows, skulkers between the trees, loathe to speak. The fact of their losses always loomed the largest, it seemed, when they made camp. A kind of desolation haunted them. They would eat with the vacant look of those thrown from the grooves of a kinder life.

Each night, Cleric wandered among them, wordlessly dispensing miniscule smudges of Qirri. He seemed taller without his cloak. Cracked blood still clotted the nimil links of his hauberk. The Nail of Heaven threw lines of blue and white across the polish of his scalp and skin. His eyes, when they blinked, seemed more animal than otherwise.

Afterward he would sit, head bowed, next to the Captain, who either sat like a stone or leaned forward to lecture the Nonman in a continuous, growling whisper. No one could fathom what was said.

The Qirri would soak into their veins, a touch of bitter on the tongue that became a slow-spreading warmth, stretching revival. And their thoughts, relieved of bodily deprivations, would climb into remembered moulds.

The shadows would begin to mutter, like children testing the absence of a violent father.

The Nonman's voice would rise from the hushed chorus, Sheyic spoken with foreign accents and deep, alien intonations. A different kind of silence would fall across them, the Skin Eaters as well as the Wizard and the girl. A silence, not of expectation, but of men who awaited tidings of themselves. Places faraway.

And the sermon would begin, every bit as disordered and beautiful as the speaker.

'You have wandered out of light and life,' he began one night. They still picked their way through the foothills, following ridges flanged by innumerable ravines, so they had camped high. Cleric sat upon a bare stone shelf, his face toward the blackening bulk of Aenaratiol, the Ziggurat. By some fluke of happenstance, Achamian and Mimara found themselves sitting a stage higher, so they could see the mountain shadows encompass the forested tracts over his shoulders. It almost seemed they had *found* him thus, sitting cross-legged before the wilderness they would dare cross, a sentinel waiting to judge their folly.

'You have *seen* what so few of your kind have seen. *Now*, no matter where you walk, you will be able to look about and see the *piling of powers*. Empires of the sky. Empires of the deep . . .'

His great head leaned forward, white and waxen as a candle against the dark.

'Ever are Men stranded on the surface of things. And ever do they confuse what they see with the sum of what matters. Ever do they forget the rank *insignificance* of the visible. And when they do honour the beyond – the *beneath* – they render it according to what is familiar . . . They *disfigure* it for comfort's sake.'

The old Wizard sat rigid.

'But you . . . you *know* . . . You know that what lies beyond resembles us no more than the potter resembles the urn . . .'

A sudden mountain gust swept the high ridges, whisked through the gnarled jack pine that crooked the stone about them. Mimara raised a hand to brush the hair from her face.

'You who have glimpsed Hell.'

'The Slog!' Sarl exclaimed in hoary tones. 'The Slog of Slogs – just as I told you!' His laugh was half gurgle and half rasp.

But the company had ceased to hear these intrusions, let alone glance at their former Sergeant.

'All things have a place,' Cleric said. 'Death has its place. You have plumbed the depths, passed beyond the gates of life, and you have been where only the dead have been, seen what only the dead have seen . . .'

The Wizard found himself flinching from the Nonman's black-glittering gaze.

'May it greet you as an old friend when you return.'

A moment of pondering silence.

'The Coffers!' Sarl croaked, his face raisin-wrinkled with hilarity. 'The *Coffers*, lads!'

Darkness claimed the wild horizon.

———∞∞∞———

Kiampas dead. Oxwora dead. Sarl deranged. And dozens of other Skin Eaters the Wizard had never known outside the continuity of their presence . . . Dead.

The toll Achamian had feared had become real. Blood had been let, lives had been lost in the deep tumble, all in the name of *his* convictions . . . and the lie he had told in their dread service.

Distance and abstraction are ever the twin lures of disaster. When he paused to recollect it, that first step from his tower seemed absurd with ease. What was one step? Two? And all the walking that followed, across the wild, into the Obsidian Gate, step after step . . . Down into mountainous nethers.

All for the sake of finding Ishuäl . . . The name spoken by a mad barbarian so many years ago. The cradle of Anasûrimbor Kellhus. The hidden refuge of the *Dûnyain*.

Now, wrecked and heartbroken, they continued the long march to Sauglish, the ruined City of Robes, in the hope of plundering the Coffers, the famed sorcerous vault beneath the Library of Sauglish. Achamian had promised them riches, baubles that would make them princes. He had told them nothing of the map he hoped to find there, nor of the capricious Dreams that guided him.

He had glimpsed the Whore's shadow from the very beginning – from the moment he had set eyes on Mimara, it seemed. All along he had known the toll of his mad mission. And yet, he had let his lies and transgressions accumulate, taking heart in flabby rationalization.

The *truth*, he had told himself. The truth demanded sacrifice, from him and from others.

Could a man be called murderer when he killed in the name of truth?

Come nightfall, Achamian often peered at them through the gloom, these men who had risked all in the name of his lies. Scalpers hugging themselves against the chill. Foul. Ragged. Eyes pricked with madness. Not so much broken as disfigured – crippled strong. Only yesterday, it seemed, he had watched them strut and caper, trade jokes and boasts in the manner of men in the shadow of imminent battle. They were going to follow their Captain across the ends of the earth to loot a treasury out of legend. They were going to return princes. Now, scarcely anything remained of that bombast – save Soma, whose peculiar idiocy had rendered change-less, and Sarl, who had gone insane. The old Wizard watched them and he mourned what he had done almost as much as he feared what he was about to do.

One night he caught Mimara watching his watching. She was one of those women with a canny gift for seeing into masculine faces. She was forever guessing his chaotic humours.

'You feel remorse,' she said in reply to his quizzical look.

'Cil-Aujas has made you right,' he replied under his breath. She had called him a murderer on the far side of the mountains, had threatened to reveal his lies to the others if he turned her away.

'It has wronged me more,' she replied.

In the absence of consequences, lies were as easy as breathing, as simple as song. During his days as a Mandate Schoolman, Achamian had told innumerable falsehoods to innumerable people, and a fair number of fatal truths as well. He had destroyed reputations, even lives, in the pursuit of an abstraction, the Consult. He had even killed one of his beloved pupils, Inrau, in the name of what could not be touched or seen. He found himself wondering what it must be like for his former brothers now that the Consult had been revealed. What would it be like to belong to an *Imperial* School, to have princes and kings stammer in your presence? According to Mimara, they even carried Shrial Warrants, holy writs that exempted them from the laws of the lands that hosted them.

Mandate Schoolmen with *Shrial Warrants*! What would that be like?

He would never know. On the day the Consult had ceased being mere abstraction, the day Anasûrimbor Kellhus had been declared Aspect-Emperor, he had decided to hunt another obscurity: the origins of the man who had revealed them – and in his *Dreams*, no less. Maybe that was his doom. Maybe that would be the tragic irony that defined the lay of his life. Hunting smoke. Throwing the number-sticks of damnation. Sacrificing the actual for the possible.

The eternal outcast. Doubter and Believer.

With more men to kill.

Dreams are only possessed upon waking, which is why men are so keen to heap words upon them after the fact. They engulf your horizons, pin your very frame to turbulent unreality. They are the hand that reaches behind the mountains, beyond the sky, beneath the deepest sockets of the earth. They are the ignorance that tyrannizes our every choice. Dreams are the darkness that only slumber can illuminate.

The old Wizard walked slots beneath mighty foundations. The stones, he knew, were among the oldest in the complex, part of the original structure raised by Carû-Ongonean, the third and perhaps the greatest of the Umeri God-Kings. Here . . . This was the place where the Nonmen of the famed Tutelage, the Siqû, had come to live among the Kûniüri. This was the place where the first Quyan texts had been translated and stored, and where the first sorcerous School, the Sohonc, had been born.

Here . . . The famed Library of Sauglish.

Temple. Fortress. Granary of many things, wisdom and power foremost among them.

The walls seemed to close about him, so narrow was the way. Candles squatted in sconces along the walls. Whenever he neared one, it sparked to white life, while the one previous vanished into strings of smoke. Over and over, until it seemed there was but one flame leaping from wick to wick.

But the illumination was never quite enough. For every ten steps, five took him through absolute shadow, allowing him to see the layering of ancient Wards without the confusion of worldly sight. Ugly, the way all sorcery is ugly, and yet beautiful all the same, like the rigging of great ships, only ethereal – and as deadly as gallows. In the millennium since its construction, the Library – and the Sohonc – had never been conquered. The Cond Yoke. The Skettic invasions. No matter what the conquering nation, civilized or barbaric, they all sheathed their swords and came to terms. Whether perfumed and erudite like Osseoratha or unwashed and illiterate like Aulyanau the Conqueror, they all came to Sauglish bearing gifts instead of threats . . . They all knew.

This was the *Library*.

The corridor ended in blind walls. Holding tight the ornate map-case Celmomas had given him, the Grandmaster spoke the sorcerous words. Meaning flashed through his eyes and mouth, and he trod *through* monolithic stone. The Cant of Sideways Stepping.

Blinking, he found himself in the Upper Pausal, a narrow rostrum overlooking the Pausal proper, a dark antechamber long and deep enough to hold a war galley. Batteries of candles set below sparked to spontaneous life. Seswatha descended the right stair, map-case firmly in hand. Of all the innumerable rooms of the Library, only the Pausal could boast Nonmen artisanship because only it had been hewn out of living rock. Twining figures adorned the walls, frieze stacked upon frieze, representations of the Tutelage and the first great peace between the High Norsirai and the False Men – as the Tusk called the Cûnuroi. But like so many who entered this room, Seswatha scarcely noticed them. And how could he when the stigmatic blemish of sorcery so assaulted his gaze?

It was always the same whenever one of the Few, those who could see the mark that the sorcerous cut into the natural, walked the Pausal. One thing and one thing only commanded their gaze . . . the Great Gate of Wheels. The portal that was a lock, and the lock that was a portal.

The entrance to the Coffers.

To mundane eyes it was a wonder of scale and machination. To arcane eyes it was nothing less than a miracle of interlocking deformities: enormous incantation wheels carved from milk-white marble, turning through a frame of bronze set with constellations of faces carved of black diorite, instilled animata – or proxies, as they called them – enslaved souls, whose only purpose was to complete the circuit between watcher and watched that was the foundation of all reality, sorcerous or not. So hideous was the Mark of the thing, so metaphysically disfigured, that bile bubbled to the back of his throat whenever he found himself before it.

Quya magic. Deeper than deep.

Seswatha paused on the stair, warred with his stomach. He looked down and for some reason felt no surprise, no alarm, to see that the golden map-case had become an infant's inert form. Blue and grey. Mottled with black bruising, as if it had perished while lying on its face. Slicked with the sweat of the dead.

Such is the madness of dreams that we can assume the continuity of even the most jarring things. An infant corpse, it seemed, had

always been what he carried. Achamian followed the grooves of
the Dream thoughtful only of what had been thought, oblivious
to the discrepancies. Only when he came to a halt beneath the
arcane machinery of the Gate, only when he commanded
the proxies to roll back the Gate, did he find himself skidding
across unlived life . . .

Squirming. The dead baby was twisting and straining against
his hands.

The Great Gate of Wheels rumbled to cracking life. At last the
Archmage gazed down in horror.

Black eyes shining up with newborn bleariness. Fat-webbed arms
reaching out, tiny fingers clutching.

Revulsion. Flailing panic. He cast the thing the way a boy might
throw off a spider or a snake, but it simply hung in the air before
him, made a cradle of empty space. Behind it, the wheels of the
Gate continued their groaning tumble.

'This,' Seswatha gasped, 'is not what hap—!'

The last of the great bronze cogs had ceased their clacking. The
Gate of Wheels was drawing open . . .

The infant had dropped from the air. A golden tube clattered
where it had fallen. Beyond it, the ponderous bronze machinery
of the Gate folded into blackness. A gust swept out across the
antechamber.

Achamian stood immobile.

Wind roiled and twisted. His gown tugged at his limbs. A rumble
shivered through the walls and lintels, deep, as if a tempest lashed
some world inside the world. The Gate, which stood within the
Library's deepest heart, now opened onto the sky – not the Coffers,
the sky! And he could see the *Library*, as though the Pausal hung
from a great height above it. Bastions collapsing. Walls flying
outward in strings of sand. And he could see *it* . . . the horror of
horrors within billowing skirts of dust and debris, a mountain

of black-spinning wind that linked wrecked earth to flickering clouds. Existence itself howled.

TELL ME . . . the Whirlwind said.

WHAT DO YOU SEE?

WHAT AM I?

The Mandate libraries in Atyersus possessed many maps, some old, others new. On all save the most ancient, the land the Skin Eaters dared cross was called the Meorn Wilderness, a name that carried many implications for the learned squints that regarded it.

The scalpers, however, simply called it the Long Side. They had heard the stories, of course. They knew the vast forests they plumbed had once been cultivated horizons. Even more, they had seen the ruins: the stone-stumped grottos that were the lost city of Teleol, and the fortress of Maimor – or Fatwall, as they called it. They knew of the Meori Empire. They knew that once, so very long ago, the wilderness and savagery had lain to the *south* of the Osthwai Mountains. And the thoughtful among them would wonder at the way the slow leakage of years could bring about such grand and dramatic reversals.

When the first companies of Scalpoi had crossed into the Wilderness some ten years previous, they had been overwhelmed by the numbers and the ferocity of the Sranc clans they had found. The 'Stick Days,' the old veterans called them, because every slog seemed a throw of the number-sticks. But the game was plentiful. And the foothills offered endless possibilities for ambush – the key to nearly every Captain's success. Within a matter of five years, the Scalpoi had driven the Sranc into the lowland forests, the Great Mop, taking so many scalps that the Holy Bounty had to be halved, lest the New Empire go bankrupt.

The reconquest of the Great Meori Empire had begun, albeit by Men who resembled the Sranc more than otherwise. When Fatwall, or Maimor, was discovered, the Holy Aspect-Emperor even sent a Judge and a company of Ministrate Pikemen to occupy the abandoned fortress over the summer months. Many among the Imperial Apparati spoke of reclaiming all the ancient Meori provinces – from the Osthwai Mountains to the Sea of Cerish – within ten scant years. Some even argued the Holy Bounty should take precedence over the Great Ordeal. Why wage war against one, they dared ask, when with mere gold you could battle against *all*?

But the forests, vast and deep and dark, made a mockery of these hopes. No matter how many companies filed into them, no matter how many bales of scalps they carried out, the frontier ceased its creeping retreat and remained fixed, year after year. For the first time since the calling of the Holy Bounty the Sranc did not dwindle and withdraw. One Imperial Mathematician, the notorious Mepmerat of Shigek, claimed that the Scalpoi had at last encountered a population of Sranc that could reproduce as fast as they could slaughter – that the Bounty had become *futile*, in effect. He would be imprisoned for his impious accuracy.

For their part, the Scalpoi cared nothing for squint-eyed calculations or petty political aspirations. One need only probe the verges of the Great Mop to understand why the skinnies had stopped running. The Mop was like no forest known to Men of the Three Seas. Trees so vast and hoary they had raised berms about their bases, creating troughs like the swells of a stormy sea. The thatching of the canopy so dense that little more than grey-green light attenuated the filtered gloom. The ground devoid of undergrowth, broken only by the colossal bones of trees long dead. For Sranc, the Mop was a kind of paradise: perpetually dark with easy earth rich in grubs. It provided for all but their most dread appetites.

That is, until the coming of Men.

———⊗⊗⊗———

Xonghis had led them down from the mountains into the foothills at a northwest tangent, so nearly a week passed before the expedition entered the Mop. The plan was to skirt the forest's edges and march to Fatwall, ancient Maimor, with the hope of resupplying. Mimara fairly clung to the Wizard during this time, sometimes actually leaned against him, even though she possessed no real wounds of consequence. Her mother had done the same, years before in the First Holy War, and the memories would have struck Achamian deep – pain deep – had not the pandemonium of the previous days been so complete. He could scarce blink without glimpsing some shredded glimpse of their ordeal.

When he asked her what happened at the bottom of the Great Medial Screw, she never answered, at least not satisfactorily. According to her, the Wight-in-the-Mountain had been driven away by her Chorae and that was that. When he reminded her that the Captain also carried a Chorae, one that apparently made no difference, she would simply shrug as if to say, 'Well, *I'm* not the Captain, am I?' Time and again, Achamian found himself circling back to the issue. He could not do otherwise. Even when he ignored her, he could sense her Chorae against her breast, like a whiff of oblivion, or the scratch of some otherworldly burr.

The School of Mandate had long eschewed the Daimotic Arts: Seswatha had believed Ciphrang too capricious to be yoked to human intent. Still, Achamian had some understanding of the metaphysics involved. He knew that some agencies could be summoned shorn of the Outside, plucked whole as it were, while others bore their realities *with them*, swamping the World with porous madness. The shade of Gin'yursis, Achamian knew, had been one of the latter.

Chorae only negated violations of the Real; they returned the world to its fundamental frame. But Gin'yursis had come as *figure and frame* – a symbol wedded to the very Hell that gave it meaning . . .

Mimara's Chorae should have been *useless*.

'Please, girl. Indulge an old man's confusion.'

It involved the Judging Eye . . . somehow. He knew it in his bones.

'Enough. It was madness, I told you. I don't know what happened!'

'More. There has to be something more!'

She fixed him with her damning glare. 'What an old hypocrite you are . . .'

She was right, of course. As hard as he pressed her about what had happened, she pressed him harder for details of the Judging Eye – and he was even more evasive. A part of him suspected that she refused to answer out of some peevish desire for retribution.

What does one say to the doomed? What could knowing provide other than the air of an executioner's vigil? To know one's doom was to know futility, to walk with a darkened, deadened heart.

To forget hope.

The old Wizard knew this as much from his Dreams as from his life. Of all the lessons he had learned at life's uncaring knee, perhaps this was the most hard won. So when she pestered him with questions – gazing at him with Esmenet's eyes and airs – he would bristle. 'The Judging Eye is the stuff of witches lore and old wives' tales! I have no *knowledge* to share, only rumours and misapprehensions!'

'Then tell me those!'

'Bah! Leave me in peace!'

He was *sparing* her, he told himself. Of course his refusal to answer simply stoked her fears, but fearing and knowing were two different things. There is mercy in ignorance; Men are born appreciating this. Scarce a day passes when we do not save others from things – small and great – they would be worse for knowing.

The old Wizard wasn't the only one to suffer Mimara's rancour. Somandutta drew abreast of them one morning, his manner at once pensive and breezy with false good humour. He began by asking her questions, then plied her with various inane observations when she refused to reply. He was trying, the old Wizard knew, to rekindle something of their old banter, perhaps hoping to find unspoken forgiveness in the resumption of old ways and manners. His approach was at once cowardly and eminently male: he was literally asking her to *pretend* that he had not abandoned her in Cil-Aujas. And she was having none of it.

'Mimara . . . please,' he finally hazarded. 'I know . . . I know I wronged you . . . down . . . down *there*. But everything happened so . . . so quickly.'

'But that's the way it is with fools, isn't it?' she said, her tone so light it could only be scathing. 'The world is quick and they are slow.'

Perhaps she had happened upon an old and profound fear of his. Perhaps she had simply shocked him with the summary ease of her condemnation. Either way, the young Nilnameshi caste-noble came to an abrupt stop, stood dumbfounded as the others trudged past. He ducked away from Galian and his teasing attempt to pinch his cheek.

Afterward Achamian joined him on the trail, moved more by the memory of Esmenet and the similarities of *her* pique than by real pity. 'Give her time,' he said. 'She's fierce in her feelings, but her heart is forgiving . . .' He trailed, realizing this wasn't quite true. 'She's too quick not to appreciate the . . . difficulties,' he added.

'Difficulties?'

Achamian frowned at the petulance of the young man's tone. The fact was he agreed with Mimara: He did think Soma was a fool – but a well-meaning one. 'Have you ever heard the saying, "Courage for men is fodder for dragons?"'

'No,' the fulsome lips admitted. 'What does it mean?'

'That courage is more complicated than simple souls credit . . . Mimara may be many things, Soma, but simple isn't one of them. We all need time to build fences about what . . . what happened.'

The wide brown eyes studied him for a moment. Even after everything they had endured, the same affable light illuminated his gaze. 'Give her time . . .' Soma repeated in the tone of a young man taking heart.

'Time,' the old Wizard said, resuming his march.

Afterward he found himself hoping the daft fool didn't confuse his advice for paternal permission. The thought of the man wooing Mimara made him bristle as if he really *were* her father. The question of why he felt this way plagued him for a good portion of the afternoon. For all her capricious strength, something about Anasûrimbor Mimara demanded protection, a frailty so at odds with the tenor of her declarations that it could only seem tragic . . . beautiful. The air of things too extraordinary to long survive the world's rigour.

This realization, if anything, made her company more irritating.

'The woman saved your life,' Pokwas told him one evening, when the to-and-fro of men milling found them side by side. 'That means deep things in my country.'

'She saved *all* our lives,' Achamian said.

'I know,' the towering Sword-dancer replied with a solemn nod.

'But *yours* in particular, Wizard. Several times.' A look of wonder crept into his face.

'What?' Achamian could feel the old scowl building, the one that had aged into his expression.

'You're so *old*,' Pokwas said with a shrug. 'Who risks everything to pluck an *empty* wineskin from a raging river? Who?'

Achamian snorted in laughter, wondered how long it had been since he had laughed. 'An empty wineskin's daughter,' he replied. And even as a part of him flinched from the lie – for it seemed sacrilegious to deceive men with whom he had shared utter and abject hardship – another part of him slumped backward in a kind of marvelling anxiousness.

Maybe this lie had also come true.

———

She watches the Wizard by moonlight, reviews his features the way a mother reviews her children: the counting of things beloved. The eyebrows like moustaches, the white hermit beard, the hand that clutches his breast. Night after night she watches.

Before, Drusas Achamian had been a riddle, a maddening puzzle. She could scarce look at him without railing in anger. So stingy! So miserly! There he sat, warm and fat with knowledge, while she haunted his stoop, begging, starving . . . *Starving!* Of all the sins between people, few are so unforgivable as being needed.

But now.

He looks every bit as wild as before, hung in wolf-pelts, stooped with years. Despite bathing in the chill blast of mountain streams (an episode that would have occasioned hilarity had the expedition not been so battered), he still carries the stain of Sranc blood across his knuckles and his cheek. They all do.

And still he denies her. Still he complains, upbraids, and rebukes. The only difference is that she loves him.

She remembers her mother's first descriptions of him, back when the Andiamine Heights had been her home, when gold and incense had been her constant companions. 'Have I ever told you about Akka?' the Empress asked, surprising her daughter in the Sacral Enclosure. There was always this twitch, a body-wide plucking of tendons, whenever her mother caught her unawares. Her jaw would tighten, and she would turn to see *herself* – as she knew she would be in twenty years' time. Mother, draped in white and turquoise silks, a gown reminiscent of those worn by Shrial Nuns.

'Is he my father?' she had replied.

Her mother shrank from the question, recoiled even. Asking about her father was Mimara's weapon of choice. Questions of paternity were at once accusations of whorishness. Woe to the woman who did not know. But this time the question seemed to strike her mother particularly hard, to the point where she paused to blink away tears.

'Your f-father,' she stammered. 'Yes.'

Stunned silence. Mimara had not expected this. She knows now that her mother lied, that Esmenet said this simply to rob her daughter of the hateful question. Well . . . perhaps not simply. Mimara has learned enough about Achamian to understand her mother's passion, to understand how she might name him her daughter's father . . . in her soul's heart, at least. Everyone tells lies to dull the world's sharper, more complicated edges – some more pretty than others.

'What was he like?' she asked.

Her mother never looked so beautiful as when she smiled. Beautiful and hateful both. 'Foolish, like all men. Wise. Petty. Gentle.'

'Why did you leave him?'

Another question meant to injure. Only this time, Mimara found herself flinching instead of celebrating. Hurting her mother where she herself was concerned was one thing: victims have rights over criminals – do they not? Hurting her for things entirely her own, however, said more about Mimara than Mimara cared to hear.

Few passions require quite so much certainty as spite.

'Kellhus,' Esmenet replied, her voice dim and damaged. *You win*, her eyes conceded as she turned to leave. 'I chose Kellhus.'

Now, watching the Wizard by moonlight, Mimara cannot stop thinking about her mother. She imagines the wrack that had to have been her soul, coming to her daughter again and again, each time with new hope, only to be punished and rebuked. Guilt and remorse crash through her, for a time. Then she thinks of the little girl who had shrieked in the arms of slavers, the child sobbing, 'Mumma!' into the creaking dark. She remembers the stink and the pillows, the child who wept within her still, even though her face had become as flat and chill as new fallen snow.

'Why did she leave you?' she asks the old Wizard the following afternoon on the trail. 'Mother, I mean.'

'Because I died,' the old Wizard says, his brown eyes lost in the fog of distant seeing. He refuses to say anything more specific. 'The world is too cruel to wait for the dead.'

'And the living?'

He stops and fixes her with that curious stare of his, the one that makes her think of artisans reviewing the work of more gifted rivals.

'You already know the answer to that one,' he says.

'I do?'

He seems to catch his smile, condense it into pursed lips. Galian and Sutadra file between them, the former frowning, the latter intent and oblivious. There are times when they all become strangers to one another, and now is one of them – though it seems that Sutadra has been a stranger all along. Bald stone ridges flange the distances beyond the Wizard, promising toil and arms bundled against high wind.

'Why . . .' the Wizard begins, then trails. 'Why didn't you leave me back in the pit?'

Because I lov—

'Because I need you,' she says without breath. 'I need your knowledge.'

He stares at her, his beard and hair trembling in the breeze. 'So the old wineskin has a few swallows left,' he says inexplicably.

He ignores her glare, turns to follow the others. More riddles! She fumes in silence for the remainder of the afternoon, refuses to even look at the old fool. He laughs at her, she decides – and after acknowledging that she had saved him! Bent-back ingrate.

Some starve. Some eat. Disparity is simply the order of things. It's only when fat men make sauce out of other's starvation that it becomes a sin.

She belongs.

The others have shown this to her in ways numerous and infinitesimal. The pitch of their talk does not change when she enters their midst. They tease her with brotherly skepticism instead of masculine daring. Their eyes are less inclined to linger on her limbs and more inclined to remain fixed on her gaze.

The Skin Eaters are less and they are more. Less because of what Cil-Aujas has taken, more because *she* has become one of them. Even the Captain seems to have accepted her. He now looks through her the way he looks through all his men.

They make camp on a ridge that falls in a series of gravel sheaves into the Mop. She stares at the forests for a time, at the play of sunlight across the humped canopy. Birds like floating dots. She thinks of how the expedition will crawl across the landscape, like lice picking their way through the World's own pelt. She has heard the others mutter about the Mop, about the dangers, but after Cil-Aujas, nothing seems particularly dangerous, nothing that touches sky.

They dine on what remains of Xonghis's previous kill, but she finds herself more eager for the smudge of Qirri that Cleric dispenses. Afterward, she keeps to herself, makes a point of avoiding Achamian's many looks, some questioning, others . . . searching. He does not understand the nature of his crime – like all men.

Somandutta once again tries to engage her, but she simply glares at the young caste-noble until he slouches away. He had saved her in Cil-Aujas, actually carried her for a mad term, only to abandon her when her need was greatest – and this she cannot forgive.

To think she had thought the fool charming.

She watches Sarl instead: he alone has not bathed since climbing out of the Ziggurat's bowel, so he sometimes seems more shade than man. Sranc blood has soaked into the very texture of his skin. His hauberk is intact, but his tunic is as foul as rags worn by a latrine beggar. He huddles against a rust-stained boulder the size of a cart, huddles in a way that suggests hiding one moment, conspiring the next. The boulder is his friend, she realizes. Sarl now sits with everything as if it were his closest friend.

'Ah, yes . . .' he murmurs in the gurgle that is his voice. His small black eyes glitter. 'Ah . . . yesss . . .' The dusk carves his wrinkles so deep that his face looks woven of bundled string.

'The fucking Mop . . . The *Mop*. Eh, lads? *Eh?*'

Viscous laughter, followed by a snapping cough. The back of his thought is broken, she realizes. He can only kick and claw where he has fallen.

'More darkness, yes. *Tree* darkness . . .'

She does not remember what happened at the bottom of the Great Medial Screw, and yet she knows nonetheless, knows with the knowledge that moves limbs and drums hearts.

Something was open that should not have been open. She closed it . . .

Somehow.

Achamian, during one of his many attempts to sound her out on the matter, mentions the line between the World and the Outside, of souls returning as demons. 'How, Mimara?' he asks with no small wonder. 'What you accomplished . . . It should not have been possible. Was it the Chorae?'

No, she wants to say, *it was the Tear of God* . . . But she nods and shrugs instead, in the bored manner of those who pretend to have moved on to more decisive things.

She has been given something. What she has always considered a blight, a deformity of the soul, has become fraught with enigma and *power*. The Judging Eye opened. At the moment of absolute crisis, it opened and saw what needed to be seen . . .

A tear *of the God*, blazing in her palm. The God of Gods!

She has been a victim her whole life. So her instinct is the immediate one, to raise a concealing hand, to turn a shoulder in warding. Only a fool fails to hide what is precious.

Precious – and of course utterly incompatible with the one thing she desperately wants. Chorae and witches, as the Ainoni would say, rarely prosper beneath the same roof.

She finds a sour comfort in this – even a kind of warrant. Had it been pure and simple she would have shunned it out of jaded, melancholy reflex. But now it is something that demands to be understood – on *her* terms . . .

So of course the old Wizard refuses to tell her anything.

More comfort. Frustration and torment is the very shape of her life. The one thing she trusts.

That night she awakens to the sound of Sarl crooning in a low, lilting voice. A song like smoke, quickly drawn into soundlessness by the ridge's height. She listens, watching the Nail of Heaven as it peeks through the tattered garments of a cloud. The words to the song, if there are any, are incomprehensible.

After a time, the song trails into rasping murmur, then a moan.

Sarl is old, she realizes. He left more than his wits in the bowel of the mountain.

Sarl is dying.

A pang of terror bolts through her. She turns to look for the Wizard among the rocks, only to find him immediately behind her, bestial with hair. He had crept to her side after she had fallen asleep, she realizes.

She stares into the shadow of his rutted face and smiles, thinking, *At least he does not sing.* She crinkles her nose at his smell. She drifts back asleep to the fluttering image of him.

I understand, Mother . . . I finally see . . . I really do.

She dreams of her stepfather, wakes with the frowning confusion that always accompanies dreams too sticky with significance. With every blink she sees *him*: the Aspect-Emperor, not as he is but as he would be were *he* the shade that haunted the accursed deeps of Cil-Aujas . . .

Not a man but an emblem. A living Seal, rising on tides of hellish unreality.

'You are the eye that offends, Mimara . . .'

She wants to ask Achamian about the dream but finds the memory of their feud too sharp to speak around. She knows what everybody knows about dreams, that they are as likely to deceive as to illuminate. On the Andiamine Heights, the caste-noble wives would consult augurs, pay outrageous sums. The caste-menials and the slaves would pray, usually to Yatwer. The girls in the brothel used to drip wax on pillow-beetles to determine the truth of their dreams. If the wax trapped the insect, the dream was true. She has heard of dozens of other folk divinations besides. But she no longer knows what to believe . . .

It's the Wizard, she realizes. The damned fool is rubbing off on her.

'The eye that must be plucked.'

They breakfast on the last of a juvenile buck. The sky is cloudless, and the morning sun is chill and sharp. An air of renewal surrounds the scalpers; they talk and prepare the way they used to, the animation of men reacquainting themselves with old and arduous tasks.

The Captain sits on a boulder overlooking the forested vista below, sharpening his blade. Cleric stands below him, shirtless beneath his nimil hauberk. He nods as though in prayer, listening as always to the grinding mutter of the Captain. Galian huddles in close conference with Pokwas and Xonghis, while Soma hovers over them. Sutadra has withdrawn up the trail to pray: he is always praying of late. Conger speaks to his countrymen in avid tones, and though Gallish defeats her, she knows that he attempts to rally them. Sarl mutters and cackles to himself as he shaves tiny slices no bigger than a fingernail from his breakfast cut, which he then chews and savours with absurd relish, as if dining on snails or some other delicacy.

Even Achamian seems to sense the difference, though he says nothing. The Skin Eaters have returned. Somehow, they have recovered their old ways and roles. Only the worried glances exchanged between jokes and declarations betray their fright.

The Mop, she realizes, the famed primeval forests of the Long Side. They fear it – apparently enough to forget Cil-Aujas for a time.

'Skinnies,' Sarl cackles, his face flushed red. 'Chop and bale them, boys . . . We have *skin* to eat!'

The cheer raised is so winded, so half-hearted, that the shadow of Lost Mansion seems to leap across them anew . . . There are so few left.

And Sarl is not one of them.

A tin clank alerts the company, tells them that their Captain has slung his battered shield over his back – what has become the signal for them to resume their march. The slopes are treacherous, and twice she infuriates the old Wizard by offering him a steadying hand. They wend their way down, descending lower and lower, picking and barging their way through massed ranks of scrub. It seems she can feel the mountains climbing into sky-high absurdity behind her.

The Mop grows beneath and before them, becoming larger and larger, until she can make out the vying of individual limbs across the tossed canopy. Despite the descriptions she has heard, she finds herself gawking in wonder. The trees are nothing short of monumental, such is their size. Through screens of leaves she glimpses soaring trunks and spanning limbs and the dark that is the world beneath the canopy.

The air fairly shivers with the sound of birds singing, screeching, hooting, creating a vast and shrill chorus that reaches, she knows, across the horizon to the shores of the Cerish Sea. They find themselves following a shelf that runs parallel to the forest edge about a length or so taller than the canopy. Her glimpses take her deeper now, though still far from the gloom-shrouded floor. She sees limbs reach like sinuous stone, bearing barn-sized shags of greenery and sheets of moss hanging like a mendicant's rags. She sees the piling on of shadows that makes blackness out of the forest depths.

It will swallow us, she thinks, feeling the old panic buzzing through her bones. She has had her fill of lightless bellies. Small wonder the scalpers were anxious.

Tree darkness, Sarl had said.

For the first time, it seems, she understands the sheer *enormity* of the task the Wizard has set for them. For the first time she understands that Cil-Aujas was but the beginning of their trial – the first in a parade of unguessed horrors.

The shallow cliff dips and collapses into a rugged slope, spilling gigantic stones into the forest verge. The expedition picks its way down and files into the Great Mop . . .

Into the green darkness.

CHAPTER TWO

The Istyuli Plains

We belittle what we cannot bear. We make figments out of fundamentals, all in the name of preserving our own peculiar fancies. The best way to secure one's own deception is to accuse others of deceit.

—HATATIAN, EXHORTATIONS

It is not so much the wisdom of the wise that saves us from the foolishness of the fools as it is the latter's inability to agree.

—AJENCIS, THE THIRD ANALYTIC OF MEN

Spring, 20 New Imperial Year (4132 Year-of-the-Tusk), The High Istyuli

The Sakarpi tell of a man who had two puppies in his belly, the one adoring, the other savage. When the loving one nuzzled his heart, he became joyous, like the father of a newborn boy. But

45

when the other gored it with sharp puppy teeth, he became desperate with sorrow. Those rare times the dogs left him in peace, he would tell people he was doomed. Bliss can be sipped a thousand times, he would say, whereas shame need only cut your throat once.

The Sakarpi called him Kensooras, 'Between Dogs,' a name that had since come to mean the melancholy suffered by suicides.

Varalt Sorweel was most certainly between dogs.

His ancient city had been conquered, its famed Chorae Hoard plundered. His beloved father had been killed. And now that he found himself in the Aspect-Emperor's fearsome thrall, a *Goddess* accosted him, the Dread Mother of Birth, Yatwer, in the guise of his lowly slave.

Kensooras indeed.

The cavalry company that was his cage, the Scions, had been called to the hazard of war. The collection of young hostages who composed the Scions had long feared their company was naught but ornamental, that they would be cozened like children while the Men of the Ordeal fought and died around them. They pestered their Kidruhil Captain, Harnilas, endlessly. They even petitioned General Kayûtas – to no apparent avail. Even though they marched with their fathers' enemy, they were boys as much as men, and so their hearts were burdened with the violent longing to prove their mettle.

Sorweel was no different. When word of their deployment finally arrived, he grinned and whooped the same as the others – how could he not? The recriminations, as always, came crashing in afterward.

The Sranc had ever been the great foe of his people – that is, before the coming of the Aspect-Emperor. Sorweel had spent the better part of his childhood training and preparing for battle against the creatures. For a Son of Sakarpus, there could be no higher calling. Kill a Sranc, the saying went, birth a man. As a boy he had spent innumerable lazy afternoons mooning over imagined glories, chieftains brained, whole clans annihilated. And he had spent as many taut nights praying for his father whenever he rode out to meet the beasts.

Now, at long last, he was about to answer a lifelong yearning and to embark on a rite sacred to his people . . .

In the name of the man who had murdered his father and enslaved his nation.

More dogs.

He gathered with the others in Zsoronga's sumptuous pavilion the night before their departure, did his best to keep his counsel while the others crowed in anticipation. 'Don't you see?' he finally cried. 'We are *hostages!*'

Zsoronga watched with an air of frowning dismissal. He reclined more than the others so that the crimson silk of his basahlet gleamed across his cheek and jaw. Plaits of his jet medicine-wig curled across his shoulders.

The Zeümi Successor-Prince remained as generous as always, but there could be no denying the chill that had climbed between them since the Aspect-Emperor had declared Sorweel one of the Believer-Kings. The young King desperately wanted to explain things, to tell him about Porsparian and the incident with Yatwer's spit, to assure him that he still *hated*, but some inner leash always pulled him up short. Some silences, he was learning, were impossible *not* to keep.

To Sorweel's left sat Prince Charampa of Cingulat – the '*true* Cingulat,' he would continually insist, to distinguish his land from the Imperial province of the same name. Though his skin was every bit as black and exotic as Zsoronga's, he possessed the narrow features of a Ketyai. He was one of those men who never ceased squabbling, even when everyone agreed with him. To his right sat the broad-faced Tzing of Jekkhia, a land whose mountain Princes paid grudging tribute to the Aspect-Emperor. He never spoke save through an enigmatic smile, as though he were privy to facts that made a farce out of all conversations. Opposite Sorweel, beside the Successor-Prince, sat Tinurit of the Akkunihor, a Scylvendi tribe whose lands lay no more than two weeks' ride from the New Empire's capital. He was an imperious, imposing character and the only one who knew less Sheyic than Sorweel.

'Why should we celebrate fighting our captor's war?'

No one understood a word, of course, but enough desperation had cracked through his tone to capture their attention. Obotegwa, Zsoronga's steadfast Obligate, quickly translated, and Sorweel was surprised to find himself understanding much of what the old man said. Obotegwa rarely had a chance to complete any of his translations of late – primarily because of Charampa, whose thoughts flew from soul to tongue without the least consideration.

'Because it is better than rotting in *our captor's* camp,' Tzing replied through his perpetual smirk.

'Yes!' Charampa cried. 'Think of it as a *hunting* expedition, Sorri!' He turned to the others, seeking confirmation of his wit. 'You can even scar yourself like Tinurit here!'

Sorweel looked to Zsoronga, who merely glanced away as though in boredom. As fleeting as the wordless exchange had been, it stung as surely as a slap.

So says the Believer-King, the Zeümi's green eyes seemed to say.

As far as Sorweel could tell, the single thing that distinguished their group from the other Scions was geography. Where the others hailed from recalcitrant tribes and nations *within* the New Empire, they represented the few lands that still exceeded its grasp – at least until recently. 'Between us we have the Aspect-Emperor surrounded!' Zsoronga would sometimes cry in joking terms.

But it was no joke, Sorweel had come to realize. Zsoronga, who would one day be Satakhan of High Holy Zeüm, the only nation that could hope to rival the New Empire, was cultivating friendships according to the interests of his people. He avoided the others simply because the Aspect-Emperor was renowned for his devious subtlety. Because spies had almost certainly been planted among the Scions.

He had to know Sorweel was no spy. But why would he tolerate a Believer-King?

Perhaps he had yet to decide.

The young Sakarpi King found himself brooding more than contributing as the night wore on. Obotegwa continued translating the others for his benefit, but Sorweel could tell that the white-haired Obligate sensed his despondency. Eventually, he could do little more than gaze at their small flame, plagued by the sense that something *stared back*.

Was he going mad? Was that it? The earth speaking, spitting. And now flames watching . . .

He had been raised to believe in a living world, an *inhabited* world, and yet for the brief span of his life dirt had always been dirt, and fire had always been fire, dumb and senseless. Until now.

Charampa accompanied him on the walk back to his tent, speaking far too fast for Sorweel to follow. The Cingulat Prince was one of those oblivious souls who saw only excuses to chatter and nothing of what his listeners were thinking. 'It's a poor hostage,' Zsoronga had once joked, 'whose father is *relieved* to see him captive.' But in a sense, this made Charampa and Sorweel ideal companions, one from the New Empire's extreme southern frontier, the other from the extreme north. The one talking without care of comprehension, the other unable to comprehend.

The young King walked, scarcely pretending to listen. As always, he found himself awed by the scale of the Great Ordeal, that they could come to blank and barren plains and within a watch raise a veritable city. He groped for a memory of his father's face but could see only the Aspect-Emperor hanging in shrouded skies, raining destruction down upon Holy Sakarpus. So he thought of the morrow, of the Scions winding into the wastes, a frail thread of some eighty souls. The other Scions talked of battling Sranc, but the real purpose of their mission, Captain Harnilas had told them, was to find game to supply the host. Even still, they rode far beyond the Pale – who could say what they would encounter? The prospect of battle fluttered like a living thing in his breast. The thought of riding down Sranc screwed tight his teeth, hooked his lips into a broad grin. The thought of *killing* . . .

Mistaking his expression for agreement, Charampa grabbed his shoulders. 'I knew it!' he cried, his Sheyic finally simple enough to understand. 'I *told* them! I told them!'

Then he was off, leaving Sorweel dumbfounded behind him.

The Sakarpi King paused in momentary dread before entering his tent, but he found his slave, Porsparian, sleeping on his reed mat, curled like half-starved cat, his breath caught between a wheeze and a snore. He stood over the diminutive man, hanging in confusion and anxiousness. He need only blink to see Porsparian's knob-knuckled hands moulding Yatwer's face in the soil, the impossible vision of spit bubbling to her earthen lips. His cheeks burned at the memory of the slave's rough touch. His heart lurched at the thought of the Aspect-Emperor declaring him one of his Believer-Kings.

A slave – a *slave* had done this! More Southron madness,

Sorweel found himself thinking. In the story and scripture of Sakarpus, the Gods only treated with the heroic and the highborn – those mortals who resembled them most. But in the Three Seas, he was learning, the Gods touched Men according to the *extremity* of their station. The abject were as apt to become their vessels as the grand . . .

Slaves and kings.

Sorweel crept into his cot as silently as he could manage, tossed in what he thought was the beginning of another sleepless night, only to dissolve into a profound slumber.

He awoke to the tolling of the Interval. With his first breath, he could taste the wind his people called the Gangan-naru – too warm for dawn, tinged with dust. The troubling glamour that Porsparian had possessed the previous night had evaporated. The slave scuttled about with nary a significant look, readied Sorweel's packs and saddle as he ate his meagre morning repast. The little man dragged the gear outside his tent, where he helped load the young King. The tablelands swirled with industry and purpose about them. Horns scored the brightening sky.

'You return . . .' Porsparian began, pausing to search for some word his owner might understand. '*Hatusat . . .*' he said, scowling with old-man concentration. 'Exalted.'

Sorweel frowned and snorted. 'I will do my best.'

But Porsparian was already shaking his head, saying, 'She! *She!*'

The young King stepped back in terror, turned away, his thoughts buzzing. When the Shigeki slave clutched at his arm, he yanked himself free with more violence than he intended.

'She!' the old man cried. '*Sheeee!*'

Sorweel strode away, huffing beneath his gear. He could see the others, the Scions, a small eddy of activity in an ocean of seething detail – an army that extended into the colourless haze. Tents falling. Horses screaming, their caparisons flashing in the early dawn light. Officers bawling. The dip and wave of innumerable Circumfix banners.

The great host of the Aspect-Emperor . . . The other dog.

Yes, the young King of Sakarpus decided. He needed to kill something.

That or die.

~~~

Grassland roamed the horizon, every direction the eye could see, rising in chaotic tiers, panning into bowls, and tumbling into ravines. The greening of spring could be glimpsed in its contours, but it was little more than a haze beneath the sheets of dead scree. For the plainsmen who had taken up the Circumfix – Famiri and Cepalorans, who were used to seeing the detritus of winter swallowed in flowers and surging grasses – this was as ominous as could be. Where others were oblivious, they saw emaciated cattle, horizons burnt into long brown lines, horned skulls in summer dust.

The clouds that baffled the northwest never sailed toward them. Instead a breeze, preternatural for its constancy, swept in from the south, drawing the thousands of Circumfix banners into one rippling direction. The Sakarpi scouts called it the Gangan-naru, the 'Parching Wind,' a name they spoke with the flat look of men recalling disaster. The Gangan-naru, they said, came but once every ten years, culling the herds, forcing the Horselords to abandon the Pale, and all but transforming the Istyuli into a vast desert. The Kianene and Khirgwi among the host swore they could smell the dusty scent of their home, the faraway Carathay.

When the hour was late, and the Judges no longer walked the

encampment, the grizzled Veterans of the First Holy War murmured stories of woe. 'You think the path of the righteous is one of certainty and ease,' they said to younger faces, 'but it is *trial* that separates the weak from the holy.' Only the most drunk spoke of the Trail of Skulls, the First Holy War's catastrophic march along the desert coasts of Khemema. And without exception their voices became murmurs, overcome by memories of the weak and the fallen.

Arrayed in great roping lines, the Men of the Circumfix trudged onward with dogged resolution, travelling ever northward. They formed a veritable sea, one churning with many-coloured currents – the black shields of the Thunyeri, the silvered helms of the Conriyans, the crimson surcoats of the Nansur – and yet the emptiness continued to open and open, vast enough to even make the Great Ordeal small. A cloud of horsemen encircled the host, companies of household knights riding beneath the banners of the Three Seas caste-nobility – Ainoni Palatines, Galeoth Earls, Kianene Grandees, and many more. They probed the distances, searching for an enemy who never appeared, save for the ever greater swathes of raked earth they galloped across.

At the Council of Potentates, the Believer-Kings finally petitioned their Holy Aspect-Emperor, asking whether he knew anything of their elusive foe. 'You look about you,' he said, stepping luminous among them, 'see the greatest host of Men ever assembled, and you yearn to crush your enemies, thinking yourself invincible. Heed me, the Sranc *will* scratch that yearning from you. A time *will* come when you look back to these days and wish that your eagerness had gone unrequited.'

He smiled, and they smiled, finding levity in his wry humour, wisdom in his sober heart. He sighed, and they shook their heads at their juvenile foolishness.

'Fret not about the *absence* of our foe,' he admonished. 'So long as the horizon remains empty, our way is secure.'

Grassland roamed the horizon, drying beneath a succession of cool spring suns. The rivers dwindled, and the dust rose to shroud the farther pageants. The Priests and Judges organized mass prayers, fields of warlike men abasing themselves for want of rain. But the Gangan-naru continued to blow. At night, the plains twinkling with innumerable fires, the Men of the Three Seas began to murmur about thirst – and rumours of discord back home.

The horizon remained empty, and yet their way no longer seemed secure.

The Holy Aspect-Emperor declared a day of rest and consultation.

The quartermasters became ever more stingy. The Men of the Circumfix had exhausted the bulk of their supplies, and they had outrun the supply-trains that chased them from the south. The rivers they tramped across had become too slight to readily fill their skins with clean water. They had come as far as their beasts and their backs could take them, which meant they had indeed passed beyond the limits of civilization. From this point, they had to fend for themselves.

The time had come for the Great Ordeal to break into foraging columns.

———∞∞∞———

Stark.

That was the only way to describe the Aspect-Emperor's bed chamber. A simple cot for sleeping, no different than those issued to low-ranking officers. A knee-high work table, without so much as a single cushion to sit upon. Even the room's leather walls, which were swagged with decoration elsewhere throughout the

Umbilicus, were bare. No gold could be seen. No ornament. The only symbols visible were those inscribed, column after meticulous column, about the octagonal circuit of the small iron hearth set in the room's heart.

King Nersei Proyas had known and served Anasûrimbor Kellhus for more than twenty years, and still he found himself regularly perplexed by the man. As a youth he had often watched his tutor, Achamian, and his sword master, Xinemus, play benjuka – an ancient game, famed for the way the pieces determined the rules. Those had been sunny days, as the days of privileged youth often are. The two men would draw a table over to one of the seaside porticos and call out curses across the Meneanorean wind. Careful to be quiet, for tempers would flare more often than not, Proyas would watch them contest the plate, a winking partisan of whoever happened to be losing – Achamian usually. And he would wonder at decisions he could rarely understand.

This, he had come to learn, was what it meant to serve the Holy Aspect-Emperor: to be a witness to incomprehensible decisions. The difference was that Anasûrimbor Kellhus took the World as his benjuka plate.

The World and the Heavens.

To act without understanding. This, this he had decided, was the essential kernel, the spark that made worship *worship*. In High Ainon, during the fevered height of the Unification Wars, he had overseen the Sack of Sarneveh, an act of brutality that still jarred him from sleep from time to time. Afterward, when the Mathematicians reported that more than five thousand children had been counted among the dead, Proyas began shaking, a flutter that began with his fingers and bowel but soon climbed through his every bone. He dismissed his staff and vomited, wept, only to find *him* standing in the gloom of his pavilion, watching. 'You *should* grieve,' the Aspect-Emperor said, his figure etched in a faint glow. 'But do not think you have sinned. The World overmatches us, Proyas, so we make simple what we cannot otherwise comprehend. Nothing is more complicated than virtue and sin. All the atrocities you have committed in my name – all of them *have their place*. Do you understand this, Proyas? Do you understand why you will never understand?'

'You are our father,' he had sobbed. 'And we are your headstrong sons.'

Zaudunyani.

The chamber was vacant. Even still, Proyas fell to his knees and lowered his face to the simple reed mats. He suffered a pang of shame, realizing that his own quarters possessed at least four times the baggage and so exacted four times the burden on the collective host. That would change, he resolved. And he would challenge all his officers to follow his parsimonious example.

'My Lord and Salvation?' he called to the empty air. The wheeze and pop of the hearth's fire filled the silence. Its light mottled the hanging walls with wavering patterns of light and dark. It almost seemed he could glimpse images in the dancing blur. Cities burning. Faces.

'Yes . . . Please, Proyas. Share my fire.'

And *there he was*, sitting cross-legged before the octagonal hearth. Anasûrimbor Kellhus. The Holy Aspect-Emperor.

He sat with the slack repose of someone who had not moved for some time. The outer edges of his plaited beard and shoulder-length hair gleamed in counterpoint to the fire. He wore a simple robe of grey silk embroidered only about the hems. Aside from the faint haze of illumination about his hands, only his eyes seemed extraordinary.

'Is everything—?' Proyas began, only to catch himself in embarrassment.

'Ours has always been a convoluted bond,' Kellhus said smiling. 'Clad in ritual armour one moment, naked the next. The time has come for us to recline side by side as simple friends.'

He gestured for Proyas to sit beside him – on his right, the place of honour. 'Truth be told,' he said in his old, joking way. 'I prefer you *clothed*.'

'So all is well?' Proyas asked, crouching and crossing his legs.

'I remember when you laughed at my jokes,' the Aspect-Emperor said.

'You were funnier back then.'

'Back when?'

'Before you beat the World to the last laugh.'

The Aspect-Emperor grinned and frowned at once. '*That* remains to be seen, my friend.'

Proyas often was astonished by the way Kellhus could, utterly and entirely, just *be* what he needed to be given the demands of circumstance. At this moment, he was simply an old and beloved friend, nothing more or less. Usually Proyas found it difficult – given all the miracles of might and intellect he had witnessed – to think of Kellhus as a creature of flesh and blood, as a man. Not so now.

'So all is *not* well?'

'Well enough,' Kellhus said, scratching his brow. 'The God has allowed me glimpses of the future, the *true* future, and thus far everything unfolds in accordance with those glimpses. But there are many dark decisions I must make, Proyas. Decisions I would rather not make alone.'

'I'm not sure I understand.'

A twinge of shame accompanied this admission, not for the fact of his ignorance, but for the way he had hedged in confessing. Proyas *most certainly* did not understand. Even after twenty years of devotion, he still succumbed to the stubborn instinct to raise his pride upon little falsehoods and so manage the impressions of others.

How hard it was to be an absolutely faithful soul.

Kellhus had ceased correcting these petty lapses; he no longer needed to. To stand before him was to stand before *yourself*, to know the warp and woof of your own soul, and to see all the snags and tears that beggared you.

'You are a king and a general,' Kellhus said. 'I would think you know well the peril of guesses.'

Proyas nodded and smiled. 'No one likes playing number-sticks alone.'

His Lord-and-God raised his eyebrows. 'Not with stakes so mad as these.'

By some trick of timing, the golden flames before them twirled, and again Proyas thought he glimpsed fiery doom flutter across the leather-panelled walls.

'I am yours, as always my Lor . . . Kellhus. What do you need of me?'

The leonine face nodded toward the fire. 'Kneel before my hearth,' the Aspect-Emperor said, the flint of command hardening his voice. 'Bow your face into the flame.'

Proyas surprised himself with his lack of hesitation. He came to his knees before the edge of the small iron hearth. The heat of the fire pricked him. He knew the famed story from the Tusk, where the God Husyelt asked Angeshraël to bow his face into his cooking fire. He knew, *verbatim*, the Sermon of the Ziggurat, where Kellhus had used this story to reveal his divinity to the First Holy War twenty years previous. He knew that 'Bowing into the Fire' had since become a metaphor for Zaudunyani revelation.

And he knew that innumerable madmen wandered the Three Seas, blinded and scarred for taking the metaphor literally.

Even still, he was on his knees, and *he was bowing*, doing exactly as his Prophet and Emperor commanded. He even managed to keep his eyes *open*. And a part of him watched and wondered that a devotion, any devotion, could run so deep as to throw a face into the furnace . . .

Across the crazed bourne of opposites. Into the lapping glitter. Into the needling agony.

Into the light.

His beard and hair whooshed into tinder. He expected agony. He expected to scream. But something was tugged from him, sloughed like flesh from overboiled bone . . . something . . . *essential*.

And he was *looking out* from the fire, into a thousand faces – and a thousand more. Enough to wrench the eyes, dazzle and bewilder the soul. And yet somehow he focused, turned from the battering complexity and took refuge in a single clutch of men, four long-bearded Men of the Ordeal, one gazing directly at him with a child's thoughtless fixity, the others bickering in Thunyeri . . . Something about rations. Hunger.

Then he was out, on his rump in Kellhus's gloomy chamber, blinking and sputtering.

And his Lord-and-God held him, soothed his face with a damp cloth. 'The absence of space,' he said with a rueful smile. 'Most souls find it difficult.'

Proyas padded his cheeks and forehead with fumbling finger-tips, expecting to feel blasted skin, but found himself intact. Embarrassed, he bolted upright, squinting away the last of the fiery brightness. He glanced about and for some unaccountable reason felt surprised that the iron hearth burned exactly as before.

'Does it trouble you that I can watch men from their fires?' Kellhus asked.

'If anything, it *heartens* me . . .' he replied. 'I marched with you in the First Holy War, remember? I know full well the capricious humour of armies stranded far from home.'

Afterward, he would realize that his Aspect-Emperor had already known this, that Anasûrimbor Kellhus knew his heart better than he himself could ever hope to. Afterward, he would question the whole intent of this intimate meeting.

'Indeed you do.'

'But why show me this? Do they speak of mutiny already?'

'No,' Kellhus replied. 'They speak of the thing that preoccupies all stranded men . . .'

The Aspect-Emperor resumed his position before the hearth, gestured for Proyas to do the same. A moment of silence passed as Kellhus poured him a bowl of wine from the wooden gourd at his side. Gratitude welled through the Exalt-General's breast. He drank from the bowl, watching Kellhus with questioning eyes.

'You mean home.'

'Home,' the Aspect-Emperor repeated in assent.

'And this is a problem?'

'Indeed. Even now our old enemies muster across the Three Seas. As the days pass they will grow ever more bold. I have always been the rod that held the New Empire together. I fear it will not survive my absence.'

Proyas frowned. 'And you think this will lead to desertion and mutiny?'

'I know it will.'

'But these men are *Zaudunyani* . . . They would *die* for you! For the truth!'

The Aspect-Emperor lowered his face in the *yes-but* manner Proyas had seen countless times, though not for several years.

They had been far closer, he realized, during the Unification Wars . . .

When they were killing people.

'The hold of abstractions over Men is slight at best,' Kellhus said, turning to encompass him in his otherworldly scrutiny. 'Only the rare, ardent soul – such as yours, Proyas – can throw itself upon the altar of thought. These men march not so much because they believe in me as they believe what I have told them.'

'But they *do* believe! *Mog-Pharau returns to murder the world.* They believe *this*! Enough to follow you to the ends of the World!'

'Even so, would they choose me over their *sons*? How about you, Proyas? As profoundly as you believe, would you be willing to stake the lives of your son and daughter for *my throw* of the number-sticks?'

A kind of strange, tingling horror accompanied these words. According to scripture, only Ciphrang, demons, demanded such sacrifices. Proyas could only stare, blinking.

The Aspect-Emperor frowned. 'Stow your fears, old friend. I don't ask this question out of vanity. I do not *expect* any man to choose me or my windy declarations over their own blood and bones.'

'Then I don't understand the question.'

'The Men of the Ordeal do not march to save the World, Proyas – at least not first and foremost. They march to save their wives and their children. Their tribes and their nations. If they learn that the world, *their* world, slips into ruin behind them, that their wives and daughters may perish for want of *their* shields, *their* swords, the Host of Hosts would melt about the edges, then collapse.'

And in his soul's eye Proyas could see them, the Men of the

Ordeal, sitting about their innumerable fires, trading rumours of disaster back home. He could see them prod and stoke one another's fears, for property, for loved ones, for title and prestige. He could hear the arguments, the long grinding to and fro of faith and incessant worry. And as much as it dismayed him, he knew that his Lord-and-God spoke true, that Men truly were so weak.

Even those who had conquered the known world. Even the Zaudunyani.

'So what are you proposing?' he asked, nodding in sour agreement.

'An embargo,' the Aspect-Emperor replied on a pent breath. 'I will forbid, on pain of death, all Cants of Far-calling. Henceforth, the Men of the Ordeal shall march with only memories to warm them.'

Home. This, if anything, was the abstraction for the Exalt-General. There was a place, of course. Even for beggars, there was a place. But Proyas had spent so many years campaigning that home for him possessed a wane and fleeting character, the sense of things attested to by others. For him, home was his wife, Miramis, who still wept whenever he left her bed for the wide world, and his children, Xinemus and Thaila, who had to be reminded he was their father upon his rare returns.

And even they seemed strangers whenever melancholy steered his thoughts toward them.

No. *This* was his home. Dwelling in the light of Anasûrimbor Kellhus.

Waging his endless war.

The Aspect-Emperor reached out, grasped his shoulder in unspoken acknowledgment. Never, in all their years together, had he promised any reprieve, any respite, from the toil that had so burdened his life. Never had he said, 'After this, Proyas . . . After this . . .'

Warmth sparked through the Exalt-General, the tingle of grace.

'What will you tell them?' he asked roughly.

'That Golgotterath has the ability to scry our scrying.'

'Do they?'

Kellhus arched his eyebrows. 'Perhaps. *Twenty centuries* have they prepared – who could say? It would terrify you, Proyas, to know how *little* I know of our enemy.'

A resigned smile. 'I have not known terror since I have known you.'

And yet he had known so many things just as difficult.

'Fear not,' Kellhus said sadly. 'You will be reacquainted before all this is through.'

The Seeing-Flame fluttered and twirled before them, caught in some inexplicable draft. Even its warmth seemed to spin.

'So,' Proyas said, speaking to ward against the chill falling through him, 'the Great Ordeal at last sails beyond sight of shore. I see the wisdom – the *necessity*. But surely *you* will maintain contact with the Empire.'

'No . . .' Kellhus replied with an uncharacteristic glance at his haloed hands. 'I will not.'

'But . . . but *why*?'

The Warrior-Prophet looked to the dark leather panels rising about them, gazed as if seeing shapes and portents in the wavering twine of light and shadow. 'Because time is short and all I have are fragmentary visions . . .'

He turned to his Exalt-General. 'I can no longer afford backward glances.'

And Proyas understood that at long last the Great Ordeal had begun in earnest. The time had come to set aside burdens, to shed all complicating baggage.

Including home.

Only death, war, and triumph remained. Only the future.

—∞∞∞—

Anasûrimbor Kellhus, the Holy Aspect-Emperor of the Three Seas, declared the Breaking of the Great Ordeal at the Eleventh Council of Potentates. The same concerns echoed through the ensuing debates, for such is the temper of many men that they must be convinced several times before they can be convinced at all. The Believer-Kings understood the need to disperse: without forage there was no way the Great Ordeal could reach its destination. But even so early in the year, the rivers were languishing, and the new growth of spring still slept beneath the detritus of the old. As the plainsmen among them knew, game followed the rain in times of drought. What use was dividing the host when all the game had fled in search of greener pasture?

But as the Aspect-Emperor and his planners explained, they had no choice but to pursue the route they had embarked upon. Any deviation from their course would force them to winter in the wilds, rather than Golgotterath, and so doom them. Tusullian, the senior Imperial Mathematician, explained how everything was knitted to everything, how forced marches meant more food, which in turn meant diminishing supplies, which in turn meant more foraging, which in turn meant slower progress.

'In all things,' the Aspect-Emperor said, 'I urge you to walk the Shortest Path. The road before us is no different, save that it is also the *only* path. We will be tried, my friends, and many of us will be found wanting. But we *will* prove worthy of salvation! We shall deliver the World from destruction!'

And so the lists were drawn, and the nations of the Believer-Kings were allotted to what would be called the Four Armies.

Prince Anasûrimbor Kayûtas, General of the Kidruhil, was given command of the Men of the Middle North, the Norsirai sons of the kings who had ruled these lands in Far Antiquity, ere

all was lost in the First Apocalypse. They consisted of the fractious Galeoth under King Coithus Narnol, the elder brother of
King Coithus Saubon; the black-armoured Thunyeri under King
Hringa Vûkyelt, the impetuous son of Hringa Skaiyelt, who had
fallen in glory in the First Holy War; the long-bearded Tydonni
under King Hoga Hogrim, the quick-tempered nephew of the
sainted Earl Hoga Gothyelk and awarded the throne of Ce Tydonn
for service in the Unification Wars; and the far-riding Cepalorans
under Sibawul te Nurwul, a man noted only for his silence during
councils.

With them would march the Swayal Sisterhood and their
Grandmistress, Anasûrimbor Serwa, the younger sister of General
Kayûtas, and widely thought to be the most powerful witch in the
world.

Of the Four Armies, the Men of the Middle-North marched
what was perhaps the most perilous path, since it skirted the
westward marches of the plain, a route that would take his host
near the vast forests that had overgrown ancient Kûniüri. 'This
is the land of your ancient forefathers,' the Aspect-Emperor
explained. 'Hazard is your inheritance. Vengeance is your
birthright!'

King Nersei Proyas, Exalt-General, Veteran of the First Holy
War, was given command of the Ketyai of the East, the sons of
ancient Shir. They consisted of the javelin-armed Cengemi under
indomitable General Couras Nantilla, famed for championing the
independence of his long-oppressed people; the silver-mailed
Conriyans under Palatine Krijates Empharas, Marshal of the fortress
of Attrempus; the bare-chested Famiri under the tempestuous
General Halas Siroyon, whose mount, Phiolos, was rumoured to
be the swiftest in the world; the Xiangol-eyed Jekki under Prince
Nurbanu Ze, the adopted son of Lord Soter, and the first of his
people to be called kjineta, or caste-noble; and the white-painted

Ainoni under cold-hearted King-Regent Nurbanu Soter, Veteran of the First Holy War, renowned for his pious cruelty through the Unification Wars.

Two Major Schools were assigned to this column: the Scarlet Spires under Heramari Iyokus, the so-called Blind Necromancer, and another Veteran of the First Holy War. And the Mandate, the School of the Aspect-Emperor himself, under their famed Grandmaster, Apperens Saccarees, the first Schoolman to successfully recite one of the Metagnostic Cants.

King Coithus Saubon, Exalt-General, Veteran of the First Holy War, was charged with leading the Ketyai of the West, the sons of ancient Kyraneas and Old Dynasty Shigek. They consisted of the disciplined Nansur under the young General Biaxi Tarpellas, Patridomos of House Biaxi, a shrewd tactician; the spear-bearing Shigeki levies under the indomitable General Rash Soptet, hero of the interminable wars against the Fanim insurrectionists; the desert-born Khirgwi under the mad Chieftain-General Sadu'waralla ab Daza, whose epileptic visions confirmed the divinity of the Aspect-Emperor; the mail-draped Eumarnans under General Inrilil ab Cinganjehoi, son of his famed father in both limb and spirit and an ardent convert to Zaudunyani Inrithism; and the celebrated Shrial Knights under Grandmaster Sampë Ussiliar.

Two Major Schools were also assigned to this column: the Imperial Saik, the School of the old Nansur Emperors, under the aged Grandmaster Temus Enhorû, and the rehabilitated Mysunsai under the irascible Obwë Gûswuran, a Tydonni who behaved more like a Prophet of the Tusk than a sorcerer.

As the heart of the Great Ordeal, both these columns would march within one or two days of each other, utilizing the far greater gap between the outer columns to gather what forage the Istyuli offered. In this way, the Aspect-Emperor hoped to concentrate a greater part of the Believer-Kings' strength, should some calamity overtake either of the flanking columns.

King Sasal Umrapathur was made Marshal of the Ketyai of the South, the sons of Old Invishi, the Hinayati, and the southern Carathay. They consisted of the dusky-skinned Nilnameshi under the brilliant Prince Sasal Charapatha, the eldest son of Umrapathur, and called the Prince of One Hundred Songs in the streets of Invishi because of his exploits during the Unification Wars; the half-heathen Girgashi under the fierce King Urmakthi ab Makthi, a man giant in limb and heart, said to have felled a rampaging mastodon with a single blow of his hammer; the shield-bearing Cironji Marines under the eloquent King Eselos Mursidides, who during the Unification Wars stole his island nation from the Orthodox with a legendary campaign of bribery and assassination; and the regal Kianene under the sober-hearted King Massar ab Kascamandri, youngest brother of the Bandit Padirajah, Fanayal, and rumoured to be as devoted to the Aspect-Emperor as his eldest brother was devoted to his destruction.

With them marched the Vokalati, the feared Sun-wailers of Nilnamesh, under the Grandmaster known only as Carindûsû, notorious for his insolence in the presence of the Aspect-Emperor and for his rumoured theft of the Mandate Gnosis.

Umrapathur was given the most uncertain route, in that he would march into the great vacant heart of the Istyuli, into a land so blank that it bore no witness to the ages but simply remained. If the Consult contrived to strike from the east, then he would bear the brunt of that fury.

The Men of the Circumfix spent the following day trudging to their new assignations, mobs cutting across mobs, columns tangling through columns. The chaos was good humoured for the most part, though it was inevitable that some tempers would be thrown out of joint. A dispute at one of the watering tributaries between

Galeoth Agmundrmen and Ainoni Eshkalasi knights lead to blood-shed – some twenty-eight souls lost, another forty-two sent to the lazarets. But other than several isolated incidents between individuals, nothing untoward marred the day.

When the Interval tolled and camp was broken the following morning, the Breaking was complete, and four great tentacles, dark with concentrated motion, twinkling as though dusted with diamonds, reached out across the endless plate of the Istyuli. Songs in a hundred different tongues scored an indifferent sky.

Thus began the longest, most arduous, and most deadly stage of the Great Ordeal's bid to destroy Golgotterath and so prevent the Second Apocalypse.

CHAPTER THREE

The Meorn Wilderness

The bondage we are born into is the bondage we cannot see.
Verily, freedom is little more than the ignorance of tyranny.
Live long enough, and you will see: Men resent not the
whip so much as the hand that wields it.

—TRIAMIS I, JOURNALS AND DIALOGUES

**Spring, 20 New Imperial Year (4132 Year-of-the-Tusk),
the 'Long Side'**

Birds permeate the soaring canopies, but their chorus is distant somehow, muffled, as if they sing from the bottom of a sock. The air is close, thick with the absence of breeze. An earthen reek clings to her every breath: the smell of detritus pounded into mush by the seasons, into earth by the years, and into stone by the ages. When she looks up she sees pinpricks of white shining through pockets of ragged green. Otherwise, there is a quality to the filtered gloom that makes the darkness palpable, viscous, as if they trudge through a fog. The pillared depths are uniformly black. The parallax

of intervening trunks slowly scissors a thousand grottoes into invisibility. It almost seems a game, the accumulation of hidden spaces.
Enough to conceal nations.

Though heaped about the massive trunks and roots, the ground
is soft and easy to tread. They follow a winding line between the
monstrous trees, but even still they are continually climbing and
descending. Often they are forced to hack their way through
hanging veils of moss.

It seems unthinkable that men had once taken hoe and plough
to this earth.

The scalpers fear the Mop for good reason, she supposes, but
for some reason her fear has left her. It is strange the way trauma
deadens curiosity. To suffer cruelty in excess is to be delivered from
care. The human heart sets aside its questions when the future is
too capricious. This is the irony of tribulation.

To know the world will never be so bad.

She fairly jumps at the sound of her name, so intent and absent
is her concentration. The old Wizard is beside her. Somehow he
seems of a piece with their new surroundings, no different than
when crossing the wild mountain heights or passing through
Cil-Aujas before that. He has spent too many years among the
wild and the ruined not to resemble them.

'The Judging Eye . . .' he begins in his curious Ainoni. There
is something embarrassed in his apologetic look. 'You will be furious
when you realize how little I know.'

'You tell me this because you are afraid.'

'No. I tell you this because I truly know very little. The Judging
Eye is a folk legend, like the Kahiht or the White-Luck Warrior,
notions that have been traded across too many generations to
possess any clear meaning . . .'

'I can see the fear in your eyes, old man. You think me cursed!'

The Wizard regards her for several unblinking heartbeats. Worry. Pity.

'Aye . . . I think you are cursed.'

Mimara has told herself this from the very beginning. *There is something wrong with you. There is something broken.* So she assumed hearing the same from Achamian would leave her intact, confirmed more than condemned. But for some reason tears flood her eyes, and her face rebels. She raises a hand against the gaze of the others.

'But I do know,' Achamian hastily adds, 'that the Judging Eye involves *pregnant* women.'

Mimara gawks at him through tears. A cold hand has reached into her abdomen and scooped away all warring sensation.

'Pregnant . . .' she hears herself say. 'Why?'

'I don't know.' He has flecks of dead leaf in his hair, and she squelches the urge to fuss over him. 'Perhaps because of the profundity of childbirth. The Outside inhabits us in many ways, none so onerous as when a women brings a new soul into the world.'

She sees her mother posing before a mirror, her belly broad and low with the twins, Kel and Sammi.

'So what is the curse?' she fairly cries at Achamian. 'Tell me, old fool!' She rebukes herself immediately afterward, knowing that the Wizard's honesty would wither as her desperation waxed. People punish desperation as much out of compassion as petty malice.

Achamian gnaws his bottom lip. 'As far as I know,' he begins with obvious and infuriating care, 'those with the Judging Eye give birth to dead children.'

He shrugs as if to say, *See? You have nothing to fear . . .*

Cold falls through her in sheets.

'What?'

A scowl knits his brow. 'The Judging Eye is the eye of the Unborn . . . The eye that watches from the God's own vantage.'

A cleft has opened about their path: a runoff that delivers them to a shallow ravine. They follow the stream that gurgles along its creases – the water is clear but seems black given the gloom. Monstrous elms pillar the embankments, their roots like great fists clenched about earth. The stream has wedged the trees far enough apart for white to glare through seams in the canopy. Here and there the water's meandering course has gnawed hollows beneath various trees. The company ducks beneath those that had fallen across the ravine, trees like stone whales.

'But I've had . . . had this . . . for as long as I can remember.'

'Which is my point exactly,' Achamian says, sounding far too much like someone taking heart in invented reasons. He frowns, an expression Mimara finds horribly endearing on his shaggy old features. 'But things are always tricky where the Outside is concerned. Things do not . . . happen . . . as they happen here . . .'

'Riddles! Why do you constantly torture me with riddles?'

'I'm just saying that in a sense your life *has already been lived* – for the God or the Gods, that is . . .'

'Which means?'

'Nothing,' he says, scowling.

'Tell me what it means!'

But that cool glint has sparked in his eyes. Once again her words have cut through the fat of the old Wizard's patience and struck the bone of his intolerance. 'Nothing, Mimara. Noth—'

A blood-curdling cry. She finds herself against sloped ground, tackled in the Wizard's wiry grasp. She senses the whisper of incipient sorceries – Wards strung out and around them. Cleric is booming something incomprehensible. She glimpses Sutadra staggering, a shaft and fletching jutting from his cheek. He's trying to scream but can only cough.

Again, she realizes. The Skin Eaters are dying again.

———∞∞∞———

'Hold my belt!' Achamian cries to her, jerking himself to a crouch. 'Don't let go!'

'In the trees!' someone shouts – Galian.

'Stone Hags! Stone Hags!'

Cleric's laughter booms through the hollows.

In her thirst for all things sorcerous, Mimara has read much about Mandate Schoolmen, and more still regarding the Gnosis and the famed War-Cants of the Ancient North. She knows about the incipient Wards they use to secure their person in event of surprise attacks. Even back at Achamian's collapsed tower, she had sensed them hanging about him, like faint child-scribbling marring the art of the immediate world. Now they crackle with life-preserving ugliness.

Arrows pelt the Wizard's Wards, sparking into nothingness. She throws her gaze to and fro, trying to make sense of the surrounding madness. She hears shouts beyond those of her companions. She glimpses shadowy figures ducking along the heights to either side: bowmen, possessing the rangy gait and mien of scalpers. The ravine has delivered them to a *human* ambush. Galian and Pokwas squat behind a heaped deadfall nearby. Sutadra is down. Soma she cannot see. Cleric has a sorcerous bulwark of his own. The Captain stands tall at his side.

'To me!' Achamian cries to the others. He's standing now, his feet braced in water and muck, and she has pulled herself beside him. 'Close about me!'

Other shouts, other voices, across the heights and through the gloom. Their attackers, crying out in alarm. '*Gur-gurwik-wikka!*' she hears a broken chorus cry, one of the few Gallish words she understands.

Gurwikka. Sorcerer.

Achamian has already begun his otherworldly mutter. His eyes and mouth flare white, painting the figures crowding about them in shades of blue.

She senses a rush of shadows above, sees men shimming down trees. They drop to the forest floor, scramble for earthen cover. They're running – fleeing.

'Stone Hags!' Pokwas booms, crying out the name like a curse. Only Galian's scarred grip prevents the Sword-dancer from bolting after them.

A thunderous crack – somewhere to the fore of their small column. She sees Cleric's silhouette against the glare of roiling fire. A *sorcerer* assails him. A man hangs between vaulting branches, dressed in black, his limbs like rag-bound sticks. An ethereal dragon head rears from his hands, vomits fire . . .

She squints against sunset brilliance.

A whooshing hiss returns her gaze to things more immediate. Achamian stands rigid, his hands raised, his face a mask of grizzled skin across sunlight. He sweeps a line of blinding white across the heights of the ravine. She throws a forearm across her eyes, glimpses her shadow as it chases a circle across the ground . . . The Compass of Noshainrau.

Fire laves barked surfaces. Wood explodes into char.

But where the trees on the Galeoth side of the mountains toppled, the leviathans of the Mop merely groan and crack. Leaves shower across the ravine. A burning clutch of branches crashes into the creek, bursts into steam. Flutters of deeper movement catch her eye: more men fleeing . . .

Stone Hags.

She looks again to the Nonman. He stands unharmed before flashing breakers of fire, crying out in his mundane voice but in a tongue she does not understand. '*Houk'hir!*' he shouts in a booming laugh. '*Gimu hitiloi pir milisis!*' The sorcerous mutter of his opponent continues to rise up out of space and substance. The figure still hangs above the ravine, black against swatches of sky and levels of brightening green . . .

Achamian is gripping her arm, as if holding her back from some ill-advised rush.

Smoke blooms from nothingness, piles outward from the heart of every hollow. Within heartbeats a pall has obscured the over-matched sorcerer.

Cleric simply stands as before, both feet planted in the shining course of the stream. His laughter is strange, like a murder of crows crying across thunder.

For several moments no one does anything more than stare and breathe.

The Captain climbs alone to the crest of the ravine, lifts himself onto the back of a long-fallen tree, one that reaches across the gully like a collapsed temple column. A lone shaft of sunlight illuminates him and the tattered remnants of his dress. Light hooks about the dents in his shield and armour.

'Knife our bales?' he roars into the crotched depths. 'Our bales?'

Sarl starts cackling, hard enough to begin hacking phlegm.

Lord Kosoter turns, rakes the surrounding dark with a look of preternatural fury. 'I will stab out your eyes!' he bellows. 'Gut your peach! *I will kick vomit from your teeth!*'

Mimara finds herself kneeling beside Sutadra – she is not sure why. The Kianene has curled onto his side, hissing breaths that end in grunts, holding riven hands to either side of the arrow embedded in his cheek.

They have shared no words, she and this man. They have lived shoulder to elbow on the trail for weeks, and yet they have scarcely exchanged glances. How could such a thing be? How could this life dwindling beneath her be little more than scenery one moment and . . . and . . .

'Please-please,' she mumbles. 'Tell me what to do . . .'

The heathen scalper fixes her in his gaze – a look of absurd urgency. He sputters something but can only speak blood. His goatee, which has become a full beard since Cil-Aujas, is clotted with it.

'Stone Hags,' she hears Galian say in explanation to Achamian. 'Bandits. A scalper company that preys on its own. They saw our numbers, I'm guessing, thought we were low-hanging fruit.' A wry laugh.

'Aye,' Pokwas says. '*Sorcerous* fruit.'

Hands held out and helpless, she stares down at the dying stranger. *Why are you doing this?* something cries within her. *He's dying. There's nothing to be done! Why—*

The Judging Eye opens.

'But have we seen the end of them?' the old Wizard asks.

'Depends,' Galian replies. 'No one knows what they do over the winter months, where they go. They could be desperate.'

And she learns what it means to stare into the moral sum of a man's life. Sutadra . . .

Soot, the others had called him.

You can count the bruises on your heart easily enough, but numbering sins is a far trickier matter. Men are eternally forgetting for their benefit. They leave it to the World to remember, and to the Outside to call them to harsh account. *One hundred Heavens*, as Protathis famously wrote, *for one thousand Hells*.

She can see it all, intuitions bundled into the wrinkled architecture of his skin, the squint about his eyes, the cuts across his knuckles. Sin and redemption, written in the language of a flawed life. The oversights, the hypocrisies, the mistakes, the accumulation of petty jealousies and innumerable small selfish acts. A wife struck on a wedding night. A son neglected for contempt of weakness. A mistress abandoned. And beneath these cankers, she sees the black cancer of far greater crimes, the offences that could be neither denied nor forgiven. Villages burned on fraudulent suspicions. Innocents massacred.

But she also sees the clear skin of heroism and sacrifice. The white of devotion. The gold of unconditional love. The gleam of loyalty and long silence. The high blue of indomitable strength.

Sutadra, she realizes, is a good man broken down, a man forced, time and again, to pitch his scruples against the unscalable walls of circumstance – *forced*. A man who erred for the sake of mad and overwhelming expediencies. A man besieged by history . . .

Regret. This is what drives him. This is what delivered him to the scalpers. The will to suffer for his sins . . .

And she *loves* him – this mute stranger! One cannot see as much as she sees and not feel love. She loves him the way one must love someone with such a tragic past. She knows as a lover knows, or a wife.

She knows he is damned.

He kicks against the mud of the stream, gazes with eyes pinned to sights unseen. He makes fish mouths, and she glimpses the arrow digging into the back of his throat. A small cry escapes him, the kind you would expect from a dying child or dog.

'Shhh . . .' she murmurs through burning lips. She's been weeping. '*Paradise*,' she lies. 'Paradise awaits you . . .'

But a shadow has fallen across them, a darker gloom. The Captain – she knows this without looking. Even as she turns her face up, the Judging Eye closes, but still she glimpses blasted back, coal-orange eyes leering from a charred face . . .

He raises his boot and kicks the arrow down. Wood popping in meat. Sutadra's body jerks, flutters like a thread in the wind.

'You rot where you fall,' the Captain says with a queer and menacing determination.

Mimara cannot breathe. There is a softness in the Kianene's passing, a sense of fire passing into powdery ash. She raises numb fingers to brush the bootprint from the dead man's nose and beard but cannot bring herself to touch the greying skin.

'Weakness!' the Captain screams at the others. 'The Stone Hags struck because they could smell our weakness! No more! No more wallowing! No more womanish regret! *This is a slog!*'

'The Slog of Slogs!' Sarl screeches out, chortling.

'And I am the Rule of Rules,' the Captain grates.

<hr>

Xonghis altered their course, leading them away from the Stone Hags and their flight. They left Sutadra behind them, sprawled across the muck, the broken arrow jutting like a thumb from his swelling face. Scalpers lie where they fall – such was the Rule. The cyclopean trunks were not long in obscuring him.

Sutadra had always been a mystery to Achamian – and to the others, from what he could tell. Galian sometimes made a show of asking the Kianene his opinion, then taking his silence as proof of agreement. 'See!' he would crow as the others laughed. 'Even Soot knows!'

This was the way with some men. They sealed themselves in, bricked their ears and their mouths, and spent their remaining days speaking only with their eyes – until these too became inscrutable. Many, you could wager, held chaos in their hearts, shrill and juvenile. But since ignorance is immovable, they seem immovable, imperturbable. Such is the power of silence. For all Achamian knew, Sutadra was little more than a weak-willed fool, a peevish coward behind the blind of an impassive demeanour.

But he would always remember him as strong.

None of this, however, explained Mimara's reaction. Her tears. Her subsequent silence. After the debacle in the mines of Cil-Aujas, he had assumed she would be immune to terror and violence. He tried to sound her out, but she simply looked away, blinking.

So he paced Galian and Pokwas for a time, asking about the Stone Hags. The bandits had haunted the Mop for some five years now, long enough to become the scourge of the Long Side. Pokwas absolutely despised them: preying upon one's own was an outrage for the Zeümi, apparently. Galian regarded them with the same wry contempt he took to everything. 'It takes figs to do what they do!' he cried at one point, obviously trying to bait his towering friend. 'As big and black as your own!' Achamian was inclined to agree. Hunting Sranc was one thing. Hunting *Men* who hunted Sranc was something else entirely.

They told him the story of the Stone Hag captain, Pafaras, the Mysunsai Schoolman who had assailed Cleric. According to rumour, he was a notorious Breacher, someone who failed to expedite his arcane contracts: a cardinal sin for a School of mercenaries. He had been chased into the wilds more than a decade ago.

'He was the first spitter to chase the Bounty,' Galian explained. 'Pompous. One of those fools who turns the world upside down when he finds himself at the end of the line. Arrogant unto comedy. They say he was outlawed for burning down an Imperial Custom House in one of the old camps.'

And so the Stone Hags were born. Scalper companies always vanished in skinny country, swallowed up as if they had never been. 'It's chop-chop-chop with the skinnies,' Pokwas said. 'Runners always die.' But the Stone Hags invariably left survivors, and so word of their atrocities spread and multiplied.

'More famous than the Skin Eaters,' Galian said cheerfully. 'The one and only.'

Achamian stole several glances at Mimara over the course of

their account, still puzzled by her blank face and distracted gait. Had she somehow come to know Sutadra?

'He died the death allotted to him,' he said, resuming his place at her side. 'Sutadra . . .' he added in response to her sharp look.

'Why? What makes you say that?' Her eyes gleamed with defensive tears.

The old Wizard scratched his beard and swallowed, reminded himself to take care, that it was *Mimara* he was speaking to. 'I thought you mourned his loss.'

'The *Eye*,' she snapped, her voice cracking about a bewildered fury. 'It opened. I saw . . . I saw *him* . . . I saw his-his *life* . . .'

It seemed he should have known this.

'It's his *damnation* I mourn,' she said. *The damnation you will share*, her look added.

Drusas Achamian had spent the bulk of his life knowing he was damned. Stand impotent before a fact long enough and it will begin to seem a fancy, something to be scorned out of reflex, denied out of habit. But over the years the truth would creep upon him, steal his breath with visions of Schoolmen in their thousands, shades, shrieking in endless agony. And even though he had repudiated the Mandate long ago, he still found himself whispering the first of their catechisms: '*Though you lose your soul, you shall gain the World.*'

'The damnation you want me to teach you,' he said, referring to the sorcery – the *blasphemy* – she desperately wanted to learn.

She ignored him after that – so damned mercurial! He fumed until he realized that *days* had passed since their last Gnostic lesson. Everything had seemed half-hearted after Cil-Aujas, as if sand had been packed into the joints of all the old motions. He scarce had the stomach to teach, so he simply assumed that she scarce had the stomach to learn. But now he wondered whether there was more to her sudden disinterest.

Life's harder turns had a way of overwhelming naïve passions. He found himself recalling his earlier advice to Soma. She had been given something, something she had yet to understand.

Time. She would need time to discover who she had become – or was becoming.

———

The Captain called them to a halt in what seemed a miraculous clearing. An oak had been felled in its hoary prime, leaving a blessed hole in the otherwise unbroken canopy. The company milled about, blinking at the clear blue sky, staring at the remains of the titanic oak. The tree had crashed into the arms of its equally enormous brothers and now hung propped and skeletal above the forest floor. Much of the bark had sloughed away so that it resembled an enormous bone braced by scaffolds of winding branches. Timbers had been set across several forks, creating three platforms at different heights.

'Welcome to Stump,' Pokwas said to Achamian with a curious grin.

'This place is known to you?'

'All scalpers know of this place.' With a gesture, the Sword-dancer led him up to the tree's base. A knoll rose about it, stepped and knotted with roots. The stump itself was as broad as a caste-menial's hovel but only as high as the Wizard's knees. The bulk of the severed trunk loomed just beyond, rising into the confusion of the surrounding forest.

'For the longest time,' Pokwas explained, 'the legend was that these trees were crypts, that each of them had inhaled the dead from the earth. So several years ago, when it seemed the Fringe would retreat into the Deeper Mop, Galian and I hacked this very tree to the ground. We worked in shifts for three days.'

The old Wizard scowled in camaraderie. 'I see.'

A jovial wink. 'Look what we found.'

Achamian saw it almost instantly, near the peak of the rough-hewn cone. At first he thought it had been carved – the product of some morbid scalper joke – but a second look told him otherwise. A skull. A human skull embedded in the coiled heartwood. Only a partial eye socket, a cheek, and several teeth – molars to canine – had been chiselled clear, but it was undeniably human.

A shudder passed through the old Wizard, and it seemed he heard a voice whisper, 'The heart of a great tree does not burn . . .'

Memories from a different age, a different trial.

'Some,' Pokwas was saying, 'will tell you the skinnies own the Mop.'

'What do you say?'

'That they're tenants, same as us.' He frowned and smiled, as if catching himself in the commission of some rank Three Seas folly. 'The dead own this land.'

The oblong of bare sky quickly darkened. After a sombre repast, the company spread across the three platforms built into the fallen giant, relishing what was likely a false sense of security even as they cursed the unforgiving edges that crooked their backs and poked their shoulders.

That night was a difficult one. The surrounding darkness was every bit as impenetrable as in Cil-Aujas, for one. And the threat of the Stone Hags had them 'on the sharp,' as Sarl might say. But the real problem, Achamian eventually decided, lay with the trees.

In the wild lore of witches – those scraps that Achamian had encountered, anyway – great trees were as much living souls as they were conduits of power. One hundred years to awake, the maxim went. One hundred years for the spark of sentience to catch and burn as a slow and often resentful flame. Trees begrudged the quick, the old witches believed. They hated as only the perpetually confused could hate. And when they rooted across blooded ground, their slow-creaking souls took on the shape of the souls lost. Even after a thousand years, after innumerable punitive burnings, the Thousand Temples had been unable to stamp out the ancient practice of tree-burial. Among the Ainoni, in particular, caste-noble mothers buried rather than burned their children, so they might plant a gold-leaf sycamore upon the grave – and so create a place where they could sit with the presence of their lost child . . .

Or as the Shrial Priests claimed, the diabolical simulacrum of that presence.

For his part, Achamian did not know what to believe. All he knew was that the Mop was no ordinary forest and that the encircling trees were no ordinary trees.

Crypts, Pokwas had called them.

A legion of sounds washed through the night. Sighs and sudden cracks. The endless creak and groan of innumerable limbs. The hum and whine of nocturnal insects. Eternal sounds. The longer Achamian lay sleepless, the more and more they came to resemble a language, the exchange of tidings both solemn and dire. *Listen*, they seemed to murmur, *and be warned* . . .

Men trod our roots . . . Men bearing honed iron.

According to Pokwas, nightmares were common in the Mop. 'You dream horrors,' the towering man said, his eyes waxy with unwelcome memories. 'Wild things that twist and throttle.'

The Plains of Mengedda occurred to the old Wizard, and the Dreams he had suffered marching across them with the Men of the Tusk. Could the Mop be a topos, a place where trauma had worn away the hard rind of the world? Could the trackless leagues before them be soaked in Hell? He had been forced to flee the

First Holy War some twenty years previous, so crazed had been his nightmare slumber. What would he suffer here?

Aside from his one nightmarish dream of the finding the No-God, he had dreamed of naught but the same episode since climbing free of Cil-Aujas: the High-King Celmomas giving Seswatha the map detailing the location of Ishuäl – the birthplace of Anasûrimbor Kellhus – telling him to secure it beneath the Library of Sauglish . . . In the Coffers, no less.

'Keep it, old friend. Make it your deepest secret . . .'

He lay on the crude platform, his back turned to Mimara. A warmth seeped through the exhausted weight of his body. Pondering rose out of pondering, thought out of thought. He drifted ever further from the mighty trees and their conspiracies, ever further from the ways of the wakeful. And as so often happened when he stood on the threshold of slumber, it seemed he could see, actually see, things that were no more than wisps, shreds of memory and imagination. The golden curve of the map-case. The twin Umeri inscriptions – token curses common to ancient Norsirai reliquaries – saying, *'Doom, should you find me broken.'*

And he thought, *Strange . . .*

Finding knowledge in sleep.

He stood shackled, one among the gloom of many . . .

A line of captives, wrist chained to wrist, ankle to ankle, wretched for abuse . . .

Standing encased in horror and ignorance, a file running the length of a shadowy tunnel . . .

His eyes rolled in equine panic. *What now? What-what now?*

He saw walls, which for an instant seemed golden but formed of mangled thatch, scrub and undergrowth, surging and twining to weave a black corridor about their miserable passage. He could even discern the terminus, over shoulders slouched in woe and capitulation, an opening of some kind, a clearing . . .

Bright with things he did not want to see.

His teeth were missing . . . Beaten?

Yes . . . Beaten from his skull.

'N-no,' Achamian sputtered, awareness rising like a fog within him. The trees, he realized.

Trees! Crypts, the scalpers called them . . .

'Cease!' Achamian cried. But not one of the chained shadows raised their heads in acknowledgment. 'Cease!' he raged. 'Cease, or I *shall* burn you and your kin! I will make candles of your crowns! Cut trails of ash and black through your heart!'

And somehow he knew that he screamed with the wrong lips in the wrong world.

Gagging shrieks filtered down the hall, ringing as though across iron shields.

Something blared, a sound too engulfing, too guttural to be a mere horn. Without warning the chains yanked him and the shadowy procession forward, one stumbling step toward the light . . . the *clearing*.

And though all the world's terror loomed before him, the brutalized stranger thought, *Please* . . .

Let this be the end.

Achamian found himself sitting, gripping his bony shoulders with bony fingers. His ears roared, and the blackness spun. He panted, gathering his wits and wind. Only then did the other sounds of the night creep into his hearing. The distant howl of wolves. The creak of sentience through vaulting limbs. The sound of Pokwas and his gentle snore. Sarl's mumbling growl . . .

And someone wailing without breath . . . on the platform below him. '*N-no* . . .' he heard a hitching, glutinous voice murmur in Gallish. '*Please* . . .' Then again, hissed through teeth clenched against returning waves of terror, '*Please!*'

Hameron, he realized. The one most broken by Cil-Aujas.

There was a time when Achamian had thought himself weak, when he had looked on men such as these scalpers with a kind of complicated envy. But life had continued to heap adversity upon him, and he had continued to survive, to overcome. He was every bit the man he had been, too inclined to obsess, too ready to shoulder the burden of trivial sins. But he no longer saw these ingrown habits as weaknesses. To think, he now knew, was not a failure to act.

Some souls wax in the face of horror. Others shrink, cringe, bolt for an easy life and its many cages. And some, like young Hameron, find themselves trapped between inability and the inevitable. All men cry in the dark. Those who did not were something less than men. Something dangerous. Pity welled through the old Wizard, pity for a boy who had found himself stranded on scarps too steep to climb.

Pity and guilt.

Achamian heard the whine and scuff of someone on the platform above him. He blinked against the dark. The limbs of the fallen tree forked black across the stars. The Nail of Heaven glittered above, higher on the horizon than he had ever seen it before – with his waking eyes at least. The clearing lay bare and silent about them, a swatch of wool soaked in the absolute ink of shadows at night. Mimara lay curled at his side, as beautiful as porcelain in the bluing light.

The platform above formed a ragged rectangle shot with strings of luminance between the timbers. The figure who climbed down from its edge looked a wraith, his clothing was so shredded about the edges. Starlight rippled across the unrusted splints of his hauberk.

The Captain, Achamian realized with dim horror.

The figure shimmed along the trunk, black sheets of hair swaying. He had scarcely set foot on the corner of Achamian's platform before swinging down to the next as nimble as a monkey. The two men regarded each other – for scarce a heartbeat, but it was enough. Ravenous, was all Achamian could think. There was something starved about the eyes that glared from the disgusted squint, something famished about the grin that cut the plaited beard.

The man dropped out of sight. Still staring at the point where their eyes had connected, Achamian heard him land on the platform below, heard the knife whisk from the sheath . . .

'*Sobber!*' a voice hissed.

There were three thuds in quick succession, each carrying the dread timbre of flesh.

Gasping. The choking rattle of pierced lungs. The sound of a heel scraping across barked wood – a feeble kicking.

Then nothing.

A poisonous fog seemed to fill the Wizard, steaming out from his gut into his extremities, something that at once burned and chilled. Without thinking he lay back beside Mimara, closed his eyes in the pretense of sleep. The noise of Lord Kosoter climbing back to his platform seemed scabrous thunder in his ears. It was all Achamian could do not to raise warding hands against the sound.

For several moments he simply breathed against the fact of what had happened – against the absence of the life that had been weeping below him only moments before. He had sat immobile and listened to it happen. Then he had pretended to sleep. He had sat there and watched a boy murdered in the name of his lie . . . The lie of a Wizard who had made benjuka pieces out of men.

The obsession.

Strength, Achamian told himself. *This! This is what Fate demands of you . . . If* his heart had not yet hardened to flint, he knew it would before this journey was done. You could not kill so many and still care.

Fail or succeed, he would become something less than a man. Something dangerous.

Like the Captain.

Nothing was said about the dead man in the morning. Not even Mimara dared speak, either because the atrocity was too obvious or too near. They simply gnawed and stared off in random directions while Hameron's blood dried to a rind along the bottom of his platform's timbers. Even Sarl seemed loathe to breach the silence. If any looks were exchanged, Achamian found Lord Kosoter's presence too oppressive to watch for them.

The fact that nothing was said about *anything* – including the Stone Hags and their attack – said everything: the Captain's new-found faith in the Rules did not sit well with his men. The company resumed its march through the deep forest gloom, somehow more desolate, more lost and exposed, for the absence of just two souls.

Once again they struck at a tangent to the mountains, down, so that walking at once seemed easier and harder on the knees. They skirted the banks of a swift-flowing tributary for a time, eventually crossing where it panned across boulder-chocked shallows. The elms and oaks, if anything, were even more gigantic. They threaded a makeshift path between the trunks, some of them so immense and hoary they seemed more natural formations than trees. All of their lowermost limbs were dead, shorn of bark, radial tiers stacked upon radial tiers, creating a false, skeletal canopy beneath the canopy proper. Whenever Achamian glanced up at them, they resembled black veins, networks of them, wending and forking across higher screens of sun-glowing green.

As the day wore on, the gaps between the walkers seemed to expand. This was when Pokwas and Galian, doing their best to shun Somandutta, happened to find themselves abreast Achamian and Mimara. They walked in guarded silence for a time. Pokwas softly hummed some tune – from his native Zeüm, Achamian decided, given its strange intonations.

'At this rate,' Galian finally ventured, 'it'll just be him sitting on a pile of bones by time the skinnies get to us.' The Nansur spoke without looking at anyone.

'Aye,' Pokwas agreed. '*Our* bones.'

They were not so much searching for an understanding, it seemed, as they were acknowledging one that already existed. If anything proves that Men are bred for intrigue, it is the way conspiracies require no words.

'He's gone mad,' Achamian said.

Mimara laughed – a sound the old Wizard found shocking. Ever since the Stone Hags and their abortive ambush, she had seemed bent on silent brooding. '*Gone* mad, you say?'

'No one's survived more slogs,' Galian said.

'Yes,' Pokwas snorted. 'But then no one has a pet Nonman either.'

'Things are topsy out here,' Galian replied. 'You know that. Crazy is sane. Sane is crazy.' The former Nansur Columnary fixed his canny gaze on Achamian.

'So what do we do?' Achamian asked.

Galian's eyes roamed the surrounding gloom, then clicked back. 'You tell me, Wizard . . .' There was anger in his tone, a resolution to voice hard questions. Achamian found his gaze as piercing as it was troubling – a fellow soldier's demand for honesty. 'What are the chances a company this small will make your precious Coffers? Eh?'

This was when Achamian realized that he stood *against* these men. Mad or not, Lord Kosoter showed no signs of wavering. If anything his most recent acts of madness displayed a renewed resolve. As much as Achamian hated to admit it, Hameron *had* been a liability . . .

The old Wizard found himself warding away thoughts of Kellhus and his ability to sacrifice innocents.

'We've scarce reached the Fringe,' Pokwas exclaimed, 'and we're three-quarters dead!'

The Fringe, the Wizard recalled, was what scalpers called the boundary of Sranc country.

'As I said,' Galian replied. 'At this rate.'

'Once we clear the Meorn Wilderness,' Achamian declared with as much certitude as he could muster, 'we'll be marching in the wake of the Great Ordeal. Our way will be cleared for us.'

'And the Coffers?' Galian asked with a kind of sly intensity – one that the old Wizard did not like. 'They are as you say?'

Achamian could feel Mimara watching his profile. He could only pray her look was not too revealing.

'You will return princes.'

--- ∞ ---

Cleric was the first to hear the cries. The sound was distant, small, like the wheeze at the bottom of an old man's breath. They had to look to one another to be sure others had heard it. The land was rutted with wandering slopes and gullies, yet no matter how steep the grade, the canopy remained unbroken above them, and nothing save a dim shower of gold and green filtered to the forest floor. This made determining the distance, let alone the direction, of the cries all but impossible. Then they heard a crack of thunder, too unnatural to be anything other than sorcerous. The scalpers all looked to Cleric – a reflex borne of previous slogs, Achamian imagined.

'The Mop,' the Nonman said, raking the surrounding gloom with his gaze. 'The trees play games with sounds . . .' A blink belonging to things nocturnal. 'With us.'

'Then we need to be free of them,' Achamian said. With scarce a look at the Captain, he began intoning the inconceivable and dug fingers of spoken meaning into the soft muck of the World.

Heedless of the wondering looks, he trod into the open air.

He climbed through the lower regions of the canopy, using his hands to pull himself around the dead limbs blocking his sorcerous ascent. Vertigo tipped his stomach. Even after so many years, so many Cants, his body still resented the impossibility. He threw his forearms across his face to fend lashing branches as he approached the greenery. He found himself fighting, embroiled in nets of foliage, then the veils fell away . . .

Pointed wind. Naked sunlight. He blinked against the brightness, savoured the daub of sun across his rutted cheeks.

He could scarce step above the crowns, so immense were the trees. He found himself walking around and between the stacked heights to gain a better view. On and on, as far as his old eyes could see, mighty shags of leaves, heaped and hanging, fluttering pale silver in the breeze, all the way to the horizon. Were it not for the way the leafy surface followed the summits and troughs of the underlying land, he would have likened what he saw to the slow-tossing surface of a sea.

The cries were clearer, but their direction escaped him until he glimpsed the flash of sorcery in the corner of his eye – to the *north*. A scarp of bald stone rose across the distance, rising and falling so as to resemble a young woman slumbering on her side. He mouthed a quick Cant of Scrying, and the air before him became watery with distorted images. Then he glimpsed *them* . . .

Men. Scalpers. Running through the foliage along plummet's edge.

They ran as fleet as children, a scattered file of them, flashing between screens of leaves and mighty trunks, in and out of shadow. A stand of strangler oaks dominated the waist of the escarpment, monsters who clenched the living rock of the edge and sent skeins of roots, interlocking fans of them, roping down the cliff face. This was where the scalpers clustered, throwing panicked glances back the way they had come. Several had already begun their perilous descent . . .

A second party of scalpers abruptly appeared on the edge, farther back, high on the hip. Achamian had assumed the company was being chased along the ledge, but now he realized they fled the forest deeps *behind* them – that they were running *toward* the Skin Eaters. The Men hesitated for a moment, their mouths shouting holes in their beards. Whatever pursued them, Achamian realized, was *close*, too close for them to join their comrades among the oaks. Numb and blinking, he watched them begin leaping . . . tiny human figures dropping along sheer stone faces, vanishing into the canopies below. It seemed he could feel the plummet of each tingling through his gut.

Then *they* appeared, rising from the gloom, engulfing those who had elected to stand and fight.

Sranc. Raving multitudes of them.

Shrieking white faces. A cacophony of miniature cries, human and inhuman, threaded the air. Men hacked at the white-skinned rush, stumbling, falling. One wild-haired scalper, obviously a Thunyeri, stood on a raised thumb of stone, wielding a great axe in each hand. He cut and hammered the first wave to ruin, managed to cow a second before black shafts began jutting from his unarmoured extremities. A stagger, then a misstep sent him skidding and jerking down the cliffside.

A kind of breathless remorse struck the old Wizard. This was how scalpers died, he realized. Lost. Thrown over the edge of civilization. A crazed death – not simply violent. Unwitnessed. Unmourned.

The scalpers down among the strangler oaks seemed to be making good their escape. A dozen of them were now clinging to hanging skirts of roots, daring a breakneck descent. More fugitives crowded the lip, tossing what gear they still carried below. Then one of them simply stepped out over the ledge . . . and *continued walking*, though he wobbled and almost fell. The Mysunsai Schoolman, Achamian realized. Pafaras. Too high to use the ground, the fool was trying to negotiate the arcane echo of a promontory that jutted outward about half the height of the cliffs proper. Even from this distance his Mark was clear.

The Stone Hags . . . He was watching the very Men who had tried to murder them – watching them die.

Achamian could see the Sranc high on the scarp's hip exulting in the flesh of those they had overcome. Others raced toward the remaining scalpers on the waist below, individuals dog-loping along the ledge, masses surging through the parallel deeps. Helpless, Achamian watched more suicidal leaps and another round of desperate, hopeless battles.

Then, with several stalwarts still roaring and battling, the floating Mysunsai set the cliff ledge alight. Even from such a distance his sorcerous cry tickled edges that could not be seen. A great horned head rose before the Mysunsai's slight figure, real enough for sunlight to glint from black scales yet stamped in smoke all the same: the Dragonhead, the dread mainstay of Anagogic sorcery. Golden fire spewed out over the bristling ledge, washed into the avenues between the great trees, making burning shadows of Sranc and Men alike. A chorus of screams climbed across the bowl of the sky.

The scalpers hanging from the roots below raised arms against the shower of burning debris. The Dragonhead dipped again, and more fire washed across the carpets of smoking dead. The Sranc retreated, howling and screaming, vanished into the safety of the deeper forest. There was a blinking pause. The Mysunsai struggled with his arcane footing, seemed to stumble, then simply dropped . . .

Achamian hung in indecision. Gone were the shouts, the cries. Fires smouldered along the length of the scarp's waist, trailing long plumes of black smoke. Miles of canopy swayed and rebounded in the open wind.

'We should return . . .'

The old Wizard fairly soiled his wolfskin robes, such was his shock. He whirled. Cleric hung in the air a mere span behind him, yet the old Wizard had heard nothing, sensed nothing.

'Who?' he cried before his wits returned to him. 'Who are you?'

A Mysunsai Schoolman keeping company with scalpers seemed mad enough, but a *Nonman*?

A Quya Mage?

'The Sranc. They move in force,' the ageless Ishroi said, his face white and immaculate in the high sun. The Mop swayed and tossed to the horizon beyond him. 'The others must be warned.'

Back to the gloom, to the reek of moss and earth.

Cleric began describing what they had seen, only to falter as his memories outran him. Achamian finished, doing his best to sound indifferent even though his heart still hammered.

'Fucking Hags!' Pokwas exclaimed, his eyes bright with imagined mayhem. 'Serves them. *Serves* them!'

'You're missing the point,' Galian said, staring at Achamian with solemn concentration.

'Pox is right,' Soma chimed in. 'Good riddance!' He turned, grinning.

'I say we run them,' Pokwas cried. 'Lop them and bale them.' He looked to Soma and laughed. 'Repay the favour in their own ski—!'

'*Fools!*' Lord Kosoter spat. 'Nothing will be run. Nothing!'

The black-skinned giant turned to regard his Captain with round-eyed outrage. Lord Kosoter's scrutiny, which was angry at the best of times, narrowed into a murderous squint.

'Don't you see?' Galian said, imploring. Achamian could see the warning in the look he shot his Zeümi friend, as if to say, *Too soon! You press too soon!* The question was whether the Captain had seen it as well.

Achamian glanced at Mimara and somehow knew that she had sensed it as well. New lines had been drawn, and for the first time they were being tested.

'The Hags are bigger than any company – harder,' Galian continued explaining. 'That's how they can hunt the likes of us. If those skinnies lopped *them*, then those skinnies can *lop us* . . .' He let his voice trail into the significance of what he had just said.

'If they catch our scent . . .' Xonghis said, nodding. 'Did you say the skinnies were chasing the Hags *this* way?' he asked the Wizard.

'Almost directly.'

The implication was plain. Sooner or later the Sranc would cross their trail. Sooner or later they would start hunting them. According to what Achamian had learned from the others, scent was what made the creatures at once so deadly and so vulnerable. Laying trails to gull the Sranc into ambushes was the primary way scalpers hunted. But if the skinnies caught a company's spoor before they had time to prepare . . .

'Fatwall,' the Captain said after a moment of furious meditation. 'Same as before, except we slog it day and night. If we lose them, we lose them. If not, we chop it out there!'

'Fatwall!' Sarl cackled, his gums blood red and glistening. His grins had seemed to eat up his whole face as of late. 'Latrine of the Gods!'

⁂

They skip-marched – as the scalpers called it – after that, hiked at a trot brisk enough to steal the wind for words. Once again Achamian found himself fearing his age, so exhausting was the pace. For him, the years had accumulated like dry rot: the fabric of his strength seemed healthy enough, but only so long as it wasn't pressed or stretched. By the time evening's shroud climbed across the Mop, the march had become a fog of petty miseries for him: reeling breathlessness, stitches in his side, cramps in his left thigh, needles in the back of his throat.

Dinner provided him with a brief respite. In truth, Cleric and his dispensation of Qirri was the only thing that interested him. Mimara slumped between the crooks fluting the base of the nearest trunk, propped her elbows on her knees, and laid her face in her palms. Xonghis, who seemed as tireless as Cleric or the Captain, set about preparing their measly repast: rank strips from a kill he had made three days ago. Others flopped across the soft humus, using fallen limbs and the like to support their heads.

Achamian leaned against his knees, did his best to spit away the nausea welling through him. He peered through the darkness, searching for Cleric and the Captain. For whatever reason, the two of them always retreated a short distance from the others when they made camp. He would see them, whether high on a

promontory or in a depression on the far side of a tree, Cleric
sitting, but with his head bowed in such a manner that he seemed
to be kneeling, while the Captain – who so rarely spoke otherwise – muttered over him, grinding out words that he could
never quite hear.

Just one of many mysteries.

The old Wizard hacked out the last of the fire pooled in his
lungs, then shuffled toward the two figures. Cleric crouched on
his toes, his cheek pressed against his knees while he listened
with eyes both empty and black. The last of the remaining light
seemed to linger along the bare-skin contours of his head and
arms. Aside from his leggings and the tattered remains of a ceremonial kilt, he wore only his shirt of nimil mail, its intricate links
always shining no matter how clotted with filth they became.
The Captain stood above him, discoursing in the same scarcely
audible mutter. His hair hung listless across the splinted sections
of his hauberk, ropes of black shot with grey. His pleated Ainoni
tunic, threadbare at the beginning of their expedition, fairly reeked
to look at – though Achamian could scarce smell anything above
his own rotting garb.

They both looked up, fixed him with twin gazes – one unearthly,
the other not quite sane.

A kind anxiousness seized the moment.

'Qirri . . .' Achamian said, shocked by the croak that was his
voice. 'I'm . . . I'm too old for this . . . this pace.'

Without a word, the Nonman turned to rummage through his
satchel – one of the few things any of them had managed to carry
out of Cil-Aujas. He withdrew the leather pouch, and Achamian
found himself hefting the thing in his soul, divvying pinches into
the near and distant future. Cleric unknotted the drawstring,
reached in with thumb and forefinger.

But Lord Kosoter stayed him with a wave of his hand. Another pang plucked through the old Wizard, this one coloured with intimations of panic.

'We need to speak first,' the Captain said. 'Holy Veteran to Holy Veteran.'

Achamian had the impression of a sneer over and above the contempt that generally ruled the man's expression. Something, a demoralizing wave, crashed through him. What now? Why? Why did this mad fool insist on beating complexity and confusion out of simple things?

He needed his pinch.

'By all means,' the old Wizard said stiffly.

What could be more simple than that?

The Captain regarded him with dead eyes. 'The others,' he finally asked. 'What do they say?'

Achamian did his best to match the madman's glare. 'They worry,' he admitted. 'They fear we no longer possess the strength to reach the Coffers.'

The Captain said nothing. Thanks to the Chorae beneath his armour, void and menace throbbed where his heart should have been.

'So?' Achamian asked crossly. All he wanted was his pinch! 'Does talk violate some Rule of the Slog as well?'

'Talk,' the Captain said, spitting to the left of his feet. 'I care nothing for your talk . . .' The man's smile reminded Achamian of the dead he had seen on the battlefields of the First Holy War, the way the sun would sometimes shrink the flesh of the face, drawing cadaverous grins on the fallen.

'So long as you don't weep.'

Sranc. The North means Sranc.

She fled them in Cil-Aujas, and now she flees them here, in

the Mop. On the Andiamine Heights, where everything turned on the Great Ordeal and the Second Apocalypse, scarce a day passed without hearing something about the Ancient North – so much so that she openly scoffed at its mention. She would actually say things like, 'Oh, yes, the *North* . . .' or 'Sakarpus? You don't say?' There was an absurdity to places far, a sense of insignificant people scratching meaningless earth. Let them die, she would sometimes think, whenever she heard tidings of famine in Ainon or plague in Nilnamesh. What are these people to me? These places?

A fool . . . that's what she had been. A pathetic little slit.

Their souls and their wind fortified with Qirri, the company fairly sprints across the pitching ground – even Achamian, who had been in obvious straits before Cleric and his medicinal pinch. The Nonman leads, a Surillic Point floating low and brilliant above his right brow. The illumination pulls their scissoring shadows out into the dark, alternately revealing the sinuous arch of limbs and falling into pockets too deep to reach. Where Cil-Aujas had encased them at every turn, sealed them in impenetrable stone, now it seems they race through a void, that nothing exists beyond narrow corridors of earth, trunk, and branching lattices. Nothing. No murdering Stone Hags. No obscene Sranc. No prophecies or armies or panicked nations.

Just the Skin Eaters and rushing shadows.

For no reason she can fathom, images from her old life on the Andiamine Heights plague her soul's eye. Gilded folly. The farther she travels from her mother, it seems, the more a stranger she becomes to herself. She cringes at the thought of her former self: the endless straining to stand aloof, the endless posturing, not to convince *others* – for how could they not see through her in some measure? – but to assure herself of some false moral superiority . . .

Survival, she realizes, is its own kind of wisdom. *Scalper* wisdom.

She almost snorts aloud at the thought. But running, it seems nothing could be more true. All things perish. All things are weak, execrable. Nothing more so than the conceits of the perpetually wronged.

'A smile?' someone says.

She turns and sees Soma pacing her. Caste-noble tall. Lean and broad-shouldered. With his gowns torn and twisted, he resembles the Disowned Prince that the other girls used to dream about in the brothel – the fabled customer who would rescue rather than abuse.

His dark-lashed eyes seem to laugh. There is a relentlessness to him that she does not quite trust, she realizes. A strength out of proportion to his foppish character.

'We all . . . start laughing . . . at some point . . .' he says between breaths.

She turns away, concentrates on what shreds of ground she can glimpse between shadows. On the long and hard trail, she knows, a twisted ankle means death . . .

'Knowing how to stop . . .' the man persists. 'That is . . . the real trick . . . of the slog.'

Unlike her sisters in the brothel, Mimara had despised men like Soma, men who continually apologized with grand gestures and false concerns. Men who had to smother their crimes beneath pillows of silken guilt.

She much preferred those who sinned with sincerity.

'Mimara . . .' the man begins.

She keeps her eyes averted. Soma is nothing to her, she tells herself. Just another fool who would grope her in the dark, if he could. Sticky his fingers with her peach.

The world rises into the sphere of Cleric's light, then pours into oblivion. She peers at the oncoming ground as it vanishes into the shadows of those before her. Running. There is *peace* in flight, she realizes, a kind of certainty she has never understood, though she has known it her entire life. Running from the brothel, running from the mother who abandoned her there: these are fraught with doubt and worry and regret, the heart-cracking recriminations of those who run to punish as much to flee.

But running from Sranc . . .

Her lungs are bottomless. The Qirri tingles through her thought, her limbs. She is little more than a feather, a mote, before the forces that inhabit her. And there is a thickness to it, an eroticism, being the plaything of enormities.

I have the Judging Eye!

Anasûrimbor Mimara marvels and laughs. Galian joins her, then Pokwas, then the rest of the company, and for some reason it seems right and true, laughing while fleeing Sranc through a cursed forest . . .

Then Cleric stops, his head bent as though listening. He turns to them. His face burns so bright beneath the Surillic Point that he seems an angel – an inhuman angel.

'Something comes . . .'

Then they all hear it . . . to their right, the dull scuff and drum of someone running. The air whisks to the sound of drawn weapons. Squirrel is in her hand.

A stranger staggers as much as leaps into existence. His hair is tied into a Galeoth war-knot. Blood slicks his right arm. Exhaustion has beaten his panic into resignation – you can see it on his face. And Mimara realizes that *her* flight has yet to begin. To flee, to truly run, is to throw yourself as this man has thrown himself, past effort and determination to the convulsive limit of endurance.

To run as they ran in Cil-Aujas.

The man crashes into Galian's arms, bawling out something inarticulate.

'What's he saying?' the Captain barks at Sarl.

'Skinnies!' the withered Sergeant cackles. 'The skinnies are on them!'

'Sweet Seju!' someone cries.

'Look!' Pokwas cries, peering into the blackness that had delivered the man. 'Look! Another light!'

Everyone, the newcomer included, turns in the direction the Sword-dancer indicates. At first they see nothing. Then it materializes, a floating point of white, appearing and disappearing to the rhythm of intervening obstructions. *Sorcerous* light. They glimpse figures as it nears, at least a dozen.

More men – surviving Stone Hags . . .

Even from this distance you can see their fear and haste, but something slows them . . . A litter, she realizes. They carry someone on a litter. The small mob passes behind the grand silhouette of a tree and she glimpses the man they carry – the sorcerer . . .

Galian and Pokwas are shouting. They've thrust the sobbing Stone Hag to his knees as if preparing to execute him. 'No!' Achamian is crying. 'I for—'

'He's a *Hag*!' Galian cries as if mystified, as if summary execution is a courtesy compared with what the man deserves – a scalper who hunts scalpers.

The Captain pays no attention whatsoever, instead mutters to Cleric, who peers into the blackness behind the approaching party. She watches the bald head turn, the white face smile. She sees the glint of fused teeth.

'Haaaaags!' Sarl gurgles. His eyes are squeezed into crescents above his cheeks.

The fugitives begin calling out as they approach, a cracked chorus of relief and desperate warning. Within heartbeats they blunder into the greater light of Cleric's Surillic Point, terrified and bleeding. The litter is dropped. Some skid to their knees. Others raise abject hands before the weapons brandished by the Skin Eaters.

Mimara feels someone clutch her sword arm, turns to see Soma standing grim beside her. He means to give reassurance, she knows, yet she finds herself offended all the same. With a jerk she pulls her arm free.

'No time!' someone is screeching – one of the Hags. 'No time!'

All is argument and confusion. In the gaggle of shouts and voices they fail to hear the loping approach. Now they stand rigid and peering, their ears pricked to the invisible rush. Twigs snapping. Throats grunting. Feet kicking.

Mimara is dead. She knows this absolutely. She and Soma are standing on the periphery, several paces from the commotion of the latest arrivals – from Achamian and his life-preserving Wards.

'To meee!' she hears the old Wizard cry. She hears the inside-out mutter of sorcery, sees shadows tossed, lights plumbing the barked blackness.

They come howling out of the black. Crude weapons held high and wide. Faces twisted into ravenous sneers. Streaming between trunks. Unshod feet kicking up humus.

The first flies at her like a thrown dog. She parries its crazed swing, ducks and strings the thing as it sails past her. Others follow a mere heartbeat behind. Too many blades. Too many teeth!

Then something impossible happens. Soma . . .

Somehow before her, when he had stood behind. Somehow catching each raving creature in its instant. He does not fight as scalpers fight, matching skill against ferocity, hammering strength against wild velocity. Nor does he dance as Pokwas dances, trusting ancient patterns to parse the surrounding air. No. What he does is utterly unique, a performance written for each singular moment. He throws and snaps his body. He moves in rings and lines, so fast that only inhuman screams and slumping bodies allow her to follow the thread of his attack.

Then it's over.

'*Mimara!*' Achamian is crying. She sees him fighting his way toward her.

He clutches her tight against his rank robes, but she is as numb to the smell as she is to everything else. She returns his hug out of reflex, all the while watching Soma standing above the twitching dead, watching her.

∞∞∞

She survived. He had glimpsed her stranded, had expected the worst, yet there she stood, utterly untouched. Holding her, the old Wizard did his best not to sob in relief. He blinked at the panicked burning in his eyes . . .

Exhaustion. It had to be.

They turned to the roar of the Captain, who held the prostrate Hag sorcerer upright. The infamous Pafaras. The man was at least as old as Kosoter, but he possessed nowhere near the stature and strength. He was Ketyai, though his unkempt beard lent him a barbaric, Norsirai countenance. His accent suggested Cengemis or northern Conriya. He swayed in the Captain's grip, capable of standing on his left foot only. His right was bootless – bare and purpling. His foul leggings had been sawed open to the thigh, revealing blood-sopped bandages about his shin. When Achamian had first glimpsed him on the litter, he had assumed the man was simply wounded. But now he could see the leg was broken – severely broken. The length of his right shin was only two thirds that of his left.

'*Tell me!*' Lord Kosoter roared. With his left hand, he held the man up as much by the hair as by the scruff of the neck. With his right, he held his Chorae before the ailing Schoolman's face. The fact that the Stone Hag scarcely glanced at the thing told Achamian he was already dying.

The other Hags, some eleven of them, milled in gasping shock.

They looked more like beggars than warriors. Most had shed their armour in their haste to flee, leaving them with only winter-rotted tunics and leggings. Several were thin to the point of bulbous elbows and knees. These were the men he had seen descending the cliff face, Achamian realized.

'Four clans . . . maybe more,' the swaying Hag was saying. 'Numerous . . . Very aggressive.'

'*More* than one clan?' Galian interjected. 'Are they mobbing?' The horror was plain in his voice.

A moment of silence. 'Maybe . . .' Pafaras said.

'Mobbing?' Achamian asked aloud.

'A scalper's greatest fear,' Pokwas replied in low tones. 'The skinnies usually war clan against clan, but sometimes they unite. No one knows why.'

'There was a cliff . . .' Pafaras managed between gasps. 'Some climbed down after us . . . the ones you k-killed . . . But the rest . . . backtracked . . . we think.'

'Your sort,' the Captain grated in disgust. He bent his face back to show the mayhem in his eyes. 'Come to flee the Ordeal, is that it? Come to lord your power?'

'N-no!' the man coughed.

The Captain raised his Chorae as though inspecting a jewel, then, with a kind of casual malice, slammed the thing into the Hag's mouth.

Sparking light. The whoosh of transubstantiation.

Achamian stood blinking, a burning pang where his breath should have been. He watched the salt replica of Pafaras fall backward. It thudded hard against the sponge-soft turf. The Captain crouched, hunched over the petrified sorcerer. He seemed little more than an apish shadow given the war of light and after-image in the Wizard's eyes. He pulled a knife from his boot, wedged the point in the salt cavity that had been the Hag's mouth. He raised his elbow in a prying motion, cracked off the alabaster jaw.

He retrieved his Chorae, then stood, glaring at everyone but Cleric.

'What's he doing?' Mimara whispered with alarm.

'I think he's recruiting,' the old Wizard replied, bracing himself against a deep shudder. As much as he despised Mysunsai Schoolmen as mercenaries, he could not help but feel a certain kinship with the man. Nothing instills brotherhood like the sharing of vulnerabilities. 'Witho—'

He fell silent, feeling the bite of the Captain's lunatic gaze.

Lord Kosoter prowled about the fugitive scalpers, scrutinizing them with a slaver's indifference. As miserable as the Skin Eaters appeared, the Stone Hags seemed even more wretched. Starved and wounded and absolutely terrified.

'You dogs have a *choice*,' he grated. 'You can let the *Whore* play number-sticks with your pitiful lives . . .' A rare grin, sinister for the murder in his eyes.

'Or you can let *me*.'

And with that, the Stone Hags ceased to exist, and the Skin Eaters were reborn.

Fugitive, they ran, a bubble of light falling through pillared blackness.

The trees seemed to claw at them with stationary malice, slow them with insinuations of frailty and doom. The Hags, who had no Qirri to brace them, cried out from time to time, begging them to stop, or to at least slow their pace. But no one, not even Achamian or Mimara, listened, let alone answered their pleas. This was the Slog of Slogs. The sooner they understood that, the greater their prospects for survival.

The lesson was dear. Two of them fell behind, never to be seen again.

Dawn rose in sheets of brightening green. The impenetrable black yielded to the murk of deep forest hollows. They encountered a surging river the scalpers called the Throat. It fairly raged with spring melt, the water brown with sediment, spouting white plumes where the current crashed against the boulders it had rolled down from the mountains. The sunlight it afforded was welcome, but the glimpse of smoke in the distance apparently was not. 'Fatwall,' Xonghis explained to Achamian and Mimara. 'It burns.' They were forced to follow the river's thundering course several miles before finding a crossing. Even still, they lost another of the Hags to the kicking waters.

They plunged back into the Mop and its temple gloom, the mossed ground wheezing beneath their feet. As always they found themselves craning their necks from side to side as if to catch some secret observer. Achamian need only glance at the others to know they suffered the same plaguing sense he did, as if they were the people hated, like the mummer tribes that migrated across the Three Seas.

Some fluke of the terrain delivered them back to the Throat, this time opposite the point they had first encountered it. Cleric bid them pause. 'Listen,' he called over the white roar. Achamian could hear nothing, but like the others he could see . . . On the far bank, through the screens of foliage stacked beneath the canopy's verge, he glimpsed shadows running. *Hundreds* of them, following the path they had taken downriver.

'Skinnies, boys!' Sarl cried with a gurgling laugh. '*Mobs* of them! Didn't I promise you a chopper? Eh? *Eh?*'

They continued climbing, the grades at times so steep that thighs burned and sputum flew. If the Qirri failed to whip them forward, then the glimpse of the Sranc who pursued them certainly did. Despite the profundity of their exhaustion, the sight of sunlight through the gallery ahead spurred them to a run.

They found themselves at the Mop's blinking edge, squinting across a slope of felled trees.

Fatwall. The long-dead fortress of Aenku Maimor.

Maimor was a name that Achamian had encountered only a few times in his dreams. The ancient Meori Empire had been little more than a tarp thrown across the fractious tribes of the Eastern White Norsirai, and Maimor had been one of several nails that had held it in place over the generations, a High Royal Fastness, which would house the High-King during his seasonal tour of his more rebellious provinces. Like everything else during the First Apocalypse, it had come crashing down in a hail of fire and Sranc.

The old Wizard wondered whether a Meorishman of yore would recognize what remained. The Maimor lost versus the Maimor cut from the Wilderness some two thousand years later . . .

Fatwall.

Trees had overgrown the ruined outer defences, strangler oaks mostly. The great stumps yet stood, as tall as towers, clutched like fists about the foundations. The scalpers had incorporated them in their reclamation of the fortress, using them as ad hoc bastions. Elsewhere they had raised palisades across the gaps and timber hoardings along the ruined heights. This was what smoked and burned, the flames all but invisible in direct sunlight.

The Skin Eaters lingered in the shadows, panting and peering. Something had attacked the fortress – and recently.

Achamian heard Galian murmur, '*Bad . . .*' to Pokwas, who towered at his side. Catching the old Wizard's look, the former Columnary said, 'Skinnies behind us and now skinnies before us? This is more than just a mobbing.'

'Then what is it?'

Galian shrugged in the scalper manner, as if to say, *We're all dead anyway*. Achamian thought of these men, Skin Eater and Stone Hag alike, spending season after season letting blood in these wastes. They feared for their lives, certainly, but not the same as other men feared. How could they? Coin lost to the number-sticks is far different from coin lost to thieves, even if the penury that resulted was the same.

Scalpers knew the gamble.

When nobody could discern any sign of friend or foe, the Captain instructed Cleric to scout ahead. The Nonman strode into the sky, his skin shining, his nimil hauberk gleaming. The mongrel company watched with exhausted wonder. He walked high over the slope of felled trees, receding until he was little more than a thin dash of black hanging over Maimor's ruined precincts.

Veils of smoke wafted about him, drawn to the lazy west. The Osthwai Mountains loomed in the distance beyond, clouds massing about their summits. After several moments of peering, Cleric waved them forward.

The company set across the boneyard of trees, following the zigzag of trunks like beached whales, picking their way through wickets of skeletal branches. At times it seemed a labyrinth. Open daylight offered Achamian another opportunity to appraise the newcomers, the Hags, who seemed even more mangy and forlorn. They had the watchful look of captives and the voices of slaves living in fear of a violent and mercurial master. Like the Skin Eaters, they hailed from across the Three Seas. But who they were did not seem to matter, at least not to Achamian. They were Stone Hags, bandit scalpers who killed Men to profit from Sranc. In a real sense they were no better than cannibals and perhaps even more deserving of death. But they were *human*, and in a land of mobbing Sranc, that kinship trumped all other considerations.

Any reckoning of their crimes would have to come after.

Maimor's gate had collapsed into utter ruin long, long ago. A makeshift replacement had been raised across its uneven remains, a timber palisade untouched by the fires that smouldered else-where. The doors stood open and unmarked. The company filed beneath the crude fortifications, gazing about in different direc-tions. Achamian had braced himself for the sight of slaughter within – few things were more disturbing than the aftermath of a Sranc massacre. But there was nothing. No dead. No blood. No seed.

'They've fled,' Xonghis said, referring to the Ministerial contin-gent that was supposed to be stationed here. 'The Imperials . . . This is their work. They've evacuated.'

In some places the ruins spilled into gravel, while elsewhere they seemed remarkably intact. Hanging sections of wall. Alleyways through waist-high remnants. Blocks breached the interior turf, scattered and heaped, creating innumerable slots and crevices for rats. Several more massive stumps hunched over and across the stonework, their roots splayed out in veinlike skirts – two storeys high in some places. The fundamental layout of the fortress followed the ancient sensibility, where recreating some original model trumped more practical considerations. Even though the heights formed a distended oval, the walls were rectilinear. The citadel, in contrast, was round, forming the circle-in-square pattern that Achamian immediately recognized from his dreams of ancient Kelmeol, the lost capital of the Meori Empire, when Seswatha had stayed at the fortress of Aenku Aumor.

The stone was pitted and multicoloured, here black with moulds, there frosted with white and turquoise lichens. What ornamenta-tion that survived, though plain in comparison to Cil-Aujas, seemed exceedingly elaborate by human standards. Every surface had been worked in patterns, animal totems for the most part, beasts standing, their arms articulated in humanlike poses. As numerous as the reliefs were, Achamian found only one intact representation of Meori's ancient crest: seven wolves arrayed like daisy petals about a shield.

His whole body hummed, at once scraped of all strength and steeped in giddy vigour. Qirri. Despite everything, Achamian found himself gazing and wandering as he had so many years ago, lost in thoughts of times long dead. He had always found sanctuary in ruins, freedom from the demands of his calling as well as connection with the ancient days that so tyrannized his nights. He had always felt whole in the presence of fragments.

'Akka . . .' Mimara called, her voice so like her mother's that goose-pimples climbed the old Wizard's spine. A plaintive echo.

He turned, surprised by his smile. This was her first time, he realized, her first glimpse of the ancient Norsirai and their works.

'Remarkable, isn't it? To think ruins like this are all that remain of . . .'

He trailed, realizing that she looked at the others, not the ruined pockets climbing about them.

She turned to him, her eyes pinned with indecision. 'Skin-spy . . .' she said in Ainoni.

'What?'

She blinked in momentary indecision. 'Skin-spy . . . *Somandutta* . . . He's a . . . a skin-spy.'

'What? What are you saying?' Achamian asked, struggling to collect his thoughts. She was a Princess-Imperial, which meant she had doubtless received extensive training regarding Consult skin-spies: who they were inclined to replace, how they were apt to reveal themselves.

She probably knew more about the creatures than he did.

'When the Sranc attacked,' she continued under her breath, watching the Nilnameshi caste-noble where he stood with the others. 'Earlier . . . The way he moved . . .' She turned to the

Wizard, fixed him with a look of utter feminine certainty, as serious as famine or disease. 'What he did was impossible, Akka.'

Achamian stood dumbstruck. A skin-spy?

Half-remembered passions galloped through him. The heat and misery of the First Holy War. Images of old enemies. Old terrors . . .

He turned to where the Nilnameshi stood. 'Soma . . .' he called, his voice rising thin.

'He saved my life,' she murmured beside him, obviously every bit as bewildered as he was. 'He revealed himself to save me . . .'

'Soma!' Achamian called again.

The man spared him a sideways glance before turning back to the mutter of those about him. Conger. Pokwas. Achamian blinked, suddenly feeling very feeble and very old. The Consult? Here?

The entire time.

'He revealed himself to save me . . .'

The confusion did not so much lift as part about necessity, leaving only naked alarm and the focus that came with it.

'*Somandutta!* I am speaking to you!'

The affable brown face turned to him, smiling with . . .

An Odaini Concussion Cant was the first thing to the old Wizard's lips.

Without warning, Soma leapt *over* the milling scalpers, boggling eyes and snuffing voices. He twisted mid-air with an acrobat's grace, landed with the scuttling fury of a crab. He was two-thirds across the courtyard before Achamian had finished. He leapt, sailing over the ruined wall as the Cant smashed stone and scabbed mortar.

The company stood pale and uncomprehending.

'Let that be a warning!' Sarl cackled in abject glee. He turned to the Hags as if they were unkempt cousins requiring lessons in jnanic etiquette. 'Steer clear the *peach*, lads!' He glanced at

Achamian, his eyes possessing enough of the old canniness to unnerve the old Wizard.

'What the Captain doesn't gut, the Schoolman blasts!'

——◦◦◦——

They slept in bare sunlight.

As was proper, since nothing was as it should be. Battling men instead of Sranc. Taking refuge in a fallen fortress. Finding a skin-spy in their midst, then saying nothing of it.

The Qirri had faded and, despite the longing looks, the Nonman kept his pouch hidden in his satchel. Of exhaustion's many modalities, perhaps none is so onerous as apathy, the loss of sense and desire, where you wish only to cease wishing, where mere breathing becomes a kind of thoughtless toil.

Achamian's sleep was fitful, plagued by flies – the biting kind – and worries, too numerous and inchoate to resolve into anything comprehensible. Soma. The Sranc pursuing them. The Captain. Cleric. Mimara. The dead in Cil-Aujas. His lies. Her curse . . .

And of course Kellhus . . . and Esmenet.

Fire and their lack of numbers had convinced Lord Kosoter that the outer walls were indefensible, so they had retreated to the shattered citadel. At some point the structure had collapsed inward, leaving only the great blocks of the foundation intact. Centuries of vegetation had choked the inner ruin with uneven earth so that the remaining walls, which towered the height of three men along their outer faces, climbed only chest high for those standing within. The scalpers salvaged what they could find, those few trifles left behind by the retreating 'Imperials,' as they called them. Then they climbed into the citadel's earthen gut to await the inevitable.

The subsequent vigil was as surreal as it was forlorn. While the rest dozed in what shade they could find, Cleric took a position on one of the great blocks, sitting cross-legged, gazing over the ruins below, across the field of felled trees, to the Mop's black verge. Achamian actually found comfort in the sight of him, a being who had survived who knew how many sieges and battles, back into the mists of history.

The Nonman waited until late afternoon to begin his sermon, when the air had cooled enough and the shade had grown enough to provide the possibility of real sleep. He stood on the lip and turned to regard them below, his slim and powerful figure bathed in light. The sky reached blue and infinite beyond him. Achamian found himself watching and listening the way the others watched and listened.

'Again, my brothers,' he said in impossibly deep tones. 'Again we find ourselves *stranded*, trapped in another of the World's hard places . . .'

Stranded. A word like a breath across a dying coal.

Stranded. Lost with none to grieve them. Trapped.

'Me,' the Nonman continued, letting his head sag. 'I know only that I have stood here a thousand times over a thousand years – more! This . . . this is *my* place! My *home* . . .'

When he looked up, his eyes glittered black for fury. A snarl hooked his colourless lips.

'Wreaking destruction on these perversions . . . Atoning . . . *Atoning!*'

This last word rang metallic across the stone, sent ever-dwindling echoes across the heights. Roused, several of the Skin Eaters mouthed their approval. The Stone Hags simply gaped.

'And this is *your place as well*, even if you loathe numbering your sins.'

'Yes!' Sarl coughed out over the rising clamour. His eyes were slits for his grin. 'Yes!'

That was when the inhuman baying began, a few throats

cascading into a hundred, a thousand, rising from the Mop below . . .

Sranc.

Achamian and the others leapt to their feet. They crowded the wall beneath Cleric, and to a man peered at the forest verge a half-mile or so to the south.

And saw nothing save lengthening shadows and boundaries of scrub bathed in sunlight. The inhuman chorus dissolved into a cacophony of individual shrieks and cries. Birds bolted from the canopy.

'A thousand times over a thousand years!' Cleric cried. He had turned to face the Mop, but otherwise stood as exposed as before. Achamian glimpsed his shadow falling long and slender across the ruins below.

'You live your life squatting, shitting, sweating against your women. You live your life fearing, praying, begging your gods for mercy! *Begging!*' He was ranting now, swaying and gesticulating with a kind of arrhythmic precision. The setting sun painted him with lines of crimson.

Unseen throats howled and barked across the distance – a second congregation.

'You think secrets dwell in these mean things, that truth lies in the toes you stub, the scabs you pick! Because you are small, you cry, "Revelation! Revelation *hides in the small!*"'

The black gaze fixed Achamian – lingered for a heartbeat or two.

'It does not.'

The words pinched the old Wizard deep in the gut.

'Revelation rides the back of history . . .' Cleric said, sweeping his eyes to the arc of the horizon, to the innumerable miles of wilderness. 'The *enormities*! Race . . . War . . . Faith . . . The truths that *move the future*!'

Incariol looked down across his fellow scalpers, his awestruck supplicants. Even Achamian, who had *lived* among the Cûnuroi as Seswatha, found himself staring in dread and apprehension. Only the Captain, who simply watched the Mop with grim deliberation, seemed unmoved.

'Revelation rides the back of history,' the Nonman cried, bowing his head to the failing sun. The light etched the links and panels of his nimil so that he appeared garbed in trickles of glowering fire.

'And it does not hide . . .'

Incariol. He seemed something wondrous and precarious, Ishroi and refugee both. Ages had been poured into him, and poured, overflowing his edges, diluting what he had lived, who he had been, until only the sediment of pain and crazed profundity remained.

The sun waxed against the distant peaks, hanging in reluctance – or so it seemed – sinking only when the watchers blinked. It rode the white-iron curve of a mountain for a moment, then slipped like a gold coin into high-stone pockets.

The shadow of the world rose and descended across them. Dusk.

All eyes turned to the ragged crescent of the treeline, to the grunting hush that had fallen across the distance. They saw the first Sranc creep pale and white from the bowers, like insects feeling the air . . . A savage crescendo rifled the air, punctuated by the moan of urgent horns.

Then the rush.

They came as they always came, Sranc, no different from the first naked hordes that had surged across the fields of Pir-Pahal in an age that made Far Antiquity young. They came, over the slope of felled trees, sluicing between the trunks, racing across barked backs. They came, through the palisade gate, thronging across the ancient courtyards, braiding the wall's ruined circuit with gnashing teeth and crude weapons. They came and they came, until they seemed a liquid, streaming and breaking, spitting an endless spray of arrows.

The blue and violet of the evening sky faded into oblivion, leaving only the starry dome of night. The Nail of Heaven glittered from raving eyes, gleamed from notched iron. The scalpers huddled behind what few shields they possessed, shouted curses, while Cleric and the Wizard stood upon the wall's disordered summit.

All was screaming destruction below. Monochrome madness. The Men gagged on the porcine smoke. And they watched, knowing that they witnessed something older than nations or languages, a Gnostic sorcerer and a Quya Mage, singing in impossible voices, wielding looms of incandescence in wide-swinging arms. They saw hands glow about impossible dispensations. They saw light issue from empty air. They saw bodies pitched and prised, and *burned*, burned most of all, until the ground became croaking charcoal.

Incariol had spoken true . . . It was a mighty thing, a sight worthy of the pyre.

A revelation.

CHAPTER FOUR

The Istyuli Plains

All ropes come up short if pulled long enough. All futures end in tragedy.

—CENEIAN PROVERB

And they forged counterfeits from our frame, creatures vile and obscene, who hungered only for violent congress. These beasts they loosed upon the land, where they multiplied, no matter how fierce the Ishroi who hunted them. And soon Men clamoured at our gates, begging sanctuary, for they could not contend with the creatures. 'They wear your face,' the penitents cried. 'This calamity is your issue.' But we were wroth, and turned them away, saying, 'These are not our Sons. And you are not our Brothers.'

—ISÛPHIRYAS

Spring, 20 New Imperial Year (4132 Year-of-the-Tusk), The High Istyuli

The Company of Scions picked its way across the broad back of Eärwa. The days passed without any visible sign of having travelled whatsoever. They had been charged with trolling the grasslands to the southwest with the hope of finding game they could drive back to the Army of the Middle-North. They did not see so much as a hoofprint. They could scarce feed themselves as the days passed, let alone an army.

The Parching Wind continued to blow, kneading scalps and hair with warm fingers, hissing through the dead scrub that bristled the endless plate of the Istyuli. Even though they rode with purpose, it seemed they drifted, such was the expanse surrounding them. The land was devoid of track or direction and so vast that Sorweel often found himself hunching in his saddle – cringing in the dim way of bodily fears. He was bred to the plains, to open endless skies, and even still he felt shrunken, soft, and exposed. Men tend to forget the World's true proportion, to think the paltry measure of their ambition can plumb the horizon. It is a genius of theirs. But some lands, by dint of monumental heights or sheer, stark emptiness, contradict this conceit, remind them that they are never so big as the obstacles the World might raise against them.

For watch after watch, Sorweel rode with the itch of this reminiscence floating within him. No distraction could scratch it away, not even Eskeles at his worst. To his chagrin, the rotund Schoolman insisted on practising language drills no matter who was in their vicinity – Zsoronga and Obotegwa more often than not. On one occasion, the entire company took up his chant, shouting Sheyic numerals across the plains while Sorweel gazed about in despair and disgust. Eskeles seemed to find the spectacle horribly amusing – as did Zsoronga, for that matter.

The Mandate Schoolman proved as much a source of embarrassment as irritation. His mere presence rendered Sorweel a schoolboy, though the man insisted he had been sent as much to

chaperone the entire company as to tutor the woefully ignorant
King Sorweel of Sakarpus. 'The Holy Aspect-Emperor takes his
enemies seriously,' the sorcerer said with a glib twinkle in his eye,
'and his enemies take their *children* seriously.' Sorweel found the
comment at once laughable and troubling. Eskeles, with his foppish
Three Seas beard and portly stature, not to mention his lack of
armour or weaponry, seemed almost absurdly defenceless and ineffectual – another soft-pawed leuneraal. And yet Sorweel had no
reason to doubt the truth of what he said, that he had been sent
to safeguard their company – especially after witnessing the
sorcerous destruction of Sakarpus.

At night, Sorweel could almost pretend, when he kept his eyes
hooked to the starry heavens, that none of what happened had
happened, that the droning voices belonged to his father and his
uncles, not the sons of exotic lands and distant kings. This was
the time of the Lioning, when the Saglanders planted their crops,
and when the male members of House Varalt and their boonsmen
rode out into the mountains in search of puma. Since his twelfth
summer he had accompanied his father and his uncles, and he
adored every moment of it, even though his youth chained him
to the hunting camp with his cousins. And he loved nothing more
than lying with his eyes closed, listening to his father speak before
the late-night fire, not as a king but as a man among others.

The Lioning was how he learned his father was truly funny . . .
and genuinely beloved by his men.

So he would lie with these memories, curl about their warmth.
But whenever it seemed he could believe, some dread would lurch
out of the nethers and the pretense would blow away like smoke
before gusting apprehensions. Zsoronga. The Aspect-Emperor. And
the *Mother* – the Mother most of all.

One question more than any other dominated the crowded
commons of his soul. *What? What does She want?* And it would be

the 'She' who appalled him the most, who filled his bowel with nervous water. She. *Yatwer*. The Mother of Birth . . .

He spent many sleepless watches simply hefting the vertiginous weight of this fact in his thoughts. He found it strange the way one could kneel, even pray with sobbing intensity, and yet never ponder, let alone comprehend, what lay behind the ancient names. Yatwer . . . What did that holy sound mean? The priests of the Hundred were dark and severe, every bit as harsh as the Tusk Prophets they took as their examples. They brandished the names of their Gods the way stern fathers raised whips: obedience was all they asked for, all they expected. The rest fell out of their hard readings of hard scriptures. For Sorweel, Yatwer had always been dark and nebulous, something too near the root of things, too aboriginal, not to be filled with the sense of peril belonging to sudden knives and fatal falls.

All children come to temple with a fear of smallness, which the priests then work and knead like clay, shaping it into the strange reconciliation-to-horror that is religious devotion, the sense of loving something too terrible to countenance, too hoary to embrace. When he thought about the world beyond what his eyes could see, he saw souls in their innumerable thousands with only frayed threads to hold them, dangling over the gaping black of the Outside, and the shadows moving beneath, the Gods, ancient and capricious, reptilian with indifference, with designs so old and vast that there could only be madness in the small eyes of Men.

And none were so old or so pitiless as the dread Mother of Birth.

That was what her name was: childhood terror.

To be pinched between such things! Yatwer and the Aspect-Emperor . . . Gods and Demons. Somehow he had been pulled into the world's threshing wheels, the grinding immensities – small wonder he had been so eager to escape the clamour of the Great

Ordeal! Small wonder the travelling sway of his pony, Stubborn, carried the promise of deeper escape.

He posed the question to Zsoronga and his impromptu court one night, careful to conceal the intensity of his interest. Fires were of course forbidden, so they sat side by side facing south, alternately staring into their hands and into the starry heavens: the Kings and Princes of lands cowed but not quite conquered by the New Empire, yearning for homes thrown far over the night horizon. Obotegwa sat dutifully behind them, translating when needed. If anything spurred Sorweel in his language lessons with Eskeles, it was the burden his stupidity had become for the wise old Obligate.

They had been discussing omens and portents, how more and more signs seemed to inveigh against the Aspect-Emperor – none more so than the persisting drought. Charampa, in particular, was convinced that the Anasûrimbor Dynasty's doom was imminent. 'They *overreach*! Think of their gall! How could they *not* be punished? I ask you! I ask you!'

Tzing seemed inclined to agree, and as always, no one could fathom Tinurit's opinion – or whether his smile was in fact a sneer, for that matter. Zsoronga, however, remained skeptical.

'What happens,' Sorweel finally ventured, 'if we fail the Gods simply because we don't know what they demand?'

'*Ka sircu alloman . . .*' Obotegwa began droning from behind him.

'Damnation,' Tzing replied. 'The Gods care nothing for our excuses.'

'No,' Zsoronga snapped, loud enough to pre-empt Charampa's eager reply. 'Only if we fail to properly honour our ancestors. The Heavens are like palaces, Horse-King. One does not need the *King's* permission to enter.'

'Pfah!' Charampa cried, as much to avenge his interruption as otherwise, Sorweel suspected. 'Here I thought the Zeümi were too sensible to believe that Inrithi nonsense!'

'No. It is *not* Inrithi nonsense. Honouring ancestors is far older than the Thousand Temples. You Cingi are as bad as the sausages . . .' Zsoronga turned to the young King of Sakarpus. 'Family *survives* death. Don't let this fool tell you different.'

'Yes . . .' Sorweel replied, listening far too keenly to what was said. This was what it meant to be a conquered people, a part of him realized: to turn to the foreign beliefs of foreign peoples. 'But what if your . . . your family is *damned?*'

The Successor-Prince watched him appreciatively. '*Trempe us mar—*'

'Then you must do everything in your power to discover what the Gods *do* want. *Everything.*'

Though Zsoronga was not overtly pious, Sorweel knew from previous discussions that the Zeümi had a far different way, not so much of conceiving life and death, as valuing them, a way that made them seem zealots on occasion. Even the peculiarities of Obotegwa's interpretations revealed as much: the Zeümi used two versions of the *same* word to speak of life and death, words that roughly translated into 'small life' and 'great life,' with death being the latter.

'Otherwise?'

The Successor-Prince looked at Sorweel as if he were searching for something.

Grounds for trust?

'Otherwise you are lost.'

The World seems greater in the morning, and Men smaller. The ground shrank beneath the rising sun, scalded into white blindness, so that it seemed they woke on the very edge of creation. Raised hands shielded eyes. Broke-back grasses cast shadows like black wire.

Sorweel had grown up in this country; its imprint lay deep in his soul, so deep that simply looking at it braced him, like legs and a wide stance for his soul. Even still, it dizzied him to think how far they had ridden beyond the Pale. He had been educated, of course, and so knew the Pale for what it was: the northern terminus of Sakarpic power, and not the point where waking reality tipped into nightmares. But the superstitions of the rabble had a way of steaming upward, of soaking the more worldly understanding of the nobility. Despite his tutors, the Pale remained a kind of *moral* boundary in his imagination, the line that marked the fading of the good and the gathering of what was evil. Enough to catch his breath when he thought of the miles between him and his holy city. For a company as small as theirs to ride the emptiness as they did, a nagging part of him insisted, was nothing short of madness.

If anything silenced these worries, it was his growing respect for Captain Harnilas. He had not thought much of Old Harni at first. Like many other Scions, he had tried to detest the man, if not for who he was, then for what he represented. Diminishing others is ever the way men raise themselves, and the might of the Aspect-Emperor was such, the glory and the competence of the Kidruhil so obvious, that petty targets like Harnilas seemed to be the only ones remaining.

But the Captain was nothing if not dogged in his warlike wisdom. Gruff. Bearded in manner, even though he shaved like so many of his Nansur countrymen. His scars picked up where his wrinkles left off so that his face seemed tattooed with different sigils depending on the angle and intensity of the light. He so obviously cared so little for what his wards thought of him that they could not but esteem him.

'In Zeüm,' Zsoronga once said, 'we call men like him *nukbaru*, masons . . . stone-hewers . . .' After Obotegwa finished translating, the Successor-Prince nodded toward the head of their small column. 'Our Captain.'

When Sorweel asked him why, Zsoronga smiled and said, 'Because to hew stone you must be stronger than stone.'

'Or smarter,' Eskeles had added.

Riding as they did had a way of nursing and smothering conversations. Sometimes they chattered as loudly as wives filing from Temple. Sometimes they rode in desert silence, with only the arrhythmic gait of their ponies to punctuate the perpetual wind. Usually their talk would be momentary, sparking here, fading there, as though a single animate spirit drifted through them all, drawing thought into voice one by one.

The morning of their tenth day of ranging, they embarked in silence and continued riding that way.

They sighted the elk trail before noon, a mottled water-stain across the linen distances, as broad as a valley. They did not reach it until early afternoon, a thin file of cavalrymen picking their way across land battered by a thousand thousand hoofs, a trail as great as any of the World's enormities.

Sorweel cursed himself for a fool, such was his relief.

The following day began the same as any other. The elk trail continued its southern arc, resembling the imprint of a curved sword left overlong in the grass, only writ across the entire landscape. The Scions filed through its great trampled heart, silent save for the clank of gear and the warbling of one or two desultory conversations. Even Charampa seemed disinclined to speak. Sorweel rocked in his saddle like the others, listening to the sweep of wind and the low ghost noises it made when it caught his ears.

The first shouts came from the head of the column: a pair of vultures had been sighted to their left. The entire company rode perched in their saddles, fingers pointing, eyes scanning the wandering line of the eastern horizon. The plain seemed to curl and fold more and more as it diminished in the haze, like a mangy carpet kicked against a wall. The sky rose high and endless above.

'We've found our herd!' Obotegwa cried, translating Zsoronga's jubilant words.

Sorweel blinked and squinted, his face angled against the sun's glare. He found and tracked the two floating specks – even glimpsed the bar of wings riding faraway winds. Before he knew what he was doing, he spurred Stubborn into a gallop. The pony leapt into its stride with almost doglike exuberance. The Scions watched with curiosity and amusement as he pounded to the fore of the line. Captain Harnilas was already scowling at him when he reined Stubborn to a reluctant halt.

'*Merus pah veuta je ghasam!*' the old cavalryman shouted.

'Captain!' Sorweel cried in Sheyic. With a sweeping gesture he directed the man's grizzled attention toward the horizon. Then as emphatically as he could he spoke the one word that transcended all the languages of Men.

'Sranc.'

He matched the officer's hard gaze, noticing, not for the first time, the scar on his left cheek, burn-puckered as though he had once shed a fiery tear. For the first time he saw the small soapstone figurines hanging about his neck: three children joined at the hands and feet, chipping across his cuirass. A strange sense of recognition welled through the young King, a realization that Harnilas, despite his exotic complexion and furious brown eyes, was not so different than his father's boonsmen, that he chambered his heart, as so many warlike men did, to keep his sense clear of his compassion. Harnilas loved, as all men loved, in the cracks and crevices of a warring world.

Eskeles finally trotted into earshot, gasping as though his pony had ridden him instead of otherwise. Sorweel turned to the Schoolman. 'Tell him to study those birds carefully. Tell him that they're *storks* – the most holy of birds. Tell him that storks *only follow Sranc* on the plain.'

Eskeles frowned in his thoughtful way, then relayed the information to Captain Harnilas. Aside from a quick glance at the sorcerer he continued to watch Sorweel intently.

'Sranc,' the Captain repeated. The leathery face turned to squint at the specks floating in the distant sky.

Sorweel pursed his lips and nodded.

'The bird is holy.'

'Your tutor argues that the Sranc should be left to him,' old Obotegwa explained, 'so that no lives need be lost. Harnilas disagrees. He thinks the Scions need . . . practice, even at the cost of lives. Better to begin with an easy blooding, he says, than a hard one.'

They had gradually closed on the high-circling storks over the course of the afternoon, taking care to remain upwind and to use the creases in the broken plain to keep their approach hidden. If Sorweel had entertained any fears regarding Harnilas, they had been allayed by the patient sensibility of his tactics and the thoughtless ease with which he exercised his command. After ascertaining the direction of their march, he angled their pursuit to better intercept their trail: they now knew they followed a warband of some three hundred – a number too small to suggest a migrating clan. They had almost been sighted twice now, crossing the crest of some knoll at the same time as their inhuman quarry, but they had managed to close within a mile of the warband. The sun had smouldered into evening, scorching the western horizon gold and crimson. Now the Company of Scions sheltered in a trough of cool shadow, watching Eskeles argue with their Captain.

The afternoon had been tense, certainly, but far more thrilling than anything else. With the possible exception of the Scylvendi, Tinurit, the Scions rode with grins whipped across their face. A kind of glee had possessed them, one that sparked low snorts of laughter whenever glances were exchanged, childlike in that sneaking way, murderous in its ultimate intent. For his own part, Sorweel felt none of the fear, not a whisper of the cowardice that he had thought would unman him. A limb-gripping eagerness filled him instead, a will to ride down and kill. Even his pony, Stubborn, seemed to sense the impending violence – and to welcome it.

Of course Eskeles was intent on ruining everything. *Blasphemer*, Sorweel found himself thinking.

Sorweel had no real idea how much influence his tutor wielded; Mandate Schoolmen were rumoured to be more powerful than Judges, but whether this extended to the field, or to Kidruhil Companies particularly, he did not know. He could only hope that their surly old Captain prevailed. Harnilas did not strike him as a particularly political man – which was probably why he had been given the Scions in the first place. Sorweel's father had told him several times that intriguing killed far more men on the field than otherwise.

The two middle-aged men waved hands and shouted for several moments more, then Eskeles apparently said something either too clever or too impertinent. Harnilas stood in his stirrups and began thundering at the sorcerer, who fairly wilted before the savage display. Sorweel found himself laughing with Zsoronga and Obotegwa.

'Fool!' Eskeles cried in corpulent exasperation as he rejoined them. 'The man is a fool!'

'Practice-practice,' Sorweel sang, mimicking the tone the Schoolman took whenever he groaned about language drills. 'You're the one always saying the easy way is never the proper way.'

Zsoronga chortled at Obotegwa's translation. The Schoolman glared at Sorweel for an angry moment, then collected himself with a harried smile. He looked up to the storks circling high above a crest that bowled the earth before them. Their white spans carried sunset gold. 'I pray you prove me right, my King. I really do.'

A chill seemed to creep into the shadow.

Once decided, their pursuit became determined. At Harnilas's gestured command they fell into wedge formation, rode the rising and falling knolls like a loose-jointed raft on ocean swells. They trotted to prevent winding their horses, a pace that allowed for more than a little excited chatter, though the anxiousness of cresting each rise knocked them into gazing silence.

'They don't move,' Zsoronga said through Obotegwa. 'Why? Have they seen us?'

'Could be,' Sorweel replied, fighting against the breathlessness that pinched his voice. 'Or they could be resting . . . Sranc prefer the night. Sun exhausts them.'

'Then why not use the high ground, where they can keep watch?'

'The sun,' he repeated, speaking through a pang of sudden apprehension. 'They hate the sun.'

'And we hate the night . . . which is why we *double* our watches.'

The Sakarpi King nodded. 'But no Man has walked this land for thousands of years, remember. Why should they keep watch for myths and legends?'

His earlier eagerness seemed to slip out of him, plummet through the soles of his boots. They climbed a slope, riding into their shadows at an angle to the dust that pealed away from them. Everywhere he looked he saw ground, and yet it seemed he rode the lip of a perilous chasm. Vertigo leaned out from him, threatened to pull him from his saddle. There was no certainty, he realized. Anything could happen on the field of war.

Anything.

A keening noise climbed into the earthen thunder of their advance, high and ragged, as though cutting the throats that were its crying origin. The storks seemed to hang in the air directly above them, lines of virgin white etched in the sun. The Scions swung through the shadow of the shallow basin, scraping through a haze of brush and dead grasses, then raced upward. The knoll's crown met their rush. The sun broke across their backs, crimson flashing from silver and crimson.

The shrieking chorus collapsed into squeals and yammering alarums.

The Sranc mobbed the spaces below them, a putrid congregation scattered across the gap between sunlit summits. Thin white arms yanked at weapons. Faces collapsed into squints of fury. Clan standards – human skulls haired with bison hide – jerked and wagged.

Sorweel did not need to look down the line of his fellows to know their faces. Disbelief is ever the door between young men and murder.

An impossible moment followed, one Sorweel had heard various Horselords mention from time to time. The line of lancers, their helms and mailed sleeves gleaming in the sunlight, stood motionless save for the most anxious of ponies. The Sranc band roiled with shriek and gesture but likewise did not move. The two parties simply regarded each other, not out of hesitation and certainly not for calculation's sake. It was more a warlike equipoise, as if the encounter were a coin spinning in the air, needing only the hard ground of murder to judge.

Sorweel lifted himself forward to whisper in Stubborn's ear: '*One and one are one . . .*'

And they were off, shouting the war cries of a dozen heathen nations, a thundering, trampling line. A flying rake of lance-points. From the stories his father's boonsmen told him, he had expected each heartbeat to last an age, but in fact everything happened fast – far too fast to be terrifying, or exhilarating, or anything, for that matter. One heartbeat, the Sranc were a tangle of sprinting forms before him, skin white, armour black with filth, iron weapons wild in the air. The next heartbeat, he was crashing through them like something thrown. His lance glanced off the corner of a shield, skewered the throat of a wagging creature he had not even seen, let alone intended to kill. The heartbeat after, he was drawing his sword, reining Stubborn about, and hacking. Shrieks and cries and shouts pealed skyward. The dreadful clatter of war.

Seven, maybe eight, threshing heartbeats passed. He wondered at the ease with which sword points punctured faces – no different from practice melons. Otherwise, he *was* his blade, his horse, dancing between the jabber of pale shadows, raining ruin and destruction. Purple blood jetted, flew black across the dead scrub.

Then it was just the low dust, the clutch of the maimed and the dying, and the cacophony had moved beyond him – continued moving.

He spurred Stubborn in pursuit, glimpsed Zsoronga grinning from a passing saddle.

The surviving Sranc ran before an uneven wave of horsemen, a kind of jerking scramble. Sorweel seized a lance jutting from the ground as he galloped past, leaned into Stubborn's exertions. He quickly overtook the laggards among the Scions, soon found himself in the pounding fore of the pursuit. A crazed grin seized his lips. He howled his people's ancient war cry, the lung-cracking sound that had marked innumerable such pursuits through the ages.

The Sranc ran, bolting through dead scrub like wolverines, opening the interval between them and the slowest of the Scions – only the quickest of the quick overtook them.

There was joy in the race. His legs and hips had become mere extensions of Stubborn's leaping gallop The ground pouring away like water. His hand gripping his lance, loosely as he had been taught from childhood, floating, tingling as if he held a thunderbolt. He was a Son of Sakarpus, a Horselord, and this – this! – was his calling. He struck with a viciousness that seemed holy for its thoughtlessness. One in the neck, rolling limbs akimbo into caged bracken. Another in the heel, left limp-running, mewling like a knifed cat. Anything he overran he instantly forgot, knowing that the pounding wall behind him would eat them up.

They scattered and he followed – there was no hiding beneath the shining plains sun. They bent their white faces back to him as he closed, black eyes glittering, features pinched ancient with fear and fury. Their limbs little more than a flutter of shadows in the grass-thatched dust. They coughed. They screamed as they spun falling.

There was joy in the race. Ecstasy in the kill.

One and one were one.

Their victory was complete. Among the Scions, three were fallen, and some nine others were wounded, including Charampa, who took a spear in his thigh. Despite the dark looks thrown by Eskeles, Old Harni was obviously satisfied with his young wards, perhaps even proud of them. Sorweel had witnessed death enough during his city's fall. He knew what it meant to watch familiar faces spit their final breath. But for the first time he experienced the jarring of elation and regret that comes with *triumph* on the field. For the first time he understood the contradiction that blackens the heart of all martial glory.

His fellows cheered him, clapped his back and shoulders. Zsoronga even embraced him, a kind of madness cackling in his wide green eyes. Stunned, Sorweel climbed the hump of the nearest knoll, stared out across the plains. The sun lay on the horizon, burning crimson through a band of violet, dousing the innumerable crests and low summits in pale orange. He stood and breathed. He thought of his ancient fathers wandering as he did across these lands – killing those who did not belong. He thought of the way his boots rooted him to the earth.

The darkening sky was so broad that it seemed to spin with slow vertigo. The Nail of Heaven glittered.

And the World towered beneath.

That night Harnilas indulged them, knowing that they were boys drunk on the deeds of men. The last of the Ainoni rum was uncorked, and each of them was granted two burning swallows.

They took one of the surviving abominations and staked it to the turf. At first scruples held them back, for among the Scions were more than a few youths of gentle breeding. They would do no more than kick the shrieking creature. Disgusted, Sorweel finally knelt over the Sranc's white head and put out one of its eyes. Some among the Scions hooped and cheered, but more cried out in consternation, even outrage, saying that such torture was a crime against jnan – what they called their effeminate and obscure laws of conduct.

The young King of Sakarpus turned to his fellows in disbelief. The creature thrashed across the ground immediately behind him. Captain Harnilas strode to his side, and all fell silent in expectation.

'Tell them,' he said to Sorweel, speaking slowly so that he might understand. 'Explain their foolishness to them.'

More than eighty faces watched, a moonlit congregation. Sorweel swallowed, glanced at Obotegwa, who simply nodded and stepped to his side . . .

'They-they come . . .' he began, only to falter at the sound of Eskeles translating in Obotegwa's stead. 'They come in winter, mostly, especially when the ground freezes too hard for them to scrounge the grubs that are their staple. Sometimes in single clans. Sometimes in shrieking hordes. The Towers of the Pale are strong for this reason, and the Horselords have become reavers beyond compare. But every year at least one Tower is overcome. At least one. The Men are slaughtered, mostly. But the women – and the children particularly – are taken for sport. Sometimes we find their severed heads nailed to doors and walls. Little girls. Little boys . . . Infants. We never find them whole. And their blood is always . . . thrust from them. Instead of crimson the dead are smeared black . . . black' – and his voice broke upon this word – 'with . . . seed . . .'

Sorweel stopped, his face flushed, his fingers trembling. In his fourteenth winter, his father had brought him north on a punitive expedition to see their ancient and implacable enemy first-hand. Hoping to find supplies and accommodation, they had come to a Tower called Grojehald, only to find it sacked. The horrors he had seen there haunted his dreams still.

'We could torment a thousand of these creatures for a thousand years,' his father had told him that night, 'and we would have repaid but a droplet of the anguish they have visited upon us.'

He repeated these words now.

Sorweel was not accustomed to addressing men in numbers, and so he took the silence that followed as a kind of condemnation. When Eskeles continued speaking, he simply assumed the

Schoolman tried to undo his foolishness. Then Obotegwa, translating the sorcerer, muttered, 'King Sorweel speaks as eloquently as he speaks true.' Sorweel was shocked to find he could follow much of what the Mandate Schoolman said.

'*Shus shara kum* . . .'

'These are beasts without souls. They are flesh *without spirit*, obscenities like no other. Each of them is a pit, a hole in the very fundament. Where we possess feelings, where we love and hate and weep, they are void! Cut them. Rend them. Burn and drown them. You can sooner wrong dirt than sin against these vile abominations!'

As strong as these words sounded, Sorweel noticed that most of the Scions continued to regard *him* rather than the Schoolman, and he realized that what he had thought was condemnation was in fact something entirely different.

Respect. Admiration, even.

Only Zsoronga seemed to watch him with troubled eyes.

The sport began in earnest after that. The Mannish laughter was as shrill as the inhuman screams were crazed.

What was left twitched and glistened in the blood-sodden grasses.

They broke camp discussing the strange absence of vultures, then rode out into the broad light of the plains. To a soul they discussed the previous day's battle, boasting of kills, comparing nicks, and laughing at gaffes. The Scions thought themselves veterans, but their talk remained that of boys. Easy victories, as a Horselord would say, grow no beards.

They recovered the elk trail without difficulty, followed it beneath an afternoon sun rendered small for the gaping horizon. They caught the reek on the wind before seeing anything. It was a *wide* smell, a rot that reached as far as the air. The vista rose into view in inexorable stages, the far corners, swathes of dun and black and bone, buttressing the line of the horizon, then the welter of nearer regions, too still, too silent. The Company of Scions assembled along the crest of a low ridge, eighty-seven of them abreast, the men slack-faced, the ponies nodding and stamping in equine anxiousness. Their Kidruhil standard, the Black Circumfix and Golden Horse, flapped and waved against endless blue. Aside from coughs and curses, none possessed the will to speak.

Carcasses. *Fields* of them, dead elk, soaking the dust black.

Vultures hunched like priests beneath cowls or raised wings in imperious accusation. In any given heartbeat, dozens could be seen dropping from the skies across points near and miles away. Their cries rose hoarse through a great buzzing hum: flies, so many they appeared as living smoke across the distances.

An elk carcass lay gutted not far from Sorweel, its gut strewn like rotted clothes. Several feet beyond lay a clutch of three more, ribs cracked out from articulated spines. Beyond that lay another, and yet another, ribs opened like gigantic traps, on and on and on, a thousand circles of gore across the wasted pasture.

Captain Harnilas called out, and the Company of Scions descended the slope in formation, opening only to skirt the carcasses. The nearest vultures screeched at their approach, a kind of reptilian outrage, then took to the wind. Sorweel watched them anxiously, knowing that others could use their ascent to track their progress from miles away.

'What kind of madness is this?' Zsoronga murmured from his side. Sorweel did not need Eskeles's translation to understand.

'Sranc,' the Schoolman said, his voice curiously tight. 'A Hording . . .'

Sorweel glimpsed the creatures in his soul's eye, hacking and tearing, stabbing the beasts still living, then coupling with shining wounds. A shrieking landscape of them.

'In ancient days,' his Mandate tutor continued, 'before the coming of the No-God, the Sranc would continually retreat before hosts too powerful for any one clan to assault. Back and back, clan heaped upon clan. Until their hunger forced them to take game, until their numbers blackened the very earth . . .'

'And then?' Sorweel asked.

'They attacked.'

'So all this time . . .'

A grim nod. 'The clans have been driven before the Great Ordeal and its rumour, accumulating . . . Like water before the prow of a boat . . .'

'Hording . . .' Sorweel repeated, weighing the term on his tongue. 'Does Harni know about this?'

'We shall know soon enough,' the corpulent Schoolman said. Without further word, he spurred his overtaxed pony to overtake the Kidruhil Captain.

Sorweel allowed his gaze to range across the ground before the Company, saw strings of blood flung across the scree, welters of cracked bone, and skulls, some with the eyes sucked out, others with cheeks chewed away to the snout. No matter where he looked he saw another gory circle.

The largest Sranc clans the Horselords battled rarely numbered more than several hundred. Sometimes a particularly cruel and cunning Sranc chieftain would enslave his neighbours and open warfare would range across the Pale. And the legends were littered with stories of Sranc rising in nations and overcoming the Outermost Holds. Sakarpus itself had been besieged five times since the days of the Ruiner.

But this . . . slaughter.

Only some greater power could have accomplished this.

Meat sweated in open sunlight. Flies steamed about the scrub and grasses. Cartilage gleamed where not chapped with gore. The stink was raw unto gagging.

'The war is real,' he said with dull wonder. 'The Aspect-Emperor . . . His war *is real*.'

'Perhaps . . .' Zsoronga said after listening to Obotegwa's translation. 'But are his reasons?'

———∞———

'Otherwise you are utterly lost . . .'

So Zsoronga had said.

Despite the clamour and triumph of the past days, these words continued to sink and to surface through the young King's turbulent soul. He had no reason to doubt them. For all his youth, Zsoronga possessed what the Sakarpi called *thil*, salt.

The fact was, Yatwer, the patroness of the weak and dispossessed, had chosen him, even though he had been trothed to her brother Gilgaöl since his fifth summer, even though he possessed the blood of warriors – even though he was what the Yatwerians called *weryild*, a Taker, a thief by virtue of his bones. Railing against the absurdity, let alone the *shame*, of her choice did nothing but prove him worthy of the humiliation. He had been chosen. Now he only needed to know why.

Otherwise . . .

Porsparian was the obvious answer. It seemed clear now that the slave was a secret priest of some kind. Sorweel had always thought that only women attended to the worldly interests of the Ur-Mother, but he scarce knew anything of the low and mean peoples of his own nation, let alone the ways of those a world away. The more he considered it, the more he felt a fool for not realizing as much earlier. Porsparian had come to him bearing this terrible burden. *He* was the one to tell him what that burden was and whither it should be borne.

That was, if Sorweel could learn to wrap his tongue and ears around Sheyic.

That night, while the others slept, the young King of Sakarpus rolled to his side on his sleeping mat and, in the way anxious bodies choose small tasks of their own volition, started picking at the grasses before him. Porsparian – his cheeks rutted like withered apples, his eyes like wet chips of obsidian – floated beneath his soul's eye the entire time, spitting fire into his palm, rubbing mud into his cheeks . . .

Only when he had bared a small patch of earth did Sorweel realize what he was doing: moulding the dread Mother's face the way Porsparian had the day the Aspect-Emperor had declared him a Believer-King. It seemed a kind of crazed game, one of those acts that send the intellect laughing even as the stomach quails.

He could not pinch and mould the way the Shigeki slave had because the earth was so dry, so he raised the cheeks by cupping dust beneath his palms, sculpted the brow and nose with a trembling fingertip. He held his breath clutched and shallow, lest he mar his creation with an errant exhalation. He fussed over the work, even used the edge of his fingernail to render details. It was a numb and loving labour. When he was finished, he rested his head in the crook of his arm and gazed at the thing's shadowy profile, trying to blink away the deranged impossibility of it. For a mad moment, it seemed the whole of the World, all the obdurate miles he had travelled, multiplied on and on in every direction, was but the limbless body of the face before him.

King Harweel's face.

Sorweel hugged his shoulders with a wrestler's fury, grappled with the sobs that kicked through him. 'Father?' he cried on a murmur.

'*Son . . .*' the earthen lips croaked in reply.

He felt himself bend back . . . as if he were a bow drawn by otherworldly hands.

'*Water,*' the image coughed on a small cloud of dust, '*climbs the prow . . .*'

Eskeles's words?

Sorweel raised a crazed fist, dashed the face into the combed grasses.

He neither slept nor lay awake.

He waited in the in-between.

'*So all this time?*' he heard himself ask Eskeles.

'*The clans have been driven before the Great Ordeal and its rumour, accumulating . . . Like water before the prow of a boat . . .*'

'*Hording . . .*'

Sorweel had seen few boats in his life: fishing hulls, of course, and the famed river galley at Unterpa. He understood the significance of the sorcerer's description.

The problem was that the Scions tracked game to the southwest of the Great Ordeal.

So very far from the prow.

He bided his time in turmoil. His body had lost its instinct for breathing, so he drew air in its stead. Never did the sun seem so long in climbing.

'With all due respect, my King . . .' the sorcerer said with a waking sneer. 'Kindly go fuck your elbows.'

Eskeles was one of those men who never learned to bridle their temper simply because it was so rare. The sun had yet to breach the desolate line of the east, but the sky was brightening over the scattered sleepers. The sentries watched with frowning curiosity, as did several of the horses. Harnilas was awake as well, but Sorweel did not trust his Sheyic enough to go to him directly.

'The Sranc war-party we destroyed,' Sorweel insisted. 'It had *no sentries posted.*'

'Please, boy,' the corpulent man said. He rolled his bulk away from the young King. 'Let me get back to my nightmares.'

'It was *alone*, Eskeles. Don't you see?'

He raised his puffy face to blink at him over his shoulder. 'What are you saying?'

'We lie to the southwest of the Great Ordeal . . . What kind of water piles *behind* a boat?'

The Schoolman stared at him for a blinking, beard-scratching moment, then with a groan rolled onto his rump. Sorweel helped haul him to his cursing feet and together they went to Harnilas, who was already ministering to his pony. Eskeles began by apologizing for Sorweel, something the young King had no patience for, especially when he could scarce understand what was being said.

'We're tracking an *army*!' he cried.

Both men looked to him in alarm. Harnilas glanced at Eskeles for a translation, which the Schoolman provided with scarce a glance in the Captain's direction. 'What makes you say that?' he asked Sorweel on the same breath.

'These Sranc, the ones who cut down the elk, they are being *driven.*'

'How could you know that?'

'We know this is no Hording,' the young King replied, breathing deep to harness his thoughts, which had become tangled for a long night of horror and brooding. 'The Sranc, as you said, are even now fleeing *before* the Great Ordeal, clan bumping into clan, gathering into a hor—'

'So?' Eskeles snapped.

'Think about it,' he said. 'If you were *the Consult* . . . You would know about the Hording, would you not?'

'More than any living,' the Schoolman admitted, his voice taut with alarm. For Sorweel, the word *Consult* as yet possessed little meaning beyond the fear it sparked in the eyes of the Inrithi. But after the incident with the skin-spy in the Umbilicus, he had found it increasingly difficult to dismiss them as figments of the Aspect-Emperor's madness. As with so many other things.

'So they would know not only that the Great Ordeal will be attacked, but *when* as well . . .'

'Very possibly,' Eskeles said.

Sorweel thought of his father, of all the times he had heard him reason with his subjects, let alone his men. *'To be a worthy King,'* Harweel had once told him, *'is to lead, not to command.'* And he understood that all the bickering, all the discourse he had considered wasted breath, 'tongue-measuring,' was in fact *central* to kingship.

'Look,' he said. 'We all know this expedition is a farce, that Kayûtas sent us to patrol a rear flank that would never have been patrolled otherwise simply because we are the Scions – the sons of his father's enemies. We cover territory that a host would otherwise be blind to, territory a cunning enemy could exploit. While patrolling this imaginary flank, we stumble across a war-party with no sentries posted, oblivious enough to find respite in the shade. In other words, we find *proof* that for this corner of the Istyuli, at least, the Great Ordeal does not exist . . .'

He trailed to let the Schoolmen complete his translation.

'Then we find the slaughtered elk, something you say Sranc only do when Hording – which we know cannot be the case . . .'

Sorweel hesitated, looked from man to man, the stern old veteran and the square-bearded sorcerer.

'You have our attention, my King,' Eskeles said.

'All I have are guesses . . .'

'And we are dutifully astounded.'

Sorweel looked out over the milling ponies to the vast elk trail, which was little more than the mottling of darker greys across the predawn landscape. Somewhere . . . Out there.

'My guess,' he said, reluctantly turning back to the two men, 'is that we've stumbled across some kind of Consult army, one that—' He paused to gulp air and swallow. 'One that *shadows* the Great Ordeal using the elk both to feed itself and to conceal their trail. My guess is they plan to wait until the Great Ordeal comes against the Hording . . .' He swallowed and nodded as if suddenly recalling some adolescent insecurity. He flinched from an image of his father, speaking dust from the dirt. 'Then . . . then attack the host from behind . . . But . . .'

'But what?' Eskeles asked.

'But I'm not sure how this could be possible. The Sranc, they . . .'

Eskeles and Harnilas exchanged a worried glance. The Captain looked up, gazed at the young King in the fixed manner officers use to humble subordinates. Without breaking eye contact, he said, '*Aethum souti sal meretten,*' to the Mandate Schoolman beside him. Then he continued in Sheyic spoken slowly enough for Sorweel to follow. 'So. What would *you* do?'

The young King of Sakarpus shrugged. 'Ride hard for the Aspect-Emperor.'

The old officer smiled and nodded, slapped him on the shoulder before bawling for camp to be broken.

'So it *is* possible?' Sorweel asked Eskeles, who remained beside him, watching with a strange, almost fatherly gleam in his eyes. 'The Sranc could be doing what I think?'

The Schoolman crushed his beard into his barrel chest, nodding. 'In ancient times, before the coming of the No-God, the Consult would harness the Sranc, chain them into great assemblies that the Ancient Norsirai called Yokes . . .' He paused, blinking as though to pinch away unwanted memories. 'They would drive them the way we drive slaves in the Three Seas, starve them until their hungers reached a fever pitch. Then, when they reached a position where the Sranc could smell Mannish blood on the wind, they would strike the chains and let them run.'

Something within the Sakarpi King, a binding of fear and hope, slumped in relief. He almost reeled for exhaustion, as if alarm alone had sustained him through all the sleepless watches.

The Schoolman steadied him with a hand on his shoulder.

'My King?'

Sorweel shook his head to dismiss the sorcerer's worry. He looked out across the morning plain: Sakarpus could be directly behind him instead of weeks away, for all the difference the horizon made.

'The Captain . . .' he said, returning the sorcerer's gaze. 'What did he say to you just then?'

'That you possess the gifts of a great king,' Eskeles replied, squeezing his shoulder the way his father had, whenever he took pride in his son's accomplishments.

Gifts? something within him wanted to cry. *No . . .*

Only things that the dirt had told him.

CHAPTER FIVE

The Western Three Seas

As death is the sum of all harms, so is murder the sum of all sins.

—CANTICLES 18:9, THE CHRONICLE OF THE TUSK

The world has its own ways, sockets so deep that not even the Gods can dislodge them. No urn is so cracked as Fate.

—ASANSIUS, THE LIMPING PILGRIM

Late Spring, 20 New Imperial Year (4132 Year-of-the-Tusk), somewhere south of Gielgath . . .

That which comes after determines what comes before – in this World.

The Gift-of-Yatwer walked across ordained ground. His skin did not burn, thanks to the swarthiness he had purchased with his seed. His feet did not blister, thanks to the calluses he had purchased with his youth. But he grew weary as other men grew weary, for like them, he was a thing of flesh and blood. But he always tired when he should grow tired. And his every slumber delivered him to the perfect instant of waking. Once to the sound of lutes and to the generosity of travelling mummers. Another time to a fox that bolted, leaving the goose it had been laboriously dragging.

Indeed, his every breath was a Gift.

He crossed the exhausted plantations of Anserca, drawing stares from those slaves who saw him. Though he walked alone, he followed a file of thousands across the fields, for he was always the stranger he pursued, and the back before him was forever his own. He would look up, see himself walking beneath a solitary, windswept tree, vanishing stride by stride over the far side of a hill. And when he turned, he would see that same tree behind him, and the same man descending the same slope. A queue of millions connected him to himself, from the Gift who coupled with the Holy Crone to the Gift who watched the Aspect-Emperor dying in blood and expressionless disbelief.

He was the ripple across dark waters. The bow of force thrown across a length of a child's rope.

He saw the assassin gagging on his own blood. He saw the besieging armies, the hunger in the streets. He saw the Holy Shriah turn oblivious and bare his throat. He saw the Andiamine Heights crashing upon itself, the Empress's eyes flutter about her final breath . . .

And he walked alone, following a road of fields, stranded in the now of a mortal soul.

Day after day, across mile after mile of tilled earth – the very bosom of his dread Mother. He slept between the rising stalks, the nascent heads, listening to his Mother's soothing whisper, staring at stars that were silver lines.

He followed his footprints across the dust, witnessing more than plotting the murder of the dead.

The River Sempis

At least, Malowebi thought to himself as he swayed in his saddle, he could say he had seen a *ziggurat* before he died. What could that fool, Likaro, say? There was more to travel than bedding Nilnameshi slave boys, just as there was more to diplomacy than wearing an ambassador's wig.

Cohorts of horsemen fanned across the land, filing along irrigation dikes, filtering through groves and across millet fields. Hills like broken molars fenced the north, marking the arid frontier of Gedea. The River Sempis lay to the immediate south, black and green and placid, broad enough to shroud the South Bank in blue-grey haze. Five plumes of smoke rose from disparate points on the horizon before them.

One of those plumes, Malowebi knew, led the dusty army to Iothiah.

'It is a dangerous thing,' Fanayal ab Kascamandri said from his side, a sharp grin drawing wide his elaborate goatee, 'to parlay with the enemies of dangerous men. And in the whole wide world, my friend, no man is so dangerous as Kurcifra.'

Despite the Padirajah's smile, something shrewd and quite humourless glinted in his eyes.

Second Negotiant Malowebi, Emissary of High Holy Zeüm, matched the man's gaze, careful to conceal his frown. 'Kurcifra . . .' he repeated. 'Ah . . . you mean the Aspect-Emperor.'

The Mbimayu sorcerer was old enough to remember the days when Kian ruled the Eastern Three Seas. Of all the outland peculiarities to leak into Zeüm, few proved more vexing than the Fanim missionaries who trickled across the frontier, bearing their absurd message of fear and damnation. The God was Solitary. The Gods were in fact devils. And all their ancestors had been damned for worshipping them – *all of them!* You would think that claims so preposterous and repulsive would require no rebuttal, but the very opposite had been the case. Even the Zeümi, it turned out, were quick to embrace tales of their own iniquity, so universal is self-loathing among Men. Not a month passed, it sometimes seemed, without some public flaying.

Even still, when Fanayal's Padirajah father had sent an embassy to attend the coronation of Malowebi's cousin, Nganka'kull, the Kianene Grandees had caused a sensation among the kjineta. High Holy Zeüm had always been an inward nation, too distant and too vain to concern itself with events or peoples beyond its sacred frontier. But the Kianene's pale skin, the stark luxury of their dress, their pious reserve – everything about them had hummed with exotic allure. Over night, it seemed, the Zeümi fondness for elaborate image and ornamentation had become dowdy and obsolete. Many caste-nobles even began cultivating goatees – until, that is, his cousin reinstated the ancient Grooming Laws.

Malowebi could scarce imagine *these* Kianene inspiring an upheaval in fashion. Where the Grandees of Kascamandri's embassy possessed the dress and bearing of heroes, Fanayal's men were little more than desert bandits. He had expected to ride with the likes of Skauras or Cinganjehoi, men terrible in war and gracious in peace, not a ragtag army of horse-thieves and rapists.

Fanayal alone reminded him of those ambassadors from long ago. He wore a helm of shining gold, five spikes rising from the peak, and perhaps the finest coat of mail Malowebi had ever seen – a mesh of inhuman manufacture, he eventually decided. His yellow-silk sleeves hung like pennants from his wrists. His curved sword was obviously a famed heirloom. The instant he had noticed it, Malowebi had known he would say, 'That glorious blade – was that your father's?' He even knew the solemn way he would pitch his voice. It was an old diplomat's trick, making a conversational inventory of the items his counterparts wore.

Relationships went much smoother, Malowebi had learned, in the absence of verbal holes.

'Kurcifra . . .' the Padirajah repeated with a curious smile, as if considering the way the name might sound to an outsider. 'The light that blinds.'

Fanayal ab Kascamandri was nothing if not impressive. Handsome, in the hard way of desert breeding. His falcon eyes set close about a hooked nose. Arrogant to the point of being impervious to insult and slight – and being quite agreeable as a result.

The Bandit Padirajah he might be, but he was no bandit, at least.

'You said no *man* is so dangerous,' Malowebi pressed, genuinely curious. 'Is this what you think? That the Anasûrimbor is a man?'

Fanayal laughed. 'The Empress is a *woman* – I know that much. I once spared a Shrial Priest for claiming he had bedded her when she was a whore. The Aspect-Emperor? I know only that he *can* be killed.'

'And how do you know this?'

'Because I am the one doomed to kill him.'

Malowebi shook his head in wonder. How the World revolved about the Aspect-Emperor. How many times had he poured himself some unwatered wine just to drink and marvel at the simple fact of the man? A refugee wanders into the Nansurium from the wilderness – with a Scylvendi savage, no less! – and within twenty years, he not only commands the obedience of the entire Three Seas but its *worship* as well.

It was mad. Too mad for mere history, which was, as far as Malowebi could tell, every bit as mean and as stupid as the men who made it. There was nothing mean or stupid about Anasûrimbor Kellhus.

'This is how Men reason in the Three Seas?' he asked. He repented the words even as he spoke them. Malowebi was *Second*

Negotiant for no small reason. He was forever asking blunt questions, forever alienating instead of flattering. He had more teeth than tongue, as the menials would say.

But the Bandit Padirajah showed no outward sign of offence. 'Only those who have seen their doom, Malowebi! Only those who have seen their doom!'

Fanayal, the Mbimayu sorcerer noted with no small relief, was a man who relished insolent questions.

'I notice you ride without bodyguards,' he ventured.

'Why should that concern you?'

Though horsemen clotted the fields and berms about them, he and the Padirajah rode quite alone – aside from a cowled figure who trailed them by two lengths. Malowebi had assumed the man was a bodyguard of some description, but twice now he had glimpsed – or thought he had glimpsed – something resembling a *black tongue* within the cowl's dun shadows. Even still, it was remarkable, really, that someone like Fanayal would treat with *anyone* face to face, let alone an outland *sorcerer*. Just the previous week the Empress had offered another ten thousand gold kellics for the Bandit Padirajah's head.

Perhaps it spoke to the man's desperation . . .

'Because,' the Mbimayu sorcerer said with a shrug, 'your insurrection would not survive your loss . . . We would be fools to provoke the Aspect-Emperor on the promise of a *martyr*.'

Fanayal managed to rescue his grin before it entirely faltered. He understood the power of belief, Malowebi realized, and the corresponding need to project confidence, both fatuous and unrelenting.

'You need not worry.'

'Why?'

'Because I cannot die.'

Malowebi was beginning to like the man but in a way that

cemented, rather than softened, his skepticism of him. The Second Negotiant always had a weakness for vainglorious fools, even as a child. But unlike the *First* Negotiant, Likaro, he never let his sympathies make his decisions for him.

Commitments required trust, and trust required demonstrations. The Satakhan had sent him to *assess* Fanayal ab Kascamandri, not to parlay with him. For all his failings, Nganka'kull was no fool. With the Great Ordeal crawling into the northern wastes, the question was whether the New Empire could survive the absence of its Aspect-Emperor and his most fanatical followers. As the first real threat to the Zeümi people and nation since Near Antiquity, it needed to fail – and decisively.

But wishing ill and doing actual harm were far different beasts. Care had to be taken – extreme care. High Holy Zeüm could ill afford any long throws of the number-sticks, not after Nganka'kull had so foolishly yielded his own son as a hostage. Malowebi had always been fond of Zsoronga, had always seen in him the makings of a truly great Satakhan. He needed some real assurance that this desert outlaw and his army of thieves could succeed before recommending the monies and arms they so desperately needed. To take isolated fortresses was one thing. But to assail a garrisoned *city* – that was quite another.

Iothiah, the ancient capital of Old Dynasty Shigek. Iothiah would be an impressive demonstration. Most assuredly.

'Kurcifra was sent as punishment,' Fanayal continued, 'an unholy angel of retribution. We had grown fat. We had lost faith with the strict ways of our fathers. So the Solitary God burned the lard from our limbs, drove us back into the wastes where we were born . . .' He fixed the sorcerer with a gaze that was alarming for its intensity. '*I am anointed*, Outlander. *I am the One.*'

'But Fate has many whims. How can you be sure?'

Fanayal's laughter revealed the perfect crescent of his teeth. 'If

I'm wrong, I always have Meppa.' He turned to the enigmatic rider trailing them. 'Eh, Meppa? Raise your mask.'

Malowebi twisted in his saddle to better regard the man. Meppa raised bare hands, pulled back the deep cowl that had obscured his face. The mask Fanayal referred to was not so much a mask as a kind of blindfold: a band of silver as wide as a child's palm lay about his upper face, as if a too-large crown had slipped over his eyes. The sun flashed across its circuit, gleamed across the innumerable lines etched into it: water rushing sideways, around and around in an infinite cataract.

His cowl thrown back, Meppa raised the band from his head. His hair was as white as the peaks of the Atkondras, his skin nut brown. No eyes glinted from the shadow of his sockets . . .

Malowebi fairly gasped aloud. Suddenly, it seemed absurd that he had missed the hue of ochre in the man's dust-rimmed robes or that he had mistaken the serpent rising from the folds about the man's collar for a black tongue.

Cishaurim.

'Look about you, my friend,' Fanayal continued, as if this revelation should settle the Second Negotiant's every misgiving. He gestured to the pillars of smoke bent across the sky before them. 'This land simmers with rebellion. All I need do is *ride fast*. So long as I ride fast, I outnumber the idolaters everywhere!'

But the sorcerer could only think, *Cishaurim!*

Like every other School, the Mbimayu had assumed the Water-Bearers were extinct – and like every other School, they had been happy for it. The Tribe of Indara-Kishauri was too dangerous to be allowed to live.

Small wonder the Bandit Padirajah had such a talent for survival.

'Then what need do you have of Zeüm?' Malowebi asked quickly. He had hoped Fanayal would overlook his obvious fluster, but the sly glint in the man's eye confirmed what the Second

Negotiant had already known: very little escaped the claws of Fanayal's acumen. Perhaps he was the first foe worthy of the Aspect-Emperor.

Perhaps . . .

'Because I am but one,' the Padirajah said. 'If a second strikes, then a third will join us, and a fourth . . .' He flung out his arms in an expansive gesture, setting alight the innumerable links of his nimil mail. 'The New Empire – *all of it*, Malowebi! – will collapse into the blood and lies from which it was raised.'

The Zeümi Emissary nodded as though acknowledging the logic, if not the attraction, of his argument. But all he really could think was, *Cishaurim*.

So . . . the accursed Water still flowed.

———∞———

Discord is the way of imperial power. Triamis the Great once described empire as the perpetual absence of peace. 'If your nation wars,' he wrote, 'not at the periodic whim of aggressors both internal and external, but *always*, then your people continually imposes its interests upon other peoples, and your nation is no longer a nation, but an empire.' War and empire, for the legendary Near Antique ruler, were simply the same thing glimpsed from different summits, the only measure of power and the only surety of glory.

In the Hoshrut, the Carythusali agora famed for the continuous view it afforded of the Scarlet Spires, the Judges publicly lashed a slave they had apprehended for blasphemy. She was lucky, they reasoned, since they could have charged her with sedition, a capital crime, in which case the dogs would already be lapping her blood from the flagstones. For some reason the unruly temper of the crowds that surrounded them escaped their notice. Perhaps because they were true believers. Or perhaps because the Hoshrut Pole, like the thousands of others scattered across the Three Seas, was so often used for matters of expedited justice. Either way, they were entirely unprepared for the mob's rush. Within a matter of moments they had been beaten, stripped, and hung from the hanging stone gutters of the Imperial Custom House. Within a watch, a greater part of the city rioted, slaves and caste-menials mostly, and the Imperial Garrison found itself engaged in pitched battles in the streets. Thousands died over the days following. Nearly an eighth of the city burned to the ground.

In Oswenta, Hampei Sompas, a high-ranking Imperial Apparati, was found in bed with his throat cut. He was but the first of many – very many – assassinations. As the days passed more and more Shrial and Imperial functionaries, from the lowest tax-farmers to highest judges and assessors, were murdered, either by their body-slaves or by the bands of armed menials that had taken to revenge killings in the streets.

There were more riots. Seleukara burned for seven days. Aöknyssus was only wracked for two, but tens of thousands were killed, so savage were the Imperial reprisals. The wife and children of King Nersei Proyas were removed to Attrempus for safety's sake.

Long-running insurrections flared into renewed violence, for there was no shortage of old and sequestered foes eager to take advantage of the general discord. In the southwest, the Fanim under Fanayal ab Kascamandri stormed and seized the fortress of Gara'gûl in the province of Mongilea, and in numbers so alarming that the Empress ordered four Columns rushed to defend Nenciphon, the former capital of the Kianene Empire. In the east, the wilder Famiri tribes from the steppes below the Araxes Mountains overthrew their Imperial administrators and massacred the Zaudunyani converts among them: sons of the families that had ruled them from time immemorial. And the Scylvendi raided the Nansur frontier with a daring and viciousness not seen for a generation.

Middle-aged veterans were called up. Militias were levied. A dozen small battles were fought across lands famous and obscure. Curfews were extended. The Yatwerian temples were closed, and those priestesses who did not flee were imprisoned and interrogated. Plots and conspiracies were uncovered. In more orderly provinces, the executions were celebrated in garish spectacles. Otherwise, they were carried out in secret, and bodies were buried in ditches. The Slave Laws, which had afforded protections the enslaved had not known since the days of Cenei, were repealed. In a series of emergency sessions, the Greater Congregate passed several laws curtailing congress according to caste. Speaking at public fountains became punishable by immediate execution.

The caste-nobility of all nations suddenly found unity in their general terror of their servants and slaves. Suits were dropped, freeing the courts for more pressing prosecutions. Old and honourable enmities were set aside. The Shriah of the Thousand Temples summoned high-ranking Cultic priests from across the Three Seas for what would be called the Third Pan-Sumni Council, urging them to set aside their parochial worship, to recall the God behind the Gods. Shrial Priests everywhere inveighed on behalf of their Prophet and Sovereign. Those Zaudunyani who had not joined the Great Ordeal raised their voices to harangue their peers and their lessers. Groups of them took to murdering in the dark of night those they deemed unfaithful.

Sons and husbands simply vanished.

And though the New Empire tottered, it did not fall.

∞

Momemn

Anasûrimbor Kelmomas sat where he always sat when attending the Imperial Synod, in the Prince's Box on a bench cushioned with plush red leather: the same place where his older siblings had

sat when they were young – even Thelli before she had joined
Mother beneath the Circumfix Throne.

'Recall *who* it is you address, Pansulla,' Mother called down in
a tight voice.

Though positioned relatively low on the palace heights, the
chamber, the Synodine, was one of the more luxurious ones in the
palace, and certainly among the most curious. Unlike other council
chambers, it possessed no gallery for visiting observers and absolutely no windows. Where airy grandeur was the rule elsewhere,
the chamber was long and narrow, with elaborately panelled boxes
– the Prince's Box one of them – lining the short walls and with
steep benches stepping the entire length of the long walls, as if
an amphitheatre had been straightened and then snapped in half,
forcing the audience to confront itself.

To accommodate the Circumfix Throne, a deep marble recess
shelved the stepped slope to Kelmomas's left, blue-white stone
trimmed with bands of black diorite. A scale replica of the
Circumfix as it had hung in Caraskand, including his father hanging
spread-eagled and upside down, rose in sinuous gold from the
throne's back. His mother's chair and Thelli's had been cut into
the marble tier immediately below it, their simple design concen-
trating the glory of the throne above. Some thirty identical seats
had been set into the steps rising opposite, one for each of the
Great Factions, whose interests governed the New Empire.

The floor lay well below all the seats, forcing those who walked
it to continually crane their heads up and around to meet the gaze
of their interlocutors. It was a narrow strip of bare floor, no bigger
than several prison cells set end to end. Kelmomas had heard
several functionaries refer to it – and with no little dread – as the
Slot.

Because the man who now paced its length was so fat, Cutias
Pansulla, the Nansur Consul, it looked even more narrow than

usual. He had been strutting back and forth for several moments now, long enough for dark stains to bloom from his armpits.

'But I must . . . I must dare speak it!' he cried, his shaved jowls trembling. 'The people are saying that *the Hundred are against us!*'

The Imperial Synod, his mother had told Kelmomas, was a kind of boiled-down version of the Greater Congregate, what other kings in other lands often called a privy council, the place where representatives of the New Empire's most important interests could confer with their divine ruler. Of course, he always pretended to forget this explanation when he spoke to his mother and to always whine as he accompanied her to the sessions, but he secretly adored the Synod and the games within games it invariably revealed – at least when his father failed to attend them. Elsewhere, the words always seemed to be the same, glory this and glory that, and the lofty tone seemed to drone on and on and on. It was like watching men dual with bars of iron. But in the Synodine, both the words and the voices were honed to a cutting edge.

Real disputes instead of pantomime. Real consequences instead of heavenly petitions. *Lives*, sometimes in the thousands, were decided in this place as in no other. The young Prince-Imperial could almost smell the smoke and blood. This was where *real* cities were burned, not ones carved of balsa.

'Ask yourself,' Mother cried to the assembled men. 'Who will you be when the scripture of these days is written? The craven? The weak-kneed doubter? All of you – *All of you!* As the trial deepens, and the trial always deepens, all of you will be judged. So stop thinking of me as *his* weaker vessel!'

Kelmomas jammed his mouth into his forearms to conceal his smile. Though his mother angered often, she only rarely expressed it as anger. The boy wondered whether the fat Consul below understood the peril of his situation.

He certainly hoped not.

'Holy Empress, please!' Pansulla exclaimed. 'This . . . this talk
. . . it does not answer our fears! At the very least you must give
us something to tell the *people!*'

The Prince-Imperial sensed the power in these words, even
though he did not fully understand their import. He certainly
could see the indecision in Mother's eyes, the realization she had
erred . . .

That one, the secret voice whispered.

Pansulla?

Yes. His breathing offends me.

Ever keen to exploit weakness, the round-bellied Consul pressed
his advantage. 'All we ask, Most Holy Empress, is for the *tools* to
work your will . . .'

Mother glared at him for a moment, then glanced nervously
across the assembly. She seemed to flinch from the gravity of their
regard. At last she waved a loose-wristed hand in weariness and
capitulation. 'Read *The Sagas* . . .' she began but without breath.
She paused to firm her voice. 'Read *The Sagas*, the history of the
First Apocalypse, and ask yourself, Where are the Gods? How can
the Hundred *allow* this?'

And the little boy could see the craft behind his mother's manner
and words. Silence had seized the Imperial Synod, such was the
force of her question.

'Thelli . . .' his mother said, gesturing to her daughter who sat
gowned in absurd intricacy at her side. Dreadfully thin, she looked
like a bird stranded between too many crumbs and the inability
to choose. 'Tell them what the Mandate Schoolmen say.'

'The Gods are-are finite,' Theliopa declared in a voice that
contradicted the stark angularity of her frame. 'They can only
apprehend a finite por-portion of existence. They fathom the future-
future, certainly, but from a vantage that limits them. The No-God
dwells in their blind spots, follows a path-path they are utterly

oblivious to . . .' She turned, looking from man to man with open curiosity. 'Because he *is* oblivion.'

Mother rested her hand atop Thelli's in a thoughtless gesture of thanks. Behind the panels of his box, the young Prince-Imperial fairly cut open his palms for balling his fists.

She loves me more! he thought.

Yes, the voice agreed, *she loves you more.*

The Empress spoke with renewed confidence. 'There is a world, my Lords, a *world concealed*, a world of shadow that the Gods cannot see . . .' She looked from Consul to Consul. 'I fear we now walk that world.'

A wall of bewildered looks greeted her. Even Pansulla seemed taken aback. Kelmomas almost chirped in glee, so proud was he of his mother.

'And the Hundred?' old Tûtmor, the Consul for King Hoga Hogrim of Ce Tydonn croaked, his eyes rimmed with real fear. Alarmed voices clamoured in his wake.

Their Empress graced them all with a sour smile. 'The Gods chafe, because like all souls, they call evil what they cannot comprehend.'

More astounded silence. Kelmomas found himself squinting in hilarity. Why anyone should fear the Gods was quite beyond him, let alone fools as privileged and powerful as these.

Because they are old and dying, the secret voice whispered.

Pansulla still held the Slot. He now stood directly beneath his Empress.

'So . . .' he said, looking to the others with a strategically blank face. 'So it *is* true, then? The Gods . . .' – his gaze wandered – 'the almighty *Gods* . . . are against us?'

Disaster. It fairly slapped the blood from Mother's painted face. Her lips retreated, the way they always did during such moments, into a thin line.

He offends me . . . the secret voice cooed. *The fat one.*

'Now . . .' she began, only to halt to master the emotion in her voice. '*Now* . . . Pansulla, is the time for care. Heretical superstition will be the end of us all. Now is the time to recall the *God of Gods* and his Prophet.'

The threat was clear – enough to trigger another exchange of whispers among the tiered men. Smiling with greasy insincerity, Pansulla knelt to the floor, so big and so floridly gowned that he looked more a heap of laundry than a man.

'But of course, Holy Empress.'

For the slightest instant, his mother's hatred lay plain on her face.

'Courage, Pansulla,' she said. 'And you too, loyal Tûtmor. You must find courage, not in the Hundred, but, as Inri Sejenus and my divine husband have taught, *in their sum.*'

The Nansur Consul struggled back to his feet.

'Indeed, Empress,' he said, smoothing his silk robes. '*Courage* . . . Of course . . .' His eyes strayed to the others. 'We must remind ourselves that we know better . . . than the Gods.'

Kelmomas grappled with the squeal of joy clawing at his throat. He so *loved* his mother's fury!

We've never killed someone so fat before.

'Not "we," Cutias Pansulla. Not you, and certainly not me. Your Holy Aspect-Emperor. Anasûrimbor Kellhus.'

The young Prince-Imperial understood what his mother was trying to achieve with these appeals to his father. Always using him as a goad. Always trying to vanish into the might of his name. But he could also see, with a kind of child-cunning, how this undermined her authority.

Once again the obese Consul nodded in jowl-quivering exaggeration. 'Ah, yes-yes . . . When the Cults fail us, we must turn to the Thousand Temples.' He glanced up as if to say, *How could I be such a fool?* He made of a show of turning to Maithanet's vacant seat, then looked to his Empress with mock confusion. 'But when can we hope to hear our *Holy Shriah's* most wise couns—?'

'Tidings!' a voice pealed. 'Tidings, Empress! Most dire tidings!'

All eyes in the Synodine turned to the figure gasping on the chamber's threshold: an Eothic Guardsman, red-faced for exertion.

'Most Holy Empress . . .' The guardsmen swallowed against his wind. 'The Kianene – the loathsome bandit, Fanayal!'

'What of him?' Mother demanded.

'He has struck Shigek.'

Kelmomas watched his mother blink in confusion.

'But . . . he's marching on Nenciphon . . .' A frantic note climbed into her voice. 'Don't you mean *Nenciphon?*'

The messenger shook his head in sudden terror.

'No, most Holy Empress. *Iothiah.* Fanayal has taken Iothiah.'

<hr />

The Andiamine Heights was a city in its own right, albeit one enclosed beneath a welter of rooftops, with gilded concourses instead of processional avenues and mazed dormitories instead of alley-riddled slums. Any number of routes could be taken between any two points, allowing the inhabitants to travel in celebrity or discretion. Unlike his father, Kelmomas's mother almost always chose the most discreet route possible, even if it made the journey twice as lengthy. Though some might think this was yet one more sign of her general insecurity, the young boy knew otherwise. Anasûrimbor Esmenet simply despised the sight of people falling to their faces.

The Imperial Synod dissolved, the Empress led her small retinue down into the Apparatory before turning to climb the rarely used stairs and halls that threaded the palace's eastward reaches. She clutched Kelmomas's hand with the too-tight desperation he so adored, tugging him when his pace faltered. Theliopa followed close behind with Lord Biaxi Sankas breathing hard at her side.

'Will Uncle Maithanet get mad at you again?' Kelmomas asked.

'Why would you say that?'

'Because he blames you for everything that goes wrong! I hate him!'

She ignored him after that, visibly angered.

Glutton, the secret voice reproached. *You need to take care.*

'Most Holy Empress,' Lord Sankas said into the ensuing silence. 'I fear the situation with your brother-in-law grows untenable . . .' Kelmomas glanced back at the man. He almost looked like Thelli's grandfather, he was so tall and slender. Decked in full martial regalia – a ceremonial Kidruhil cuirass and the purple cloak of a retired general – and clean-shaven in the traditional way, he resembled the old Nansur that Kelmomas so often saw engraved or painted in the original parts of the palace.

'Fanayal is in *Shigek*,' she replied testily. 'If you haven't noticed, Sankas, I have more pressing concerns.'

But the Patridomos was not so easily silenced. 'Perhaps if you were to speak with hi—'

'No!' the Empress exclaimed, wheeling around to glare up at the man. The wall to their left had yielded to an open colonnade that overlooked the Imperial Precincts and the east more generally. The Meneanor heaved dark beneath the sun on the horizon beyond.

'He must never see my face,' she said more evenly. The shadow of an arch divided her from waist to shoulder so that her lower gown shimmered with light. Kelmomas pressed his face into the warm, scented fabric. She combed his scalp out of maternal reflex. 'Do you understand, Sankas? *Never.*'

'Forgive me, Most Holy!' the caste-noble fairly cried. 'It-it was not my intent to cause offence . . .'

He trailed awkwardly, looking as though he had tripped across some disastrous suspicion. 'Most Holy Empress . . .' he said tightly. 'May I ask *why* the Shriah must not see your face?'

Kelmomas almost chortled aloud, saved himself by looking away in the appearance of little-boy boredom. Over a jumble of roof and structure, he glimpsed a formation of distant guardsmen doing drills on one of the seaward campuses. More soldiers were arriving every day, so many it was becoming impossible for him to adventure in the old way.

'Thelli,' his mother said from above. 'Please, would you assure Lord Sankas that *I am not* a skin-spy.'

The Patridomos blanched. 'No . . . No!' he blurted. 'That is certainly no—'

'Mother is not-not a skin-spy,' Theliopa interrupted.

His mother's hands and presence slipped away from the boy. Ever conscious of her menial stature, the Empress used the view as an excuse to step clear of the looming Patridomos. She gazed out over the Meneanor. 'Our dynasty, Sankas, is a . . . a complicated one. I say what I say for good reason. I need to know that you have faith enough to trust that.'

'Yes – certainly! But . . .'

'But what, Sankas?'

'Maithanet *is the Holy Shriah* . . .'

Kelmomas watched his mother smile her calm, winning smile, the one that told everyone present that she could feel what they felt. Her ability to communicate compassion, he had long since realized, was easily her strongest attribute – as well as the one most likely to send him into jealous rages.

'Indeed, Sankas . . . He is our Shriah. But the fact remains: my divine husband, his *brother*, decided to *trust me* with the fate of the Empire. Why might that be, you wonder?'

The man's pained squint relaxed in sudden comprehension. 'Of course, Most Holy! Of course!'

Men cast their lots, the Prince-Imperial realized. They gambled time, riches, even loved ones, on those great personages they thought would carry the day. Once the gambit was made, you need only give them reasons to congratulate themselves.

His mother dismissed both Sankas and Theliopa shortly afterward. Kelmomas's heart cartwheeled for joy. Again and again and again, *he* was the one she brought with her to her apartments.

He was the one! Again and again. The only one!

As always, they passed the ponderous bronze door to Inrilatas's room with their ears pricked. Kelmomas's older brother had ceased screaming of late – like the seasons he had his tempests and his idylls – leaving the young Prince-Imperial with the troubling sense that he was there, his cheek pressed against the far side of his door, *listening* to their comings and goings. The fact that he never heard Inrilatas doing this troubled him even more, for he was quite fond of hearing things. Theliopa once told him that of all his brothers and sisters, Inrilatas possessed his father's gifts in the greatest measure, so much so they continually overwhelmed his mortal frame. Though Kelmomas did not begrudge Inrilatas his insanity – he celebrated it, if anything – he did resent his greedy share of Father's blood.

And so he hated Inrilatas as well.

Mother's body-slaves rushed from their antechambers to line the hall to either side, kneeling with their faces to the floor. The Empress brushed past them in distaste, pushed open the bronze doors to her apartments herself. Kelmomas never understood why she disdained using people – Father certainly never hesitated

– but he adored the way it gave them more time alone. Again and again, he got to hug her and to kiss her and to cuddle-cuddle . . .

Ever since he had murdered Samarmas.

Sunlight rafted through the airy interior, setting the white-gossamer sheers aglow. A sycamore stood dark and full in the light beyond the balconies, close enough to glimpse the limbs forking through the shadows behind the bushing leaves. Sandalwood scented the air.

Capering across lavish carpets, the Prince-Imperial breathed deep and smiled. He swept his gaze across the frescoes of Invishi, Carythusal, and Nenciphon. Around a corner's fluted edge, he glimpsed the tall silvered mirror in her dressing-room. He saw the chest with the toys he pretended to play with when she was preoccupied. Through the propped doors to her sleeping chamber, he saw her great bed gleaming in the murk.

This, he thought as he always thought. This was where he would live forever!

He assumed she would seize him in a hug and spin in a pirouette. A mother finding strength in the *need* to be strong for a beautiful son. A mother finding respite in the *love* of a beautiful son. She always held him when she was frightened, and she literally reeked with fear. But instead she wheeled him about by the arm and slapped him hard across the cheek.

'You are never to say such things!'

A tide of murderous hurt and outrage swamped him. Mummy! Mummy had struck him! And for what? The truth? Scenes flickered beneath his soul's eye, strangling her with her own sheets, seizing the Gold Mastodon set upon the mantle and—

'But I do!' he bawled. 'I do hate him!'

Maithanet. Uncle Holy.

She was already holding him in a desperate embrace, shushing and kissing, pressing her tear-slicked cheek against his own.

Mommeee!

'You shouldn't,' she said, a thumb's breadth from his ear. 'He's your uncle. Even more, *he's the Shriah*. It's a sin to speak against the Shriah – don't you know that?'

He fought her until she pressed him back.

'But he's against you! Against Father! Isn't that a si—?'

'Enough. *Enough*. The important thing, Kel, is that you never say these things. You are a Prince-Imperial. An *Anasûrimbor*. Your blood is the very blood that flows in your uncle's veins . . .'

Dûnyain blood . . . the secret voice whispered. *What raises us above the animals.*

Like Mother.

'Do you understand what I'm telling you?' the Blessed Empress continued. 'Do you realize what others think when they hear you disputing your own blood?'

'No.'

'They hear dissension . . . discord and weakness! You embolden our enemies with this talk – do you understand me, Kel?'

'Yes.'

'We have come upon fearful times, Kel. Dangerous times. You must always use your wits. You must always be wary . . .'

'Because of Fanayal, Mommy?'

She held him tight to her breast, then pressed him back. 'Because of many things . . .' Her gaze became suddenly absent. 'Look,' she continued. 'There's something I need to show you.' She stood and with a rustle of silk moved across the bed chamber, paused before the frieze on the far wall, belts of mythic narrative piled one atop the other.

'Your father raised *two* palaces when he rebuilt the Andiamine Heights,' she said, gesturing to the sun slanting through the unshuttered balcony. 'A palace of light . . .' She turned, leaning forward on her toes to peer at the top panel of the marble frieze. She pressed the bottommost star of a constellation Kelmomas had never seen before. Something clicked elsewhere in the room. The Prince-Imperial literally swayed with vertigo, so surprised were his senses. The marble-gilded wall simply dropped away and swooped out, rotating on a perfect central hinge.

Light only filtered several feet into the black passage beyond.

'And a palace of shadow.'

—✻—

'Your uncle,' Mother said. 'I don't trust him.'

They sat where they always sat when the Empress took her 'morning sun,' as she termed it: on divans set near the heart of the Sacral Enclosure between two of the taller sycamore trees. A thin procession of clouds rode high in the blue sky above. The Imperial Apartments surrounded them on all sides, colonnaded walkways along the ground, verandas on the upper floors, some with their canopies unfurled, all forming the broad, marmoreal octagon that gave the Enclosure its famous shape.

Theliopa sat immediately next to Mother, a distance that suggested mother-daughter intimacy but was really an artefact of the girl's blindness to the rules that governed proximity. Her face, as always, was pale and sunken – skin stretched across the tent-poles of her bones. She wore what looked like several luxurious gowns sown into a florid motley, as well as dozens of jewelled broaches set end to end along the sleeve of either arm. Tree shadows waved across her, so that she seemed continually ablaze with reflected sunlight.

Wearing only a morning robe, Mother looked plain and dark in comparison – and all the more beautiful for it. Kelmomas played in the adjacent garden. With blackened fingers, he had started forming walls and bastions, a small complex of dirt structures he could strike down, but had quickly stopped when he discovered a stream of ants crawling from the earth to the blue-tiled walkway, hundreds of them. He began executing them, one by one, using his thumbnail to chip off their heads.

'Wha-what do you suspect?' his sister asked, her voice as dry as the air.

A long breath. A hand drawn to the back of her weary neck. 'That he is somehow behind this crisis with the Yatwerians,' his mother replied. 'That he intends to use it as a pretext to seize the Empire.'

Of all the games he played, this was the one the young Prince-Imperial relished the most: the game of securing his mother's constant attention while at the same time slipping beneath her notice. On the one hand, he was such a sad little boy, desolate, scarred for the tragic loss of his twin. But he was also *just* a little boy, too young to understand, too lost in his play to really listen. There was a time, not so long ago, when she would have sent him away for conversations such as this . . .

The *real* ones.

'I see,' Theliopa said.

'Are you not surprised?'

'I'm not sure surprise-surprise is a passion I can feel, Mother.'

Even watching from his periphery, Kelmomas could see his mother's expression dull. It troubled her, the little boy knew, filling in what was missing in her children. Perhaps this was why he didn't despise Theliopa the way he had that bitch, Mimara. Mother's feelings for Thelli would always be stymied by the girl's inability to reciprocate her love. But Mimara . . .

Some day soon . . . the secret voice whispered. *She will love you as much . . . More!*

'Have you conferred with Father-Father?' Theliopa asked.

His sister was a face reader. She had to see Mother's bewildered heartbreak as easily as he could. Did Thelli lack the heart to grieve this as well? Kelmomas had never been able to read much of anything in his sister. She was like Uncle Maithanet that way – only harmless.

If Mother were to ever look at *him* with those eyes . . .

'The Far-callers . . .' Mother said with the reluctant air of admission. 'They've heard nothing for two weeks now.'

The merest flicker of horror slackened Theliopa's pale face. Perhaps she could feel surprise after all – as crippled as her heart was. 'What?'

'Do not fear,' Mother said. 'Your father lives. The Great Ordeal continues its march. I am certain of that much at least.'

'Then-then what has happened?'

'Your father has declared an Interdiction. He has forbidden every Schoolmen in the Great Ordeal, on pain of *execution*, from contacting any soul in the Three Seas.'

Kelmomas recalled his lessons on Cants of Far-Calling well enough. The primary condition of contacting someone in their dreams was to know, *precisely*, where they were sleeping. This meant the Great Ordeal had to contact *them*, since it travelled day by day.

'He suspects spies among the Schools?' Theliopa asked. 'Is this some kind of ruse to draw them out?'

'Perhaps.'

His sister was generally averse to eye contact, but those rare times she deigned to match someone's gaze, she did so with a peculiar intensity – like a bird spying worms. 'You mean Father hasn't told you anything?'

'No.'

'He *abides* by his own embargo? Mother . . . has Father deserted us?'

The young Prince-Imperial abandoned the pretense of his garden play. He even held his breath, so profound was his hope. For as long he could remember, Kelmomas had feared and hated his divine father. The Warrior-Prophet. The Aspect-Emperor. The one true Dûnyain. All the native abilities possessed by his children, only concentrated and refined through a lifetime of training. Were it not for the demands of his station, were he more than just a constantly arriving and departing shadow, Father would have certainly seen the secret Kelmomas had held tight since his infancy. The secret that made him strong.

As things stood, it was only a matter of time. He would grow as his brothers and sisters had grown, and he would drift, as his brothers and sisters had drifted, from Mother's loving tutelage to Father's harsh discipline. And one day Father would peer deep into his eye and see what no one else had seen. And that day, Kelmomas knew, would be his doom . . .

But what if Father *had* abandoned them? Even better, what if he were *dead*?

He has the Strength, the voice whispered. *So long as he lives, we are not safe . . .*

Mother raised a finger to scoop tears from either eye. This, the young Prince-Imperial realized. This was why she had struck him the previous day! This was why the fat fool, Pansulla, had so easily goaded her, and why the tidings from Shigek had so dismayed her . . .

If Father is gone . . . the secret voice dared whisper.

'It would appear so,' she said, speaking about a crack in her voice. 'I fear it has something to do with your uncle.'

Then we are finally safe.

'Maithanet,' Thelli said.

The Empress mastered her feelings with a deep breath. 'Maybe this is a . . . a *test* of some kind. Like the fable of Gam . . .'

Kelmomas recalled this from his lessons as well. Gam was the mythical king who faked his own death to test the honour of his four sons. The boy wanted to shout this out, to bask a moment in Mother's pride, but he bit his tongue. For the briefest of instants, he thought he saw his sister glance at him.

'It need not have anything to do with Uncle,' Theliopa said. 'Maybe the Consult has discovered some way of eavesdropping on our communications . . .'

'No. It has something to do with Maithanet. I can feel it.'

'I can rarely fathom Father,' Theliopa admitted.

'You?' the Empress cried with pained hilarity. 'Think about your poor mother!'

Kelmomas laughed precisely the way she wanted.

'Ponder it, Thelli. Your father assuredly *knows* about the strife growing between us, his wife and his brother, so then why would he choose *this moment* to strand us each with the other?'

'That much is simple-simple, at least,' Thelli replied. 'Because he believes the best solution will be the one you find on your-your own.'

'Exactly,' Mother said. 'Somehow he thinks my ignorance will serve me in this . . .' Her voice trailed into pensive thought. For several moments she let her gaze wander across points near and far within the Sacral Enclosure, then shook her head in sudden outrage and disgust.

'Damn your father and his machinations!' she cried, her voice loud enough to draw looks from the nearby Pillarian Guardsmen. She glanced skyward, her eyes rolling with something like panic. 'Damn him!'

'Mother?' Theliopa asked.

The Empress lowered her head and sighed. 'I am quite all right, Thelli.' She spared her daughter a rueful look. 'I don't give a damn what you think you see in my face . . .' She trailed, her mouth hanging on these words. Kelmomas held his breath, so attuned had he become to the wheel of his mother's passion.

'Thelli . . .' She began, only to hesitate for several heartbeats. 'Could . . . Could *you* read his face?'

'Uncle's? Only Father has that-that ability. Father and . . .'

'And who?'

Theliopa paused as if weighing the wisdom of honest answers. '*Inrilatas*. He could see . . . Remember Father trained-trained him for a time . . .'

'Father trained who?' Kelmomas cried, the way a jealous little brother might.

'Kel – please.'

'*Who?*'

Esmenet raised two fingers to Theliopa, turned to Kelmomas, her manner cross and adoring. 'Your older brother,' she explained. 'Your father hoped teaching him to read passions in others would enable him to master his own.' She turned back to her daughter. 'Treachery?' she asked. 'Could Inrilatas see *treachery* in a soul so subtle as Maithanet's?'

'Perhaps, Mother,' the pale girl replied. 'But the real-real question, I think, is not so much *can* he, as *will* he.'

The Holy Empress of all the Three Seas shrugged, her expression betraying the fears that continually mobbed her heart.

'I need to know. What do we have to lose?'

<hr>

Since Mother had to attend special sessions with her generals, the young Prince-Imperial dined alone that evening – or as alone as possible for a soul such as his. He was outraged even though he understood her reasons, and as always he tormented the slaves who waited on him, blaming his mother for each and every hurt he inflicted.

Later that night he pulled the board from beneath his bed and resumed working on his model. Since his uncle's treachery had loomed so large that day, he decided to work on the Temple Xothei, the monumental heart of the Cmiral temple complex. He began cutting and paring miniature columns, using the little knives that Mother had given him in lieu of a completed model. 'What a man makes,' she had told him, 'he prizes . . .' Unerringly, without the benefit of any measure, he carved them, not only one identical to another, but in perfect proportion to those structures he had already completed.

He never showed his work to Mother. It would trouble her, he knew, his ability to see places just once, and from angles buried within them, yet to grasp them the way a bird might from far above.

The way Father grasped the world.

But even worse, if he showed his little city to her, it would complicate the day when he finally burned it. She did not like the way he burned things.

Bugs, he thought. He needed to fill the streets of his little city with bugs. Nothing really burned, he decided, unless it moved.

He thought of the ants in the garden.

He thought of the Pillarian Guardsmen patrolling the Sacral Enclosure. He could even hear their voices on the evening breeze as they whiled away the watches with fatuous talk . . .

He thought about the fun he could have, sneak-sneaking about them, more shadow than little boy.

He thought about his previous murders and the mysterious person he saw trapped in the eyes of the dying. The one person he loved more than his mother – the one and only. Convulsing, bewildered, terrified, and beseeching . . . *beseeching* most of all.

Please! Please don't kill me!

'The Worshipper,' he declared aloud.

Yes, the secret voice whispered. *That's a good name.*

'A most *strange* person, don't you think, Sammi?'

Most strange.

'The Worshipper . . .' Kelmomas said, testing the sound. 'How can he travel like that from body to body?'

Perhaps he's locked in a room. Perhaps dying is that room's only door . . .

'Locked in a room!' the young Prince-Imperial cried laughing. 'Yes! Clever-clever-cunning-clever!'

And so he slipped into the gloom-gloomy hallways, dodging and ducking and scampering. Only the merest shiver in the shining lantern-flames marked his passing.

Finally he arrived at the Door . . . the high bronze one with seven Kyranean Lions stamped into its greening panels, their manes bent into falcon wings. The one his mother had forbidden the slaves to polish until the day it could be safely opened.

The door to his brother Inrilatas's room.

⊸∞⊷

It stood partially ajar.

Kelmomas had expected, even hoped to find it such. The slaves who attended to his brother generally did so whenever lulls in his tantrums permitted. During his brother's calm seasons, however, they followed an exact schedule, cleansing and feeding Inrilatas the watch before noon and the watch before midnight.

The boy mooned in the corridor for several moments, alternately staring at the stylized dragons stitched in crimson, black, and gold across the corridor's carpet and stealing what glimpses the narrow slot provided of the cell's bare floor interior. Eventually his curiosity mastered his fear – only Father terrified him more than Inrilatas – and he pressed his face to the opening, peering past the belt of brushed leather that had been tacked to the door's outer rim to better seal in the sound and smell of his mad brother.

He could see an Attendant to his left, a harried-looking Nilnameshi man soaping the walls and floor with a rake-mop. He saw his brother sitting hunched like a shaved ape to the right of the room, his edges illuminated in the light of a single brazier. Each of his limbs were shackled to a chain that ran like an elongated tongue from the mouth of a stone lion head, one of four set into the far wall, two with their manes pressed against the ceiling, two with their chins across the floor. A winch-room lay beyond that wall, Kelmomas knew, with wheels and locks for each of the chains, allowing the Attendants to pull his brother spread-eagled against the polished stone, if need be, or to grant him varying degrees of freedom otherwise.

From the look of the links curled across the floor, they had afforded him two lengths or so of mobility – enough both to relieve and to embolden the boy. Inrilatas usually howled and raged without some modicum of slack.

At first, Kelmomas thought him absolutely motionless, but he was not.

He sat making faces . . . expressions.

Not any faces, but those belonging to the slave who bent to and fro with his mop a mere toss away, scrubbing away urine and feces with a perfumed astringent. Periodically the deaf-mute would cast a terrified glance in his prisoner's direction, only to see his face reflected back to him.

'Most of them flee,' Inrilatas said. Kelmomas knew he addressed him even though he did not so much as glance at the boy. 'Sooner or later, they choose the whip over my gaze.'

'They are simple fools,' Kelmomas replied, too timid to press open the door, let alone cross the threshold.

'They are exactly what they appear to be.'

The shaggy mane turned. Inrilatas fixed the young Prince-Imperial with wild and laughing blue eyes. 'Unlike you, little brother.'

Save for his long face, Inrilatas looked utterly unlike the brother Kelmomas remembered from his infancy. His growth had come, gilding his naked form in a golden haze of hair. And years of warring against his iron restraints had strapped his frame in luxurious muscle. A beard stubbed his chin and the line of his jaw but had yet to climb his cheeks.

His voice was deep and beguiling. Not unlike Father's.

'Come, little brother,' Inrilatas said with a comradely grin. He leapt toward the entrance so suddenly that the deaf-mute fumbled the handle of his mop and tripped backward. He landed at a point just shy of where the chains would bring him up short.

Kelmomas watched his brother squat and defecate, then retreat to his previous position. Still smiling, Inrilatas waved his little brother forward. He possessed a man's wrists now: the hands of a thick-fingered warrior.

'Come . . . I want to discuss the shit between us.'

With anyone else, Kelmomas would have thought this a mad joke of some kind. Not so with Inrilatas.

The boy pressed the door inward, strode into the stench, pausing but two steps from the coiled feces. The slave glimpsed Kelmomas in his periphery, wheeled in sudden alarm. But the man was quick to resume his cleaning when he recognized him. Like so many palace slaves, terror kept him welded to the task before him.

'You show no revulsion,' Inrilatas said, nodding at the feces.

Kelmomas did not know what to say, so he said nothing.

'You are not like the others, are you, little brother? No . . . You . . . are like *me*.'

Remember your face, the secret voice warned. *Only Father possesses the Strength in greater measure!*

'I am nothing like you,' the little Prince-Imperial replied.

It seemed strange, standing on the far side of the Door. And *wrong* . . . So very wrong.

'But you are,' Inrilatas chuckled. 'All of us have inherited our Father's faculties in some mangled measure. Me . . . I possess his sensitivities, but I utterly lack his unity . . . his control. My natures blow through me – hungers, glorious hungers! – unfettered by the little armies of shame that hold the souls of others in absolute captivity. Father's reason mystifies me. Mother's compassion makes me howl with laughter. I am the World's only unbound soul . . .'

He raised his shackled wrists as he said this, gestured to the polluted floor before him.

'I shit when I shit.'

A ringing filled the boy's ears, such was the intensity of his older brother's gaze. He began to speak, but his voice caught as though about a hook in his throat.

Inrilatas grinned. 'What about you, little brother? Do you shit when you shit?'

He sees me . . . the secret voice whispered. *You have become reckless in Father's abse—*

'Who?' Inrilatas laughed. 'The shadow of hearing moves through you – as it so often does when no one is speaking. *Who whispers to you*, little brother?'

'Mommy says you're mad.'

'Ignore the question,' his older brother snapped. 'State something insulting, something that will preoccupy, and thus evade a prickly question. Come closer, little brother . . . Come closer and tell me you do not shit when you shit.'

'I don't understand what you mean!'

He knows you lie . . .

'Of course you know . . . Come closer . . . Let me peer into your mouth. Let me listen to this whisper that is not your voice. Who? Who speaks inside of you?'

Kelmomas fell backward a step. Inrilatas had managed to creep forward somehow, to steal slack from his chains without the boy noticing.

'Uncle is coming to see you!'

A heartbeat of appraising silence.

'Again you ignore the question. But this time you state a *truth*, one that you know will intrigue me. You mean Uncle *Holy*, don't you? Uncle Holy is coming to visit me? I smell Mother in that.'

The boy found strength in her mere mention.

'Y-yes. Mother wants you to read his face. She fears that he plots against Father – against us! She thinks only you can see.'

'Come closer.'

'But Uncle has learned how to *fool* you.'

Even as he spoke the words, Kelmomas cursed them for their clumsiness. This was an *Anasûrimbor* crouched before him. Divinity! Divinity burned in Inrilatas's blood as surely as in his own.

'Kin,' Inrilatas crowed. 'Blood of my blood. What love you possess for Mother! I see it burn! Burn! Until all else is char and ash. Is *she* the grudge you bear against Uncle?'

But Kelmomas could think of nothing else to say or do. To answer any of his brother's questions, he knew, was to wander into labyrinths he could not hope to solve. He had to press forward . . .

'He has learned to disguise his disgust as pity, Uncle Holy. His treachery as concern!'

There was no other way through the monstrous intellect before him.

This is a mistake . . .

'The whisper *warns* you!' Inrilatas laughed, his eyes bright, not for the twin flames they reflected, but something more incendiary still: apprehension. 'You do not like sharing . . . Such a peevish, devious little soul! Come *closer*, little brother.'

He sees me!

'You cannot let him fool you!' the boy cried, trying to goad a pride that did not exist.

'I see *him* – the one you hide, oh yes! The other one, the whisperer. I *seeeeeeee* him,' Inrilatas crooned. 'What does he tell you? Is he the one who wants Uncle Holy dead?'

'You will want to kill him, Brother, when he comes. I can *help* you!'

More laughter, warm and avuncular, at once teasing and protective. 'And now you offer the beast candy. Come closer, little brother. I want to stare into your mouth.'

'You will want to *kill* Uncle Holy,' Kelmomas repeated, his thoughts giddy with sudden inspiration. 'Think, brother . . . The *sum of sins.*'

And with that single phrase, the young Prince-Imperial's dogged persistence was rescued – or so he thought.

Where his brother had fairly radiated predatory omniscience before, his manner suddenly collapsed inward. Even his nakedness, which had been that of the rapist – lewd, virile, bestial – lapsed into its chill and vulnerable contrary. He actually seemed to shrink in his chains.

Suddenly Inrilatas seemed as pathetic as the human shit breathing on the floor between them.

The young man's eyes flinched from the boy's gaze, sought melancholy reprieve in the shadowy corners of his cell's ceiling.

'Do you ever wonder, Kel, why it is I do what I do?'

'No,' the boy answered honestly.

Inrilatas glanced at his brother, then down to the floor. Breathing deep, he smiled the sad smile of someone lost in a game pursued too far for too long. Too long to abandon. Too long to continue.

'I do it to heap damnation upon myself,' he said as if making an absurd admission.

'But why?' the boy asked, genuinely curious now.

Be wary . . . the secret voice whispered.

'Because I can think of no greater madness.'

And what greater madness could there be, exchanging a handful of glorious heartbeats for an eternity of anguish and torment? But the boy shied from this question.

'I . . . I don't understand,' he said. 'You could leave this room . . . anytime you wished! Mother would release you – I know it. You just need to follow the *rules*.'

His brother paused, looked to him as if searching for evidence of kinship beyond the fact of their blood. 'Tell me, little brother, what *rules* the rule?'

Something is wrong . . . the voice warned.

'The God,' the boy said, shrugging.

'And what rules the God?'

'Nothing. No one.'

He breaths as you breathe, the secret voice whispered, *blinks as you blink – even his heartbeat captures your own! He draws your unthinking soul into the rhythms of his making. He mesmerizes you!*

Inrilatas nodded in solemn affirmation. 'So the God is . . . unconstrained.'

'Yes.'

Inrilatas stood with sudden grace, walked to the limit of chains. He seemed godlike in the gloom, his hair falling in flaxen sheets about his shoulders, his limbs bound in veined muscle, his phallus laying long and violet in a haze of golden down. He placed his foot upon his feces, and using his toes, smeared it in a foul arc across the floor below him.

'So the God is like *me*.'

And just like that, the boy *understood*. The senseless sense of his brother's acts. The miraculous stakes of his mad exchange.

Suddenly this little room, this shit-stained prison cell hidden from the light of shame, seemed a *holy place*, a temple to a different revelation, the nail of a darker heaven.

'Yes . . .' the boy murmured, lost in the wisdom – the heart-breaking wisdom! – of his brother's constant gaze.

And it seemed his brother's voice soaked into the surrounding walls, cupped everything that could be seen. 'The God punishes us according to the degree we resemble him.'

Inrilatas towered before him.

'And you resemble him, little brother. You resemble . . .'

What was this trap he had set for him? How could understanding, *insight*, capture?

'No!' the boy cried. 'I am not mad! I am not like you!'

Laughter, warm and gentle. So like Mother when she is lazy and wishes only to tease and cuddle her beautiful little son. '*Look,*' Anasûrimbor Inrilatas commanded. 'Look at this heap of screams you call the world, and tell me you would not *add* to them – pile them to the sky!'

He has the Strength, the secret voice whispered.

'I would . . .' Anasûrimbor Kelmomas admitted. 'I would.' His limbs trembled. His heart hung as if plummeting through a void. What was this crashing within him? What was this release?

The Truth!

And his brother's voice resonated, climbed as if communicating up out of his bones. '*You think you seek the love of our mother, little brother – Little Knife! You think you murder in her name. But that love is simply cloth thrown over the invisible, what you use to reveal the shape of something so much greater . . .*'

Memories tumbled into his soul's eye. Memories of his Whelming, how he had followed the beetle to the feet of the Grinning God, the Four-horned Brother, how they had laughed when he had maimed the bug – laughed *together*! Memories of the Yatwerian priestess, how she had shrieked blood while the Mother of Fertility stood helpless . . .

And the boy could feel it! An assumption of glory. A taking possession of a certainty that had possessed him all along – possessed him in ignorance . . . Yes!

Godhead.

'*Come closer,*' Inrilatas said in a whisper that seemed to boom across all creation. He nodded to the arc smeared across the floor between them. '*Wander across the line others have etched for you . . .*'

The young Prince-Imperial watched his left foot, small and white and bare, step forward—

But a gnarled hand caught him, held him with gentle insistence. Somehow the deaf-mute Attendant had circled around without the boy noticing. The man wagged his face in alarm and horror.

Inrilatas began laughing.

'Flee, little brother,' he said, passion fluting through his voice. 'I can feel the . . .' He dandled his tongue on his lips as if savouring his own sweetness, even as his eyes widened in animal fury. A coital shudder passed through him. 'I feel the *rage*!' he roared to the stone vaults. '*The furies!*' He seized the slack chains, wrenched them savagely enough to make the links screech for biting one another. Saliva swung from his mouth when he jerked his face back to Kelmomas. 'I can feel it come . . . come upon me . . .' His phallus climbed into a grinning arc.

'*Diviniteeeeeee!*'

The boy stood astounded. At last he yielded to the Attendant and his shoulder-tugging hands, allowed the wretch to pull him from his brother's cell . . .

He knew Inrilatas would find the little gift he had left for him, lying along the seam between floor-stones.

The small file he had stolen from the palace tinker . . . not so long ago.

Iothiah

Fire, fierce enough to sting the skin from paces away. Smoke, rolling in oily sheets, acrid enough to prick the eyes, needle the throat. Screams, violent enough to cramp the heart. Screams. Too many screams.

Dizzy and nauseated, Malowebi rode close beside Fanayal ab Kascamandri as the Padirajah toured the streets, some raucous, others abandoned. The Second Negotiant had never witnessed the sacking of a village, let alone a city as vast and mighty as Iothiah. It reminded him that High Holy Zeüm, for all its high holy bluster, knew very little about war. The Men of the Three Seas, he had come to realize, warred without mercy or honour. Where the dynastic skirmishes his Zeümi kinsmen called war were bound by ancient code and custom, Fanayal and his men recognized no constraints that he could see, save that of military expediency and exhaustion.

They fought the way Sranc fought.

The Mbimayu sorcerer saw entire streets carpeted in bodies. He saw several rapes, the victims either vacant or shrieking, and more summary executions than he cared to count. He saw a pale-skinned Columnary holding a squalling babe in one arm while trying to battle two laughing Kianene with the other. He saw an old man jumping from a rooftop, his clothing afire.

Perhaps glimpsing something of his dismay, Fanayal was at pains to describe the atrocities suffered by his own people during the First Holy War and the subsequent Wars of Unification. A kind of madness warbled through his outrage as he spoke, condemnation spoken in the tones of divine revelation, as if nothing could be more right and true than the slaughter and rapine about them. The Bloodthirsty Excuse, the sage Memgowa had called it. Retribution.

'But there is more to this than crude vengeance,' Fanayal explained, as if suddenly recalling the learning of the man he addressed. The Padirajah was proud of his own youthful education, Malowebi knew, but found the posture difficult to recover after decades of brutality and fugitive insurrection. 'You make an example of the first,' the man continued, 'then you show mercy to the second. First, you teach them to fear you, then you earn their trust. *Nirsi shal'tatra*, we call it. The Honey and the Goad.'

Malowebi could not but reflect on how easily the whip and the honey became confused. Everywhere they rode, the Kianene turned from their sordid labours and called out to their lord in exultation and gratitude – cheered as if famished guests at a sumptuous feast.

Savages, Cousin. You have sent me out among savages.

Something, Malowebi's silence, perhaps, convinced the Bandit Padirajah to cut their tour short. They reversed direction, rode for what seemed an entire watch plagued by the sound of a babe crying – Malowebi could almost believe someone followed them torturing a cat. Silence haunted the empty windows. Smoke sheeted the west in gauze rags, lending an eerie, watery timbre to the sunlight that slanted across the dying city. Finally they returned to the wrack and ruin of the city's northwestern walls – the section brought down by Meppa.

Once again, Malowebi found himself gawking.

'It frightens you, no?' Fanayal said, watching his profile. 'The spilling of the Water.'

'What do you mean?'

The Padirajah graced him with an upside-down smile. 'I've been told that Schoolmen find the Cishaurim Psûkhe troubling. You see a violation with your mundane eyes – the glare of sorcery – when your *other* eye, the one that itches, sees only mundane creation.'

Malowebi shrugged, thinking of the brief dual between Meppa and the lone Saik sorcerer – a decrepit and dishevelled old man – who had defended the hapless city. The rogue Cishaurim floating, impervious to the fire of the Schoolman's Anagogic dragonhead, disgorging cataracts of blue-twinkling light as pure as it was beautiful. As awesome as Meppa's power had been – there was no doubting he was a Primary – it had been the *beauty* that had most astounded, and mortified, the Second Negotiant.

To be a sorcerer was to dwell among deformities.

'It is extraordinary,' Malowebi admitted, 'to see the Work without the Mark.' He smiled the wise and slippery smile of an old diplomat. 'But we Schoolmen are accustomed to miracles.'

He said this last more in bitter jest than anything. What he witnessed had left many profound impressions. The power of Meppa, certainly. The martial acumen of the Padirajah. The cunning and the bravery of the Fanim, not to mention their barbarity . . .

But nothing loomed so large as the *weakness* of the New Empire.

The rumours were absolutely true: the Aspect-Emperor had boned his conquests to pursue his mad invasion of the northern wilds. Disaffected populations. Ill-equipped soldiers, poorly trained and even more poorly led. Infirm and doddering Schoolmen. And perhaps most interestingly, *absolutely no Chorae* . . .

Nganka – nay, *Zeüm* – needed to be informed. This night would be filled with far-calling dreams.

'The people call him Stonebreaker,' Fanayal said. 'Meppa . . . They say he was sent to us by the Solitary God.'

Malowebi turned to him, blinking.

'What do *you* say?'

'I say he was sent to *me*!' the hawk-faced Padirajah cried laughing. '*I am* the Solitary God's gift to his people.'

'And what does *he* say?' the Second Negotiant asked, now genuinely curious.

'Meppa? He does not know who he is.'

CHAPTER SIX

The Meorn Wilderness

Everything is concealed always. Nothing is more trite than a mask.

—AJENCIS, *THE THIRD ANALYTIC OF MEN*

If you find yourself taken unawares by someone you thought you knew, recall that the character revealed is as much your own as otherwise. When it comes to Men and their myriad, mercenary natures, revelation always comes in twos.

—MANAGORAS, *ODE TO THE LONG-LIVED FOOL*

Late Spring, 20 New Imperial Year (4132 Year-of-the-Tusk), the 'Long Side'

It tracked their blundering flight through the Wilderness. It watched and it hungered and it hated . . .

How it hated.

It remained in the trees for the most part, running with glee along the dead limbs of the under-canopy. It fed on squirrels, eaten raw, and once upon a wildcat that had tried to feed on it. It supped on the mewling litter afterward, laughed at their miniature hisses and struggles. Their tiny skulls cracked like delicacies.

Days. Weeks.

Over gnarled miles, through rain falling in sheeted fury. It watched them trudge and it watched them sleep. It watched them feud and bicker. Three times it saw them battle the errant children of the Old Fathers, the Sranc, and it crouched, its eyes wide and wondering as tangles of sorcerous light and shadow fluttered through the forest's mangled depths.

And sometimes it dared crawl close, like a serpent worming toward prey. Grinding its phallus against hoary bark, it would watch *her*, the girl who had saved them in the ancient-old deeps. And it would know lust, malice. It would gaze with a singularity unknown to Men.

The thing called Soma.

Each night it sought some tree greater than the others, a tower among lesser pillars, and it climbed, leaping and swinging through the canopies, from dead to living, following fork and branch to the wiry limit, until it breached the final leafy weave. There, gently creaking side to side in the breeze, it stared across an ocean of arboreal crowns.

It would bend its neck back until its head pressed its spine, and it would scream.

And scream.

Watch after watch, night after night, shrieking in tones that not even dogs could hear. Only rats.

Screaming. Until its mouth filled with blood.

The Hags could not keep up.

They would begin complaining around midday – at least at first.

Belmorn, the particularly brutish Galeoth who had become their de facto leader, even went so far as to accuse the Skin Eaters of devilry. With a kind of immovable indifference, Achamian watched the Captain stroll up to the arm-waving giant and plunge a knife in his armpit.

'Your lives are mine!' he screamed at the others. 'Mine to beat! Mine to torture! Mine to murder!'

That night two of the Hags disappeared – Achamian could not remember their names. Nothing was said of them the next day or any of the days following. Scalpers did not speak of the dead, even ones so despicable as the Stone Hags.

The rains began after that, and below dark skies the world beneath the forest canopies was darker still. Lightning strikes were little more than sparks and glows glimpsed through the gauze of a million leaves, but the thunder crashed undulled through the brachiated gloom. Guttered by the trees, the rainwaters fell in the form of countless hanging rivulets, a pissing army of them, soaking the ground to wheezing muck. And if the way became more arduous for the Skin Eaters with their nightly ration of Qirri, it became harder still for the Hags.

One, a ritually scarred Thunyeri named Osilwas, they lost to a river crossing. With a wound festering in his arm, the man had staggered as much as marched for days. One evening Achamian had watched him cut his hair away, lock by lock – to shed weight, he supposed. Despite the man's condition, the old Wizard had thought Osilwas would survive, perhaps mistaking the gleam of fever in his eyes for the light of determination. One stumble in roiling waters was all it took to sweep him away.

Another, a bow-legged Cepaloran the others called Scroll – apparently because of the elaborate blue tattooing across his limbs – simply began wailing like a madman one night and had to be put down as a sobber. The day after, Erydides, who continually claimed to be a Cironji pirate in the chaotic days preceding the New Empire, developed a limp. No matter how hard he laboured, he fell ever farther behind. Achamian's last memory of him was his grimace: a kind of panicked grin stretched across expressions of abject pain. A look that urged wild effort in the utter absence of strength.

Then there was the dispute between Pokwas and Wulgulu, the strutting Thunyeri who for a time had assumed titular command of his brothers. Achamian did not know what caused the altercation, only that it occurred in the course of dividing a joint of wild boar. Pokwas, in particular, was inclined to heap abuse on the Hags, alternately calling them dogs, wretches, and 'mibus' – apparently a mibu was a kind of Zeümi jackal renowned for eating its own kind during the dry season. 'Be a good mibu,' Achamian had overheard him say on more than one occasion, 'and we will feed your dead to you.' One moment everything was gloom and milling exhaustion, the next the two men were grappling, their heels kicking up leaves and dirt as they heaved at each other. Pokwas was easily the stronger: the green-eyed giant twisted Wulgulu around, wrenched him to the ground. Then he began pounding the prostrate Thunyeri about the head and face. Again and again, while everyone gnawed and chewed their dinner, their hands and faces gleaming with grease. Nothing was said, and aside from the black giant's laboured breathing, nothing was heard beyond the slapping thud of his fists. Again and again. The Sword-dancer continued striking the man long after he was dead, while Achamian and the others continued watching and eating. Only Mimara turned away.

Afterward Sarl began cackling in his strange, inward way, muttering, 'I *told* you, Kiampas! Eh? Yes!'

Something was happening . . .

Achamian could feel it in his bones – catch glimpses of it in the eyes of the others. Mimara especially. He had watched a human head hammered into a wineskin, and he had felt nothing more than . . . curiosity?

It was the Qirri. It had to be. The medicine seemed to numb their conscience as much as it quickened their limbs and stretched their wind. Even as Achamian felt himself becoming closer to Mimara, he found himself caring less for the surviving Skin Eaters and not at all for the wretched Hags.

The old Wizard had enough experience with hashish and opium to know the way drugs could alter the small things, stretch and twist the detailed fabric of life. In the fleshpots of Carythusal, he had seen the way the poppy, especially, could conquer the myriad desires of men, until their hunger for the drug eclipsed even lust and love.

He knew enough to be wary, but the fact was they were moving *fast*, far faster than Achamian had dared hope. Several days into the rains they had found the ruins of a bridge on the banks of a great river, a bridge that Achamian recognized from his dreams as the Archipontus of Wûl, a work famed across the Ancient North in Seswatha's day. That meant they had travelled over half the distance from Maimor to Kelmeol, the ancient capital of the Meori Empire, in the space of two weeks – a spectacular distance. If they could maintain this pace, they would easily reach Sauglish and the Coffers before summer's end.

But it was a pace that was killing the newcomers. More and more the remaining Hags took on the vigilant aspect of hostages, a look at once surly, bewildered, and terrified. They ceased speaking, even among themselves, and as much as the Skin Eaters found their gaze inexorably drawn to Cleric, their eyes continually circled about the Captain and the threat of his discipline. Night would fall, the rains would thread the dark with lines of silver, and the Hags would huddle in shivering clutches, while Galian, Conger, and the others would bare their arms and marvel at their steaming skin.

'Where we going?' the youngest of them, a Galeoth adolescent with the strange name of Heresius, began shrieking one evening. 'What madness?' he screamed in broken Sheyic. 'What madness you do?' Staring was the most any of the original company could manage, so sudden and crazed was the young man's outburst. Finally, with the same murderous deliberation Achamian had seen many times, the Captain stood. The youth, who was no fool, bolted like a spooked doe into the murk . . .

Afterward, Galian insisted he had seen something – arms, he thought – hook out of the dead undercanopy and yank the young wretch into oblivion.

No one mourned him. No one, Stone Hag or Skin Eater, so much as spoke his name. The dead had no place in their history. They were scalpers. As much as they feared their mad Captain, none of them disputed his simple and dread logic. Death to sobbers. Death to loafers. Death to limpers, bellyachers, and bleeders . . .

Death to *weakness*, the great enemy of enmity.

So day after day they threw themselves at horizons they could not see, trudged with bottomless vigour into lands obscured and obscure, whether the sky cracked and poured water or the sun shone through sheets of green luminescence. And day after day the Stone Hags dwindled – for they were weak.

As the Skin Eaters were strong.

There was no place for pity, even less for regret, on the slog. And this, as Sarl continually slurred under his breath, was the *Slog* of Slogs. You could not be wholly human and survive the Long Side, so you became something less and pretended you were more.

In subsequent days Achamian would come to look at this leg of their journey with a peculiar horror, not because he had lived necessary lies, but because he had come to *believe* them. He was a man who would rather know and enumerate his sins, bear the pain of them, than cocoon himself in numbing ignorance and flattering exculpation.

You can only believe so many lies before becoming one of them.

What began as a remedy in the Cil-Aujan deeps had somehow transcended habit and become sacred ritual. 'The Holy Dispensation,' Mimara once called it in a pique of impatience.

Each night they queued before the Nonman, awaiting their pinch of Qirri. Usually Cleric would sit cross-legged and wordlessly dip his index finger into his pouch, darkening the pad with the merest smear. One by one the Skin Eaters would kneel before him and take the tip of his outstretched finger into their mouths – to better avoid any waste. Achamian would take his place among the others, kneel as they did when his time came. The Qirri would be bitter, the finger cold for the spit of others, sweet for the soil of daily use. A kind of euphoria would flutter through him, one that stirred troubling memories of kneeling before Kellhus during the First Holy War. There would be a moment, a mere heartbeat, where he would buckle beneath the dark gaze of the Nonman. But he would walk away content, like a starving child who had tasted honey.

Thoughtless, he would sit and savour the slow crawl of vitality through his veins.

The first and only Stone Hag to dare ridicule the act was found dead the following morning. Afterward, the renegade scalpers restricted their opinions to sullen looks and expressions – fear and disgust, mostly.

Sometimes the Nonman would climb upon some wild pulpit, the mossed remains of a fallen tree, the humped back of a boulder, and paint wonders with his dark voice. Wonders and horrors both.

Often he spoke of war and tribulation, of loves unravelled and victories undone. But no matter how the scalpers pressed him with questions, he could never recall the *frame* of his reminiscences. He spoke in episodes and events, never ages or times. The result was a kind of inadvertent verse, moments too packed with enigma and ambiguity to form narrative wholes – at least none they could comprehend. Fragments that never failed to leave his human listeners unsettled and amazed.

Mimara continually pestered the old Wizard with questions afterward. 'Who is he?' she would hiss. 'His stories must tell you something!'

Time and again Achamian could only profess ignorance. 'He remembers the breaking of things, nothing more. The rest of the puzzle is always missing – for *him* as much as for us! I know only that he's old . . . exceedingly old . . .'

'How old?'

'Older than iron. Older even than human writing . . .'

'You mean older than the Tusk.'

All Nonmen living were impossibly ancient. Even the youngest of their number were contemporaries of the Old Prophets. But if his sermons could be believed, Cleric – or Incariol, Lord Wanderer – was far older still, in his prime *before* the Ark and the coming of the Inchoroi.

An actual contemporary Nin'janjin and Cû'jara Cinmoi . . .

'Go to sleep,' the Wizard grumbled.

What did it matter who Cleric had been, he told himself, when the ages had battered him into something entirely different?

'You look upon me and see something whole . . . singular . . .' the Nonman said one night, his head hanging from his shoulders, his face utterly lost to shadow. When he looked up tears had silvered his cheeks. 'You are mistaken.'

'What did he mean?' Mimara asked after she and the Wizard

had curled onto their mats. They always slept side by side now. Achamian had even become accustomed to the point of absence that was her Chorae. Ever since that first Sranc attack, when she had been stranded with Soma beyond the protective circuit of his incipient Wards, he had been loathe to let her stray from his side.

'He means that he's not a . . . a *self* . . . in the way you and I are selves. Now go to sleep.'

'But how is that possible?'

'Because of memory. Memory is what binds us to what we are. Go to sleep.'

'What do you mean? How can somebody not be what they are? That makes no sense.'

'Go to sleep.'

He would lay there, his eyes closed to the world, while the image of the Nonman – mundane beauty perpetually at war with his arcane disfiguration – plagued his soul. The old Wizard would curse himself for a fool, ask himself how many watches he had wasted worrying about the Erratic. Cleric was one of the *Pharroika*, the Wayward. Whatever the Nonman once was, he was no longer – and that should be enough.

If he had ceased pondering Incariol altogether in the days following the battle in the ruins of Maimor, it was because of the skin-spy and what its presence implied. But time's passage has a way of blunting our sharper questions, of making things difficult to confront soft with malleable familiarity. Of course, the Consult had been watching him, the man who had taught the Gnosis to the Aspect-Emperor, and so delivered the Three Seas. *Of course*, they had infiltrated the Skin Eaters.

He was Drusas Achamian.

But the further Soma fell into the past, the more Cleric's presence irked his curiosity, the more the old questions began prickling back to life.

Even his Dreams had been affected.

He had lost his inkhorn and papyrus in the mad depths of Cil-Aujas, so he could no longer chronicle the particulars of his slumbering experience. Nor did he need to.

It almost seemed as if he had become unmoored when he pondered the transformations. First he had drifted from the central current of Seswatha's life, away from the tragic enormities and into the mundane details, where he had been delivered to knowledge of Ishuäl, the secret fastness of the Dûnyain. Then, as if these things were too small to catch the fabric of his soul, *he slipped from Seswatha altogether*, seeing things his ancient forebear had never seen, standing where he never stood, as when he saw the Library of Sauglish burn.

And now?

He continued to dream that he and nameless others stood shackled in a shadowy line. Broken men. Brutalized. They filed through a tube of thatched undergrowth, bushes that had grown out and around their passage, forming vaults of a thousand inter-locking branches. Over the stooped shoulders of those before him, he could see the tunnel's terminus, the threshold of some sunlit clearing, it seemed – the spaces beyond were so open and bright as to defeat his gloom-pinched eyes. He felt a dread that seemed curiously disconnected from his surroundings, as if his fear had come to him from a far different time and place.

And he did not know who he was.

A titanic horn would blare, and the line would be pulled stumbling forward, and peering, he would see a starved wretch at the fore, at least a hundred souls distant, stepping into the golden light . . . vanishing.

And the screaming would begin, only to be yanked short.

Again and again, he dreamed this senseless dream. Sometimes

it was identical. Sometimes he seemed one soul closer to the procession's end. He could never be sure.

Was it the Qirri? Was it the deathless rancour of the Mop, or a cruel whim of Fate?

Or had the trauma of his life at last unhinged him and cast his slumber to the wolves of grim fancy?

For his whole life, ever since grasping the withered pouch of Seswatha's heart deep in the bowel of Atyersus, his dreams had possessed *meaning* . . . logic, horrifying to be sure, but comprehensible all the same. For his whole life he had awakened with *purpose*.

And now?

'So what was it like?' Achamian asked her as the company filed through the arboreal maze.

'What was *what* like?'

They always addressed each other in Ainoni now. The fact that only the Captain could comprehend them made it seem daring somehow – and curiously proper, as if madmen should oversee the exchange of secrets. Even still, they took care that he did not overhear.

'Life on the Andiamine Heights,' he said, 'as an *Anasûrimbor*.'

'You mean the family you're trying to destroy.'

The old Wizard snorted. 'Just think, no more running.'

At last she smiled. Anger and sarcasm, Achamian had learned, were a kind of reflex for Mimara – as well as a fortress and a refuge. If he could outlast her initial hostility, which proved difficult no matter how much good humour he mustered, he could usually coax a degree of openness from her.

'It was complicated,' she began pensively.

'Well then, start at the beginning.'

'You mean when they came for me in Carythusal?'

The old Wizard shrugged and nodded.

They had slackened their pace enough to fall behind the others, even the dour file of Stone Hags, who stole longing glances as Mimara drifted past. Despite the chorus of birdsong, a kind of silence reared about them, the hush of slow growth and decay. It felt like shelter.

'You have to understand,' she said hesitantly. 'I didn't know that I had been wronged. The brutalities I endured . . . But I was a child . . . and then I was a brothel-slave – that's what I was . . . Something *made* to be violated, abused, over and over, until I grew too old or too ugly, and they sold me to the fullery. That was just the . . . the way . . . So when the Eothic Guardsmen came and began beating Yappi . . . Yapotis . . . the brothel master, I didn't understand. I *couldn't* understand . . .'

Achamian watched her carefully, saw a rare strand of sunlight flash across her face. 'You thought you were being attacked instead of saved.'

A numb nod. 'They took me away before the killing began, but I knew . . . I could tell from the soldiers' manner, cold, as merciless as any of these scalpers. I knew they would kill anyone who had a hand in my . . . my *fouling* . . .'

She had the habit of slipping into Tutseme when she became upset, the rough dialect peculiar to menials and slaves from Carythusal. The clipped vowels. The singsong intonations. Achamian would have teased her for sounding like an Ainoni harlot, had the subject matter been less serious.

'They brought me to a ship – you should have seen them! Stammering, bowing and kneeling, not the soldiers, but the Imperial Apparati who commanded them. They asked me – *begged* me! – for some kind of request, for something they could do, for my health and my ease, they said. For my glory. I'll never forget that! My whole life my only prize had been the lust my form incited in men – the face of an Empress, the hips and slit of a young girl – and there I stood, the proud possessor of what? *Glory?* So I said, "Stop. Stop the killing!" And they looked at me with long faces and said, "Alas, Princess, that is the one thing we cannot do." "Why?" I asked them . . .'

'"Because the Blessed Empress has commanded it," they said . . .

'So I stood on the prow and watched . . . They had moored on the high river, on the quays typically reserved for the Scarlet Spires – you know those? – so I could see the slums rise to the north, all the Worm laid out for inspection. I could see it burn . . . I could even see souls trapped on their roofs . . . Men, women, children . . . jumping . . .'

The old Wizard watched her, careful to purge any hint of pity from his frown. To be a child-whore one moment and a Princess-Imperial the next. To be plucked from abject slavery and hurtled to the heights of the greatest empire since Cenei. And then to have your old world burned down around you.

Esmenet, he understood, had tried to undo her crime with the commission of another. She had mistook vengeance for reparation.

'So you understand,' Mimara continued, swallowing. 'My first years on the Andiamine Heights were hateful . . . shameful, even. You understand why I did everything I could to punish Mother.'

Achamian studied her for a moment before nodding. The company had crested a gradual slope and now descended, using webs of bared roots as steps. A rare glimpse of the sun flashed above, making silhouettes of shagged leaves.

'I understand,' he said as they picked their way down, feeling the raw weight of his own story, his own grievances, press through the tone of his reply. They were both victims of Esmenet.

They walked in silence, their strides as thoughtless as they were quick.

'Thank you,' Mimara said after a time, fixing him with a curious gaze.

'For what?'

'For not asking what all the others ask.'

'Which is?'

'How I could have *stayed* all those years. How I could have allowed myself to be used as I was used. Apparently everyone would have run away, slit their master's throat, committed suicide . . .'

'Nothing makes fools of people quite like a luxurious life,' Achamian said, shaking his head and nodding. 'Ajencis says they confuse decisions made atop pillows for those compelled by stones. When they hear of other people being deceived, they're certain *they* would know better. When they hear of other people being oppressed, they're certain *they* would do anything but beg and cringe when the club is raised . . .'

'And so they judge,' Mimara said sourly.

'They certainly picked the wrong woman in your case!'

This coaxed another smile – another small triumph.

She began talking about her younger siblings, haltingly at first, then with more confidence and detail. She seemed surprised by her own reminiscences, and troubled. She had foresworn her family – he knew that much. But watching and listening to her describe the embittered object of her anger, he came to suspect she had gone so far as to *deny* her family, to tell herself that she was in fact alone, without the guy ropes of kith and kin to prop her.

Small wonder she had been so reluctant to tell him anything. People are generally loathe to describe what they need to forget, especially the small things, the loving things that contradict their precious sense of injustice.

She started with Kayûtas, the child Esmenet had carried in her womb the day Achamian had repudiated her before the assembled Lords of the Holy War. He would have seemed a kind of god to her, she said, had her stepfather not been Kellhus – a real God. 'He is the very image of his father,' she said, nodding as if agreeing with her own description. 'Not so remote, certainly . . . More . . .'

'Human,' the old Wizard said, scowling.

She then turned to Moënghus, whom she described as the most normal and difficult of her younger siblings. Apparently he was quite the terror as a youth, given to episodes of inconsolable anger and continually brooding, if not sulking. Esmenet regularly left the boys in her care – with the hope of fostering some tenderness for her younger siblings, Mimara presumed. She despised the swimming expeditions most of all.

Apparently Moënghus enjoyed diving under the water and not reappearing for the longest time. The first incident was the worst – she even called on their bodyguards to help her, only to watch Moënghus's head break the flashing water several spans away. He ignored her commands and curses, and repeated the stunt again and again. Each time she would tell herself he was simply playing, but her heart would continue counting beats, and the panic would well higher and higher – until she was fairly beside herself with fear and fury. Then his head would magically pop into sight, his black hair glazed in white sunlight, and he would glare at her shouting antics before descending again. Finally she turned on his brother, demanding an explanation.

'Because,' Kayûtas said with a detachment that clammed her skin, 'he wants people to think him dead.'

The old Wizard responded with a nodding snort. When he asked her whether anyone knew about his true parentage, she merely frowned and said, 'Questioning our holy parentage is sacrilege.'

Lies, Achamian mused. Deceit heaped atop deceit. In the early days of his exile, he would sometimes lie awake at night, convinced that sooner or later someone would see through Kellhus and his glamour, that the truth would win out, and all the madness would come crashing down . . .

That he could come home and reclaim his wife.

But as the years passed he came to see this for the rank foolishness that it was. He – a student of Ajencis, no less! Truths were carved from the identical wood as were lies – words – and so sank or floated with equal ease. But since truths were carved by the *World*, they rarely appeased Men and their innumerable vanities. Men had no taste for facts that did not ornament or enrich, and so they wilfully – if not knowingly – panelled their lives with shining and intricate falsehoods.

Mimara's eldest sister, Theliopa, would be the only one of her siblings to occasion a true smile. According to Mimara, the girl was almost incapable of expressing passion of any sort and was oblivious – sometimes comically so – to all but the most obvious social graces. She was also dreadfully thin, famine thin, and had to be continually cajoled and bullied to eat. But her intellect was nothing short of a miracle. Everything she read, she remembered, and she read voraciously, often to the point of forgetting to sleep. Her gifts were so prodigious that Kellhus made her an Imperial Adviser at the tender age of twelve, after which she became a continual presence in her mother's entourage: pale, emaciated, decked in absurd gowns of her own design and manufacture.

'It's hard not to pity her,' Mimara said, her gaze flat with memories, 'even as you marvel . . .'

'What do people say?'

'Say?'

'About her . . . peculiarities. What do they think caused them?' Few things inspired more malicious speculation than deformities. Conriya even had a law – back before the New Empire, anyway – rendering misshapened children the property of the King. Apparently the court diviners thought a careful reading of their deformations could reveal much about the future.

'They say my stepfather's seed is too heavy for mortal women to bear,' Mimara said. 'He took other wives, "Zikas" they call them, after the small bowls they pass out for libations on the Day of Ascension. But of those who became pregnant, none carried to term – either that or they died . . . Only Mother.'

Achamian could only nod, his thoughts roiling. Kellhus had to have known this, he realized. From the very beginning *he had known* Esmenet possessed the strength to survive him and his progeny. And so he had set out to conquer her womb as one more tool – one more *weapon* – in his unceasing war of word, insight, and passion.

You needed her, so you took . . .

Regarding her sister Serwa, Mimara said very little, save that she was cold and arrogant.

'She's the Grandmistress of the Swayali, now. *Grandmistress!* I don't think Mother ever forgave Kellhus for sending her away . . . I saw very little of her, and when I did my teeth fairly cracked for envy. Studying with the Sisters! Attaining the only thing I truly desired!'

Inrilatas, on the other hand, she discussed for quite some time, partly because Esmenet had sought to involve her in the boy's upbringing. According to Mimara, none of her siblings possessed more of their father's gifts – or more of their mother's all too human weaknesses. Speaking long before any infant should. Never forgetting. And seeing deeper, far deeper, than any human could . . . or should.

His subsequent madness, she said, was inevitable. He was perpetually at a loss, perpetually overwhelmed by the presence of others. Unlike his father, he could only see the brute truths, the facts and lies that compelled the course of lives, but these were quite enough.

'He would look into my eyes and say impossible things . . . hateful things . . .'

'How do you mean?'

'He told me once that I punished mother not to avenge my slavery, but because . . . because . . .'

'Because what?'

'Because I was broken inside,' she said, her lips set in a grim and brittle line. 'Because I had suffered so much so long that *kindness* had become the only cruelty I could *not* endure – kindness! – and so suffering would be all I . . . all I would ever know . . .'

She trailed, turned her face away to swat at the tears clotting her eyes.

'So I *told* him,' she continued, avoiding Achamian's gaze. 'I told him that I had *never known* kindness because everything – everything! – I had been given had been just another way to take – to steal! "You cannot stroke a beaten dog," he replied, "because it sees only the raised hand . . ." A beaten *dog*! Can you believe it? What kind of little boy calls his grown sister a *beaten dog*?'

A Dûnyain, the old Wizard thought in unspoken reply.

She must have glimpsed something of his sorrow in his eyes: the outrage in her expression, which had been helpless in the face of memory, turned in sudden fury upon him.

'You pity me?' she cried, as if her pain were something with its own outrage and volition. 'Pity?'

'Don't, Mimara. Don't do this . . .'

'Do what? *What?*'

'Make Inrilatas true.'

This smacked the fury from her expression. She stared at him speechless, her body jerking as her legs carried her thoughtlessly forward, her eyes wide with a kind of desolate horror.

'What about the others?' the old Wizard asked, snipping all memory of her outburst from his tone. The best way to retrieve a conversation from disaster, he often found, was to speak as if the disaster had never happened. 'I know there's more – the twins. Tell me about them.'

She marched in silence for a time, collecting herself, Achamian supposed. The footing had become even more treacherous: a stream had gullied the forest floor, cutting away the loam beneath the feet of several massive elms so that roots hung in tentacled sheets to their right. Achamian could see the rest of the party below, picking their way under a toppled giant with the same haste that was taking such a toll on the Hags. He glimpsed Cleric behind the Captain, white and bald and obviously not human. Even from a distance, his Mark blotted out his inhuman physical beauty, stained him with gut-wrenching ugliness.

The stream glittered, a ribbon of liquid obsidian in the gloom. The air smelled of clay and cold rot.

'They were the only ones, really . . .' she finally said. 'The twins. I was *there*, you know . . . there from the beginning with them. I saw them drawn squalling from Mother's womb . . .' She paused to watch her booted feet pick steps across the ground. 'I think that was the only moment I truly . . . truly *loved* her.'

'You've never stopped loving her,' Achamian said. 'You wouldn't care to hate her otherwise.'

Anger shrouded her eyes once again, but to her credit she managed to purge it from her voice. She was *trying*, the old Wizard realized. She wanted to trust him. Even more, she wanted to understand what *he* saw when he looked upon her – perhaps too desperately. 'What do you mean?'

'No love is simple, Mimara.' Something hooked his voice while saying this, something like weak eyes and a burning throat. 'At least no love worth the name.'

'But . . .'

'But nothing,' he said. 'Far too many of us confuse complexity for impurity – or even pollution. Far too many of us mourn what we should celebrate as a result. Life is unruly, Mimara. Only tyrants and fools think otherwise.'

She frowned in a mock here-we-go-again manner. 'Ajencis?' she asked, her eyes bright and teasing.

'No . . . Just wisdom. Not everything I say is borrowed, you know!'

She walked in silence for a time, her smile fading into a look of puzzled concentration. Achamian paced her in silence.

She resumed her account, describing the Imperial twins, Kelmomas and Samarmas. The latter was indeed an idiot, as Achamian had heard. But according to Mimara, the Imperial Physicians had feared both children were idiots in the beginning. Apparently the two infants would simply stare into each other's eyes, day after day, month after month, then year after year. If separated, they ceased to eat, as if they shared but one appetite between the two of them. It was only after Esmenet contracted a celebrated physician from Conriya that their two souls were finally pried apart and the idiocy of Samarmas was revealed.

'It was a wonder,' Mimara exclaimed, as if reliving the memories of their cure in a rush. 'To be so . . . so *strange*, and then to waken as, well, beautiful little boys, normal in all respects.'

'You were fond of them.'

'How could I *not* be? They were innocents born into a labyrinth – a place devious beyond compare. The others could never see it, no matter how much they complained and clucked, they could never see the Andiamine Heights for what it was.'

'And what was that?'

'A prison. A carnival. And a temple, a *temple* most of all. One where sins were counted according to harms *endured* rather than inflicted. It was no place for children! I told Mother as much, told her to take the twins to one of the Refuge Estates, some place where they could grow in the light of the sun, where things were . . . were . . .'

They had stooped to make their way beneath the fallen tree he'd seen earlier, so he supposed she had trailed to better concentrate. The limbs of the giant had folded and snapped, either bending back or prying deep into the earth. Dead leaves hung in rasping sheets. Finding passage was no easy task.

'Where things were what?' he asked when it became apparent she did not care to continue.

'Simple,' she said dully.

Achamian smiled in his wise old teacher way. The thought occurred to him that she had sought to protect the memory of her own childhood as much as the innocence of her two little brothers. But he said nothing. People rarely appreciate alternative, self-serving interpretations of their conduct – especially when suffering ruled the balance of their lives.

'Let me guess,' he ventured. 'Your mother refused, said that they would need to learn the perils and complexities of statecraft to survive as Princes-Imperial.'

'Something like that,' she replied.

'So you trusted him. Kelmomas, I mean.'

'Trusted?' she cried with open incredulity. 'He was a child! He adored me – to the point of annoyance!' She fixed him with a vexed look, as if to say, *Enough, old man* . . . 'He was the reason I ran away to find you, in fact.'

Something troubled the old Wizard about this, but as so often happens in the course of heated conversations, his worries yielded to the point he hoped to press home. 'Yes . . . But he was a child of *Kellhus*, an Anasûrimbor *by blood*.'

'So?'

'So, that means he possesses *Dûnyain* blood. Like Inrilatas.'

They had sloshed across the stream and were now climbing the far side of the gully. They could see the rest of the company above them, a string of frail forms labouring beneath the monumental trunks.

'Ah, I keep forgetting,' she said, huffing. 'I suppose he simply *must* be manipulative and amoral . . .' She regarded him the way he imagined she had regarded countless others on the Andiamine Heights: as something ridiculous. 'You've been cooped in the wilds too long, Wizard. Sometimes a child is just a child.'

'That's all they know, Mimara. The Dûnyain. They're bred for it.'

She dismissed him with a flutter of eyelids. She had no inkling, he realized – like everyone else in the Three Seas. For her, Kellhus was simply what he appeared to be.

In the first years of his exile, the hardest years, Achamian had spent endless hours revisiting the events of the First Holy War – his memories of Kellhus and Esmenet most of all. The more he pondered the man, the more obvious the Scylvendi's revelatory words came to seem, until it became difficult to remember what it was like living *within* the circuit of his glamour. To think he had still loved the man *after* he had lured Esmenet to his bed! That he had spent sleepless hours wrestling with excuses – excuses! – for him.

But even still, after so many years, the appearances continued to argue *for* the man. Everything Mimara had described regarding the preparations for the Great Ordeal – even the scalpers accompanying him! – attested to what Kellhus had claimed so many years previous: that he had been sent to *prevent* the Second

Apocalypse. Achamian had suffered that old sense several times now while feuding with Mimara, the one that had plagued him as a Mandate Schoolman travelling the courts of the Three Seas arguing the very things Kellhus had made religion (and *there* was an irony that plucked, if there ever was one). The anxious urge to throw words atop words, as if speaking could plaster over the cracked expressions that greeted his claims. The plaintive, wheedling sense of being disbelieved.

Maybe you need it, old man . . . Need to be disbelieved.

He had seen it before: men who had borne perceived injustices so long they could never relinquish them and so continually revisited them in various guises. The world was filled with self-made martyrs. Fear goads fear, the old Nansur proverb went, and sorrow, sorrow.

Perhaps he was mad. Perhaps everything – the suffering, the miles, the lives lost and taken – was naught but a fool's errand. As wrenching as this possibility was, and as powerful as the Scylvendi's words had been, Achamian would have been entirely prepared to accept his folly. He was a true student of Ajencis in this respect . . .

Were it not for his Dreams. And the coincidence of the Coffers.

The old Wizard continued on in silence, mulling the details of Mimara's tale. The picture she had drawn was as fascinating as it was troubling. Kellhus perpetually distracted, perpetually absent. His children possessing a jumble of human and Dûnyain attributes – and half-mad for it, apparently. Games heaped upon games, and sorrow and resentment most of all. Esmenet had fetched her broken daughter from the brothel only to deliver her to the arena that was the Andiamine Heights – a place where no soul could mend.

Not hers, and certainly not her daughter's.

Was this not a kind of proof of Kellhus? Pain followed him, as did tumult and war. Every life that fell into his cycle suffered some kind of loss or deformation. Was this not an outward sign of his . . . his *evil*?

Perhaps. Perhaps not. Suffering had ever been the wages of revelation. The greater the truth, the greater the pain. No one understood this quite so profoundly as he.

Either way, it was proof of *Mimara*. Our words always paint two portraits when we describe our families to others. Outsiders cannot but see the small peeves and follies that wrinkle our relationships with our loved ones. The claims we make in defensive certainty – that we were the one wronged, that we were the one who wanted the best – cannot but fall on skeptical ears since everyone but everyone makes the same claims of virtue and innocence. We are always more than we want to be in the eyes of others simply because we are blind to the bulk of what we are.

Kellhus had taught him that.

Mimara had wanted him to see her as a victim, as a long-suffering penitent, more captive than daughter, and not as someone embittered and petulant, someone who often held others accountable for her inability to feel safe, to feel anything unpolluted by the perpetual pang of shame . . .

And he loved her the more for it.

Later, as the murk of evening steeped through the forest galleries, she slowed so that he could draw abreast, but she did not return his questioning gaze.

'What I told you,' she eventually said, 'that was foolish of me.'

'What was foolish?'

'What I said.'

This final exchange left him sorting through melancholy thoughts of his own family and the wretched Nroni fishing village where he had been born. They seemed strangers, now, not simply the people who inhabited his childhood memories, but the passions as well. The doting love of his sisters . . . Even the tyranny of his father – the maniacal shouts, the wordless beatings – seemed to belong to some soul other than his own.

This, he realized . . . This was his true family: the mad children of the man who had robbed him of his wife. The New Anasûrimbor Dynasty. These were his brothers and sisters, sons and daughters. And this simply meant that he had *no* family . . . that he was alone.

Save for the mad woman trekking beside him.

His little girl . . .

Back when he had been a tutor in Aöknyssus, he took up the antique Ceneian practice of considering problems while walking – peripatetics, the ancients had called it. He would trudge down from his apartment by the Premparian Barracks, through the wooded pathways of the Ke, and down to the port, where the masts made a winter forest of the piers. There was this defunct temple where he would always glimpse the same beggar through a breach in the walls. He was one of those unravelled men, unkempt and withered, slow-moving and speechless, as if dumbfounded at where the years had delivered him. And for some reason it always knocked Achamian from his stride seeing him. He would pass gazing, his walk slowing to a numb saunter, and the beggar would simple stare off, beyond caring who did or did not watch. Achamian would forget whatever problem he had set off to ponder and brood instead about the cruel alchemy of age and love and time. A fear would clutch him, knowing that this, *this*, was true solitude, to find yourself the feeble survivor, stranded at the end of your life, your loves and hopes reduced to remembered smoke, hungering, suffering . . .

And waiting. Waiting most of all.

His mother was dead, the old Wizard supposed.

Making water or mud has always been an irritating challenge for her. She cannot simply retreat behind a tree as the others might, not for the sake of modesty – a sentiment that had been pummelled from her in childhood – but out of a keen awareness of men and their lustful infirmities. She has to plunge deeper, beyond the possibility of craning looks. 'A glimpse is a promise,' the brothel masters used to say. 'Show them what they would steal, and they will spend – *spend!*'

She squats, her breeches crowded about her knees, stares up into the veined complexities of the canopy as she relieves herself. She follows the dark lines of silhouetted limbs scrawling across foliated stages, ragged screen set across ragged screen, each brighter than the next. She doesn't see the figure . . . not at first.

But then its shape is unmistakable: *human* limbs clutched and hanging about arboreal. Unlike other forests, where trees branch and thicken according to their exposure to the sun, the trees of the Mop fork into the low nethers, as though begrudging all open space. The creature hangs from the lowermost skein, unnaturally still, intent with scrutiny and malice.

The thing called Soma.

Her fear falls short of reason. If it had wanted to kill her, she would already be dead. If it had wanted to steal her, she would already be missing.

No. It wants something.

She should cry out, she knows, send it fleeing into the sepulchral depths, chased by the crack and thunder of sorcerous lights. But she does not. It wants something, and she needs to know what. Slowly, deliberately, she stands and draws up her leggings, winces at her own humid reek.

Its face hangs down just far enough to be discernable in the murk. Soma, as if glimpsed through a veil of black gauze. The canopy's high-hanging glow paints his edges with traceries of green.

'He's killing you,' it coos. 'The Nonman.'

She stares up, breathless, immobile. She *knows* this thing, she reminds herself, knows it as surely as scalpers know Sranc. Assassins. Deceivers. Sowers of resentment and mistrust. Discord arouses them. Violence spills their cup. They are, as her mother once told her, the consummate union of viciousness and grace.

'Then I shall kill him first,' she says, shocked by the resolute tenor of her voice. Her whole life she has been surprised by her ability to appear strong.

This is not the reply it was expecting. She's not sure how she knows this: its hesitation, perhaps, or the click of indecision that passes like smoke across its false expression. Regardless, she knows that it does not want the Nonman dead . . . at least not yet.

'No . . .' it whispers. '*Such a thing is beyond your power.*'

'My fath—'

'*He too would certainly perish.*'

She glares upward, peering, trying to discern the folding digits that compose its face. She cannot.

'*There is only one way to save yourself,*' it rasps.

'And how is that?'

'*Kill the Captain.*'

⸺◦⸺

She rejoins the company as if nothing has happened. She should tell Achamian. She knows this without *wanting* to know. Her reflex is to hide and to hoard – a product of the brothel, no doubt. Too much had been stolen.

Soma came to me . . .

She circles this thought, stalks it, returns to it the way she continually reaches for her Chorae where it hangs about her neck. As troubled as she is, as frightened as she is, a part of her soul exults – in the mystery of it, certainly, but also because it had chosen her before any of the others.

Why had it saved her during the Stone Hag attack? At the cost of revealing itself, no less!

Why was it following them in the first place?

And why was it reaching out to *her*?

After the nightmare of Maimor, Achamian spent long miles verbally pondering the skin-spy and its presence among the Skin Eaters. From the outset he made assumptions, forgivable assumptions: that the skin-spy had infiltrated the Skin Eaters immediately after *he* had contracted them. That *he*, the outcast inheritor of their ancient and implacable enemy, Seswatha, was the motive for the infiltration. That it was charged with killing him, lest *he* discover something too decisive . . . And so on.

More than anything else, what prevents her from telling the old Wizard is the fear that *he is wrong* – utterly and catastrophically. The suspicion that the Consult has sent the skin-spy, not to assassinate Achamian or to sabotage the expedition, no. Her fear is that the Consult has sent it to assist them . . . to *ensure* they reach Sauglish and the Coffers.

And why not, when Drusas Achamian is the enemy of their enemy? According to her mother, the Consult waited months before finally attacking Kellhus during the First Holy War. 'The only thing they found more terrifying than your stepfather,' she said, 'was the possibility there could be *more like him*.'

The possibility of Ishuäl.

The origin of the Aspect-Emperor. As much as Achamian desires this knowledge to *judge* Anasûrimbor Kellhus, would not the Unholy Consult covet it even more?

She has seen the Wizard with the Judging Eye – seen his damnation. At the time she simply assumed that sorcery was the cause, that contrary to her stepfather's claims, sorcery *remained* the unpardonable sin. And this seemed to lend credence to Achamian and his desperate case against the man who had stolen his wife. But what if this wasn't the case? What if this very quest was the ground of his damnation? There is poetry in the notion, as perverse as it is, and this more than anything else is what hones her fear to a cutting edge. To strike out in the name of love, only to inadvertently unleash the greatest terror the world has ever seen. When she mulls the possibility, it seems to smell of the Whore through and through . . . at least from what she has seen of Her.

This is what makes telling the Wizard all but impossible. What was she supposed to say? That his life and the lives of all those his deceptions have killed have been in vain? That he is a tool of the very apocalypse he hopes to prevent?

No. She will not speak what cannot be heard. Soma would have to remain her secret, at least for the immediate future. She needs to discover more before going to the Wizard . . .

Kill the Captain . . .

She knows this creature. She can number the bones in its false face. She even knows the questions that will confuse it, hint at the absence that is its soul. It stands upon a different field of battle, vast and spectral and devious with a thousand years of patient calculation. And for some reason, it needs Lord Kosoter to be a casualty of that cryptic battle.

Kill the Captain. Understand this command, she realizes, and she will understand Soma's design.

She has watched the slow transformation of loyalties and rivalries within the company. She has seen the glint of sedition in Galian's eyes. She has noticed the way Achamian has come to accept, even prize, the Captain and his ruthless methods. Lord Kosoter *will* deliver them to the Library of Sauglish – despite all the perils and uncertainties. He is simply one of those men, possessed of a will so cruel, so domineering, that the world could not but yield.

He was the *Captain*. The harsh shadow, bloodthirsty and pitiless, forever standing in her periphery.

She has always watched, and her eyes are nothing if not critical, but she has never probed, never *tested*. According to Soma something was happening, something that would eventually imperil their lives. According to Soma things transpired that neither she nor the old Wizard could see.

So she will squint against the glare of the obvious, peer into the gloom of implication. She will pretend to sleep while pondering possibilities and assembling questions. She will solve this one mystery . . .

She will become a spy.

So far the Mop has climbed and conquered every terrain they have encountered, scaffolding the sides of hills, braiding the heights above rivers, pillaring broad plains. She has peered through the green murk and trod across root-heaved earth for so long that sometimes she forgets the arid smell of open places, the flash of sunlight, and the kiss of unobstructed wind. All is humid and enclosed. She feels like a mole, forever racing beneath the thatch, always wary of flying shadows. When she thinks of the Stone Hags who have fallen in exhaustion, they are already buried in her soul's eye.

Finally they come to a stone formation jutting like a great fractured bone from the earth. Scrub clings to its scarped shelves, but nothing else, and peering up they actually catch ragged glimpses of sky where its bulk breaches the canopy. Standing aloof from their curious peering, the Captain bids them to find a way to the summit. Though hours of daylight remain, they will camp.

The sun glares. The air chills. The Mop tosses on and on, an endless ocean of swaying crowns. Whatever relief they hope to find in wind and sunlight is snuffed when they look to one another. Squinting. Eyes glittering from blackened faces. Ragged like beggars. In the gloom below, they seemed as true to their surroundings as the moss or the humus. Here on the heights, there is no overlooking either their straits or their desperation.

They look like the damned. Achamian, in particular, given the Mark.

They make camp on the formation's rump, where enough soil has accumulated to sustain a thin wig of foliage. They sit in scattered clots, watching the setting sun fall crimson into distant canopies. The Mop seems to mock and to beckon in turn, a susurrus unlike any she has heard, a horde of a million million leaves rattling in the dying breeze.

Opposite their camp, the formation rears into a promontory, stone horned like a bent-back thumb. The Captain stands in the dying light, beckons Cleric to follow him. Mimara pretends not to watch them vanish about the treacherous ledges. She counts fifty heartbeats, then strikes out along the opposite face, where they have designated their latrine. She continues past the putrid smell, literally risks life and limb scaling a serrated pitch. Then she creeps forward in a crouch, moving toward the sound of muttered voices.

The breeze or the play of echoes across chaotic stone fools her, for she almost blunders upon them. Only some instinct to freeze saves her from discovery. She breathlessly shrinks behind the cover of a tortoise-humped outcropping.

'They remind you . . .'

The Captain's voice. It shocks her as surely as a knife point pressed against the back of her neck.

She creeps along the outer circuit of the tortoise stone, nearer,

nearer . . . As shallow as it is, her breath burns against the tightness of her high chest. Her heart thumps.

'*What's happening?*' the Nonman says. '*I don't . . . I don't understand . . .*'

'*You are truly a blasted idiot.*'

She steps from behind the rising shell of rock, finds herself standing almost entirely exposed. Only the direction of their gazes prevents them from seeing her. Cleric sits in a pose of dejected glory, at once beautiful and grotesque for the blasted depths of his Mark. The Captain stands over him, a vision of archaic savagery, his Chorae so close to the Nonman that she can see a faint husk of salt rising across his scalp.

'Tell me!' Incariol cries in hushed tones. 'Tell me why I am here!'

A moment of glaring impatience. 'Because they *remind* you.'

'But who? They remind me of who?' Even as Cleric says this his glittering black eyes wander toward her.

'Someone you once knew,' the Captain grates. 'They remind you of someone you once—'

He whirls toward her. His hair swings in broken sheets of black and grey.

'What are you doing?' he barks.

'I-I . . .' she stammers. 'I think I need more . . . more Qirri.'

A moment of murderous deliberation, then something like a grin hooks his eyes. He turns wordlessly to the Nonman, who remains seated as before.

'No,' Cleric says with a strange solemnity. 'Not yet. I apologize . . . Mimara.'

This is the first time he has spoken her name. She retreats, flinching from the Captain's manic glare, her skin buzzing with the shame of her exposure. Afterward she remembers the Nonman's lips more than his voice, their fulsome curves, white tinged with too-long-in-the-water blue. She sees them moving to the rhythm of consonant and vowel.

Mim . . . araa . . .

Like a kiss, she thinks, her arms bundled against a curious sense of chill.

Like a kiss.

——◦◦◦◦——

She keeps to herself the following day. The Wizard seems only too happy to oblige her. The trail has its rhythms, its own ebb and flow. Sometimes everyone seems to be engaged in low conversation, while other times everyone appears sullen and wary or simply lost in their own labouring breaths, and naught can be heard above the whistling chorus of birdsong. Their descent back into the Mop has replaced their anxiousness with melancholy.

She is quite lost in thought when Cleric comes alongside her, senseless ruminations, more a collage of recriminations and pained memories than anything meaningful.

She smiles at her shock. The unearthly beauty of his face and form unsettles her, almost as much as the horrid depth of his Mark. Something wrenches at the inner corners of her eyes whenever she allows her gaze to linger. He is contradiction incarnate.

'Is it true,' he inexplicably asks, 'that being touched by another and touching oneself are quite distinct sensations for Men?'

The question bewilders and embarrasses her, to the point of drawing even more heat to her flushed face. 'Yes . . . I suppose . . .'

He walks in silence for a time, eyes tracking the ground before his booted feet. There is something . . . overwhelming about his stature. The other men, with the possible exception of Sarl, exude the same aura of physical strength and martial brutality as had so many warlike men on the Andiamine Heights. But Cleric possesses a density beyond intimations of force and threat, one that reminds her of her stepfather and the way the world always seemed to bow about his passage.

She thinks of all the skinnies he has killed, the legions incinerated in the existential thunder of his voice. And he seems *hardened* for the multitudes that flicker shrieking before her soul's eye – in Cil-Aujas, on Maimor, across the Mop – as if murder draws flesh to stone. She wonders what it would be like, dying beneath his black-glittering eyes.

Beautiful, she decides.

'I think I once knew this,' he finally says. At first she cannot identify the passion twining through his voice. Achamian has told her much about the Nonmen, how their souls often move in ways counter to the tracks of human passion. She wants to say sorrow, but it seems *more* somehow . . .

She wonders if tragedy could be a passion.

'Now you know it again,' she says, smiling at the frigid gaze.

'No,' he replies. 'Never again.'

'Then why ask?'

'There is . . . comfort . . . in rehearsing the dead motions of the past.'

She finds herself nodding – as if they were peers discussing common knowledge. 'We are alike in this way.'

'Mimara,' he says, his tone so simple with astonishment that for an instant he seems a mortal man. 'Your name is . . . *Mimara* . . .' He turns to her, his eyes brimming with human joy. She shudders at the glimpse of his fused teeth – there is something too dark about his smile. 'Ages have passed,' he says wondering, 'since I have remembered a human name . . .'

Mimara.

Afterward, her thoughts racing, she ponders the absurdity of memory, the fact that so simple a faculty can make a being so powerful so pathetic in its faltering. But the Wizard has been watching, of course. He's *always* watching, it seems. Always worried. Always . . . trying.

Like Mother.

'What did he want?' he rasps in heated Ainoni.

'Why do you fear him?' she snaps in return. She is never sure where this instinct comes from, knowing how to throw men on their heels.

The old Wizard walks and scowls, frail against a murky background of colossal trunks and mossed deadfalls. Trees growing in a graveyard of trees.

'Because I'm not sure that I could kill him when the time comes,' he finally says. He speaks as much to the matted ground as to her, his beard crowded against his breastbone, his eyes unfocused in the manner of men making too-honest admissions.

'When the time comes . . .' she says in mocking repetition.

He turns to her profile, studies her.

'He's an *Erratic*, Mimara. When he decides he loves us, he will try to kill us.'

The words she overheard the previous night seem to clutch with their own fingers, to scratch with nails like quills . . .

'But who? They remind me of who?'

'Someone,' the Captain replies in his grinding voice, *'you once knew . . .'*

She composes her face into the semblance of boredom. 'How can you be so sure?' she asks the Wizard.

'Because that is what Erratics do. Kill those they love.'

She holds his gaze for an instant, then looks down to her trudging feet. She glimpses the skull of some animal – a fox, perhaps – jutting from the humus.

'To remember.'

She doesn't mean this as a question, and apparently understanding, the old Wizard says nothing in reply. He always seems preternaturally wise when he does this.

'But his memory . . .' she says. 'How could he be more powerful than you when he can barely follow the passage of days?'

Achamian scratches his chin through the wiry mat of his beard. 'There's more than one kind of memory . . . It's events and individuals he forgets, mostly. Skills are different. They don't pile on the same way across the ages. But like I told you, sorcery depends on the purity of the meanings. What makes magic so difficult for you to learn turns on the same principle that makes him so powerful – even if he has forgotten the bulk of what he once knew. *Ten thousand years*, Mimara! The purity that escapes you, the purity that I find such toil, is simply a reflex for the likes of him.'

He stares at her the way he always does when trying to press home some crucial point: his lips slightly parted, his eyes beseeching beneath a furrowed brow.

'A Quya Mage,' she says.

'A Quya Mage,' he repeats, nodding in relief. 'Few things in this world are more formidable.'

She tries to smile at him but looks away because of the sudden threat of tears. Worry and fear assail her. Over Cleric and the Captain, over the skin-spy and what it has insinuated. She draws a deep breath, risks looking at the old man. He grins in melancholy reassurance, and suddenly it all seems manageable, standing here at his gruff and tender side.

Akka. The world's only sorcerer without a School. The only Wizard.

'Akka . . .' she murmurs. A kind of gentle beseeching.

She understands now why her mother still loves him – even

after so many years, even after sharing her bed with a living God. The uniform teeth behind his smile. The sheen of compassion that softens even his most hostile glare. The heart and simple passion of a man who, despite all his failings, is capable of risking everything – life and world – in the name of love.

'What?' he asks, his voice querulous, his eyes twinkling.

An unaccountable shyness climbs into her face. He is, she realizes, the first man to have ever made her feel safe.

'May our dooms be one,' she says with curt nod.

The old Wizard smiles. 'May our dooms be one, Mimara.'

The pebble it throws is round and chipped, drawn down from the high mountains, its surface cracked and polished by ages of blasting water and migrating gravel. It threads the sieve of dead branches, climbing its low-thrown arc, before sailing into the midst of supine company, over the slumbering form of Pokwas, into the tangle of hair about her head.

She awakens instantly, knows instantly.

Soma.

She recoils from the thought, knowing that Soma, the real Soma, lies dead somewhere near Marrow – that what awaits her in the black has no name because it has no soul.

She wanders from the camp, following a rare lane of low light, beyond the first ring of towering sentinels, beyond the reach of any incipient Wards. She feels more than sees the shadow atop the blunt limb above her. Breathless, she looks up . . .

The shadow leans down and forward, and she sees it, staring at her with wide, expectant eyes . . .

Her own face.

'I can smell the fetus within you . . .' she hears her voice say.

'Kill the Captain, and it will be saved.'

No. No. No.

Deceit! Devilry and deceit!

All her life she has thought in whispers. A habit of slaves, who must practise within what will save them without.

But her heart shouts as she tries to find her way back to sleep.

Lie. This is what they do, skin-spies. Uncertainty is their contagion; fear and confusion are their disease. 'They seduce,' her mother once told her. 'They play on your fears, your vulnerabilities, use them to craft you into their tool.'

But what if . . .

Coupling. It was something she did . . . A kind of blankness rose within her, an absence where human feeling should have been. Men always wanted her, and she almost always despised them for it. Almost always. Sometimes, when she needed things or when she simply wanted to feel dead, her body answered their want, and she took them into her. She held them while they laboured and trembled, she bore them as a burden upon her back. And she almost never thought about it afterward, simply continued running through her running life.

She had endured innumerable suitors while on the Andiamine Heights, an insufferable parade of dandies and widowers, some cruel, others despondent, all of them hungry for the peach of Imperial power. To a man she had spurned them, had even managed to provoke a handful of formal protestations. One, the Patridomos of House Israti, even brought a suit before the Judges, claiming that she should be forced to marry him as punishment for her slander. Mother had seen to that fool.

But she had been bedded nonetheless. And despite years of carrying a whore-shell, despite the chaos of her menstrual cycle, pregnancy was not impossible. The strong seed forces the womb . . .

Her mother was proof of that.

Three, she tells herself. There are only three occasions she can think of that would make the accursed creature true. There was the darling body-slave – little more than a boy – who attended to her ledgers before her flight. As absurd as it is, she owns estates across the Three Seas – as does everyone in the Imperial Family. There was Imhailas, the vain Captain of the Eothic guard, who helped her escape in exchange for a taste of her peach.

Then there was Achamian, who yearned so for the mother she so resembled. She had yielded and he had taken – their 'first mistake together,' he had called it – in exchange for a sorcery she no longer desired.

Three, she tells herself, when in fact there is only one.

She dwells on the skin-spy and its revelation, makes adversaries of its words and an arena of her soul.

'I can smell the fetus within you . . .'

She battles it with unvoiced denunciations. *Liar!* she rails within. *Obscene deceiver!* But hers is a treacherous heart, forever miring what should be simple with unwanted implications. So she hears the Wizard speaking in rejoinder . . .

'The Judging Eye is the eye of the Unborn . . .'

Trying to explain away the horror of her accursed sight.

'The eye that watches from the vantage of the God.'

On and on the voices tangle, until it seems they are one and the same, the sorcerer and the spy.

'Kill the Captain, and it will be saved.'

No, she tells herself. No. No. No. The brothel has taught her the power of pretense, the way facts will sometimes fade into oblivion, if you deny them with enough ferocity.

This is what she will do.

Yes. Yes. Yes.

—∞∞∞—

Several days pass without sign of the thing called Soma. She tells herself she is relieved, yet she lingers in the lonely dark nonetheless, gazing up through the dead branches, listening to the blackness croak and creak.

One night she finds a small pool bathed in a miraculous shaft of moonlight. She crouches beside it, stares up through the hanging tunnel to consider the moon. She gazes at her image poised between floating leaves and finds herself troubled. The skin-spy, she realizes, was the last time she saw her own face. She wants to fret over her appearance in the old way, to primp and preen, but it all seems so foolish, life before this, the Slog of Slogs.

Then, in the empty interval between breaths, the Judging Eye opens.

For a time she gazes in stupefaction, then she weeps at the transformation.

Her hair cropped penitent short. Her clothing fine, but with the smell of borrowed things. Her belly low and heavy with child . . .

And a *halo* about her head, bright and silver and so very holy. The encircling waters darken for its glow.

She convulses about breathless sobs, falls clutching her knees for anguish . . .

For she sees that *she is good* – and this she cannot bear.

The old Wizard pesters her with questions when she returns. He wonders at her swollen eyes – worries. She withdraws the way she always withdraws when dismay overwhelms her ability to think clearly. She can see the hurt and the confusion in the Wizard's eyes, knows that he has treasured the gradual intimacy that has grown between them – that he truly has come to think of her as his daughter . . .

But this can never be, for fathers do not lie with their daughters.

So she spurns him, even as she allows him to curl about her.

To shelter.

Weeks pass. Weeks of marching gloom and touches of Qirri. Weeks of battling clans of Sranc.

Weeks of tracing the line of her stomach in the murk.

At last they walk clear of the Mop, and it seems like climbing, setting foot on land open to the sun. They gather in a line across a low ridge, thirteen of them including the Hags, their skin and clothes black from sleeping across mossy earth, the splint and chainlinks of their armour rusted for rain and torn for battling Sranc. The Skin Eaters remain intact, but the Hags have dwindled to three: the Tydonni thane, Hurm, who remains as hale as any; the Galeoth freeman, Koll, whose body seems to be wasting about his will; and the deranged Conriyan, Hilikas – or Grinner, as Galian calls him – who seems to draw sustenance from madness.

The ground collapses into broad skirts of rock and gravel below the company's feet. A smattering of trees cling to the base, hedged by surging nettles and sumac, a tangle of stem and colour that abruptly ends in blue-green swathes of reed, a kind of papyrus, hazy miles cut by black-water channels. Salt marshes. The Cerish Sea forms a featureless plate across the northern horizon, iron dark save where the sun silvers its faraway swells.

They watch ripples of lighter green sweep over the marshes – the apparition of the wind across the rushes. And then they see it, the bones of once-mighty walls, the scapular remains of a gate, and the fields beyond clotted with ruins. She gazes in silent wonder, watches the shadow of a cloud soundlessly soak the distances grey and blue.

'Behold!' the old Wizard calls out from her side. 'Ancient Kelmeol. Home to the Sons of Meori. The Far Antique capital of these wastes ere the First Apocalypse.'

She gazes at him, unaware of the palm that has strayed to her belly.

Your father.

She bites her lip, hard, as proof against getting sick.

Achamian could scarce believe his fortune.

Until sighting Kelmeol, he had not realized just how little he had believed in his own mission. Ever since Marrow, some seditious faction within his soul had doubted he would survive even this far. And it seemed a kind of miracle that Men could suffer such trials in the absence of belief, that deeds worthy of wonder and song could be accomplished on the strength of a doubting will.

Unable to find the causeway, the company waded through the mire, beset by clouds of mosquitoes and biting flies. Several actually cried out in relief when they finally clambered onto hard ground and into the wind. After a mere watch Sarl looked poxed, he was covered with so many welts.

Kelmeol lay before them, the terrain humped with tells, the grasses so high it seemed a field in Massentia save for the grand remains of towers and temples breaching the near distance. Achamian had wandered the ruins of antique cities before, but never one so vast or so old. Seswatha had come to Kelmeol in 2150, one more refugee of the fall of the High Norsirai nations. And though those dreamed glimpses were two thousand years old, Achamian could not shake the sense that Kelmeol had fallen in his lifetime, that he was witness to a miraculous obliteration. With every glance a part of him wanted to cry out in disbelief.

There, where the mighty twin statues of Aulyanau had looked down the processional and out across the harbour and over the turquoise sea. Later he would find one of the great heads staring out of the high grasses, more than half-buried and yet still taller than a man. The harbour itself had been swallowed by waving miles of reeds, its very shape lost to the creep of earth and ages.

There, where the Hull, the white-washed curtain walls, had traced the circuit of the city. In some places nothing more than a berm remained of the once-celebrated fortifications, whereas in others sections remained remarkably intact, missing only the polished bronze spikes that had once adorned the crenulations.

There, where the ponderous lines of the Nausk Mausoleum had loomed over the lesser structures of the Pow, the low harbour district – a place of drawn blades and bared breasts. He could still see the rear walls of the Nausk rising like a husk from the ruins of the facade, the stone black save where matted with white and green lichens. The Pow, however, had utterly vanished beneath the waving sheets of green.

And *there*, the Heilor, the sacred acropolis where the Three Auguries once read the future in the blood of stags, rising like a low-hewn tree stump against the blue band of the Cerish Sea. The citadel had been razed to its foundations. The palace, where Seswatha had taken refuge from the Whirlwind, was little more than a mouth of ruined teeth behind the marble-pillared porticoes.

The decision was made to camp on the ruined acropolis, where they could defend against whatever Sranc clans ranged the marshes. In the Mop, they had slogged in a loose file. Now they spread out across the fields, walked in a ragged rank. They opened and closed about fragments of structure and ornamentation, heaps of spilled masonry, and square columns fallen for so long that the ground had climbed to encompass all but their leaning crowns. In some places, the ruins crowded thick enough to break their formation altogether.

A sadness welled through the old Wizard as he walked and peered, a mourning that possessed the airy clutch of premonition. There was poetry in loss and ruin, a wisdom that even children and idiots understood. For a time he suffered the eerie sense that he walked one of the great capitals of the Three Seas, that these were the ruins of Momemn, Carythusal, or Invishi, and they were the Last Men, thirteen instead of the one hundred and forty-four thousand of legend, and that no matter how far they travelled, how many horizons they outran, all they would find was soot and broken stone.

The world became strange with loneliness. And quiet, very quiet.

Insects whirred to and fro. Fluff scribbled across the back of warring gusts.

Without thinking he reached out for Mimara's hand. He did not answer her wondering gaze.

By happenstance, he found himself abreast Galian and one of the remaining Stone Hags, the dispossessed Tydonni thane, Tûborsa Hurm.

Hurm was perhaps the strangest of Stone Hags, both in appearance and behaviour. He continued to shave, for one, long after even Galian had abandoned his bare chin. At the close of the day's march, when his brothers could scarce speak for exhaustion, he would set to sharpening his dagger, which he had worn as narrow as a fish knife, for use on his cheeks at first light. Apparently this was a kind of ritual protest among the ordinarily long-bearded Tydonni, a way to proclaim the theft of one's honour.

Either way, it spoke to the man's stamina: even without Qirri he seemed to have little difficulty matching the company's pace. He had one of those lean physiques, with powerful shoulders perpetually angled forward as if in anticipation of a sprint. His face, which remained ruddy even in the perpetual gloom of the Mop, was shaped like the outward curve of a bow, with close-set eyes and a tiny, even womanish mouth beneath a shark-fin nose.

Galian was pressing the man with questions about the Stone Hags and the scalpers they robbed and murdered – an indelicate topic even given the crude standards of the slog.

'Gali . . .' Achamian heard Pokwas murmur in warning.

The former Columnary scowled up at the towering Zeümi. 'I want to know what moves a man to kill his own kind when skinnies are stacked to the horizon.'

'*Scalps,*' Hurm said, grinning. 'The Custom House counts. It makes no distinction between the likes of you and the likes of me.'

'I don't understand,' Galian said, his voice lowered in mock caution. Somewhere, somehow, Achamian realized with more than a little dismay, the man had lost his fear of their Captain. 'The Bounty is the *Holy* Bounty, is it not?'

'Holy, is it?'

'What else would it be?'

A phlegmatic snort. '*Gold,*' Hurm said after spitting a string of phlegm. 'Gold for mead. Gold for pork-and-onion stew . . .' His porcine gaze clicked from place to place, then settled on Mimara, appraised her with a kind of milky viciousness. His lips parsed about rotted teeth. 'Gold for pretty, pretty peaches.'

Perhaps this was when Achamian first sensed the madness about to happen.

'You would wager *damnation* for these things?' Galian asked.

'Damnation?'

A sly grin. 'The Holy Bounty is Holy because it has been decreed by the Aspect-Emperor.'

'The Aspect-Emperor, is it? Would you like to know what *I* think of our glorious tyrant?'

Achamian recognized the triumph in the Columnary's look. Galian used the same baiting manner with Soma, only with more mischief than malice in his eyes.

'Very much.'

What was happening here?

The Tydonni thane grinned with alehouse cruelty. 'I think his gold was *born* to burden my purse. I think he overlooks the likes of me . . . and of you! I think all those prayers, all those little wire circumfixes, are naught but wasted effort! Because *in the end*,' he continued with a conspiratorial lean, 'I think he's *no different* than you or me. A sinner. A dog. A demon when too deep in his cups! A fool. A fraud. A scalper of sou—!'

Lord Kosoter materialized at the man's side, his knife out . . . Achamian blinked in confusion. A stabbing motion. Hurm crushed his cheek against his shoulder, as if plagued by a mosquito in his ear.

Mimara cried out for shock. Achamian stood dumbfounded.

Gripping a nest of black hair, the Captain – impossibly – *held the man upright* while he hacked at the man's neck with his free hand. For an instant there was no blood. Then it seemed to gush from the jerking form.

'Blasphemer!' Sarl chortled, his teeth and gums shining, his eyes squeezed into creases. 'No *blasphemers* on the slog!'

Galian had *known* this would happen, the old Wizard realized.

The Captain continued his savage work, grimacing in yellow-toothed disgust. He did not so much cut the head from the body as hack the body from under the head. The Hag's black-stained limbs flumped senseless between the grasses. His head yanked high like a freed kite.

'Anasûrimbor Kellhus!' the Captain raved at the survivors. '*He is the God!* And *this*' – he swung Hurm's head so that blood flew from the crimson lobes of its mouth – 'is *His* work!'

Achamian could only watch with detached wonder, the kind that afflicts the survivors of sudden catastrophes. He saw well enough. He knew well enough. And yet none of it made the slightest sense.

He found himself wondering how long before Cleric called on them to dispense the Qirri. He needed it. To the point of wringing hands and clenched teeth, he needed it.

The Captain, it seemed, was a Believer.

Zaudunyani.

The pretense of thought twined through the fraud that was its soul . . .

It ran like a dog, bent, so that the grasses whipped in wet shags about its face and shoulders. The morning sun hung low, a pale orb in the mists that always greeted the dawn on the shore of a great sea. Gold limned any stonework bared to the sky. The acropolis rose from the ink of its own shadow, a silhouette without depth in the haze. There was beauty in the destruction, as well as thunderous proof of the Old Fathers and their power. Here, the will and might of Men had perished before the rapacious hunger of the Derived. Here, the glorious multitudes had coupled with the screaming, the broken and the dead.

These were holy facts – sacred. But the thing called Soma did not raise its head to contemplate or to consider. It did not da~
There was the tracker, Xonghis, whose almond eyes misse~
And there was the Nonman, whose senses almost riva~
in some respects.

There was the *mission*.

It paused over the headless corpse of the Stone Hag, listened to the music of carrion flies. It lingered for a moment, long enough to savour the thickness between its thighs, the arching bloat. Then it continued racing along the company's blundering trail.

On the heights of what had once been called the Heilor, it dashed through concentric shells of ruin, crept along debris-choked foundations. It ignored the vista: the city scattered like bones, the steaming marshes, the plate of the Cerish Sea. Instead it rooted through the remains of the scalper camp, sniffing the sweet where their anuses had pressed against the grasses. It found the spot where the female had made water, only to flee from the reek of her fetus.

It paused over the sour musk of the Nonman.

Something was happening . . . Something unanticipated by the Old Fathers.

It cringed, swatted its face in slouching fear. Had anyone happened upon it at that moment, they would have seen a crazed creature, limbed like a man but possessing a woman's beautiful face, greased with blood and filth, rocking from foot to foot like a bereaved ape.

It bent back its head until the base of its skull pressed against the crown of its spine, unsheathed its second voice . . .

And screamed.

'There's no need . . .' a small voice piped from above. 'I have followed you since sunrise.'

It whirled in feral alarm.

A series of ruined walls fenced the ground behind, each rising and falling like miniature mountain ranges. A bird perched on the summit of the nearest, its body glossy black, shot with strains of violet, its head white with marmoreal translucence – and human.

A Synthese . . . vessel of the Old Fathers. Flowering weeds trembled in the wind beside its clicking feet. A daylight moon, a blind cat's eye, rose above its obsidian back.

The thing called Soma fell to its false face.

'You were to watch him,' the bird said, a miniature scowl creasing its expression.

'Things have changed.'

Eyes like blue beads closed then opened. 'How so?'

The thing called Soma dared raise Mimara's face. 'A sorcerer, a *Gnostic* sorcerer, hired the company several weeks ago . . . He hopes to find the Coffers.'

A moment of palm-sized confusion.

'The *Mandate*? The Mandate has hired the Skin Eaters?'

'No . . . I'm not sure . . . He claims *to be a Wizard*, a sorcerer without a School. Even still, Chigra burns strong in him. Very strong.'

The Synthese bent its tiny head down in momentary meditation. 'So the old fool has found his way back to the benjuka plate . . . And *he* discovered you? *Drusas Achamian?*'

'No . . . There is a woman with him – one who has been taught how to recognize us. A *pregnant* woman . . .'

A sharp puppet nod. 'The face you wear . . . I see.' Shadows fluttered around the bird form, as if some greater eye blinked about the world. An intimation of rage and power. 'Mimara.'

The thing called Soma cringed and retreated. 'Yes.'

'She's pregnant. You are certain of this?'

'The stench is unmistakable.'

Another moment of bird-hesitation, as if each thought had to be untangled . . . It was no small matter planting a soul so mighty into a skull the size of an eggshell.

'Then she cannot be harmed. *All* the prophecies must be respected, the false as much as the true.'

'Yes, Old Father. I anticipated this, which is why I . . . refrained.'

A sideways twitch of the head. 'She leaves the safety of the others?'

'To piss and shit. I have spoken with her twice now. She will yield their secret in time.'

'And the Schoolman has not intervened?'

'He does not know.'

The small head flicked back. Laughter tinkled like glass. The Consult Synthese looked from the Heilor, its gaze ticking between points across the fields of papyrus out to the featureless reaches of the Cerish Sea. The wind combed its feathered tailings, blowing wide with the inaudible roar of absence and ruin.

The thing called Soma breathed deep the scent of ash become earth.

'*Brave* girl . . .' the Old Father cooed, still considering the crumbs of the age-long feast that was the Meorn Empire. 'Continue tracking them, Tsuör. At the very least, they will take you home.'

CHAPTER SEVEN

The Istyuli Plains

. . . and they scoff at heroes, saying that Fate serves disaster to many, and feasts to few. They claim that willing is but a form of blindness, the conceit of beggars who think they wrest alms from the jaws of lions. The Whore alone, they say, decides who is brave and who is rash, who will be hero and who will be fool. And so they dwell in a world of victims.

—QUALLAS, ON THE INVITIC SAGES

Ever do Men use secrets to sort and measure those they love, which is why they are less honest with their brothers and more guarded with their friends.

—CASIDAS, ANNALS OF CENEI

Late Spring, 20 New Imperial Year (4132 Year-of-the-Tusk), The High Istyuli

They had fled and they had gathered, like sawdust before the sweep of the carpenter's hand.

Sranc.

The clans that infested the Sakarpi Pale had fled long before the Great Ordeal trod their nourishing earth. They, unlike their wilder cousins to the north, had long, hard experience with the cunning ways of Men. They knew the folly of closing for battle absent overwhelming numbers, so they fled where other clans would have raced gibbering to their doom. They fled, bearing word of the dread *Israzi'horul*, the Shining Men, who marched with world-cracking strength behind them.

Their cousins to the north heeded them, as did their cousins in turn. Hundreds became thousands became tens of thousands. So the clans fell back, ever back, wincing from chance encounters with Mannish pickets, forming a rind that grew ever more raucous with numbers as it retreated across the empty leagues. And growing ever more hungry.

What began as the flight of a few scattered clans soon became a shrieking migration. The Parching Wind whipped high the dust of their discord, raised veils of arid filth to the arch of Heaven. The sun was blotted. The Sranc teemed as insects across the obscured flats and shallows, so many the land became desert waste in their wake, stamped and scratched into lifelessness.

And as their numbers swelled so did their fear of the Shining Men dwindle.

Shortly after the Breaking of the Ordeal, General Sibawul te Nurwul, intent to demonstrate the skill and daring of his Cepalorans, disobeyed the orders of Prince Kayûtas and rode far ahead of his fellow Kidruhil pickets. He would be the first among Men to lay eyes on the storm brewing in the Istyuli wastes. There was no question of giving battle, for the inhuman multitudes blackened the circuit of all that could be seen. A full third of his riders fell that day, for the fleetest among the Sranc were quicker than the slowest among the Cepaloran riders. Sibawul and his Cepalorans raced fleeing toward their fellow pickets, drawing thousands in pursuit, and a running battle, the first since the Fall of Sakarpus, was fought as the Kidruhil companies scrambled to fend them. Several hundred cavalrymen were lost before the day's end – a needless waste.

When Sibawul was brought before Kayûtas, the Prince-Imperial rebuked him in the harshest terms, saying that the Aspect-Emperor had known of the Hording all along, but realizing the ardour this knowledge would spark in the hearts of his men, he waited for the most opportune time to inform the Sacred Host.

'How do you, a master of men, punish those who disobey your commands?' Kayûtas asked.

'Flogging,' Sibawul fearlessly replied.

So was the first Lord of the Ordeal whipped for a martial transgression.

And so did the Zaudunyani learn that beyond the northern horizon, their foe roiled in numbers that encompassed the horizon – numbers far greater than their own. About the campfires, those who had argued a bloodless march to Golgotterath were silenced.

None could deny that a grievous toll was about to be paid.

King Nersei Proyas had seen the way hosts accumulate infirmities more times than he cared to remember. Supplies dwindled, spirits flagged, diseases multiplied, and so on, until armies that once appeared invincible came to resemble doddering old men. There was the war against the Tydonni Orthodox, of course, and the disastrous campaign across the Secharib Plains, where he had almost succumbed to the Fevers. But more and more, he found himself thinking of the First Holy War, the way it had marched into Fanim lands the mightiest host the Three Seas had even seen, only to be starved into cannibalism in a matter of months.

The Great Ordeal, he had come to realize, was no different. The cracks had opened, and Fate had set the wedges as surely as shipbuilders striking boards from felled trees. What was cracked could be hammered asunder. The Army of the Middle-North, especially, seemed to be marching under a pall of imminent disaster.

And yet, time and again, at least once every week, his Lord-and-God called him to his spare, leather-panelled bedchamber in the Umbilicus to sit and discuss . . . madness.

'It troubles you often, that day in Shimeh.'

That day in Shimeh, when Kellhus had been acclaimed Aspect-Emperor. Proyas found himself clearing his throat and looking away. Twenty years had passed, twenty years of toil and strife, and yet the image of his old tutor standing derelict before his Holy Aspect-Emperor plagued him as insistently as ever. A memory like a childhood burn, not quite stinging but too puckered not to probe with idle fingertips.

'I loved Achamian.'

How could a boy, especially one as curious and precocious as he had been, not love his first true teacher? Children can smell the difference between duty, which is merely a form of self-regard, and the temper of genuine concern. Achamian taught not to serve, but to *teach*, to arm an errant boy against a capricious world. He taught young master *Proyas*, and not the Conriyan King's second son.

'But it troubles you . . .' Kellhus said, 'that a soul so wise and gentle would so condemn me.'

'He was a man *spurned*,' Proyas replied on a heavy breath. 'No cuckold possesses a wise and gentle soul.' He remembered Achamian coming to him – coming back from the presumption of death – when the First Holy War lay besieged in Caraskand.

He remembered his own cowardice, how he spared himself the heartbreak of watching the sorcerer absorb tidings of the impossible . . .

News that Esmenet, his wife, had abandoned hope and turned to the Warrior-Prophet's bed.

'Even still, it troubles you.'

The Exalt-General gazed at his Lord-and-God, pursed his lips against the difficulty of admission.

'Yes.'

'So much so that you read his *Compendium*.'

Proyas smiled. For years he had wondered when Kellhus would call him out on this small secret. 'I read a summary of its charges against you.'

'Did you believe those charges?'

'Of course not!'

The Holy Aspect-Emperor frowned as if troubled by the vehemence of his denial. He lowered his gaze to the fire twirling in the arcane octagon of his hearth.

'But why would that be, when they are true?'

The small Seeing-Flame wheezed into the silence.

The Exalt-General stared at his Lord-and-God in breathless bewilderment. The simplicity of his garb. The scriptural profile of his face, long featured, profound for the archaic cut of his beard and hair, wise for the clarity of his gaze. The lingering glow about his hands, as if unseen clouds were forever breaking above them.

'What . . . What are you saying?'

'That Men are children to me, precisely as Achamian claims.'

'As you are father to us!'

Anasûrimbor Kellhus regarded him with the utter absence of expression.

'What father murders so many of his sons?'

What was this melancholy? What was this doubt? After

campaigning so long, surviving so much calamity, how could the man *who gave meaning to it all* ask such corrosive questions?

'A *divine* one,' the Exalt-General declared.

The Sranc waxed ever more bold in measure with their hunger. Soon, not a day passed without word of some violent encounter. When they dared scout or patrol at all, the Kidruhil did so in force, stung by the loss of two entire companies, one of them captained by King Coithus Narnol's youngest son, Agabon. The Army of the Middle-North began marching and camping on the ready. During the day they assembled into a vast, mile-long chevron, with the heavily armoured Thunyeri at the point, the Galeoth on the left flank, the Tydonni on the right, and all the baggage scattered behind and between. During the night, they arrayed their camps in tight, concentric circles, with a full quarter of their numbers assigned to defend the perimeter in rotating shifts. Drills were scheduled at irregular intervals to ensure that each man knew his place. Habitual laggards were publicly whipped. The last companies to the line were assigned to the latrines.

Despite their growing exhaustion, the Men of the Ordeal took to singing as they marched, Zaudunyani hymns for the most part, but folk songs from faraway homes as well. Some were ribald and merry, others melancholy, but one song in particular, the 'Beggar's Lament,' became especially popular. In some cases groups more than a thousand strong would cry out, bemoaning everything from the boils on their rumps to the pox on their members, only to be answered by thousands more complaining of even more outrageous afflictions. One man in particular, a Galeoth Agmundrman named Shoss, became famous for the hilarity of his lyrics.

And so the Army of the Middle-North marched into the Horde's shadow laughing.

No such humour could be found in Kayûtas's evening councils. The Prince-Imperial always began by insisting he had no news of home, so pre-empting the inevitable parade of questions. His conferences with his Holy Father, he explained, were too rare and too brief to permit such questions – especially when the challenges they faced were so grievous.

The supply situation had become perilous, so much so that rationing had reduced the slaves who marched with the Ordeal to less than half the fare they needed to recoup their daily expenditures. Indeed, diseases of malnutrition were beginning to claim them in ever greater numbers; dozens were lost every day, either to death outright or to the straggling wastes behind them.

The presence of slaves, Kayûtas reminded his commanders, was but one of many concessions his Holy Father had made to appease the caste-nobility – *them*. Soon, he would demand they sacrifice in return. The Prince-Imperial bid them to recall the First Holy War and the infamous Slaughter of the Camp-followers.

'When the time comes, each will kill his own,' he said. '*Each*. Those who fail to do so will be executed in their slave's stead. Remember, my brothers: cruelty is only injustice in the *absence* of Necessity. Compassion. Generosity. These are fast becoming gluttonous sins.'

He did not need to speak the obvious, that unless their foraging began providing game in far greater quantities, Necessity would be upon them in a matter of days. They did not even possess pasture enough for their ponies and beasts of burden, thanks to the drought and the scourging of the land.

As always, the discussion returned to the reason for their straits: the Horde. Kayûtas polled his cavalry commanders, one by one, drawing martial wisdom from their observations: tactics to draw them out for easy slaughter, how the relative starvation of the creatures predicted their aggression, and the like.

There was no doubt, the Prince-Imperial informed his charges, that the Sranc were becoming more desperate and therefore more bold. He explained the way the snows accumulated in the high mountains, week after week, season after season, until the snow beneath could no longer hold the snow above.

'They will come crashing down upon us,' he said. 'And when they do, they will not be cowed so easily as they are now. They will come and they will come, until you cry out to the Gods for respite.'

'How many are they?' King Hogrim asked. There was no missing the Imperial Mathematicians, as pale as sorcerers beneath their parasols, riding out with Anasûrimbor Moënghus on their daily forays.

'More than us, my friend. Far more.'

King Narnol, who still grieved the loss of his beloved son, chose this moment to voice a sentiment common among his peers: that the Breaking of the Great Ordeal had been ill advised. 'We should stand together!' he protested. 'Shoulder to shoulder with our brothers! Divided, they can engulf and overwhelm us one by one. But if the Great Ordeal confronts this Horde entire . . .'

'We cannot feed ourselves as it is,' the Prince-Imperial answered. 'We are gathering far more fare as four than we could as one, and still we hunger. To stand together is to starve together.'

Though his reasoning was sound, Kayûtas could see that Narnol, in the course of framing his argument, had sparked real fear in the hearts of his commanders.

'Trust in my *Father*,' he pressed, 'who has foreseen and planned for all of these dilemmas. Think of how fifty of your knights can rout a mob of thousands! The Sranc battle in crazed masses, bereft of design or coordination. You need not fear for your flanks, only stand your ground! Hack and hew!' He turned to gesture to his sister, Anasûrimbor Serwa, the Grandmistress of the Swayali, whose beauty was ever a lodestone for idle eyes. 'Most importantly, recall the *Schools* and the destruction they can rain down upon our foes! Have no fear, my brothers. We will cobble the *horizon* with their carcasses!'

And the Lords of the Ordeal filed from the council striking their chests and crying out in renewed resolution. So easy it was to kindle the lust for blood in the hearts of Men. Even those thrown more than a thousand miles from their home.

———

To look at skies bright and arid and to sense a darkness unseen.

The Men of the Ordeal marched, little more than shadows in the sheeted dust. Knowing what gathered in the distance, they gazed ever forward, pondering what they could not see. There is an exhaustion peculiar to hanging threats, a needing-to-confront that tires the soul the way overstuffed packs sap the limbs. They would look out across the blasted plate of the Istyuli, and they would wonder at the rumour of their enigmatic foe. The Horde. They would argue numbers, exchange speculations, discuss battles waged by long-dead men. It became a game for some, counting the hundreds of dust plumes that marked the Kidruhil and the various companies of knights that patrolled ahead of them. They would wager rations on which plume marked who, a practice that became so common that some companies found themselves returning to the shouts of uproarious thousands.

For the pickets themselves, it seemed they had come to the ends of the earth. The ground was all but gutted dust by this time, so the Horde always appeared as a peculiar dust storm that spanned the horizon, one tethered to the irregularities of the earth. Ochre clouds piled upon billowing foundations, a great curtain that climbed into a haze that stained the northern sky, obscuring the lower constellations at night. Streamers preceded it, tails of gauze hooked as though on nails, marking those clans that had fled the longest, starved the longest. On and on it extended, powder raised into sinuous mountains, beautiful for its slow-blooming complexities, wondrous for its mad scale. A sense of impunity had grown upon many of the riders, one of those thoughtless convictions that arise when something expected perpetually fails to arrive. They rode their trackless circuits, and the unseen hordes before them retreated, always retreated. This was simply the way.

Then some trick of the Gangan-naru would kick open a door across the distance, and the windy hush would suddenly tingle with *sound* of the Horde, a roar that was at once booming and thin. 'Like shrieking children,' one of the Kidruhil Captains would explain to General Kayûtas. 'For the life of me, they sound like shrieking *children*.'

Or, more rarely, given the sheer number of companies pacing the Horde, one of the retreating streamers would reverse direction and begin racing toward one of the slender fingers of dust that marked the pursuing cavalry companies. Then the choreographed race would begin, with the company pursued turning back to the main host, drawing the reckless clan ever farther from the Horde and so delivering it to the lances of those companies flanking. The battles would be so one-sided as to scarce be battles at all. Ghostly riders pounding out of the smoke of powder-dry earth, riding down the shadows of screeching Sranc, some so starved as to be little more than dolls of knotted rope. Men with chalked faces would congratulate one another, exchange petty news, then ride on with whatever trophies they so prized.

Originally, they tallied the dead, thinking this a means of measuring the Sranc's defeat. And squads would always be sent back for the gratification of the host, their lances heavy with severed heads. The counting was abandoned after they reached some ten thousand – for who bothers to count inexhaustible things? The practice was forsaken when the trudging infantrymen began jeering at the lancers' approach. The hearts of men are like buoys: the more water you give them, the higher their expectations swim. All that would survive of the custom was the use of *lance* as a term for twelve Sranc – the average number of heads that could be carried on a standard Kidruhil shaft.

And so did a kind of unspoken accord arise between the Men of the Ordeal and the Sranc of the Horde, a truce whose falseness lay in the meagreness of the former's rations – the footmen of most nations had been reduced to gnawing amicut. Every morning, the number of slaves abandoned to die climbed a handful of souls. Camp would be broken, and the Army would begin crawling toward the northern horizon, leaving several dozen forlorn and broken souls sitting amid the detritus, waiting to be claimed by whatever it was that ailed them. Many just vanished, and the vassals of different lords began trading rumours of midnight murder. Some tales, like the story of Baron Hunrilka demanding his thanes dip their beards in the blood of their slaves, transcended bounds of kin and vassalage and were traded through the Ordeal as a whole.

Fewer and fewer fires glittered at night, for the Sranc Horde had so raked the earth that the Judges forbade the binding of grasses – or anything else that could be used as fodder – for fuel. Here and there enterprising souls would raise fires of thistles and scrub, but for the most part men whiled away the watches in apprehension and gloom, uncounted thousands of them, sitting in small, shadowy bands, with only the Nail of Heaven to reveal the worry in the eyes around them. It was a soldier's nature to accumulate grievances over the course of a campaign. In civilized lands, where marches were brief and battles quick in coming, a commander could rely on either victory to cleanse the ledgers or defeat to render them moot. But this march was unlike any other, and the surrounding wastes offered nothing to ease the frustrations of a warlike heart.

They believed still, for they were Zaudunyani, and they feared the Judges enough to stay their tongues, but they were simple men and so thought the solution to their travails was simple.

Battle. They need only close with their inhuman foe and hack them to the ground.

Earlier, when the Horde had been more novelty than existential threat, the Lords of the Ordeal had hoped that one of the Istyuli's many rivers would catch the Sranc as though in a bottle, forcing them to close. But the severity of the drought had choked even the greatest of the Istyuli's rivers into muddy channels. The Horde fled across them as though they scarce existed, fouling the waters with their waste as they did so.

And so was the Great Ordeal thrown open to Disease, dread Akkeägni, who reached through the host seizing men in his pestilent hands. Sick Columns were formed, ever growing formations that trailed each of the Four Armies. They quickly became pageants of death and misery, men marching with heads slumped, many of them naked from the waist down, their backsides stained with blood and feces. Hemoplexy was far and away the most common ailment – as well as the most deadly, given the lack of clean water. Only in the madness that is war could men die of thirst through drinking. And so did many learn what the poets and historians left unspoken: that more warriors die in offal than in blood.

And still the Sranc continued to fall back, a mad seething that scarred the very curve of the world. More and more clans fell upon the companies of horsemen that shadowed them throughout the day, attacks that fooled several Captains into thinking the Horde *itself* descended on the Ordeal. Miles were lost to their false alarms.

Of the innumerable skirmishes, two in particular became famous. General Siroyon was already notorious because of the way he and his Famiri rode into battle bare-chested and because of the legendary beauty and speed of his mount, Phiolos. Since his Famiri could easily outdistance the Sranc, he began riding ever closer to the Horde, threading the dust streamers that marked the straggling clans, so close his men's necks were pained for gazing up at the mountainous skirts of dust that obscured their foe.

'It is like riding into canyons of smoke,' he told King Proyas and his war-council, 'a land where storm clouds war directly with the earth. The shrieks are too . . . too many to sound of shrieking . . . The world simply . . . *rings*. And then you see them, like a plague of insects clotting the ground, leaping, sprinting, massing without order or reason . . . Madness. Threshing madness! Only the outermost are visible, so they seem frail, at first, such is the proportion of the dust piling above them. But then you catch glimpses of the countless thousands swirling beyond . . . and you know, just know, that what you see is but the edge of screaming miles . . .'

The edge of screaming miles. This phrase in particular would find itself passed from lip to lip, until fairly every soul in the Army of the East had heard it.

Knowing that he would arouse the creatures, the Famiri General took care to coordinate his expeditions with King-Regent Nurbanu Soter and his Ainoni. Arrayed some miles in advance of the Army, Soter's heavily armoured Palatines and their household knights would await Siroyon's howling return. They would wonder at the thin thread of half-naked Famiri flying across the waste and the mobs of leaping shadows that pursued them. They would open alleys for the men to flee between, then they would close ranks and begin thundering forward . . .

And so were the Sranc felled in the thousands.

When these tales reached Sibawul te Nurwul in the Army of the Middle-North, he commanded his Cepalorans to strip off their armour, reckoning this was what enabled Siroyon and his Famiri to outrun the creatures. Bent on redeeming his earlier failure, he passed informal word to several caste-nobles and Kidruhil Captains that he planned on repeating Siroyon's tactics, allowing them to destroy the creatures by the thousands. What he failed to realize was that the uneven accumulation of Sranc before the Army of the Middle-North meant his horses had far less fodder than General Siroyon's. The Cepalorans rode into the smoke canyons as the Famiri had, wheeled as they had wheeled when the Sranc began racing toward them. And fled as they fled, howling out with the same exhilaration.

But their ebullient mood quickly faltered. Once again, the Sranc *closed* upon the laggards among them. Sibawul commanded his hornsmen to signal for assistance, but the General had not discussed contingencies with any of the lords or captains who commanded the jaws of his trap. The inhuman masses gained on the rearmost horsemen, shrieked in obscene triumph as the first stragglers were pulled down. Men crouched in their saddles, whipped their ponies bloody, wept as the slavering masses engulfed them . . .

Some two thousand of Sibawul's kinsmen were lost to the gibbering pursuit. It would be the first true disaster suffered by the Great Ordeal. And so did the ill-fated General earn a second flogging, as well as everlasting shame in the scripture that would survive.

As the days passed, the shape of what had been an unthinkable fate had become clear to anyone who pondered the Ordeal's straits. They faced a more mobile enemy on open terrain – and this meant doom. They could not close with their foe, and as a result they could not secure the supplies they needed to survive. Tales of various historical battles, especially those involving the Scylvendi, the famed People of War, began filtering through the host, traded between shrugging men and pensive looks. More than one antique emperor, the Men of the Ordeal learned, had led the pride of his people to doom on distant plains.

'Fear not,' Kayûtas assured his commanders. 'They will attack, and soon.'

'How?' King Narnol asked. Bent by the death of his son, he had grown ever more bold in his questioning, ever more insolent. 'How could you know?'

'Because as much as we hunger, they *starve*.'

'Ha!' the greybeard Galeoth cried. 'So they will come to steal food we don't possess?'

Kayûtas said nothing, content to allow Narnol's own harsh intonations condemn him.

'We!' King Vûkyelt erupted. '*We* are the food, fool!'

At some point, each of the Marshals of the Four Armies petitioned the Aspect-Emperor, asking that he address their host and so silence the growing presentiment of doom. He rebuked each of them in turn, saying, 'If your nations cannot endure trials so paltry without my intervention, then truly the Great Ordeal is doomed.'

And so the Men of the Ordeal roused themselves at the Interval's morning toll. They tightened their belts and war-girdles, shouldered packs that always seemed one stone heavier than the day previous. And they trudged to their assembling formations, wondering at the dust that puffed from their steps. Some continued blinking long into the morning, whether from weariness or airborne grit, like men trapped in nightmares.

Sorweel had no brothers, a fact that had caused him no little shame in his childhood. He had no clue as to why he should feel responsible for his mother's failure to bear a second son, or for his father's refusal to take another wife after his mother died. From time to time he would hear his father arguing with some wizened adviser about the frailty of the dynastic line: *'But if the boy should die, Harweel!'* He would slink away numb and bewildered, oppressed by a curious sense of urgency, as if he should don his toy armour, do everything he could to safeguard his precious pulse. And he would think how much easier it would be if he had a younger brother, *someone to protect* – someone to share the future's terrible burdens.

And so he grew up searching for brothers, an asking-for-more that dogged his every friendship. He was the Prince. He was the one ordained to ascend the Horn-and-Amber Throne. *His* was the indispensable soul, and yet it always seemed otherwise. And now, when he needed a brother more than at any time in his life, he was not even sure he possessed a friend.

What Sorweel had feared had come to pass: the Scions had in fact stumbled across a Sranc host shadowing the Great Ordeal. They only glimpsed it a few times, from what rare heights the landscape provided: a column of vast squares marching in perfect formation. Twice Eskeles had cast an air-bending spell that allowed them to scry the host in greater detail. While others busied themselves counting heads, Sorweel watched with breathless wonder: the tiny figures become liquid and large, executing soundless errands utterly oblivious to the Scions and their sorcerous observation.

Nonmen, the first the young King had ever seen, policed the column's flanks, riding black horses and wearing elaborate gowns of chainmail. Erratics, the Mandate Schoolman called them, Nonmen who had gone mad for immortality. Sorweel found the appearance of them disconcerting – their faces especially. Since time immemorial, his people had battled the Sranc. And so, for him, the Sranc were the rule and the Nonmen the perversions.

He could not look at them without seeing the heads of Sranc stitched onto the bodies of statuesque Men.

Scarcely a hundred of them accompanied the host. Far more numerous were what Eskeles called Ursranc, a species bred for obedience. 'Like dogs to wolves,' the Schoolman said. They seemed somewhat taller and broader than their wild cousins, but aside from their freedom, they were really only distinguished by the uniformity of their armour: hauberks of black iron scale. The Scions could only guess at their numbers, since they not only crawled throughout the column whipping and beating their more wolfish kin, but also patrolled the surrounding plains in loose companies of a hundred or so – the way Men would.

No matter what their numbers, they were but a pittance compared with their unruly relatives. At first Sorweel could scarce credit his eyes, gazing at the great square formations through the Schoolman's lens of air. Sranc chained to Sranc chained to Sranc. On and on. Snapping. Soundlessly howling. Shambling through screens of dust. Eskeles counted one hundred heads a side, which meant that each square contained some *ten thousand* of the creatures. Arguing glimpses through the endless veils of dust, he and Captain Harnilas decided that no less than ten squares composed the column. Which meant that Sorweel witnessed something his people knew only from legend: a horde whipped and shackled into the form of a great army.

A Yoke Legion, Eskeles had said, speaking with a survivor's dread. The Erratics and Ursranc, he explained, would drive their wretched captives until the scent of the Ordeal sang on the clear wind, then simply strike the chains that threaded their shackles. Hunger would do the rest. Hunger and diabolical lust . . .

The Consult was *real*. If the unmasking of the skin-spy in the Umbilicus had not entirely convinced Sorweel, this most certainly did. The Aspect-Emperor warred against a *real* enemy. And unless the Scions could find some way to warn Kayûtas, the Army of the Middle-North was doomed.

They had spent a crazed fortnight trying to catch the Army – without dying. They had struck eastward, slowly bending their course to the north, riding day and night in the hope of skirting, then outdistancing, the Consult host. Within three days they found the great track the Army of the Middle-North had beaten into the dusty waste. But the urgency that spurred their flight was easily matched by the dread host. Day after day, no matter how hard they pushed their ponies, the smear of dun haze that marked the Ten-Yoke Legion on the horizon stubbornly refused to fall behind them.

After the first week, the miraculous endurance of their Jiünati ponies began to fail, and Harnilas had no choice but to leave more and more of their company hobbling on foot behind them. The rule he used was simple: those he deemed strong riders went on, while those he deemed weak were left behind, regardless of whose pony failed. Obotegwa was among the first to be so abandoned: Sorweel need only blink to see the old Satyothi smiling in philosophic resignation, trudging through the dust of their trotting departure. Charampa and other Scions who were not bred to horses were quick to follow. Eskeles was the sole exception – even though the others began calling him 'Pony-killer.' Every other day, it seemed, his paunch broke another pony's strength and so doomed another Scion to trudge alone on foot. He felt the shame keenly, so much so that he began refusing his rations. 'I carry my pack on my waist,' he would say with a forced laugh.

The remaining Scions began watching him in exasperation – and, in some cases, outright hatred. The fifth pony he lamed, Harnilas chose a tempestuous Girgashi youth named Baribul to yield his mount. 'What?' the young man cried to the Mandate Schoolman. 'You cannot walk across the sky?'

'There are *Quya* on the horizon!' the sorcerer exclaimed. 'We are all dead if I draw their eye!'

'Yield your shag!' Harnilas bellowed at the youth. 'I will not ask again!'

Baribul wheeled about to face the commander. 'There will be *war* for this!' he roared. 'My father will sound the High Shi—'

Harnilas hefted his lance, skewered the young man's throat with a blurred throw.

The Kidruhil veteran spurred his pony in a tight circle about the dying youth. 'I care not for your fathers!' he called to the others, resolution like acid in his eyes. 'I care not for your laws or your customs! And apart from my mission, I care not for *you*! Only *one* of us needs to reach the Holy General! *One of us!* and the Great Ordeal will be saved – as will your fathers and their fool customs!'

The huffing Schoolman clambered onto Baribul's pony, his face dark with the rage that weak men use to overmatch their shame. The remaining Scions had already turned their backs to him, resumed their northward drift. Baribul was dead, and they were too tired to care. He had been insufferably arrogant, anyway.

Sorweel lingered behind, staring at the body in the dust. For the first time, he understood the mortal stakes of their endeavour – the mission his insight had delivered. The Scions could very well be doomed, and unless he set aside his cowardice and pride, he would die not only without brothers but without friends as well.

The Company rode in haphazard echelon across the plain, each pony hauling skirts of spectral dust. Zsoronga rode alone, relieved of his Brace by the steady loss of their mounts. He hung his head, his blinks so sticky as to become heartbeats of sleep. His mouth hung open. They had ridden past exhaustion, into mania and melancholy, into the long stupor of mile stacked upon endless mile.

'I'm next,' the Successor-Prince said with offhand disgust as Sorweel approached. 'The fat man eyes my Mebbee even now. Eh, Mebbee?' He raked affectionate fingers through his pony's plumed mane. 'Imagine. The Satakhan of High Holy Zeüm, stumping alone through the dust . . .'

'I'm sure we'll fi—'

'But this is good,' Zsoronga interrupted, raising a hand in a loose *but-yes* gesture. 'Whenever my courtiers air their grievances, I can say, "Yes, I remember the time I was forced to hobble alone through Sranc-infested wastes . . ."' He laughed as if seeing their faces blanch in his soul's eye. 'Who could whine to such a Satakhan? Who would dare?'

He had turned to Sorweel as he said this, but he spoke in the inward manner of those who think their listeners cannot understand.

'I'm not one of the Believer-Kings!' Sorweel blurted.

Zsoronga blinked as though waking.

'You speak Sheyic now?'

'I'm *not* a Believer-King,' Sorweel pressed. 'I know you think I am.'

The Successor-Prince snorted and turned away.

'Think? No, Horse-King. *I know.*'

'How? How could you know?'

Exhaustion has a way of parting the veils between men, not so much because the effort of censoring their words exceeds them, but because weariness is the foe of volatility. Oft times insults that would pierce the wakeful simply thud against the sleepless and fatigued.

Zsoronga grinned in what could only be called malice. 'The Aspect-Emperor. He *sees* the hearts of Men, Horse-King. He saw yours quite clearly, I think.'

'*No.* I . . . I don't know what happened at the-the . . .' He had assumed his tongue would fail him, that his Sheyic would be so rudimentary that it would only humiliate him, but the words were there, cemented by all those dreary watches he had spent cursing Eskeles. 'I don't know what happened at the council!'

Zsoronga looked away, sneering as though at a younger sister. '*I* thought it plain,' he said. '*Two* spies were revealed. *Two* false faces . . .'

Sorweel glared. Frustration welled through him and with it an overwhelming urge to simply close his eyes and slump from his saddle. His thoughts sagged, reeled into nonsensical convolutions. The ground looked cushion soft. He would sleep such a sleep! And his pony, Stubborn – Eskeles could have him. He was strong. Zsoronga could keep Mebbee, and so lose the moral high-ground to his whining courtiers . . .

The young King was quick in blinking away this foolishness.

'Zsoronga. Look at me . . . Please. I am the enemy of your enemy! *He murdered my father!*'

The Successor-Prince pawed his face as though trying to wipe away the exhaustion.

'Then why—?'

'To sow . . . *thrauma* . . . discord between us! To sow discord in my own heart! Or . . . or . . .'

A look of flat disgust. 'Or?'

'Maybe he was . . . mistaken.'

'What?' Zsoronga crowed, laughing. 'Because he found your soul too subtle? A *barbarian*? Spare me your lies, shit-herder!'

'No . . . *No!* Because . . .'

'Because . . . Because . . .' Zsoronga mocked.

For some reason this barb found its way through the numbness, stung enough to bring tears to his eyes. 'You would think me mad if I told you,' the young King of Sakarpus said, his voice cracking.

Zsoronga gazed at him for a long, expressionless moment – a look of judgment and decision.

'I've seen you in battle,' he finally said, speaking with the semblance of cruelty that men sometimes use to make room for a friend's momentary weakness. He smiled as best his heart could manage. 'I already think you mad!'

A single teasing accusation, and the rift of suspicion between them was miraculously healed. Often men need only speak around things to come together and so remember what it means to speak through.

Too weary to feel gratified or relieved, Sorweel began telling the Successor-Prince everything that had transpired since the death of his father and the fall of his hallowed city. He told him of the stork who had alighted on the walls the instant before the Great Ordeal attacked his city. He told him how he had wept in the Aspect-Emperor's arms. He confessed everything, no matter how shameful, how weak, knowing that for all the aloofness of Zsoronga's gaze, the man no longer judged him with a simple rule.

And then he told him about the slave, Porsparian . . .

'He . . . he . . . made a face, *her face*, in the earth. And – I swear to you, Zsoronga! – he gathered . . . mud . . . *spit*, from her lips. He rubbed it across my chee—'

'*Before* the council?' Zsoronga asked, astonished eyes shining from a dubious scowl. 'Before the Anasûrimbor named you one of the faithful?'

'Yes! Yes! And ever since . . . Even *Kayûtas* congratulates me on my . . . my turning.'

'Conversion,' Zsoronga corrected, his head slung low in concentration. 'Your conversion . . .'

So far the young King of Sakarpus had spoken through the weariness that hooks lead weights to each and every thought, making the effort of talking akin to that of lifting what would rather sink. Suddenly speaking felt more like trying to submerge air-filled bladders – holding down things that should be drowned.

'Tell me what you think!' Sorweel cried.

'This is bad *rushru* . . . The Mother of Birth . . . For us, she is the *slave* Goddess. Beneath our petitioni—'

'It *does* shame me!' Sorweel blurted. 'I am one of the warlings! Born of blood both ancient and noble! Trothed to Gilgaöl since my fifth summer! *She* shames me!'

'But not beneath our *respect*,' Zsoronga continued with an air of superstitious concern. Dust had chalked his kinked hair, so that he resembled Obotegwa, older and wiser than his years. 'She is among the eldest . . . the most powerful.'

'So what are you saying?'

The Successor-Prince absently stroked his pony's neck rather than answer. Even when hesitating, Zsoronga possessed a directness, a paradoxical *absence* of hesitation. He was one of those rare men who always moved in accordance with themselves, as though his soul had been cut and stitched from a single cloth – so unlike the patched motley that was Sorweel's soul. Even when the Successor-Prince doubted, his confidence was absolute.

'I think,' Zsoronga said, 'and by that I mean *think* . . . that you are what they call *narindari* in the Three Seas . . .' His body seemed to sway about the stationary point of his gaze. 'Chosen by the Gods to kill.'

'Kill?' Sorweel cried. 'Kill?'

'Yes,' the Successor-Prince replied, his green eyes drawn down by the frightful weight of his ruminations. When he looked up, he gazed with a certain blankness, as if loathe to dishonour his friend with any outward sign of pity. 'To avenge your father.'

Sorweel already knew this, but in the manner of men who have caged their fears. He knew this as profoundly as he knew anything, and yet somehow he had managed to convince himself it wasn't true.

He had been chosen to kill the Aspect-Emperor.

'So what am I to do?' he cried, more honest to his panic than he intended. 'What does She expect of me?'

Zsoronga snorted with the humour of the perpetually over-matched. 'What does the *Mother* expect? The Gods are children and we are their toys. Look at you sausages! They cherish us one day, break us the next.' He held out his arms as if to mime Mankind's age-old exasperation. 'We Zeümi pray to our *ancestors* for a reason.'

Sorweel blinked against mutinous eyes. 'Then what do *you* think I should do?'

'Stand in front of me as much as possible!' the handsome Successor-Prince chortled. A better part of Zsoronga's strength, Sorweel had learned, lay in his ability to drag good humour out of any circumstance. It was a trait he would try to emulate.

'Look at these past days, Horse-King,' the black man continued when Sorweel's lack of amusement became clear. 'With every throw of the number-sticks you *win*! First, She disguised you. Now She *exalts* you with glory on the field, raises you in the eyes of men. Can't you see? You were little more than a foundling when you first joined the Scions. Now old Harni can scarce sneeze without begging your advice . . .' Zsoronga appraised him with a kind of cocked wonder.

'She is *positioning you*, Sorweel.'

More truths he had already known yet refused to acknowledge. Suddenly, the young King of Sakarpus found himself regretting his confession, repenting what was in fact his first true conversation since the death of his father. Suddenly it seemed pathetic and absurd, searching for a brother in a Son of Zeüm, a nation the Sakarpi used to refer to things too distant or too strange to be credited.

'What if I don't *want* to be disguised or positioned?'

Zsoronga shook his head with a kind of bemoaning wonder. *You sausages . . .* his eyes said.

'We Zeümi pray to our ancestors for a reason.'

Clouds climbed the horizon, and the Men of the Middle-North rejoiced, thinking the Gods had relented at long last. They sailed across the sky with the grace of whales, ever more crowded, ever more bruised about their bellies, but aside from brief showers of spittle, the rain did not come. A windless humidity rose in its stead, the kind that makes sodden cloth of limbs and lead of burdens. The day ended in weariness and indecision, the same as any other, save that the Zaudunyani's exhaustion was total and their unslaked thirst extreme. The absence of dust was their only reprieve.

Night brought near absolute darkness.

The attack came during the first watch. A Sranc war-party some twenty lances strong simply leapt out of the blackness and fell upon the Galeoth flank. Men who muttered among themselves to while away the boredom cried out in sudden horror and were no more. The Sranc swept over the outermost sentries, raced caterwauling toward the ranks of the night defenders proper. Men locked shields against the blackness, lowered their pikes. Some cursed while others prayed. Then the obscenities were upon them, hacking and howling, their limbs wasted, their stomachs pinned to their spines. Heaving and hewing along the length of their shallow line, the Galeoth held their ground. Crying out hymns, they struck the maniacal creatures down.

Horns and alarums rang through the rest of the host. Men raced to their positions, some hopping to pull on their boots, others with their hauberks swinging. Agmundrmen with their war knots,

Nangaels with their blue-tattooed cheeks, Numaineiri with their great hanging beards: ironclad men drawn from all the great tribes of Galeoth, Thunyerus, and Ce Tydonn, arrayed across a mile of flats and shallow ravines. They readied themselves with cursing bravado, and then, when every strap was buckled and every shield raised, they peered across the dark plain. Behind their gleaming ranks, the Kidruhil and caste-noble knights loitered in mounted clots, many standing in their stirrups to gaze as well.

No one saw anything, such was the darkness. During the following watch, news of the Sranc war-party's easy defeat circulated through the ranks. The cynics among them predicted weeks of blaring horns and sleepless, pointless vigils.

General Kayûtas sent out several Kidruhil companies to reconnoitre the plain. The cavalrymen loathed few things more than riding pickets at night – for fear of ambush, certainly, but more for fear of being thrown. Since Sakarpus, some eighty souls had perished ranging the dark and hundreds more had been injured or crippled. After the Judges executed a Kidruhil captain for deliberately laming his ponies to feed his men, the companies were even denied the tradition of feasting on the crippled mounts.

The Northmen became complacent, and soon the host boomed with impatient chatter. Several pranksters broke ranks to dance and gesticulate before the pitch-black distances. The thanes could not silence them, no matter how hard they bawled. So when reports of cries heard on the plain reached General Kayûtas, he was not immediately inclined to believe them . . .

He summoned his sister, Serwa, only when the first of the scouting parties failed to return.

As with the other Schools, the Swayali Witches had remained largely cloistered within the host. Apart from chance encounters in the camp, the Zaudunyani saw them only during the Signalling, when one of the Swayali would climb the night sky to flash coded messages to their Saik counterparts in the Army of the East.

The reasons for this discretion were manyfold. The Swayali were *witches*, for one. Despite the Aspect-Emperor, many held their old prejudices fast – how could they not, when so many of their words for sorcery and its practitioners were also words for wickedness? They were *women*, for another. Several men had already been whipped, and one even executed, for acting out deranged infatuations. But most importantly, the Aspect-Emperor wished to deny the Consult any easy reckoning of the power he brought against them. For in truth, all the Men of the Ordeal in their countless, shining thousands were little more than a vehicle for the safe conveyance of the Schools.

Prince Anasûrimbor Kayûtas decided the time for discretion was at an end.

At her brother's command, Serwa deployed her witches behind the common line, holding forty-three of the most senior and accomplished in reserve. A profound hush accompanied their appearance throughout the camp. The 'Nuns,' the Men called them. With their yellow billows – the immense silken gowns they wore as protection against Chorae – wrapped and bound about them, the Swayali indeed resembled Jokian Nuns.

Sorcerous utterances cracked the gloom, and one by one the witches stepped into the air. They strode out over the deep ranks of the common line. Men in their thousands craned their necks to follow their soundless course. Some murmured, a few even called out, but most held their breath for wonder. Given the youth of the School, the women were young as well, with faces of smooth alabaster and teak, lips full about the lights that flashed from them. Free of the ground, they unbound their billows, spake the small Cant that animated them. The fabric dropped, unfurled in arcs that twined in the glow of the Nuns' arcane voices. One by one the Swayali bloomed, opened like flowers of golden silk, and the Men of Ordeal were dumbstruck.

Swayali, the School of Witches.

They climbed out beyond the common line, a second chevron, like a mathematical apparition of the first, two hundred lights flung into the blackness of the plain. They stopped, hung like wickless candle lights. Arcane chanting, eerie and feminine, shrugged away the cavernous heights of the night and found ears in the form of intimate whispers.

Prompted by some inaudible signal, they lit the world in unison.

Bars of Heaven, lines of blinding white rising from the wasted ground to the shrouded sky, some two hundred of them, like silver spokes across the near horizon.

Their faces slack above the rims of their shields, the Men of the Middle-North squinted across a lightning-illuminated world, one devoid of sound, bleached of colour. At first, many could not credit their eyes. Many stood blinking as if trying to awaken.

Instead of earth, Sranc. Instead of *distance*, Sranc.

Fields upon fields of them, creeping on their bellies like worms.

They had come as locusts, where the lust of the one sparks the lust of the other, until all is plague. They had come, answering a cunning as old as the age of their obscene manufacture. They had come to feast and they had come to couple, for they knew of no other possibility.

The Nuns' chanting chorus crumbled into an arcane cacophony. One glowing figure sparked with furious light. Then another. Then all was glare and blinking hell.

The air whooshed and cracked, sounds so great that many flinched behind their shields – sounds that blew through the roar of burning Sranc. The Men of the Ordeal stood dazzled. Seven heartbeats Fate would grant them. Seven heartbeats to see their foe thrash in the fire of their burning. Seven heartbeats to wonder at the girls hanging alone in the sky, setting the earth alight with glowing song.

Seven heartbeats, for even though the beasts died in untold thousands before their eyes, *all the world* beyond the witches was Sranc. And far more creatures heaved and scrambled between the circuits of their sorcerous destruction than within. Arrows chipped at the Nuns' Wards, a few that quickly became an obscuring rain, until the witches were naught but blue-glowing marbles beneath clattering black. Far more missed their mark than otherwise so that the creatures fell in great arcs below.

And the Horde *howled*, a noise so savage, raised in so many ulcerated throats, that many Men of the Ordeal dropped their weapons to clasp their ears. A cry that pinched the nape of even the bravest man's neck . . .

And sent the very landscape rushing.

Not a man who had boasted failed to repent his words. The Swayali seemed to move for the fields of Sranc surging beneath them. Many men stumbled for vertigo. Shrieks warbled through the all-encompassing roar. No word that Men traded could be heard. No horn that sounded. No drum.

But the Believer-Kings had no need of communication; they had but one inviolable order . . .

Yield no ground.

Mouthing soundless shouts, the Men of the Middle-North watched the cyclopean charge. They saw the ground vanish beneath waves of howling faces. They glimpsed silhouettes against cauldrons of destroying light. Notched blades held high. Figures kicking in starved-dog fury.

They watched the *Horde* descend upon them . . .

No words, no training could prepare them for the fact of their enemy. Many glanced to the horizon, thinking they would see their Holy Aspect-Emperor striding across the back of a shrouded world – not realizing that the Horde had beset each of the Four Armies, that he battled faraway with Proyas and the Army of the East.

The fleetest among the Sranc struck first, a scattering of mad, individual assaults. They clawed and thrashed like cats thrown from rooftops. But the Men scarcely noticed them, such was the deluge that followed . . .

The scrambling herd of limbs. The flying line of blades and axes. The crazed white faces, those intent startling for their inhuman beauty, those that shrieked appalling for their infernal deformity. Glimpses rimmed in the light of Swayali destruction . . . Stick-limbed apparitions.

The Men of the Middle-North raised their shields and spears against them.

So did the Horde crash against the Army of the Middle-North. The dead could scarce fall, so packed, so violent was the melee. Men grimacing in thrusting panic. Nonmen faces squealing and snapping. Sranc, crushed by the heave of their countless brothers. Sranc, their every bestial instinct bent to ferocity. Men cringed from their eye-blink speed, gasped against their gut-twisting stink: the rot of fish mongers clothed in fecal rags.

But the Shining Men stood their stubborn ground. Heavily armoured, stout of heart, and mighty of limb, they knew that flight would be their destruction. Torrents of arrows and javelins blackened the deranged vista, falling upon the ranks in a sound-less clatter, but only those foolish enough to raise their faces were wounded or killed. Heeding the lessons of the ancients, they fought in deep phalanxes, arrayed so that those forward could brace their backs or shoulders against the shields of those behind, so that the entire formation must be clawed like a burr from world's hair before moving. The Galeoth and Tydonni wielded their thrusting spears and *nansuri*, short-swords designed

for close-quarters fighting, to great effect, stabbing at the abominations pinioned against their shields. The Thunyeri, who were
weaned on the blood of Sranc, used the hatchets long favoured
by their fathers.

The host's bowmen maintained their positions immediately
behind the common line, loosing shaft after shaft on shallow arcs
over the heads of their countrymen. All of them, even the famed
Agmundrmen, fired blind, knowing their arrows killed and yet
despairing the insignificance of their toll.

For the knights and thanes stranded on their ponies behind
the common line, it seemed a kind of mad performance, like
those staged by the great troupes of dancers who frequented the
courts of kings. For weeks they had skirmished with the Sranc,
had grinned the pulse-pounding grin of the chase and kill. But
now they could only watch in astonished frustration, for the
Sranc had swallowed the very ground they would ride. Hundreds
abandoned their mounts, hoping to shoulder their way to the
fore of their men-at-arms, but the Judges stayed them with
threats of doom and damnation, reminded them of the Aspect-
Emperor and his Martial Prohibitions. For each phalanx was a
kind of abacus, and each man a bead bound by strict rules of
substitution.

Earl Hirengar of Canute spurned the Judges. He was one of
those belligerent souls who could not abide watching while his
lessers fought, let alone consider the consequences of his acts.
When the Judges tried to seize him, he killed two and grievously
injured a third. Then, because no signal could be heard above the
clamour, he rode unopposed into the phalanx of his countrymen
with his thanes in grim tow. His company managed to hack their
way some thirty yards beyond the common line, great-bearded
Tydonni, their mouths howling inaudible war cries, their swords
and axes swinging on wild arcs. But the Sranc engulfed them,

climbed the backs of their brothers, leapt to tackle the hapless knights. Hirengar himself was dragged from his saddle by the beard. Death came swirling down.

Dismayed and disorganized, his kinsmen faltered. But even as panic leapt like wildfire among them, four Nuns floated above, their billows flaring golden, their sorcerous mutter fluting through the ringing deafness. Hanging as high as treetops, they decimated the Sranc with scythes of crackling light, and so provided the Canutishmen a desperate respite.

Wherever Men faltered, the Swayali witches were there above them, their silk billows cupping the light of their dread dispensations, glowing like jellyfish in the deep. Their mouths flashing lanterns. Their hands working looms of killing incandescence. After the initial shock, the Men of the Middle-North embraced their training, realizing with a kind of wonder that this was what they had prepared for all along. How to yield ten paces whenever the dead piled too high. How to draw their own wounded and dead through their line. Even how to *fight the sky*, for in their frenzy, the Sranc would claw across the backs and shoulders of their brothers and leap over the forward ranks.

Battle became a kind of dread harvest. Sranc died burning. Sranc died punctured and trampled. Sranc died scratching at shields. Yet they came and they came, surging beneath the witches and their comb of brilliant destruction, a shrieking chorus that wetted ears with blood. Men who faltered for exhaustion rotated with men from the rearward ranks. Soon gored figures could be seen stumbling behind the common lines, crying out for water, for bandages, or simply crashing to the dust. The Judges paced the line, their gilded Circumfixes held high, their mouths working about exhortations no one could hear. Hell itself seemed to churn but a keel away. And they wondered that mere Men could hold such wickedness at bay.

And then, slowly, inexorably, a different sound climbed into the deafening clamour, a more human intonation, tentative at first, but constant in its slow swelling . . . *Singing.*

The Shining Men crying out, rank upon rank, nation upon nation, until every soul bellowed in miraculous unison, a shout that climbed high upon the back of the Horde's bedlam roar . . .

The 'Beggar's Lament.'

I have boils like little titties,
I have feet like stumps of beef,

And the Men of the Middle-North began laughing as they hacked and hewed, weeping for the joy of destruction.

Every coin that falls for me,
gets snatched by another thief!

The same lyric, hollered out over and over, like a sacred intonation. It became a banner, a scrap of purity hoisted high above a polluted world, and none would relinquish it. A call and a promise. A curse and a prayer. And the Shining Men matched the Sranc and their preternatural fury, roared singing as they stove skulls and spilled entrails. In one mad voice they fumbled for their faith, raised high the shield of their belief . . .

And became unconquerable.

———— ∞ ————

The Scions fled across the black, the earth little more than liquid shadows sweeping beneath. Sorweel continually found himself sagging to his right, such was his exhaustion. His eyes would roll between pasty blinks, and his head would loll like a tipping weight. The dark world would tilt, and for a heartbeat he would float on the border of unconsciousness . . . before catching himself with a panicked jerk. At least his pony, Stubborn, remained true to his moniker and showed no sign of faltering.

Periodically he would shout mock encouragement to Zsoronga, who would always reply by wishing him ill. Neither paid attention to what was said: the saying was all that mattered, the reminder that other souls endured the same congealed misery and somehow persevered.

Finally, after days of tacking across the wastes, they had flanked and outdistanced the Ten-Yoke Legion – though they had been reduced to fifteen mounted souls doing so. Now with their last sip of strength, they raced toward the smear of flickering lights on the horizon, what they would have thought a thunderstorm were it not for the tin-distant clamour . . .

They could hear it over the broken percussion of hooves tumbling across the dust, over the pinched complaints of their ponies. A sound, high and hollow, ringing as if the world were a cistern. It was a sound that grew and grew – impossibly, they realized, guessing the distance of its origin. Crooning like a thousand wolves, hacking like warring geese. An immeasurable sound, or at least one beyond Men and their mortal rule.

The Horde.

A sound so titanic that Harnilas, for all his ruthless determination to reach General Kayûtas, called the ragged company to a halt. The Scions sat rigid in their saddles, squinting at their shadowy companions, waiting for their dust to outrun them. Sorweel peered ahead, struggling to make sense of the flash and flicker that now extended across a good swathe of the horizon.

He looked to Zsoronga, but the man hung his head, grimacing and thumbing his eyes.

At the Captain's bidding, Eskeles cast another of his sorcerous lenses. The light of his incantation seemed a jewel, so dark the world had become. Sorweel glimpsed the others, their faces drawn and gaunt, eyes bruised with the sorrow and fury that is manhood. Then soundless images crowded the air before the Schoolman . . .

The Scions gasped and cried out, even those too exhausted to speak.

A screeching world. Heaving, howling masses, pale and silvery like fish schooling through dark waters. Sranc, raving and thronging, so many as to seem singular, their rushing like the slow curl of scarves warring across the horizon. The Men of the Middle-North could be barely glimpsed, arrayed in bristling, segmented bars, defending barricades of stacked carcasses. Only the Swayali Witches could be clearly seen, hanging like slips of gold foil, drawing skirts of flashing Gnostic destruction . . . never enough.

With twists of his fingers, Eskeles turned the lens on a shallow arc, revealing more and more of the madness that awaited them. For all its power and the glory, the Army of the Middle-North was but a shallow island in dark-heaving seas. No one need speak the obvious.

The Northmen were doomed.

Real, Sorweel once again found himself thinking in dumb wonder. *His war is real* . . .

He turned from the spectacle to the Schoolman, saw the ribs of his ailing pony carved in light and shadow.

'A sight from my Dreams . . .' Eskeles murmured. And Sorweel worried for the brittle cast of his eyes, the promise of panic.

Without thinking, he reached out to squeeze the man's round shoulder in reassurance – the way King Harweel might. 'Remember,' he said, speaking words he suddenly *wanted* to believe. 'This time the God marches with us.'

'Yes . . .' the square-bearded sorcerer replied with a throat-clearing *harrumph*. 'Of-of course . . .'

And then they heard it, like an echo floating through howling winds, *human* voices, shouting out human sounds: hope, fury, and *defiance*, defiance most of all.

'The "Beggar's Lament"!' someone called from behind them. 'The crazy bastards!'

And with that, they all could hear it, word for hoarse word, a *drinking* song bellowed out to the heavens. Suddenly the throat-pricking frailty fell away from the distant Men, and what had seemed a vision of doom became legendary – *glorious* – more indomitable than overmatched. The gored Northmen, their lines unbroken, reaving . . .

A massacre of the mad many by the holy few.

That was when they heard another sound, another ear-scratching roar . . . one that came shivering through the dark and dust and grasses.

More Sranc.

Behind them.

<hr>

A miraculous slaughter, on a scale too demented to be celebrated.

Kayûtas and his Believer-Kings knew their flanks would be quickly enveloped, but they also knew, thanks to the ancients, that their encircling would be the product of happenstance, a consequence of the Sranc and their mobbing desperation. Whipped by their lunatic hunger, each simply ran toward Men and their porcine smell, a course continually deflected by the mobbing of their brothers before them. In this way, the Horde spilled ever outward like water chasing gutters. But the process was such that those who reached the ends of the Galeoth flanks would be but trickles compared with the torrents above.

'The Horde will strike the way Ainoni courtesans pile their hair,' Kayûtas had explained to his laughing commanders. 'Locks will spill down our cheeks, make no mistake. But only a few curls will tickle our chin.'

And so was the ignominious task of defending the camp and rear delegated to the Lords of the Great Ordeal. So-called 'Cornice Phalanxes' occupied the ends of the common-line, formations of courageous souls trained to battle in all directions. Triunes of Swayali hung above, scourging the endless flurries of Sranc that sluiced around them. And with the Kidruhil, the assembled thanes and knights policed the darkling plains between.

If the Prince-Imperial's descriptions had led them to expectations of easy slaughter, they were quickly disabused. Many were lost to the mundane treachery of burrows and ant mounds. Earl Arcastor of Gesindal, a man renowned for his ferocity in battle, broke his neck before he and his Galeoth knights encountered a single Sranc. Otherwise all was darkness and racing madness, conditions that favoured the lust-maddened Sranc clans. Companies would ride down one cohort in effortless slaughter, only to be surprised by the shrieking assault of another. Company after company limped back to the precincts of the camp, their numbers decimated, their eyes vacant with vicious horrors. Lord Siklar of Agansanor, cousin of King Hogrim, would be felled by a stray arrow out of nowhere. Lord Hingeath of Gaenri would fall in pitched battle with his entire household, as would Lord Ganrikka, Veteran of the First Holy War – a name that would be mourned by many.

And so death came swirling ever down.

Despite the toll, not one of the obscenities lived to trod the alleys of the darkened camp.

Fleeing into a world illumined by faraway sorcery.

Riding as if chased by the world's own crumbling edge.

Gouged hollow, a stack of tin about a papyrus fire. Light enough to be blown by terror. Dull and heavy enough to die, to tumble dirt against dirt.

The intellect overthrown. The eyes rolling, seeking non-existent lines, as if trying to peer around the doom encircling them.

Stubborn coursed beneath him, galloping like a dog across invisible earth, scoring the thirsty turf. Zsoronga glanced at him, sobs kicking through the monkey-terror of his grin. The others were less than shadows . . .

The world flew in shreds beneath them. And the whole was delivered to Sranc.

The Ten-Yoke Legion.

A shriek, a sound heard only for its humanity, and the Scions were fourteen.

'They would drive them the way we drive slaves in the Three Seas,' the Schoolman had said, *'starve them until their hungers reached a fever pitch. Then, when they reached a position where the Sranc could smell Mannish blood on the wind, they would strike the chains, and let them run . . .'*

Sorweel tossed a panicked glance over his shoulder, toward the inscrutable black that gnashed and grunted behind them . . .

Saw Eskeles yanked to earth on the back of his tumbling pony, slapped like a fish onto the gutting-table.

And he was reining, crying out to Zsoronga, leaping to the turf, sprinting to the motionless Schoolman. The Scions were nothing but streamers of fading dust. He gasped shrieking air, skidded to a halt. He heaved the sorcerer onto his back, cried out something he could not hear. He looked up, felt more than saw the rush, raving and inhuman . . .

And for a heartbeat he smiled. A King of the Horselords, dying for a leuneraal . . .

One last humiliation.

The beasts *surfaced*, as if looking back had become looking down. Faces of pale silk, crushed into expressions both crazed and licentious. Slicked weapons. Glimpses piled upon glimpses, terror upon terror.

Sorweel looked to them, smiling even as his body tensed against hacking iron. He watched the nearest leap . . .

Only to crash into a film of incandescent blue – *sorcery* – wrapped into a hemisphere about them.

The booming roar swept into them, over them, and Sorweel found himself in a mad bubble, a miraculous grotto where sweat could be wiped from sodden brows.

Sand and dust shivered and danced between leather threads of grass. Beyond, howling faces, horned weapons, and knobbed fists crowded his every glimpse. He watched with a kind of disembowelled wonder: the white-rope limbs, the teeth like broken cochri shells, the covetous glitter of innumerable black eyes . . .

Breathing required will.

Eskeles thrashed his way back to blubbering consciousness. Moaning, he threw his gaze this way and that, flailed with his fists. Sorweel hugged his shoulders, tried to wrestle the panic from him. He thrust the portly man back, pinned him, crying, 'Look at me! *Look* at me!'

'*Noooo!*' the man howled from his dust-white beard. Urine blackened the man's trousers.

'Something!' Sorweel cried through the scratching, pounding racket. The heave of crazed wretches encompassed everything. The first luminous cracks scrawled across the Ward, wandering like the flight of flies. 'You *have* to do something!'

'It's happening! Sweet Seju! Sweet-swe—!'

Sorweel cuffed him full on the mouth.

'*Eskeles!* You have to do something! Something *with light!*'

The Mandate Schoolmen squinted in confusion.

'The *Ordeal*, you fat fool! The Great Ordeal *needs to be warned!*'

Somehow, somewhere in Sorweel's cry, the sorcerer seemed to encounter himself, the stranger who had sacrificed all in the name of his Aspect-Emperor. The Zaudunyani. The *Believer*. His eyes found their focus. He reached out to squeeze the young King's shoulder in assurance.

'L-light,' he gasped. 'Light – *yes!*'

He pressed Sorweel to the side, tottered to his feet even as his incipient Ward began to crumble. The glow of his chanting gleamed across swatches of madness. Screeching faces, jerking, trembling like strings in the wind. Bleeding gums. Diseased skin, weeping slime and algae. Notched edges flying on arcs both cramped and vicious. Eyes of glittering black, hundreds of them *fixing* him, weeping and raging for hunger. Lips shining for slaver . . .

Like a nightmare. Like a mad fresco depicting the living gut of Hell, bleached ever whiter for the brilliance of the Schoolman's unholy song. Words too greased to be caught and subdued by the Legion's vicious roar, echoing through invisible canyons.

And there it was . . . striking as straight as a geometer's line from the ground at the fat sorcerer's feet, dazzling the eyes, stilling the inhuman onlookers with salt-white astonishment . . .

Reaching high to illuminate the belly of the overcast night.

A Bar of Heaven.

—∞∞∞—

General Kayûtas was the first to glimpse it out across the tumult, the Northmen but rafts of discipline in a tossed sea of Sranc, the Swayali like columns of sunlight breaking through tempest clouds, burning the inexhaustible waters. He saw it, between pelting arcs of arrows, a needle of glittering white on the southern horizon . . .

Where nothing but dead earth should be.

He turned to his sister, who had followed his gaze out to the distant and inexplicable beacon. Others in his cortege noticed also, but their shouts of alarm were soundless in the thrumming roar.

Serwa need only glimpse her brother's lips to understand – they were children of the Dûnyain.

She stepped into the sky, summoned the nearest of her sisters to rise with her.

***

The world smelled of burning snakes.

Sorweel saw clouds knotted into woollen plates, flickering in and out of edgeless illumination. His head lolled and he saw the earth reeling, pricked with infinite detail, a thousand thousand mortal struggles. Ironclad men hacking and hollering. Sranc and more Sranc – twitching and innumerable. He saw women hanging in the air with him, far-gowned Swayali, singing impossible, incandescent songs.

And he jerked his lurching gaze to the hook that had lifted him so high . . .

A *Goddess* held him, carried him like a child across the surfaces of Hell.

'Mother?' he gasped, thinking not of the woman who had borne him but of the divinity. Yatwer . . . the Mother of Wombs, who had cursed him with murdering the most deadly man to ever walk her parched earth.

'No,' the glorious lips replied. It seemed a miracle that she could hear him, such was the guttural clamour. A roar so knotted with violence, that the very air seemed to bleed. 'Worse.'

'*You . . .*' he gasped, recognizing the woman through the fiery veil of her beauty.

'Me,' Anasûrimbor Serwa replied, smiling with the cruelty of the peerless. 'How many hundreds will die,' she asked, 'for saving you?'

'Drop me then,' he croaked.

She recoiled from the floating fury of his gaze, looked out across the threshing darkness, frowning as if finally understanding she bore a king in her arcane embrace. Through acrid veils of smoke, he breathed deep the scent of her: the myrrh of glory and privilege, the salt of exertion.

Let me fall.

CHAPTER EIGHT

The Western Three Seas

*Complexity begets ambiguity, which yields in all ways to
prejudice and avarice. Complication does not so much defeat
Men as arm them with fancy.*

—AJENCIS, THE THIRD ANALYTIC OF MEN

**Late Spring, 20 New Imperial Year (4132 Year-of-the-Tusk),
Nansurium, somewhere south of Momemn**

In Gielgath, two thieves assailed him, and the White-Luck Warrior
watched them scuffle, drunk and desperate, with the man who was their
doom. They lurched out of alleyway shadows, their cries choked to
murmurs for fear of being heard. They sprawled dead and dying across
cobble and filth, the one inert, the other twitching. He wiped his
Seleukaran blade clean across the dead one, even as he raised the sword
to counter their manic rush. He stepped clear of the one who stumbled,
raised his blade to parry the panicked swing of the other . . . the swing
that would notch the scimitar's honed edge – as thin as an eyelid.

The notch that would shatter his sword, so allowing the broken blade to plunge into the Aspect-Emperor's heart. He could even feel the blood slick his thumb and fingers, as he followed himself into the gloomy peril of the alley.

Unholy blood. Wicked beyond compare.

No one noticed him in the subsequent hue and cry. He watched himself slip unnoticed through gathering crowds of onlookers – for even in these lawless times, the murder of two men was no small thing. He followed himself through an ancient and impoverished maze that was Gielgath. One of the priestess beggars called, 'You! You!' as he passed a fullery. He saw her sob for joy a million times.

The slave plantations were more severe in their discipline, more grand in extent, in the lands he subsequently crossed, following his following. He watched himself lean so that he might draw his bloody hands across the crowns of surging millet and wheat. Across the span of ages, the Goddess watched and was pleased, and it was Good.

He came across a cow calving, and he knelt into his kneeling so that he might witness his Mother made manifest. He watched himself draw his fingers through the afterbirth, then redden the lobes of his ears.

He found a fugitive child hiding in an overgrown ditch, watched himself give all that remained of his food. 'There is no greater Gift,' he overheard himself say to the wide brown eyes, 'than to give unto death.' And he caressed the dark-tanned cheek that was also a skull decaying between grass and milkweed.

He saw a stork riding invisible gusts across the sky.

He walked, forever trailing the man who walked before him and forever leading the one who walked behind. He watched his form, dark for the brilliance of the sun, sink over cultivated summits, even as he turned to see his form, dark within its own shadow, rising from the crest behind.

And so he stepped into his stepping, walked into his walking, travelled into his journey, a quest that had already ended in the death of the False Prophet.

Until at last he paused upon a hill and for the first time gazed across the walls and streets he had seen innumerable times.

Momemn. The Home City. Great Capital of the New Empire.

He saw all the lanes he had never travelled. He saw the Temple Xothei with its famed domes, heard the riotous cries that would shiver its stone. He saw the Imperial Precincts along the seaward walls, the campuses hazy and deserted. He saw the piling of structure and marble beauty that was the Andiamine Heights, his eyes roaming until they found the famed veranda behind the Aspect-Emperor's throne-room . . .

Where the Gift-of-Yatwer glimpsed himself peering back, the Holy Empress beside him.

Momemn

'Why should it trouble a mother to see her child love himself so?' Inrilatas said from his shadow. He exhaled a breath pent in hungry pleasure. 'Fondle himself?'

Sunlight streamed through the cell's one small window, drawing a fan of illuminated surfaces from the smoky gloom. A stretch of her son's hair, the outer lines of his left shoulder and arm. Thankfully, she could not so much see him masturbate as infer it.

She fixed him with a mother's flat gaze. Perhaps it was her old life as a whore, or perhaps he had simply exhausted her with his antics; either way she was unimpressed. There was very little Inrilatas could do that would shock or dismay her anymore.

A small carpet had been laid across the floor, with an oak chair, cushioned and elaborately carved, set upon it for her comfort. White-clad body-slaves stood ready to either side with wicker screens – shields, really – ready to shelter her if her son decided to begin pelting her with feces or any other fluid that caught his fancy. It had happened before. After they were done, she knew, the chains would be drawn to fix her son across the wall, and the Attendants would scour the floor looking for anything dropped or forgotten. The boy – young man, now – was simply too ingenious not to devise tools for some kind of mischief. Once he managed to make a shiv, which he used to kill one of his attendants, using only the fabric of his tunic and his seed.

'I want Maithanet brought here . . . to you.'

She could feel him peering into her face, the strange tickle of being known. She experienced some sense of exposure with almost all her children by Kellhus, but it differed with each one. With Kayûtas, it simply seemed to render her irrelevant, a problem easily dismissed or solved. With Serwa, it raised her ire because she knew the girl could see the pain she had caused her mother and yet chose to ignore it. With Theliopa, it was simply a fact of the time they spent together, and a convenience as well, since it allowed the girl to more completely subordinate herself to her mother's wishes.

But with Inrilatas it always seemed more profound, more intrusive, somehow . . .

Like the way she felt in her husband's eyes, only without the sense of . . . resignation.

'Uncle Holy,' he said.

'Ye—'

'They smell it on you, you know,' he interrupted. 'Fear.'

'Yes,' she replied in a long breath. 'I know.'

Kellhus once told her that Inrilatas's soul had been almost perfectly divided between the two of them, his intellect and her heart. *'The Dûnyain have not so much mastered passion,'* he had explained, *'as snuffed it out. My intellect is simply not robust enough to leash your heart. Imagine bridling a lion with string.'*

'You are blackened by Father's light,' the adolescent said, his voice straying across resonances only her husband used. 'Rendered pathetic and absurd. How could a *mere whore* presume to rule Men, let alone the Three Seas?'

'Yes . . . I know, Inrilatas.'

What was the power that a mother wielded over her son? She had watched Inrilatas reduce her flint-hearted generals to tears and fury, yet for all the cutting things he had said to her, for all the truths, he managed only to increase her pity *for him*. And this, it seemed to her, kindled a desperation in him while rendering her a kind of challenge, a summit he must conquer. For all the labyrinthine twists of his madness, he was just an anguished little boy in the end.

It was hard to play God in the eyes of a heartbroken mother.

Inrilatas grunted and huffed air. She tried to ignore the strings of semen that looped across the oblong of sunlit floor several paces from her feet.

He was always doing this, marking the spaces about him with his excretions. Always staining. Always defacing. Always desecrating. Always expressing bodily what he sought to do with his mastery of word and expression. All men gloried in transgression, Kellhus had told her, because all men gloried in power, and no power was more basic than the violation of another's body or desire. '*Innumerable rules bind the intercourse of Men, rules they can scarce see, even if they devote their lives to the study of jnan. Our son lives in a world far different than yours, Esmi – a visible world. One knotted and stifled and choked with the thoughtless customs we use to pass judgment one upon another.*'

'Aren't you curious?' she asked.

Her son raised a finger to his mouth. 'You think Father left the Empire to you because he feared the ambition of his brother. So you suspect Uncle Holy of treachery. You want me to interrogate him. Read his face.'

'Yes,' she said.

'No . . . This is simply the rationale you use. The truth is, Mother, *you know you will fail.* Even now, you can feel the New Empire slip from your grasp, topple over the edge. And because you know you fail, you know Maithanet will be forced to wrest the Empire *from you*, not for his own gratification, but for the *sake* of his brother . . .'

And so the game began in earnest. *'You must be forever wary in his presence,'* Kellhus had warned her. *'For truth will be his sharpest goad. He will answer questions that you have never asked yet lay aching in your heart nonetheless. He will use* enlightenment *to enslave you, Esmi. Every insight you have, every revelation you think you have discovered, will be his.'*

Thus had her husband, in the course of arming her against their mad son, also warned her against himself. As well as confirmed what Achamian had said so very long ago.

She leaned forward, braced her elbows against her knees to watch him the way she had when he was but a babe. 'I *will not fail*, Inrilatas. If Maithanet assumes my eventual failure, then he's mistaken. If he acts on this assumption, then he has broken the Aspect-Emperor's divine law.'

Inrilatas's chuckle was soft, forgiving, and so very sane.

'But you *will* fail,' he asserted with a slaver's nonchalance. 'So why should I do this for you, Mother? Perhaps I should side *with Uncle*, for in truth, *only he* can save Father's Empire.'

How could she trust him? Inrilatas, her and her husband's monstrous prodigy . . .

'Because my heart beats in your breast,' she said out of rash maternal reflex. 'Because half of your madness is mine . . .' But she trailed, troubled by the way Inrilatas could, merely by listening, reveal the falsehood of sentiments that seemed so simple and true otherwise.

A jerk and rattle of iron chains. 'Things *heave* in me, Mother. Be. Quick.'

'Because I know that you *want* the Empire to fail.'

His laughter was curious, as though crazed forces sheered the humour underpinning it.

'And you will trust . . . what I tell you?' he said, his voice cracked by inexplicable exertions. 'The words . . . of a madman?'

'Yes. If only because I know that *Truth* is your madness.'

A kind of jubilation accompanied these words – one that she immediately repented, knowing her son had already seen it, and fearing he would deny her for simple perversity's sake. Even as a young child, he had always sought to quash whatever was bright within her.

'Inspired words, Mother.' His tone was thin and blank, almost as if he mocked his older sister, Theliopa. 'The very kind Father has warned you not to trust. You cannot see the darkness that precedes your thoughts, but unlike most souls you *know* it exists. You appreciate how rarely you are the author of what you say and do . . .' He raised his shackled hands for a clap that never came. 'I'm impressed, Mother. You understand this trick the world calls a soul.'

'A trick that can be saved . . . or damned.'

'What if redemption were simply another form of damnation? What if the only true salvation lay in seeing *through* the trick and embracing oblivion?'

'And what if,' Esmenet replied with more than a little annoyance, 'these questions could be debated endlessly without hope of resolution?'

In a wink, Theliopa's manner vanished, replaced by a hunched ape, leering and laughing. 'Father has been rubbing off on you!'

Perhaps she should have been amused. Perhaps she would have been, despite the utter absence of trust. But her heart had been bludgeoned, her hope battered beyond the possibility of amusement.

'I tire of your games, Inrilatas,' she said, speaking a fury that seemed to gather strength in the sound of her voice. 'I *understand* that you can see my thoughts through my voice and face. I *understand* your abilities as well as anyone without Dûnyain blood can. I even understand the predicaments I face in merely speaking to you!'

More laughter. 'No, Mother. You most certainly *do not* understand. If you did, you would have drowned me years ago.'

She fairly leapt to her feet, such was the sudden violence of her anger. But she caught herself. '*Remember, Esmi,*' Kellhus had warned her, '*never let your passions rule you. Passions make you simple, easy to master. Only by twisting, reflecting upon your reflections, will you be able to slip his grasp . . .*'

Inrilatas had leaned forward from his hunch, his face avid with a shifting mélange of contradictory passions, a face like a pick, sorting through tumblers of her soul.

'You lean heavily on Father's advice . . .' he said, his voice reaching for intonations that almost matched Kellhus's. 'But you should know that I am your husband *as he really is*. Even Uncle, when he speaks, parses and pitches his words to mimic the way others sound – to conceal the inhumanity I so love to flaunt. We Dûnyain . . . we *are not human*, Mother. And you . . . You are *children* to us. Ridiculous and adorable. And so insufferably stupid.'

The Blessed Empress of the Three Seas could only stare in horror.

'But you know this . . .' Inrilatas continued, his gaze fixed upon her. 'Someone else has told you this . . . And in almost precisely the same words! Who? The Wizard? The legendary Drusas Achamian – yes! He told you this in a final effort to rescue your heart, didn't he? Ah . . . *Mother!* I see you so much more *clearly* now! All the years of regret and recrimination, torn between terror and love, stranded with children – such wicked, gifted children! – ones you can never hope to fathom, never hope to love.'

'But I do love you!'

'There is no love without trust, Mother. Only need . . . hunger. I am a reflex, nothing more, nothing less.'

Her throat cramped. The tears welled to her eyes, spilled in hot threads across her cheeks.

He had succeeded. At last he had succeeded . . .

'Damn you!' she whispered, swatting at her eyes. Battered and exhausted – that was how she felt after mere moments with her son. And the words! What he had said would torment her for nights to come – longer. 'This was a mistake,' she murmured, refusing to glance at his lurid figure.

But just as she turned to signal the slaves to leave, he said, 'Father has cut off all communication.'

She slumped in her seat, breathing, staring without focus at the floor.

'Yes,' she said.

'You are alone, lost in a wilderness of subtleties you cannot fathom.'

'Yes . . .'

At last she raised her gaze to meet his. 'Will you do this for me, Inrilatas?'

'Trust. Trust is the one thing you seek.'

'Yes . . . I . . .' A kind of resignation overwhelmed her. 'I *need* you.'

Invisible things boiled through the heartbeats that followed. Portents. Ruminations. Lusts.

'There can only be three of us . . .' Inrilatas finally said. Once again, unnameable passions creaked through the seams of his voice.

The Blessed Empress blinked more tears, this time for relief. 'Of course. Just your uncle and myself.'

'No. Not you. My brothers . . .' A heaving breath swallowed his voice.

'Brothers?' she asked, more alarmed than curious.

'Kel . . .' he said with a bestial grunt, 'and Sammi . . .'

The Holy Empress stiffened. If Inrilatas had been seeking a fatal chink, he had discovered it. 'I don't understand,' she replied, swallowing. 'Sammi is . . . Sammi, he . . .'

But the figure she spoke to was scarce human anymore. Anasûrimbor Inrilatas rose with a dancer's slow deliberation, then threw himself forward, his arms and legs outstretched, straining against the limits of his chains. He stood there, all spittle and squint-eyed passion, his naked limbs heaving, trembling with veins and striations. Her shield-bearers, Esmenet could not help but notice, had shrunk behind the wicker screens meant for her.

'Mother!' her son shrieked, his eyes shining with murder. 'Mother! Come! Closer!'

Something of her original imperviousness returned. This . . . This was her son as she knew him best.

The beast.

'Let me see your mouth, Mother!'

⬥

Iothiah

The woman called Psatma Nannaferi was brought before the Padirajah and his loutish court the same as all the other notable captives, stripped naked and shackled in iron. But where other attractive women had been greeted with lascivious hoots and calls – humiliation, Malowebi had realized, was as much as part of the proceedings as the Padirajah's judgment – a peculiar silence accompanied Psatma Nannaferi's short march to the floor below Fanayal. Rumours of this woman, the Mbimayu sorcerer decided, had spread quickly among the desert men. The fact that he had not heard these rumours simply served to whet his curiosity, as well as to remind him that he remained an outsider.

Fanayal had seized one of the few temples not burned, a great domed affair that abutted the Agnotum Market – the ironic point of origin for many luxury goods that found their way to Zeüm. The altar had been broken down with sledges and hauled away. The tapestries with panels drawn from the Tractate and the Chronicle of the Tusk had been burned. Those representing the First Holy War, Malowebi was told, had been carted out of Iothiah to line the horse stalls seized by Fanayal's growing army. The frescoes had been defaced, and graven images everywhere had been smashed. Several green-and-crimson banners bearing the Twin Scimitars of Fanimry had been roped and tacked across the walls. But the Tusks and Circumfixes were simply too ubiquitous to be completely blotted. No matter where his eye strayed, along the columns, over the cornices and vaults of the flanking architraves, Malowebi glimpsed unscathed evidence of the Aspect-Emperor and his faith.

Nowhere more so than the dome itself – whose height and breadth alone were a kind of miracle to Malowebi, hailing as he did from a nation without arches. A great wheel of frescoes hung in the high gloom above the unbelievers, five panels representing Inri Sejenus in some different pose, his face gentle, his hands haloed in painted gold, his silvered eyes glaring endlessly down.

Fanayal's desert Grandees betrayed no discomfort that the Second Negotiant could see. But then Malowebi always found himself surprised by men's general blindness to irony and contradiction. If the Kianene had looked vicious and impoverished before, they looked positively absurd now, decked in the eclectic spoils of a great imperial city. The desert mob seethed with jarring mixtures of clothing and armour: the high conical helms from Ainon, black

Thunyeri hauberks, a couple of silk gowns that Malowebi suspected belonged to a woman's wardrobe, and in one case, the baggy crimson pantaloons typically worn by caste-slave eunuchs. One man even sported a Nilnameshi feather-shield. Most of them, Malowebi knew, had spent the bulk of their lives hunted like animals across the desert wastes. Until now, they had counted sips of water and shelter from sun and wind as luxury, so it made sense they would feast in all ways possible, given the crazed rewards Fate had heaped upon them.

Even still, they looked more a carnival of dangerous fools than a possible ally of High Holy Zeüm.

Once again Fanayal alone embodied the elegance and reserve that had once so distinguished his people. A wooden chair had been set behind the forward ridge of the altar's shattered base, where the Padirajah sat, agleam even in temple gloom, wearing a coat of golden mail over a white silk tunic: the armour and uniform of the Coyauri, the famed heavy cavalry he had commanded as a young man during the First Holy War.

Meppa stood at his right hand, his cowl drawn back, his eyes hidden as always behind the silver band about his head. The Cishaurim's serpent rose like a black iron hook from his neck, tasting the air with its tongue, wagging from voice to voice.

Malowebi had been assigned the shadows behind and to the left of the Padirajah, where he had watched perhaps a hundred naked woman and men dragged beneath Fanayal and his vengeful whims, a piteous train of them, some proud and defiant, but most abject and broken, wheezing and weeping for a mercy that was never shown. The captive men, no matter what their station, where asked whether they would curse their Aspect-Emperor and embrace the truth of the Prophet Fane. Those who refused were dragged off for immediate execution. Those who agreed were taken away to be auctioned as slaves. As far as the Mbimayu sorcerer could tell, the women – the bereaved wives and orphaned daughters of the caste-nobility – were simply brought out to be divided as spoils.

On and on the proceedings continued, becoming more sordid and more farcical, it seemed, with the passing of every doomed soul, dull enough for an old scholar to ponder the perversities of faith, long enough for an old man's feet to ache and itch.

Something about Psatma Nannaferi, however, instantly dispelled his boredom and discomfort.

The guardsmen threw her to the prayer tiles beneath the Padirajah. But where they had delighted in wicked little flourishes with the others, they did so this time with mechanical reluctance – as if trying to hide behind their function.

Fanayal leaned forward, petted his braided goatee as he studied the captive. This too was unprecedented.

'My Inquisitor has told me a most interesting tale . . .'

The woman slowly pulled herself upright, graceful despite her iron shackles. She betrayed neither fear for her future nor shame for her captive nudity. She was not without a certain, diminutive beauty, Malowebi thought, but there was a hardness to her that belied the soft brown curves of her skin. And there was something about her posture and her squint that suggested the habits of someone older – far older – than her apparent thirty years.

'He says,' Fanayal continued, 'that you are *Psatma Nannaferi*, the Mother-Supreme of the Yatwerian Cult.'

A grim and condescending smile. 'I am.'

'He also says *you* are the reason we found these lands afire when we arrived.'

She nodded. 'I am but a vessel. I pour only what has been poured.'

Even after so few words, Malowebi knew her for a formidable woman. Here she stood, naked and manacled, yet her gaze and bearing communicated a confidence too profound to be named pride, a majesty that somehow upended the stakes between her and the famed Bandit Padirajah.

'And now that your Goddess has betrayed you?'

'Betrayed?' she snorted. 'This is not a sum. This is not a wager of advantages over loss. This is a *gift*! Our Mother Goddess's will.'

'So the Goddess wills the destruction of her temples? The torment and execution of her slaves?'

The longer Malowebi gazed at the woman, the more a weight seemed to press against his brow. Her eyes seemed bright with moist vulnerability, her body fetching in the lean way of peasant virgins. And yet watching her, an impression of something hoary, hard, and old continued to plague him. Even the downy curve of her sex . . . She seemed a kind of visible contradiction, as if the look and promise of virgin youth had eclipsed the *sight* of a hag but not the corona of meaning that hung like a haze about it.

So even now, as she glared at Fanayal, it seemed something reptilian peered through *her peering*, the look of something vicious and remorseless with age, flashing from the gaze of a woman, flushed and breathless and so very inviting.

'We take such gifts that come,' she crooned. 'We suffer this worldly trifle, and She will save us! From oblivion! From those demons our iniquities have awakened! This is but the arena where souls settle *eternity*. Our suffering is dross compared to the glory to come!'

Fanayal laughed, genuinely amused. But his humour cut against the obvious unease of his court.

'So even your captivity . . . You think this a *gift*?'

'Yes.'

'And if I were to deliver you to the lust of my men?'

'You will not.'

'And why is that?'

In a twinkling, she became coy and whorish. She even glanced down at her breasts, which were firm with improbable youth. 'Because I have been reborn as black earth, as rain and sweating sun,' she said. 'The Goddess has cast me in *Her image*, as sweet, sweet Fertility. You will not allow other men to trade me, so long as your loins bur—'

'My loins?' Fanayal cried out with forced incredulity.

Malowebi gazed and blinked. She literally *tingled* with nubile promise, yet still she carried the air of old stone. Something . . . Something was *wrong* . . .

'Even now,' she said, 'your seed rises to the promise of soft earth deeply ploughed.'

Masculine laughter rumbled through the chamber, only to falter for want of breath. Even old Malowebi could feel a tightness in his chest and a matching thickness crawling across his thighs . . .

With no little horror the Mbimayu sorcerer realized the Goddess *was among them*. There was peril, here – great peril. This woman walked with one foot on the Outside . . .

He opened his mouth to call out in warning but caught himself on the very hinge of his voice.

He was no friend to these savage people. He was an observer, interpreter. The question was whether Zeüm's interests would be served if Fanayal were alerted. Ally or not, the fact remained that the man was a fanatic of the worst kind, a believer in a creed, Fanimry, that made devils out of the Gods and hells out of the Heavens. To strike an alliance that earned the enmity *of the Mother of Birth* would be a fool's exchange. The Zeümi might not pray to the Hundred, given their intercessory faith, but they certainly revered and respected them.

'"Soft earth deeply ploughed,"' Fanayal repeated, gazing upon her form with frank hunger. He turned to the lean and warlike men of his court. 'Such are the temptations of evil, my friends!' he called, shaking his head. 'Such are the temptations!'

More laughter greeted these words.

'Your sisters are dead,' the Padirajah continued as if immune to her wiles. 'Your temples are pulled down. If these are *gifts*, as you say, then I am in a most generous mood.' He paused to make room for a few frail guffaws from his assembled men. 'I could give you a noose, say, or a thousand lashes. Perhaps I will have Meppa show you what kind of prison your body can be.'

Malowebi found himself wondering whether the woman had even blinked, so relentless was her gaze. The fact that Fanayal weathered it with such thoughtless ease actually troubled the Mbimayu sorcerer. Was the man simply oblivious or did he possess a heart every bit as hard as her own?

Either possibility would not bode an alliance well.

'My soul has already left and returned to this body,' she said, her girlish voice scratched with the harsh intonations of a crone. 'There is no torment you could inflict upon me.'

'So hard!' Fanayal cried laughing. 'Stubborn! Devil-worshipping witch!'

Again the desert court rumbled with laughter.

'I would not ply your body,' Meppa said without warning. So far he had stood silent and motionless at his sovereign's side, his face directed forward as always. Only the asp, which curved like a onyx bow across his left cheek, faced the lone woman.

Psatma Nannaferi regarded the Cishaurim with a sneer. 'My soul is beyond your devilry, Snakehead. I worship the Dread Mother.'

Never had Malowebi witnessed an exchange more uncanny, the blinded man speaking as if to a void, the shackled woman as if she were a mad queen among hereditary slaves.

'You worship a demon.'

The Mother-Supreme laughed with the bitter hilarity. The cackle rang across distant walls, echoed through the high crypt hollows, gelding all the humour that had come before it. Suddenly the assembled men were nothing but ridiculous boys, their pride swatted from them by the palm of a shrewd and exacting mother.

'Call her what you will!' Psatma Nannaferi exclaimed. 'Demon? Yes! *I worship a demon!* – if it pleases you to call her such! You think we worship the Hundred because they are *good*? *Madness* governs the Outside, Snakehead, not gods or demons – or even the God! Fool! We worship them because *they have power over us.* And we – we Yatwerians – worship the one with the most power of all!'

Malowebi squelched another urge to call out, to urge the Fanim to spare her, to set her free, then to burn a hundred bulls in Yatwer's honour. The *Mother* was here! Here!

'Gods are naught but greater demons,' the Cishaurim said, 'hungers across the surface of eternity, wanting only to taste the clarity of our souls. Can you not see this?'

The woman's laughter trailed into a cunning smile. 'Hungers indeed! The fat will be eaten, of course. But the high holy? The faithful? They shall be *celebrated*!'

Meppa's voice was no mean one, yet its timbre paled in the wake of the Mother-Supreme's clawing rasp. Even still he pressed, a tone of urgent sincerity the only finger he had to balance the scales. 'We are a narcotic to them. They eat our smoke. They make jewellery of our thoughts and passions. They are beguiled by our torment, our ecstasy, so they collect us, pluck us like strings, make chords of nations, play the music of our anguish over endless ages. We *have seen this*, woman. We have seen this with our missing eyes!'

Malowebi scowled. Fanim madness . . . It had to be.

'Then you *know*,' Psatma Nannaferi said in a growl that crawled across Malowebi's skin. 'There will be no end to your eating, when She takes you. Your blood, your flesh – they are inexhaustible in death. Taste what little air you can breathe, Snakehead. You presume your Solitary God resembles you. You make your image the form of the One. You think you can trace lines, *borders*, through the Outside, like that fool, Sejenus, say what belongs to the God of Gods and what does not – errant abstractions! Hubris! The Goddess waits, Snakehead, and you are but a mote before her patience! Birth and War alone can seize – and seize She does!'

The Mbimayu sorcerer glanced out over the festooned court, his attention drawn by gasps and murmurs of outrage. The desert men watched, their faces caught between fury and horror. Several of them even signed small folk charms with their fingers. The oddities had been piled too high for them not to realize something profound was amiss.

'Stay your curses!' Fanayal cried, his humour finally beaten into fury.

She cackled in a manner far too savage for lips as young as hers. Dust plumed through a rare shaft of sunlight, star-scapes rolling on temple drafts. 'Yes, Mother!' she shouted to the air the way Meppa might. 'Seizing him would be a delight! Yes!'

'*Demoness!*' the Last Cishaurim bellowed. He descended the steps toward her, his face held forward as stiff as a doll's. 'I know the true compass of your power. You are written across ages and yet you need *tools* – Men. And all Men can fail. It is the foundation of what we are! You will be broken with your tools! And you will starve in your pit!'

'Yes!' Psatma Nannaferi cackled once again. 'All Men *save one!*'

Meppa lowered his face, as if only now seeing her through the etched silver of his band. 'The White-Luck,' he said.

'White-Luck?' Fanayal asked.

Malowebi stood breathless in the wake of the question. These

Fanim barbarians could not fathom the disaster they courted. The Hundred. The Hundred rode to war!

'There are infinite paths through the tumble of events,' Meppa explained to his sovereign. 'The White-Luck, the idolaters believe, is that perfect line of action and happenstance that can see any outcome come to pass. The White-Luck *Warrior* is the man who walks that line. Everything that he needs, happens, not because he wills it but because his need is *identical* to what happens. Every step, every toss of the number-sticks, is a . . .' He turned back to the fierce glare of the Yatwerian Mother-Supreme.

'Is a what?' Fanayal demanded.

Meppa shrugged. 'A gift.'

The diminutive woman cackled and rattled her chains for stamping her feet. 'You are but a temporary blight! A trial that sorts the faithful from the thieves. A far greater war has seized the Three Seas. The Goddess has broken the yoke of the Thousand Temples. The Cults arm themselves for battle. Ride, Fanim fool! Ride! Conquer what you can! Death and horror will *eat you all* ere this ends!'

Fanayal ab Kascamandri raised his hand as if trying to snatch words she had tossed aside. 'So this White-Luck Warrior of yours,' he snapped, 'he *hunts* the Aspect-Emperor?'

'The *Goddess* hunts the Demon.'

Fanayal turned to his Cishaurim and grinned. 'Tell me, Meppa. Do you like her?'

'Like her?' the blind man responded, obviously too accustomed to his jokes to be incredulous. 'No.'

'Well I *do*,' the Padirajah said. 'Even her curses please me.'

'So she is to be spared?'

'She *knows* things, Meppa. Things we need to know.'

But Malowebi, his skin crawling with gooseflesh, understood, as did every man present save perhaps the Cishaurim: the Bandit

Padirajah simply made excuses. For all her provocations, for all her *deadliness*, Psatma Nannaferi remained, as she had said, soft earth deeply ploughed . . .

And the dread Mother of Birth would work her inscrutable will.

Momemn

Grief had crippled her. Grief for the death of her youngest, her sweetest and most vulnerable, Samarmas. Grief for the loss of her oldest, her bitterest and most wronged, Mimara.

Anger had saved her. Anger at her husband for stranding her. Anger at her servants for failing her and for doubting her – doubting her most of all.

Anger and the love of dear little Kelmomas.

She had taken to stalking the palace halls those nights that sleep eluded her. Twice now she had caught guardsmen throwing number-sticks, and once, slaves making love in the Hepatine Gardens – sins she knew her husband would have punished but that she feigned to overlook. Almost inevitably, she found herself padding alone through the cavernous heart of the Imperial Audience Hall. She would gawk as she walked, crane her neck like the caste-menial she was, thinking of all the peoples behind the panoply of symbols hanging between the polished pillars. She would climb the dais, run her fingers across the arm of her husband's great throne, then sashay out onto the veranda beyond, where she would gaze across the labyrinthine expanse of her capital.

How? How did a low and mean whore, the kind who would sell her daughter in times of famine, become the Blessed Empress of all the Three Seas? This, she had always thought, was the great question of her life, the remarkable fact that historians would ponder in future generations.

She had been the rut, the track long mudded, and now she found herself the charioteer.

There was a mystery and a beauty in great inversions. This was the genius and the power of the Circumfix, the paradox of the God Almighty hanging naked from an iron ring. All men are born helpless, and most men simply grow into more complicated forms of infancy. And yet, since they are the only summit they know, they constantly find themselves *looking down* even as they grovel at the knees of the mighty. 'All slaves become emperors,' Protathis had written with canny cynicism, 'the instant the slaver looks away.'

Her rise – as impossible, as *miraculous*, as it had been – expressed a conceit native to all men. And so the wild anomaly of her life had become a kind of human beacon. For the caste-nobility, long used to beating aspiration from their slaves, her mere existence triggered an instinct to punish. For slaves and menials, long accustomed to eating their imperious judgments, her rise reminded them of their daily indignity.

But their question was essentially the same. Who was *she* to be exalted so?

This. This was the real question of her life, the one the historians would never think to ask. Not how could a whore become Empress, but how could a whore *be* an Empress.

Who was she to be exalted so?

She would show them.

She had laboured tirelessly since word of Iothiah's fall had reached her. Emergency sessions with Caxes Anthirul, her Home Exalt-General, as well as the ever-irascible Werjau, Prime Nascenti of the Ministrate. Apparently activity along the Scylvendi frontier, which had surged in previous weeks, had now dwindled to nothing, a fact that at once heartened her, because of the redeployment it allowed, and troubled her. She had read *The Annals*, and though

Casidas had died long before the Scylvendi sacked Cenei, she could not but recall throughout that reading how all the far-flung glory he described had been swept away by the People of War.

Mercurial. Merciless. Cunning. These were the words that best described the Scylvendi. She knew this because she had known Cnaiür urs Skiötha, and because she had raised his son, Moënghus, as her own.

Though her generals had eyes only for the prospect of avenging their fellows in Shigek, she knew stripping the Scylvendi frontier was a risk – a mad risk. Despite denuding the Empire otherwise, Kellhus had left three crack Columns to guard the Gap, and for no small reason.

But Fanayal and the cursed Yatwerians had left her no choice. The plan was to garrison Gedea as best as they could while the Imperial Army of the West assembled at Asgilioch. Hinnereth could be supplied by sea. General Anthirul assured her that they would have five full Columns ready to retake Shigek by summer's end. Though everyone present understood what Fanayal intended, none dared speak it in her presence. The Bandit Padirajah had not so much attacked the Empire as her legitimacy.

He would suffer for that. For the first time in Esmenet's life, she actually found herself gloating over the prospect of destroying another. And it did not trouble her in the slightest, even though she knew her former self would recoil in horror from such malevolent passions. Fanayal ab Kascamandri would scream for her mercy before all was said and done. Nothing could be more simple.

She also met regularly with both her Master of Spies, Phinersa, and her Vizier-in-Proxy, Vem-Mithriti. She had feared that Phinersa, who always seemed brittle for his nervous intensity, would fold under the extraordinary demands she made of him. But if anything the man thrived. Within a week of Iothiah's fall, Phinersa had almost entirely rebuilt their network of spies throughout

Shigek. When she asked him for pretexts she could use to arrest Cutias Pansulla, he had the man imprisoned by the following evening, allowing her to install Biaxi Sankas in his place in the Imperial Synod.

Likewise, she had feared that Vem-Mithriti would literally die, so feeble did he seem. But he too flourished, organizing cadres of Schoolmen, students, and those, like Vem-Mithriti, too frail to participate in the Great Ordeal, for the defence of the Empire. All the world had thought the Cishaurim exterminated by the First Holy War. The stories of their return had sparked a new, almost fanatical, resolve in those Schoolmen who remained.

It seemed miraculous, when she paused to think about it, the way her husband's ministers rallied about her. From the outset, she had understood that the greatest strength of an empire, its size, was at once its greatest weakness. So long as its population *believed* in its power and purpose, an empire could bring almost limitless resources to bear against its foes, be they internal or external. But when that belief waned, its tendency was to dissolve into warring tribes. The very resources that had been its strength became its enemy.

This was what made the fall of Iothiah so disastrous. Yes, Fanayal had cast all of Shigek into lawless turmoil. Yes, he had cut the western Empire in half. But Shigek was but one province out of many, and the links between north and south had always been maritime thanks to the Great Carathay. Strategically, the loss of Iothiah was little more than a nuisance.

Symbolically, however . . .

The crisis she faced was a crisis in *confidence*, nothing more, nothing less. The less her subjects believed in the Empire, the less some would sacrifice, the more others would resist. It was almost arithmetic. The balance was wobbling, and all the world watched to see which way the sand would spill. Anasûrimbor Esmenet had made a resolution to act as if she believed to spite all those who doubted her as much as anything else, and paradoxically, they had all started *believing with her*. It was a lesson Kellhus had drummed into her countless times and one she resolved never to forget again.

To know is to have power over the world; to believe is to have power over *men*.

With *belief* then, belief and craft, she would heave on the great chain of empire and haul the balance to the benefit of her children. Esmenet had no more illusions. She understood that if she failed, her sons and daughters would all be doomed.

And she simply would not – could not! – tolerate another . . . Another Samarmas.

As always, her Seneschal, Ngarau, proved indispensable. The longer she had been involved in the New Empire's administration, the more she had come to realize that it possessed its own codes and dialects – and the more she had understood not only why men such as Ngarau were so indispensable, but also why Kellhus, no matter how bloody his conquests, never failed to spare the functionaries of each nation he conquered. Everything required translation. The more fluent the Apparati, the fewer the misinterpretations, the quicker the findings, the more decisive the Empire's actions.

The only wheel she could not turn in concert with the others was the Thousand Temples. But soon, very soon, she would have a resolution to that dilemma.

She gazed out across the dark landscape of Momemn, slowly stalking the perimeter of the veranda. She thought about how all the jumbled structures were in fact hollow, how their walls seemed little more than parchment when viewed from so far. She thought of all the thousands slumbering like miniature, innumerable larva, soft in their crisp cocoons. And she plotted their survival.

'*We walk the Shortest Path*,' her divine and heartless husband had told her the last time she had seen him, '*the Labyrinth of the Thousandfold Thought. This is the burden the God has laid upon us, and the burden the Gods begrudge . . .*'

Expediency would be her rule. As ruthless as it was holy.

Kelmomas, she knew, would be awake and waiting when she returned – he always was. Simply because she was so busy, she allowed him to sleep with her in her bed.

Save for those nights she called for Sankas or Imhailas to comfort her.

———◦◦◦———

The day itself seemed daring. The wind was constant and thin. The sky was nearly empty, the horizon scraped clean. The Meneanor Sea was stone-coast dark beneath the sunlight sparking across its perforations.

She sat at a small table with Theliopa at her side, watching the Shriah of the Thousand Temples step from the shadow of the Imperial Audience Hall into the glare of the veranda. Anasûrimbor Maithanet. Because of the innumerable golden slivers – tusks – woven up and down its length, his white robe twinkled gold with every step. His hair piled high and rich upon his head, the same improbable black as his braided beard.

'This is madness, Esmi,' he called. 'The Empire *burns*, yet you spurn my counsel?'

She hoped she looked as impressive, with her stark grey gown beneath an ankle-long vest of gold rings. And of course, she had her smoke-hazed city as her mantle, an intricate mottling of white and grey that reached to the horizon. But she was sure it would be her porcelain mask, glazed white with features as fine and as beautiful as her own, that would most weigh against his eyes.

'And now you wear a *mask*? An Ainoni mask?'

She had long pondered how he would begin. Before conferring

with Inrilatas, she had thought he would be conciliatory, that he would use wise and self-effacing words to move her. *'Do this, Esmi. Confidence awaits . . .'* But she had reconsidered in the light of what her crazed son had told her. He would affect injury and outrage, she eventually decided, thinking her native doubts would grease his way.

And she had been right.

'This is about Sharacinth . . .' he continued in the same indignant tones, his voice striking resonances that seemed to warble about her heart. 'You think I was involved in her murder!'

She did not reply simply because she did not trust her voice. She could only speak when she felt the 'cold' within her – as Theliopa had instructed.

He took the seat waiting for him in apparent fury. Even out of doors the scent of him, myrrh and a kind of musk, bloomed invisible.

'Or has the loss—?'

He paused as if catching himself, but the implication was clear. *'Or has the loss of your son driven you mad . . .'*

He had not meant, she realized, to say this only to halt out of some compassionate instinct. He had meant for her to complete the thought . . . Her! Then he could commiserate, and slowly pry open her trust the way he had so many times in the past.

But she had already decided the path this conversation would take.

She peeled a section of flat-cake, used it to grasp a pinch of spice-shredded pork. She dipped both into the cinnamon and honey, then passed it to him, searching for any sign of hesitation.

There was none.

He had not extended her any of the traditional greetings or honorifics, so neither would she. 'Proyas . . .' she said, taking heart in the coldness she felt beneath the clarity of her voice. 'Shortly after Carythusal fell, he took me hunting kanti, a kind of antelope, on the Famiri . . . Have I ever told you that story, Maitha?'

He gazed at her with unsettling intensity. 'No.'

The mask tingled against her cheeks. She found herself wondering if this was how skin-spies felt behind the digits of their false faces. Safe.

'This was after the conquest of Ainon,' she said. 'We had tracked a mother and her foal for the better part of an afternoon. But when we finally sighted them, we discovered we weren't the only hunters. Wolves. Wolves had tracked them as well. We had climbed a shallow ridge, so we could see it all, the kanti mother and her child watering at a black stream . . . and the wolves closing about her . . .' She glimpsed the predators in her soul's eye, sleek as fish, tunnelling through the grasses. 'But the cow either heard them or caught their scent on the wind. She bolted before the noose could be knotted – bolted directly toward us! It was astonishing enough to watch from a distance. She backed her foal against the earthen drop – immediately below us – turned to battle her pursuers. The wolves flew at her, but kanti are strong, like vicious horses, and she kicked and stamped and butted, and the wolves veered away. I almost cried out for jubilation, but Proyas clutched my arm and pointed directly down . . .'

She paused to lick her lips behind the porcelain.

'The wolves, Maitha. The wolves *had known* what she would do, even where she would run. So even as the cow seemed to frighten off the pack, two others, who had concealed themselves in the thickets at the ridge's base, leapt upon the foal and tore out its throat. The mother shrieked, chased them away, but it was too late. The pack simply waited until she abandoned her child's body.'

Esmenet really had no idea how much he could infer from the sliver of her voice. She had rehearsed this story to baffle his penetration. She had struggled to purge all sign of the passions that moved beneath her voice and intent – but how does one conceal what is already hidden?

'Do you understand, Maitha? *I need to know* you aren't a wolf waiting in the thicket.'

For a heartbeat, anger and compassion seemed to war for the high ground of his gaze. 'How could you think such a thing?' he exclaimed.

She breathed deep. How *had* she come by her suspicions? So often the past seemed a cistern sloshing with dissolved voices. Inrilatas had said she feared Maithanet because she despised herself. How could he not try to save the Empire from her incapacity? But something in her balked at the possibility. Her entire life, it seemed, she had fended fears without clear origin.

Just a tactic . . . she told herself. *An attempt to engage me* morally *– make me defensive.* She tapped the Ainoni mask with a lacquered nail – a gesture meant for herself as much as for him.

'How?' she replied. 'Because you are Dûnyain.'

This occasioned a long silence between them. Watching his pained look lapse into blank scrutiny, Esmenet could not shake the nagging sense that her brother-in-law actually considered murdering her there and then.

'Your *husband* is Dûnyain,' Maithanet finally said.

'Indeed.'

She wondered if it would be possible to count all the unspoken truths that hung between them, all the devious grounds for their mistrust. Was there ever a family so deranged as theirs?

'If I condescend to this, this *test*, it will be only to reassure *you*, Esmi,' he finally said. His tone was devoid of pride or resentment, a fact that simply made him more inhuman in her eyes. 'I am your brother. Even more, I am your husband's willing slave, no different than you. We are bound together by blood *and faith.*'

'Then *do* this for me, Maitha. I will apologize if I'm wrong. I will wash your feet on the Xothei steps – anything! *Wolves* pursue me . . .'

It was all a game for them, she realized. No word, no expression, simply was. Everything was a tool, a tactic meant to further some occult and devious goal.

Even love . . . Just as Achamian had said.

She had known this for years, of course, but in the way of all threatening knowledge: at angles, in the shadowy corners of her soul. But now, playing that game with one of them, with a *Dûnyain*, it seemed she understood that knowledge down to its most base implication.

She would be overmatched, she realized, were it not for her mask.

Maithanet had paused in the semblance of a man at his wit's end. His jet beard looked hot in the sunlight – she wondered what dye he used to conceal the Norsirai blond. 'And you are willing to trust the judgment of a mad adolescent?'

'I am willing to trust the judgment of my son.'

'To read my face?'

He was trying to extend the conversation, she realized. To better scrutinize her voice? Had something in her tone hooked his interest?

'To read your face.'

'And you realize the training this requires?'

Esmenet nodded toward her daughter. For all her deficits, Theliopa had been her reprieve. She too was Dûnyain, but as Kelmomas possessed his mother's capacity to love, so too she possessed her mother's need to please. This, Esmenet had decided, was what she could trust: those fractions of her that had found their way into her children.

She would count all the world her enemy otherwise.

'The ability to re-read *passions* is largely native,' Theliopa said, 'and save for father-father, none can see so deep as Inrilatas. Inferring *thoughts* requires training, Uncle, a measure of which Father pro-provided.'

'But you know this,' Esmenet added, trying to hide the accusation in an air of honest confusion.

Gasping in exasperation, the Shriah of the Thousand Temples fell back in his chair. 'Esmi . . .'

The tone and pose of an innocent bewildered and bullied by another's irrationality. *'If his actions conform to your expectations,'* Kellhus had told her, *'then he deceives you. The more unthinkable dissembling seems, Esmi, the more he dissembles . . .'* Even though her husband had been referring to their son, the words, she knew, applied all the same to Maithanet. Inrilatas had said it himself: the Dûnyain were not human.

And so she would play her own mummer's role.

'I don't understand, Maitha. If you're innocent, what do you have to lose?'

She already knew what Inrilatas would see in his uncle's face – what he would say.

'The boy . . . He could say anything. He is mad.'

All she needed were grounds.

'He loves his mother.'

—∞∞∞—

Before, the young Prince-Imperial had run about the bones of the Andiamine Heights; now he ran through them.

The more Kelmomas thought about it, the more it seemed he always knew that these tunnels existed, that all the subtle discrepancies between dimensions – shortened rooms and too-wide walls – had scratched and whispered at the edges of his notice. He did not like to think that ways had been hidden from him.

He wandered through the dark. He held a small hand about his candle flame to protect against drafts where he could, but he was not so afraid of losing his way as missing something of interest were the light to flicker out. All eyes, he padded through narrow corridors, a bubble of light slipping through black pipes. Everything he saw bore the strict stamp of his father. Bare surfaces. Crude stonework. Simple iron. Here and there he came across walls adorned with chapped paint, and once, an entire hall that had been vaulted and corniced: sections of the old Ikurei palace, he realized, that Father had bent to his own design. He quickly realized the stairs and halls composed but a small fraction of the complex. For every stair there were at least five tubes set with iron rungs, some climbing, others plumbing depths he had yet dared to go. And for every hallway there were at least a dozen chutes, accessing, he imagined, the palace in its entirety.

But there were too many locked doors and grates and hatches. He could almost see Mother or Father sending agents into these halls, using these portals to control how many bones could be explored.

He resolved to teach himself how to pick their locks.

Even though he knew he risked his mother's wrath, he decided to explore one of the few unbarred chutes – one leading through the Apparatory, he soon discovered. He passed innumerable voices, laughing and gossiping for the most part. He even glimpsed several shadows through tight marble and bronze fretting. He heard a couple making like dogs, and rooting around, he found a crease through which he could watch their sweaty backs heave.

'This is the way you are to me,' he whispered to the secret voice.

This is how I am to you.

'One bright.'

One dark.

His eyes little more than slits, Kelmomas watched the plunging mystery for a time. The smell of it intrigued him, and it seemed he had caught some whiff of it on every man and woman he had met in his entire life. Including Mother. Finally, answering to a rising urgency, he began retracing his steps. He happily let his candle gutter out, knowing the route step for step, rung for rung. The musty darkness blew like a breeze through his hair and across his cheeks, so fleet was his passage back to the Empress's apartment.

But Mother was waiting for him, her face as immobile as stone for fury.

'*Kel!* What did I tell you?'

He could duck her strike. He could catch her hand and break any one of her fingers. And while she winced for pain, he could snatch one of the pins fixing her hair and drive it deep into her eye. Death deep.

He could do any of these things . . .

But it was better to lean his cheek into her swatting palm, allow the blow to crack far harder than she intended, so that he could weep in false misery while she clutched him, and glory in her love and regret and horror.

———— ✵ ————

Psatma Nannaferi rose from him, skin peeling from skin. She stood, savoured the kiss of cool air across her breasts, felt his seed flush her inner thighs – for her womb would have none of it. His post-coital slumber was deep, so deep he did not stir when she spat her contempt upon him. She could strike him dead and he would never know. He would writhe in agony for all eternity, thinking he need only awaken to escape.

Fanayal ab Kascamandri, blasted to charcoal, time and time again.

She barked in laughter.

She wandered the gloom of his pavilion, gazed upon the heirlooms of a destroyed empire. A fire-scorched standard, leaning
negligently against a chair panelled in mother-of-pearl. Glittering
coats of mail hanging from mahogany busts. The Padirajah's body-
slave, a solemn Nilnameshi as old as she had once been, cowered
in a slot between settees, watching her the way a child might
watch a wolf.

She paused before the pavilion's small but sumptuous shrine.
'You are one of Her children,' she said without looking at the man.
'She loves you despite the wickedness your captors have forced
upon you.' She drew a finger along the spine of the book nestled
in crimson crushed velvet upon the small altar: the *kipfa'aifan*, the
Witness of Fane.

The leather cracked and pimpled at her touch.

'You *give*,' she murmured, turning to fix the old man with her
gaze. 'He *takes*.'

Tears greased his cheeks.

'She will reach for you when your flesh stumbles, and you are
pitched into the Outside. But you must reach *for Her* in turn. Only
then . . .'

He shrank into his refuge as she stepped toward him.

'Will you? Will you reach for Her?'

He shook his head in affirmation, but she had already turned
away, knowing his answer. She sauntered toward the draped
entrance, glimpsed herself in the long oval of a standing silver
mirror. The Mother-Supreme paused in the lantern gloom, allowed
her eyes to roam and linger across the supple lines of her reborn
body. She made a tongue of her image, savoured the honey of
what she saw . . .

To be *returned*, to experience the unfathomable loss, to shrink
and wither – and then to bloom anew! Psatma Nannaferi had
never suffered the vanities of her sisters. She did not hunger, as

the others hungered, for the thieving touch of Men. Only in the execution of the rites would her flesh rise to the promise of congress. Even still, she exulted in this Gift as she had no other. There was glory in middle-youth, the tested limb and will of maturity, clothed in firm silk years away from the sackcloth it would become.

Her temples looted and burned. So many of her sisters raped and put to the sword, and here she stood, drunk with joy.

'Are you such a dog?' she asked the open air. 'Eh, Snakehead?'

She turned to where Meppa stood on the pavilion's threshold. The ornate flaps swayed into motionlessness behind him. Highland cool wafted through the interior.

'*You,*' he said with muttering intensity. His face remained directed forward, but the black finger of his salt asp had turned directly toward the cringing body-slave. The Mother-Supreme smiled, knowing the old man would not live to see dawn. He would die for her sake, she knew, and he would reach . . .

'Always guarding his master's portal,' she cackled.

'Cover yourself, Concubine.'

'You do not like what you see?'

'I see the withered old crone that is your soul.'

'So you are a man still, eh, Snakehead? You judge my beauty, my worth, according to the youth of my womb . . . My *fertilit—*'

'Still your tongue!'

'*Bark*, dog. Rouse your master. Let us see whose snout he will strike.'

The shining snake finally turned to regard her. The lips beneath the silver band tightened into a line.

Psatma Nannaferi resumed her appraisal of her miraculous twin in the mirror. 'You bear the Water within you,' she said to the Last Cishaurim. She drew a palm across the plane of her abdomen. 'Like an ocean! You can strike me down with your merest whim! And yet you stand here bandying threats and insults?'

'I serve my Lord Padirajah.'

The Mother-Supreme laughed. This, she realized, was her new temple, a heathen army, flying through lands where even goatherds were loathe to go. And these heathen were her new priests – these Fanim. What did it matter what they believed, so long as they accomplished what needed to be done?

'But you lie,' she croaked in her old voice.

'He has been anoin—'

'He *has* been anointed!' she cackled. 'But not by whom you think!'

'Cease your blasphem—'

'Fool! All of them. All these *Men* – all these *Thieves*! All of them think themselves the centre of their worlds. But not you. You *have seen.* You alone *know* how small we are . . . mere specks, motes in the gusting black. And yet you place your faith in errant abstraction – the Solitary God! Pfah! You throw number-sticks for your salvation, when all you need do is *kneel!*'

The Cishaurim said nothing in reply. The salt-asp, lantern light gleaming along the cross-hatching of its scales, hooked away from her toward a point over her shoulder.

She turned to see Fanayal standing naked in a kind of stationary lurch behind her. He seemed insubstantial for the play of shadow and gloom.

'Do you see now?' Meppa asked. 'Her treachery. Her *devilry*! My Lord, please tell me that you see!'

Fanayal ab Kascamandri wiped his face, breathed deep, his nostrils whistling. 'Leave us, Meppa,' he said roughly.

A moment of equipoise followed, the mutual regard of three overbearing souls. Their breathing abraded the silent air. Then with the merest bow, the Cishaurim withdrew.

The Padirajah loomed behind the diminutive woman.

He flung her about, cried, '*Witch!*' He clamped callused hands about her neck, bent her back, crying, '*Accursed witch!*'

Groaning, the Mother-Supreme clutched his hard muscled arms, hooked a naked calf about his waist.

Thus he ravished her.

Still huddled between the settees, the doomed body-slave wept for watching . . .

Soft earth deeply ploughed.

∞∞∞

Scant ceremony greeted Uncle Holy's arrival at the Andiamine Height's postern gate, only sombre words and unspoken suspicion. Slaves raised embroidered tarps against the rain, forming a tunnel with upraised arms, so Maithanet was spared the indignity of soaking in his own clothes. Kelmomas was careful to observe and mimic the attitude of his mother and her retinue. Children, no matter how oblivious otherwise, are ever keen to their parent's fear and quick to behave accordingly. Kelmomas was no different.

Something truly momentous was about to happen – even his mother's fool ministers understood as much. Kelmomas actually glimpsed crooked old Vem-Mithriti shaking his head in disbelief.

The Shriah of the Thousand Temples was about to be interrogated by their God's most gifted, destructive son.

Uncle Holy paced the dripping gauntlet in the simulacrum of fury. He fairly shouldered aside Imhailas and Lord Sankas to stand before Mother, who even so diminutive seemed imposing for the strangeness of her shining white mask. For not the first time, Kelmomas found himself hating his uncle, not simply because of his stature, but because of the way he *occupied* it. No matter what the occasion, be it a blessing or a marriage or an exhortation or the Whelming of a child, Anasûrimbor Maithanet cultivated an aura of neck-breaking strength.

'Dispense with the frivolities,' he snapped. 'I would be done with this, Esmi.'

He wore a white robe with gold-embroidered hems – stark, even by his staid standards. Aside from the heavy Tusk-and-Circumfix that hung above his sternum, his only concessions to ornament were the golden vambraces that sheathed his forearms in antique Ceneian motifs.

Rather than speak, the Empress lowered her head a degree short of what was demanded by jnan. Kelmomas felt her hand tighten about his shoulder as she did so.

The young Prince-Imperial savoured the way they carried the scent of rain into the closeted halls of the palace. Moist creases of silk and felt. Feet squishing in sandals. Wet hair growing hot.

Neither party spoke a word the entire trek, save Vem-Mithriti, who begged his mother's pardon as soon as they climbed beyond the Apparatory, asking whether he could continue on his own at a pace more suitable to ancient bones. They left the frail Saik Schoolman behind them, following a path of stairs and corridors cleared in advance and guarded at every turn by stone-faced Eothic Guardsmen. The wall sconces were idle despite the darkness of the day, so they passed through pockets of outright gloom. Despite his mother's fixed, forward glare, the young Prince-Imperial could not resist craning about, matching the ways he could see with the ways he could not – comparing the two palaces, visible and invisible.

At long last they gained the Imperial Apartments and reached the Door.

It seemed taller and broader than the boy remembered, perhaps because his mother had finally ordered it polished. Normally chalked in green, the Kyranean Lions now gleamed in florid majesty. He wanted to ask Mother whether this meant Inrilatas would be set free, but the secret voice warned him to remain silent.

The Empress stood before them, her masked face lowered as if in prayer. All was silent, save for the creak of Imhailas's gear. Kelmomas reached about her silk-girdled waist to press his cheek into her side. She ran thoughtless fingers through his hair.

Finally Maithanet asked, 'Why is the boy here, Esmi?'

No one could miss his tone, which twisted the question into, *What is this morbid fixation?*

'I don't know,' she replied. 'Inrilatas refused to speak to you unless he was present.'

'So this is to be a *public* humiliation?'

'No. Only you and my two sons,' she replied, still gazing at the Door. 'Your nephews.'

'*Madness* . . .' the Shriah muttered in feigned disgust.

At last she turned her mask toward him. 'Yes,' she said. '*Dûnyain* madness.'

She nodded to Imhailas, who grasped the latch and pushed the great door inward.

The Shriah of the Thousand Temples looked down to Kelmomas, clasped his small white hand in the callused immensity of his own. 'Do you fear me as well?' he asked.

Rather than reply, the boy looked to his mother in the appearance of anxious yearning.

'You are a *Prince-Imperial*,' his mother said. 'Go.'

He followed Uncle Holy into the gloom of his brother's cell.

The cell's lone window was unshuttered, revealing a slot of dark sky and flooding the room with chill and moist air. Rain was all the boy could hear at first, roaring across complicated rooftops, gurgling and slurping down the course of zigzag gutters. A single brazier warmed the room, pitching an orange glow into the dark. An elaborately carved chair had been set facing the wall where Inrilatas's chains hung from the four stone lion heads. The brazier had been positioned, the boy noticed, to fully illuminate the chair's occupant and no one else.

Inrilatas crouched naked some four paces from the chair, his arms about his knees. The dim light did not so much illuminate as *polish* him, it seemed. The young man watched them with a kind of blank serenity.

We must discover what he wants us to do, the secret voice whispered.

For certainly Inrilatas wanted *something* from him. Why demand his presence otherwise?

His uncle released his hand the instant the Door creaked shut behind them. Without so much as looking at either brother, he reached into his left sleeve and extracted a wooden wedge from beneath the antique vambrace. He dropped it clattering to the floor, then kicked it beneath the base of the door . . .

Locking them in.

Inrilatas laughed, flexing arms as smooth and hard as barked branches. 'Uncle Holy,' he said, bending his head to press his left cheek against his knees. 'Truth shines.'

'Truth shines,' Maithanet replied, taking the seat provided for him.

Kelmomas peered at the wooden butt jammed into the black seam between the floor and the portal. What was happening? It had never occurred to him that Uncle Holy might have plans of his own . . .

Shout, the secret voice urged. *Call for her!*

The boy shot a questioning look at his older brother – who simply grinned and winked.

Raw for the rain, distant thunder reverberated through the cell window. But for the little boy, the crazed proportions of the circumstances that seized them rattled louder still. What was happening?

'Do you *intend* to murder Mother?' Inrilatas asked, still staring at Kelmomas.

'No,' Maithanet replied.

We have missed something! the voice exclaimed. *Something has—*

'Do you intend to *murder* Mother?' Inrilatas asked again, this time fixing his uncle in a cartwheeling gaze.

'No.'

'Uncle Holy. Do you intend to murder *Mother*?'

'I said, no.'

The boy breathed against the iron rod of alarm that held him rigid. Everything was explicable, he decided. Inrilatas played as he always played, violating expectations for violation's sake. His uncle had stopped the door for contingency's sake . . . The little boy almost laughed aloud.

They were all Dûnyain here.

'So many years,' Inrilatas continued, 'piling plots atop plots – could it be you have simply forgotten how to stop, Uncle?'

'No.'

'So many years surrounded by half-witted peoples. How long have you toiled? How long have you suffered for these malformed children with their stunted intellects? How long have you suffered their ignorance – their absurd vanity? And then Father, that slovenly ingrate, raises one of them *above* you? Why might that be? Why would Father trust a *whore* over the pious Shriah of the Thousand Temples?'

'I know not.'

'But you suspect.'

'I fear my brother does not fully trust me.'

'Because he *knows*, doesn't he? He knows the secret of our blood.'

'Perhaps.'

'He knows *you*, knows you better than you know yourself.'

'Perhaps.'

'And he has seen the flicker of sedition, the small flame that awaits the kindling of circumstance.'

'Perhaps.'

'And have the circumstances arrived?'

'No.'

Laughter. 'Oh, but Uncle Holy, they *have* arrived – most certainly!'

'I do not understa—'

'*Liar!*' the wild-haired figure screeched.

The Shriah did not so much as blink. His face bathed in wavering orange light, Maithanet enveloped Inrilatas in Dûnyain scrutiny, a gaze that seemed to tinkle like coals. It was a profile Kelmomas had seen thousands of times, stitched into banners if not in flesh. High of cheek, virile, the strength of his jaw obvious despite the thickness of his beard.

He is our first true *challenge*, the voice whispered. *We must take care.*

Inrilatas's eyes glittered in the gloom. He crouched the same as before, his chains hanging in arcs across the floor. If their uncle's scrutiny discomfited him, he betrayed no sign of it.

'Tell me, Uncle Holy. How many children did grandfather sire?'

'Six,' the Shriah replied. There was a toneless brevity to the exchange now, as if they had shed the disguises they used when interacting with normal men.

'Were any of them like me?'

A fraction of a heartbeat.

'I have no way of knowing. He drowned them at the first sign of peculiarities.'

'And you were the only one that expressed . . . balance?'

'I was the only one.'

'So grandfather . . . He would have drowned me?'

'Most certainly.'

The stark appraisal of a Dûnyain, directly to the point, careless of pride or injury. In an arena packed with the blind and the beggared, he and his family were the only sighted players. They played as the blind played – goading, commiserating, flattering – simply because these were the moves that *moved the blind*. Only when they vied one against another, the young Prince-Imperial realized, could they dispense with the empty posturing and play the game in its purest, most rarefied form.

'So why,' Inrilatas asked, 'do you think Father has spared me?'

The Shriah of the Thousand Temples shrugged. 'Because the eye of the World is upon him.'

'Not because of Mother?'

'She watches with the rest.'

'But you do not believe this.'

'Then enlighten me, Inrilatas. What do I think?'

'You think Mother has *compromised* Father.'

Another fraction of hesitation. Maithanet's gaze drifted in and out of focus.

Inrilatas seized the opportunity. 'You think Mother has blunted Father's pursuit of the Shortest Path time and again, that he walks in arcs to appease her heart, when he should cleave to the ruthless lines of the Thousandfold Thought.'

Again the Holy Shriah of the Thousand Temples hesitated. Perhaps Inrilatas had found the thread. Perhaps Uncle *could* be unmasked . . .

Perhaps Maithanet should be counted weak in their small tribe.

'Who has told you these things?' his uncle demanded.

Inrilatas ignored the distraction. 'You think Father *risks the very world* for his Empress's sake – for the absurdity of love!'

'Was it her? Did *she* tell you about the Thousandfold Thought?'

'And you see *me*,' the naked adolescent pressed, 'the fact that

I have been caged rather than drowned, as the most glaring example of your elder brother's folly.'

Again Kelmomas watched his uncle's eyes fall out of focus then return – an outward sign of the Probability Trance. It wasn't fair, he decided, that he should be born with all these gifts yet be denied the training required to forge true weapons out of them. What *use* was Father to him, so long as he let him flounder? How could the Aspect-Emperor be anything but his son's greatest threat, greatest foe, when he always saw more, more deeply?

'I *fear* that you might be . . .' the Shriah said. 'I admit as much. But if *you* can see this, Inrilatas, then your *father* has seen it also – and far more completely. If he sees no sedition in my fearing, why should you?'

Once again his uncle tried to seize the initiative with questions of his own. Once again, Inrilatas simply ignored him and pressed on with his interrogation.

'Tell me, Uncle, how will you have me killed when you seize power?'

'These tricks, Inrilatas. These tactics . . . They only work when they are hidden. I see these things the same as you.'

'Strange, isn't it, Uncle? The way we Dûnyain, for all our gifts, can never *speak*?'

'We are speaking now.'

Inrilatas laughed at this, lowered his beard-hazed cheek to his knees once again. 'But how can that be when we *mean nothing* of what we say?'

'You conf—'

'What would they do, you think, if Men could *see* us? If they could fathom the way we don and doff them like clothes?'

Maithanet shrugged. 'What would any child do, if they could fathom their father?'

Inrilatas smiled. 'That depends upon the father . . . This is the answer you want me to speak.'

'No. That is *the* answer.'

More laughter, so like the Aspect-Emperor's that goose-pimples climbed across the boy's skin.

'You really believe that we Dûnyain differ? That, like fathers, some can be good and some bad?'

'I know so,' Maithanet replied.

There was something *coiled* about his brother, Kelmomas decided. The way he lolled his head, flexed his wrists, and rocked on his heels created an impression of awkward, effeminate youth – a *false* impression. The more harmless he seemed, the young Prince-Imperial understood, the more lethal he became.

All of this, the secret voice warned, *is simply for show.*

And that was the joke, Kelmomas realized: Inrilatas truly meant nothing of what he said.

'Oh, we have our peculiarities, I grant you that,' the adolescent said. 'Our hash of strengths and weaknesses. But in the end we all suffer the same miraculous disease: reflection. Where they think, one thought following hard upon the other, tripping forward blindly, we *reflect*. Each thought *grasps* the thought before it – like a starving dog chasing an oh-so meaty tail! They stumble before us, reeling like drunks, insensible to their momentary origins, and we *unravel* them. Play them like instruments, plucking songs of love and adoration that they call their own!'

Something was going to happen.

Kelmomas found himself leaning forward, such was his hanker. When? *When?*

'We all *deceive*, Uncle. All of us, all the time. That is the gift of reflection.'

'They make their choices,' Maithanet said in a head-shaking tone.

'Please, Uncle. You must speak before me the way you speak before Father. I *see your lies*, no matter how banal or cunning. No choices are made in our presence. Ever. You know this. The only freedom is freedom *over*.'

'Very well then,' the Holy Shriah replied. 'I tire of your philosophy, Inrilatas. I find you abhorrent, and I fear this entire exercise simply speaks to your mother's failing reason.'

'Mother?' his older brother exclaimed. 'You think *Mother* arranged this?'

A heartbeat of hesitation, the smallest crack in Maithanet's false demeanour.

Something is wrong, the voice whispered.

'If not her, then who?' the Shriah of the Thousand Temples asked.

Inrilatas at once frowned and smiled, his expression drunk with exaggeration. His eyebrows hooked high, he glanced down at his little brother . . .

'Kelmomas?' Maithanet asked, not with the incredulity appropriate to a human, but in the featureless voice belonging to the Dûnyain.

Inrilatas gazed at the young Prince-Imperial as if he were a puppy about to be thrown into a river . . .

Poor boy.

'A thousand words and insinuations batter them day in and day out,' the youth said. 'But because they lack the memory to enumerate them, they forget, and find themselves stranded with hopes and suspicions not of their making. Mother *has always loved you*, Uncle, has always seen you as a more human version of Father – an illusion you have laboured long and hard to cultivate. Now, suddenly, when she most desperately needs your counsel, she fears and hates you.'

'And this is *Kelmomas's* work?'

'He isn't what he seems, Uncle.'

Maithanet glanced at the boy, who stood as rigid as a shield next to him, then turned back to Inrilatas. Kelmomas did not know what he found more terrifying: the unscalable surfaces of his uncle's face or his brother's sudden betrayal.

'I have suspected as much,' the Shriah said.

Say something . . . the voice urged.

Inrilatas nodded as if ruing some tragic fact. 'As mad as all of us are, as much heartbreak we have heaped upon our mother, he is, I think, the *worst* of us.'

'Surely you—'

'You know *he* was the one who killed Samarmas.'

Another crack in his uncle's once-impervious demeanour.

It was all the young Prince-Imperial could do to simply stand and breathe. All his crimes, he had committed in the shadow of assumption. Were his Uncle to suspect him capable – of murdering Samarmas, Sharacinth – he would have quickly seen his guilt, such were his gifts. But for all their strength, the Dûnyain remained as blind to ignorance as the world-born – and as vulnerable.

And now . . . Never in his short life had Kelmomas experienced the terror he now felt. The sense of flushing looseness, as if he were a pillar of water about to collapse in a thousand liquid directions. The sense of binding tension, as if an inner winch cranked at every thread of his being, throttled him vein by vein . . .

And he found it curious, just as he found this curiosity curious.

'Samarmas died playing a foolish prank,' Maithanet said evenly. 'I was there.'

'And my little brother. He was *there* also?'

'Yes.'

'And Kelmomas, does he not share our gift for leading fools?'

'He could . . . in time.'

'But what if he were *like me*, Uncle. What if he were *born* knowing how to use our gifts?'

Kelmomas could hear all three of their hearts, his beating with rabbit quickness, his uncle's pounding as slow as a bull's – his brother's dancing through the erratic in-between.

'You're saying he murdered his own brother?'

Inrilatas nodded the way Mother nodded when affirming unfortunate truths. 'And others . . .'

'Others?'

Kelmomas stood, immobilized by astonishment. How? *How?* How could everything turn so quickly?

'Turn to him, Uncle. Use *your* portion. Gaze into his face and ask him if he is a fratricide.'

What was the mad fool doing? His uncle was the one! He was the one who needed to be humiliated – *destroyed!*

The Shriah of the Thousand Temples turned to the boy, not as a human might, frowning, questioning, but with the glint of void in his eyes. As a Dûnyain.

'The *sum of sins*,' Inrilatas continued. 'There is nothing more godly than murder. Nothing more *absolute*.'

And for the first time Kelmomas found himself trapped within the dread circuit of his Uncle's scrutiny.

Hide! the secret voice cried. *He glimpses . . . glimpses!*

'Come now, Kelmomas,' his mad brother cackled. 'Show Uncle Holy why you should be *chained in my place*.'

'*Liar!*' the boy finally shrieked in blubbering denial. '*Lies!*'

'Kelmomas!' the Shriah shouted, his voice yanking on every string of authority, from parental to religious. 'Turn to me! Look to me and tell me: Did you murd—'

Two clicks, almost simultaneous. Two screeches – a noise as small as mice trampled underfoot. The whirr of flying iron. Links snapping. File-weakened links snapping. One chain whooshed over the boy's head, while the other hooked behind his uncle . . .

They intersected, lashed in opposing directions about the post of Uncle Holy's neck. Wound like whips.

Kelmomas had scarcely torn his eyes away from his uncle, when his brother heaved, throwing his arms out and back like wings, his spine arched like a bow. Maithanet flew headlong to his feet.

Then Inrilatas *had* him, pulled him, for all his stature, like a child, against his chest. He roared in bestial exultation, wrenched at the chains again and again . . .

And Kelmomas watched the Shriah of Thousand Temples strangle.

Maithanet was on his knees, his face darkening, frantic hands grubbing at the chains. His silken sleeves had dropped down, revealing the fine-wrought beauty of his vambraces.

Inrilatas screamed and twisted, his arms, chest, and shoulders grooved with exertion. Maithanet surrendered his breath, fought only to protect his carotid artery. Inrilatas wrenched once, twice, violently enough to lift Uncle from his knees. But in a heartbeat of dropping slack, Maithanet's left hand fluttered across the vambrace on the forearm opposite. A blade appeared, jutting a finger's length beyond his elbow. It gleamed as though wet.

The first strike puffed the spark from Inrilatas's eyes. The second, low on his ribs, occasioned no more than a flinch. The chain slipped from the adolescent's grasp. Maithanet fell forward to his hands. He choked for air as would any mortal but recovered far more quickly. In mere heartbeats, it seemed, he had cast aside the chains and whirled to confront his dying nephew.

Inrilatas had staggered back two steps, his mouth gaping, his hand pawing the blood welling from his side. No words needed to be exchanged. Muffled shouts and hammering could already be heard at the door. The Shriah of the Thousand Temples could not trust a madman's dying words. He raised his fist. His strike caught the adolescent utterly unprepared. His left brow and socket collapsed like bread crust.

The Prince-Imperial fell back. The clink of iron accompanied the slap of his nude body across the floor. He jerked as if possessed by fire. Blood chased the creases between floor-stones.

'Soft . . .' Maithanet said, as if noting a natural curiosity. He turned to the dumbstruck boy, his right sleeve crimson with blood. 'And you?' he asked without a whisper of passion.

'Do you have your *mother's* bones?'

The bronze door burst open. Both uncle and nephew whirled to the faces massed beyond the threshold. Angry and astounded eyes probed the gloom, sorted the living from the dead.

'Mommy-mommy-mommy!' Kelmomas shrieked to the lone porcelain mask in the crowd's midst. 'Uncle moves against you! He killed Inri to keep you from knowing!'

But his mother had already caught sight of her prostrate son, had already jostled her way to the fore.

'Esmi . . .' Maithanet began. 'You have to und—'

'I don't care how it happened,' she interrupted, drifting more than walking toward the form of her son on the floor, his flushed nakedness becoming ever more grey. She teetered over him as if he were a fatal plummet.

'Did you do this, Esmi?' the Shriah persisted, his voice imperious. 'Did you plan this to—'

'Did I do what?' she said in a voice so calm it could only be crazed. *'Plan for you to murder my son?'*

'Esmi . . .' he began.

But some sights commanded silence – even from a Dûnyain. For several giddy, horrifying moments, Kelmomas did not so much see his mother slump to her knees as he saw the Empress of the Three Seas collapse. A stranger. He told himself it was the mask, but when she pulled it from her face, the profile of cheek and brow did not seem familiar to him.

Holding the thing in ginger fingers, she set it upon Inrilatas's shattered brow.

Low thunder rumbled through the cell. Rain hissed and thrummed.

'Before,' she said, her head still down. 'Before, I knew I could defeat you . . .'

The Holy Shriah of the Thousand Temples stood imperious and scowling. 'How?'

She shrugged like someone weary beyond all suffering. 'A story Kellhus once told me about a wager between a god and a hero . . . a test of courage.'

Maithanet watched her with the absolute absence of expression.

She looked up to him, her eyes red and welling. 'I sometimes think he was *warning* me . . . Against him. Against my children . . . Against you.'

She turned back to her dead son.

'He told me this story revealed the great vulnerability of the Dûnyain.' She brushed a lock of hair from the mask upon Inrilatas's face. Blood had continued to drain, pooling, chasing the seams, soaking the nethers of her gown. 'You need only be willing to sacrifice yourself . . .'

'Esmi . . . You have been decei—'

'*I was so willing, Maitha.* And I knew you would see . . . see this in me, realize that I would let all the Empire burn to war against you, and that you would capitulate the way all the others have capitulated to my sovereign will.'

'Esmenet . . . *Sister*, please . . . Relinquish this madn—'

'But what . . . what you have done . . . here . . .' Her head dropped like a doll's, and her voice faded to a whisper. 'Maitha . . . You have killed my *boy* . . . my . . . my son.'

She frowned, as if only now grasping the consequences, then glared at her Exalt-Captain.

'Imhailas . . . Seize him.'

They crowded about the entrance, a small mob of astounded souls. Until now, the statuesque Norsirai officer had stood motionless, watching with a horrified pallor. Now Kelmomas almost giggled, so comic was his shock. 'Your Glory?'

'Esmi . . .' Maithanet said, something dark growling through his voice. 'I will not be taken.'

He simply turned and began striding down the marmoreal halls.

Silence, stunned and panting.

'Seize him!' the Holy Empress screeched at Imhailas. She turned back to the corpse of her son, hung over him, murmuring, '*No-no-no-no-no . . .*' against the shudders that wracked her slender frame.

Not another one, the secret voice whispered, laughing.

—✦—

Her body-slaves had only attended to a handful of lanterns before she chased them from her apartments. Darkness ruled the clutch of interconnected rooms as a result, punctuated by pools of lonely illumination. In the boy's eyes, the world seemed soft and warm with secrets, all the edges rounded with shadow. The belly of an urn gleaming here, the combed planes of a tapestry hanging there – familiar things, made strange for the scarcity of light.

Yes, he decided. A different world. Better.

They lay together on the broad bed, she with her back partially propped on pillows, he within her sheltering curve. Neither of them spoke. For the longest time, the gauze sheers drawn across the balcony were all that moved, gently teasing the marble shadows.

The Prince-Imperial had set an idle fraction of his soul the task of counting heartbeats so that he might know the measure of his bliss. Three thousand, four hundred and twenty-seven passed before

Lord Sankas appeared from the darkened depths, his face drawn for worry.

'He simply walked out of the palace.'

The Empress stiffened but did not move otherwise.

'*No one* would dare raise arms against him?'

'No one.'

'Not even Imhailas?'

Sankas nodded. 'Imhailas, yes, but none of his men assisted him . . .'

Kelmomas fairly squirmed for excitement. *Please-please-please let him be dead!*

Inrilatas gone. Uncle Holy banished from the palace. Imhailas dead would make this a most perfect of perfect days!

But his mother had gone rigid behind him. 'Is he . . . Is he okay?'

'The fool's pride will be splinted for a month, but his body is intact. May I suggest, Your Glory, that he be relieved of his command?'

'No, Sankas.'

'His men *mutinied*, Your Glory – and for all eyes to see. His hold over them, his command, is now broken.'

'I said, no . . . More than *his* command has been broken. All of us have been damaged this day.'

The patrician's eyes widened in acknowledgment. 'Of course, Your Glory.'

A forlorn moment passed, filled with all the things that rise into the place of hopes dashed. Paroxysms had swept through her, rising and falling with the swells of her grief. She had clutched and released him, clutched and released, as if something had groped *through* her, making a glove of her skin, fingers of her limbs. Now her hold on him relaxed, and her breathing slowed. Even the rhythm of her heart became thick and swollen.

And somehow the boy just knew that she had found peace in a fatal resolution.

'You're a Patridomos, Sankas,' she said. He could feel the heat of her breath on his scalp, so he knew that she stared down at him, melancholy and adoring. 'You belong to one of the most ancient houses. You have ways . . . *resources*, utterly independent of the Imperial Apparati. I am sure you can provide me with what I need.'

'Anything, Your Glory.'

Kelmomas closed his eyes, floated in the luxurious sensation of her fingers twining through his curls.

'I need someone, Sankas,' she said from the darkness immediately above him. 'I need someone . . . Someone who can kill.'

A long, appreciative pause.

'Any man can kill another, Empress.'

Words. Like flakes of poison, a mere handful could overturn the World.

'I need someone with skills. *Miraculous* skills.'

The Patridomos went rigid. 'Yes,' he said tightly. 'I see . . .'

Lord Biaxi Sankas was a son of a different age, possessing sensibilities that never quite fit the new order Father had established. He continually did things that struck the boy as odd – like the way he not only dared approach his Empress but actually sat upon the edge of her bed. He gazed at her with bold candour. The play of dim light and shadow did not flatter him, drawing deep, as it did, the long ruts of his face.

'Narindar,' he said with a solemn nod.

The young Prince-Imperial struggled to preserve the drowsy sorrow of his gaze. He had heard no few tales about the Narindar, the Cultic assassins whose name had been synonymous with dread – that is, before Father had unmasked the first of the Consult skin-spies.

Funny, how men had only so much room for their fears.

'I can arrange everything, if you wish, Your Glory.'

'No, Sankas. This I must command myself . . .' She caught her breath by biting her lower lip. 'The damnation must be mine alone.'

Damned? Did Mother think she would be damned for murdering Uncle Holy?

She doesn't believe this, the secret voice whispered. *She doesn't believe a Dûnyain can be a true* anything, *let alone the Holy Shriah* . . .

'I understand, Your Glory.' Biaxi Sankas said, nodding and smiling a humourless smile that reminded the boy of Uncle Proyas and his melancholy devotion. 'And I admire.'

And the boy craned his head up to see the tears at last overwhelm her eyes. It was becoming ever more difficult, finding ways to make her cry . . .

She clutched her boy tight, as if he were her only limb remaining.

The gaunt Patridomos bowed precisely as low as jnan demanded of him, then withdrew to afford his Empress the privacy that all anguish required.

CHAPTER NINE

The Istyuli Plains

The shape of virtue is inked in obscenity.

—AINONI PROVERB

Early Summer, 20 New Imperial Year (4132 Year-of-the-Tusk), The High Istyuli

'I am the smoke that hangs from your cities!' the Nonman screams. 'I am the horror that captivates! The beauty that chases and compels!'

And they gather before him, some kneeling, others hanging back with reluctance and terror. One by one they open their mouths to his outstretched finger.

'I am the plummet!'

———⊷⊷⊷———

Twelve walkers, little more than grey shadows in the veils of dust, lean to the rhythm of their exertions. The forests, vast and haunted, are behind them. The Sea, trackless and heaving, is behind them. The dead who mark their path are long rotted.

The plains pass like a dream.

Food becomes scarce. Xonghis continually scans the ground for sign of voles and other rodents, leads them on a winding course, toward this or that high-circling bird of prey. Whenever he finds a warren, he directs the Wizard to tear up the ground while the others stand ready with their weapons. Arcane lights prise the earth in broad sheets. When the Imperial Tracker guesses true, most are killed outright, while the others are stunned or lamed enough to easily skewer. Fat-limbed rats, Mimara can not help but think as she devours them, her face and fingers greased in the evening gloom. Because finding the warrens is uncertain, they heap uneaten carcasses on their backs.

This is what kills Hilikas: sickness from spoiled meat.

The twelve become eleven.

Starlight provides their sole illumination at night. The Captain speaks only to Cleric, long murmuring exhortations that no one can quite hear. The others gather like shipwreck survivors, small clots separated by gulfs of exhaustion. Galian holds court with Pokwas and Xonghis. The three gripe and joke in low, suspicious tones and sometimes watch the others, only to look away when the subject of their scrutiny turns to question them. Conger and Wonard rarely speak but remain shoulder to shoulder whether walking, eating, or sleeping. Sarl sits alone, skinnier, and far less inclined to ape his former role as Sergeant. Mimara catches him glaring at the Captain from time to time, but she can never decide whether she glimpses love or murder in his eyes.

Of the Stone Hags, only Koll remains. Never has Mimara witnessed a man so gouged. But he awakens, wordlessly, joins their long striding march, wordlessly. It seems he has forsworn all speech and thought as luxuries belonging to the fat. He has abandoned his armour and his girdle. He has tied a string from the pommel of his broadsword, which he slings about his forehead so he can carry the blade naked across his back.

Once she catches him spitting blood. His gums have begun bleeding.

She avoids all thought of her belly.

Sometimes, while walking in the dusty cool of the morning, or the drought-sun glare of the afternoon, she catches herself squeezing her eyes shut and opening them, like someone warding much needed sleep. The others are always *there*, trudging through their own dust in a scattered file.

As are the plains, stretching dun and white to the limit of the bleached sky . . .

Passing like a dream.

'How I loved you!' the Nonman weeps. 'So much I would have pulled down mountains!'

Stars cloud the sky in sheets, vaulting the night with innumerable points of light. In the shadow of the False Man, the scalpers bend back their heads, open their mouths in infant need, infant wonder.

'Enough to forswear my brothers!'

They wave their arms in exultation, cry out in laughing celebration.

'Enough to embrace damnation!'

Koll watches them from the dark.

The Wizard recites long-dead poets, his voice curiously warm and resonant. He argues metaphysics, history, even astrology.

He is a wild old man, clad in rancid hides. He is a Gnostic Mage from days of old.

But he is a teacher most of all.

'The Qirri,' he says to her one evening. 'It sharpens the memory, makes it seem as if . . . you *know* everything you know.'

'It makes me happy,' she replies, resting her cheek on her raised knees.

A beaming smile splits his beard. 'Yes . . . sometimes.'

A momentary frown clenches his brow.

He shakes it into another smile.

———

The plains pass like a dream.

———

She sits with herself in the high grasses, thinking, *Could I be this beautiful?*

She finds herself fascinated by the line of her jaw, the way it curves like a chalice to the soft hook of her earlobe. She understands the pleasure that mirrors hold for the beautiful. She knows vanity. In the brothel, they endlessly primped and preened, traded fatuous compliments and envious gazes. Beauty may have been the coin of their subjugation, but it was the only coin they possessed, so they prized it the way drunks prize wine and liquor. Take away enough and people will treasure their afflictions . . . If only to better accuse the world.

'I know what you're doing,' she whispers to the thing called Soma.

'And what am I doing?'

There are differences to be sure. It wears the rags that were once Soma's gowns, for one. And the thing is filthier than she – something she would have not thought possible before encountering it here, away from the others. Especially about the face and neck, where the remains of multiple raw feedings have sheathed and stained its skin . . .

Her skin.

'Surrogation,' she says. 'Consult skin-spies typically begin with a servant or a slave – someone who allows them to study their real target, learn their mannerisms, voice, and character. Once they've learned enough, they begin transforming themselves, sculpting their flesh, moulding their cartilage bones, in preparation for the subsequent assassination and replacement of the target.'

It has even replicated the lean, starved look that has begun to afflict them all.

'Your father has told you this?'

'Yes.'

And the growing curve of her lower belly . . .

'You think this is what I'm doing?'

'What else could you be doing?' A sudden sharpness pokes through her manner. She will show this thing . . . this beautiful thing.

'Declaring your beauty,' it replies.

'No, Soma. Do not play games with me. Nothing human passes through your soul because *you have no soul*. You're not real.'

'But I speak. How could I speak if I had no soul?'

'Parrots speak. You are simply a cunning parrot.'

'I fear I am far more.'

'I can even prove it to you.'

'Can you now?'

Now *she's* playing games, she realizes, games when she has so many burning questions – ones crucial to their survival. Every night she rehearses them, but for some reason they no longer seem . . . pertinent. If anything, they suddenly feel absurd, bloated with unreality, the kinds of questions fat priests might ask starving children. Even the central question, when she thinks of it, leaves her leaden with reluctance . . .

And yet she *needs* to ask it, to lean heedless into the thing's menace and *demand* an answer, to blurt, *'What do you mean, the Nonman is trying to kill us?'*

But she cannot.

And it has become as proper as proper can be, avoiding things troubling and obvious. To play games with inhuman assassins.

'A man comes to you saying,' she begins with a sly smile, '"Do not believe anything I say, for I am liar . . ."' She pauses to allow the words to resonate. 'Tell me, *thing*, why is this a *paradox?*'

'Because it's strange for a liar to say such things.'

The response occasions a small flare of triumph. It's remarkable, really, witnessing things learned in the abstract happen in actuality – and yet further proof of her stepfather's divinity. She can even see the Aspect-Emperor's luminous face, smiling and gentle, saying, *'Remember, Mimara . . . If you fear, simply ask this question . . .'*

The thing before her truly possesses *no soul*. But as dread as the fact is, it seems . . . a farce.

'There. That is my proof.'

'Proof? How?'

She feels as if she pretends the water has boiled even though the fire has long since guttered, as if everyone raises stone-cold bowls, smacks their lips, and spouts some homily about the way tea warms the soul even as they shudder at the chill lining their collective gut.

'Only a soul can hold a paradox,' she explains. 'Since the true meaning of paradox escapes you, you can only grasp non-paradoxical approximations. In this case, "strange." Only a *soul* can comprehend contradictory truths.'

'If I'm not a soul, then what am I?'

How? How has everything become such a farce?

'An abacus crafted of skin, flesh, and bone. A monstrous, miraculous tool. A product of the Tekne.'

'That too is something *special*, is it not?'

Something is wrong, she realizes. Their voices have waxed too loud. And the Wizard, she knows, will be peering into the darkness after her, wondering. Worrying.

'I must go . . . I've tarried too long.'

Cleric saw it first, scooped along distant tentacles of wind. A scarf of white and gold – the colours of the Thousand Temples – floating, coiling and uncoiling. The first sign of humanity they had encountered since passing the last of the Meori ruins weeks previous.

Of course Achamian was among the last to pick it out against the dun monotony of the distance. 'There,' Mimara repeated time and again, pointing. '*There* . . .' At last he glimpsed it, twisting like a worm in water. He clenched his teeth following its meandering course, balled his fists.

The Great Ordeal, he realized. Somewhere on this very plain, the host of Kellhus and his Believer-Kings marched the long road to Golgotterath. How close would they pass?

But this worry, like so many other things, seemed uprooted, yet another scarf floating across parched ground. Everything seemed to float lately, as if yanked from its native soil and carried on a slow flood of invisibility.

Few men returned the same after months or years of travel – Achamian knew this as well as anyone. Sheer exposure to different sights, different customs, different peoples, was enough to alter a man, sometimes radically. But in Achamian's estimation, the real impetus, what really changed men, was the simple act of walking and *thinking*, day after day, week after week, month after month. Innumerable thoughts flitted through the soul of the long traveller.

Kith and kin were condemned and pardoned. Hopes and beliefs were considered and reconsidered. Worries were picked to the point of festering – or healing. For those who could affirm the same thoughts endlessly, men like the Captain, the trail typically led to fanaticism. For those with no stomach for continuous repetition, men like Galian, the trail led to suspicion and cynicism, the conviction that thought was never to be trusted. For those who found their thoughts never quite repeating, who found themselves continually surprised by novel angles and new questions, the trail led to philosophy – to a wisdom that only hermits and prisoners could know.

Achamian had always considered himself one of the latter: a long-walking philosopher. In his younger days, he would even take inventory of his beliefs and scruples to better judge the difference between the man who had departed and the man who had arrived. He was what the ancient Ceneian satirists called an *aculmirsi*, literally, a 'milestone man,' one who would spend his time on the road forever peering at the next milestone – a traveller who could not stop thinking about travelling.

But *this* journey, arguably the most significant of his long life . . . was different somehow. Something was happening.

Something inexplicable. Or something that wanted to be . . .

———

His Dreams had changed as well.

The night they had camped atop the Heilor, he once again found himself one of many captives chained in an ever-diminishing line, still toothless for scarce-remembered beatings, still nameless for the profundity of what he suffered – and yet everything was different. He glimpsed the flash of memories when he blinked, for one, images of ghastly torment, obscenities too extreme to be countenanced. The glimpse of Sranc hunched in frenzied rutting. The taste of their slaver as they arched and drooled across him. The stench of their black seed . . .

Degradations so profound that his soul had kicked free his body, his past, his sanity.

So he pinned his eyes wide in false wakefulness, stared over the wretches before him with a kind of mad glaring, toward the opening that marked his destination. Where scrub and brush had enclosed the file before, he now saw gleaming bulkheads and curved planes of gold: a corridor of metal, canted as though part of an almost toppled structure or some great boat dragged ashore. Where the tunnel had ended in a clearing of some kind, he now saw a *chamber*, vast in implication, though he could see naught but the merest fraction, and illuminated with a kind of otherworldly light, one that rinsed the walls in watery arrhythmia, and sickened for staring.

The Golden Room, he called it. And it was the sum of all horrors.

The unseen horn would blare, scraping across intonations no human ear was meant to suffer. Shadows would rise from the threshold, and the procession would be heaved staggering forward – two steps, never more. He would listen to the shrieks, infant in their intensity, as the Golden Room devoured yet another damaged soul.

Thinking, *Please . . . Let it end here.*

The trees, he had realized upon awakening. The Dream had been refracted through their lethargic wrath, distorted. A forest tunnel. A forest clearing. Now the barked skin of the Mop had fallen away, revealing the true locus of his dream captivity, one that he recognized instantly, yet was long in admitting . . .

The Dread Ark. Min-Uroikas. He now dreamed the experiences of *some other soul*, a captive of the Consult, shuffling to his doom in the belly of wicked Golgotterath.

And yet, despite the mad significance of this latest transformation, despite all the care and scrutiny he had heaped upon his Dreams over the years, he found himself dismissing these ethereal missives with an inexplicable negligence. Even though their horror actually eclipsed his old dreams of the Apocalypse, they simply did not seem to matter . . . for some reason . . . for some reason . . .

The old Wizard laughed sometimes, so little did he care.

<hr>

Seventeen days into the Istyuli Plains, the day following the scarf, Mimara suddenly asked him why he had fallen in love with her mother.

Mimara was forever talking about the 'Empress,' as she called her, always describing her in ways that lampooned and criticized. Often she would adopt her mother's tone and voice – lips pulled into a line, eyelids wary and low, an expression that strove to look impervious yet seemed brittle instead. It was a habit that amused and alarmed the old Wizard in equal measure.

Although Achamian was forever defending Esmenet, as well as chiding Mimara for her lack of charity, he had always managed to avoid revealing his true feelings. His instinct was to keep his counsel when talking mothers to their children – even when adult. Motherhood, it seemed, meant too much to be trusted to something as sordid as truth.

So he would tell her pleasant lies, the kind of polite observations designed to discourage further discussion. If she insisted or, worse yet, pestered him with direct questions, he would bark and bristle until she relented. *Too much pain,* he would tell himself. And besides, he had become quite fond of acting the crabby old Wizard.

But this time he did neither.

'Why?' she asked. 'Out of all the women you had lain with, why love *her*?'

'Because she possessed a sharp wit,' he heard himself reply. 'That was why I . . . why I *returned*, I think. That and her beauty. But your mother . . . She was always asking me questions about things, about the world, the past – even my Dreams fascinated her. We would lie in her bed sweating, and I would talk and talk, and she would never lose interest. One night she interrogated me until dawn gilded the cracks of her shutters. She would listen and . . .'

He trailed into the marching silence, not so much stymied by the difficulty of what he wanted to say as astonished by the fact he spoke at all. When had confession become so easy?

'And what?'

'And she . . . she *believed* me . . .'

'Your stories, you mean. About the First Apocalypse and the No-God.'

He glanced about, as though wary about being overheard, when in truth he really did not care.

'That . . . But it was more, I think. She believed *in* me.'

Could it be so simple?

And so he continued. He heard himself explaining things he never knew he understood, how doubt and indecision had so ruled his soul and intellect that he could scarce act without lapsing into endless recriminations. Why? Why? Always why? He heard himself explaining the horrors of his Dreams, and how they had frayed his nerves to the quick. He heard himself telling her how he had come to her mother *weak*, a man who would sooner hatch plots in his soul than take any real action . . .

How Drusas Achamian, the only Wizard in the Three Seas, had been a cringer and a coward.

The strange thing is that he found himself actually *yearning* for those days – missing not so much the fear, perhaps, as the simple anguish of needing another. Living with her in Sumna while she continued taking custom, sitting and waiting in the bustling agora, watching the to and fro of innumerable Sumnites while images of her coupling with strangers plagued him gut and soul. Perhaps this explained what happened later, when she had climbed into Kellhus's bed, believing that Achamian had perished in the Sareotic Library. If there was any fact from his past that caused Achamian to both flinch and marvel, it was the way he had continued to love *both* of them after their joint betrayal. Despite the years, he never ceased balling his fists at the pageant of memories, his awe of Kellhus and the godlike ease with which he mastered the Gnosis, and his impotent fury when the man retired . . . to lie with his wife – his *wife*!

Esmenet. Such a strange name for a whore.

'Fear . . .' the old Wizard said in resignation. 'I was always afraid with your mother.'

'Because she was a whore,' Mimara said with more eagerness than compassion.

She was right. He had loved a whore and had reaped the wages accordingly. Perhaps the final days of the First Holy War simply had been a continuation of those early days in Sumna. The same hurt, the same rage, only yoked to the otherworldly glamour that was Anasûrimbor Kellhus.

'No . . .' he said. 'Because she was so beautiful.'

It seemed a proper lie.

'What I don't understand,' Mimara exclaimed with the air verbalizing something she had long debated in silence, 'is why you refuse to hold her *accountable*. She was a caste-menial, not sold into slavery like me. She *chose* to be a whore . . . just as she chose to betray you.'

'Did she?' It seemed that he listened to his voice more than he spoke with it.

'Did she what? Choose? Of course she did.'

'Few things are so capricious as choice, girl.'

'Seems simple to me. Either she chooses to be faithful or she chooses to betray.'

He glared at her. 'And what about you? Were you chained to your pillow in Carythusal? No? Does that mean you chose to be there? That you *deserved* everything you suffered? Could you not have jumped off the ship when the slavers she sold you to put out to sea? Why blame your mother for *your wilful refusal to run away?*'

Her look was hateful but marred by the same hesitation that seemed to dog all of their heated conversations of late, that moment of searching for the proper passion, as if willing away some reptilian fragment of self that simply did not care. Mimara, part of him realized, was injured because he had said something injurious, not because she felt any real pain. That capacity, it seemed, had been lost in the dark bowels of Cil-Aujas.

'There are chains,' she said dully, 'and then there are *chains*.'

'Exactly.'

A kind of humility haunted her manner after that, but one that seemed more motivated by weariness than any real insight. Even so, he welcomed it. Arrogance is ever the patron of condemnation. Though most all men lived in total ignorance of the ironies and contradictions that mortared their lives, they instinctively understood the power of hypocrisy. So they pretended, laid claim to an implausible innocence. To better sleep. To better condemn. The fact that everyone thought themselves more blameless than blameworthy, Ajencis once wrote, was at once the most ridiculous and the most tragic of human infirmities. Ridiculous because it was so obvious and yet utterly invisible. Tragic because it doomed them to unending war and strife.

There is more than strength in accusation, there is the presumption of *innocence*, which is what makes it the first resort of the brokenhearted.

During the first years of his exile, Achamian had punished Esmenet in effigy innumerable times in the silent watches before sleep – too many times. He had accused and he had accused. But he had lived with his grievances too long, it seemed, to perpetually condemn her for anything she might have done. No one makes the wrong decisions for reasons *they* think are wrong. The more clever the man, as the Nroni were fond of saying, the more apt he was to make a fool of himself. We all argue ourselves into our mistakes.

And Esmenet was nothing if not clever.

So he forgave her. He could even remember the precise moment. He had spent the bulk of the day searching his notes for the specifics of a certain dream, one involving a variant of Seswatha's captivity in Dagliash – he could no longer remember why it was important. Furious with himself, he had decided to climb down from his room to assist Geraus with his wood chopping. The odd blister, it seemed, helped focus his thoughts as well as steady his quill. The slave was doggedly hacking away at one of the several shorn trunks he had drawn to the crude hutch where they stored their wood. Grabbing what turned out to be the dull axe, Achamian began chopping as well, but for some bizarre reason he could not strike the wood without sending chips spinning up into Geraus's face. The first one went unmentioned. The second occasioned a frowning smile. The third incited outright laughter and a subsequent apology. The fifth chip caught the man in the eye, sent him to the water-bucket blinking and grimacing.

Once again Achamian apologized, but only so far as was seemly between master and slave. Strangely enough, he had come to prize the jnanic etiquette he so despised when travelling the fleshpots of the Three Seas. Afterward he stood there, watching the man he owned rinse his left eye time and again, feeling somehow guilty and wronged at the same time. After all, he had *meant* to assist the man . . .

Geraus turned toward him, ruefully shook his head, and commended him for his supernatural aim. Achamian's vague ire evaporated, as it always did in the face of the man's relentless good nature. And then, impossibly, he caught the scent of the *desert*, as if somewhere just beyond the arboreal screens that fenced his tower, he would find the dunes of the mighty Carathay.

And just like that, *she* was forgiven . . . Esmenet, the whore become Empress.

Numb to his fingertips, Achamian returned the axe to its nook. 'Better to heed the Gods,' Geraus had said in approval.

Of course habits, like fleas, are not so easy to kill, especially habits of thought and passion. But she was forgiven, nonetheless. Even if he wasn't finished accusing her, she was forgiven.

And somehow, while walking with a band of killers through the empty heart of a dead civilization, he managed to explain this to Mimara.

He told her about their very first meeting, about the bawdy way her mother had accosted him from her window.

'Hey, Ainoni,' she had shouted down. It was the custom in Sumna to call all bearded foreigners Ainoni. 'A man so swollen needs to take his ease, lest he bursts . . .'

'I was quite fat in those days,' he said, answering Mimara's dubious look.

And he told her about herself – or at least the memory of her that continued to haunt her mother.

'This was the summer after the famine. Sumna, the whole Nansur Empire had suffered grievously. In fact, the poor had sold so many of their children into slavery that the Emperor issued an edict voiding all such sales between Nansur citizens the previous summer. Like most caste-menials, your mother was too poor to afford citizenship, but Exceptions were being issued by various tax farmers throughout the city. Your mother would have never told me about you, I think, were it not for the law . . . the Sixteenth Edict of Manumission, it was called, I think. She needed the gold, you see. She was mad for gold – for anything she might use as a bribe.'

'You gave it to her.'

'Your mother never dreamed she could get you back. In fact, she never thought she would survive the famine. She literally believed she was sparing you her doom. You simply cannot imagine the straits she was in, the *chains* that shackled her. She sold you to Ainoni slavers, I think, because she thought the farther she could deliver you from the Nansurium the better.'

'So the Emperor's edict was useless.'

'I tried to tell her, but she refused to listen . . . *Really* refused,' he added with a chuckle, drawing a finger to the small scar he still sported on his left temple. 'Even still, she managed to secure the Exception . . . from a man, a monster, named Polpi Tharias – someone I still dream of killing. The first day the law went into effect she went down to the harbour. I don't know about now, but back then the Ershi district – you know? the north part of the harbour, in the shadow of the Hagerna – was where the slavers held their markets. She refused to let me accompany her . . . It was something . . . something she needed to do on her own, I think.'

It was a strange thing for a man to enter the world of a damaged woman. The apparent disproportion between event and evaluation. The endless sinkholes that punished verbal wandering. The crazed alchemy of compassion and condemnation. It was a place where none of the scales seemed balanced, where the compass bowl never settled and the needle never showed true north.

'You know, girl, I think that was when I *truly* fell in love with her . . . that day, so very hot, as humid as any day in the Sayut Delta. I sat on the very sill she used to accost men on the street below, watched her slender form swallowed by the mobs . . .'

For some reason, he could not conjure the image in his soul's eye. Instead he glimpsed the eunuch-fat man she had vanished behind in the press: his smile hooking his jowls, empires of dark soaking his armpits.

Such is the perversity of memory. Small wonder the Nonmen lapsed into madness.

'She wasn't the only one,' he continued. 'Apparently thousands of Exceptions had been sold, almost all of them counterfeit. Not that it would have mattered, given that you were in Carythusal, far beyond the sway of the Emperor and his ill-considered law. The slavers had hired mercenaries in anticipation. There were riots. Hundreds were killed. One of the slaver's ships was set alight. When I saw the smoke I went out into the city to try to find her.'

He idly wondered whether anyone had seen as many smoking cities as he. Many, he decided, if the rumours he had heard regarding the Wars of Unification were true.

Sarl and the Captain among them.

'Men are fools at the best of times,' he continued, 'but when they gather in mobs they lose whatever little reason they can claim when alone. Someone cries out, they all cry out. Someone bludgeons or burns, and they all bludgeon and burn. It's remarkable really, and terrifying enough to send kings and emperors into hiding.

'I was forced to resort to the Gnosis twice just to reach the harbour, and this in a city where Chorae were rife and sorcerers had their tongues scraped out with oyster shells. I actually remember little, just smoke, shadows running, bodies in the dust, and this . . . this *cold* that seemed to burn in the bottom of my gut.'

Even after so many years, the phantasmagoric feel of that

afternoon still tickled. It had been one of the first times
his waking life had approximated the shrieking madness of his
Dreams.

'Did you find her?' Mimara asked. She had been walking with
her head slouched, almost slung, from her shoulders. It was a
unlikely posture, a peculiar combination of reflection and defeat.

'No.'

'No? What do you mean, no?'

'I mean *no*. I remember *thinking* I found her. Along one of the
Hagerna's walls, lying face first in her own blood . . .' The moment
came back to him unbidden. He had been nauseated for smoke
and worry, leaning his then fat body against what seemed a
laborious incline. The sight of her struck all thought and breath
and motion from him. He just stood there, teetering, while the
screams and shouts continued to pipe in the near distance behind
him. At first, he had simply *known* it was her. The same girlish
form and piling black hair. Even more, the same mauve cloak –
though it struck him now that it might have only *seemed* the same
cut and colour. Fear has a way of rewriting things to suit its purposes.
She had fallen facing uphill, pigeon-toed, one arm slack along her
side, the other bent beneath her torso. The blood had streamed
along her edges, outlining her in black and crimson. He remembered horns sounding across the harbour – the Shrial Knights
signalling – and how in their blaring wake a hush had fallen,
allowing him to hear the tap-tap of her blood directly into the
heart of the earth: she had fallen across one of Sumna's famed
gutters.

'But it wasn't her?' Mimara was asking.

Several young men had raced past without so much as seeing
them. With nerveless fingers he had reached down, certain she
would be as light as bundled rags. She was not, and it reminded
him of pulling stones out of wet beach sand as a child. He heaved

the woman onto her back, revealed her sodden face, and stumbled back against the wall, falling to his rump.

Joy and relief . . . unlike anything he would experience until the First Holy War.

'No,' he replied. 'Just some other unfortunate. Your mother had found her way back with nary a scrape.' She had been sitting on her sill when he returned, staring down the slots between the opposing tenements, toward the harbour. The room was dark, so that she seemed to glow from where he stood in the doorway.

'She never spoke of you again . . . Not to me or anyone.'

Not until she succumbed to Kellhus.

They both fell silent for a trudging time, as though struggling to absorb the sideways significance of his tale. They stared at the sparse crowd of scalpers before them: Pokwas with a vole carcass slung across his great tulwar, which he wore holstered diagonally across his back. Galian bobbing at his side, his stride as quick and nimble as his tongue. Conger and Wonard shuffling like hurried ghosts, their Galeoth war-knots so haphazard that their hair fell in filthy rags to their shoulders. Koll lurching and limping, his shoulders as sharp as sticks.

'Your mother is a *survivor*, girl,' Achamian finally hazarded. 'Same as you.'

He found himself thinking that perhaps she *had* died that day in the harbour – or a part of her. The Esmenet he had found was not the Esmenet who had left him, that much was certain. Her melancholy had lifted, if anything. He remembered thinking that she had actually *healed* in some way. Before that day, a kind of inward lethargy had always blunted the appetite of her curiosities, the wicked edge of her witticisms. Or so it seemed at the time.

'Let the Outside sort her sins,' he added.

He typically shied from this kind of talk. The World seemed too much a rind pulled across something horrific, and death loomed as the only terror. Someday his sins would be sorted as well, and he did not need Mimara and her Eye to know his ultimate fate.

He walked, waiting for Mimara to pinch him with more questions and unflattering observations. But she kept her face turned to the distances before them, the wind-whisking openness, the endless lines. You would not know the world was crooked, he thought, living on the plains.

Perhaps because they had been speaking Ainoni, he found himself recalling the time he had spent in Carythusal spying on the Scarlet Spires, and of this old drunk – Posodemas, he called himself – who would ply him with stories at a tavern called the Holy Leper. The man, who claimed to have survived seven naval battles and no less than five years as a captive of the Shirise pirates, would speak of nothing but his wives and mistresses. He would describe, in excruciating detail, how each had betrayed him in this or that humiliating respect. Achamian would sit listening to the cow-eyed wretch, alternately scanning the crowd and nodding in false encouragement, telling himself that few things were more precious to a man than his *shame* – the very sense endless drink stripped from him.

And that, he realized with no small amount of dismay, was what seemed to be happening here, on the long road to Ishuäl.

Endless intoxication. And with it, the slow strangulation of shame.

What good was honesty when it carried no pain?

⎯⎯∞⎯⎯

Dust on the horizon. Human smells on the hot wind.

Fleet, they sprinted across the grasses, running low so that the weeds clawed their shoulders, their numbers scattered wide so that the dust of their approach would not alert their prey. They howled insults at the hated sun. They were sleek creatures, tireless and unrelenting in the prosecution of their dread appetites. They took dirt for sustenance, violence for bliss. They wore the faces of their enemy, inhumanly beautiful when calm, twisted grotesqueries when aroused.

Sranc . . . Weapons of an ancient war, ranging a dead world.

They could smell them, the trespassers. They could see the lobes of flesh, the bloody pockets they would cut for their coupling, the eyes wide with unspeakable horror. Though generations had passed since their ancestors had last encountered Men, the fact of them had been stamped into their flesh. The aching splendour of their screams. The heat of their bleeding. The twitching glory of their struggles.

They loped like wolves, scuttled like spiders. They ran for truths they did not know, for verities written in their blood. They ran for the promise of violation . . .

Only to be astonished by a human figure rising from wicks of scrub and grass.

A woman.

Baffled, they tripped to a walk, closed about her in a broad arc. The wind flowed over her limbs, rifled through her hair, her rags, drawing with it the sediment that was her scent.

Man, rot, feces, and . . . and something else . . .

Something at once alarming and alluring.

They formed fences about her, swaying and screeching, brandishing crude weapons, or mewling in confused apprehension. Their Chieftain approached, his arms thrown down and back to drag knives through the powdery turf. He stood before her, nearly as tall, flies buzzing about the rotted leathers that clothed him.

'*What are you?*' he barked.

'A child of the same father,' she said.

The Chieftain began stomping. He bared his teeth, gnashed them for the woman to see. '*Father . . . father! We have no fathers save the earth!*'

She smiled a mother's smile. 'But you do. And they deny you this path.'

'*Kill! Kill you! Kill-murder-fuck the others!*'

'Yet you have no hunger for me . . .'

'*No hunger . . .*'

'Because we are children of the same fathers.'

'*Kill!*' the Chieftain shrieked. '*Kill-murder-fuck!*' He shook his jaws like a wolf disputing a bone, raised his pitted knives to the featureless sky.

The thing called Mimara leapt high over the Chieftain's wagging head. Sunlight sparked from bared steel. It somersaulted with preternatural languor, landed in a warrior stance. Behind its back the Chieftain jerked, shrieked, clawed the air, as if trying to snatch at the violet blood spouting from his neck. The beast spun into the dust, little more than a twitching shadow behind screens of chalk.

'We are children of the same fathers,' the woman said to the others. 'Do you smell the truth-power of this?'

A raucous swell of howls . . .

'The Black Heaven will call you very soon.'

She smiled at the grovelling obscenities.

'He will call you very soon.'

'What was it like?' she asks. 'Meeting Kellhus for the first time, I mean.'

The old Wizard's reply is typically long-winded.

Ajencis, he tells her, was fond of chiding his students for confusing assent with intellect. Apparently this confusion was what made obviously profound souls so troubling – and so rare. 'You, my girl, are the ground of your assumptions. No matter how bent your cubit may be, it is the very definition of straight for you. So when another comes to you with their carpenter's string . . . Well, let's just say they will necessarily come up short the degree to which their assumptions deviate from yours – and it will strike you as *obviously* so. No matter how wrong, how foolish you are, you will think you know it "in your stomach," as the Galeoth say.'

'So true wisdom is invisible? You're saying we can't see it when we encounter it.'

'No. Only that we have great difficulty recognizing it.'

'Then what made my stepfather different?'

The old Wizard walked in silence for what seemed a long while, pondering the kick of his boots through the leathery grasses. 'I've spent many hours mulling this. *Now*, you see, he possesses the authority . . . He is the mighty, all-knowing Aspect-Emperor. His listeners come to him with their yardsticks in hand, actually *seeking* his correction. But back then . . . Well, he was little more than a beggar and a fugitive.'

His tone is halting, pensive. He has the manner of a man surprised by things so familiar they have become thoughtless.

'He had a gift for showing you the *implications* of things . . .' he says, then trails into the silence of second thoughts. His brow furrows. His lips purse within the shaggy profile of his beard. 'Ajencis was forever saying that ignorance is invisible,' he begins again, 'and that this is what fools us into thinking we know the truth of *anything*, let alone complicated matters. He thought certainty was a symptom of stupidity – the most destructive one. But at the risk of offending the Great Teacher – or his ancient shade, anyway – I would say that not all ignorances are . . . are *equal*. I think there are truths, profound truths, that we somehow know without knowing . . .'

Mimara glances around the way she often does when they have

conversations like this. Pokwas is the nearest, his harness sagging, his black skin chalked by dust. Galian trudges nearby – the two have become inseparable. Cleric strides more than walks several paces ahead, his scalp gleaming white in the wide-sky sun. Sarl lags with Koll, his face pulled into a perpetual grimace. The Skin Eaters. They look more like a scattered mob of refugees than a warlike company on a quest.

'This . . .' Achamian says, still gazing into his reminiscences, 'this was Kellhus's *noschi*, his genius. He could look into your eyes and pluck these . . . half-known truths from you . . . and so, within heartbeats of speaking with him, you would begin doubting your own cubit, and begin looking more and more toward *his* measure . . .'

She feels her eyes arch wide in comprehension. 'A deceiver could ask for no greater gift.'

The Wizard's look is so sharp that at first she fears she has offended him. But he has that appreciative gleam in his eyes, the one she has come to prize.

'In all my years,' he continues, 'I have never quite understood worship, what happens to souls when they prostrate themselves before another – I've been a sorcerer for too long. And yet I *did* worship him . . . for a time. So much so I even forgave him the theft of your mother . . .'

He shakes his head as if trying to ward away bees, looks away to the stationary line of the horizon. A cough kicks through him.

'Whatever worship is,' he says, 'I think it involves surrendering your cubit . . . opening yourself to the perpetual correction of another . . .'

'Having faith in ignorance,' she adds with a wry grin.

His laughter is so sudden, so mad with hilarity, that fairly all the scalpers turn toward them.

'The grief you must have caused your mother!' he cries.

Even though she smiles at the joke, a part of her stumbles in errant worry. When has she become so clever?

The Qirri, she realizes. It quickens more than the step.

Wary of the sudden attention, they stay their tongues. The silence of endless exertion climbs over them once again. She stares out toward the northern horizon, at the long divide between sky and earth. She thinks of Kellhus and her mother making love in a distant desert. Her hand drifts to her belly, but her thoughts dare not follow . . . Not yet.

She has the sense of things bending.

—◦∞∞◦—

The World is old and miraculous and is filled with a deep despair that none truly know. The Nonman, Mimara has come to understand, is proof of this.

'There was a time,' he says, 'when the world shook to the stamping chorus of our march . . .'

Dusk rolls the plain's farther reaches into darkness and gloom. The wind buffets, hard enough to prickle with grit. Thunderheads scrawl across the sky, dark and glowing with internal discharges, but rainless save for the odd warm spit.

The Nonman stands before them, naked to the waist, one held in the eyes of ten. His hairless form is perfect in cast and proportion, the very image of manly grace and strength, a statue in a land without sculptors.

'There was such a time. . .'

Thunder rolls across the mocking skies, and the scalpers crane their gazes this way and that. It alarms the soul, thunder on the plain. The eyes turn to shelter when the heavens crack, and plains are naught but the absence of shelter, exposure drawn on and on across the edge of the horizon. The plains offer no place to hide – only directions to run.

'A time when we,' Cleric says, 'when *we*! – were many, and when these depravities – these *skinnies* – were few. There was a time when your forefathers wept at the merest rumour of our displeasure, when you offered up your sons and daughters to turn aside our capricious fury!'

She cannot yank her gaze from him – Incariol. He is a mystery, a secret that she must know, if she and Achamian were to be saved. His aspect has become a compulsion for her, like a totem or even an idol: something that rewards the ardour of its observation.

'The most foolish among us,' Cleric continues, 'has forgotten more than your wisest will ever know. Even your Wizard is but a child stumbling in his father's boots. You are but twig-thin candles, burning fast and bright, revealing far more than your span allows you to fathom.'

He bends back his head until the line of his jaw forms a triangle above the banded muscle of his neck. He shouts heavenward, mouthing words that pool blue and brilliant white . . . Then, miraculously, he steps into the sky, arms out, rising until the clouds become a kind of mantle about his shoulders, a windblown cloak of smoke and warring, interior lights.

'But now look at us,' he booms down to their astonished shadows. 'Diminished. Perpetually foundering. Lost without memories. Persecuted as false. Hunted by the very depths we warred to uncover, the very darkness we sought to illuminate.'

He hangs above them. He lowers his radiant gaze. His tears burn silver with refracted light. Thunder crashes, a thousand hammers against a thousand shields.

'This is the paradox – is it not? The longer you live, the smaller you become. The past always dwarfs the present, even for races as fleeting as yours. One morning you awaken to find now . . . *this very moment* . . . little more than a spark in a cavern. One morning you awaken to find yourself so much . . . less . . .'

Incariol, she thinks. *Ishroi . . .*

'Less than what you wanted. Less than what you once were.'

She is in love, she realizes. Not with him, but with the power and wonder of what he was.

'One day you, who have never been mighty or great, will ask where the glory has gone. Failing strength. Failing nerve. You will find yourself faltering at every turn, and your arrogance will grow brittle, defensive. Perhaps you will turn to your sons and their overshadowed ardour. Perhaps you will seal yourself in your mansion, as we did, proclaiming contempt for the world rather than face its cruel measure . . .'

She is *more* in his presence, she decides. She will always be more, whether he flees or dies or utterly loses himself in the disorder that is his soul. For knowing him . . . Cleric.

'One day you, who have never been mighty or great, will peer through the maze of your depleted life, and see that *you are lost . . .*'

He abandons his mantle of clouds, sinking as though on a wire. He sets foot upon powder-dry earth.

Mimara leans forward with the Wizard and the other scalpers. Their mouths hang slack with drool.

'Lost like us,' he murmurs, reaching for the wonder that hides in his pouch.

The thunderheads continue their march into the obscurity of night.

The rain, as always, refuses to fall.

Cil-Aujas, she decides. Something broke in Cil-Aujas. Something between them, something within. And now sanity is abandoning them, drip by lucid drip.

There's a new Rule of the Slog, and even though it has never been spoken, Mimara knows with utter certainty that violators will be punished as lethally as all the others. A rule that ensuites no mention shall be made of the madness slowly possessing them.

No questions. No *doubters* on the slog.

The extraordinary thing about insanity, she has come to realize, is the way it seems so normal. When she thinks of the way the droning days simply drop into their crazed, evening bacchanals, nothing strikes her as strange – nothing visceral, anyway. Things that should make her shudder, like the nip of Cleric's nail as his finger roams the inside of her cheek, are naught but part of a greater elation, as unremarkable as any other foundation stone.

It is only when she steps back and reflects that the madness stares her plain in the eye.

'He's killing you . . .' the thing called Soma had said. 'The Nonman.'

She finds herself drifting to the rear of their scattered mob and approaching Sarl, thinking that someone *wholly* broken might know something about the cracks now riddling their souls. According to the old Wizard, the Sergeant has known Lord Kosoter since the Unification Wars – a long time, as far as life is measured by scalpers. Perhaps he can decipher the skin-spy's riddle.

'The Slog of Slogs,' she says lamely, not knowing where to begin with a madman. 'Eh, Sarl?'

The others have long since abandoned him to his crazed musings. No one dares glance at him, for fear of sparking some kind of rambling tirade. For weeks she has expected, and a couple of times even *hoped*, that the Captain would silence him. But no matter how long his harsh voice rattles on into the night, nothing is done, nothing is said.

Sarl, it seems, is the lone exception to the Rules.

'She talks to me,' he says, staring off to her right as if she were a phantasm that had plagued his ruminations too long to be directly addressed. 'The second most beautiful thing . . .'

He was easily one of the most wrinkled men she had ever seen when she first saw him. Now his skin is as creased as knotted linen. His tunic has rotted to rags, his hauberk swings unfastened from his knobbed shoulders, and his kilt has somehow lost its backside, baring withered buttocks to open daylight.

'Tell me, Sergeant. How long have you known the Captain?'

'The Captain?' The hoary old man wags a finger, shaking his head in cackling reproach. 'The *Captain*, is it? He-heeee! There's no explanation for the likes of him. He's not of this world!'

She flinches at the volume of his voice, reflexively lowers her own tone to compensate.

'How so?'

He shudders with silent laughter. 'Sometimes souls get mixed up. Sometimes the dead *bounce*! Sometimes old men awaken behind the eyes of babes! Sometimes wolves . . .'

'What are you saying?'

'Don't *cross* him,' he rasps with something like conspiratorial glee. 'He-he! Oh, no, girl. Never cross him!'

'But he's such a friendly fellow!' Mimara cries.

He catches her joke but seems to entirely miss the humour. So much of his laughter possesses the dull hollow of reflex. More and more he seems to make the sound of laughter without laughing at all . . .

And suddenly she can feel it, the lie that has been burrowing through all of them, like a grub that devours meaning and leaves only motions. Laughter without humour. Breath without taste. Words said in certain sequences to silence words unsaid – words that must never be said.

Her whole life she has lived some kind of lie. Her whole life she has charted her course about some contradiction, knowing yet not knowing, and erring time and again.

But this lie is different. This lie somehow eludes the pain of those other lies. This lie carves the world along more beautiful joints.

This lie is bliss.

She needs only look to the others to see they know this with the same deathless certainty. Even Sarl, who had long since fled the world's teeth, content to trade fancy for mad fancy, seems to understand that something . . . false . . . is happening.

'And Cleric . . . How did you fall in with him?'

There's something about the Sergeant's presence that winds her. His gait is at once vigorous and wide, his arms swinging out like a skinny man pretending to be fat.

'Found him,' he says.

'Found him? How? Where?'

Mischief twinkles in his gaze.

'Found him like a coin in the dirt!'

'But where? How?'

'After we took Carythusal, when they disbanded the Eastern Zaudunyani . . . they sent us north to Hûnoreal, he-he!'

'Sent you? *Who* sent you?'

'The Ministrate. The *Holies*. Stack skinnies, they said. Haul the bales and keep the gold – they don't care about gold, the Holies. Just stay on the southeastern marches of Galeoth, they said. Nowhere else? No. No. Just *there* . . .'

This confuses her. She has always thought that scalpers were volunteers.

'But what about Cleric?' she presses. 'Incariol . . .'

'*Found him!*' he explodes with a phlegmatic roar. 'Like a coin in the dirt!'

More eyes have turned to them, and she suddenly feels

conspicuous – even *guilty* in a strange way. Aside from other madmen, only thieves trade jokes with madmen – as a way of playing them. Even the old Wizard watches her with a quizzical squint.

Simply talking to the man has compromised her, she realizes. The others now know that she's seeking something . . . The *Captain* knows.

'The Slog of Slogs,' she says lamely. 'They'll sing songs across the Three Seas, Sergeant – think on it! The Psalm of the Skin Eaters.'

The old man begins weeping, as though overwhelmed by the charity of her self-serving words.

'Seju bless you, girl,' he coughs, staring at her with bleary, blinking eyes. For some reason he has started limping, as if his body has broken with his heart.

Suddenly he smiles in his furrow-faced way, his eyes becoming little more than deeper perforations in his red-creased face. 'It's been lonely,' he croaks through rotted teeth.

They see the plume of dust shortly after breaking camp. It rises chalk-white and vertical before being drawn into a mountainous, spectral wing by the wind. The plains pile to the north in desiccated sheets, some crumpled, others bent into stumps and low horns. The plumb line of the horizon has been raised and buckled, meaning some time will pass before the authors of the plume become visible. So they continue travelling with a wary eye to the north. Mimara hears Galian and Pokwas muttering about Sranc. The company has yet to encounter any since crossing into the Istyuli, so it stands to reason.

The plume waxes and wanes according to unseen terrain but grows ever nearer. The Captain barks no instructions, even when the first of the specks appear crawling across the back of a distant knoll.

Hands held against the spiking sun, they peer into the distance.

Riders. Some forty or fifty of them – just enough to defend themselves against a single clan of skinnies. A motley assemblage of caste-menials, wearing crude hauberks of splint over stained tunics of blue and gold. Their beards hang to their waists, sway to the canter of their ponies. They ride beneath a standard she has never seen before, though she recognizes the checkered black shields of Nangaelsa.

'Nangaels,' she says aloud. 'They're Tydonni.'

The Wizard hushes her with an angry glance.

The Great Ordeal, she realizes. At long last they have crawled into its mighty shadow . . .

A kind of trembling anticipation suffuses her, as if she has stumbled into the gaze of something monstrous with power. And she wonders when she became terrified of her stepfather, when for so long he seemed the only sane voice, the only understanding soul.

'A lost patrol?' Galian asks.

'Supply cohort,' Xonghis says with authority. 'They must have abandoned their wains.'

Even though they can see the approaching riders discussing and debating them, the Skin Eaters remain silent. They have outrun civilization, these men, so far and for so long they no longer need fatuous words to bind them.

The Nangael commander is a greybeard with a long, craggy face and a low, prominent brow. His left arm hangs in a sling. The Captain gestures for Galian to accompany him. The two men walk out several paces to greet the nearing man.

The aging officer does them the courtesy of dismounting, as do

the two riders nearest him. But his eyes linger on Cleric for several
heartbeats. He does not like the looks of him.

'*Tur'il halsa brininausch virfel?*' the officer calls.

'Tell him we don't speak gibberish,' the Captain instructs the
former Columnary.

Mimara looks to the old Wizard, suddenly afraid. He wags his
head almost imperceptibly, as if warning her against anything rash.

'*Manua'tir Sheyarni?*' Galian calls back.

The Nangaels are sunburned and travel-worn, their kilts frayed,
the lines of their faces inked in sweat-blackened dust. But the
contrast between them and her companions horrifies Mimara.
The scalpers' clothing has been reduced to black rags, waxy with
filth. Conger's tunic has all but disintegrated into shags of foul
string. They look like things that should shamble . . . like things
dead.

The officer comes to a halt before the two men. He is Tydonni
tall, but stooped with years, so that he seems of a height with Lord
Kosoter. The Captain seems more shade than man in his presence.
'Who are you?' he asks in passable Sheyic.

'Skin Eaters,' Galian says simply.

'*Scalpers?* This far? How is that possible?'

'The skinnies were mobbing. We had no choice but to flee
northwest.'

A moment of canny blankness dulls the officer's eyes.

'Unlikely.'

'Yes,' the Captain says.

He pulls his knife, thrusts it into the man's eye socket. 'Unlikely.'

The body slumps forward. Cries rifle the arid sky, and somehow
Mimara knows the commander was beloved. The men to either
side of the officer stumble back in horror. Lord Kosoter glares and
grins, his knife braced against his right thigh. His eyes shine above
the tangled fury of his teeth and beard. Weapons are drawn in the

clamour. Beneath shouts of alarm and outrage, a different voice strums the strings of a different world . . .

Cleric is singing.

He stands pale and bare-chested. Brilliance glares through the apertures of his face. He reaches out, his hands crooked into empty claws. Lariats of white light scribble across the rear of the ragtag column . . .

The Seventh Quyan Theorem – or something resembling it.

Shrieks, both equine and human. The glimpse of shadows in high sunlight. Men are thrown. Horses roll and thrash, kicking up clouds of dust. Mimara sees a man on his knees screaming. At first he's little more than a shadow in the dust, but by some miracle a tunnel of clarity opens through the sheets. He howls, his beard aflame beneath scalded cheeks.

Then the battle crashes over her.

Nangael war-cries wrack the air. The nearest Tydonni kick their ponies forward, shields braced, broadswords swinging high. The scalpers meet their charge with eerie calm. They step around the hurtling forms, hacking riders, stringing horses. Pokwas leaps, pivoting to the weight of his great tulwar. A pony blunders into exploding dust. A rider's head spins high, then falls, trailing its beard like a comet. Xonghis ducks between charging Tydonni, gores a thigh. The Captain draws another in an elusive half-circle before lunging high to pierce the man's throat. The wretch falls backward, is dragged choking from his right stirrup.

Chaos and obscurity. Figures emerge then vanish into the tan fog. Sorcerous light flickers and glows, like lightning in clouds. An injured Nangael lurches out of the curtained madness, a cudgel raised in a bloody fist. Mimara is astonished to find Squirrel in her hand, bright and sharp. His face is blank with mortal determination. He swings at her, but she easily ducks to one side, scores the inside of his forearm to the bone. He roars and wheels, his

beard pendulous for blood. But the cudgel slips from his hand – she
has cut him to the tendon. He leaps to tackle, but again she is
too nimble. She steps aside, brings Squirrel flashing down, chops
the back of his neck. He drops like a nerveless sack.

The clamour fades. The dust is drawn up and out like milk
spilled into a stream. The scalpers stand in what should have been
gasping disbelief but more resembles blinking curiosity. The fog
clears, revealing chalked figures crawling or writhing across the
parched grasses. They have tar for blood.

Mimara gazes at the man she has killed. He lies motionless on
his stomach, blinking as he suffocates. The tattoo of a small
Circumfix graces his left temple. She cannot bring herself to end
his suffering the way the others do. She turns away, blinking at
the dust, looking for Achamian. . . .

She finds him several paces from Koll, who stands exactly as
he had before the battle began, his sword still hanging from the
string that creases his forehead. She tries to secure the Wizard's
gaze, but he's peering somewhere beyond her, squinting into the
distance.

'No,' Achamian croaks, as though jarred from a profound stupor.
'No!'

At first Mimara thinks he refers to the murder of innocents
before them, but then she realizes that his gaze follows the escaping
riders. She can scarce see them for the dust – some eight or nine
men, riding hard for the north.

'Noooooo!'

Gnostic words rumble out from all directions, as if spoken with
the sky's own lungs. Bluish light flares from the Wizard's eyes and
mouth . . . Meaning – unholy meaning. He steps out into the open
sky, climbing across spectral ground. Wild, hoary, old – he seems
a doll of rags flung high against the distance.

She stands dumbstruck, watches as he gains on the fleeing

horsemen, then rains brilliant destruction down upon them. Dust steams and plumes, the mark of tumult on the horizon.

The others scarce seem interested. A quick glance reveals that almost all of them are intact, save for Conger, who sits in the dust grimacing, his hands clutched about a crimson welling knee. He watches his Captain's approach with dull horror. The shadow of Lord Kosoter's sword hangs across his face for a breathless heartbeat, then Conger is no more.

'No limpers!' the Captain grates, his eyes at once starved and bright.

And that is the sum of their plunder. It seems sacrilege, for some reason, to don the possessions of others – things so clean they can only be filthy. The old Wizard returns on weary foot, framed by seething curtains of smoke. He has set the plains afire.

'I'm damned already,' is all he says in reply to Mimara's look.

He stares at the ground and says nothing for the next three days.

⌘

His continuing silence does not trouble her so much as her own indifference to it. She understands well enough: in running down the Tydonni, the old Wizard has murdered in the name of rank speculation. But she knows his guilt and turmoil are as much a matter of going through the motions as is her compassion. His silence is the silence of falsehood, and as such, she sees no reason why she should care.

She has the weight of her own murder to bear.

The morning of the third day passes like any other, save that the tributaries they cross have all dried to dust and their skins have grown flabby enough for the Captain to institute rationing. When the old Wizard finally chooses to speak, he does so without spit.

'Have you ever seen Kellhus with it?'

Kellhus. Hearing the name pricks her for some reason, so much so she resists the urge to make one of the signs of warding she learned in the brothel. Before Achamian, she had never heard anyone refer to her stepfather in the familiar before, not even her mother, who always referred to him as 'your father.' Not once.

'Seen my *stepfather?*' she asked. 'You mean with my . . . other eyes?'

She can tell by his hesitation that this is a question he had feared to ask for a long time.

'Yes.'

Absolution, she realizes. He killed the Tydonni to prevent any word of their expedition from reaching the Great Ordeal. Now he seeks to absolve himself of their deaths through the righteousness of his cause. Men murder, and men excuse. For most the connection is utterly seamless: those killed simply *have* to be guilty, otherwise why would they be dead? But Achamian, she knows, is one of those rare men who continually stumble over the seams in their thought. Men for whom nothing is simple.

'No,' she replies. 'You must believe me when I tell you I've only seen him a handful of occasions. Prophets have scarce the time for *real* daughters, let alone the likes of me.'

This is true. For most of her years on the Andiamine Heights, the Aspect-Emperor was scarce more than a dread rumour, an unseen presence that sent hoards of perfumed functionaries scurrying this way and that through the galleries. And in a manner, she realizes with a peculiar numbness, very little has changed. Was he not the hidden tyrant of this very expedition?

For the first time, it seems, she sees things through Drusas Achamian's eyes: a world bound to the machinations of Anasûrimbor Kellhus. Looking out, she has a sudden sense of loads borne and stresses diffused, as if the world were a wheel spoked with mountains, rimmed with seas, one so vast that the axle lay perpetually over the horizon – perpetually unseen. Armies march. Priests tally contributions. Ships leave and ships arrive. Emissaries howl in protest and wriggle on their bellies . . .

All at the pleasure of the Holy Aspect-Emperor.

This is the world the old Wizard sees, the world that frames his every decision: a singular thing, a *living* thing, nourished by the arteries of trade, bound by the sinew of fear and faith . . .

A leviathan with a black cancer for a heart.

'I believe you,' he says after a time. 'I was just . . . just wondering.'

She ponders this image of the Aspect-Emperor and his power, this hellish seal. It reminds her of the great Nilnameshi mandala that hangs in the Allosium Forum below the Andiamine Heights. For more than a thousand years, the artisan-sages of Invishi sought to capture creation in various symbolic schemes, resulting in tapestries of unparalleled beauty and manufacture. The Allosium Mandala, her mother had told her once, was famed for being the first to use concentric *circles* instead of nested squares to represent the hierarchies of existence. It was also notorious for containing no image whatsoever in its centre, the place typically reserved for the God of Gods . . .

Innovations that, her mother explained, saw the artisan stoned to death.

Now Mimara sees a mandala of her own manufacture in her soul's eye, one more temporal than cosmological but every bit as subversive in its implications. She sees the million-panelled extremities, the tiny lives of the mob, each enclosed in ignorance and distraction. And she sees the larger chambers of the Great Factions, far more powerful but just as oblivious given their perpetual scramble for prestige and dominance. With terrifying clarity she sees it, *apprehends* it, a symbolic world thronging with life yet devoid of nerves, utterly senseless to the malignancy crouched in their absent heart . . .

A dark world, one battling a war long lost.

As thin as her passions have become, it seems she can feel it: the impotence, the desolation, the gaping sense of hopelessness. She walks for a time, tasting, even savouring, the possibility, as if doom were a kind of honey-cake. A world where the Aspect-Emperor is *evil* . . .

And then she realizes that the *opposite* could just as easily be true.

'What would you have thought,' she asks the old Wizard, 'if I had told you he was wreathed in *glory* when I saw him, that he was, without any doubt, the Son of Heaven?'

This is it, she realizes. The rat that hides in his gut, gnawing and gnawing . . .

'Hard questions, girl. You have a talent for them.'

The overthrowing fear.

'Yes. But the dilemmas remain *yours*, don't they?'

He glares at her, and for the merest heartbeat, she glimpses hatred. But like so much else, it drops away without residue. Simply another passion too greased with irrelevance to be clutched in the hands of the present.

'Strange . . .' he replies distantly. 'I see *two* sets of footprints behind me.'

There is this sense of unravelling.

A sense of threads worn and abraded, until snipped by their own tension. A sense of things hanging, as if they were nothing more than fluff skipping across the wind. A sense of things tying, of newborn anchors, novel tautnesses yanked across old seams, old straps, as if they were spiderwebs become kites, soaring high and free, batted by falcon winds, pinned to the earth by a singular string . . .

Qirri.

Qirri the holy. Qirri the pure.

Each night they queue before the Nonman, suck from the teat that is his finger. Sometimes he clasps their cheek with his free hand, gazes long and melancholy into their eyes, while his finger probes their tongue, their gums and teeth.

And it is right and proper to taste the spittle of another.

They have found a new Tusk to guide them, a new God to compel their hearts and to bend their knees. Qirri, as rationed and apportioned by its prophet, Incariol.

During the day they walk, utterly absorbed in the blessed monotony. Like beetles, they walk with their faces to the earth, step after step, watching their boots hooking through haloes of dust.

During the night they listen to Cleric and his incoherent declarations. And it seems they grasp a logic that binds disjointed absurdities into profound wholes. They revel in a clarity indistinguishable from confusion, an enlightenment devoid of claim or truth or hope . . .

And the plains pass like a dream.

'The Qirri . . .' she finally manages to blurt. 'It's beginning to frighten me.'

The Wizard's silence has the character of a breach. She senses his alarm, the effort of will it takes for him to stifle his rebuke. She knows the words warring for control of his voice because they are the same words that continue to nag and accuse the corners of her thought. *Fool. Why throw stones at wolves? Everything is as it must be. Everything will turn out fine . . .*

'How so?' he says coldly.

'In the brothel . . .' she hears herself reply and is amazed because she is usually so loathe to speak of the place. 'Some of the girls, the one's who broke, mostly . . . They would feed them opium – force them. Within weeks they would . . . would . . .'

'Do whatever they needed to get more,' the Wizard says dully.

Trudging silence. Coughing from somewhere ahead of them.

'Could that be what the Nonman is doing to us?'

Speaking this question is like rolling a great stone from her chest. How could it be so difficult to stand square in the light of what was happening?

'Why?' the Wizard asks. 'Has he been making . . . making *demands?*'

'No,' she answers. *Not yet.*

He ponders the ground, his stride, and the resulting exhalations of dust.

'We have nothing to fear, Mimara,' he finally says, but there is something false in his manner, as if he were a frightened boy borrowing the assured tone and posture of a priest. 'We're not the same as the others. We *understand* the dangers.'

She does not know how to reply, so she simply continues pacing the Wizard in silent turmoil. *Yes!* something cries within her. *Yes! We know the danger. We can take precautions, refuse the Qirri anytime we wish! Anytime!*

Just not now.

'Besides . . .' he eventually continues, 'we need it.'

She has anticipated this objection. 'But we've travelled so far so fast already!'

Why so harsh? a voice – her voice – chides her. *Let the man speak at the very least.*

'Look at the Stone Hags,' he replies. 'Men bred for the slog, eaten up in the matter of weeks. How well do you think an old man and a woman would fare?'

'Let the others go ahead then. Or even better, we could steal away in the heart of night!'

Or best of all, it occurs to her, *just* take *the Nonman's pouch . . . Yes! Steal it!* This makes so much sparkling sense to her that she almost laughs out loud – even as a more sober part of her realizes that one does not take *anything* from a Quya Mage – ever. As quick as her smile leaps to her lips, her eyes tear in frustration.

'No,' the old Wizard is saying. 'There's no breaking the covenant we've struck with these men. They would hunt us down, and well they should, given what they've sacrificed.'

He is warming to the ingenuity of his rationalizations – as is she.

'Maybe we should confront Cleric,' she offers. 'Drag the issue before the whole company.' Even as she utters this, she can feel her resolution leach away. *See? Why bother?*

You never had the heart for this . . .

Achamian shakes his head as if at a truth so old and fat it cannot but be weary. 'I don't trust Galian. I fear the Qirri is the only thing keeping him here . . .'

'Let him leave then.' Her shrug is directed more at her words than at the man, it seems.

'If Galian leaves,' Achamian replies, his self-assurance relentless now, 'he will take Pokwas and Xonghis with him. We need Xonghis. To eat as much to find our way.'

Though they smile at each other, their gazes are too slicked with apprehension to truly lock. And so it ends, a conversation that began so real it sent burning coals skidding through her gut, become a pantomime, a shadow-play of numbing words and self-serving reasons.

As she had hoped all along.

They walk, the nine, their backs bent to an exhaustion only the remaining Stone Hag can feel. Mimara actually cries, softly, so that the others cannot hear above the wind batting their ears. She sobs, once, twice, so profound is her relief. Her thighs blush and her mouth waters at the thought of the coming darkness . . .

And of the soot smudged across the tip of Cleric's white finger.

There is a vastness to the wind on the nocturnal plain, a sense of heaven-spanning enormities, one drawn roughly across the other. All things are seized. All things are lifted and bent. And when the gusts are violent enough, all things kneel – or are broken.

She has crept from the others into the night. Gusts scour the ground, galloping like the outriders of an infinite horde. She turns her face away from the prick of flying sand, gazes without surprise at herself wearing the tattered rags that had once belonged to Soma.

It seems she had known she would find it here waiting – the Consult skin-spy. The company had continued marching past dusk, stopping only when they found the protection of a meagre depression. She set out the way she always set out, instinctively choosing the line of sight and wind most favourable to a stalking predator . . .

And found one.

'How?' she hisses. There is something frantic within her, something that would fly into pieces were it not for her skin. 'How is the Nonman killing us?'

The thing mimics her crouching posture. It seems at once harmless, nothing more than an image without depth, a mere reflection, and as deadly as a bolt cocked in a ballistae. Fear tickles her, but she feels it with a stranger's skin.

'Tell me!'

It smiles with the same condescension she has felt across her face innumerable times. One both beautiful and infuriating.

'Your Chorae,' it says with her voice. 'Give it to me and I can save you.'

What? She clasps the pouch where it hangs between her breasts. 'No! No more games! Tell me how!'

Her vehemence surprises both of them. She watches her eyes click to the darkness of the camp behind her, her face imperceptibly bent to the needs of a sharper ear.

Then she hears it herself. The mutter of sorcery, effortlessly stepping around the buffeting wind, climbing up out of the substance of dust and earth.

'The Qirri . . .' the other her says. The other spy. 'Ask him what it is!'

Then the thing is gone, leaping high and deep into the darkness and running like no human can run. Yanking her head about, Mimara sees the old Wizard scaling the gusting heights, his eyes and mouth alight with brilliant meaning. His voice echoes deep across the angles and surfaces of a different plane. Lines of blinding light needle the dark, carving trails of white across plain. She glimpses fire and exploding earth, swathes of ground clawed into black by the shadow of grasses.

She glimpses herself running with gazelle beauty, leaping with serpentine grace. Then the spewing dust sweeps up to obscure him and so secure his escape.

———— ∞ ————

Koll. The last of the Stone Hags.

She stares at him while the Wizard rails at her.

'What? What were you doing so far away?'

The man sits hunched, the only one not watching her and her father. He was a large man, a powerful man, when they had rescued the surviving Stone Hags in the Mop. Now he is scarce more than a knob-jointed rack. He has long ceased caring about his war-knot, so his hair falls in mats about his face and shoulders. Whatever armour he possessed, he has lost to the trail – and were it not for the Captain, he would have cast away his broadsword as well, she imagines. His beard is matted with grime, making a sphincter of his mouth, which hangs perpetually open. His eyes stare down, always down, but even still they possess the glint of desperation.

'It just came to me,' she lies, for in truth, she came to it. 'It had my face . . .'

'You could have been killed! Why? Why would you wander so far?'

Koll. Only Koll. Of all his brother Hags, only he has yet to succumb to the rigours of the trail. He is, she realizes, the last *pure thing* in their mad company.

The measure, the cubit of their depravity. The only one who has not tasted Qirri.

'It meant to *replace* you!'

As she watches, the man's shaggy head jerks as if to a gnat's sting. The bleary eyes squint and struggle, as if trying to sort shadows from the darkness . . .

He can't see, she realizes. Not because his eyes fail him, but because it is a moonless night and clouds obscure the Nail of Heaven. He can't see because his eyes remain *human* . . .

Unlike theirs.

'Fool! Fool of a girl! It would have strangled you. Stripped and *replaced* you!'

At last she turns to look up at the Wizard. He stands with his back to the wind so the edges of him – rotted hide and tangled hair – seem to fly toward her.

'What is it?' she asks in Ainoni.

He blinks, and even though his fury continues to animate him, she somehow knows that a kernel of him simply does not

care, that a hunger lies balled like a greased marble in his soul,
waiting for the watches to pass and for the pouch to be drawn
again.

'What is *what*?' he cries. He is troubled, she knows, because she
has spoken in Ainoni, the tongue of their conspiracy. 'I'm talking
to you, girl!'

In her periphery she can see the hoary aspect of the Captain,
his hair and caste-noble braid lashing the air above his right
shoulder, his eyes as bright as Seleukaran steel. His knife slumbers
in its scabbard, hanging high on his girdle, but she sees its curve
glint above his bloodstained knuckles nonetheless.

'Nothing,' she says to the Wizard, knowing that he does not
know.

Qirri is Qirri . . .

The desire that forever slips the leash of your knowing. The
hunger that leaves no trace in your trammelled soul.

'Water before food,' Xonghis says to them.

They walk an undeviating line now that their water-skins are
empty. Nothing can be more simple, it seems, than walking straight
across never-ending flatness. And yet all is turmoil and confusion,
not the kind that quickens hearts or wrings hands, but the kind
that simply hangs like a chrysalis in her soul, suspended, motionless. Everything, it seems – her voice, her scissoring step, her
expression – is as assured as it has ever been, save that the world
they confront has become a dream.

Everything possesses a nagging lightness. The colours, the
maroon swirls of different weeds drying and dying, the patches of
sienna dust, the black of some recent grass fire. The swagger of
the land piling without height, as if some god had poured mud
atop mud just to watch the edges spread over the horizon. The

drama of the sky, the clouds climbing in ranges, here tangled into luxuriant locks, there swept up and around in a snowy mélange of wings. A kind of disbelief plagues everything she sees, as if existence were foam, and the world nothing more than a titanic bubble . . .

What was happening?

'You have the look,' a voice gurgles from behind.

She turns and sees teeth and gums, eyes pinched into besotted creases. Sarl, somehow shadowy though all the world is bright, looking like a filthy gnome.

'You have the look . . . Aye!'

She can hear phlegm snap in his cackle. The peril of speaking to madmen, she realizes, is that it permits them to speak to you.

'Don't dispute me, girl, it's true. You have the look of a path long mudded. Am I wrong? Am I? Tell me, girl. How many men have marched 'cross your thighs?'

She should hate him for saying this, but she lacks the inner wind. When has feeling become an effort?

'Many fools. But *men* . . . Very few.'

'So you admit it!'

She smiles out of some coquettish reflex, thinking she might use his carnal interest to learn more about Lord Kosoter.

'What am I admitting?'

The grin drops from his face, enough for her to glimpse a sliver of his bloodshot eyes. He leans close with a kind of wonder – too close. She fairly gags at his buzzing reek.

'She *burned a city* for you – didn't she?'

'Who?' she replies numbly.

'Your *mother*. The Holy Empress.'

'No,' she laughs in faux astonishment. 'But I appreciate the compliment!'

Sarl laughs and nods in turn, his eyes once again squeezed

into invisibility. Laughs and nods, trailing ever farther behind her . . .

What was happening?

———⊶∞∞⊷———

She is not who she is . . .

She is already two women, each estranged from the other. There is the Mimara who knows, who watches the old motives, the old bonds, gradually disintegrate. And there is the Mimara who has gathered all of the old concerns and set them in a circle about an unspeakable pit.

She is already two women, but she needs only touch her bowing abdomen to become *three*.

They laugh at her for all the food she eats. More and more, she is ravenous come evening. She chides the Wizard for loitering when he should be preparing the humble field Cants he uses to cook their spoiling game. She scolds Xonghis when he fails to secure them enough game.

Whatever speech they possess leaks away as the sun draws down the horizon. They sit in the dust, their beards lacquered with grease, the entrails of their victims humming with flies. Vultures circle them. They sit and they wait for rising darkness . . . for the melodious toll of Cleric's first words.

'I remember . . .'

They gather before him. Some come crawling, while others shuffle, kicking up ghostly trails of dust that the wind whips into quick oblivion.

'I remember coming down from high mountains, and treating with Mannish Kings . . .'

He sits cross-legged, his forearms extended across his knees, his head hanging from his shoulders.

'I remember seducing wives . . . healing infant princes . . .'

Stars smoke the arch of Heaven paint the Nonman's slouching form in strokes of silver and white.

'I remember laughing at the superstitions of your priests.'

He rolls his head from side to side, as if the shadow he cradles possesses hands that caress his cheeks.

'I remember frightening the fools among you with my questions and astounding the wise with my answers. I remember cracking the shields of your warriors, shattering arms of bronze . . .'

And it seems they hear distant horns, the thunder of hosts charging, clashing.

'I remember the tribute you gave to me . . . The gold . . . the jewels . . . the babes that you laid at my sandalled feet.'

A hush.

'I remember the love you bore me . . . The hatred and the envy.'

He raises his head, blinking as if yanked from a dream inhumanly cruel for its bliss. Veins of silver fork across his cheeks . . . Tears.

'You die so easily!' he cries, howls, as if human frailty were the one true outrage.

He sobs, bows his head once more. His voice rises as if from a pit.

'And I never forget . . .'

One of the scalpers moans in carnal frustration . . . Galian.

'I never forget the dead.'

Then he is standing, drawn like a puppet by invisible strings. The Holy Dispensation is about to begin. Strange shouts crease and crumple the windy silence, like the yelping of leashed dogs. She can see hunger leaning in their avid eyes. She can see manly restraint give way to clutched arms and rocking gesticulations. And she does not know when this happened, how awaiting the pouch had become a carnival of fanatic declarations, or how licking a smudged fingertip had become carnal penetration.

She sits rigid and estranged, watching Cleric, yes, but watching

his *pouch* even more. As meagre as their rations are – scarce enough
to blacken the crescent of a pared fingernail – she wonders how
long they have before the purse fails them altogether. Finally he
towers before her, his bare chest shining with hooks of light and
shadow, his outstretched finger glistening about the nub of precious
black.

She cannot move.

'Mimara?' the Ishroi asks, remembering her name.

He calls to both of her selves, to the one who knows but does
not care and to the one who cares but does not know.

But for once it is the *third* incarnation that answers . . .

'No,' it says. 'Get that *poison* away from me.'

Cleric gazes at her for a solemn moment, long enough for the
others to set aside their singular hunger.

There is horror in the Wizard's look.

Lord Incariol gazes at her, his eyes watery white about coin-sized
pupils. 'Mimara . . .'

She repeats herself, finding new wind in her unaccountable
resolution. 'No.'

Desire, she has come to understand, is not the only bottomless
thing . . .

There is motherhood.

She dreams that an absence binds her, a hole that claws at her
very substance. Something is missing, something more precious
than jewels or celebrated works, more sustaining than drink
or love or even breath. Something wonderful that she has
betrayed . . .

Then she is gasping, swallowing at sour consciousness, and
blinking at the visage of Incariol leaning over her.

She does not panic, for everything seems reasonable.

'What are you doing?' she coughs.

'Watching you.'

'Yes. But *why?*'

Even as she asks this, she realizes that only sorcery, subtle sorcery, could have made this visitation possible. She thinks she can even sense it, or at the very least guess at its outlines, the warping of the Wizard's incipient Wards. It was as if he had simply bent the circumference of Achamian's conjuring, pressed into his arcane defences as if they were no more than a half-filled bladder.

'You . . .' the flawless face said. 'You remind me . . . of someone . . . I think . . .'

There is something old about this reply. Not dead nation old, but *doddering* old . . . frail.

'What is it?' she asks. She does not know where this question comes from, nor which traitor gives voice to it.

'I no longer remember,' he replies with a grave whisper.

'No . . . The Qirri . . . Tell me what it is!'

The Wizard murmurs and stirs beside her.

Cleric stares at her with ancient, ancient eyes. The Nail of Heaven traces a perfect white sickle along the outer rim of his brow and skull. He has a smell she cannot identify, a deep smell, utterly unlike the human reek of the Wizard or the scalpers. The rot that softens stone.

'Not all of my kind are buried . . . Some, the greatest, we burn like you.'

And she understands that she has been asking the wrong question – the wrong question all along. Not what, but *who?*

'Who?' she gasps. Suddenly his hand is all that exists. Heavy with power, gentle with love. Her eyes track its flying path to his hip, to the rune-stitched pouch . . .

'Taste . . .' he murmurs in tones of distant thunder. 'Taste and see.'

She can feel the weight of him, the corded strength, hanging above her, and a part of her dreams she is naked and shivering.

His finger lowers toward her, pointing to something that cannot be seen . . .

She leans back her head, parts her lips. She closes her eyes. She can taste her breath, moist and hot, passing from her. The finger is hard and cold. She closes the pliant lobes of her mouth about it, warming and wetting its stubborn white skin. It comes alive, pressing down the centre of her tongue, tracing the line of her gums. It tastes of strength and dead fire.

In the corner of her eye she glimpses the Captain through overlapping lattices of dead grass – a wraith watching.

Above her, Cleric's face dissolves into a porcelain blur. Relief tunnels like lightning through her, swelling the slack hollows about her heart, flushing her extremities. Thin clouds race overhead, black trimmed in starlight, swept into the shapes of wings and scythes. They lend the illusion of surface across the infinite plummet of Heaven like froth drawn along a stream.

He draws his finger back, and a reflex rises within her. She clamps her lips about his knuckle, takes the tip between her teeth, pad and nail. Her tongue soaks whatever residue remains.

He places his hand across her face, thumb against her chin, fingers along her jaw and cheek. He withdraws the penetrating finger slowly, rolling down her lower lip. The Nail of Heaven gleams along its glazed edges. He stands in a single motion, at once swift and utterly soundless. She cannot tear her eyes from him, nor can she smother the longing that wells through her – so profound the ground itself seems to move.

Her mouth tastes of ash and soot and glory . . .

Glory everlasting.

The old Wizard walked.

Once, while travelling between Attrempus and Aöknyssus, he saw a child of no more than ten summers fall from the willow he had climbed in the hope of stealing honey from a great hive. The child broke his neck, died in his father's arms, mouthing inaudible words. Another time, while walking the endless paddies of the Secharib, he saw a woman accused of witchcraft stoned to death. They had bound her with rose wicks so that her struggles scored her skin. Then they cast stone after laughing stone, until she was little more than a crimson worm writhing through the mud her bleeding had conjured from the dust. And once on the road between Sumna and Momemn, he camped at the ruins of Batathent, and in the cool of morning, glimpsed the shadow of Fate cast across the First Holy War.

Adversity lay in all directions, the Nilnameshi were fond of saying. A man need only walk.

'I know what it is,' Mimara said from his side. The sun spiked his eyes when he turned to her. Even when he squinted and raised his hand, it framed her with fiery white, blackened her with encircling brilliance. *She is a shadow. A judging shadow.*

'The Qirri . . .' her silhouette continued. 'I *know* what it is . . .'

An angel-of-the-sun delivering tidings of woe.

'What is it?' he asked. But not because he cared. *He had outrun all caring.*

'*Ashes* . . .' she almost whispered. 'Ashes from the pyre.'

Something in this stirred him, as if she had kicked a long-gutted fire and discovered coals – deep burning coals.

'Ashes? Who?'

He slowed, allowing her to outrun the sun's glare. He blinked at the immobility of her expression.

'Cû'jara Cinmoi . . . I think . . .'

A name drawn from the root of history.

There was nothing to say, so he turned to the trackless world before them. Great flocks of tern rose like steam from the far-ranging folds of dust and grasses.

The plains . . .

They passed like a dream.

CHAPTER TEN

The Istyuli Plains

There is morality and there is cowardice. The two are not to be confused, even though in appearance and effect they are so often the same.

—EKYANNUS I, 44 EPISTLES

If the Gods did not pretend to be human, Men would recoil from them as from spiders.

—ZARATHINIUS, A DEFENCE OF THE ARCANE ARTS

Late Spring, 20 New Imperial Year (4132 Year-of-the-Tusk), The High Istyuli

The shadows of missing things are always cold. And for Varalt Sorweel so very much was missing.

Like the way his mother would read to him in bed or how his father would pretend to lose finger-fights to him. Like laughter or hope.

Loss is at once memory – that is the kernel of its power. If you were to lose the memory with the person – the way Eskeles had said Nonmen lose – then loss would be complete, utter, and we could carry on oblivious. But no. The pain dwells in the balance of loss and retention, in losing and knowing what was lost. In being *two* incommensurate people, one with a father and mother, and one without. One with pride and honour . . .

And one without.

So the old him had continued to come up with jokes, questions, and observations to share with his father. Harweel had talked often with his son. While the new him, the orphan, would shiver, teeter, inner fingers groping for lost handholds. And that recognition, the crashing, all-encompassing cold, would strike him as if for the first time . . .

Your father is dead. Your people are slaves.

You are alone, a captive in the host of your enemy.

But the paradox, some would say tragedy, of human existence is that we so easily raise our lives about absence. We are bred for it. Men are forever counting their losses, hoarding them. There is meaning to be found in victimization, and no small justification. To be wronged is to be *owed*, to walk among debtors wherever you go.

But now even that embittered and self-righteous persona was missing . . . that *boy*.

Sorweel awoke tangled in fragmentary glimpses of the previous night. The last frantic moments with Eskeles, stranded in the very gut of Hell, the face of Serwa, hanging above a world painted in light and the shadows of spitting, gibbering violence . . .

Then Zsoronga's dark and handsome face, smiling in haggard joy.

'You took a knock on the head, Horse-King. Good thing you have more skull than brain!'

White-weathered canvas framed the Successor-Prince with dull brilliance. Sorweel raised a hand as if to block out the sight of him, tried to say something snide but choked on his own throat instead. His entire body buzzed with the deprivations of the previous weeks. He felt like a wineskin squeezed to its final pulpy dregs . . .

The alarm, when it came, wrenched him upright . . .

The Horde. The Ordeal. Eskeles.

'Ho!' Zsoronga cried, nearly toppling backward from his stool.

Sorweel glanced about the stifling confines of his tent, glaring with the urgent stupor of those worried they still dream. The canvas planes glowed with heat. The entrance flap wagged in the breeze, revealing a sliver of baked earth. Porsparian huddled in the corner next to the threshold, watching with a look that was at once wary and forlorn.

'Your slave . . .' Zsoronga said with a dark look at the Shigeki. 'I fear I tried to beat the truth out of him.'

Sorweel tried to focus on his friend, felt his eyes bulge for the effort. Something malodorous hung in the air, a smell he had breathed too long to identify. 'And?' he managed to cough.

'The wretch fears powers greater than me.'

The young King of Sakarpus rubbed his eyes and face, lowered his hands to consider the blood worn into the whorls of his palms. 'The others?' he asked roughly. 'What happened to the others?'

The question snuffed what remained of his friend's hilarity. Zsoronga explained how he and the others had continued riding hard for General Kayûtas, how the treachery of the ground and fugitive exhaustion pulled them down one by one. Captain Harnilas was among the first to fall. A burst heart, Zsoronga assumed, given the way his pony had seized mid-stride. He never saw what became of Tzing. Only he, Tinurit, and four others managed to outdistance the Ten-Yoke Legion, only to be assailed by more Sranc – these from the Horde. 'That was when the longbeards saved us . . .' he said, his voice limping about his disbelief. 'Zaudunyani Knights. Agmundrmen, I think they were.'

Sorweel regarded his friend in the silence that followed. Zsoronga no longer wore the crimson tunic and golden cuirass of a Kidruhil officer. He had donned, rather, the apparel and regalia of his native Zeüm: a battle-sash cinching a jaguar-skin kilt and a wig consisting of innumerable oiled ringlets – symbolic of something, Sorweel imagined. The fabric and accoutrements seemed almost absurdly clean and unused, entirely at odds with the starved, battered, and unwashed form they clothed.

'What about those we left behind,' Sorweel asked. 'What about Obotegwa?'

'Nothing . . . But perhaps that's for the best.'

The young King wanted to ask what he meant, but it seemed more important to ignore the man's tears.

'The Scions are no more, Sorweel. We are all dead.'

They both paused to ruminate. The bindings of the tent complained in a mellow wind. The clamour of the camp seemed to wax and wane with its breezy pulses, as if the sky were a glass that alternately blurred and focused the world's sound.

'And Eskeles?' Sorweel asked, realizing he had only assumed his tutor's survival. 'What about him?'

Zsoronga scowled. 'He's a fat man in times of famine.'

'What?'

'A Zeümi proverb . . . It means men like him never die.'

Sorweel pursed a thoughtful lip, winced at a sudden pain lancing through his sinuses. 'Even though they *should*.'

Zsoronga dropped his gaze as if regretting glib words, then looked up with a helpless smile. 'Zeümi proverbs tend to be harsh,' he said. 'We have always preferred the wisdom that cracks heads.'

Sorweel snorted and grinned, only to find himself tangled in recriminations of his own. So many dead . . . Friends. Comrades. It seemed obscene that he should feel amusement, let alone relief and gratification. For weeks they had strived, warred against distance and frailty to accomplish a mortal mission. They had faltered and they had feared. But they had persevered. They had *won* – and despite the grievous proportions of the toll exacted, that fact cried out with its own demented jubilation.

The Scions had died in glory . . . undying glory. What was a life of bickering and whoring compared with such a death?

Zsoronga did not share his celebratory sentiment.

'Those who fell . . .' Sorweel said in the tentative way of friends hoping to balm guessed-at pains. 'Few are so *lucky*, Zsoronga . . . Truly.'

But even as he spoke, the young King understood he had guessed wrong. The Successor-Prince did not grieve those who had fallen, he grieved his own *survival* . . . or the manner of it.

'There is another . . . saying,' Zsoronga said with uncharacteristic hesitancy. 'Another proverb that you need to know.'

'Yes?'

The Successor-Prince levelled his gaze. 'Courage casts the longest shadow.'

Sorweel nodded. 'And what does that mean?'

Zsoronga flashed him the impatient look people give when called upon to elaborate embarrassing admissions. 'We Zeümi are a people of *deeds*,' he said on a heavy breath. 'We live to honour our dead fathers with wisdom in the court, valour on the fiel—'

'The back door to the heavenly palace,' Sorweel interrupted, recalling the man's explanation of Zeümi religion as a kind of spiritual influence-peddling. 'I remember.'

'Yes . . . Exactly. The saying means that the courage of one man is the *shame* of the other . . .' He pursed his fulsome lips. 'And you, Horse-King . . . What you did . . .'

The night, the dark, the flurry of passion and dim detail came back to Sorweel. He remembered crying out to his friend the instant after Eskeles crashed to earth . . .

'Are you saying I *shamed* you?'

A dour grin. 'In the eyes of my ancestors . . . most certainly.'

Sorweel shook his head in disbelief. 'I apologize . . . Maybe if you're lucky, they'll smuggle you in the slave entrance.'

The Successor-Prince scowled. 'It was a thing of *wonder* . . . what you did,' he said with disconcerting intensity. 'I saw you, Horse-King. I *know* you called to me . . . And *yet I rode on.*' He glared like someone speaking against a mob of baser instincts. 'I will be forever finding my way out from your shadow.'

Sorweel flinched from the look. His eyes settled on Porsparian where he sat humbled and huddled in the airy grey light . . .

'Time to seek the company of cowards,' he offered weakly.

'The *longest* shadow, remember?' Zsoronga said, with an air of someone humiliated for his admission of humiliation. 'The only way – the *only way* – to redeem myself is to stand at your side.'

Sorweel nodded, did his best to shrug away the clamour of adolescent embarrassment, and to comport himself as a man – as a king of a proud people. Zsoronga ut Nganka'kull, the future Satakhan of High Holy Zeüm, was at once apologizing – which was remarkable in and of itself – and begging the most profound of favours: a means of recovering his honour and so securing the fate of his immortal soul.

The young King of Sakarpus offered up his hand, palm up, with his index finger alone extended. One boonsman to another.

Zsoronga frowned and smiled. 'What is this . . . You want me to *smell* it?'

'N-no . . .' Sorweel stammered. '*No!* We call it the *virnorl* . . . "finger-lock" you would say. It is a pledge of unity, a way to say that henceforth, all your battles will be my battles.'

'You sausages,' the Successor-Prince said, clasping his entire hand within the warm bowl of his own. 'Come . . . Our mighty General wishes to see you.'

⸻

Sorweel crouched next to his slave before following Zsoronga outside. 'I can *speak* to you now,' he said in Sheyic, hoping this might elicit some flicker of passion. But the old Shigeki merely regarded him with the same grieved lack of comprehension, as if he had forgotten Sheyic as promptly as Sorweel had learned it.

'More importantly,' he added before stepping clear the cloistered heat, 'I can *listen*.'

Arid sunlight seemed to shower the whole of creation, so bright he stumbled for squinting. He stood at the tent threshold, blinking the liquid from the glare, until the world finally resolved into parched vistas. The camp, the crowded tents and grand pavilions, bleached of colour for brightness . . .

And the horror that encircled it.

Swales of blackening dead humped and pitted the distances. Sranc and more Sranc, teeth hanging spitless about gaping maws, eyes fogged, heaped into an endless array of macabre deadfalls. Limbs predominated in certain places, piled like the sticks Saglanders brought to market to sell as kindle. Heads and torsos prevailed in others, cobbled into mounds that resembled stacks of rotting fish. Great smears of black scored the far-flung mats, where the witches had burned their countless thousands. They reminded him of the charcoal grounds to the south of Sakarpus, only with bodies instead of trees charred to stumped anonymity. These marked the greatest concentrations of dead.

The reek struck too deep to be smelled. It could only be breathed.

The sight unsettled him, not for the grisly detail, but because of the preposterous scale. He wanted to rejoice, for it seemed that was what a true son of Sakarpus should do seeing their ancestral foe laid out to the horizon. But he could not. Breathing the carrion wind, glancing across the carcass heights, he found himself *mourning*, not for the Sranc, whose obscenity blocked all possibility of compassion, but for the innocence of a world that had never seen such sights.

For the boy he had been before awakening.

'Even if I survive,' Zsoronga said from his side, 'none will believe me when I return.'

'We must make sure you die then,' Sorweel replied.

The Successor-Prince smirked about a worried glance. They trekked on in awkward silence, sorting through industrious crowds of Inrithi, wending down tented alleys. Fairly every man Sorweel glimpsed bore some sign of the previous night's battle, whether it be bandages clotted about appalling wounds or the divided stares of those trying to stumble clear of memories of violence and fury. Many seemed to recognize him, and some even lowered their faces – in accordance, he imagined, with some precept of jnan, the arcane etiquette of the Three Seas.

The awkward transformation of his relationship with Zsoronga, he realized with no little dismay, was but the beginning of the changes his thoughtless courage had wrought. *Courage* . . . It seemed such a foolish word, naught but the scribble of a child compared to the lunacy of the previous night. When he dared glimpse his memories, he suffered only the crowding of dread and terror. He felt a *coward*, looking back, so laughably far from the hero Zsoronga was making of him.

A mob of caste-nobles and Kidruhil officers milled about the entrance to Kayûtas's command tent, and Sorweel simply assumed that he and Zsoronga would be forced to while away the watches in listless conversation. But faces turned to regard them as they approached, across the outer rind of warriors at first, then deeper as word of their arrival passed from lip to lip. The rumble of conversations evaporated. Sorweel and Zsoronga found themselves standing dumbfounded before their accumulated gazes.

'*Huorstra kum de faul bewaren mirsa!*' a towering longbeard cried from the assembly's midst. The man shouldered his way through the others, his eyes bright with a kind of vicious joy. '*Sorweel Varaltshau!*' he bellowed, seizing him in a great, black-armoured embrace. '*Famforlic kus thassa!*'

Suddenly everyone was cheering, and the young King found himself thrust into the crowd's congratulatory heart, shaking hands, returning embraces, nodding and thanking strangers with a kind of witless, breathless confusion. He acknowledged face after bruised face, even hugged a man blindfolded with bandages. In a matter of heartbeats he was delivered to the command tent, where he fairly tripped past the Pillarian Guards and into the washed light of the interior – so flustered that it seemed a minor miracle that he remembered to fall to his knees.

'*She positions you . . .*'

Anasûrimbor Kayûtas watched him from his chair, obviously amused by the spectacle of his arrival. Even in his Kidruhil cuirass and mail skirts, he sat with feline repose, his sandalled feet stretched across the mats before him, watching with the remote, lolling manner of an opium eater. Sorweel knew instantly that the man had not slept – and that he would not be the worse for it.

The air was stifling, as much for the sunlight that frosted

the canvas ceiling as for all the exhaling mouths. Five scribes crowded the sheaf-laden table to his right, and numerous others stood milling in what little space remained: officers and caste-nobles for the most part. Sorweel saw Eskeles among them, decked in his crimson Mandate robes, his left eye swollen into a greasy purple crease. He also glimpsed Anasûrimbor Serwa standing as tall as many of the men, swanlike in gowns of embroidered white. A memory of her arcane embrace whispered through him.

Kayûtas allowed the uproar to subside before gesturing for him to stand. The Prince-Imperial was not long in waiting: something immaculate in his manner seemed to cut against all things unruly.

'Teüs Eskeles has told us everything,' he declared. 'You have saved us, Sorweel. You . . .'

A broken chorus of cheers and shouts rose from those gathered within the tent.

'I . . . I did nothing,' the Sakarpi King replied, trying to avoid the Swayali Grandmistress's gaze.

'Nothing?' The Kidruhil General frowned, scratched the flaxen plaits of his beard. 'You read the signs, like a true son of the plains. You *saw* the doom our foe had prepared for us. You counselled your commander to take the only action that could save us. And then, in the moment of utmost crisis, you lent your shoulder to Eskeles, *cast your life* on the longest of odds, so that he might alert us . . .' He glanced up toward his sister, then looked back, grinning like an uncle trying to teach his nephew how to gamble. 'Nothing has ever been so impressive.'

'I did only what I . . . what I thought sensible.'

'Sense?' Kayûtas said with scowling good nature. 'There are as many sensibilities as there are passions, Sorweel. *Terror* has a sense all its own: flee, shirk, abandon – whatever it takes to carry away one's skin. But *you*, you answered to the sense that transcends base desire. And we stand before you breathing, *victorious*, as a result.'

The Sakarpi King glanced about wildly, convinced he was the butt of some cruel joke. But everyone assembled watched with a kind of indulgent expectation, as if understanding he was but a boy still, unused to the burden of communal accolades. Only Zsoronga's solitary black face betrayed worry.

'I . . . I-I know not what to say . . . You honour me.'

The Prince-Imperial nodded with a wisdom that belied the adolescent tenderness of his beard. 'That is my intent,' he said. 'I have even sent a party of crippled riders back to Sakarpus to bear word of your heroic role to your kinsmen . . .'

'You what?' Sorweel fairly coughed.

'It's a political gesture, I admit. But the glory is no less real.'

In his soul's eye, Sorweel could see a wracked line of Kidruhil filing through the ruins of the Herders' Gate, outland conquerors, oppressors, crying out the treachery of Harweel's only son, how *he had saved* the very host that had laid Sakarpus low . . .

Nausea welled through him. Shame squirmed in his breast, clawing his ribs, scratching his heart.

'I . . . I don't know what to say . . .' he stammered.

'You need not say anything,' Kayûtas said with an indulgent smile. 'Your pride is clear for all to see.'

'*She is hiding you . . .*'

And for the first time he felt it, the impunity of standing unseen. He had stood before Anasûrimbor Kayûtas before. He had suffered his raking gaze – he knew what it meant *to be known* by an enemy, to have his fears counted, his vengeful aspirations reckoned, and so transformed into levers that could be used against him. Now he felt as if he were peeking at the man through his mother's shielding fingers. And his cheeks stung for the memory of Porsparian rubbing Yatwer's spit into them.

'I've had you entered into the lists as the new Captain of the Scions,' Kayûtas continued. 'Disbanded they may be, but their honour will be yours. We were fortunate that Xarotas Harnilas possessed wisdom enough to recognize your sense – I will not trust fortune to so favour us a second time. Henceforth, you will attend me and my staff . . . And you will be accorded all the glory and privilege that belongs to a Believer-King.'

She had placed him here. The Dread Mother of Birth . . . Was the courage even his?

It seemed an important question, but then the legends seemed littered with the confusion of heroes and the Gods that favoured them. Perhaps his hand simply was her hand . . .

He recoiled from the thought.

'May I beg one boon?'

A flicker of mild surprise. 'Of course.'

'Zsoronga . . . I would have him accompany me if I could.'

Kayûtas scowled, and several onlookers exchanged not-so-discreet whispers. For perhaps the first time, the Sakarpi King understood his friend's importance to the Anasûrimbor. Of all the world's remaining nations, only Zeüm posed a credible threat to the New Empire.

'You know that he conspires against us?' the Prince-Imperial said, switching to effortless Sakarpic. Suddenly the two of them stood alone in a room walled with strangers.

'I have my fears . . .' Sorweel began, lying smoothly. 'But . . .'

'But what?'

'He no longer doubts the truth of your father's war. No one does.'

The implication was as clear as it was surprising, for in all his life Sorweel had never counted his among devious souls.

The first son of Nganka'kull *wavered*. To bring him into the Prince-Imperial's retinue could be the very thing his conversion required . . .

And that, Sorweel suddenly realized, was the Aspect-Emperor's goal: to have a *believer* become Satakhan.

'Granted,' Kayûtas said, switching to the dismissive air of men who scarce had time for accommodations. He made a two-fingered gesture to one of his scribes, who began fingering through sheaves of vellum.

'But I fear you have one last duty to discharge,' the General said in Sheyic just as Sorweel glanced about for some cue that the audience had ended. 'A mortal one.'

The omnipresent smell of rot seemed to take on a sinister tang.

'My arm is your arm, Lord General.'

This reply occasioned a heartbeat of scrutiny.

'The Great Ordeal has all but exhausted its supplies. We *starve*, Sorweel. We have too many mouths and too little food. The time has come to put certain mouths to the knife . . .'

Sorweel swallowed against a sudden pang in his breast.

'What are you saying?'

'You must put down your slave, Porsparian, in accordance with my father's edict.'

'I must what?' he asked blinking. So there was a joke after all.

'You must kill your slave before sunrise tomorrow, or *your life* will be forfeit,' Kayûtas said, speaking in a tone as much directed to the assembled caste-nobles as to the Believer-King standing before him. *Even heroes*, he was saying, *must answer to our Holy Aspect-Emperor*.

'Do you understand?'

'Yes,' Sorweel replied, speaking with a determination utterly at odds with the tumult that was his soul.

He understood. He was alone, a captive in the host of his enemy.

He would do whatever . . . kill *whomever* . . .

'*Chosen by the Gods* . . .'

Anything to see the Aspect-Emperor dead and his father avenged.

∽∽∽

Sorweel returned to his tent alone, his back still warm for all the slapping, his ears still hot with the chorus of overwrought acclaim. Porsparian stood before the entrance, forlorn and emaciated and as motionless as a sentinel. The sight fairly winded the young King.

'Follow me,' he told the man, his gaze scratched with incredulity. The old Shigeki slave regarded him with a momentary squint, then without worry – or even curiosity – he struck out *ahead* of his master, leading him into the fields of rotting Sranc. Sorweel could only gape at the sight: a little nut-brown man, walking stooped, his limbs bowed as if bent to the bundle of his many years, picking his way across the packed dead.

So the slave led the King, and perhaps this was how it should have been, given the way Sorweel felt himself dwindle with every step. He could scarce believe what he was about to do . . . Execution. When he forced himself to confront the prospect, his body and soul rebelled the way he had once feared they would in the thick of battle. The lightness of the hands. The starlings battling in his gut, loosening his bowel. The wires that hooked his head and shoulders into a pose just shy of a cringe. The incessant murmur of dread . . .

Men often find themselves stranded in circumstance, stumbling toward goals not of their making, surrounded by absurdities they can scarce believe. They assume the little continuities that characterize their moments will carry them through their entire lives. They forget the volatility of the whole, the way tribes and nations trip like drunks through history. They forget that Fate is a whore.

Porsparian hobbled ahead, picking a path through the carapace of dead. Sorweel quickly lost sight of the camp behind the blood-slicked mounds. When he looked out, death and far-flung rot were all he could see. Sranc. When he glimpsed them in fragments – a face nestled in the crook of an arm, a hand hanging from a raised wrist – they almost seemed human. When he gazed across them en masse, they seemed the issue of a drained sea. As bad as it had been in the camp, the reek welled palpable from the sweating tangle, to the point where coughing and gagging became one and the same, until smell became a *taste* that seemed to hang against the skin – an odour that could be licked. Ravens made summits of skulls, jumped from crown to crown spearing eye sockets. Vultures hunched and squabbled over individual spoils even though all was carrion. The whine of flies was multiplied until it became a singular hum.

Porsparian walked and he numbly followed, at times skidding across offal or wincing at the crack of ribbed hollows beneath his boots. He alternately found himself studying the Shigeki slave, his shoulders crooked about hard huffing breaths, and avoiding all sight of him. He knew now that he had deceived himself, that he had failed to press the enigmatic man for answers out of *fear*, and not because the intricacies of Sheyic defeated him. He had reacted, not as a man, but as a little boy, embracing the childish instinct to skulk and to avoid, to besiege fact with cowardly pretense. All this time, they could not speak and so were strangers, each perhaps as frightful to the other. And now, when he could finally ask, finally discover what madness the Dread Mother had prepared for him, he had to kill the little . . . *priest*, Zsoronga had called him

His slave, Porsparian.

Sorweel paused, suddenly understanding Zsoronga's cryptic tone when he had asked him about Obotegwa. He had been thinking of the Aspect-Emperor's edict, the very edict behind the crime Sorweel was about to commit. If he himself balked at the prospect of murdering a terrifying stranger, what would it be like for Zsoronga to put down a beloved childhood companion – a surrogate father, even? Perhaps it was for the best that the Istyuli swallow the wise old man whole, that Obotegwa stumble into a small pile of human rubble – cloth and scattered bones – marking nothing.

Sorweel found himself blinking at the slave's form labouring through carrion ravines.

'Porsparian . . .' he called, coughing against the stench.

The old man ignored him. A clutch of ravens cried out in his stead, their caws like a small army of files scraping edges of tin.

'Porsparian, stop!'

'Not there yet!' the man hacked over his shoulder.

'Not where?' Sorweel cried, hastening after the agile slave. Bones popped in stiffening meat. Arrow shafts cracked. What was the man doing? Was this his manner of fleeing?

'Porsparian . . . Look. I'm *not* going kill you.'

'What happens to me is not important,' the Shigeki wheezed. Sorweel suffered dim memories of his grandfather in his final shameful days, how he had taken to wilful and insensible acts, if only to answer some prideful instinct to *do* . . .

'Porsparian . . .' he said, at last seizing the man's bony shoulder. He was going to tell the man that he could run, that he was free to risk the open plains, perhaps trust in the Goddess to deliver him, but instead he released the man, shocked by the immediacy of the bones beneath his tunic, by the sheer ease he had yanked him about, as if the man were naught but a doll, pigskin wrapped about desert-dry wood.

When had he last eaten?

Cursing in some harsh tongue, the slave resumed his senseless trek, and Sorweel stood, absorbing the realization that Porsparian would not survive on the plains, that to set him free was simply to condemn him to a slower, far more miserable demise . . .

That anything short of execution would be an act of cowardice.

A moment of madness ensued, one which Sorweel would remember for the rest of his life. He choked on a scream that was a laugh that was a sob that was a father's soothing whisper. A kind of macabre intensity bubbled up out of his surroundings, an inversion of seeing, so that the jutting spears and the innumerable arrow shafts that stubbled the summits of dead pinned and staked his skin. The foggy glare of hundreds from limb-thatched burrows, the tongues like hanging snails, the entrails spilling from shells of armour, drying into papyrus . . .

She is positioning you . . .

How?

As mad as it sounds, I really have come to save Mankind . . .

What?

Fuh-Fuh-Father!

And then he saw it . . . standing with the grace and proportion of an Ainoni vase, regarding him, the knife of its long beak folded against its neck. A *stork*, perched upon purpling dead as though upon a promontory of high stone, its snowy edges framed by bleached sky.

And he was racing after the diminutive slave, tripping, skidding.

'What's going on?' he cried, seizing the man. 'You *will* tell me!'

The rutted face betrayed no surprise, no anger or fear whatsoever.

'Pollution has seized the hearts of Men,' the slave rasped. 'The Mother prepares our *cleansing.*'

The slave raised warm fingers to Sorweel's wrists, gently tugged his hands from his shoulders.

'And all thi—?'

'Is deception! *Deception!*'

Sorweel stumbled, so placid had Porsparian seemed, and such was the fury of his barked reply.

'So-so his war . . .' the Sakarpi King stammered.

'He is a demon who wears men the way we don clothes!'

'But his *war* . . .' He scraped his gaze across the tossed and tangled carcasses about them. 'It is real . . .'

Porsparian snorted.

'All is false. And all who follow him are damned!'

'But his war . . . *Porsparian!* Look around you! Look around you and tell me his war *is not real!*'

'What? Because he has sent his followers against the Sranc? The world is filled with Sranc!'

'And what of the Consult Legion . . . the Sranc who killed my comrades?'

'Lies! Lies!'

'How can you know?'

'I know nothing. I speak!'

And with that he resumed his bandy march into the dead.

The slave picked his way across a swale of blasted and blackened Sranc and into a region of sorcerous destruction. In his soul's eye, the young King could see the Swayali witch hanging a hard stone's throw above, a slender beauty aglow in the curlicue bloom of her billows, dispensing lines and sheets of cutting light. He shook his head at the vision . . .

'Porsparian!'

The little man ignored him, though he did slow his pace. He peered downward as he walked, looking this way and that, as if searching for a lost kellic.

'Tell me!' Sorweel called out, his wonder giving way to irritation. 'Tell me what She *wants*!'

'A mighty lord died here . . .' he heard the man mutter.

'Yatwer!' the Sakarpi King cried, throwing the name like a cold and heavy stone from his breast. 'What does She want of me?'

'*Here* . . .' The old man's voice was thick with a kind of unsavoury relish. 'Beneath the skinnies.'

Sorweel stood dumbfounded, watching the mad fool heave at the burnt Sranc thatched beneath his feet. 'The *earth* . . .' he grunted, tossing aside an arm and attached shoulder. 'Must . . . uncover . . .'

The Sakarpi King gazed witless. When they had set out, he could scarce look at Porsparian without flinching from the madness of what he had to do. But the Shigeki slave seemed to care not in the least, even though he *had* to know he was doomed. Not in the least! Sorweel had followed him out here into carrion *to cut his throat*, and the man acted as if this were but a trifling compared to what he . . .

Cold flushed through and about the young man. He found himself casting wild looks across the surrounding dead, as if he were a murderer suddenly unsure of the secrecy of his crime.

The Goddess.

The King bent his back and joined the slave in his grisly labour.

The forms were uniformly burned; many of them possessed cauterized slices – amputations. He cleared two that had lost their legs, one at the hips, the other high on the thigh, as if they had been felled side by side, reaved as if by a single scythe. Where those on the top had been mostly scorched to husks, those below remained primarily raw and wet. Their eyes glared out with an aimless, smoky curiosity. Not knowing what the man intended, Sorweel simply grabbed the carcasses adjacent to those his slave wrenched into sunlight. He cast hooded looks over his shoulders.

He found himself troubled by the *weight* of the creatures, the way their scrawniness belied a brute density. The corpses became colder as the toil continued.

They found the earth sodden with filth – puddled. They gasped for their effort, gagged for the stench they had unleashed. Sorweel watched Porsparian fall to his knees in the heart of the muck oval they had cleared. A grave dug from the dead.

He watched him raise and kiss the polluted earth . . .

The wind tousled the King's lengthening hair, tumbled across all visible creation, troubling the emanations. The flies hummed undisturbed. Ravens punctuated the distance with random cries.

He watched his slave scallop muck clear, glimpsed a skull unearthed beneath the shadow of his hands. Peering, he willed himself to breathe through his horror. He watched the man gather putrid mud, then mould a face about the bone, all the while murmuring prayers in some harsh and exotic tongue. Then he watched as he skinned a Sranc face with terrifying economy, watched him pad the result across the earthen face he had prepared for it. The King experienced something outside horror or exaltation.

He watched his slave stroke and caress the slick surfaces: forehead, brow, lip, cheek. He watched and he listened, until the rasp that was the slave's prayer became a drifting smoke that obscured all other sound.

He watched life – impossible life – rise into the inhuman skin.

He watched Yatwer's eyes snap open.

He heard the groan of the earth.

———— ⬥ ————

The Goddess smiles . . .

The old man crouches over her, frozen like a man caught in the commission of some obscenity. Something shivers through the hideous earth. Scabrous arms burst from the soil to either side . . . Clotted bones. Knotted worms.

The slave stumbles back, staggers into the clutch of the horrified King.

They watch the Goddess exhume her own corpse. She trowels away muck and viscous slop, reveals the ivory comb of her ribs. She reaches into her muddy abdomen, excavates her cadaverous womb . . .

The very ground croaks and groans beneath them, the complaint of some cosmological hinge – existence pried too far from its essential frame.

She draws a pouch from the pit below her stomach, raises it pinched in fingers of filth and bone. She smiles. Tears of blood stream from her earthen eyes. The watching men gasp for the sorrow of a mother's endless Giving . . .

So many. So many children born . . .

So many taken.

The King trips to his knees. He crawls forward to receive her Gift, crawls with the shame of an inconstant son. He snatches the pouch as if from a leper. It lies stiff and cold in his fingers, like a dead man's tongue. He scarcely sees it for his Mother's dirt glare. He looks back to the slave, who sobs for joy and horror. . . He turns back to his Goddess . . .

But She is no more, nothing but a grotesque face, a monstrosity, moulded above an overturned grave.

'What just happened?' the King cries to the slave. 'What just happened?'

The slave says nothing. He climbs to his feet, hobbles from the macabre clearing back into the dead with an invalid's gait. He stumbles up a slope of pitched carcasses. He pauses before a spear that juts from the buzzing summit.

The King calls out to him, beseeching . . .

The slave places his chin upon the spear point, lifts his hands high in heavenly supplication.

'What the Mother gives . . .' he cries out to the King. 'You must take!'

He smiles fleetingly, as if regretting things both inevitable and criminal. Then Porsparian nesh Varalti drops. He never reaches his knees. He hangs, rather, from the inside crown of his skull, then slowly tips to his side. He seems to vanish among the strewn forms.

One more dead skinny.

The King of Sakarpus staggered back alone, trudging across mad ways of the dead. Zsoronga was waiting for him when he returned. Neither man had any words to speak, so they simply sat side by side in the dust, staring into their hands.

Zsoronga was first to break their fast of silence. He clasped his friend's shoulder and said, 'Things done are done.'

Sorweel did not reply. Each of them gazed in his own absent direction, like dogs leashed to the shade. They watched the endless to and fro of warlike men across and between the tents. The Army of the Middle-North. They watched the dust-devils spinning in and out of faint existence between the innumerable pennants and banners.

'Did he tell you?' Zsoronga asked. 'Your little priest . . . Did he tell you what . . . what *She* wants?'

Sorweel turned to regard his friend with a wide and wary glare. He knew he could trust the man – with his life if need be – and this comforted him in a way he had never known. Zsoronga was a true boonsman. But he also knew that he could not trust his *face*, that he could not risk saying anything for the shadows the Anasûrimbor would glimpse within him.

'Yes,' he replied, looking back to the Men of the Ordeal. 'What is done is done.'

When the Successor-Prince finally departed, Sorweel retreated from the setting sun into the gloom of his tent. He pulled the pouch from his belt. The muck had dried to ash about its edges. He brushed it away with trembling fingers, noticing for the first time the dizzying patterns burned into the age-old leather. Crescents. Crescents within crescents.

Broken circles, he decided, glimpsing the gold-thread circumfixes embroidered along the hem of his own tunic.

Broken circumfixes.

He tugged free the clip of chapped bronze that held its mouth closed. He already knew what it contained, for as King of Sakarpus, he was also High Keeper of the Hoard. Nevertheless, he tipped the pouch so that he might hold it in his callused palm: a sphere of ancient iron . . .

A Chorae. A holy Tear of God.

The Swayali enclave formed an encampment all its own within the greater camp. When the host set stake across rolling or broken pasture, the witches' tents always tattooed the hazy vista, an oval of shining ochre among the jumbled phalanxes of canvas. The Scions had sat and pondered the sight more than a few evenings, like every other company in the Army. Charampa, in particular, was given to dreaming aloud. The 'Granary,' he called it. Here his little brother was *starving*, and yet the Granary remained closed. Several times he had leapt to his feet to display the hook lifting his skirts, crying out for food to feed his little brother. And though everyone about Zsoronga's hearth laughed with crazed merriment, they also became exceedingly reluctant to encourage the Cingulati Prince. Charampa was far too fond of his little brother.

He was also the reason why none of the witches strayed from their enclave – save Anasûrimbor Serwa. As the days piled into months, as the memories of wives and lovers became more and more elusive, the famed Swayali witches, the Nuns, became a kind of narcotic. More than a few little brothers had been throttled for mere glimpse or rumour.

At first, Sorweel had no clue as to why he stalked the camp searching for the Granary. He had lain on his cot for watches, pinned by an exhaustion unlike any he had known, one that made slop of his centre, as if he were naught but a head and limbs sutured to a heap of entrails. He had stared at the canvas ceiling, glimpsing portents in water stains, feeling the prickle of Porsparian's continuous absence. And then he was up, answering to a restlessness he could not quite feel. And he was walking.

Initially he decided he sought out the Swayali because he needed to *thank* Anasûrimbor Serwa for saving him. But this rationale, for all its convenience, did not long survive its insincerity. The unkind fact was that Sorweel felt *no* gratitude. Of the many Three Seas peculiarities that Zsoronga called out for disgust and ridicule, none occasioned quite the same cutting vehemence as the witches. The Successor-Prince thought them worse than whores and certainly more accursed. 'They make pits of their *mouths*,' he said once, referring to the Tusk's ancient condemnation of prostitutes. But Sorweel's lack of gratitude had nothing to do with grudges against licentious women. Since the Sakarpi considered all sorcery anathema, the Swayali struck him as little more than a wicked anomaly. Yet one more Three Seas perversion.

No. He felt no gratitude because he no longer considered his life a gift.

Stars fogged the vault of Heaven in light. Clouds like wisps of tugged wool formed the illusion of a surface so that looking up seemed like gazing into waters of consummate clarity, an ocean of diamond emptiness. The ways of the camp were all but abandoned. Were it not for the odd voices and the moans of the ailing,

he would have thought it emptied of Men. Maybe it was combination of quiet and cool air, or maybe it was the stench that
soaked the edges of his every breath, but the place seemed ancient
and haunted, and the shadows seemed to boil with unseen threats.

He found the Granary more by chance than by any unerring
sense of direction. He slowed to a wary saunter when the sagging
pyramids of its roofs rose into view. The tents were of the Ainoni
parasol variety, with a single pole hoisting a square frame that
formed the tasselled edges of the roof. They were pitched one
against the other with their entrances turned inward so that their
felt backs walled in the enclave. He had heard the tale of some
Galeoth fool burning his fingers to stubs trying to slit a peephole
through one of the greased panels. But who knew whether this
rumour were true or something calculated precisely to prevent
Galeoth fools from cutting peepholes. The Grandmistress of the
Swayali was an Anasûrimbor, after all.

He followed the enclave's outer circuit, his ears pricked to voices
he could not hear, his arm hairs tingling with the anxious expectation of sorcery. In his soul's eye, he saw the witches hanging above
the oceanic heave of the Horde. For his life, he could not think
of what to do next. Twin torches on poles illuminated the entrance,
drawing shags of ochre from the otherwise blue tent walls. Two
heavily armoured men stood between them, speaking in voices as
muted as the torchlight was dim. They fell silent the instant they
spied him.

They were both clean-shaven, Nansur traditionalists, but the
insignia stamped into the plates of their hauberks were unfamiliar
to him – no surprise there. The question was whether they would
recognize him.

'I have come to see Anasûrimbor Serwa,' he blurted in answer
to their scowling gaze.

The two regarded him for a torch-lit heartbeat. The taller one smiled, an expression rendered malicious for the play of shadow across his hard face. He stepped aside, saying, 'She told us you might come.'

The guardsman led him into the Granary with the same uncanny focus – the same thoughtless *discipline* – that seemed to characterize so many Men of the Ordeal: no fatuous words, no posturing or bored bullying. A Sakarpi guard would have bickered until either cowed by threats or bribed.

The Granary's courtyard was as dusty and trampled as any other ground in the camp, and with few exceptions, the surrounding tents were every bit as dark. Several censors had been set across the expanse, their smoky issue barely visible in the starlight. He breathed deep their odour: a pungent astringent of some kind, one specifically concocted to nullify the stench rising from the rotting miles surrounding them – or so he imagined.

The tall Nansur led him to a parasol tent on the far side of the oval courtyard, one identical to the others, save that it had been physically stitched to the tents adjoining. The entrance flap had been negligently drawn, revealing a golden sickle of interior light. Sorweel's breath and ligaments tightened with every nearing step, as if he were a bow slowly drawn. The slit in the tent bobbed in his vision with erotic intensity, as though a candle had been lit beneath a courtesan's skirts and he were about to glimpse the regions between her knees.

Perhaps he had come to feed his little brother after all.

''Ware her, my King,' Eskeles had said that fateful day in the Umbilicus. 'She walks with the Gods . . .'

The Swayali guardsman bid him pause with a polite gesture, then fell to his knees and called softly into the opening. Sorweel glimpsed ornate carpets and the odd leg of furnishing, nothing more.

If anyone replied, he did not hear it. The guardsmen simply

stood and drew aside the ornately embroidered flap. 'Kneel!' he hissed as Sorweel strode into the lane of light. Ignoring him, the Sakarpi King ducked into the interior and stood blinking in the light. Three bronze lanterns hung from a three-armed bracket set high on the centre pole, all of them dark. He had once asked Eskeles why he bothered with lanterns when he could spark brighter lights with mere words. *'Because lanterns burn whether I remember them or not,'* he had said. *'Think of the way trivia weighs against your heart . . .'* Anasûrimbor Serwa, apparently, did not mind the burden of sorcerous illumination: a point of blinding white hung in the corner, twinkling like a pilfered star. Its brilliance revealed faint patterns of russet in the felt walls – sigils or plant motifs – and rendered the room's furnishings stark with shadow. Stacked chests. A cot, much the same as his own, save for the luxury of the blankets and pillows heaped across it. A worktable with canvas camp chairs. His boots felt an insult to the carpets beneath him: ranging landscapes wrought in black and silver, stylized according to exotic sensibilities. An unfamiliar perfume hung in the air.

The Grandmistress sat hunched over the worktable, wearing naught but a silken shift – her sleeping garb, Sorweel imagined. She hung her head to one side as she read, so that her hair fell in lazy blond wings across her right shoulder. She had hooked her bare feet about the forward legs of the chair – an undignified pose, and all the more erotic for it. Silk hung loose about her breasts, and pulled tight across her parted thighs. The hairlessness of her legs made her seem a little girl and so poisoned his desire with a peculiar shame.

Sin. Everything Three Seas, no matter how awe-inspiring or beautiful, had to be greased in sin.

'My brother finds you odd . . .' she said, apparently still absorbed by the inked lines before her.

'I find your brother odd.'

This occasioned a small smile – as well as her attention. She turned to regard him, careless enough with her knees to make him forget how to breathe. He struggled to remind himself that for all her wanton youth, she was the most powerful woman in all Eärwa, short of her Empress mother . . . who *had* been a whore.

'Have you come to thank me, or have you come to woo?'

The Sakarpi King scowled. 'To thank you.'

Her eyes ranged across him with a boldness that would have seen a Sakarpi wife or daughter whipped.

'That pouch . . . hanging from your hip . . . Where did you find that?'

He swallowed, at last understanding the reason for this otherwise inexplicable visitation.

'It's an heirloom. As ancient as my family.'

She nodded as if believing him.

'That motif . . . the triple crescent . . .'

'What about it?' he asked, far too aware of the proximity of her gaze to his groin.

At last her eyes climbed to meet his own. Her look was cool, remote in the way of old and prideful widows.

'That is the Far Antique mark of *my* family . . . the Anasûrimbor of Trysë.'

Sorweel struggled to speak around memories of the Goddess reaching into the muck of her womb.

'Would you like it back?'

A laugh like a sneezing cat.

'You seem more insolent than thankful.'

And in a heartbeat, Sorweel understood how the penetration of the Anasûrimbor, their godlike cunning, was as much their greatest *weakness* as their greatest strength. Men, Zsoronga had said, were like children to them.

Who fears children?

'I apologize,' he said. 'The past weeks have been . . . difficult. This afternoon I . . . I murdered my slave in your father's name.'

He saw Porsparian slump from the upright spear, hang twitching . . .

'You loved him,' she observed with something resembling pity.

He saw the light of watching fade from the slave's yellow eyes.

'Here . . .' Sorweel said, grasping the pouch. 'Take it as a gift.'

You are mad, a voice whispered in some corner of his soul.

'I would rather you keep it,' she replied with a frown almost identical to her brother's. 'I'm not sure I like you, Horse-King.'

Sorweel nodded as if in apology.

'Then I shall woo you . . .' he said, turning to step back out into the cool Istyuli night.

He had half-hoped she would call him back but was not surprised when she did not. He crossed the incense-fogged expanse of the Granary, his thoughts roiling in that strange fingerless way that prevents them from gripping your expression. He walked the way a man who had just gambled his freedom might walk: with the nimble gait of those preparing to run.

Anasûrimbor Serwa . . . She was one of the Few, among the greatest to practise the arcane arts, were the rumours to be believed.

'What the Mother gives . . .'

And he had carried a Chorae – *concealed* – within an arm's span of her embrace.

'You must take.'

⸻

The following weeks did not so much pass like a dream as they seemed like one in hindsight.

Despite Anasûrimbor Kayûtas's fine words the day following the Battle of the Horde, he did not so much as consult with Sorweel once when it came to the Sranc, let alone the mountain of trivial issues that confronted any great host on the march. Sorweel and Zsoronga spent most of their time mooning about the perimeter of the Prince-Imperial's entourage, waiting to be called into whatever the ongoing debate.

They were accorded the honour of martial advisers, but in reality they were little more than messengers – runners. This fact seemed to weigh more heavily on Zsoronga than Sorweel, who would have been a runner for his father eventually, had the past months never happened. The Successor-Prince sometimes spent entire watches cursing their lot while they supped together: the Zeümi court, Sorweel had come to realize, was a kind of arena, a place where the nobility were inclined to count slights and nurture grudges, and where politicking through the dispensation of privileges had been raised to a lethal form of art. Zsoronga did not so much despise the actual work of bearing missives – Sorweel himself genuinely savoured the freedom of riding through and about seas of trudging men. What he could not abide, Sorweel decided, was the *future*, the fact that, when he finally found his way back to Domyot, he would be forced to describe things his countrymen could not but see as indignities. That in the sly calms between official discourse, they might murmur 'Zsoronga the Runner' to one another and laugh.

More and more, Sorweel saw fractions of his former self in the Zeümi Prince – glimpses of Sorweel the Orphan, Sorweel the Mourner. Zsoronga had learned a dismaying truth about himself in fleeing when Sorweel had turned to save Eskeles. He had also lost his entire entourage – his Brace, as the Zeümi called their boonsmen – as well as his beloved Obotegwa. For all his worldly manner, the Successor-Prince had never experienced *loss* in his privileged life. Now he was stranded, as Sorweel had been stranded, in the host of his enemy. And now he was burdened, as Sorweel had been burdened, with questions of his own worth and honour.

They did not so much speak of these things as act around them, the way young men are prone to do, with only brotherly looks and warm-handed teasing for proof of understanding.

Zsoronga still asked him about the Goddess from time to time, his manner too eager for Sorweel's comfort. The Sakarpi King would simply shrug and say something about waiting for signs, or make some weak joke about Zsoronga petitioning his dead relatives. The toll Zsoronga had paid in self-respect had turned the man's wary hope into a kind of pressing need. Where before he had feared for his friend's predicament, now he *wanted* Sorweel to be the instrument of the Goddess – even needed him to be. Each day seemed to add a granule of spite to the hatred he was slowly accumulating in his soul. He even began to take risks in Kayûtas's distracted presence – insolent looks, snide remarks – trifles that seemed to embolden him as much as they alarmed Sorweel.

'*Pray* to Her!' Zsoronga began to urge. 'Mould faces in the earth!'

Sorweel could only look at him in horror, insist that he was trying to no avail, fretting all the while about what traces of his own intent the Anasûrimbor might glimpse in the man's face.

He had to be careful, exceedingly careful. He knew full well the power and cunning of the Aspect-Emperor, having lost his father, his city, and his dignity to him. He knew far better than Zsoronga.

This was why, when he finally mustered the courage to ask his friend about the narindari, those chosen by the Gods to kill, he did so in the guise of passing boredom.

'They are the most feared assassins in the World,' the

Successor-Prince replied. 'Men for whom murder is prayer. Fairly all the Cults have them – and they say Ajokli has no devotees save narindari . . .'

'But what use would the Gods have of assassins, when they need only deliver calumny and disaster?'

Zsoronga frowned as if at uncertain memories. 'Why do the Gods require devotion? Sacrifice? Lives are easy to take. But souls – souls must be *given*.'

This was how Sorweel came to think of himself as a kind of divine thief.

'What the Mother gives . . . You must take.'

The problem was that in the passage of days he felt nothing of this divinity. He ached and he hungered. He scratched his buttocks and throttled his little brother. He squatted as other squatted, holding his breath against the reek of the latrines. And he continually *doubted* . . .

Primarily because what divinity he witnessed belonged to the Anasûrimbor. As before, Kayûtas remained a lodestone for his gaze, but where Sorweel had peered after his Horse and Circumfix standard across the massing of faraway columns, now he could watch him from a distance of several spans. He was, Sorweel came to realize, a consummate commander, orchestrating the activities of numberless thousands with mere words and manner. Requests and appraisals would arrive, and responses and reprimands would be dispatched. Failures would be scrutinized, alternatives considered. Successes would be ruthlessly exploited. Of course, none of these things carried the stamp of divinity, not in and of themselves or in their sum. No, it was the *effortlessness* of the Prince-Imperial's orchestration that came to seem miraculous. The equanimity, the repose, and the ruthless efficacy of the man in the course of making a thousand mortal decisions. It was not, Sorweel eventually decided, quite human . . .

It was Dûnyain.

And there was the miracle of the Great Ordeal and its relentless northward crawl. Whatever heights the Istyuli afforded, no matter how meagre, he would find his gaze wandering across the Army of the Middle-North, the landslides of trudging men, columns drawing mountainous veils of dust. And if the vision seemed a thing of glory before, it fairly hummed with the *gravitas* of legend now, clothed as it was with crazed memories of what had been endured and with dire premonitions of what was to come.

For despite the toll the Men of the Ordeal had exacted, the Horde had not been defeated. It had reeled back, diminished, grievously wounded, too quick and too amorphous to be run down. Twice he and Zsoronga were called on to deliver missives to the forward pickets – once to Anasûrimbor Moënghus himself. The two of them had galloped ahead with abandon, relieved to be free of the dust and cramp, and wary of the tawny haze that rimmed the horizon before them. Solitary, riding hard across the desolate plain, they felt a peculiar freedom, knowing that Sranc fenced the north in unseen multitudes. Zsoronga told him about a cousin of his who captained a war galley, how he said he loved – and hated – nothing more than sailing in the shadow of an ocean tempest. 'Only sailors,' the Successor-Prince explained, 'know where they stand in their God's favour.'

The Schools had been fully mobilized by this time, so as the Horde's dust steamed mountainous above them, they glimpsed sheets of light, not high among the slow swirling veils, but low, near the darkening base – flickers of brilliance through funereal shrouds. They would crane their heads, draw their gaze from the high piling summits, floating bright beneath the sun, to the false night of the foundations, and the dread scale would humble and mortify them. Schools. Nations. Races both foul and illumined. And they understood that even kings and princes counted for nothing when thrown upon the balance with such things.

They would ride dumbstruck, until the first of the pickets became visible, the companies marked by lighter tassels of dust beneath the sky-spanning mark of the Horde. Finding Moënghus – who by this time was notorious for the daring of his exploits – forced them to ride perilously deep, until the sun became little more than a pale smear, and the haunting call of the Horde swelled into a deafening roar.

'Tell me!' the wild-eyed Prince-Imperial cried above the howl, gesturing with his clotted sword to the sunless world about them. 'What do infidel eyes see when they look upon my father's foe?'

'Hubris!' Zsoronga called before Sorweel could restrain him. 'Mad misadventure!'

'Bah!' Moënghus shouted laughing. '*This,* my friends! This is where Hell concedes Earth to Heaven! Most Men grovel because their fathers grovelled. But *you*! Simply for seeing this, you will know *why* you pray!'

And beyond the Prince-Imperial, Sorweel saw them, the Nuns, striding above obscurities, wracking the earth beneath them. A necklace of shining, warring beads, cast thin across the trackless miles, scattering the Sranc before them.

Day in and day out, burning the earth to glass.

And then there was the greatest witch of all, Anasûrimbor Serwa, who had come to seem a miracle of beauty amid the sweat and Mannish squalor of the march. She rode a glossy brown, perched with one knee drawn high on a Nilnameshi side-saddle, her flaxen hair folded about the perfection of her face, her body slender, almost waifish beneath the simple gowns she wore when not freighted with her billows. She never spoke to Sorweel even though she spent much of her time at her brother's side. She did not so much as look at him, though he could never shake the impression that out of all the shadows that crowded her periphery, she had picked him out for special scrutiny. He was not the only one bewitched by her beauty. He sometimes spent more time watching the others steal glances in her direction than watching her himself. But he did not worship her the way the Zaudunyani did. He did not see her as the daughter of a god. Though he was loathe to admit as much, he feared the yearning – and at times, the raw lust – she inspired in him. And so, as is the wont of men, he often found himself *resenting*, even hating her.

The crazed fact was that he *needed* to hate her. If he were narindari, a kind of divine executioner chosen by the Hundred to deliver the world from the Aspect-Emperor, then what struck him as divine in his enemies had to be demonic – *had* to be, otherwise *he* would be the one dancing from a demon's strings. A Narindar proper – a servant of Ajokli, the evil Four-Horned Brother.

When he was a child, Good and Evil had always *simplified* a world that was unruly and disordered otherwise. Now it vexed him to the point of heartbreak, the treachery of sorting the diabolical and the divine. Some nights he would lie sleepless, trying to *will* Serwa evil, trying to rub pollution into the image of her beauty. But as always the memories of her carrying him across heaving fields of Sranc would rise into his soul's eye, and with it the reeling sense of security and numbing gratitude.

And he would think of the murderous intent he concealed behind his mudded cheeks and of the Chorae he bore hidden in the ancient pouch bound to his hip, and he would despair.

Sometimes, during the more sombre meals he and Zsoronga shared together, he dared voice his more troubling questions, and the two would set aside their bluster and honestly consider all they had seen.

'Golgotterath is not a myth,' Sorweel ventured one night. 'The Great Ordeal marches against a real foe, and that foe *is* evil. We have seen him with our own eyes!'

'But what does that mean?' Zsoronga replied. 'Wickedness is forever warring against wickedness – you should read the annals of my people, Horse-King!'

'Yes, but only when they covet the same things . . . What could the Aspect-Emperor want with these wastes?'

'For hatred's sake, as well. For hatred's sake.'

Sorweel wanted to ask what could inspire such hatred, but he conceded the argument, for he already knew what the Successor-Prince's would say, his argument of final resort, the one that typically doomed Sorweel to watches of cringing sleeplessness.

'But what about the Hundred? Why would the Goddess raise you as a knife?'

Unless the Aspect-Emperor were a demon.

It made him feel a worm sometimes, a thing soft and blind and helpless. He would raise his face to the sky, and it would seem he could actually feel the great gears of the Dread Mother's design, churning the perpetual dust on the horizon, clacking inscrutable through the voices of innumerable men. He would feel himself carried on the arc of her epic intent, and he would feel a worm . . .

Until he remembered his father.

'Father – Father! *My bones are your bones!'*

Sorweel had always flinched from thoughts of that final day before Sakarpus fell. For so long, recollecting those events had seemed like fumbling spines of glass with waterlogged fingers. But more and more he found himself returning to his memories, surprised to find all the cutting edges dulled. He wondered at the arrival of the stork in the moments before the Inrithi assault – at the way it had singled out his father. He wondered that his father had sent him away, and so *saved his life*, almost immediately after.

He wondered if the Goddess had chosen him even then.

But most of all he pondered their last moment alone together, before they had climbed to man the walls, when they had stood father and son warming themselves over glowering coals.

'There are many fools, Sorwa, men who conceive hearts in simple terms, absolute terms. They are insensible to the war within, so they scoff at it, they puff out their chests and they pretend. When fear and despair overcome them, as they must overcome us all, they have not the wind to think . . . and so they break.'

King Harweel had known – even then. His father had known his city and his son were doomed, and he had wanted his son, at least, to understand that fear and cowardice were *inevitabilities*. Kayûtas had said it himself: sense was the plaything of passion. The night of the Ten-Yoke Legion, Zsoronga had fled when Sorweel called because stopping seemed the height of madness. He simply did what was *sensible*, and so found himself standing in the long shadow of his friend's bravery.

But Sorweel had stopped on that darkling plain. Against all instinct and reason, he had cast his life across the altar of necessity.

'. . . *they have not the wind to think* . . .'

All this time, he had mourned his manhood, had made a flag of his humiliation. All this time he had confused his lack of certainty with the lack of strength and honour. But he was strong – he knew that now. Knowing his ignorance simply made his strength that much more canny.

'. . . *and so they break.*'

As ever, the world was a labyrinth. And his was a complicated courage.

'Are you such a fool, Sorwa?'

No, Father.

———

The Men of the Ordeal marched, answering to the toll of the Interval day in and day out, until at long last they had chased the arid emptiness to its dregs. Despite its greatness the Istyuli was not inexhaustible.

For the first time they awoke to horizons different from those they had greeted the previous morn. The ground was just as gutted by the retreating Horde, and the distances were just as devoid of game or any other kind of forage, but the earth bent to a different sensibility. The rolls became deeper, the summits became more pinched, almost as if the hosts crossed the transitions wrought by age, from the smooth swales of youth to the creases of middle age. Bare rock scraped clear the turf with ever-greater regularity. And the tepid rivers, which had snaked brown and lazy, quickened into white, carving ever-deeper ravines.

The Army of the West, the host commanded by the mercurial King Coithus Saubon, came to the ruins of Suönirsi, a trading entrepot once famed as a link between the High Norsirai of Kûniüri and the White Norsirai of Akksersia. The Men of the Ordeal were astounded. After so many months of shambling waste, they walked the buried ways of a different, *human* age, struck by how time makes swamps of scabrous earth. They wondered at the contradiction of ruins, the way some structures are smashed to dust while others are granted the immortality of geological formations. For the first time they could connect the tales and rumours that stirred them to take up the Circumfix with the stumped earth beneath their feet, and they would stare in their weary, shuffling thousands, the tragedy of lost ages reflected in their eyes.

The land had lost its anonymity. Henceforth, they knew, the

earth, for all its desolation, would carry the stamp of long-dead intentions. Where the High Istyuli had been barren, a land impervious to the generations who had once ranged across it, its northwestern frontiers were soaked in human history. Ruins teethed the heights, mounded the shallow valleys. The learned told tales of Sheneor, the least of the three nations divided between the sons of the first ancient Anasûrimbor King, Nanor-Ukkerja I. Names were debated by firelight. Names were invoked by the Judges in their sermons. Names were called out in curses and in prayers. Everywhere the Men of the Ordeal looked, they glimpsed ghosts of ancient meaning, the apparitions of ancestors, raising arms, leaning beneath burdens. If they could decode the land, it seemed, see it with *ancient* eyes, they could reclaim it in the name of Men.

It passed through them as a shiver, the coincidence of souls antique and new.

Though hunger had become a crisis, the numbers who succumbed to sickness declined. The rivers were simply too swift to hold the pollution of the retreating Horde, and in some cases, they fairly teemed with fish. Nets borne all the way from Cironj and Nron and Cingulat were cast across the narrows, and the issue was heaved onto the crowded shores: pike, bass, pickerel, and others. Men ate them raw, such was their hunger. But it was never enough. No matter how much they slowed their progress to throw their nets, they could do no more than prolong the host's starvation.

Meanwhile the Horde withdrew and congregated.

Day and night, the Schools assailed the gathering masses, striding into earthbound clouds of grey and ochre, burning and blasting the screeching shadows that fled beneath them. The Scarlet Spires strode alone through the shrouds with their Dragonheads, scourging the wasted earth beneath. The Vokalati worked with the cunning of wolves, driving swathes of the creatures into traps of golden flame. And the Mandati and the Swayali arrayed themselves in lines miles long, like threads beaded with stars, wracking the earth with combs of blinding Gnostic light.

The massacre was great, but never great enough. For all their feral simplicity, the Sranc possessed an instinctive cunning. They could hear the Schoolmen sing through the world-wringing roar, the unearthly rattle of sorcerous meaning, and so they scattered, ran with speed of fire-maddened horses, scooping up dust both to obscure their foe's vision and to blunt their incandescent dispensations.

The Culling, the Men riding the pickets came to call it. Every evening knights returned with stories of arcane violence glimpsed from afar, and the Men of the Ordeal wondered and rejoiced.

The Imperial Mathematicians tallied numbers, estimates of slain versus the inexorable accumulation of more and more clans, but they knew only that it was never enough, no matter how devious the tactics or how powerful the sorceries. The Horde grew and bloated, an assembly of shrieking mobs that encompassed more and more of the horizon – until all the North screamed.

The only tally they knew with certainty was the number of Schoolmen lost.

The first sorcerer to go missing, a Scarlet Schoolman named Irsalfus, had been dismissed as a fluke. The prevailing assumption was that the Sranc, even if they had somehow managed to keep Chorae through the wild tide of generations, would have no clue as to their purpose. After the fifth Schoolman was lost they realized they were mistaken. Either certain clans had managed to preserve the artefacts (along with some understanding of their use), or, what was more likely, the Consult had managed to infiltrate the Horde. Perhaps they had scattered contingents of Ursranc throughout the Sranc host. Or perhaps they had simply spread *word* of the Chorae and how they could be used.

The possibility occasioned no small amount of debate in the Aspect-Emperor's councils. Heramari Iyokus, the sightless Grandmaster of the Scarlet Spires, argued that the Schools should abandon the Culling, retire from the field. 'Otherwise,' he said, 'we shall be halved before we reach the Gates of Golgotterath.'

But Nurbanu Soter, the King-Regent of High Ainon, scoffed, saying the Great Ordeal would scarce survive to reach the Neleost Sea, let alone Golgotterath, unless the Schoolmen continued. 'How many battles?' he cried to the Blind Grandmaster. 'How many contests such as the last can we endure? Two? Four? Eight? For that is the *real* question.' What made Culling so essential, the Holy Veteran argued, was the degree to which it *slowed* the Horde's cycle of retreat, starvation, and assault. To abandon it altogether would be to invite more skirmishes with disaster. 'With each battle we toss the number-sticks,' the old man said, his voice indomitable, his eyes as dark and cruel as they had been during the First Holy War. 'Should we risk *all* for a few dozen wizard-skins?'

Tempers flared, a rarity in the presence of the Anasûrimbor, with the Schoolmen generally arguing against, and the caste-nobility generally arguing for, the Culling. In the end, the Aspect-Emperor declared the Culling would continue, but with the Schoolmen deployed in tandems to minimize losses. With their billows, he explained, the odds were good that any one Chorae strike could be survived, so long as someone uninjured could carry the one struck away from the Horde. 'In all things we must conserve and we must sacrifice,' he admonished. 'We must be acrobats and rope-walkers, both in intellect and in heart. Far worse dilemmas confront us, my brothers. Far more dreadful decisions.'

And so the Horde reeled back, shrank from the pricks of a thousand lights. And the Four Armies marched into the desolation that was its wake, across lands painted with the horror and glory of the Holy Sagas.

Into the gloom of the Ancient North.

⸺⸱⸺

King Nersei Proyas would much rather discuss arms, the dilemmas of the field, and the strategies to overcome them. Instead, his Lord-and-God turned to him and asked, 'When you look into yourself, when you look *into your soul*, how much do you see?'

'I see . . . I see what I see.'

The Exalt-General had spent many sleepless watches on his cot, pondering their discussions while listening to the camp and its dwindling murmur. Recollections from his long years of service and devotion would cycle through his soul's eye, a lifetime of war and ultimatum, and the worrisome sense that something *had changed*, that these talks were utterly unprecedented both in tenor and content, would grow ever more leaden with dread certainty. As much as he would marvel at the privilege – to sit and speak plain truth with a *living prophet!* – he would fear the implications more.

Anasûrimbor Kellhus waged more than one war, he had come to realize. One far beyond the meagre intellects of his followers. One fought across fields of maddening abstraction . . .

'But you *do* see. I mean, you do possess an inner eye.'

'I suppose . . .'

The Aspect-Emperor smiled, rubbed his bearded chin like a carpenter assessing problematic wood. He wore the same plain white gown he always wore – the one Proyas imagined he slept in. The Ainoni silk was so fine as to be crushed into a thousand wrinkles at his every joint, creases that resembled the forking of twigs in the dim light of the octagonal hearth.

Proyas sat freighted as always in his Imperial armour, his golden cuirass biting his hips, his blue cloak wrapped about his waist in the ceremonial fashion.

'What if some people lacked that eye?' Kellhus asked. 'What if some people could see nothing more than the outline of their passions, let alone the *origins* of those scribbles? What if most people were blind to themselves? Would they know as much?'

Proyas stared into the luminous gauze of the fire, rubbed his cheeks against the memory of its sorcerous bite. People insensible to their own souls . . . It seemed he had known many such men over the course of his life, when he considered it. Many such fools.

'No . . .' he said meditatively. 'They would think they see everything there is to be seen.'

Kellhus smiled in affirmation. 'And why's that?'

'Because they know nothing different,' Proyas replied, daring his sovereign's gaze. 'You need to glimpse *more* to know that you see less.'

Kellhus raised a wooden decanter to refill Proyas's dwindling bowl of anpoi. 'Very good,' he said as he poured. 'So you understand the difference between you and me.'

'I do?'

'Where you are blind,' his Lord-and-God said, 'I can see.'

Proyas paused in hesitation, drank deep from his bowl. The tang of nectar, the bite of liquor. At a time when clear water had become a luxury, sipping anpoi seemed an almost obscene extravagance. But then everything had the taste of miracles in this room.

'And this . . . *this* is why Achamian speaks true?'

Simply asking the question loosed a queasiness in his gut. As much as the topic of his old tutor and his heresy troubled Proyas, the fact that Kellhus *knew* the unruly thoughts the man occasioned disturbed him even more. Proyas had not so much buried Drusas Achamian as turned his back on him, the way men are want to do with matters too acidic to honestly consider. He had grown into manhood in the sorcerer's critical shadow, clinging to his convictions in a fog of nagging questions. He could not think of him without suffering some flutter of spiritual insecurity, without hearing his warm and amiable voice saying, 'Yes, Prosha, but how *do you know?*'

And now, twenty years after Achamian's famed denunciation and subsequent exile, Kellhus had inexplicably raised the spectre of the man and his questions. Why?

Proyas *had been there*. He had clenched his teeth in shame, squinted through tears of heartbreak, watching the portly sorcerer condemn the first true prophet in a thousand years! Condemn the Holy Aspect-Emperor as *false* . . .

Only to be told now, on the very threshold of apocalypse, that he had spoken true?

'Yes,' Kellhus said, watching him with unnerving concentration.

'So even now, you're . . . *manipulating* me?'

The Exalt-General could scarce believe he had asked the question.

'There is no other way for me to be with you,' the Aspect-Emperor replied. '*I see what you do not*. The origins of your thought and passion. The terminus of your fear and ambit. You experience but a *fragment* of the Nersei Proyas that I see. With every word, I speak to you in ways you cannot hear.'

Some kind of test – it *had* to be . . . Kellhus was sounding him, *preparing* him for some kind of trial.

'But . . .'

The Aspect-Emperor downed his bowl in a single draught. 'How could that be when you *feel* free, to say, to think, any way you please?'

'Yes! I never feel so free as I feel when I am with you! In all the world, wherever I go, Kellhus, I sense the jealousies and judgments of others. With you, I know I have no cause for wari-ness or concern. With you, I am my own judge!'

'But that is only the man *you* know, the Lesser Proyas. The man I know, the Greater Proyas, I hold in shackles of iron. I am *Dûnyain*, my friend, exactly as Achamian claimed. To merely stand in my presence is to be enslaved.'

Perhaps *this* was the golden kernel, the whole point of these thought-bruising sessions. To understand how little he was himself . . .

There was no revelation without terror and overturning.

'But I am your *willing* slave. I *choose* a life of bondage!'

And he felt no shame in saying this. Ever since childhood he had understood the exaltation that was submission. To be a slave to truth is to be a master of men.

The Aspect-Emperor leaned back into the glow of his unearthly halo. As always the hearth's twirling light sketched smoky glimpses of doom across the canvas walls behind him. For a heartbeat, the Exalt-General could swear he saw children running . . .

'Choice,' his Lord-and-God said smiling. 'Willing . . . Your shackles are cast from this very iron.'

Sorweel and Zsoronga sat unceremoniously in the dust at the entrance of the tent they now shared, gnawing on their ration of amicut. Gone was the Successor-Prince's garish pavilion. Gone were the ritual wigs. Gone were the sumptuous cushions, the ornate decorations. Gone were the slaves who had borne all this pointless luxury.

Necessity, as Protathis famously wrote, makes jewels of lack and turns poverty into gold. For the Men of the Ordeal, wealth was now measured in the absence of burdens.

They sat side by side gazing with a kind of numb incredulity as the figure wobbled toward them through the haze of knee-high dust. They recognized him immediately, though it did not seem so at the time, so quick is the heart to deny what it cannot bear. Limbs like black ropes. Hair white as the sky. He staggered as much as he walked, a gait that spoke of endless miles, a thousand steps too many. Only his gaze remained steady, as if all that remained of him had been concentrated into his sense of sight. He did not blink once the entirety of his approach.

Swaying, he stood before them.

'You were supposed to be dead,' Zsoronga said, looking up with a peculiar terror, his voice wavering about some contest of dismay and gratitude.

'*I am told . . .*' Obotegwa rasped, his smile more a lipless grimace, '*my death . . . is your duty . . .*'

Sorweel made to leave, but the Successor-Prince cried out for him to stay.

'I beg you . . .' he said. 'Please.'

So he helped the old man into the tent, shocked, nauseated even, by his kindling weight. He watched his friend chew his food, then offer up the resulting paste. He watched him raise Obotegwa's feet so that he might wash them, only to wash his shins instead because of the ulcerations that cankered his toes and heel. He listened to him whisper to the ailing servant in the warm, resonant tones of their native language. He understood none of it, and yet grasped all of it, for the tones of love and gratitude and remorse transcend all languages, even those from different ends of the world.

Sorweel watched Obotegwa blink two tears, as if they were all that remained, and somehow he just knew: the man had lived so long only to obtain permission to die. With fingers of trembling teak, the Obligate reached beneath his tunic and withdrew a small golden cylinder, which Zsoronga clasped with solemn disbelief.

He watched his friend take a knife to the old man's wrists.

He watched the lantern oil of his life leak into the earth, until the guttering flame that was Obotegwa shined no more. He stared at the inanimate body, wondered that it could seem as dry as the earth.

Zsoronga cried out as if freed of some long-suffering obligation to remain strong. He wept with outrage and shame and sorrow. Sorweel embraced him, felt the anguish kick through his powerful frame.

Afterward, when night had drawn its chill shroud over the world beyond their tent, Zsoronga told a story about how, in his eighth summer, he had come, for no reason he could fathom, to covet his older cousin's Battle-Sash – so much so he actually crept into his quarters and stole it. 'Things glitter in the eyes of a child,' he said, speaking with the blank manner of the bereaved. 'They *shine*, more than is seemly . . .'

Thinking himself clever, he had taken care to hide the thing in Obotegwa's annex to his room – in his matins satchel. Of course, giving the ceremonial importance of the Sash, a hue and cry was raised the instant it was discovered missing. By some stroke of disastrous fortune, it was found among Obotegwa's effects shortly after, and the Obligate was seized.

'Of course they knew *I* was the culprit,' Zsoronga explained, staring down at his thieving palms. 'This is an old trick among my people. A way to peel past the bark, as they say. Someone else is accused of your crime, and unless you confess, you're forced to witness their punishment . . .'

Seized by the terror and shame that so often makes puppets of children, Zsoronga had said nothing. Even as Obotegwa was whipped, he said nothing – and to his everlasting shame, the Obligate said nothing as well. 'Imagine . . . the *whole* of the Inner Court, watching him be whipped and knowing full well that I was the one!'

So he did what most children do when cornered by some fact of failure or weakness: he made believe. He told himself that Obotegwa *had* stolen the Sash, out of spite, out of fascination – who knew what moved lesser souls? 'I was a child!' Zsoronga cried, his voice pinched eight summers short.

One day passed. Two. Three. And still he said nothing. The whole world seemed bent to the warp of his fear. His father ceased speaking to him. His mother continually blinked tears. And so the farce continued. At some level, he knew that the world knew, but the stubbornness would not relent. Only Obotegwa treated him precisely as before. Only Obotegwa, the one bearing his welts, *played along*.

Then his father summoned him and Obotegwa to his apartments. The Satakhan was furious, to the point of kicking over braziers and spilling fiery coals across the floor. But Obotegwa, true to character, remained amiable and calm.

'He assured Father that I felt shame,' the Successor-Prince recalled with a vacant stare. 'He bid him recall my eyes and take heart in the *pain* he had seen there. Given this, he said, my silence should be cause for *pride*, for it is the curse of rulers to bear the burden of shameful secrets. "Only weak rulers confess weakness," he said. "Only wise rulers bear the full burden of their crimes. Take heart knowing your son is both strong and wise . . ."'

Zsoronga hung upon these words for a time. He glanced at the shadowy corpse at their feet, sat blinking at the impossibility. And Sorweel knew precisely what he felt, the way you lose so much more than simply another voice and gaze from an otherwise crowded life. He knew that many things in Zsoronga's life had some history peculiar to him and Obotegwa alone – that they had shared a world *between* them, a world that was gone.

'And what do you think?' Sorweel dared ask.

'That I was foolish and weak,' Zsoronga said.

They spoke of Obotegwa long into the night, and it seemed indistinguishable from speaking about life. They said things wise and foolish by turns, as young, intelligent men are prone. And at last, when weariness and grief overcame them, Zsoronga told the Sakarpi King how Obotegwa had insisted that he befriend Sorweel, how the old Obligate had always believed he would surprise them all. And then the Successor-Prince told him how, on the morn, he would add the name *Harweel* to his ancestor list.

'A *brother*!' the Successor-Prince whispered with startling violence. 'Sakarpus has a brother in Zeüm!'

They slept with the beloved dead, as was the custom in High Holy Zeüm. Their breathing pulled deep with rhythmic life, a garland about the breathless.

They awoke before the Interval, buried Obotegwa without marker on the grey, desolate plain.

———

Sorweel and Zsoronga hung about the edges of the General's retinue, witless for the lack of sleep and the expenditure of passion. The sun had climbed past the precincts of noon, drawing the shadows of things to the east. The line of the land, which for so long reached out in a monotonous crescent before them, had been broken and multiplied. Low knolls rose against low ridges. Ravines rutted mounded distances. Gravel spilled from wandering defilades. The Army of the Middle-North mobbed the horizon immediately behind them, its innumerable pennants little more than shadows lolling through the steaming dust. They rode as they always did at this time of day, their brows angled away from the sun's glare, their thoughts wandering on the slack leash of midday boredom.

Sorweel was the first to glimpse the speck hanging low over the western horizon. He had fallen into the habit of *reading* the world as much as watching it, so he said nothing, convinced he witnessed some kind of sign. Was it another stork come to communicate the inexplicable?

He was quickly disabused of this conceit. The speck, whatever it was, hung in the faraway air more like a bumblebee than a bird, like something too cumbersome to fly . . .

He peered, squinted as much out of disbelief as against the high sun. He saw black *horses* – a team of four. He saw wheels . . .

A *chariot*, he realized. A flying chariot.

For a time he simply watched stupefied, rocking in rhythm to his mount's dogged trot.

A chorus of alarums cracked the air. The General's Pillarian escort leapt into formation about their flanks, their armour and tunics shining green and gold. The Nuns who accompanied Serwa cried out in arcane unison, let out their billows as they strode glimmering into the sky.

The sorcerous chariot rode a low arc over the churned landscape. Sunlight flashed across panels laden with graven images. Sorweel saw three pale faces swaying above the gilded rail – one of them shouting light.

Kayûtas, for his part, betrayed no surprise or urgency whatsoever. 'Silence!' he cried to those in his immediate circle. 'Decorum!' Then, without a word of explanation, he tore off, galloping on a long plume of dust.

The witches hung motionless in the air, their billows winding and waving about them.

The retinue, which typically rode in a loose mass, flattened into a crescent as the officers and caste-nobles jostled for vantages. Sorweel and Zsoronga watched from the centre of the press. The sky-chariot banked toward the Prince-Imperial and swung to earth. The hooves of the blacks bit hard into the denuded turf, and wings of dust and gravel sprawled about their glossy flanks. Golden wheels gleamed about spokes spun into invisibility. The centre figure leaned back, pulling hard on the reins.

Standing in his stirrups, Kayûtas raced out to meet them, hailed them with a raised arm.

The three strangers turned toward him in unison.

'They're not human,' Zsoronga said. His tone was ragged, and not for exhaustion. He sounded like a man who had had his fill of miraculous things. Like a man straining to believe.

The Kidruhil General reined his pony to a dusty halt, exchanged what seemed cryptic greetings. Nothing could be heard on the arid wind. Then, with scarce a breath expended, he wheeled his mount about and began trotting back toward his astonished command. The sky-chariot lurched into motion behind him, trundling across the earth . . .

And for some reason, of all the awe-inspiring sights Sorweel had seen and would see, none would be so arresting as the sight of the gilded chariot wheeling back into open sky. He understood his friend's beseeching tone, for it had made a beehive of his own breast as well.

Nonmen.

So many miracles. All of them speaking for his enemy's cause.

For reasons he could scarce fathom, the Exalt-General found himself pondering the siege and fall of Shimeh – the final night of the First Holy War – as he walked the short distance from his pavilion to the black silhouette of the Umbilicus. Fleeing the streets of the Holy City, he had climbed onto the pediment of an ancient fullery, where he had watched his Holy Aspect-Emperor battle the last of the heathen Cishaurim. There had been five of them, Primaries, mightier, despite the crudity of their art, than the most accomplished Schoolmen. Five hellish figures floating high above the burning city, their eyes gouged so they might see the Water-that-was-Light – and Anasûrimbor Kellhus had slain them all.

Such was the power of the man he had come to worship. Such was the might. So how had his soul let slip the ardour of his faith? Why had hope and inflexible determination become foreboding and gnawing worry?

The Men of the Ordeal hailed him as they always did when he walked the interior ways of the camp, but for once he did not return their salutations. He fairly knocked over Lord Couras Nantilla, the General of the Cengemi, at the entryway to the Umbilicus, such was the depth of his walking reverie. He squeezed the man's shoulder in lieu of an apology.

At long last the plains had yielded. At long last the Great Ordeal, the sum of his lifelong hope and toil, trod the fabled lands named in the Holy Sagas. At long last they marched into the shadow of foul Golgotterath – *Golgotterath!*

For all the perils facing them, for all the privations, this should be a time of *jubilation*. For who, in all the world, could withstand the might of Anasûrimbor Kellhus?

No one.

Not even the dread Consult of Mog-Pharau.

So why did his heart pound air into his veins?

He resolved to make *this* his question. He resolved to set aside his pride, and to reveal the full extent of his misgivings . . .

To ask his Prophet how he could doubt his Prophet.

But for once the Aspect-Emperor was not alone in his chamber. He stood arms out while two body-slaves attended to him, cinching and fussing robes freighted with ceremonial splendour: the costume of a Ketyai warrior-king from Far Antiquity. He wore a full-length gown whose hems had been bound into his ankle-wraps. Golden vambraces encased his forearms and matching greaves his shins.

Opposing Kyranean Lions gleamed across his breast-plate. With his stature and haloed mien, he seemed a vision from some ancient relief – save for the two severed demon heads hanging from his girdle . . .

'You are troubled, I know,' Kellhus said, grinning at his Exalt-General. 'For all your yearning, for all your *faith*, yours remains a pragmatic soul, Proyas.' The slaves continued their silent labour, binding straps and laces. The Aspect-Emperor glanced down at his garb, rolled his eyes as if offering himself up as a poor example. 'You have little patience for tools you cannot immediately use.'

As a young child, one of Proyas's duties had been to bear his mother's train at public ceremonies. All he remembered of the toddling farce was stumbling after the long-dragging hems, clutching embroidery, losing it, then stumbling after the hems again, while all the Conriyan court roared in adoring laughter around him. In so many ways, Kellhus made him feel the same tender fool, always chasing, always stumbling . . .

'If I have fail—'

Kellhus interrupted him with a warm hand on his shoulder. 'Please, Proyas. I'm just saying we grapple with *earthly* things tonight . . .'

'Earthly things?'

A broad smile cracked the flaxen curls of the Aspect-Emperor's moustache and beard.

'Yes. The Nonman King has finally answered our call.'

Earthly, Proyas reflected, was not a term many would accord the ghouls.

'Even now his embassy waits here in the Umbilicus,' his Lord-and-God continued. 'We will receive them in the Eleven Pole Chamber . . .'

Within a matter of heartbeats, Proyas found himself immersed in the organizational carnival that perpetually characterized life behind the veils of power. Slaves took him in hand, washing his hands, brushing and perfuming his field armour, oiling and combing his hair and beard. A part of him always found it remarkable, the degree of coordination required for even the simplest and most impromptu of state occasions. An Imperial Eunuch festooned in insignia from across the Three Seas led him out into the airy chill of the Eleven Pole Chamber. Kellhus already stood on the low dais, dispensing trivial instructions to a small mob of functionaries. The Ekkinû, the sorcerous arras that framed the throne, writhed gold on black with the utter absence of motion. Glimpsing Proyas, Kellhus gestured for him to stand at his side.

His thoughts racing, the Exalt-General took his place next to the throne, convinced he could feel the sinuous, symbolic twine of the Ekkinû in the air behind him. He had never been able to fathom the significance of the Nonmen to the Ordeal – especially since whatever strength they could muster would be but a fraction of their former glory – and scarcely anything at all compared with the might of the Great Ordeal – at least in his humble, human opinion. But Kellhus had sent hundreds to their death, if not thousands, in his perpetual attempts to contact Nil'giccas: small fleets charged with leaving the Three Seas and running the coasts of Zeüm, thence into the mists of the Ocean and the legendary shores of Injor-Niyas.

All in the name of striking an alliance with a ten-thousand-year-old king.

Another question to trouble their discussions.

Proyas gazed up into the gloom of the tented heights. Only three braziers had been lighted, so they seemed a small island of illumination surrounded by half-glimpsed Circumfix banners and walls and panels so dim as to be nothing more than the ghosts of structure.

The slaves and functionaries withdrew, taking the air of carnival bustle with them. Save for the shadowy guards posted about the chamber's perimeter, it was just the two of them.

'I have pulled aside the harem beads,' Kellhus said. 'And you find my wives ugly . . .'

The Exalt-General coughed aloud, such was his consternation. 'What?'

'Your *question*,' Kellhus said, chuckling. He spoke in the wry, warm tones of a friend who has always dwelt several paces closer to the peace that truth delivers. 'You wonder how it is you can *doubt* after so many years of witness and miracle.'

'I . . . I'm not sure I understand.'

'There's a reason Men prefer their prophets *dead*, Proyas.'

Kellhus stared askance at his Exalt-General, one eyebrow hooked in *Do-you-see?* curiosity.

And Proyas did see – he realized that he had understood all along. His question, he suddenly realized, was no question at all but instead a complaint. He did not doubt so much as *yearn* . . .

For the simplicity of simple belief.

'We begin believing when we are children,' Kellhus continued. 'And so we make childish expectations our rule, the measure for what the holy *should* be . . .' He gestured to the ornamentation about them, spare as it was compared with the fleshpots of the South. 'Simplicity. Symmetry. Beauty. These are but the *appearance* of the holy – the gilding that deceives. What is holy is difficult, ugly beyond comprehension, in the eyes of all save the God.'

Just then, the Pillarian Seneschal announced the visitors.

'Remember,' Kellhus murmured as a mother might. 'Forgive them their peculiarities . . .'

Three striding figures resolved from the gloom, hooded in black cloaks that shone as though slicked in rain.

'And beware their beauty.'

The foremost figure paused immediately below them, threw

back his cloak, which slipped into a pool of kneaded folds about the heels of his boots. His scalp gleamed with the pallor of cold mutton fat. His face was alarming, as much for its perfection as for its resemblance to the Sranc. He wore a hauberk that was at once a gown, one that baffled the eyes for the wrought delicacy of the chain: innumerable serpents no larger than the clippings of a child's nails.

'I am Nin'sariccas,' the Nonman announced in High Kûniüric, a language Proyas had spent years mastering so he could read *The Sagas* in their original tongue. 'Dispossessed Son of Siol, Emissary of his Most Subtle Glory, Nil'giccas, King of Injor-Niyas . . .' His bow fell far short of what jnan demanded. 'We have ridden long and hard to find you.'

Kellhus regarded him the way he regarded all penitents who found their way to his feet: as someone who had stumbled out of wintry desolation into the warm, sultry glow of summer.

'You are surprised,' he said in a voice that easily matched the melodious resonance of the Nonman's. 'You thought us doomed.'

A serpentine blink. The preternatural eyes clicked to the Aspect-Emperor's right – to the sorcerous arras, Proyas realized. He understood what Kellhus had meant by peculiarities. Something about the ghoul's manner followed unexpected lines. For the first time he noticed that the Nonman stood nude beneath the gleam of his nimil hauberk.

'Nil'giccas sends his greetings,' Nin'sariccas said. 'Even in an age so dark, the light that is the Aspect-Emperor shines for all to see.'

A leonine nod.

'Then Ishterebinth is with us?'

The Emissary's air of vague distraction lapsed into outright insolence. Rather than answer, Nin'sariccas peered across the Eleven Pole Chamber's airy interior, then, with the remote reserve of those careful to conceal their disgust, considered Proyas and the Pillarian Guards flanking him. Weathering the inhuman scrutiny, Proyas suffered a strange twinge of inadequacy, one he imagined caste-menials felt in the presence of nobles: a presentiment of bodily and spiritual inferiority.

Like the angels of a long-dead god, the Nonmen stood rigid with a pride that had outlived their glory. Only the mien and manner of the Aspect-Emperor dwarfed them – a sun to their moon.

'The memory of your forefather's treachery . . .' the Emissary finally replied, his gaze lingering on Proyas, 'burns bright with us. For some, *Anasûrimbor* is the very name of Mannish arrogance and disorder.'

At this, several Pillarians loosened their broadswords in their scabbard. Proyas was quick in raising his hand to restrain them, knowing the Nonman spoke from the vantage of *ages*, that for them, generations of Men were as fleeting as mice. They had no grave to swallow their ancient grudges.

Kellhus betrayed no consciousness of the affront. He leaned forward in a familiar way, rested his elbows on his knees, clasped his haloed hands.

'Is Ishterebinth *with* us?'

A long, cold gaze. For the first time Proyas noticed how the two Nonmen accompanying Nin'sariccas held their eyes down as though in ritual shame.

'Yes,' the Emissary said. 'The Sacred Ishroi of Injor-Niyas will add voice and shield to your Ordeal . . . If you retake Dagliash. If you honour the Niom.'

Proyas had never heard of the Niom. Dagliash, he knew, was the fortress the ancient High Norsirai had raised to guard against Golgotterath. It stood to reason that the ghouls would want some guarantee of success before casting their lot.

'Have you seen the massacre we have wrought?' Kellhus cried in the semblance of a more impassioned ruler. 'No Horde so great has been overcome. Not Pir-Pahal. Not Eleneot. No age of Man or Nonman has seen a host such as the one I have assembled!' He stood to peer into the Emissary's inhuman face, and somehow the World seemed to lean with him, milky with the roar of intangible things.

'The Great Ordeal *will* reach Golgotterath.'

The Exalt-General had seen innumerable men – strong, proud men – shrivel beneath the Aspect-Emperor's divine scrutiny, so many that it had come to seem a law of nature. But Nin'sariccas remained as remote as before.

'If you retake Dagliash. If you honour the Niom.'

Proyas took care not to look at his Lord-and-God directly, knowing that the sight of subordinates watching their rulers would be taken as a sign of weakness. But he found himself desperately curious as to the intricacies of Kellhus's expression – the art. Proyas had witnessed many men deny the Aspect-Emperor through the years, either through *him*, as was the case with King Harweel of Sakarpus, or directly. But never in circumstances so extraordinary.

Daring souls, and foolish, given that so few yet breathed.

'Agreed,' the Aspect-Emperor said.

A concession? Why did he need these inhuman ghouls?

Once again, Nin'sariccas's bow fell far short of what jnan demanded. He lifted his aquiline face. His glittering black gaze fell to Kellhus's waist, to the abominations hanging from his hip.

'We are curious . . .' the Nonman said. 'The Ciphrang bound about your girdle. Is it true you have walked the Outside and *returned*?'

Kellhus resumed his seat, leaned back with a single foot extended. 'Yes.'

An almost imperceptible nod. 'And what did you find?'

Kellhus propped his face with his right hand, two fingers pressed to his temple. 'You worry that I never truly returned,' he said mildly. 'That the soul of Anasûrimbor Kellhus writhes in some hell and a demon Ciphrang gazes upon you instead.'

The Decapitants, as the demonic heads had come to be called, were something wilfully ignored by many among the Zaudunyani. A kind of indigestible proof. Proyas was one of few who knew something about their acquisition, how Kellhus, during one of the longer truces that punctuated the Unification Wars, spent several weeks studying with Heramari Iyokus, the Grandmaster of the Scarlet Spires, learning the darkest ways of Anagogic sorcery, the Daimos. Proyas had been among the first to see them when he returned from Carythusal and perhaps the first to dare ask Kellhus what had happened. His reply loomed large among the many unforgettable things the man had told him over the years: *'There are two species of revelation, my old friend. Those that seize, and those that are seized. The first are the province of the priest, the latter belong to the sorcerer . . .'*

Even after so many years, his skin still prickled in revulsion when he glimpsed the Decapitants. But unlike many of the faithful, Proyas never forgot that his prophet was also a mage, a Shaman, not unlike those so piously condemned by the Tusk. His was the New Covenant, the sweeping away of all the old measures. So many former sins had become new virtues. Women had claimed the privileges of men. Sorcerers had become priests.

Obscenity *should* hang from the waist of Salvation, or so it had come to seem.

'Such thefts . . .' Nin'sariccas said with passionless tact. 'Such *substitutions*. They have happened before.'

'Why should you care,' Kellhus said, 'if your hatred is satisfied, your ancient foe at last destroyed? Ever have Men been ruled by tyrants. Why should you care what soul lies behind our cruelty?'

A single inhuman blink. 'May I touch you?'

'Yes.'

The Emissary instantly stepped forward, sparking cries and the baring of weapons throughout the gloom.

'Leave him,' Kellhus said.

Nin'sariccas had paused immediately above the Aspect-Emperor, the hem of his chain gown swaying. For the first time he betrayed something resembling indecision, and Proyas realized the creature was, in his own inhuman manner, *terrified*. The Exalt-General almost smiled, such was his gratification.

The Emissary extended a sallow hand . . .

Which the Aspect-Emperor clasped in a firm, human grip. For a heartbeat, it seemed that worlds, let alone the shadowy confines of the Eleven Pole Chamber, dangled from their grasp.

Sun and moon. Man and Nonman.

The clasp broke with the gliding of fingers.

'What did you see?' Nin'sariccas asked with what seemed genuine curiosity. 'What did you find?'

'God . . . broken into a million warring splinters.'

A grim nod. 'We worship the spaces between the Gods.'

'Which is why you are damned.'

Another nod, this one strangely brittle. 'As False Men.'

The Aspect-Emperor nodded in stoic regret. 'As False Men.'

The Emissary retreated from the dais, resumed his place at the fore of his voiceless companions. 'And why should the False Men lend their strength to the True?'

'Because of Hanalinqu,' the Holy Aspect-Emperor of the Three Seas declared. 'Because of Cû'jara Cinmoi. Because four thousand years ago, all your wives and daughters were murdered . . . and you were cursed to go mad in the shadow of that memory, to live forever, dying their deaths.'

Nin'sariccas bowed yet again, this time deeper, yet still far short of honouring jnan.

'If you retake Dagliash,' he said. 'If you honour the Niom.'

As he had every morning since the Battle of the Horde, Sorweel awoke before the Interval's toll. He lay aching in his cot, more pinched than warmed by his woollen blanket, blinking at the impossibility of his straits. Other than a residue of warmth that made cold dismay of his every waking, nothing sensible remained of his dreams. He knew only that he dreamed of better places. He could only dream of better places.

Zsoronga lay on his side as he always did, one arm thrown askew, his face the image of boyish bliss. Sorweel regarded him for a bleary moment, thinking as he often thought that the man's future wives would love him best like this, in the innocence of his mornings. The young King crept from his cot, fumbled with his gear in the dawning pallor, then slipped outside so as to not disturb his brother from Zeüm.

He savoured the chill of breathing open sky, rubbed his bearding chin as he gazed out across the encampment. He felt the clamour to come, the rousing of thousands about him, and the warring of doubts within. Another day marching with the Great Ordeal. The discomfort of long watches in the saddle. The ligatures of sweat. The ache of perpetual squinting. The anxiousness of the accumulating Horde. And for a fleeting moment, he knew the peace of those first to awaken – the gratitude that accompanies solitary lulls.

He sat on his rump to labour with his riding boots.

'Truth shines . . .' a voice chimed.

'Truth shines,' habit replied for him.

Anasûrimbor Serwa stood before him, her silken billows knotted tight about her slight form. She had appeared without the merest inkling. From his first glimpse, Sorweel knew he would crouch peering after her departure, looking for her footfalls across the trampled dust. She stood to his left, beneath the arch of the bluing sky. Crimson gilded the edges of the tents jumbled behind her.

She drew back a lick of flaxen hair from her cheek.

'The Charioteer you and my brother found . . . Father has met with them.'

'The Embassy . . .' Sorweel said, squinting up at her. 'Kayûtas said your father hopes to forge a treaty with Ishterebinth.'

She smiled. 'You know of Ishterebinth in Sakarpus?'

He scowled and shrugged. 'From *The Sagas* . . . None thought it real.'

'The mightiest among the Quya dwell there still.'

He did not know what to say so he turned back to his boots. He never felt the Goddess so fiercely as when he found himself before Serwa or Kayûtas. His cheeks literally prickled. And yet at the same time, he never felt so unworthy of the Mother's dread design. To stand before the Anasûrimbor was to doubt . . . things old.

'The Nonmen have invoked Niom,' she said. 'An ancient ritual.'

Something in her tone seized his attention. She had sounded almost embarrassed.

'I don't understand.'

Her gaze had recovered its remote vantage. She considered him with a serenity that he yearned to muddy with his passion . . .

Evil. How could someone so beautiful be evil?

'The ancient Nonmen Kings found Men too mercurial,' she explained, 'too proud and headstrong to be trusted. So in all their dealings they demanded hostages as a guarantee: a son, a daughter, and a captive enemy. The two former as a surety against treachery. The latter as a surety against deception.'

The sun broke behind her. Light unfurled in a burning fan about her silhouette.

'And I am to play the enemy,' he said, holding a hand out against her glare.

What new twist was this?

'Yes,' her shadow replied against the high drone of the Interval.

He had expected her to vanish, to wink out of existence the same way she had winked in. But she simply turned and began walking at an angle to the eastern sun. Her shadow floated across the trampled earth, drawn as long and slender as a felled sapling. With every step she became smaller, a mere wisp before the enormity of dawn . . .

Ever more lonely and afraid.

CHAPTER ELEVEN

Momemn

This one thing every tyrant will tell you: nothing saves more lives than murder.

—MEROTOKAS, THE VIRTUE OF SIN

No two prophets agree. So to spare our prophets their feelings, we call the future a whore.

—ZARATHINIUS, A DEFENCE OF THE ARCANE ARTS

Early Summer, 20 New Imperial Year (4132 Year-of-the-Tusk), Momemn

'I gutted a dove in the old way,' the long-haired man said, 'with a sharpened stone. And when I drew out the entrails, I saw you.'

'Then you know.'

The Narindar assassin nodded. 'Yes . . . But do you?'

'I have no need of knowing.'

The Gift-of-Yatwer leaned against the door he had already entered.
The way was not barred.

The room was little more than a cellar, even though it hung some
four storeys above the alleyway. The plaster had sloughed from the
walls, leaving bare stretches of cracked brick. Near the slot that served
as a window, he saw himself speaking with a man, his tunic grimed
about the armpits. A cloak of road-beaten leather lay crumpled upon
the spare bed. His hair was waist long, a peculiarity among the Ketyai.
The only thing extraordinary about his dress was his war-girdle: a wide
belt stamped with the images of bulls. A variety of knives and tools
gleamed from holsters along the back.

'I gutted a dove in the old way,' the long-haired man was saying,
'with a sharpened stone. And when I drew out the entrails, I saw you.'

'Then you know.'

'Yes . . . But do you?'

'I have no need of knowing.'

The Narindar frowned and smiled. 'The Four-Horned Brother . . .
Do you know why he is shunned by the others? Why my Cult and my
Cult alone is condemned by the Tusk?'

The White-Luck Warrior saw himself shrug.

He glanced back, saw himself climbing stairs that had crumbled into
a narrow slope.

He glanced back, saw himself pressing through packed streets,
faces hanging like bulbs of garlic in shifting fields of cloth, soldiers
watching from raised stoops, slave-girls balancing baskets and urns
upon their heads, teamsters driving mules and oxen. He glanced back,
saw the immensity of the gate climbing above him, engulfing sun and
high blue sky.

He glanced back, one pilgrim among others braiding the roadway,
watching Momemn's curtain walls wandering out to parse the hazy
distances. A monumental fence.

He looked forward, saw himself rolling the long-haired man through *his blood into the black slot beneath the bed rack. He paused to listen through the booming of the streets, heard tomorrow's prayer horns yaw deep across the Home City.*

'The Four-Horned Brother . . .' the long-haired man was saying. 'Do you know why he is shunned by the others? Why my Cult and my Cult alone is condemned in the Tusk?'

'Ajokli is the Fool,' he heard himself reply.

The long-haired man smiled. 'He only seems such because he sees what the others do not see . . . What you do not see.'

'I have no need of seeing.'

The Narindar lowered his face in resignation. 'The blindness of the sighted,' he murmured.

'Are you ready?' the Gift-of-Yatwer asked, not because he was curious, but because this was what he had heard himself say.

'I told you . . . I gutted a dove in the old way.'

The White-Luck Warrior glanced back, saw himself standing upon a distant hill, looking forward.

The blood was as sticky as he remembered.

Like the oranges he would eat fifty-three days from now.

Esmenet felt a refugee, hunted, and yet somehow she also felt free.

Twenty years had passed since she had trod through the slots of a city as great as Momemn. When she married Kellhus, she had exchanged her feet for palanquins borne on the backs of slaves. Now that she walked again, alone save Imhailas, she felt as naked as a slave dragged out for auction. Here she was, easily the most powerful woman in the Three Seas, and she felt every bit as power-less and persecuted as she had as a common whore.

Once Biaxi Sankas had provided him with the time and loca-tion, Imhailas had plotted their course with the thoroughness of a military planner – even sending out soldiers, a different one for each leg of the journey, to count paces. She had dressed as the wife of a low Kianene functionary, cloaked in modest grey with a hanging half-veil that rested diagonally across her face, then she and Imhailas, who had disguised himself as a Galeoth caste-merchant, simply slipped out of the Imperial Precincts with the changing of the watches.

And she walked the streets – *her* streets – the way those she owned and ruled walked.

Sumna, where she had lived as prostitute, should have been a far different city, dominated as it was by the Hagerna, the city within the city that administered all the Thousand Temples. But power was power, whether clothed in the ecclesiastical finery of the Hagerna or the marshal regalia of the Imperial Precincts. Both Sumna and Momemn were ancient administrative centres, overrun with the panoply of peoples that served or seduced power. All that really distinguished them was the stone drawn from their respective quarries. Where Sumna was sandy and tan, as if one of the great Shigeki cities had been transplanted north, Momemn was largely grey and black – 'the child of dark Osbeus,' the poet Nel-Saripal had called it, referring to the famed basalt quarries that lay inland on the River Phayus.

She walked now the way she had walked then, her step brisk, her eyes shying from every passerby, her hands clutched before her. But where before she had passed through the fog of threat that surrounded every young and beautiful woman in low company, now she traversed the fog of threat that surrounded the powerful when they find themselves stranded among the powerless.

Imhailas had balked at the location Sankas had provided, but the Patridomos had assured him there was nothing to be done, that the kind of man they wanted to contract was as much priest as assassin, and so answered to his own unfathomable obligations. 'You must understand, all of this is a kind of prayer for them,' Sankas explained. 'The penultimate . . . act . . . does not stand apart from the acts that feed into it. In their eyes, this very discussion is an integral component of the . . . the . . .'

'The assassination,' Esmenet said.

For her part, she did not resent the prospect of sneaking across her city. *Something* had to be given, it seemed to her, for her mad design to have the least chance of succeeding. What was the risk and toil of walking mere streets compared with what she wanted – *needed* – to accomplish?

They walked side by side where the streets permitted, otherwise she followed Imhailas like a child – or a wife – taking heart in his high, broad shoulders. Even relatively affluent passers-by stepped clear of his arm-swinging stature. They followed the Processional toward the Cmiral temple-complex, turned after crossing the Rat Canal. They skirted the River District, then crossed what was called the New Quarter, presumably because it had come to house itinerant communities from across her husband's far-flung empire. The clamour waxed and waned from street to street, corner to corner. Tutors crying out to their classes. Blue-skinned devotees of Jukan, chanting and crashing their cymbals. Beggars, cast-off galley or fuller slaves, calling out Yatwer's name. Violent drunks, raging against the jostle.

Even the smells ebbed and flowed, too pungent and deep, too acrid and sharp, and too many – an endless mélange of the noxious and the perfumed. The canals revolted her so much with their flotsam and stench that she resolved to legislate their cleaning when she returned to the palace. When she travelled as Empress, a company of slaves flanked her passage, each bearing blue-steaming censers. Absent them, she found herself alternately holding her breath and gagging. Ever attentive, Imhailas purchased an orange at the first opportunity. Cut in half and held about the mouth and nose, oranges and lemons provided a relatively effective remedy against urban reek.

She saw mule-drawn wains swaying with firewood heaped so high she and Imhailas quickened their step whenever they passed them. She tried hard not to glare at the Columnaries they passed playing number-sticks on the steps of the Custom House they were supposed to be guarding. They passed an endless variety of vendors, some walking the streets bent beneath their wares, others occupying the stalls that slotted the first floor of most buildings. She even saw prostitutes sitting on the sills of second-floor windows, hanging their legs so that passersby could chase glimpses along their inner thighs.

She could not but reflect on the miracle that had raised her from the warp and woof of the sordid lives surrounding her. Nor could she avoid the great wall that years, luxury, and innumerable intermediaries had thrown between her and them. She was one of them, and she was not one of them – the same as with the caste-nobility that showered her with flattery and insolence day in and day out.

She was something in-between – apart. In all the world the only person like her, she realized in a pique of melancholy, the only other member of her lonely, bewildered tribe, was her daughter, Mimara.

Even though she knew that countless thousands made journeys no different from the one she and Imhailas had undertaken, it seemed miraculous they should gain their destination without some kind of challenge. The streets became more narrow, less crowded, and odourless enough for her to finally discard her orange. For the span of a dozen heartbeats she even found herself alone with her Exalt-Captain, fending a sudden, unaccountable suspicion that he and Sankas conspired to kill her. The thought filled her with shame and dismay.

Power, she decided, was a disease of the eyes.

Esmenet studied the ancient tenement while Imhailas consulted the small map Sankas had provided him. The structure had four floors, built in the Ceneian style with long, fired bricks no thicker than three of her fingers. Pigeon droppings positively mortared the ledges above the ground floor. A great crack climbed the centre of the facade, a line where the bricks had been pulled apart by settling foundations. She could tell most of the apartments were abandoned by the absence of shutters on the windows. Given the clamour and hum they had passed through, the place seemed almost malevolent for its silence.

When she glanced back at Imhailas, he was watching her with worried blue eyes.

'Before you go . . . May I speak, Your Glory? Speak *freely*.'

'Of course, Imhailas.'

He seized her hand with the same urgency she allowed him during the deep of night. The act startled her, at once frightened and heartened her.

'I beg you, Your Glory. Please, I *beseech*! I could have ten thousand soldiers break ten thousand curse-tablets on the morrow! *Leave him to the Gods!*'

The gleam of tears rimmed his eyes . . .

He loves me, she realized.

Even still, the most she could say was, 'The Gods are against us, Imhailas,' before turning to climb the rotted stairs into darkness.

The smell of urine engulfed her.

Another one of her boys was dead. This was simply the skin of the unthinkable, the only thought her soul could countenance when it came to justifying what she was about do. Far darker, more horrifying realizations roiled beneath. The closest she could come to acknowledging them was to think of poor Samarmas, and how his sweet innocence guaranteed him a place in the Heavens.

But Inrilatas . . . He had been taken too early. Before he could find his way past . . . himself.

Inrilatas was . . . was . . .

It is a strange thing to organize your life about the unthinkable, to make all your motions, all your words, expressions of absence. Sometimes she felt as though her arms and legs did not *connect* beneath her clothing, that they simply hung about the memory of a body and a heart. Sometimes she felt little more than a cloud of coincidences, face and hands and feet floating in miraculous concert.

A kind of living collapse, with no unifying principle to string her together.

The stairwell had been open to the sky at some point in the structure's past: she could see threads of light between boards high above. The landlord had decided to keep the rain out, she imagined, rather than repair the drainage. The steps had all but crumbled, forcing her to claw the bricked wall to ascend safely. She had known many tenements like this, ancient affairs, raised during glory days that no one save scholars remembered. Once, before Mimara had been born, a catastrophic roar had awakened her in the dead of night. The curious thing was the totality of the ensuing silence, as if the entire world had paused to draw breath. She had stumbled to her window and for a time could see only the dull glow of torches and lanterns through the blackness and dust. Only morning revealed the ruins of the tenement opposite, the heaps, the hanging remains of corner walls. In a twinkling, hundreds of faces she had known – the baker and his slaves, the souper who spent his day bellowing above the street's clamour, the widow who would venture out with her half-starved children to beg in the streets – had simply vanished. Weeks passed before the last of the bodies were recovered.

The stench had been unbearable, toward the end.

She paused on the second floor, peering and blinking. She breathed deep, tasted the earthen rot that soaks into mortar and burnt brick – and felt young, unaccountably young. Of the four doors she could discern, one stood ajar, throwing a lane of grey light across the dirty floor.

She found herself creeping toward it. Despite the crude cloth of her cloak, a kind of fastidious reluctance overcame her, the worry of staining what was fine and beautiful. What was she thinking? She couldn't do this . . . She had to flee, to race back to the Andiamine Heights. Yes . . .

She wasn't appropriately dressed.

Yet her legs carried her forward. The door's outer edge drew away like a curtain, revealing the room beyond.

The assassin stood staring out the window, but from the centre of the room, where he could scarce hope to see anything of interest. Indirect light bathed his profile. Aside from a certain solemn density in his manner, nothing about him suggested deceit and murder. The line of his nose and jaw was youthful to the point of appearing effeminate, yet his skin possessed the year-brushed coarseness of someone hard beyond his years. His jet hair was cropped short, which surprised her, since she had thought the assassin-priests always wore their hair long, as long as an Ainoni caste-noble's, but without the braids. His beard was trim, as was the present fashion among certain merchants – something she knew only because fanatical interests in the Ministrate had petitioned her to pass beard laws. His clothing was nondescript. Brown stains marred his earlobes.

She paused at the threshold. When she was a child, she and several other children would often swim in the Sumni harbour. Sometimes they made a game of holding heavy stones underwater and walking across the mud and debris of the bottom. She had the same sense stepping into the room, as if some onerous weight gave her traction, that she would pop from the floor otherwise, breach the surface of this nightmare . . .

And breathe.

The man did not turn to regard her, but she knew he scrutinized her nonetheless.

'My Exalt-Captain frets below,' she finally said, her voice more timid than she wished. 'He fears you will murder me.'

'He loves you,' the Narindar replied, jarring her with memories of her husband. Kellhus was forever repeating her thoughts.

'Yes . . .' she replied, surprised by a sudden instinct to be honest. To enter into a conspiracy is to commit a kind of adultery, for nothing fosters intimacy more than a shared will to deceive. What does clothing matter, when all else is shrouded? 'I suppose he does.'

The Narindar turned to regard her. She found his gaze unnerving. Rather than latching upon her, his focus seemed to float over and through her. The result of some ritual narcotic?

'Do you know what I want?' she asked, joining him in the indeterminate light. Her breath had climbed high and tight in her breast. She *was* doing this. She was seizing fate.

'Murder. To seek the Narindar is to seek murder.'

He smelled of mud . . . mud cooking in the sun.

'I will be plain with you, assassin. I appreciate the peril I represent. I know that even now you hedge, knowing that only something . . . something *extraordinary*, could deliver a woman of my exalted station to a man . . . a man . . . such as you. But I want you to know, it is *honesty* that has brought me here, alone . . . to you. I am simply not willing to see another damned for sins that are my own. I want you to know that you can trust that honesty. No matter what happens, I appreciate that you have placed your *very soul* upon the balance. I will make you a *prince*, assassin.'

If her words possessed effect, his gaze and expression betrayed none of it.

'Warm blood is the only gold I would hoard, Your Glory. Sightless eyes the only jewels I would covet.'

This had the sound of a catechism *believed*.

'*Maithanet,*' she said on a pent breath. 'The Shriah of the Thousand Temples . . . Kill him, and I shall compel *princes* – Do you hear me? Princes! – to kneel before you!'

It seemed utter madness, now that the words hung in the air between them. She almost expected the man to cackle aloud, but he grasped his bearded chin and nodded instead.

'Yes,' he said. 'An extraordinary sacrifice.'

'So you will do it?' she asked in unguarded astonishment.

'It is already done.'

She recalled what Lord Sankas had said about the Narindar carving events along different joints – the way this very meeting would be of a piece with raising the knife.

'But . . .'

'There is nothing more to be said, Your Glory.'

'But how will I . . . I . . .'

She trailed in flustered indecision. How could the world be so greased, so rounded, that matters this weighty could be discharged with such fugitive ease? The Narindar had turned to gaze through the slotted window. She reflexively followed his gaze, saw pillared smoke rising above the motley roofs to the east. Something was happening . . .

More riots?

She made to leave, but something intangible hooked her at the battered door, turned the tether of her gaze. He stood as if waiting for this very occurrence. He looked both old and young, as if time had lacked the tools to properly craft the clay of his skin. She wondered how she must look to him, furtive beneath her sack-cloth cloak and hood. An Empress cowering from her own Empire.

'What is your name?'

'Issiral.'

'Issiral . . .' she repeated, struggling to recall the meaning of the Shigeki word. 'Fate?' she asked, frowning and smiling. 'Who named you this?'

'My mother.'

'Your mother was cruel, to curse you with such a name.'

'We take such gifts as she gives.'

Something about this, and about the man's demeanour more generally, had blown terror into her anxiousness. But she reasoned that men who kill for hire – assassins – should be frightening.

'I thought Narindar were devotees of the Four-Horned Brother . . .'

'Devotion? The Brother cares not for our cares, only that we murder in His Name.'

The Blessed Empress of the Three Seas swallowed. That the World could accommodate such men, such designs. That even murder could become worship . . .

'The Brother and I have that much in common,' she said.

The Unaras Spur

Spaceless space . . . hanging.

Glimpses of slave-girls, shining black and naked save for a single ostrich feather between their thighs. Towering eunuchs, their ceremonial shackles gleaming in the humid gloom. Great beams of wood and bulbous pillars of marble and diorite. Pillows tossed negligently through the pleasure gardens . . .

The Palace of Plumes.

Soundless sound. Voiceless voice . . .

'Tell him, Cousin. Tell the cunning Son of Kascamandri. If he

succeeds, High Holy Zeüm will be as a brother to Kian. We will strike as he strikes, bleed as he bleeds!'

Even as he replied, Malowebi could feel himself toppling backward, plummeting into himself, so much had he dreaded these words. *'Yes, Great Satakhan.'*

The aging Mbimayu sorcerer blinked and coughed, found the infinite nowhere replaced by the squalid confines of his tent – if the wretched thing the Fanim had given him could be called such. He sat cross-legged, the twin mahogany figurines – the fetishes that made possible the Iswazi Cant – squeezed tight in his knobbed fists. He braced his elbows against his knees, buried his face in his hands.

Tomorrow, he decided. He would tell the Padirajah tomorrow.

Tonight he would groan and complain in his canvas cage, toss and obsess – do everything but sleep.

How Likaro would laugh. The ingrate.

After the Zaudunyani conquest of Nilnamesh, Malowebi and his senior Mbimayu brothers had burned whole urns of lantern oil scrutinizing and arguing the madness that was the Aspect-Emperor and the Great Ordeal. Even if their Satakhan had not demanded it, they would have set aside all things to ponder it. For years they had believed that Anasûrimbor Kellhus was simply a kind of contagion. For whatever reason, the Three Seas seemed particularly prone to prophets and their tricks. Where Zeüm had remained faithful to the old Kiünnat ways, albeit in their own elliptical fashion, the Ketyai – the Tribe entrusted with the Holy Tusk, no less! – seemed bent on tearing down their ancient truths and replacing them with abstraction and fancy. 'To better measure their ages,' Wobazul had quipped in one of their discussions. Anasûrimbor Kellhus, Malowebi and his fellow Mbimayu had assumed, was simply another Inri Sejenus, another gifted charlatan bent on delivering even more of his kinsmen to damnation.

But the man's *successes*. And the reports, both from Zeüm's spies and the Mbimayu's contact with the Schools. The Aspect-Emperor was more than a gifted demagogue, more than a cunning general or sorcerer or tyrant – far more.

The question was what?

So they debated, and debated, as is the wont of wise men pondering questions without obvious answers. Nganka'kull was often criticized for his patience and leniency, but eventually even he tired of their endless delays and demurrals. Finally he summoned his cousin, demanding to know the substance of their disagreements.

'We have considered everything of note,' Malowebi reported on a heavy breath. 'There is but one clear lesson . . .'

The Satakhan had perched his chin on his fist, such was the weight of the battle-wig – an heirloom from his beloved grandfather – that he wore. 'And what is that?'

'All those who resist him perish.'

Word that Imperial Columnaries had occupied the ruins of Auvangshei arrived later that very night – such was the perversity of Fate. The ancient fortress meant very little to Three Seas Men, Malowebi had since discovered. But for the Zeümi, it was nothing less than the sacred threshold of their nation. The one gate in the great wall the World itself had raised about High Holy Zeüm.

The Zaudunyani missionaries began arriving shortly afterward, some of them little more than paupers, others disguised as merchants. Then, of course, there was the infamous Embassy of Suicides. And during all this time, Auvangshei was rebuilt and expanded, the provinces of Nilnamesh reorganized along military lines. Their spies even reported the construction of numerous granaries in Soramipur and other western cities.

A kind of war was being waged against them, they realized. At every point of connection between Zeüm and the Three

Seas – mercantile, diplomatic, geographical – the Aspect-Emperor was *preparing* in some way.

'He fights us with pins rather than swords!' Nganka'kull exclaimed.

Malowebi had read *The Compendium* by this time. The book found its way to High Domyot more by accident than anything – or what amounted to the same, the Whore's whim. An Ainoni spice merchant named Parmerses had been seized under suspicion of spying, and the manuscript was discovered among his belongings. Of course, the man was summarily executed once his captors discovered the falsity of the charges against him, long before the importance of the work was understood, so questions regarding the book's provenance remained unanswered.

But once it was read, it was quickly traded among the wise and mighty. Malowebi had been gratified to learn that he was the *sixth* person to read *The Compendium* – no less than seven people before that fool, Likaro!

Drusas Achamian's revelations occasioned more than several sleepless nights. The wry humility of the tome, as well as the numerous references to Ajencis, convinced him the exiled Mandate Schoolman was a kindred intellect. The difficulty lay in the sheer audacity of what the Wizard alleged about the Aspect-Emperor: the idea of a man so quick, so cunning, that he, Malowebi, among the foremost sorcerers of his age – greater than Likaro by far – was nothing but a *child* in comparison. It was a thing too strange to credit. In all of the Kuburu, the accumulated legends of Zeüm, the hero's exalted trait was always strength, skill, or passion – never intellect. A miraculously accurate archer. A miraculously ardent lover . . .

Never a miraculously penetrating thinker, one who used *truth* as his primary instrument of deception.

But why? Malowebi found himself asking. It was a puzzle that deepened as more and more of his brothers expressed their skepticism of *The Compendium*. 'A cuckold's fancy,' Likaro had sneered, thus confirming its veracity in Malowebi's more discriminating eyes.

Why should the notion of a *Thought-dancer* rest so uneasy in the souls of Men?

Because, the Mbimayu sorcerer realized, they made what they *already* believed the measure of what other's believed. Not the World, and certainly not Reason. This was what rendered them blind to a being such as Anasûrimbor Kellhus, one who could play on innumerable strands of thought and weave that agreement into designs of his making. It reminded him of a passage from Ajencis, a thinker he secretly esteemed more than Memgowa: 'The world is a circle that has as many centres as it has men.' For someone who assumed he was the centre of his world, the thought of a man who occupied the *true* centre, who need only walk into a room to displace all those present within it, had to be as odious as it was incomprehensible.

Was the Aspect-Emperor a prophet as he claimed? Was he a demon as Fanayal believed – Kurcifra? Or was he inhuman in a more mundane sense, the harbinger of a *new race*, the Dûnyain, dreadful for the symmetry between their strength and human frailty . . .

A race of perfect manipulators. Thought-dancers.

If he *were* a prophet, then he and Mandate Schoolmen were right: the Second Apocalypse, despite what all the oracles and priests claimed, was evident, and Zeüm should enter into an alliance with him. If he were a demon, then Zeüm should arm for immediate war, now, before he achieved his immediate goals, for demons were simply Hungers from the abyss, insatiable in their pursuit of destruction.

And if he were Dûnyain?

Malowebi did not believe in prophets. You must first believe in Men before you could do that, and no serious student of Memgowa or Ajencis could do that. Malowebi most certainly believed in possessing demons – he had seen them with his own eyes. But demons, for all their cunning, were never *subtle*, certainly not to the degree of the Aspect-Emperor. No demon could have written the magisterial lies told in the *Novum Arcanum*.

Dûnyain . . . whatever that meant. The Aspect-Emperor had to be Dûnyain.

The problem, the Mbimayu sorcerer had realized, was that this conclusion in no way clarified the dilemma facing his nation and his people. Would not a Dûnyain bend all his effort and power to prevent his own destruction? Even without Drusas Achamian and his allegations, one could easily argue that Anasûrimbor Kellhus was among the greatest intellects to walk the earth. What could induce such a man to tip the bowl of the entire Three Seas, drain it to its dregs, in the name of warring against a nursemaid's cruel tale?

Could these *truly* be the first days of the Second Apocalypse?

Nonsense. Madness.

But . . .

When his family first yielded him to the Mbimayu, the Pedagogue of the School had been an ancient soul named Zabwiri, a legendary scholar, and a rare *true* disciple of Memgowa. For whatever reason, the old man had chosen him to be his body-servant for his final, declining years – a fact that some, like Likaro, begrudged him still. An intimacy had grown between them, one that only those who care for the dying can know. The pain had become increasingly difficult for the old man to manage, toward the end. He would sit in his little garden, shivering in the sunlight, while Malowebi hovered helpless about him. 'Question me!' he would bark with amiable fury. 'Pester me with your infinite ignorance!'

'Master,' Malowebi once asked, 'what is the path to truth?'

'Ah, little Malo,' old Zabwiri had replied, 'the answer is not so difficult as you think. The trick is to learn how to pick out *fools*. Look for those who think things simple, who abhor uncertainty, and who are incapable of setting aside their summary judgment. And above all, look for those who believe *flattering things*. They are the true path to wisdom. For the claims they find the most absurd or offensive will be the ones most worthy of your attention.'

Without fail the Mbimayu sorcerer's heart caught whenever he recalled these words: because he had loved Zabwiri, because of the way this answer embodied the wry, upside-down wisdom of the man. And now, because of the direction they pointed him . . .

The Aspect-Emperor a genuine prophet? The myths of the No-God's resurrection true?

These were the claims that *Likaro* found the most absurd and offensive. And in all the world there was no greater fool.

———

Horns were clawing the sky by the time she tripped clear of the tenement's gloom. Imhailas stood motionless in the middle of the street, his face raised in the blind way of those who peered after sounds.

The horns did not belong to either the Army or the Guard – yet she knew she had heard them before. They blared, climbed high and long enough to flush her heart with cold.

'What happens?' she asked her Exalt-Captain, who had not seen her, such was the intensity of his concentration.

He turned – looked at her with a fear she had never before seen in his face. A *soldier's* fear, not a courtier's.

'The horns . . .' he said, obviously debating his words. 'The signals . . . They belong to the Shrial Knights.'

Several heartbeats separated her soul from her dread. At first, all she could do was stare up into the man's beautiful face. She thought of the way his eyebrows arched just before he reached his bliss. 'What are you saying?' she finally managed to ask.

He looked to what sky they could see between the dark facades looming to either side of them.

'They sound like they're coming from different parts of the city . . .'

'What are they signalling?'

He stood rigid. Beyond him, she could see several others down the winding length of the street, mulling and listening the same as they did.

'Imhailas! What are they signalling?'

He looked to her, sucked his lips tight to his teeth in an expression of deliberation.

'Attack,' he said. 'They're coordinating some kind of attack.'

Running simply seized her, threw her back the way they had come.

But Imhailas was upon her in a matter of strides, clutching her shoulders, begging her to stop, to think, in hushed and hurried tones.

'Smoke!' she heard herself cry. 'From the room! I saw *smoke* to the east! The *palace*, Imhailas! They attack the palace!'

But he had known this already. 'We have to *think*,' he said firmly. 'Calculation is what sorts rash acts from bold.'

Another proverb he had memorized. Her hands fairly floated with the urge to scratch out his eyes. Such a fool! How could she conspire, let alone couple, with such a fool?

'*Unhand me!*' she gasped in fury.

He raised his hands and stepped back. Something in her tone had struck all expression from his face, and a kind of panicked regret joined the terrors flushing through her. Was he deciding where to cast his lots? Would he abandon her? Betray her? Curses spooled through her thoughts. Her foolishness. Fate. The ability of men to so easily slip the leash of feminine comprehension.

'Sweet Seju!' she heard herself cry. '*Kelmomas! My boy*, Imhailas!'

Suddenly a different horn cawed high above the roaring in her ears, one that she knew from innumerable drills – knew so well that it almost seemed a word shouted across the world. *Rally! Guardsmen, Rally!*

Then Imhailas was kneeling on the stone before her. 'Your Glory!' he said, his voice cast low. 'The Imperial Precincts are under attack. What would you have your slave do?'

And at last, reason was returned to her. To act in ignorance was to flail as though falling. Knowledge. They needed to discover what Maithanet was doing and to pray the palace could resist him.

'Keep his Empress safe,' she said.

Anasûrimbor Kelmomas would never quite understand how he knew. Funny, the way the senses range places the soul cannot follow.

He was playing in his room – *pretending* to play would be more accurate, since he was far more lost in his plots and fancies than in the crude toys he was *supposed* to be amused by – when something simply called him out to his balcony onto the Sacral Enclosure . . .

Where it seemed he could *smell* whatever it was. His nurse called out after him. He ignored her. He peered about, saw the guardsmen milling as they always milled, the slaves trotting to and fro . . .

Everything and everyone in their place.

Something *bigger* had been thrown out of joint, he realized. He turned to gaze down the line of balconies to his right, saw his older sister, Theliopa, wearing a crazed gown with coins hanging heavy from every hem, standing like a bird leaning into the breeze, her senses pricked to the same something he could neither hear nor see.

The sycamores loomed before and above them, each leaf a little whistling kite, forming mops that dipped and murmured in the sunlight. Nothing . . . He could hear nothing.

Of all his siblings, only Theliopa commanded any fondness in his heart. Kelmomas had never bothered to ponder why this might be. She ignored him for the most part and typically spoke to him only on Mother's behalf. He certainly feared her the least. And despite the time she spent with Mother, he envied her not at all.

She had never seemed quite real, his sister.

Kelmomas gazed at her chipped-porcelain profile, debating whether he should call out to her. He had opened his ears so wide that her gown fairly crashed with sound when she whirled to face him.

'Run-run,' she said without any alarm whatsoever. 'Find some-some place to hide.'

He did not move. He rarely took anything Thelli said seriously, such was his fondness for her. Then he heard it, the first faint shouts breaching the low roar of the sycamores.

The ring and clatter of arms . . .

'What happens?' he cried, but she had already vanished.

Uncle Holy, the secret voice whispered as he stood witless. *He has returned.*

Shrial horns continued signalling one another, but, ominously, they heard no more calls from the Eothic Guard aside from the first, single cry. The city seemed deceptively normal, apart from the roofs, which had become packed with onlookers. Traffic filed through the alleys and streets with greater haste, certainly. Momemnites milled here and there, exchanging fears and guesses between eastward glances. But no one panicked – at least not yet. If anything, the city *waited*, as if it were nothing more than a vast cart, sitting idle while the yoke was bound to a new mule.

For the first time, and with more than a little terror, Esmenet understood the *slipperiness* of power, the ease with which substitutions could be made, so long as the *structure* remained intact. When people kissed your knee, it was so easy to think *you* were the principle that moved them and not the position you happened to occupy. But glancing from face to face – some aged, some poxed, some tender – she realized that she could, if she wished, throw aside her veil, that she had no need whatsoever to disguise herself, simply because *she*, Esmenet, the Sumni harlot who had lived a life crazed with tumult and detail, literally did not exist for them.

What did it matter, the person hidden behind the palanquin's screens, so long as the bearers were fed?

There was doom in these thoughts, so she shied from them.

The crowds grew, as did the agitation and turmoil. The closer they came to the palace, the more complicated their passage became. Most people fought their way eastward, frantic to escape whatever was happening behind them. Others, the curious and those who, like Esmenet, had kin in the vicinity of the palace, battled their way eastward.

Twice Imhailas stopped to ask aimless Columnaries what happened, and twice he was rebuffed.

No one knew.

Even still, hope wormed ever higher into her throat as they raced, dodged, and shoved. She found herself thinking of her Pillarian and Eothic Guardsmen, how competent, how numerous, and how loyal they seemed. For years she had dwelt among them, thoughtlessly demanding the security they provided but never really appreciating them – until now. They were handpicked, chosen from across the Middle-North for their prowess and fanaticism. They had spent the greater portion of their lives preparing for occasions such as this, she reminded herself. If anything, they *lived* for just such an eventuality.

They would defend the Imperial Precincts, secure the palace. They would keep her children safe!

Breathless, she imagined them bristling along the walls, arrayed about the gates, glorious in their crimson-and-gold regalia. She saw old Vem-Mithriti standing high upon some parapet, his stooped shoulders pulled back with outrage and indignation, raining down sorcerous destruction. She saw old Ngarau waddling in walrus-armed panic, barking out commands. And her boy – her beautiful boy! – frightened, yet too young not to be exhilarated, not to think this some kind of glorious game.

Yes! The Gods would not heap this calamity upon her. She had paid their bloodthirsty wages!

The World *would* rally . . .

But the smoke climbed ever higher as they raced through the ever more raucous streets, until she felt she stared up into a tree for craning her neck. The faces of those fleeing became ever more sealed, more intent. The roaring – shouts from the crowded rooftops, from the seething streets – seemed to grow louder and louder.

'The Palace burns!' one old crone cried immediately next to her. 'The Empress-Whore is dead! *Dead!*'

And in the crash of hope into dismay, she remembered: the *Gods* hunted her and her children.

The White-Luck had turned against them.

At last they pressed their way free of the slotted streets onto the Processional with its broad views.

Were it not for Imhailas and his strength, the mobs would have defeated her, prevented her from seeing the catastrophe with her own eyes. He pulled her by the wrists, cursing and shoving, and she followed with the pendulum limbs of a doll. Then suddenly they were clear, panting, among the crowd's forward ranks.

A cohort of unmounted Shrial Knights guarded the bridges crossing the Rat Canal – as much to police the mob, it seemed, as to ward against any attempt to retake the Imperial Precincts. The fortifications rising beyond were deserted. She glimpsed pockets of battle here and there across the climbing jumble of structure that composed the Andiamine Heights: distant figures vying, their swords catching the sun. Smoke poured in liquid ribbons from the Allosium Forum. Three other plumes climbed from places unseen beyond the palace.

Imhailas need not say anything. The battle was over. The New Empire had been overthrown in the space of an afternoon.

Planning, she realized. An assault this effective required meticulous planning . . .

Time.

The Empress of the Three Seas stood breathless, an errant hand held to her veil, gazing at the loss of everything she had known for the past twenty years. The theft of her power. The destruction of her home. The captivity of her children. The overturning of her world.

Fool . . .

A thought like a cold draft in a crypt.

Such a fool!

Vying against Anasûrimbor Maithanet. Crossing swords with a Dûnyain – who knew the folly of this better than she?

She turned to Imhailas, who stood as immobile and aghast as she. 'We . . .' she murmured, only to trail. 'We have to go back . . .'

He looked down into her eyes, squinted in confusion.

'We have to go back!' she cried under her breath. 'I'll . . . I'll throw myself at his feet! Beg for mercy! Seju! Seju! I *have* to do something!'

He cast a wary glance across those packed close about them.

'Yes, Your Glory,' he said intently, speaking below the mob's rumble. 'You must do something. This is treason. *Sacrilege!* But if you deliver yourself to him, *you will be executed* – do you understand? He cannot afford your testimony!'

Threads of light tangled and distorted his face. She was blinking tears. When had she started weeping?

Since coming to Kellhus's bed, it seemed. Since abandoning Akka . . .

'All the more reason for you to leave me, Imhailas. Flee . . . while you still can.'

A smiling frown creased his face.

'Damnation doesn't agree with me, Holy Empress.'

Another one of his quotations . . . She sobbed and laughed in exasperation.

'I am not asking, Imhailas. I am *commanding* . . . Save yourself!'

But he was already shaking his head.

'This I cannot do.'

She had always thought him a fop, a thick-fingered dandy. She had always wondered what it was that Kellhus had seen in him, to raise him so high so fast. As a courtier, he could be almost comically timid – always bowing and scraping, stumbling over himself in his haste to execute her wishes. But now . . . Now she could see Imhailas as he really was . . .

A warrior. He was – at his pith – a true warrior. Defeat did not break his heart so much as stir his blood.

'You don't know, Imhailas. You don't know . . . Maithanet . . . the way I know him.'

'I know that he is cunning and treacherous. I know that he

pollutes the Holy Office your husband has given to him. Most of all, I know *you have already done* what you needed to do.

'I . . . I . . .' She trailed, wiped her nose, and squinted up at him. 'What are you saying?'

'You have loosed the *Narindar* . . .'

He was inventing his rationale as he spoke: she could see this in his inward gaze, hear it in his searching tone. He would stand by her side, die for her, not for any tactical or even spiritual reason, but because sacrificing his strength on the altar of higher things was simply what he did.

This was why Kellhus had given him to her.

'All that remains is to *wait*,' he continued, warming to the sense of what he said. 'Yes . . . We must hide and wait. And when the Narindar strikes . . . All will be chaos. Everyone will be casting about, searching for authority. That's when you reveal yourself, Your Glory!'

She so wanted to believe him. She so wanted to pretend that the Holy Shriah of the Thousand Temples was not a Dûnyain.

'But my boy! My daughter!'

'Are children of your husband . . . The *Aspect-Emperor*.'

Anasûrimbor Kellhus.

Esmenet gasped, so sudden was her understanding. Yes. He was right. Maithanet would not dare to kill them. Not so long as Kellhus lived. Even so far from the northern wastes, they dwelt in the chill shadow of the Holy Aspect-Emperor's power. As did all Men.

'Hide . . .' she repeated. 'But how? Where? They are *all against me*, Imhailas! Inrithi. Yatwerians . . .'

And yet, even as she voiced these fears, implications began assembling about the mere fact of her husband. This, she realized. This was why Kellhus had left *her* the Imperial Mantle.

She did not covet it. How could one covet what one despised?

'Not me, Your Glory. Nor any Guardsmen living, I assure you.'

Kellhus *would* succeed and he *would* return – he always conquered. Even Moënghus, his father, could not overcome him . . . Kellhus would return, and when he did, there would be a horrible accounting.

Imhailas clasped her hands in his own. 'I know of a place . . .'

She need only live long enough to see it done.

He will come back for us!

She made a litany of this thought as they fled back into the city proper.

Kellhus will return!

When despair reeled through her, the sense of skidding backward into doom . . .

He will return!

When she imagined Theliopa, sitting rigid in her room, staring into her hands as Maithanet's shadow darkened the threshold . . .

He will! He will!

When she saw Maithanet kneel before Kelmomas, grasp his slender shoulders between his hands . . .

He will kill him with his own hands!

And it seemed she could see *him*, her glorious husband, stepping from spiking light to stride across the city, calling out his brother's treacherous name. And it pulled her breath sharp, wound her teeth tight, stretched her lips into an animal grin . . .

The fury of his judgment.

Then she found herself in a lantern-lit foyer, standing and blinking while Imhailas muttered in low tones to an armed man even taller than he was. The tile-work, the frescoed ceiling, everything possessed an air of opulence, but a false one, she quickly realized, seeing the grimed corners and grouting, the myriad chips and cracks – details that shouted an inability to support slaves.

Then Imhailas was leading her up marble stairs. She wanted to ask him where they were, where they were *going*, but she could not speak around the confusion that bloated through her. At last they gained a gloomy corridor. Her breathlessness – years had passed since she had last travelled such distances on foot – became a sense of floating suffocation.

She stood blinking while he hammered on a broad wooden door. She scarcely glimpsed the face, dark and beautiful, that anxiously greeted him. A room beyond, yellow-painted, dimly illuminated.

'Imma! Sweet Seju! I was wor—'

'Naree! Please!' the Exalt-Captain cried, shouldering the woman back, hustling Esmenet into the dimly lit interior without begging permission.

He shut the door behind them, turned to the two astounded women.

The girl was no taller than Esmenet, but she was darker of complexion, younger. And beautiful. Very beautiful. Despite her appearance and accent, it was actually her costume, a gaudy, glass-beaded affair, that made Esmenet realize this . . . this Naree . . . was Nilnameshi.

Naree, for her part, appraised Esmenet with open distaste.

'This will *cost* you, Imma . . .' she said skeptically.

And Esmenet understood – the tone as much as anything else. Naree was a whore.

Imhailas had brought her to his whore.

'Stop playing the fool and grab her a bowl of water!' he cried, grabbing Esmenet by the shoulders, guiding her to a battered settee. Her eyes could not make sense of the room relative to the movements of her body – everything whirled. Breathless. Why was she so breathless?

Then she was sitting, and her Exalt-Captain was kneeling before her.

'Who is she?' Naree asked, returning with water.

Imhailas raised the bowl for her to drink. 'She's not . . . not *right* . . . The day . . .'

Naree stared, her face slack in the way of long-time victims assessing threats. Her eyes popped wide, rings of shining white about dark, dark irises. She was a whore: innumerable silver kellics had passed through her hands, each bearing the image of the woman before her.

'Sweet Mother of Birth – it's *you*!'

A wave crashed through the Andiamine Heights, swirling into the corridors, rising ever higher, foaming blood. It battered down doors. It threw itself howling into braced mobs of Eothic Guardsmen. It clutched welling wounds, grunting and crying out. It slumped dying in the corners of raucous rooms.

Slipping through hollow walls, the young Prince-Imperial tracked its grim progress. He watched men hacking and grappling, murdering in the name of symbol and colour. He saw flames leap from ornament to ornament. He watched astounded slaves beaten – and, in one instance, raped. And it seemed a miracle that he could be *alone* while witnessing such heroism and atrocity.

Never had the end of the world been so much fun.

He knew full well what he witnessed – a coup, nearly flawless in its execution. The fall of the Andiamine Heights. He knew that his Uncle would rule the Empire ere the day was done and that his mother would either be a captive or a fugitive . . .

If he did not think of the unthinkable consequence – that she would be *executed* – it was because he knew *he* was responsible, and nothing he authored could lead to anything so disastrous.

He had made this happen – there was a clenching glee to this thought, an elation that at times barked as a laugh from his lungs, such was its intensity. And it seemed the Palace itself became his model, the replica he had decided to break and burn. Uncle Holy, for all his danger, was but one more tool . . .

He was the God here. The Four-Horned Brother.

Wires of smoke coiled beneath the vaults, hazed the gilded corridors. Slaves and costumed functionaries fled. Armoured men rallied, charged, and grappled, as colourful as new toys: the gold on white surcoats of the Shrial Knights, the crimson of the Eothic Guard, the gold on green of the Pillarians. He watched a company of these latter defend the antechambers to the Audience Hall. Time and again they broke the Knights of the Tusk who assailed them, killing so many they began using their bodies as improvised barricades. Only when the Inchausti, the bodyguard of the Holy Shriah himself, assaulted them were the fanatics finally overcome.

Their willingness to die left Kelmomas breathless. For *him*, he realized. They sacrificed themselves for him and his family . . .

The fools.

He glimpsed or watched a dozen such melees moving down the Heights, isolated pockets of violence, the Palace's defenders always outnumbered, always fighting to the desperate last. He listened to the curses and catcalls they traded, the Shrial Knights beseeching their foes to surrender, to yield the 'Mad Whore,' the Pillarians and guardsmen promising doom and damnation for their foe's treachery.

Exploring the Palace's lower tracts, below the rising tide of battle, he saw rooms and corridors strewn with dead, and he witnessed the savagery that so often leaps into the void of power overthrown. He watched one of his mother's Apparati, an Ainoni named Minachasis, rape and strangle a slave-girl – assuming the crime would be attributed to the invaders, the astonished boy supposed.

And then there were the looters, Shrial Knights – pairs usually – who found themselves happily separated from their companies, ranging halls they believed already cleared. Kelmomas found one solitary fool rummaging through a room in the Apparatory, rending the mattress, rifling the wardrobe, hacking open a small chest and kicking the baubles he found in disgust.

The room was windowless, so the boy peered through a ventilation grill tucked high in a corner. He watched with fascination, realizing that he witnessed avarice in its purest, most impatient form. It almost seemed a mummer's act, as if a starving ape had been dressed in Shrial regalia, then sent scavenging for the amusement of unseen patrons.

Even before he realized his intent, Kelmomas began snuffling audibly – weeping the way a frightened little boy might. The Knight of the Tusk fairly jumped clear out of his hauberk and surcoat, such was his surprise. He whirled from side to side. Several heartbeats passed before he mastered his alarm and listened – before he realized it was a *child* that he heard – someone harmless. A leering smile cracked his beard.

'Shush,' he drawled, scanning the high corners, for he had realized the sound came from above. The Prince-Imperial continued weeping, making the sounds of a derelict child. His face ached for the manic ferocity of his grin.

The sounds hooked the man's gaze. He kicked a chair to the corner. Mounted it.

'*Moh-moh-mommeeee!*' the boy sobbed, hitching his voice into a high whine.

The man's face loomed before the iron fretting, darkened by its own shadow. His breath reeked of cheap liquor . . .

The crawlspace was so cramped that Kelmomas bungled his

strike, driving his skewer through the man's pupil rather than his tear duct. Strange sensation that – like popping the skin of a grape. The man's face clenched about the intrusion, a fist without fingers. He toppled, fell flat on his back, where he jerked in a strange parody of a fool's caper.

Like a beetle flicked onto his back.

Look at him! the secret voice chortled.

'Yes!' Kelmomas cackled. He even clapped his hands, such was his raw delight.

Afterward, when night fell and silence hardened the acrid air, he toured the labyrinth of small battlefields, taking care lest he track bloody footprints across the expansive floors. He had thought he would find glory wandering among the dead, but all he witnessed were its dregs. Nothing remained of the desperation, the shouts and cries of mortal struggle. There was no distinguishing the heroic from the craven. The dead were dead, utterly helpless and invulnerable. The more he counted them, the more they seemed to laugh.

Eventually he stood marooned, silence pricking his ears.

'Mommy?' he finally dared call. The dead did not so much as twitch.

At long last his face-cracking grin faded . . .

And a weeper's grimace rose to take its place.

There had been a heartbeat, upon awakening, when nothing seemed amiss, where she need only blink and stretch and groan her morning groan to summon her body-slaves and their soothing ministrations. A heartbeat . . .

But horror, true horror, dwells in the body as much as the soul. She needed only to raise her arms to recall the madness of the previous day. The pinioned breath. The curious mismatch between motion and effort, as if her sinews had become sand, her bones lead. The seashell roar.

Lying prostrate across a narrow cot, the Blessed Empress of the Three Seas plummeted and plummeted, clutching at thoughts too sharp with fingers too cold. Fumbling with knives . . .

The palace lost.

Her husband betrayed.

Kelmomas . . .

Sweet little Kelmomas!

She tried curling into a ball, tried weeping, but tears and sobs seemed things too heavy to be moved, so frail had her innards become. A crazed, floating restlessness inhabited her instead, where the most she could do was throw her limbs, flop them this way and that, like things, dead things, continually in the way of themselves. But even this effort defeated her, so she lay motionless, thrashed within, as if she were a greased worm, writhing against appendages too slippery to hold.

'Please . . .' a girlish voice whispered. 'Your Glory . . .'

Esmenet opened her eyes, blinking. Even though she had yet to weep, she could fell the itch of swollen lids.

Naree knelt next to the cot, her large eyes round with fear, her luxurious hair hanging in sheets about her plump cheeks. The far window shone white over her shoulder, gleamed across the yellow-painted walls. 'I n-need you to stay h-here,' the girl said, tears spilling down her cheeks. She was terrified, Esmenet realized – as she should be. Imhailas had delivered a burden she could not bear. 'Just-just stay here, yes? Keep your face . . . your face to the wall.'

Without a word the Blessed Empress of the Three Seas turned from the girl, toward the cracked paint and plaster. What else was there do?

Watches passed, and she did not move, not until the need to make water overpowered her. Only her listening roamed . . .

Between uncertain faces. Beneath damp sheets.

'Who is that?'

'My mother . . .'

'Mother?'

'Pay her no heed.'

'But I will!'

'No . . . Please . . . Heed this instead.'

Four different men visited the girl, but they seemed one and same creature in Esmenet's ears. The same half-hearted flatteries, carnal witticisms. The same nostril-pinching intakes of breath. The same moans and giggles. The same rasp of grinding hair. The same cries. The same liquid drumbeat.

Only the stench varied.

And it repelled her, even as her inner thighs grew slick. It *shamed* her. To conjure the miracle of intimacy, to become one breathless creature while still wearing the skin of strangers.

She coupled with them anew that afternoon, all the men she had known as a harlot. She saw them skulking in from the open streets, their eyes clouded with need, offering silver instead of wooing, proving, *loving*. She laughed as she teased, gagged as she choked, huddled beneath the apish rage of the impotent, gasped beneath the slow stir of the beautiful. She gloated over coins, dreamed of the food she would buy, the cloth.

She wept for the loss of her Empire.

There was a lull after the fourth man departed. The clatter and shout of the street climbed through the unshuttered windows, rang with the stark clarity of plastered walls and tiled floors. A man with a cracked voice bellowed, boasting the curative power of his sulphured cider. A dog snarled and barked, obviously old and frightened.

Esmenet finally turned from the wall, her bladder so full she could scarce contain herself. Even after all this time, the room was a mystery to her. It was far larger than any room Esmenet had been able to afford in Sumna, but then, for all her beauty, she had not been an outlander like Naree, and Sumna had never seen the wealth that had concentrated in Momemn since Kellhus's rise to power. Two windows looked onto the sun-drenched facade of the tenement across the street – one housing more prostitutes, she realized, glimpsing two pale-skinned Norsirai girls sitting on sills. The far window illuminated a small scullery: a water basin upon a wooden counter, a standing amphorae, pottery-stacked shelves, and various herbs hanging to dry. The near window showered light across Naree's bed, which was a broad, extravagant affair constructed of black-lacquered mahogany. Esmenet's cot was set parallel to the bed on the far side of the door.

The girl lay naked across the tangled covers, staring from the ridge of her pillow. The fugitive Empress of the Three Seas gazed back with numb urgency. She knew the exhaustion in Naree's eyes, the dull throb of her sex, the faint pinch of seed drying across bare skin, the peculiar sense of *having survived*. She knew the disjoint chorus that was the girl's soul: the voice counting coins, the voice fending against despair, the voice flinching from the fact of what had just happened – and the voice urging her to betray her Empress.

Naree was broken – that much was certain. Even the priestesses of Gierra, who sold themselves with the sanction of god and temple, were broken. To sell intimacy is to be turned inside out, to make a cloak of your heart, so that others might be warmed. A soul could only be inverted so many times before it all became confused, inside and outside.

Broken. Esmenet could see the cracks floating in her watery gaze. The only real question was one of *how*. Selling peaches did not so much rob a soul of trust or dignity or compassion as it robbed these words of their common meaning. Naree believed in trust, jealously guarded her dignity, felt compassion – but in ways utterly peculiar to her.

'I need to pee,' Esmenet finally said.

'Sorry-sorry-sorry!' the girl cried, leaping from her bed. She ran to the screen that flanked her settee. She pulled back one of the faded embroidered panels and, with a mummer's flourish, revealed a white porcelain chamber pot. Esmenet thanked her sheepishly.

'*Nareeee!*' an accented voice cried from out-of-doors – one of the Galeoth girls hanging her thighs from a window opposite. '*Nareeee! Who dat you hat wit you?*'

'Mind your own sheets!' the Nilnameshi girl cried, hastening to close the shutters on the near window.

The whore cackled the way Esmenet had heard countless times before. '*Brooshing rugs, eh?*'

Fairly in a terror, Naree explained how they all kept their windows unshuttered when attending to their custom – for safety.

'I know,' Esmenet said. 'I used to do the same.'

Suddenly she realized the impossibility of her circumstance. Naree, like most people of hale heart, knew all her neighbours and was known by them. Esmenet knew first-hand the way city-dwellers roped themselves into small tribes and villages, caring for one another, envying, spying, hating.

More shutters clattered and the room darkened while she attended to her bladder. When she stepped from behind the screen she found Naree in the gloom, still naked, sitting cross-legged on her bed weeping. Without thinking she took the girl's slender shoulders in her arms, pulled her into a mother's embrace.

'Shush,' the Holy Empress said.

She thought of the famine, the way Mimara had seemed to retreat further into her bones with every passing day. She thought of the way she had torn in two, walking with her to the slavers in the harbour. The hum of disbelief. The goad of numb necessity. The little fingers clasping hers in anxious trust.

And she wished, with a violence that rolled her eyes, that she had simply held on to those bones, folded them within the squalid circle of her own . . . and died with her only daughter. Mimara.

The one thing unsold.

'I understand.'

How long had it been since she had kept company with her past?

Esmenet sat with the girl until the glaring white lines that etched the shutters paled to grey. Naree did not know her age, only that five years had passed since her flowering. She had been raised a yitarissa, a ritual harem-slave popular among the Nilnameshi caste-nobility. Her owner had possessed estates both in Invishi, where they wintered, and in the Hinayati Mountains, where they spent the plague months of summer. She had loved him fiercely. Apparently he was a gentle, caring man, one who lavished her with gifts to atone for the inevitable injuries he inflicted on her. The great catastrophe in her life – her year zero – came with her first bleeding. Rather than sell her to a brothel, as was the fate of most yitarissa, her owner set her free. Almost immediately she became the mistress of another caste-noble, a trade representative who had been sent to Momemn almost four years ago. He was the one who had purchased the yellow room and its sumptuous furnishings. Naree loved him as well, but when his year-long tenure expired, he simply moved his wife and household back to Invishi without saying a word.

She began selling herself almost immediately.

Esmenet found herself listening with two souls: the one, the old whore, almost contemptuous of the cozened luxury that had characterized so much of the girl's life; the other, the aging mother, horrified at the way she had been used and cast away, only to be used and cast away again.

'I *want* to help you!' the girl cried. 'Imma, he . . . he . . . I . . .'

Thus is cruelty always explained away. A life of suffering. A life where simple survival seems an unaccountable risk. A life too damaged to countenance heroism.

Esmenet tried to imagine what she would have done those years had one of her customers come to her with a fugitive of any description – let alone the Empress of the Three Seas. She wanted to think she would be fearless, generous, but she knew that she would do what Fate demanded all prostitutes do: betray in the name of survival.

Only *Akka* could have coaxed such a risk from her, she realized.

Only love.

Suddenly she understood the girl's torment. Naree loved Imhailas. She had made him the sum of her simple hopes. Were he just another man, she would have resorted to the grim, guarded manner that prostitutes typically use to distance people they were forced to hurt. But he was not. And he had come to her demanding a *mortal* favour.

People had died – people *were dying* – because of her, Anasûrimbor Esmenet. From this moment on, she realized, she had become a mortal risk to anyone who so much as glimpsed her without alerting the Shrial Knights. From this moment on, she was the most sought-after fugitive in all the Three Seas.

'Please!' Naree cried, her voice piteous for her accent. '*Please!* Blessed Empress! You must find some *other* place! You-you're not-not . . . *safe* here! There are too many people!'

But Naree, she knew, wasn't simply asking her to hide elsewhere. The girl was asking her to take *responsibility* for leaving as well, so that she might salvage her relationship with Imhailas.

And were it not for her children, Esmenet probably would have done exactly as she asked.

'Why?' a masculine voice asked from behind them. Both women gasped, started violently enough to pop some joint in the bed. Imhailas stood by the door, cloaked as before, staring at Naree in naked outrage. The combination of gloom and surprise made him seem an apparition. 'Why are we not safe?'

The girl instantly dropped her eyes – some habit from her childhood bondage, Esmenet supposed. Imhailas strode around the bed, glaring in fury. The floorboards creaked beneath his booted feet. The girl continued staring down in submissive immobility.

'What is this?' he snapped, tugging at the blanket she had pulled about her shoulders. The girl caught an exposed breast with a forearm. 'You've been *taking custom?*' he cried in low, incredulous tones.

'Imma!' she called, at last looking up. Tears streamed from her eyes.

The blow was sudden, hard enough to send the slight girl rolling across the mattress. Imhailas hauled her upright, pinned her writhing against the wall before Esmenet could find her voice, let alone her feet. The girl clawed at the hand about her throat, gurgled and gagged. The Exalt-Captain pulled his knife, raised the point before her wide and rolling eyes.

'Should I send you to them now?' he grated. 'Should I let the Hundred judge you *now*, while you still stink for rutting before your *Holy Empress*! Should I send you to them *polluted?*'

Esmenet circled behind him as if through a dream. *When did I become so slow?* a vague portion of her soul wondered. *When had the world become so fast?*

She raised a palm to the wrist of the choking hand. Imhailas looked to her, his eyes wild and bright and clouded with the madness that is the terror of all women. He blinked, and she watched him catch himself from the murderous brink.

'Shush, Imma,' she said, using the diminutive of his name for the first time. She met his astounded gaze with a warm smile. 'Your Blessed Empress, remember, happens to be an old whore.'

The Exalt-Captain released the naked girl, who slumped to the tiles, gagging and weeping. He stepped back.

Esmenet crouched over the girl, hesitated, her soul caught on the humming threshold of compassion.

Your children! she thought with a kind of inward torsion. *No enemy is so relentless as a forgiving nature. Kelmomas! Remember him!*

'I'm your Empress, Naree . . . Do you know what that means?'

Esmenet reached toward Imhailas, gestured for his knife. *His palms are hotter than mine*, she thought as her fingers closed about the warm leather of the grip.

Even skinned in tears, there was something crisp and vigilant about the girl's eyes, a troubling alacrity in the way they clicked from the shining blade to Esmenet's own gaze. As young as she was, Esmenet realized, Naree was an inveterate survivor.

'It means,' Esmenet said, her smile as warm and motherly as the knife's edge was wicked, 'that your life – your *life*, Naree – belongs to me.'

The girl swallowed and nodded with the same air of learned submission.

Esmenet pressed the knife's point against the soft curve of her throat.

'Your *soul*,' the Blessed Empress of the Three Seas continued, 'belongs to my husband.'

'Maithanet has loosed an army of priests across the city,' Imhailas said, leaning back in exhaustion across the battered settee. Naree, now robed and almost comically meek, sat cross-legged on the floor at his feet, holding up a bowl of watered wine in yet another pose of ritual subservience. Esmenet sat on the corner of her cot watching them, hunched forward with her elbows on her thighs. The world beyond the shutters had gone black. A single lantern illuminated the room, casting haphazard shadows through ochre gloom.

'Criers,' the Exalt-Captain continued, 'only decked in full vestments, swinging censers on staffs . . .' His eyes latched on to Esmenet in the gloom, the lamplight reflected in two shining white dots low on his irises. 'He's saying you've gone mad, Your Glory. That you – *you!* – have betrayed your husband.'

The words winded her, even though she was entirely unsurprised. Maithanet need not be Dûnyain to understand the importance of legitimacy.

Kellhus had explained nations and polities to her, how they worked like the Cironji automata so prized by the more fashionable caste-nobility. 'All states are raised upon the backs of men,' he had told her after the final capitulation of High Ainon. 'Their *actions*, the things they do, day in and day out, connect like wheels and cogs, from the stonemason to the tax-farmer to the body-slave. And all actions are raised upon the back of *belief*. When men turn from their beliefs, they turn from their actions, and the entire mechanism fails.'

'So this is why I must lie?' she asked, watching him from her pillow.

He smiled the way he always did when she missed his mark in a penetrating manner. 'No. To think in these terms, Esmi, is to think *honesty* is the decision that confronts you.'

'What is the decision, then?'

He shrugged. 'Effectiveness. The masses will always be mired in falsehood. Always. Each man will *think* he believes true, of course. Many will even weep for the strength of their conviction.

So if you speak truth to their deception, they will call you liar and cast you from power. The ruler's only recourse is to speak *oil*, to communicate in ways that facilitate the machine. Sometimes this oil will be truth, perhaps, but more often it will be lies.'

Speaking oil. Of all the analogies he used to illustrate the deeper meaning of things, none would trouble her quite so much. None would remind her so much of Achamian and his fateful warning.

'But . . .'

'How did I rise to power?' he asked, seeing her thoughts as always. A rueful smile, as if remembering escapades best forgotten. 'Men make what they *already believe* the measure of what is true or false. What they call "reason" is simply apology. The masses will *always* believe false because the fancy of their forefathers is *always their rule*. I rose to power by giving them truths, little truths, for which they possessed *no rule*, one after the other. I chased the unthought implications of what they already believed, gaining ever more legitimacy, until, eventually, men *made me* their one and only rule. Insurrection, Esmi. I waged a long, hard insurrection. The petty overthrow of petty assumptions precedes all true upheavals of belief.'

'So you *lied?*'

A small smile. 'I guided. I guided them to a lesser falsehood.'

'Then what *is* the truth?'

He had laughed, shining as if anointed in oil.

'You would call me a liar if I told you,' he had said.

Both Imhailas and Naree stared at her in anxious expectation, and it seemed a miracle to her, that she could be so powerless *in fact*, and yet hold souls such as these in her thrall – simply because they believed she possessed power over them. The way countless *thousands* believed, she realized.

Maithanet had removed the New Empire's head – her. Now he was simply doing what any usurper would: speaking oil. He had to give the masses an excuse to continue acting in all the old ways. Otherwise all the wheels and cogs would cease turning in concert, and the entire mechanism would come crashing down. Every palace revolt took this form.

Only the precision and alacrity of his execution distinguished him as Dûnyain.

'The people will never believe him!' Imhailas finally cried when she failed to speak. 'I am sure of it!'

A wave of resignation washed over her. 'Yes,' she said, dropping her forehead into her palm. 'They will.'

His story was simple enough – believable enough. The machine was broken, and he, Maithanet, was the Chosen Tinker.

'How? How could they?'

'Because he has reached them first.'

The three of them soaked in the implications of this disastrous fact.

One could not dwell in the presence of Anasûrimbor Kellhus as long as she had without developing an acute awareness of one's own soul: the thoughts, the passions, and, most importantly, the *patterns*. If she lacked insight before, it was simply because she had occupied the centre of power for so long. Nothing so deadens the inner eye as habit.

But now . . . Maithanet had obliterated everything she had known, and it seemed she could see herself with a peculiar lucidity. The fugitive Empress. The bereaved mother. The cycling of dismay, desolation, hatred, and a curious in-between, a sense as relentless as it was numb. The going-through-the-motions of survival.

Numbness. This was the only strength she possessed, so she strained to hold on to it.

'He's calling himself the Imperial Custodian,' Imhailas continued, his eyes tearing for frustration and disgust.

'What of the Army?' Esmenet heard herself ask. Only the pain in her throat told her the importance of this question.

As anxious and solemn as he had appeared before, Imhailas looked to her with outright horror now.

'They say Anthirul has met with him in Temple Xothei,' he said, 'that the traitor has publicly kissed his knee.'

Esmenet *wanted* to lash out in crazed fury, to punish petty things for the epic injustices she had suffered. She wanted to shriek in imperious outrage, heap loathing and curses upon General Anthirul – everyone who had surrendered their capricious loyalty . . .

But she found herself looking at Naree upon the floor below Imhailas instead. The girl glanced at her – a bright, almost animal look – only to turn away in terror. The girl was trembling, Esmenet realized. Only the palm and arm she held posed to receive Imhailas's wine-bowl remained motionless.

And the Holy Empress of the Three Seas tasted something she had not known since the crazed day she had led her daughter to the slavers in the harbour so many years before.

Defeat.

CHAPTER TWELVE

Kûniüri

Skies are upended, poured as milk into the tar of night. Cities become pits for fire. The last of the wicked stand with the last of the righteous, lamenting the same woe. One Hundred and Forty-Four Thousand, they shall be called, for this is their tally, the very number of doom.

—ANONYMOUS, *THE THIRD REVELATION OF GANUS THE BLIND*

Know what your slaves believe, and you will always be their master.

—AINONI PROVERB

Summer, 20 New Imperial Year (4132 Year-of-the-Tusk), the Istyuli Plains

She made love to him, draping her famed hair, which was so blonde as to be white.

They despised each other, but their passion was oblivious and so did not suffer. Her final cries brought the servants scurrying in alarm, even as her thrashing cracked his loins asunder. Afterward they even laughed at the commotion. And as the drowsiness overcame him, he thought it was not such a bad thing for a man to sound a woman without heart or scruple, so long as she was his wife.

He did not pause to ask *why* she had seduced him. *Perhaps there will be peace between us,* he thought, slipping into sleep . . .

Except that he remained awake – somehow, impossibly.

Through closed eyes he watched her, Ieva, his wife of seven years, scurry naked to the cabinet across their spare room and produce a philtre, which she considered with an expression hung between terror and gloating. She turned to him, her face thin and cruel.

'How she will weep,' she growled, 'the *filthy* whore . . . And I will see it, and savour it, the breaking of her heart when she learns her beloved Prince has died in his *wife's* arms!'

He tried to call out as she leaned above him, holding the black tube with medicinal care. But he was sleeping and could not move.

'But you will not die, my heroic husband. Oh no! For I will fall upon your corpse, and I will wail-wail-wail, claiming to the Bull Heavens that you demanded to be *buried* rather than burned – like a Nonman!'

He tried to spit the foul liquid she poured between his teeth. He tried to reach up and out, seize her pale neck . . .

'Oh my husband!' she cried in a whisper. 'My dear-dear husband! How could you not see the grudge I hold against thee? But you will know it, soon enough. *When you are delivered*, when you are beaten and broken – then you will know the compass of my spite!'

Cold trickled into the back of his throat – and burned.

And at last his slumbering form answered the alarums screeching through his soul. Drusas Achamian shot upright, gasping and sputtering . . . swatting at the afterimage of another man's treacherous wife.

Gone was the ancient bedroom. Gone was the drowsy light of afternoon . . .

But he could taste the poison all the same.

He spat across the dead grasses, sat clutching his temples, incredulous and reeling.

Nau-Cayûti. He had dreamed he was *Anasûrimbor Nau-Cayûti* . . . and more.

He had dreamed not the experience, but the *fact* of his ancient assassination.

What was happening?

He turned to Mimara, who lay motionless beside him, beautiful despite the squalor of her skin and clothing. He recalled her fateful declaration the first and only night they had lain together.

'You have become a prophet . . . A prophet of the past.'

⬦⬦⬦

Never had he seen the like, not even in the darkest of Seswatha's Dreams.

They had crossed paths worn by herds of elk, vast swathes of grassland veined by innumerable trails, diverging, crossing, forking out to the limits of their vision. As gouged as they were, the scalpers could not but whistle, their souls' eyes straining to conjure a herd whose mere passing could so mark the earth. 'The ground moans at their approach,' Xonghis told them that evening. Apparently he had seen the elk herds during his days as an Imperial Tracker. 'Even the skinnies flee.'

But this . . .

They had spent the morning climbing long lobes of land piled one atop the other – a range of flattened hills. They paused to recover their wind when they finally crested the summit, only to find it stolen by the vista before them.

The Wizard's first thoughts were of the Great Carathay, that the drought had transformed the Istyuli into a northern desert. But as his aging eyes sorted through the distances he realized that he was gazing across another *trail*, one far greater than the braided immensities left by the elk . . .

'The Great Ordeal,' he called out to the others. Something clutched his throat, thinned his voice, a horror or wonder he could not feel.

That was when his eyes began picking out the points of black scattered all across the landscape that bowled out before them in swirls of dun and ochre. The dead.

A battleground, Achamian realized. They had happened upon a battleground, one so vast it would take more than a day to cross, even with their quickened limbs.

'A battle of some kind?' Galian called as if reading his thoughts.

'Not a pitched one,' Xonghis said, his almond eyes little more than slits as he peered northward. 'A *running* battle, I think . . . There're dead skinnies along the entire length of the trail.'

'The true contest was to the north,' Cleric said, peering.

Images from his dreams assailed the old Wizard. In the early days of the First Apocalypse, before the coming of Mog-Pharau, the ancient hosts of Kûniüri and Aörsi had left trails such as this whenever they marched through Sranc lands. 'A *Hording*,' he heard himself say. He turned to address the small crowd of curious looks. 'A mobbing like no other. This is what happens when you fight your way through an endless accumulation of Sranc.'

'Now we know where all the skinnies went,' Pokwas said, a great hand raised to the back of his neck.

'Aye,' Galian said nodding. 'Why chase scraps when a feast marches across your land.'

The company passed the first clutch of Sranc within a watch of its downward trek, at least a hundred of them, their skin withered to hide, their limbs jutting like sticks. Xonghis had difficulty estimating when they had been killed because of the drought. 'Dried to jerky,' he said, gazing across the blackened remains with a practised eye.

Soon they were in the midst of the battlefield, a thin file wandering across trammelled dust that was barely whiskered with grass – a barren as vast as the horizon. They saw vultures feuding, crows probing eye sockets, wolves and jackals loping in wary circles. They saw figures burned to charcoal, little more than stumps jutting from sand blasted to glass. They saw bodies hacked to the ground, tangled lines and arcs of them, and in his soul's eye the old Wizard saw the battle formations that had shaped them, the hard-armoured men fighting beneath banners drawn from across the Three Seas. They saw what looked like the remains of pyres, broad circles of gutted black. Mimara crouched to the dust, fetched a wire Circumfix from the sand. The old Wizard watched her tie the leather string, then loop the thing over her neck. By some perverse coincidence, the symbol fell directly across the Chorae that lay hidden against her breast.

Everywhere the old Wizard looked, he glimpsed the stain of sorceries, Gnostic rather than Anagogic. To the practised eye, the difference was plain, as if the world had been gored with razors instead of bludgeoned with hammers. Mimara once told him that Kellhus had largely honoured the ancient Mandate monopoly on the Gnosis, granting the secret knowledge only to the witches, the Swayali, as both a promise and a goad for other Schools. So wherever he glimpsed some Gnostic residue, he could not help but think of his erstwhile brothers and wonder why he no longer seemed to care.

'Skinnies!' Sarl cackled from somewhere behind him. 'A mobbing like no other! Think of the bales!'

The Captain said nothing. Cleric said nothing. Both walked as if the scene about them were interchangeable with any other landscape, as if mounds of dead surrounded them no matter where they walked. But the others craned their looks this way and that, pointing to various sights of grisly interest.

'He marches against Golgotterath,' Mimara murmured from the old Wizard's side. 'He slaughters Sranc . . .'

'What do you mean?'

'Kellhus . . . You *still* think him a fraud?'

He swept his gaze across the strewn carnage.

'That's for Ishuäl to answer.'

Ghosts moved in him, ghosts of who he had been. Once, before his exile, he would have celebrated fields such as this with hoots of exultation, tears of joy. An Aspect-Emperor marching against the Consult, bent on preventing the Second Apocalypse: the old him would have laughed in derision had anyone suggested he would live to see such a sight, laughed at the desperation of his longing.

But there was *another* ghost in him, a memory of who he had been mere months ago, the man who would have been aghast at the sight, not because he did not pray for Golgotterath's fall – he did with a fervour only a Mandate Schoolman could know – but because he had wagered the lives of innocents in a mad quest to prove the faith of millions wrong, and a lunatic barbarian – a *Scylvendi*, no less – right . . .

What had happened? Where had this man gone?

And if he was gone, what did that make of his quest?

He turned to scrutinize Mimara, gazed long enough to spark a curious frown.

She was right . . . He realized this as if for the first time.

The Qirri.

Flies had inherited the earth.

They crossed fields of detritus, threading the hillocks of dead, stepping over dried-out puddles skinned in cracked blood. Lines and blots of interlocking corpses reached out to knot the distances. Skin tight about grinning skulls. Innumerable hands with sunken palms, fingers drawn into claws. A thousand poses corresponding to a thousand deaths: thrown, struck spinning, flailing in fire. All of them lying inert and breathless in pools of inky shadow.

The reek was overpowering, a mélange of rot and feces. The wind raised it, powdered them in it, yet they did not care.

The Captain called a halt. They prepared camp.

The sun scorched the western horizon. Nearby, hundreds of Sranc had been piled for some unknown reason, forming a heap that had dried into a kind of grisly deadfall. Stripped to his loin-cloth, Cleric climbed to the summit, his bare feet cracking ribcages like crusts of snow. The sight of him, a Nonman burnished in the bronze and copper of sunset standing upon the compressed remains of Sranc, struck the old Wizard with peculiar force. He sat gawking at Mimara's side, fumbling with things half-remembered.

Cleric stood with regal inhumanity, his skin gleaming as if greased. 'This *war*,' he began. 'This war is older than your tongues and nations . . .'

The old Wizard found himself wondering where the gruel of rotted memory would lead the Nonman this time. Would he speak of Far Antiquity? The First Apocalypse? Or would he speak of times when the Five Tribes of Men still wandered the wastes of Eänna?

Would he reveal his true identity?

Achamian lowered his gaze, stared blinking at his hands, at his scabbed knuckles, at the grime darkening the whorls of his skin. How long had it been since he last asked this question?

When had he forgotten to wonder?

'Men bled here,' Cleric said from his macabre summit. 'Men leaned shouting into their shields.'

How long had it been since he had last *cared*? Even now he could feel it welling within him, defeat and dissolution, a knee-cracking resignation. And a voice whispered within him, *his* voice, asking, *What is there to care about?*

'So frail, so mortal,' the ancient Ishroi continued, 'yet they cast themselves before the scythes of happenstance, yielded their souls to the perversities of Fate.'

All the world seemed a burned-out pyre. All the glory gone, roaring into the hiss of failing coals. All the hope twisting into smoky oblivion.

'Dogs scavenge,' the Nonman called. 'Wolves chase the foaling mother, the aged, and the weak. Even the lion shies from clawed prey. Only *you and I* know the madness that is war. Man and Nonman. Only we pursue what lions flee.'

And who was he, Drusas Achamian, to think he could grapple Fate, pin Her to the floor of his hateful aspiration?

'We die for what we know,' the Nonman boomed, 'and *we know nothing!* Generations heaped upon generations, tossing lives after self-serving guesses, murdering nations in the name of ignorance and delusion.'

Seswatha? Was that who he thought he was? The incarnation of an ancient *hero*?

'We call our greed justice! We call our soiled hands divine! We strike in the name of avarice and vanity, and the—!'

'*Enough!*' the Captain shouted at the high-shining figure. Aside from Cleric, he alone stood, wind whipped and insane. 'Some wars are holy,' he grated in blood-raw tones. 'Some wars . . . *are holy.*'

The Nonman regarded him from his summit, blinked once before turning from his furious aspect. He climbed from the heaped Sranc, making a stair of heads and torsos, then leapt to the dust with leonine grace. The shadows of the dead crowded his naked legs.

'Yes,' he said, drawing his shoulders back to stand tall. 'Enough.'

The sky darkened. The reek of dust and death tumbled through the air. The Nonman reached for the leather pouch where it lay against his bare hip.

Yes! something cried within the old Wizard, something that leaned forward with his own shoulders, flooded his mouth with his own spit. An affirming urgency.

Yes! This is all that matters. The worries will go away. They. Will. Go. Away. And if not, clarity will come – yes! Clarity. Clarity will come, the clarity needed to honestly *consider these questions. Come. Come, old man! Out of the muck!*

Animal spirits inhabit every soul, which is why a man could attend to one thing while remaining vigilant for another, why he could converse with his neighbour while lusting after his wife. In that moment, Cleric was all that existed. *Incariol,* wild and dark and, yes, even holy. The word upon which creation's own prayer seemed to turn. The Nail of Heaven gleamed across his scalp, a crown that only the Hundred could bestow. And it was as proper as it was inevitable, for he ruled the way the moon ruled the tides, the way the sun ruled the fields . . .

Absolute. As a father among his children.

One by one he ministered to the sitting scalpers, and Achamian watched, leaning in envy and anticipation. There is closeness in ritual. There is touch. There is an intimacy that approached coupling, an iron faith that the nearing hands would not strike or throttle. Achamian watched the near-naked form loom above Mimara beside him, watched her raise her lips in eager acquiescence. The blackened finger slipped along the chute of her tongue, pressed deep into her mouth. She went rigid, pulled her shoulders back in bliss. For the first time he noticed the bow of her belly . . .

Pregnant? Was she pregnant? But . . .

Yes! his soul's voice cried. *Simplicity! You need* simplicity *to honestly ponder complications!*

Cleric loomed over him, his shoulders brushing the violet clouds, his face blank with inhuman serenity. Achamian watched his finger, still glistening with Mimara's saliva, dip into the fox-mouth opening of his pouch. A delicious moment, magical in the way of small miracles, the little pins from which all life hangs. He watched the finger reappear, tip blackened as with soot . . . ashes . . .

Cû'jara Cinmoi.

Mimara . . . pregnant?

Who? Who are you?

Yes! Honesty. Simplicity! Raise your lips – yes!

The finger rose before him, its tip a tingling black. The old Wizard bent back his face, opened his mouth . . .

'*The next time you come before me,*' the hated voice called out over fawning masses, '*you will kneel, Drusas Achamian . . .*'

Kellhus.

A coldness smoked through Achamian. The finger hesitated. He raised his eyes to the Nonman's black-glittering gaze.

Kellhus. The Aspect-Emperor.

'No,' the old Wizard said. 'No more.'

She falls asleep troubled by the wordless uproar of the evening. Her own half-hearted attempt to refuse the Qirri the previous week had occasioned little more than curiosity, it seemed to her. Who knew a women's fickle ways? But when the *Wizard* had refused, a strange species of alarm had gripped the company. Dread prickled the silence. She could sense the scalpers watching at angles to their eyes. Wariness quickened their movements as they went about otherwise thoughtless tasks. The Captain, especially, possessed the air of waiting.

'Akka . . .' she whispered in the dark. 'Something is wrong.'

'Many things are wrong,' he replied, his voice clipped, his eyes fogged with turmoil.

He was at war, she realized.

'I've been a drunkard before,' he muttered – but not to her, it seemed. 'I've even hung from the hooks of the poppy . . .' Momentary clarity sparked in his eyes. 'The burden that Mandate Schoolmen bear . . . Many of us are compelled to seek low pleasures.'

At war with the earthly residue of Cû'jara Cinmoi.

Her fear is a novelty to her, so long have her passions slipped into oblivion at the merest distraction. She struggles to keep hold of it, but she is too weary. She drifts into unsettled sleep.

She dreams of Cil-Aujas, of white throngs scratching through the black. She dreams that she runs *with them*, the Sranc, chasing her own waifish figure ever deeper into the earth.

A cry awakens her, grunts and earth-scuffing struggle.

She blinks, sucks waking air. The sounds are near – very near.

Dawn rims a blackened world. Two figures crouch over the Wizard . . . The Captain and Cleric.

What?

The Wizard kicks and pedals.

'What are you doing?' she asks with bleary curiosity. No one acknowledges her. The Wizard gags, jerks, and struggles like a landed fish.

'*What are you doing!*' she cries.

Heedless, she scrambles to her feet, throws herself across the Nonman's hunched back. He shrugs her away. 'Hold her!' the Captain barks at shadows standing in the dark. Callused hands clamp about her wrists: Galian, restraining her from behind. 'There, pretty!' he grunts, dragging her back. He twists her arms against the small of her back, thrusts her to her knees. She hears herself howling in fury. *'No! Nooooo!'* All she can see of the Wizard is his legs kicking. Crude laughter slouches from the dark – Sarl. A hand closes about the back of her neck. Her face is slammed into the dust, the wiry remains of weeds. Other hands seize the waist of her breeches. She knows what comes next.

But the Captain has turned from the struggling Wizard, sees what has happened to her. He flies to his feet, savagely kicks one of her unseen assailants. Stabs another – she sees Wonard stumble kicking to the dust. The hands vanish and she finds herself on all fours.

'Touch her,' Lord Kosoter grates to the unseen shadows behind her, 'and your *soul* is forfeit!'

She glimpses Wonard convulsing, puking blood into his beard. She scrambles forward with an instinct borne of desperation. She seizes Squirrel from her meagre belongings, draws it retreating, trips over the beehive carcass of a Sranc.

Dawn is but a corona of slate and blue across the horizon. The night sky rises black and infinite, oblivion littered with countless stars. The scalpers are naught but hunched shadows, their heads and their shoulders stuck in pale starlight. They approach her, wary and weaponless.

Achamian screams.

'Nooo!' she shrieks. 'Stop this! Stop!'

The Captain draws his blade. The rasp draws chills across her skin. He strides toward her as if she were nothing more than wood to kindle. Light soaks the horizon behind him, renders him black. She can see the murderous glint of his eyes beneath his hood of wild hair. They seem to glow for the black lines tattooed about them.

'What are you doing?' she cries. 'What madness is this?' Her voice cuts the back of her throat, such is her terror. This is how it happens, she realizes. The brothel taught her as much, but she has forgotten in all the intervening years. Your doom always outruns you. You grow complacent, fat in the company of peace, then awaken to find all safety, all hope, overthrown.

The air is windless, chill. Lord Kosoter lunges at her. He hacks with a violence that notches her blade, wrenches her wrists. She retreats. She is quick enough, skilled enough to parry his strikes. She is trained. He sweeps and swings his broadsword, brings it clanking down. His caste-noble braid swings like sodden rope.

With a kind of wonder she realizes that he *isn't* trying to kill her. The future towers dark and shrieking in her soul's eye. Images of torment and violation, of brutalities only scalpers could commit.

Her cries become a wail. She throws herself at him, fighting the way her brothers have taught her, nimble and light, pitting craft against strength. He grunts in surprise, swatting at Squirrel. He relinquishes a single step, a hoary shadow thrown onto its heels.

Gold bursts across the horizon. He sidesteps, leans, angles his shadow to her side. Sunlight crashes into her squint. She blinks, hesitates. Her sword spins from fingertips she cannot feel. A fist of stone strikes her to the ground. It's happening, she thinks. After enduring so much, surviving so much, her death is happening.

'Akka . . .' she gasps, scrambling back. Sunlight splices her tears. Blood runs hot across her lips.

And nothing happens. No hand clamps about her throat. No knife pares away her rags.

Out of instinct she falls motionless, breathless.

The Judging Eye, which had remained sealed for so long, opens.

And she *sees* them standing in a ragged arc, demons on the plain. Their hides charred, the hair of their few redeeming deeds the only light threading them. And the darkest, the most fearsome by far, lies directly before her . . . *kneeling*. The Captain.

'Princess-Imperial,' it croaks, glaring from eyes of fiery tar. 'Save us from damnation.'

———∞———

'I am *Anasûrimbor Mimara*,' she cries. 'Princess-Imperial, daughter of the Holy-Empress, wife-daughter of the *Aspect-Emperor himself*! On pain of death and damnation I command you to release the Wizard!'

They have Achamian bound and gagged, trussed like a corpse about to be raised to the pyre.

'You are apostate,' the Captain says. 'A runaway.'

They have her sword, poor Squirrel.

'No! No! I am on a . . . a . . .'

They have her Chorae . . . her Tear of God.

'Foolish girl. Did you think your disappearance went unnoticed?'

They have her.

'You presume? You presume to command me?'

'You are a *captive*. Thank your gods you are not more.'

And she recalls as much as realizes that he is completely unlike her – that in soul and sentiment he is as alien as the Nonman, if not more. There is a *wholeness* to him, a singularity of act, aspect, and intention. She can see it in his look, in his face: the utter absence of warring pieces.

For some reason this calms her. There is relief to be found in futility. She knew this once.

'So what? You're going to bring me back to Mother then?'

His gaze has strayed from her to the dawn. Crimson light illuminates his face, paints the wilder strands of his beard in tones of blood.

'We march to the Coffers . . . Same as before.'

'Why? What has my father commanded?'

He draws his knife, begins shaving the calluses about his fingernails.

'Why?' she cries. 'I demand you tell me *why*.'

He looks up from his trivial labour, gazes with a flat intensity that sets her thoughts quailing. He has always frightened her, Lord Kosoter. The threat of violence has always kindled his manner. For him, atrocity was simply one more thoughtless faculty – one more base instinct. Kindness, she knows, is mist to him, something not entirely real. The honed edge is one of only two boundaries he respects.

The other is *faith* . . . Faith in her mother's husband. Even after running so far, deep into the savagery beyond the New Empire's rim, she remains caught in the Aspect-Emperor's nets. And knowing this has made the Captain even more fearsome. The thought that he is *Zaudunyani* . . .

She does not ask again.

She rifles through the Wizard's satchel, finds only five sheaves of parchment, the writing across them illegible for some river soaking – evidence of the Qirri in that, she supposes. And a small razor, scabbed with rust, which she conceals beneath her belt.

She wants to weep as they resume their course. She wants to scream, to run, to scratch out the Captain's eyes. She slouches instead, stares at her feet for as long as boredom allows. She avoids looking at the scalpers, consigns them to her periphery, where they seem apiece with the desolate plains, little more than leering shadows.

She feels naked now that she is known.

They keep the old Wizard bound and gagged at all times. When they break for meals, either Galian or Pokwas remove the gag while the Captain dandles a Chorae – whether his own or the one he stole from her, she does not know – before the old Wizard's face. Achamian avoids any glimpse of the Trinket, invariably looks down to his right instead. He says absolutely nothing, even with his gag removed, presumably because Lord Kosoter has told him that any sound, arcane or mundane, would mean his instant death. Periodically, the thick fingers holding the Chorae stray too close, and the Wizard grimaces at the salting of his skin. After several days, a patchwork of scabs and pink skin web his face above his beard.

He reminds her of an ascetic she once saw burned alive in Carythusal when she was still young enough to feel terror for others. The Shrial Priests had marched the old man through the streets, decrying his heretical claims, and bidding onlookers to come witness his fiery cleansing. Where Achamian wears rancid furs, he wore putrid rags. But otherwise, they seem so alike that her gut flutters at the recollection. Knob-knuckled hands bound before them. Gags to stop the danger of their voice. Wild hair and beard, wiry and grey. And the distant look of men condemned long before the thugs had seized them.

The old Wizard stares at her, from time to time. A strange look, ragged, at once hopeless and reassuring. They have always shared an understanding, it seems, one as deep and cold as clay in earth. They have both been broken over the knee of Fate, and as different as their lives and catastrophes have been, their hearts have sheared along similar lines.

Be calm, girl, his eyes seem to say. *No matter what happens to me, survive . . .*

Without fail, his looks make her think of the razor hidden beneath her belts.

She only hears Achamian when he's gagged. On the afternoon of the first day, he begins roaring at the Captain through the spit-soaked cloth, shrieking with such guttural fury that the man pauses in his approach. Nostrils flaring. Eyes glaring with lunatic intensity. He screams about his own retching.

The Captain remains as imperturbable as always, simply gazes and waits until the Wizard's maniacal ire subsides. Then he cups his palm and cuffs the old man to the ground.

Mimara glimpses the smiling look exchanged between Galian and Pokwas.

Each night they force Qirri upon him.

She receives her measure willingly.

Koll hunches alone in the dusty grass, watches them with dead eyes. She cannot remember when she last heard his voice. Did he even speak Sheyic?

The Stone Hags no longer seem real.

She prays that Soma still follows them – that a *skin-spy* might save her! – but she has no way of knowing: the Captain now forces her to practise her daily indignities in plain view.

The other scalpers – Galian and Pokwas especially – regard her with forced indifference. They gambled on their lust, thinking the Wizard her only protection. Now, their intentions revealed, they behave like pious thieves, like men wronged for wronging others. They sit and eat without speaking. Aside from the rare hooded glance in her direction, it seems they look only to their hands or the horizon. The mutinous air that had festered ever since Cil-Aujas has become gangrenous. The expedition now seems more a collection of warring tribes than men bound to a singular purpose.

She finds herself stranded with the Captain and Cleric.

The first few nights she lies awake, plotting possibilities more than actions. Her body aches with sensation: the bruising ground, the prick of grasses, the tickle of fleas climbing her scalp. She can see Squirrel jutting from the beggar's bundle that is his pack. She can sense both her Chorae and the Captain's beneath his tunic, dark little twins suckling oblivion. She guesses at his slumber, only to be disabused time and again. He invariably lies on his side, his head cradled on a raised arm. But just when she thinks he has fallen into the arms of Orosis, he raises his head and lies rigid, as if probing the surrounding black with his ears. Once she even begins crawling toward him, her thoughts a mad tumble of terror and mayhem. *Grab your sword!* her thoughts cry through the tumult. *Grab your sword! Cut his throat!* But she glimpses his hand slide to his waist as she continues her feline creep, sees his fingers settle upon the grime-blackened pommel of his broadsword.

After that she decides he never sleeps. At least not the way humans sleep.

They rarely speak to each other, Cleric and the Captain. They almost never address her. For the entirety of their journey, a part of her has wondered at their relationship. The Captain's advantage seems plain enough: a scalper's kill is a scalper's profit, and she can scarce imagine a killer more formidable than Cleric. But what could induce a Nonman, an *Ishroi* no less, to submit to a mortal's will – even a will so preternatural as Lord Kosoter's? She fixates on this mystery, even becomes jealous of it, thinking that at the very least this one question will be answered. But as the days pass, as she watches them from their very midst, the relationship becomes more enigmatic if anything.

A week into the Wizard's captivity she is awakened by the sound she finds inexplicable at first until, blinking, she spies Cleric sitting cross-legged on the far side of the Captain's slumbering form. He weeps. She lies motionless across the hard ground, feeling the stamp of flattened weeds through her blanket. She battles a sudden terror of breathing. Cleric sits with his arms stretched across his knees, his head hanging so low that she can see the sinews roping the back of his neck, the humps of his spine. His breath is dog rapid, horse deep. He moans – a sound as bottomless as Cil-Aujas. He mumbles or murmurs – words she cannot decipher. Random tremors seem to fly through him, afflicting first this hand, then that shoulder, as if the ghost of some bird battles to escape him.

A sense of heroic melancholy seems to emanate from him, as onerous and grand as the ages that have birthed it . . .

A sorrow that would crack a human soul.

'Kosoter . . .' he rasps.

This is the first time she has heard Cleric refer to the Captain by name. It prickles her skin for some reason. The Captain draws himself to a seated position opposite the Nonman. She can only see the man's back, the play of starlight across the battered lines of his splint hauberk. Funnelled down the centre of his back, his hair hangs in a tangle about the rope of his caste-noble braid.

She already knows that Cleric's sanity is not a constant thing, that it ebbs and flows according to its own disordered rhythm. But she has only guessed at the role played by the Captain.

A shudder passes through the Nonman's frame. 'I . . . I struggle.'

'Good.' There is an uncharacteristic softness to the Captain's voice, one borne more out of a greed for secrecy than any tenderness.

'Who . . . Who are these people?'

'Your children.'

'What? What is this?'

'You are *preparing*.'

The Nonman lowers his bald head back into shadow.

'Preparing? What is this tongue I speak? Where did I learn this tongue?'

'You are preparing.'

'Preparing?'

'Yes. To remember.'

Cleric raises his face to the grim figure sitting before him. Then without warning, his black gaze clicks over the Captain's shoulder, finds Mimara where she pretends to sleep.

'Yes . . .' the white lips say, full in the play of blackness and starlight. 'They *remind* me . . .'

The Captain turns to follow his gaze, reveals his savage profile for no more than an instant before turning away. 'Yes . . . They remind you of someone you once loved.'

Lord Kosoter stands, shouldering the light of the stars, then draws Cleric into the windy dark.

This exchange alarms her, but more like news of growing famine overseas than any immediate threat. She recalls Achamian's description of Nonmen Erratics, how their memories of mundane life fade first, leaving only archipelagos of spectacle and intensity, the confusion of a soul hanging without foundation. And how their redemptive memories gradually follow, stranding them more and more with disconnected episodes of torment and pain, until their life becomes a nightmare lived through mist, until all love and joy sink into oblivion, become things guessed at through the shadows cast by their destruction.

This, she realizes. This is the prize the Captain has cast upon the balance of their transaction. Cleric yields up his power, and Lord Kosoter offers him *memory*. Men to love. Men to destroy . . .

Men to remember.

And yet Lord Kosoter is *Zaudunyani* – one of her stepfather's fanatics. Why else would he protect her from the bent lusts of the others? And if he is Zaudunyani, then he would never deliver his expedition into destruction unless . . . Unless his Aspect-Emperor has commanded it.

The deal he has struck with Incariol, she realizes, could be a false one. If so, the Captain plays a most deadly game.

Like all of the Few, she is accustomed to ignoring her arcane sight. But Cleric bears his mark so deeply, the residue of ages of sorcerous practice. Occult ugliness blasts him, the scars of his innumerable crimes against creation. Add to this the sheer beauty of his mundane form – the contradiction – and it sometimes seems as if the merest glance will pry her eyes from their sockets.

Even if she had not seen him warring through the sewered depths of Cil-Aujas or beneath the clawed bowers of the Meörn Wilderness, she would have known he was a power – a great power.

If he were to choose to annihilate the Skin Eaters . . .

Only Achamian could possibly hope to stand against him – were he free to speak.

⁂

The company continues its lonely walk, dwarfed by the confluence of never-ending land and sky. What features the landscape possesses are slavish and melancholy, as if they were mountains beaten into ruddy heaps and long-wandering flanges. Wild clouds feather the sky, slow-sailing immensities that promise rain that is never delivered. She often gazes into them while she walks, probing the precipices and the plummets, wondering at the way they form floating plates that seem to wheel in competing directions, pinching deep glimpses of blue into white oblivion.

The Wizard stumbles along, bound and gagged, glaring hate at everyone save her.

Survive, Mimara! Forget me!

More days pass before she is able to piece things together. Sarl, especially, provides her with pivotal insights. He tells her how Lord Kosoter, famed for his cruelty and marshal zeal, had come to the Aspect-Emperor's attention during the Unification Wars. How he had been promised a special Shrial Remission by none other than her uncle, Maithanet, for founding a scalper company and remaining in the vicinity of Hûnoreal – where he could regularly check on the Wizard.

'He is born of Hell,' the madmen tells her, his face squished into I-knew-all-along glee. 'He is born of Hell, the Captain. And he knows it – oh-ho! He knows it. He thinks your *gurwikka*, there, will pay his toll . . .' His squint pops open in mock alarm. 'Deliver him to paradise!'

'But how?' she protests.

'Because of him!' the madman cackles. '*Him!* The Aspect-Emperor *knows all* . . .'

She herself had seen the yield of the Wizard's twenty years alone in the wilderness. After Achamian absconded for Marrow, she fought her way past his slaves and broke into his tower room. Part of her had expected to be blasted, to die screaming in sorcerous fire. She could sense the residue of something arcane. But there had been no incipient Wards protecting the room, nothing . . . Because of his slaves' children, she knew.

At first she could see little save the sunlight outlining the shuttered window where she had first seen him. The smell was rancid but curiously dry and inviting. Finally she saw the wolf-pelts warming the walls and ceiling. The crude-hewn bed. And then the issue of his decades-long labour.

Pages. Scattered. Stacked into teetering piles. Scrolls piled like bones, tumbling into shadow. Dream after dream, scratched in ink and numbered – everything numbered. Pattern after pattern. Theory after theory. Seswatha this. Seswatha that. A horde of details she could never hope to decode, let alone remember.

Out of all the scribbles she peered at, only one would live on in her memory, what seemed the old Wizard's final entry, the one that would spur her to pursue him.

She has returned. Of all people!
I am awake at last.

She, he had written. *She* . . . Esmenet.
Mother.
If she could simply walk into the old Wizard's room, Mimara

reasons, then so too could her stepfather. She can even see *him* in her soul's eye, the Aspect-Emperor stepping from a point of blue-white light. She can see his face, always so remote, always so terrifying, slowly scan the slovenly gloom. What would a god think, she wonders, looking upon the low belongings of his old teacher, the obsessive issue of his wife's first abiding love?

Nothing human, she is certain.

She laughs in the course of these ruminations, loud and hard enough to draw more than one questioning look from the others. Part of her blames the Qirri, which she adores even as she hates. It continues to leach her soul, to draw water from her previous concerns. Now and again she even catches herself thinking her captivity an honest and advantageous trade . . . so long as Cleric continues to plumb her mouth with his cool and bitter finger.

But the humour is real. From the very beginning she had dismissed the old Wizard's fears regarding her stepfather. *'This is the way he sends you,'* Achamian said. *'This is the way he rules – from the darkness in our own souls! If you were to feel it, know it, that would simply mean there was some deeper deception . . .'*

She had discounted him with a smirk, with the grimace she reserved for fools. She, an Anasûrimbor by marriage, who had lived in his divine presence, who had sat riven, skinned in goose-pimples, as her stepfather merely crossed the room. Like so many she confused absence with impotence. The Andiamine Heights seemed so *distant*. Now she knows: the Aspect-Emperor transcends distance. Anasûrimbor Kellhus is everywhere.

Exactly as the old Wizard feared.

With this realization comes a new understanding of her power. She finds herself scrutinizing the Captain, guessing at the warring scales within him, the precarious balance of piety and bloodlust. She represents an infuriating complication, Mimara decides, the wrinkle marring the long silk of his ambition. He feels no worldly terror, she decides, because his fear of damnation eclipses all. Too warlike to find redemption in the Gods of Compassion. Too miserly and too cruel to secure the favour of War or the Hunter . . .

Only the Aspect-Emperor. Only he can make a virtue out of his bloodlust. Only *he* can deliver him to Paradise.

She is the variable, she thinks, remembering the algebra she learned at the knee of Yerajaman, her Nilnameshi tutor. She is the value he cannot calculate.

What Lord Kosoter does, she finally decides, depends on what he thinks his lord and master, his *god*, desires.

'I am with child,' she tells him.

A flinch passes across the implacable face.

'Are you not curious?' she asks.

His glare does not waver. Never has a man so terrified her.

'You *know* . . .' she presses. 'Don't you?'

She has spent her life, it seems, staring into the faces of bearded men, guessing at the line of their jaw, feeling their hair chafe the bare skin of her neck. She has childhood memories of bare-faced priests and caste-nobles in Sumna. Some of the older Nansur who populated the Imperial Court still clung to their womanish cheeks. But it seems that for as long as she can remember, men meant beards. And the more they adorned them, the higher their station.

Lord Kosoter looks like little more than a cutthroat to her – a beggar, even. *Think of him as that!* she cries wordlessly. *He is less than you! Less!*

'Know what?' he grates.

'Who the father is . . .'

He says nothing.

'Tell me, Captain,' she says, her voice pinched shrill. 'Why do you think I fled the Andiamine Heights?'

Even his blink seems a thing graven, as if mere flesh were too soft to contain such a gaze.

'Why does any girl flee her stepfather's home?' she asks.

The lie is a foolish one: he need only guess at the length of her term to realize there is no way she could have been impregnated in Momemn. But then, what would a man such as him know of pregnancy, let alone one borne of a divine violation? Her mother had carried all her brothers and sisters far beyond the usual term.

'You understand, don't you? You *realize* what I bear . . .'

A god . . . I carry a god in my belly. It seems she need only tell herself this for it to be true . . .

Another gift of the Qirri.

And she sees it sparking in his eyes. Wonder and horror both. She almost cries out in jubilation. She has cracked his face. At last she has cracked his face!

His lunge is so sudden, so swift, she scarcely knows what has happened until she slams across the turf. He pins her. His right hand clamps her mouth, so large it all but engulfs the lower half of her face. A kind of wild monkey rage shines from his glare. He leans close enough for her to smell rotting teeth.

'*Never!*' he says in a roaring whisper. '*Never speak of this again!*'

Then she is free, her head spinning, her lips and cheeks numb.

He turns away from her, back toward the watching Nonman. There is nothing to do, it seems, but to sit and weep.

Despair fills her after this last foolish gambit. These were *scalpers*. Implacable. These were the kind of men who never paused to reflect, who asked questions of women only so they might show them the proper answer. Even without the Qirri, they were forever trapped at the rushing edge of passion and thought, believing utterly what they needed to see their hungers appeased. Where some were set aflutter by the mere suspicion of slight, nothing but outright calamity could throw these men back into themselves. Only blood – *their* blood – could incite them to question.

What was, for these men, *was*. Lord Kosoter was a fanatical agent of the Aspect-Emperor. Drusas Achamian was his prisoner. They marched to plunder the Coffers.

If they were caught in the wheels of some greater machination, then so be it.

It is night and the scalpers argue. The voices of the others climb about the Captain's rare growl. They sit in a clutch several paces away, ragged shadows chalked in starlight. Sarl's laughter scratches the night. For some reason the substance of their feud does not concern her, even though she periodically hears the word *peach* carried on the wind. She has her razor to consider.

Achamian lies trussed beside her, his face pressed into the turf. He either sleeps or listens.

Cleric sits cross-legged nearby, his knees obscured by weedy shags. He stares at her without embarrassment. She can still feel the chill of his finger across her tongue.

She raises her waterskin high, slowly pours it over her head. She can feel the water warm as it snakes along her scalp. Her hair wet, her gaze fixed on the watching Nonman, she lifts the razor to her scalp.

She works quickly, even thoughtlessly. She has done this innumerable times: the custom of whores in Carythusal was to wear wigs. She had owned eleven by the time her mother's men had come with their swords and torches.

Galian's voice rises in disbelief. '*Slog?*' he cries. '*This is mor*—'

Her hair drops in a tangle of ribbons across her lap. Rare dry strands ride the wind, float out behind her, where they snag grasses, hang quivering.

Cleric watches, twin points of white wetting his black gaze.

She pours more water across her shorn head, works her scalp until the filth becomes a kind of lather. Raising the razor once again, she takes the remaining hair down to nothing. Then she scrapes away her eyebrows.

When she finishes, she sits blinking at the imperturbable Nonman, savours the tingle of air over unearthed skin. Several heartbeats pass – more. His mere presence seems to crackle, he remains so motionless.

She crawls into the pool of his immediate gaze. Her skin pimples, as if she has been stripped of her clothing as well.

'Do you remember me?' she finally whispers.

'Yes.'

She raises her hand to his face, draws the pad of her finger across the soft length of his lips. She presses between, touches hot spit. She gently thrusts her finger between his fused teeth, wonders at the dullness of the opposing edges. She probes deep, forces a channel down the centre of his tongue.

How many thousands of years? she wonders. How many sermons across the ages?

She withdraws her finger, wonders at the gleam of inhuman saliva.

'Do you remember your wife?'

'I remember all that I have lost.'

She is beautiful. She knows she is beautiful because she so resembles her mother, Esmenet, who was the most celebrated beauty in the Three Seas. And mortal beauty, she knows, finds its measure in the immortal . . .

'How did she die?'

A single tear falls from his right eye, hangs like a bead of glass from his jaw. 'With the others . . . *Cir'kumir teles pim'larata* . . .'

'Do I resemble her?'

'Perhaps . . .' he says, lowering his gaze. 'If you wept or screamed . . . If there was blood.'

She moves closer, into the smell of him, sits so that her knees brush his shins. His pouch hangs from his waist, partially hooked in a miniature thicket of stems. Vertigo billows through her, a sudden horror of tipping, as if the pouch were a babe set too close to a table's edge. She clutches his forearms.

'You tremble,' she whispers, resisting the urge to glance at the pouch. 'Do you want me? Do you want to . . .' She swallows. 'To *take* me?'

He draws away his arms, stares down into his palms. Beyond him, clouds pile like inky flotsam beneath the stars. Dry lightning scorches the plains a barren white. She glimpses land piling atop land, scabbed edges, woollen reaches.

'I want to . . .' he says.

'Yes?'

He lifts his eyes as if drawing them against weighted threads. 'I . . . I want to . . . to *strangle* you . . . to split you with my—'

His breath catches. Murder floats in the sorrow of his gaze. He speaks like someone marooned in a stranger's soul. 'I want to hear you shriek.'

And she can feel the musky strength of him, the impotence of her flailing arms, clawing fingers, should he simply *choose* . . .

What? a stranded fragment of her asks. *What are you doing?* She's not quite certain what she intends to do, let alone what she hopes to accomplish. Is she seducing him? For Achamian? For the Qirri?

Or has she finally broken under the weight of her suffering? Is that what it is? After all this time, is she still the child traded between sailors, weeping to the moan of timbers and men?

She glimpses herself climbing into the circuit of Cleric's arms, taking his waist into the circuit of her legs. Her breath catches at the thought of his antique virility, the union of her flower and his stone. Her stomach quails at the thought of his arcane disfigurement, the ugliness heaving against her, into her.

'Because you *love* me?'

'I . . .'

He grimaces, and she glimpses Sranc howling by the light of sorcerous fire. He raises his face to the vault of the night, and she sees a world before human nations, a nocturnal age, when Nonmen marched in hosts from their great underworld mansions, driving the Sons of Men before them.

'No!' Cleric cries. 'No! Because I . . . I need to remember! I must remember!'

And miraculously, she sees it. Her purpose and her intent.

'And so you must *betray* . . .'

His passion blows from him, and he falls still – very still. Clarity peers out from his eyes, a millennial assurance. Gone is the bewildered stoop, the listless air of indecision. He pulls his shoulders and arms into an antique pose of nobility. He draws his hands behind him, seems to clasp them in the small of his back. It is a posture she recognizes from Cil-Aujas and its innumerable engravings.

The voices of the scalpers continue to feud and bicker. The clouds continue to climb, a shroud drawing across the gaping bowl of Heaven. The Captain is speaking, but low rolling thunder obscures his voice.

The first darts of rain tap across the dust and grasses.

'Who?' Mimara presses. 'Who are you, truly?'

The immortal Ishroi watches her, his smile wry, his eyes luminous with something too profound to be mere regret.

'Nil'giccas. . . .' he murmurs. 'I am Nil'giccas. The Last Nonman King.'

<hr>

To be silent, the old Wizard discovered, is to watch.

You see more when you speak less. First your eyes turn outward, the thoughtless way they always turn outward when you have spoken your say: to await a response, to gauge the effectiveness of your lies. But when your voice is bricked over, when you are robbed of the very possibility of speaking, your eyes are left hanging. And like bored children they begin inventing things to do.

Like observing things otherwise unseen.

He noticed the way Galian would sleep apart from the others, and how he would make inexplicable little cuts on his arms when he thought no one could see him. He noticed how Pokwas would glance at the small wounds when Galian seemed distracted. He noticed how Xonghis whispered what were either prayers or folk-charms over his arrows. He noticed Koll convulsing when no one else seemed to notice him at all.

He noticed how barren life became when camp after camp was struck without making a fire. When Men sat in darkness.

To see what was unseen was to understand that blindness was always a matter of degree. To say that all men were blind in some respect – to the machinations of others, to themselves – was a truism scarcely worth noting. What was astounding was the way this truism perpetually escaped Men, the way they confused seeing mere slivers with seeing everything they needed to see.

He pondered this for days: the invisibility of the unknown.

The hook from which all deception hung.

He struggled to remember the posture of his soul before Cleric and the Captain had fallen upon him. He had been so preoccupied with his inner demons, he had utterly forgotten the outer. It had never occurred to him that Lord Kosoter, whose cruelty had become such an unwelcome ally, could be an agent of the Aspect-Emperor. He had been too confused to fear for himself when they fell upon him, but his horror for Mimara, for what might happen to her absent his power, had been immediate. Time and again he had cried out, against the gag choking him, against the leather straps binding him, but against the colossal perversity of Fate most of

524   The White-Luck Warrior

all. He could scarce see her in the subsequent scuffle of shadows, but he saw enough to know the others had seized her, that their intent was both violent and carnal. He was not heartened in the least when Lord Kosoter intervened. He remembered the early days of the expedition, how the Captain had executed Moraubon for attempting to rape Mimara. The Captain, as Sarl had said, always gets the first bite. So Achamian assumed that he simply saved her for himself. He wasn't at all surprised when the Captain fought to disarm rather than to kill her. What had stunned him, seized him with both horror and relief, was watching the Captain *kneel* before her.

He had been deceived. He had never trusted these men, these scalpers, but he had trusted their nature – or what he had assumed to be their nature. So long as they thought they marched for riches, for the Coffers, so long as they thought he was their key, he believed he could . . . manage them. Knowing. This was the great irony. Knowing was the foundation of ignorance. To think that one *knew* was to become utterly blind to the unknown.

He had been a fool. What scalper company would assent to an expedition such as this? Who would be so desperate as to wager their lives in pursuit of ancient rumour? Only fanatics and madmen would undertake such a quest. Only men like the Captain . . .

Or himself.

Thinking he knew, Achamian had blinded himself to the unknown. He had ceased asking *questions*. He had plucked his own eyes, and unless he could find some way to overcome this reversal, the daughter of the only woman he had ever loved was almost certainly doomed.

Ignorance was trust. Knowing was deception. Questions! Questions were the only truth.

This was the resolution that arose out of his first days of captivity.

To notice everything. To question everything. To take no knowledge for granted.

This was why his aggression wilted so quickly, why a kind of fatalistic calm claimed his soul.

Why he began *waiting*.

I live because Kosoter needs me, he would remind himself. *I live because of things I cannot see . . .*

Of course the absurdity of all this pondering was not lost on him. A captive of men without scruple or pity, scalpers. A captive of his foe of foes, *Kellhus . . .* Far more than his life, he knew, would be decided by this forced march across the dregs of the Istyuli. And yet here he was, whiling away the watches pondering philosophical inanities.

His lips cracked to bleeding. His throat and palette scored with ulcers. His fingers numbed to paralysis, his wrists festering. And yet here he was, smiling at the play of insight, at the assemblage of categorical obscurities in his prying soul.

Only a drug could so overturn the heart's natural order. Only the ashes of a legendary king.

Qirri. The poison that made strong.

They need only bend back their faces to drink.

The rain drums down across their heads, rolls across the distances in misty sweeps. The puddled earth sizzles, sucks at the rotting seams of their boots. Clothing sags and pinches, rubbing skin raw. Straps long rotted by sweat give way altogether. Pokwas is forced to bind his shoulder harness about his waist, so that the scythed tip of his tulwar sketches an arthritic line through the muck. Sarl even tosses away his hauberk in a bizarre tirade where he alternately argues, rages, and laughs. 'On the ready!' he cries time and again. 'This is skinny country, boys!'

On and on it falls. In the evenings they cluster together for their meagre repast, glaring into nowhere with a kind of beaten-down fury.

Only the Wizard, looking strangely young with his hair and beard flattened into sheets, seems unaffected. He watches with a canniness that Mimara finds both encouraging and alarming. It would be better, she thinks, if he were to look more defeated . . . Less dangerous.

Only Koll shivers.

On the third night, Cleric strips naked and climbs a clutch of thumb-shaped boulders. He is little more than a grey shadow in the near distance, yet all of them with the exception of Koll gaze in wonder. He does this sometimes, Mimara has learned, shouts his crazed sermons to the greater world.

They listen to him rant about curses, about ages of loss and futility, about the degradation of life's end. *'I have judged nations!'* he bellows into the curtained gloom. *'Who are you to condemn me? Who are you to deliver?'*

They watch him trade lightning with the clouds. Even sodden, the earth shivers with competing thunders.

When Mimara looks away, she finds the old Wizard staring at her.

The ground is more broken, the undergrowth more toilsome: grasses like flayed hide, shrubs still sharp from the drought. Even still, the forests seem to arrive without warning. The land pitches upward, and kinked hill country climbs out of the grey haze, guttered with gorges booming with brown waters, sloped with stands of slender poplar and crooked fir.

Kûniüri, she realizes. At long last they have *arrived*.

It is the weariness of this realization, if anything, that astonishes her. Were she the same woman who had fled the Andiamine Heights, this moment would be profound with disbelief. Kûniüri, the ancient homeland of the High Norsirai ere their destruction, the place so deeply revered by the nameless authors of *The Sagas*. How many expositions had she read, descriptions of its works, chronicles of its kings? How many scrolls authored by its enlightened sons? How many psalms to its lost glory?

It all seems little more than dross in the face of her trudging misery. The world seems too grey, too cold and sodden for glory.

But the rain stops not long after, and the uniform grey resolves into clouds balled into fists of darkness. Soon the sun presses through, and the clouds are drawn into pageants of purple and gold. The land is revealed, and she gawks across previously unseen miles, rugged hills marching to the horizon, stumps of limestone rising from gowns of gravel and earth. For the first time in days her face is warmed for looking.

And again she thinks, *Kûniüri*.

During her years as a brothel-slave the name meant little to her. It seemed simply another dead thing known by everyone older and wiser, like a grandfather who had died before she was born. That had changed when her Empress mother had burned Carythusal. For all the symbolic tempest of her revolt, she fell upon the gifts her mother lavished upon her, the clothes, the cosmetics, and the *tutors* – the tutors most of all. Who she had been, the brothel-slave, dwindled to an ignorant kernel, albeit one that refused to relinquish the heights of her soul. The world became a kind of drug. And Kûniüri became an emblem of sorts, as much a marker of her ingrown emancipation as the dead and sacred land of *The Sagas*.

And now she is *here*, on the frontier of her own becoming.

That night they camp in the ruins of an ancient fort: battered foundations glimpsed between trees, the remains of a single bastion, massive blocks arrested in their downward tumble. After their passage across the Istyuli and the endless miles of human absence, the ruins almost seemed a landmark promising home.

Game is plentiful, and thanks to Xonghis and his unerring aim they feast on a thrush and a doe. The Imperial Tracker skins and butchers the doe, which Cleric then cooks using a small and incomprehensible Cant. As his eyes dim to a dark glitter, the tip of his finger shines as bright as a candle flame, and Mimara cannot but think of the glorious soot, the Qirri, that will blacken it later in the evening. Cleric slowly draws the pad of his finger along the haunches, then the ribs, transforming crimson lobes into sizzling, smoking meat.

The thrush they boil.

Afterward, Mimara saunters along the edges of the Captain's distraction, then creeps back in a broad circle, ducking behind palms of leaning stone, slipping between throngs of undergrowth. A wall of sorts borders the inner courtyard where they have gathered, an arc of unmortared stone broken into toothlike sections. The Captain has deposited the Wizard at the far end, careful as always to keep him segregated from the others. She hurries even though she knows she risks Cleric's preternatural hearing. For a man who betrays almost no anxiety, Lord Kosoter is nothing if not a fastidious shepherd, always counting and remorselessly quick to catch strays with his crook.

She slows as she nears the wall behind the old Wizard, following the tingle of his Mark more than any visual cue. She slinks between sumac, presses against the cold stone. She stretches out onto her belly, creeps with serpent patience until she can see the Wizard's maul of hair rising before her.

'Akka . . .' she whispers.

A warmth climbs through her as she speaks, an unaccountable assurance, as if out of all her crazed burdens, confession is the only real encumbrance. Secrecy mars the nature of every former slave, and she is no different. They hoard knowledge, not for the actual power it affords, but for the *taste* of that power. All this time, even before Achamian's captivity, she has been accumulating facts and suspicions. All this time she has fooled herself the way all men fool themselves, thinking that she alone possessed the highest vantage and that she alone commanded the field.

All this time she has been a fool.

She tells him what she has learned about the Captain and his mission. 'He knows he's damned. We are his only hope of salvation – or so he believes. Kellhus has promised him paradise. So long as he needs us, we're secure . . . As soon as I discover just *why* he needs us, I promise I'll find some way to tell you!'

She tells him how Cleric is more than Ishroi – so much more. 'Nil'giccas!' she cries under her breath. 'The last Nonman King! What could that mean?'

She speaks of the terror she did not know she had. And there is something in her murmur, a despair perhaps, that bumps her from the ruts, carries her away from the tracks the previous weeks and months have worn into her thoughts. She recalls who she was.

She tells him of the incense mornings on the Andiamine Heights, when she would laze in bed watching the sheers across her balcony rise and fall with twining grace, her breath deep and even, her eyes fluttering to protest the sun.

'I dreamed of you . . . you, Akka.'

Because he wasn't real. Because a fictitious love was the only love she could bear.

She always knew he would rebuff her, that he would deny his paternity, deny her the knowledge she so desperately sought. She always knew, in the queer way of damaged souls, that she loved him because he knew *nothing about her*, and so had no grounds for casual judgment – or even worse, the watchful pity she so despised in her mother's eyes.

And it seems, somehow, impossibly, that she knew it would

come to this, rooting across sodden earth, cringing against crumbling stone, whispering desperations . . .

Clutching her belly and declaring love.

Grace is more than immortal. The more the world besieges it, the greater its significance burns. And she can feel it, this very instant, a spark shining in the God's infinite palm.

'The child is yours,' she whispers sobbing. 'Can't you see?

'I bear *my mother's* child . . .'

She reaches out with fingers that are steady even as shudders wrack her. She presses them through the matted nest of his hair, sobs aloud when she touches the hot skin of his scalp. For the first time she feels movement in her womb – an infant heel . . .

'We're here, Akka . . . *Kûniüri*. At last we're here!'

The Captain's voice, when it comes, seems to crack all hope asunder.

'Lot of bones in this ground,' he says from the far side of the stone. 'I can feel it.'

Lord Kosoter stands from an unseen crouch, looms over her and the Wizard, testing his aging knees. Her intake of breath is so sharp it sounds like an inverted shriek. An unkind coincidence of angles places the Nail of Heaven just beyond his brow, illumines the rim of his hair, so that he seems more an unholy wraith than a man, a dark god come to punish for mere perversity's sake. He holds a rib in his hands, strips the last remaining rind with his teeth. Grease slicks his beard below his mouth.

'Keep throwing the sticks like this, girl, and you *will* join them.'

He bends toward her with the leisurely cruelty of a butcher picking his slaughter. He grips the back of her neck, hauls her kicking to her feet. He throws her to the ground in the direction of the others. As she scrambles to find her footing, he kicks her to the ground once again. Weeds claw her cheeks.

'This is *my* slog!' the Captain growls, unfastening one of his belts.

Suddenly she is a little girl, one sold to foreign slavers by a starving mother. Suddenly she is flinching beneath violent shadows, cringing and cringing until she is scarce a human child at all, but a thing small, blind, and mewling, a thing to be cracked in mercantile jaws, a thing to be tasted . . .

'*Sarl!*' the merciless voice bellows. 'What's the *Rule?*'

'Pleaaase!' she weeps, scuffing backward. 'I'm-I'm sor—!'

'No *conniving!*' the madman chortles. 'No whispering on the slog!'

She raises a frantic palm in warding. The belt makes small cooing sounds as it whips through the air. It reminds her of the lariats that musicians use performing in the alleyways of Carythusal's slums. And the breathless songs they composed, haunting, as if their instruments were children crying out from sleep.

She looks past the shadows of those who laugh and catcall. She looks to *him*, the Nonman King. She calls out to the horror she sees in his great eyes. She spits blood and sobs his name, his *real* name.

But he merely watches . . .

She knows he will remember.

———

That night he comes to the little girl. He kneels beside her, offers his blackened fingertip.

'Take him,' he says. 'Cherish him. He will make you strong.'

The little girl clutches his hand, halts its descent. She clasps his finger, then presses the stained tip across his own lips. She rises into his embrace, sucks the magic from his mouth. The strength of it races across her skin, then soaks through her, rinsing away a constellation of pains.

'You could have stopped him . . .' the little girl wheezes between her sobs.

'I could have stopped him,' he says, dropping his solemn gaze. He withdraws into the dark.

⸺∞⸺

The following morning it is her Judging Eye that opens.

Lashed and bone-sore, she breakfasts with charcoal-scabbed demons. Even the old Wizard sits with his skin blistered, his edges haunted by the shadow of his soul's future thrashing. Galian glances at her and mutters to the others, and laughter jumps through them in small, peevish squalls. And it seems she can see it, the piling on of sin – wickedness in all its bestial diversity. Thievery and betrayal, deceit and gluttony, vanity and cruelty, and *murder* – murder most of all.

'About your screams . . .' Galian says to her, his face grave with mockery. 'You really should cross the Captain more often. The boys and I were quite taken.'

Pokwas laughs outright. Xonghis grins while working his bow.

She has wondered at Galian's transformation. He seemed a friend in the beginning, someone who could be trusted, if only because he was wry and sane. But as his beard grew and his clothing and accoutrements rotted, he became ever more remote, ever more difficult to trust. The burdens of the trail, she thought, recalling the way the brothel had embittered so many sweet souls.

But now, seeing him revealed in the light of God, she realizes the months of hardship – or even the Qirri – have changed him very little. He is one of those men who is lovable or despicable depending on the peevish lines of camaraderie. Gracious and generous with those he deems his friends and caring not at all about others.

'A crimson butterfly . . .' she murmurs, blinking at memories not her own.

The man's grin falters. 'A what?'

'You raped a child,' she tells the former Columnary. 'You killed her trying to stifle her screams . . . You still dream of the crimson butterfly your bloody palm left on her face . . .'

All three men go rigid. Pokwas looks to Galian for a laughing dismissal that does not come. A kind of pity wells through her, watching horror and arrogance dual in Galian's eyes.

Henceforth, she knows, his jokes will be furtive and hidden. Fearful.

Of all the Skin Eaters, none are more blasted than Cleric, whose sins run so deep she can scarce glance at him without her eyes rebelling. He is an impossible figure, a heaving motley of monstrosities, angelic beauty marred by sorcerous ugliness, blotted by ages of moral obscenity.

But the Captain is perhaps the most horrifying. She can see the hallow brilliance of the two Chorae burning white through his rag tunic and between the splints of his hauberk – a contradiction that intensifies the hoary imprint of his transgressions. Murder barks his skin, victim chapped across victim. Cruelty smokes from his eyes.

He gives the call to march, and then, inexplicably, the Eye closes. The sins vanish in a kind of inward folding, like wood unburning. The right and wrong of the world is hidden once again.

She has been beaten many times. Beatings were simply the penultimate rite in the flurry of mean and petty ceremonies that composed life in the brothel. As a child she learned that some men could find bliss only in fury, climax in degradation. And as a child she learned to flee her body, to take refuge behind wide-open eyes. A final sip. Her body would weep, moan, even shriek, and yet she would always be there, hidden in plain sight, calmly waiting for the tempest to pass. One sip remaining.

The outrage would come afterward, when she returned to find her body curled and sobbing.

'*You are a cunning little slit,*' Abbarsallas, her first owner, once told her. '*The others fear the likes of you. They fear you because you are so difficult to see . . . Your kind lurks and lurks, waiting for opportunities . . . opportunities you do not even know! A knife forgotten. A shard of glass. A throat bared in a thoughtless moment. I've seen it with my own eyes – oh yes! You don't even know it's happening. You just strike, spit all your poison, and a freeman dies.*' He laughed as if at the particulars of some crazed memory. '*That's why they would keep you shackled, or drown you in the courtyard as a moral for the others. Spare themselves the worry. But me, oh, I see gold in you, my little darling. Hard men take no pleasure in breaking what is already broken. And your kind can be broken a thousand times – a thousand more!*'

Five years later they would find him dead, his body jammed into the sewer chute behind the scullery. Apparently Abbarsallas could only be broken once.

Anasûrimbor Mimara has been beaten many times, so the coldness she feels as she walks, the numbness of a soul flinching from its own sharp edges, is a familiar one. As is the impulse that draws her to the fore of the slack-eyed company, into the glowering presence of the Captain.

'I will tell him. He *will* damn you.'

A part of her even laughs, saying such to someone already damned – irrevocably.

She has wondered what he was like in his youth. It seems absurd that he once reclined at *heteshiras*, the night-long bacchanals of eating and vomiting so popular among the Ainoni nobility, that he plotted with men too fat to walk, that he concealed his expressions with porcelain masks during negotiations, or painted his face white before riding out to war. High Ainon was a land of ringlets and perfume, where men ranked one another according to eloquence and jnanic wit. Where disputes over buttons could provoke duals to the death.

And here stands Lord Kosoter, as savage as any Kutnarmi tribesman, as hardbitten as mountain flint. More so than any of the other Skin Eaters, he seems bred to the cycle of deprivation and tribulation that rules a scalper's life. She can scarce imagine a man more at odds with the consumptive pantomime that was Carythusal. Silk, it seems, would tear for simply touching his skin.

'You argue your own doom,' he says without so much as glancing at her.

'How is that?'

He turns, seizes her with his gaze. 'Killing you would be my only recourse, if what you say is true.'

Perhaps she is too exhausted to be frightened – or too disgusted. If her smile surprises him, he shows no sign of it. 'You think he would not see such treachery within you?' she asks, using the tone her mother and the Wizard know so well. 'You think he will not see these very words when you kneel before him?'

'He'll see it. But you don't know him as I know him.'

'You know him better?'

'There is a *chasm*, girl, an abyss between the hearth and the battlefield. Your stepfather and my prophet are two very different men, I assure you.'

'You sound certain of yourself, my Lord.'

There is a *flatness* to him, an aura of immovability. When she speaks to him like this, in low tones, walking side by side, she has this nagging sense of amputation, of a soul that either has legs for hatred and fury or has no legs at all.

'We were seven days out from Attrempus,' he says, sparing her his scrutiny, 'marching on the Numaineiri Orthodox. We were naught but the jugglers – the greater parade lay with my kinsmen to the south. But still, *he* found time to inspect our bloody handi-work. The long-bearded fools only thought they *believed*. We showed them conviction – *Zaudunyani* conviction. But your stepfather, he decided we needed to show *more*, something all the blondies in Ce Tydonn could mull in their racks. So we herd up the converts, all those who had found salvation in the execution line, *and we put out their eyes*. Gropers, we called them – what they call them still.'

He does not turn to look at her, as she would expect from anyone who cared whether his words had effect. So much of what makes him unsettling, she realizes, are these violations of the innumerable small ways people anticipate one another. He is the most ruthlessly *direct* man she has ever known, and still he continually surprises her.

'So you think my stepfather's cruelty is something that *I* should fear?'

She even manages to laugh.

He sweeps his gaze about and down, swallows her with a kind of compressed regard – a look that seems to throw her whole existence on the balance, as if weighing her life against half-hearted promises.

'Besides,' she says, pressing the remnants of her anger into her glare. 'It's my *mother* you really need to consider.' She looks away in feigned disinterest.

'If she would burn down half a city to avenge me, what do you think she will do to you?'

Day after day, they walk through a dead land, a land where sons were slaughtered before they could father, where daughters were exterminated before their wombs could quicken. A land where birth itself had been murdered. And she mourns.

She mourns her lost naiveté, the girl who would be a witch, not for knowledge's sake, but to better batter an offending world. To better injure a mother she cannot forgive.

She mourns all those they have lost. Skin Eaters. Stone Hags. She whispers prayers to Yatwer, though she knows the Goddess despises warlike men as takers. She prays for Kiampas, for giant Oxwora. She even laments Soma, the unknown youth who was murdered not for gold or hate but for his face.

She mourns her captivity and the suffering of the Wizard.

She mourns her boots, which will very soon fail her feet.

She mourns the tiny black sliver that is her ration of Qirri.

She did not know what to expect coming to Kûniüri. Great journeys are often such, a matter of placing one foot before the other, again and again, for what seems a trudging eternity. Sometimes dusk and sleep are your only destination, and the trek's overarching end comes about as a kind of surprise.

She wasn't journeying to places glimpsed in ancient dreams. She wasn't *drawn* the way the Wizard was drawn.

She had been chased.

She thinks of the Andiamine Heights, of her Empress mother. She thinks of her little brother, Kelmomas, and she worries – as far as the Qirri will allow her.

At last they come to a river, every bit as great as the Sayut or the Sempis, broad-backed and slow moving, deep green with life and sediment, gleaming like a plate of silver where it catches the sun.

The Captain turns to his captive. 'Is this it?'

Gagged, the old Wizard simply gazes at him in incredulity and disgust.

The Captain yanks the gag from his mouth. '*Is this it?*'

Achamian spits, works his lips and jaw for a moment. For the first time Mimara notices the sores caking the creases of his lips. After glaring at the Captain, the old Wizard turns to the others with mock grandiloquence. 'Behold!' he cries through the sludge of a long-stopped voice. 'Behold the Mighty Aumris! The nursery of Mannish civilization! The cradle of all!'

The Captain slaps him to the ground for his insolence.

She mourns the fact that cringing has become so easy.

The old Wizard was the first to realize how near they had come.
He lay bound on his side as he had fairly every night of his captivity.
But this time the Captain had thrust him across an incline, so
that he could see the night sky through a broad gap in the canopy.
A black plate of stars. At first, he gazed with a kind of senseless
yearning, the attitude belonging to the defeated, one numbed to
things beyond the immediate circuit of his fears. But then he
glimpsed patterns . . . *ancient* constellations.

The Round of Horns, he realized. The Round of Horns as it
appeared during the height of summer . . .

From Sauglish.

After that he bore the Captain's indignities with renewed
resolution.

Stone heaved with greater regularity from the earth, until dirt
became something found only in scallops of rock. Soon the Aumris
became a booming white cataract, rushing through giant scarp-
shelved canyons that were sometimes miles wide. They followed
high lips of stone, laboriously descending and scaling the hanging
gorges that fed the river. The Mirawsul, the Kûniüri had called
these highlands – a name that meant 'Cracked Shield' in ancient
Umeri.

They found and followed what remained of the Hiril, the road
that traversed the Mirawsul and where Seswatha had once shown
a band of highwaymen the error of their ways. Three consecutive
nights the Skin Eaters camped in the shells of ruined watchtowers
– the famed Nûlrainwi, the 'Sprinting-fires,' beacons of war and
peace that had linked the cities of Aumris since the days of
Cûnwerishau.

At last they came to the Shield's end, and from high cliffs they gazed across forested alluvial plains that reached to the hazed horizon. For Achamian, the vista was like seeing a work of intricate art defaced with a child's crude strokes. Gone was the Kairil, the monumental stone road that tracked Aumris's winding course with ruler straight lines. Gone were the villages and the fields arrayed in great radial quilts. Gone were the innumerable plumes of smoke and the hearths and families that had kindled them.

The Wizard had expected a land like this, a wilderness overgrown with thronging life. But he had assumed that the Sranc would assail them time and again, an endless string of clans, and that he and Cleric would spend their nights crying out destruction. Knowing there could only be one explanation, Achamian found himself gazing into the east, wondering how many days their bent company would have to march to overtake them . . .

Kellhus and the onerous lodestone that was his Great Ordeal.

The old Wizard reflected on his days in arid Gedea, on the humble campfire he had shared with Esmenet and Kellhus more than twenty years ago. He could only marvel that Fate had brought them so far.

The company descended the cliffs using what remained of a great switchback stair. Soon they found themselves on the loamy banks of an Aumris that once again flowed wide and ponderous and brown. Great willows, some even rivalling the mighty elms and oaks of the Mop, stepped and knotted the ground they trod, trailing sheaves of yellow and green across the waters. There was a strange peace in their passage, even a sense that the land was at last awakening, having slumbered ages waiting for their return.

Flies plagued them.

That night, as always, the old Wizard dreamed of the horror

that was the Golden Room. The moaning procession. The eviscerating horn. The chain heaving him and the other wretches forward.

Closer. He was coming closer.

—∞∞∞—

They reached the ruined gates of Sauglish two nights following. The towers had become knolls and the walls had crumbled into low, earthen ridges, like the wandering dikes so common to Shigek and Ainon.

But no one needed to be told. The very air, it seemed, smelled of conclusion.

Climbing the ridge, they could even see sun-bright trees waving across the westward slopes of the Troinim in the near distance: three low hills made one by the ruins strewn across their backs. Mottled walls, here hewn to their foundations, there rising blunted. Cratered brick faces. Witch-fingers of stone rising from the clamour of growth and tumble. The silence of things distant and dead.

The Holy Library.

It did not seem possible.

We all imagine what it will be like when we finally reach long-sought places. We all anticipate the wages of our toil and suffering – the momentary sum. Achamian had assumed he would feel either heartbreak or outrage, setting eyes upon the legendary Sohonc stronghold. Tears and inner turmoil.

But for some reason it seemed just another derelict place.

Give him Qirri. Give him sleep.

The dead could keep until morning.

They made camp at the mouth of the gate. There was no sermon that night, only the rush of wind through the treetops and the sound of Sarl's cackle, gurgling through the mucus that perpetually weighted his lungs, rising and falling in the manner of drunks given to reciting grievances at the edge of unconsciousness.

'*The Cofferrrssss! Ha! Yes! Think on it, boys! Such a slog as there never was!*'

'*Kiampas!* Kiampas! *He-hee! What did I tell you . . .*'

On and on, until it seemed an animal crouched in their shadowy midst, growling with low and bestial lust.

'*The Cofferrrssss . . .*'

CHAPTER THIRTEEN

The Istyuli Plains

Gods are epochal beings, not quite alive. Since the Now eludes them, they are forever divided. Sometimes nothing blinds souls more profoundly than the apprehension of the Whole. Men need recall this when they pray.

—AJENCIS, *THE THIRD ANALYTIC OF MEN*

Summer, 20 New Imperial Year (4132 Year-of-the-Tusk), The High Istyuli

Three days Sorweel waited after learning of the Nonman Embassy and the Niom.

Zsoronga refused to even countenance the possibility of his departure. Even though he had seen the Nonman Embassy first-hand, the Successor-Prince continued insisting the entire thing was some kind of Anasûrimbor deceit. Sorweel was narindari, he insisted, chosen by the Gods to excise the cancer that was the Aspect-Emperor.

'Just wait,' Zsoronga said. 'The Goddess *will* intervene.

Something auspicious will happen. Some twist will keep you here, where you can discharge your fate! Wait and see.'

'And what if they know?' Sorweel finally asked, voicing the one alternative they had passed over in silence: that the Anasûrimbor had somehow guessed the Dread Mother's divine conspiracy.

'They don't know.'

'But wh—'

'They *don't know.*'

Zsoronga, Sorweel was beginning to realize, possessed the enviable ability to yoke his conviction to his *need* – to believe, absolutely, whatever his heart required. For Sorweel, belief and want always seemed like ropes too short to bind together, forcing *him* to play the knot as a result.

Faced with yet another sleepless night, he once again struck out through the encampment for the Swayali enclave, determined to confront Serwa with pointed questions. But the guardsmen denied him entry to the Granary, saying their Grandmistress conferred with her Holy Father over the horizon. When he refused to believe them, they called for the Nuns. 'Cap your gourd,' a spice-eyed witch teased. 'Soon the Grandmistress will be skipping you like a stone across water!'

Sorweel walked back to his tent in a stupor, at once dismayed at the capricious ways of Fate and *thrilled* – sometimes to the point of tingling breathlessness – at the prospect of spending so much time with his Enemy's daughter.

'Well?' Zsoronga cried when he returned.

'You are my brother, are you not?' Sorweel asked, pulling free the small purse that Porsparian – or the Goddess – had given him. It seemed dull and unremarkable in the sunlight, despite the golden crescents embroidered across it. 'I need you to keep this.'

As High Keeper of the Hoard, he knew enough about Chorae

to know that it would wreck whatever sorcerous contrivance Serwa had prepared for them. Concealed or not.

'So you *are* leaving,' the Successor-Prince said, taking the pouch with a blank air of incomprehension.

'It's a family heirloom,' Sorweel offered by way of lame explanation. 'An old totem. It will bring you luck only so long as you don't *know* what it contains.'

This struck the young King as plausible enough, given that he had been forced to improvise. Many charms required some small sacrifice: beans that could not be eaten or wine that could not be quaffed.

But Zsoronga scarcely looked at the thing, let alone pondered it. In his eyes, *Sorweel* was the divine weapon.

'This cannot be!' he cried. 'You! You *are the one! She* has chosen you!'

Sorweel could do no more than shrug with weary resignation.

'Apparently *He* has chosen me as well.'

—∞—

The following morning none other than Anasûrimbor Moënghus himself came to fetch him before the Interval's toll. The Prince-Imperial was predictably menacing, not merely for his glare and feral physique. Like many of the Ordeal's outriders, he had taken to ornamenting his gear with fetishes cut from the Sranc. Most riders used shrivelled digits and blackened ears, but Moënghus, for some unfathomable reason, had their *teeth* braided across the hems of his nimil hauberk. Because of the way they were fused, the things seemed peculiarly inhuman: small, curved combs of enamel with three pairs of roots to a tooth.

The Prince-Imperial watched with bored amusement as Sorweel dressed and gathered his gear. Zsoronga, who sat watching Moënghus, could not keep his peace.

'Nil'giccas is a myth,' he said with open contempt. 'There is no Nonman King.'

Moënghus shrugged, picked a curl from his wild black mane to study. 'So says Zeüm.'

'So says Zeüm.'

Something about Zsoronga's assertion – its pious confidence perhaps – hooked the Prince-Imperial's attention. 'Tell me, what has your father accomplished with all his Zeümi wisdom?'

'How to avoid marching into the wastes to die . . . among other things.'

'Other things,' Moënghus snorted. 'Like surrendering his son as a hostage?'

Zsoronga glared at the man, speechless.

Moënghus's presence seemed too oppressive for any real verbal exchange, so, heavy with pack and shield, Sorweel simply clasped fingers with his friend. He smiled in the pretense of manliness, ignored the abject worry in Zsoronga's green gaze. Then, with the giddy sense of toppling from some ledge of happenstance, he turned to follow the Prince-Imperial toward the Granary.

The Interval had tolled by this time, so the encampment roiled with activity. Anasûrimbor Moënghus paid no attention whatsoever to the warriors falling to their faces about them. He walked as though this simply were the way, the World abasing itself at his booted feet.

As though he truly were an Anasûrimbor.

The Granary seemed another world, crowded as it was with women bustling in florid silk. Given the strict apportioning of duty and labour in Sakarpus, Sorweel could not but think of the kitchens and fulleries of his father's palace – the only places, in his narrow experience, where the voices of men did not predominate. He was not scandalized, though he suffered the vague sense that he *should* be.

Anasûrimbor Serwa stood near the entrance of her pavilion, dispensing last-minute instructions to a small crowd of petitioners. She dismissed them the instant she glimpsed their approach, speaking some language Sorweel failed to recognize. The sun had climbed above the enclave's eastern rim, catching her flaxen hair in a brilliance that mimicked her father's haloed hands. A hush fell across the congregated witches, who, almost without exception, ceased their small labours to turn and watch their Grandmistress greet the newly arrived men.

Sorweel glanced from face to face, feeling more than a little conspicuous. More than a few of the Nuns, he realized, blinked tears. He suffered the sense, yet again, of blundering into dangers that only others could appreciate.

He turned to find Serwa standing nearby. Despite the craftsmanship, her leather jerkin and leggings seemed almost absurdly plain in comparison to the billows worn by her sisters. Both she and her brother shouldered packs that had been awaiting them in the dust.

'Come,' she said, her arm lowered to receive his waist. 'You must hold me tight.'

Moënghus already stood hulking in her slip embrace. Sorweel glimpsed his eyes grinning at him over the flaxen arc of her head. 'You get used to the reek,' he said when the young King hesitated. Only several of the Nuns laughed, few enough to underscore the anxiousness of the others.

They loved her, Sorweel realized. The way King Harweel's men had loved him.

He stepped into the soft sphere of her touch and perfumed scent. Despite his mail hauberk, he started like an unbroken colt at her touch. She pulled him tight to her side, and he felt her spine arch to an inexplicable exertion. She leaned her head back, and he fairly cried out for the blue-white light shining from her mouth and eyes, so brilliant as to blacken her sunburned face.

Moënghus's laughter slipped through the chinks of her arcane call.

A fog rose about them, scored with glowing parabolic lines. The dawn-shadowed world dimmed. There was a binding, a sense of straps whipping about his body, immobilizing him, heaving him in a thousand simultaneous directions . . . and then the *slip*, as if he folded along occlusions in reality. Whipping light, then a lurching *coming to be*, as if he were a thing rotted yanked clear of his grave . . .

He was on his knees, retching.

He felt the fleeting press of Serwa's hand, as if she tested his bodily integrity. He spent several moments spitting into dust and balding turf. Then he staggered toward the Imperial siblings where they sat on the crest of a low berm. He had assumed they were watching him, but their gaze remained unbroken when he stepped beyond its angle. Craning his head back he saw regions of dust steaming across the horizon. The Army of the Middle-North, he realized, preparing to resume its long march to Golgotterath. Of the Men of the Circumfix, he could only glimpse the outermost assemblies, clouds of black specks, snaking beneath the dun plumes.

He turned back to Serwa and Moënghus.

'I am my father's daughter,' she said, answering his questioning look. 'But I am *not* my father . . .' Her eyelids fluttered against some unearthly drowsiness. 'Metagnostic Cants are . . . trying for me.'

He took an unceremonious seat at her side, found himself looking down, such was the lure of her gaze.

'Fate is indignity,' he heard her say.

'What do you mean?'

'The King of Sakarpus, the city famed the world over for hoarding *Chorae*, now finds himself whisked across the sorcerous aether . . . and by a *woman*, no less'

'I hadn't considered it,' he said with fuming wariness. 'You lose track of the indignities after a while.'

She smiled in what seemed genuine humour.

The Cant of Translocation, she went on to explain, could take them only the space of horizon, less if her vision were obscured. The Cant's difficulty was such that she could successfully hold its meaning only after at least two watches of sleep. She was lucky, she said, if she could complete two Translocations a day, unlike her divine father, who could cross endless leagues in that time, stepping from horizon to horizon.

'So you will vomit,' she said, 'and I will snooze, day in and day out, until we come to Ishterebinth.'

'And while the Holy Princess snores and farts and mumbles,' Moënghus said, leaning his shaggy-maned head low to see past his sister, 'you and I will *hunt*.'

'And the Sranc?' Sorweel asked, speaking with a confidence he did not feel.

'Will do everything they can to bugger our corpses,' the Prince-Imperial replied, staring off.

Clenching his teeth against the tailings of his nausea, Sorweel turned back to regard their mighty fraction of the Great Ordeal. So many men, believing unto death . . .

<hr />

The Horde retreated, scraping the horizon, and the Four Armies marched into its desolate wake.

Thus far the Army of the Middle-North under Anasûrimbor Kayûtas, charged with the extreme left flank, had confronted the greatest concentration of the abominations. For the Sranc sustained themselves on the fruits of the grave, worms and grubs, and so multiplied according to the richness of the earth. Though Kayûtas did not so much as lay eyes on Lost Kûniüri, his Army lured innumerable clans from its forested frontiers. And so the Horde had accumulated in disproportion, mobbing to the west and thinning to the east, until, like gravel heaped upon a balance beam, it had tipped and come crashing . . .

Now it was the Army of the South under King Umrapathur of Nilnamesh that found itself most besieged. For as the Great Ordeal crawled ever northward, the Neleost, the famed Misty Sea, sheltered it to the west while the High Istyuli yawned ever more infinite to the northeast. Word of the Israzi'horul, the Shining Men, spread far among the high northern clans, and the Sranc came mobbing from over the horizon, a never-ending trickle of inhuman lust and wicked arms. They rutted and howled. They scoured the depleted earth. They battled over the carcasses of the dead, devoured their offspring. They blotted the earth with their multitudes.

For weeks the Great Ordeal had cleaved to a northern course, skirting the more broken lands to the west. But as they drew abreast the Neleost, the Four Armies had veered westward, forcing King Umrapathur to pivot with reference to his foe and so position the mad masses before him across his right flank. He understood the dangers, for as a long-time veteran of the Unification Wars he had fought many mortal campaigns. To drag your foe on your flank was to court disaster. Yet he put his faith in his Holy Aspect-Emperor, knowing that his Lord-and-God understood this risk far better than he did. But his men were not so sanguine. King Urmakthi of Girgash, especially, troubled him with dire pronouncements in council. As did the sinister Carindûsû, the Grandmaster of the sorcerous Vokalati. For they spent their days in the shadow of the Sandstorm, fencing with the shrieking multitudes.

'When we drove them before us,' Carindûsû said, his oiled face held high and imperial, 'fear was their contagion. Now that we drag them upon our boards, they answer more and more to their hunger.'

Indeed, clans assailed them with increasing frequency, and not simply those driven by the extremis of starvation, the ones they cut down as easily as howling dogs. Soon not a day passed without tidings of some Grandee or Satrap dying on the dusty fields: Tikirgal, the Grandee of Macreb, who had always carried himself with the air of an immortal in council, and so shocked all the more with his passing; Mopuraul, the bellicose Satrap of Tendant'heras, whose overbearing manner few would miss.

And not a night passed without some pitched battle across the perimeter of the camp, crazed random affairs that often roused the whole of the Army and so contributed to its mounting exhaustion. The Vokalati never ceased walking the low skies to the immediate north, their lavish billows winding like nested snakes, their mouths and eyes aglow. Kites, the Men of the Circumfix began to call them. From dusk to dawn, they cast lights across the barren tracts, and without fail they found cohorts of Sranc – sometimes thousands strong – creeping toward the camp with reptilian cunning. Many of the swarthy Schoolmen bound themselves to their mules during the day so they might slumber. Fewer and fewer mustered for the daylight Culling.

And yet Umrapathur doggedly refused calling on their Holy Aspect-Emperor. When the Signallers asked what message they should flash across the horizon each evening, he would describe their straits, for he was not so arrogant as to pretend, but he would always conclude with '*all is well with the Army of the South.*'

They exchanged horizon for horizon, winking from waste to wilderness to waste.

Since the Swayali Grandmistress had to *see* the places she delivered them to, the journey was one of stepping – if the madness of sorcery could be called such – from height to height. This made their passage a succession of breathtaking vistas, most of them densely forested after the first three days. Serwa's voice would speak from Sorweel's skin, bind the air about them with light, collapse his physical form into ash, then deliver them to an entirely novel vantage on the rim of the one previous. Usually, when she was not overcome by her arcane exertions, she would tell the two men something about the land beneath their blinking gaze.

'This was once the province of Ûnosiri, the ancient hunting grounds of the Umeritic God-Kings.'

'There . . . See that line of shadow through the trees? That was the Soholn, the great road raised by King Nanor-Ukkerja I to speed the passage of his hosts to the frontier.'

And each time, Sorweel would gaze out with a kind of perplexed wonder, trying to imagine what it would be like to possess memories of a distant age. Moënghus would typically scowl and cry, 'Bah!'

Only the Neleost remained constant, a hazy band of dark across the north. And despite the clamour of birdsong, the land seemed hushed for the fact of losses endured so very long ago.

From height to height they leapt. A ridge-line crooked like an arthritic finger. A scarp overlooking forests whose trees dwarfed the greatest Sorweel had ever seen in the arid environs of Sakarpus. Once she conveyed them to the summit of a ruined tower, one that proved impossible to climb down from. The conjuring had proven to be particularly difficult, so much that Moënghus had to catch Serwa as she teetered on the brink. The two men found themselves stranded on the ruined summit for watches waiting for her to recover. Once she conveyed them to an island of stumped rock in a river, not realizing that miles of marshland lay just beyond. The three of them were pimpled in mosquito bites before they could escape.

They typically made their 'leaps,' as Moënghus called them, twice daily, though the Swayali Grandmistress often attempted – and sometimes succeeded – delivering them a third time. Early in the morning, not long after awaking, then again in the afternoon, or later depending on what success Serwa had snoozing in daylight. They struck no fire, relying instead on Serwa's witchcraft to cook the game that Moënghus felled with his gorgeous bow. They slept every night, taking turns keeping watch. Sorweel would never forget the moonlit worlds he gazed across during his shifts, his ears pricked to the chorus of nocturnal sounds. Not a night passed where he did not steal glimpses of Serwa sleeping. She would seem a thing of polished marble beneath loose cloth, something more dense than the surrounding world. And he would wonder that loneliness could be so beautiful.

Sometimes the Princess-Imperial did not so much sleep as swoon, such was her exhaustion following certain leaps. She often whimpered, or even cried out, while unconscious, prompting Sorweel to ask Moënghus what afflicted her.

'The past,' he replied, glaring as if troubled by Sorweel's ignorance. 'Same as all those who have touched the shrivelled turd that is Seswatha's heart. She dreams of *these very lands* dying in Sranc and fire. She dreams of Father's foe.'

'The No-God,' Sorweel said numbly.

Eskeles had told him about the First Apocalypse, of course, how the shadowy force the Sakarpi called the Great Ruiner was about to return to finish the destruction of the world. Eskeles also had moaned and whimpered in his sleep, but if anything he had complained of his Dreams too much, to the point where Sorweel had made a habit of dismissing them.

For whatever reason, the fact that Serwa dreamed these very *same* dreams troubled him more.

'What was it like,' he asked her once, 'the First Apocalypse?'

'Defeat,' she replied with inward eyes. 'Horror. Anguish . . .' She looked to him with a frowning smile. 'And beauty too, in a strange way.'

'Beauty?'

'The end of nations . . .' she said with uncharacteristic hesitancy. 'Few things command the heart with such profundity.'

'Nations,' he repeated. 'Like Sakarpus.'

'Yes . . . Only exterminated instead of enslaved.' She stood as though to put distance between herself and his thin-skinned questions. 'And multiplied to the ends of the earth.'

Twice they heard Sranc horns calling, similar, yet eerily different from those heard on the Sakarpi Pale. On both occasions the three of them halted whatever it was they were doing, crooked their heads in pensive listening, and it would seem – to Sorweel at least – that the end of the world was not so far.

The death toll climbed, enough to even provoke King Umrapathur's fearless son, Charapatha, the famed Prince of One Hundred Songs, to speak out in apprehension. Every morning he led the Knights of Invishi into the roiling horizon, and every evening he returned with reports of fomenting danger. 'They no longer flee,' he told his father. 'They scatter only when they see Kites in the sky, and those have become all too rare . . . Soon they will not fear us at all, and they will fall upon us in numbers ten times greater than before – ten times or more!'

'What can we do but march?' King Umrapathur cried out in reply.

Even though the Believer-Kings understood their collective predicament, the fact that they had no choice but to continue advancing, their fear goaded them to question the *manner* of their march. Soon even King Mursidides of Cironj, who had been otherwise supportive, and Prince Massar of Chianadyni, who saw weakness in all complaints, began speaking out in council. At the very least, the Holy Aspect-Emperor had to be consulted.

'Why this stubbornness, King-Brother?' Mursidides chided. 'Do you fear you will become less in His eyes? Your faith in Him should not hang on His faith in you.'

There was no insolence in these words. All of them knew what it meant to dwell in the presence of their Holy Aspect-Emperor, to breathe air relieved of pride and shame, and they sought always to rekindle something of its tenor among themselves. They did not flinch from the prick of honesty, so long as it was well spoken.

So Umrapathur relented. He set aside his pride and commanded the Signallers to call on the Holy Aspect-Emperor with their coded pageants of light.

'The Horde waxes. Lord Most Holy, the Army of the South calls on your strength and wisdom.'

Less than a watch passed before the Signallers, hanging in the sky above the camp's eastern perimeter, saw the reply glitter along the bald night horizon.

'Assemble the Believer-Kings.'

Anasûrimbor Kellhus arrived even as they organized themselves. He wore a common cloak, striding among them without ceremony, clutching shoulders in solemn reassurance.

First, he questioned them regarding forage and supplies. They starved as the other Armies starved, but since the rivers had quickened, their position high on the Neleost watershed assured them the most plentiful catches of fish. Indeed, many companies marched with flimsy mantlets spanning the heads of dozens, covered with fish to dry in the sunlight.

Then he questioned them about the Horde, heard their multi-tudinous misgivings.

'This is the balance of perils,' he said, glaring down from his halo. 'You are exposed for the sake of sustenance. To undo the one is to undo the other . . . I will send you Saccarees. I can do no more.'

And with that, he winked out of existence.

To a man the Believer-Kings of the South rejoiced, for Apperens Saccarees was the Grandmaster of the *Mandate*, the Aspect-Emperor's own School. Only Carindûsû, who could not set aside his scholastic rivalries even here, thousands of miles from his fastness in Invishi, scoffed. What could the Mandate do that the Vokalati could not do as well, if not better?

'Double your numbers,' the ever-witty Mursidides declared to uproarious laughter.

The Grandmaster withdrew, embittered.

The Mandate Schoolmen arrived the following midday, bearing only what they could carry with them across the low sky. The great columns of infantrymen watched with wonder as the sorcerers filed across the flashing sun, their crimson-silk billows hanging like windless flags.

And so the number of Kites flown by the Army of the South was doubled. More than three hundred sorcerers of rank and some two hundred more understudies now strode through the sepulchral clouds above the Horde.

They crossed it as sparks from a grass fire – as a light leaping.

Kûniüri . . . The fabled land of his ancestors.

Not even two thousand years could undo the glory of its works. It seemed a great vessel clinging to the surface of an earthen sea, wrecked and derelict, too powerfully wrought to founder, too vast to entirely drown. Humped fortifications. Overgrown processionals. Mounded temples. It would linger for another two thousand years, Sorweel realized, even if only as featureless stones kissed by the sun. And this, he found himself thinking, was not such a bad thing, to find immortality in your bones.

'Do you ever ponder?' Serwa asked him once, watching him gaze across a field of vine-draped debris. Her voice startled him, since he had thought her asleep.

'Ponder?'

'The Apocalypse,' she said, rubbing the bridge of her nose. 'How your city survived when far greater bastions toppled.'

The young King of Sakarpus shrugged. 'Some live. Some die. My father always said it was a good thing that Men could only trust in the Whore when it comes battle. He believed Men should be wary of war.'

She smiled in appreciation.

'But you *do* see it, don't you?'

'See what?'

'*Evidence*. Proof of my Holy Father.'

Something balked within him, balked at the lies about to be told. Even in childhood, his had always been an honest, even earnest, soul. He gazed into her clear blue eyes, trusting in the mask the Dread Mother had given him.

'My friend, Zsoronga . . . He thinks your Consult is a myth, an—'

'And that Father is mad.'

'Yes.'

'But he saw the skin-spy Father unmasked in the Umbilicus.'

'Months back? Yes.'

Her scowl was quizzical enough to be alarming. 'And?'

'He thought it a trick.'

'Of course he did. The Zeümi are stubborn fools.'

Now it was Sorweel's turn to scowl. He could feel the danger – the slippery tumble of word in passion, passion in word, that prefaced every argument – yet he erred against caution once again. 'Better a fool than a slave,' he snapped in reply.

Boldness, it seemed, was its own shelter.

Her expression hung in blank equipoise, as if deciding whether to be offended or amused. 'You are not like the others. You do not *speak* as a Believer-King.'

'I am not like the others.'

Then she asked the dreaded question. 'But you *do* believe, don't you? Or has your stubborn Zeümi friend robbed you of your conviction?'

The assumption was plain. Her father had declared him a Believer-King, therefore he simply *had* to be a believer – at least at some point. Once again, Sorweel found himself marvelling at the strange *power* the Goddess and her deception had afforded him. Knowledge – this was the great fortress the Anasûrimbor had raised about themselves. And somehow he had found his way past the gates, into the very bosom of his adversary.

He *was* narindari, as Zsoronga had said. He, and he alone, was capable of murdering the Aspect-Emperor.

He need only summon the courage to die.

'Is doubt such a bad thing?' he asked, blinking to recover his concentration. 'Would you rather I be a fanatic like the others?'

She glared at him, five heartbeats of scrutiny, unnerving for the glint of preternatural canniness in her Anasûrimbor eyes.

'Yes,' she finally said. 'Most assuredly yes. I have battled *Shauriatas* in my Dreams. I have been tortured by Mekeritrig. Chased across Eärwa by Aurax and Aurang. The Consult is as real as it is wicked and deadly, Sorweel. Short of my father, the world knows no powers more ferocious. Even absent the No-God and the Second Apocalypse, they warrant the bloodthirsty fanaticism of Men.'

If anything, her voice had grown softer in speaking these words, yet the intensity of her look and intonation shocked the young King of Sakarpus. For all her allure and arcane potency, Anasûrimbor Serwa had always seemed arrogant and flip like her brothers – another child too aware of her divine paternity. Now she reminded him of Eskeles, and the way the portly Schoolman had tucked his zealotry between the folds of his wit and compassion.

This was the *true* Serwa, he realized. The earnest one. And her beauty seemed to blaze all the brighter for it.

He found himself staring at her breathless. Leaf shadows bobbed across the perfect lines of her face.

'Don't be a fool, Sorweel.'

She turned on her rump to kick her snoring brother.

⬩∞⬩

No Schoolmen was as famed as Apperens Saccarees, who had long stood high among the Empire's Exalt-Ministers. His voice proved a tonic for the Army of the South's nightly war-councils, for it carried both the authority of their Aspect-Emperor and the promise of tactical acumen. Like all Mandate Schoolmen he dreamed the First Apocalypse through the eyes of Seswatha and so could speak of their straits with the wisdom of one who had suffered them before – many times.

'In Atyersus,' he said, referring to the Mandate's famed citadel, 'we have whole libraries dedicated to warring against the Sranc. Centuries have we dreamed the battles of old. Centuries have we pondered the debacles and the successes.'

The Grandmaster of the Vokalati, however, was not impressed in the least. Such is the perversity of pride that it can drive a man to embrace contradiction, so long as some semblance of his privilege is preserved. Carindûsû, who had been among the first to warn of their growing peril, now became the first to discount the ominous declarations made by others – and Saccarees especially.

'Why do you speak of them so?' the Invitic Grandmaster asked, his oiled features gleaming with derision. 'They are naught but brutes, vicious beasts, to be herded with care, certainly, but to be *herded* nonetheless.'

'Beasts to be herded?' Saccarees replied scowling. 'They speak their own tongue. They forge their own weapons – when they cannot scavenge ours. The bliss we find in coupling, they find in the murder of innocents. They gather when we trod their earth, drawn from lands far from our stink on the wind. When over-matched they withdraw of their own nature, gouging all life from the earth before us, denying us the least sustenance. And when they come to dwarf our numbers, they assail us with suicidal ardour, throw themselves upon our spears simply to deny us our weapons!' The Grandmaster of the Mandate glanced from face to face to ensure that all present grasped the dire significance of his words. 'Do you think this a mere *coincidence*, Carindûsû?'

'They are *beasts*,' the tall Vokalati Schoolman said.

'No. Carindûsû, please, you must forgive my insistence. They are *weapons*. They were *designed* thus, hewn from the flesh of Nonmen by the Inchoroi to purge this world of souls – to exterminate Men! Beasts live to *survive*, my old friend. Sranc live to kill!'

And so was Carindûsû shamed a second time.

The Culling was reorganized under Saccarees's direction. As the Army of the South veered westward, the Vokalati had simply spread themselves across the entirety of the Horde facing them. Since the clans accumulating along their right flank posed the

greatest threat, Saccarees, with Carindûsû's grudging assent, dedicated all the Mandate and Vokalati – some three hundred sorcerers
of rank – to their extermination. For the long-suffering pickets,
the vision of so many Kites sailing into the enormous bowers of
dust was a thing of cheering joy and wonder. 'Like watching angels
drag skirts of fire,' Prince Sasal Charapatha reported to his father.

Arrayed in cadres of three – triunes – the Schoolmen walked
the high-hanging veils, their Wards turning aside flurries of arrows
and javelins, their Cants scorching the shadows that raced
shrieking beneath. The violence of the Horde's flight kicked ever
more dust into the sky, so piling obscurity atop obscurity, until
the Schoolmen could scarce see their own apparitional defences,
let alone the ground seething beneath. Since nothing singular
could be heard above the cavernous roar, they could not even
rely on their ears to guide them. So, their mouths and eyes alight,
they lashed out blindly, swept the ground with Cirroi Looms,
Dragonheads, Gotaggan Scythes, and more, destroying the
gibbering mobs they saw more in their soul's eye than in fact.
They advanced in hellish echelon, using the glow of the triunes
flanking to pace their progress into the ochre gloom. Shouting
their voices to croaks, they chased the far flank of the Horde out
into the droughted wastes . . .

Only to find it returned the following morning.

Since the Sranc cannibalized their dead, evidence of their
efficacy was difficult to find. The cavalry pickets who crossed the
sorcerer's wake counted the dead as they had been instructed.
The Imperial Mathematicians argued estimates, and the Believer-
Kings continually bent their darling ear, as the Nilnameshi put
it, to the numbers that most flattered their hopes. But Saccarees
was not fooled – no more than Carindûsû.

'The number is irrelevant!' he finally cried to King Umrapathur.
'The *effect* is all that matters.'

This put an end to their numerical speculations, for everyone knew that despite the cunning and fury of their efforts, the Schoolmen had accomplished nothing that any man could discern. Their predicament, if anything, had become more perilous. Not only did the Horde seem to be swelling along their flank, it had grown mobbing tendrils that hooked about their rear. Sranc, uncounted thousands of them, now *followed* the Army.

Once again Umrapathur was forced to set aside his pride and call upon the Aspect-Emperor.

This time their Lord-and-God came to them chalked in dust, bearing the crackling aura of sorceries dispensed. In their soul's eye, the Believer-Kings could see him striding alone into the inhuman Horde, wracking the masses that thronged about him with cataclysmic light.

'Indeed,' he said, favouring Sasal Umrapathur with a nod, 'your peril is great. You were wise to call me, Umra.'

Crisis, he told the assembled caste-nobles, was inevitable. The best they could hope to achieve was to weaken the Horde in tactically advantageous ways so they might survive its inevitable assault. 'Henceforth, you must encircle yourselves with your might, camp curled as a caterpillar, armed against all directions.'

The advance pickets were thinned to a handful of companies while the bulk of the Army's horsemen – the heavily armoured knights of Nilnamesh and the more fleet riders of Girgash and Chianadyni – concentrated on clearing the southeastern tracts of Sranc in concert with the Schoolmen. At the Aspect-Emperor's direction, they adopted the extravagant *hunting* tactics of the Far Antique Norsirai kings, who would use their hosts to encircle entire provinces and so drive all the beasts of the land to slaughter. The Schoolmen filed out into the depths of the plain, then arrayed themselves *behind* the Sranc so they could drive them into far-flung arcs of horsemen. It seemed they herded clouds with staffs of light. For the men marching in the main host, half the world was fenced in mountainous dust.

But it was like digging holes in loose sand: for every thousand they gouged clear, another thousand came collapsing in from the sides. And the losses, especially among the unarmoured ponies, rose to unsustainable levels. As ever, death came swirling down. Possu Hurminda, the even-handed Satrap of Sranayati, was lost, pulled down by a crazed Sranc chieftain. So too was Prince Hemrût, the eldest son of King Urmakthi, killed.

Despite these losses, despite the relentless heroism of their efforts, the numbers of Sranc trailing the Army of the South seemed to grow at an *increasing* rate, to the point where the cavalrymen found themselves mired in pitched battles rather than riding down panicked swarms. Then, on the sixth day of the Hunt, as it had come to be called, some five companies of Nilnameshi knights under Satrap Arsoghul were out-and-out overwhelmed, and the Cironji Marines, who were tasked with guarding the Army's rear, found themselves beset by several thousand Sranc.

'They seek each other out,' Saccarees said to the dismayed Believer-Kings, 'like schooling fish or flocking birds, so that the presence of few licenses the gathering of many.' Far from clearing the clans from their rear, he explained, they actually were pressing them farther afield and so opening ever-greater tracts for innumerable others to occupy. Their efforts to clear their flanks were leading to their encirclement.

'Could it be?' Carindûsû asked in derision. 'Have the fabled Dreams of the First Apocalypse led the illustrious Saccarees astray?'

'Yes,' the Mandate Grandmaster replied, his honesty so genuine, his humility so reminiscent of their Lord-and-God, that Carindûsû found himself shamed before his peers a third time.

'What we face . . . The world has never seen the like.'

They sat, as always, side by side before the octagonal iron hearth. Master and disciple.

'Maithanet,' the Aspect-Emperor said. 'My brother has seized control in Momemn.'

After so many years Proyas suffered only the most subtle urges to lie or save face. The merest hesitations were all that remained of his old instincts to write himself large in the eyes of others. This time it was the instinct to conceal his dismay. Before he had found Kellhus, he had made himself into Maithanet's disciple. And over the years since the First Holy War, he had come to love Esmenet as a sister, as much as he revered her as the wife of his Lord-and-God. To think the one could usurp the other . . . It seemed impossible.

'What could have happened?' he asked.

The fire seemed to sputter for the tidings as much as Proyas's heart laboured. If Maithanet, the Shriah of the Thousand Temples, had revolted against his brother . . .

The Empire itself teetered.

'For some reason Esmi suspected Maitha of sedition,' Kellhus said without the least whisper of remorse or concern, 'and so called him to account before *Inrilatas*. The interrogation went wrong, horribly wrong, and my brother ended up killing my son . . .' He looked down to his haloed palms, and Proyas found it curiously affecting, the contrast between his tone and his manner. 'I know little more than this.'

The Exalt-General breathed deep and nodded. 'What do you intend to do?'

'Gather as much knowledge as possible,' the Holy Aspect-Emperor replied, his head still bowed. 'I yet have resources in Momemn.'

Since the beginning, Anasûrimbor Kellhus had possessed a peculiar density of presence, as if he were the lone iron ingot among shards of clay and stone, invulnerable to what would smash others to powder. But with each of these remarkable sessions, the more this density seemed to leak from him . . .

So much so the Exalt-General suffered the demented urge to prick him, just to see if he would bleed. *Faith* . . . he upbraided himself. *Faith!*

'Do you—?'

Proyas paused, recognizing the implications of what he was about to ask.

'Do I fear for Esmi?' Kellhus asked. He turned his friend smiling. 'You wonder, as you have wondered your whole life, what passions bind me.' He closed his eyes in resignation. 'And whether they are human.'

So here it was, the question of questions . . .

'Yes.'

'Love,' the Holy Aspect-Emperor said, 'is for lesser souls.'

Young men are forever casting their meagre will and intellect against the tide of their passions, claiming they do not fear when they fear, insisting they do not love when they love. So the young King of Sakarpus told himself that he *despised* Anasûrimbor Serwa, cursed her as the self-important daughter of his Enemy, even as he mooned over the similarity of their names and the poetry of their conjunction: Serwa and Sorweel, Sorweel and Serwa. Even as he dreamed of their tender coupling.

Even as he began fearing more for *her* – a Gnostic sorceress – than for himself.

When he asked her whether she was worried about being a hostage, she simply shrugged and said, 'The ghouls mean us no harm. Besides, we are children of Fate. What is there for us to worry?'

And indeed, the more time he spent with her, the more this seemed to characterize her: the absence of worry.

Equanimity, soothing for its constancy, arrogant for its extent.

'So, this Nonman King, Nil'giccas, what are you to offer him?'

'Nothing. We are the *terms* of the negotiation, Horse-King, not the framers.'

'So we are to be captives? Nothing more?'

He almost always found her smile dazzling, even when he knew she laughed at him and his barbaric ignorance. 'Nothing more,' she said. 'We will languish, safe and useless, while the Great Ordeal carries the burden of Apocalypse.'

And he could not but exult at the thought of languishing with Anasûrimbor Serwa. Perhaps, he found himself hoping, she might come to love him out of boredom.

Days had passed, and her demeanour remained every bit as wry and reflective as that day when he first met her in Kayûtas's tent. She carried an aura of power, of course, as much for the miraculous way she whisked them from place to place as for the dizzying facts of her station and her blood. Grandmistress and Princess-Imperial. Archmage and Anasûrimbor.

Nevertheless, her youth and sex continually beguiled Sorweel into thinking she was a *mere girl*, someone weaker, simpler, and as much a victim of circumstances as he himself. And perhaps this was what he needed her to be, for no matter how many times her knowledge and intellect contradicted this image, it would reassert itself. Sometimes she astonished him, so subtle were her observations and so complete was her knowledge of the ancient lands they crossed. And yet, within a handful of heartbeats, she would inevitably lapse into the alluring waif, the one who would find such security in his arms, if only she would let him embrace her.

He would be long in appreciating the stamp of ancient profundity she carried in her soul.

'This Nil'giccas . . . Do you know much of him?'

'I was his friend once, ere the first end of the world . . .'

'And?'

Though they were of an age, sometimes her look made her seem a thousand years his senior.

'He was wise, powerful, and . . . unfathomable. The Nonmen resemble us too much not to continually fool us into thinking we comprehend them. But they always surprise, sooner or later.'

If Serwa embodied serenity, Moënghus was nothing short of mercurial. Sorweel had never forgotten Kayûtas's warning to beware his brother's madness. Even Serwa had mentioned Moënghus's 'foul humours,' as she called them. Sometimes *days*, as opposed to mere watches, would pass with the Prince-Imperial speaking nary a single word. Sorweel quickly learned to avoid him altogether during these periods, let alone refrain from speaking to him. The most innocuous question would spark a murderous glare, one all the more lunatic for the white-blue of his unblinking eyes and all the more frightening for the vigour of his frame. Then, over the course of a night or a day, whatever besieged him would lift, and he would resume his more sociable manner, wry and observant, quick to tease, and often outright considerate, especially when it came to his sister – to the point of risking his neck for eggs or wading through marsh muck for tubers, anything that might delight her when they took their evening repast.

'What makes *you* so worthy?' Sorweel once asked her while Moënghus crouched on the riverbank nearby, trolling the waters with a string and hook.

She drew her hair back to regard him, a gesture the Sakarpi

King had fallen in love with. 'Podi always says that aside from Mother, I'm the only Anasûrimbor he likes.'

'Podi,' Sorweel had learned, was the jnanic diminutive for 'older brother,' a term of endearment and respect.

'My sister is *sane*,' Moënghus called from his perch over the flashing water.

Serwa scowled and smiled at once. 'He thinks my family is crazy.'

'*Your* family?' Sorweel asked.

She nodded as if recognizing some previously discussed inevitability – truths they would have no choice but to share because of the intimacies of the trail. 'He's my brother, yes. But we share no blood. He is the son of my father's first wife – my namesake, Serwë. The one whose corpse they bound with Father on the Circumfix – during the First Holy War. The one everybody is loathe to speak about.'

'So he's your *half*-brother?'

'No. Have you heard of Cnaiür urs Skiötha?'

Even from a distance, Moënghus seemed to stiffen.

'No.'

She glanced at her brother with something resembling relish. 'He was a Scylvendi barbarian, famed for his martial exploits in the First Holy War, and now venerated for his service to my father. I'm told,' she called out teasingly, 'there's even a cadre of fools who scar their arms like Scylvendi in the Ordeal . . .'

'Bah!' her brother cried.

'Why does he think your blood is crazy?' Sorweel pressed, eager to sidestep the topic of Moënghus's paternity.

Serwa cast another laughing look at the dark-haired man.

'Because they think about *thoughts*,' Moënghus said, looking over his shoulder.

Sorweel frowned. He had always thought this the definition of wisdom. 'And this is crazy?'

Moënghus shrugged. 'Think about it.'

'Father,' Serwa explained, 'says that we have an *extra soul*, one that lives, and another that *watches* us living. We are prone to be at war with ourselves, the Anasûrimbor.'

Her terms were simple enough, but Sorweel suspected she understood the matter with a philosopher's subtlety.

'So your *father* thinks you crazy?'

Both siblings laughed at this, though Sorweel had no inkling as to the humour.

'My father is Dûnyain,' Serwa said. 'More human than human. His seed is strong, apt to crack the vessels that bear it.'

'Tell him about our brother Inri . . .'

She crinkled her sunburned brow. 'I would rather not.'

'What are Dûnyain?' Sorweel asked, speaking with the curiosity of those wishing to pass the time, nothing more, when in fact his breath ached for interest.

She looked to her brother once again, who shrugged and said, 'No one knows.'

Serwa leaned her head low, almost sideways, so that her hair fell in a silk sheet. It was a girlish gesture, one that again reminded the Sakarpi King that for all her worldliness and self-possession, she was scarcely older than he.

'Mother once told me they dwelt some place in the northern wastes, that they have spent thousands of years breeding themselves the way Kianene breed horses or the Ainoni breed dogs. Breeding and training.'

Sorweel struggled to recall what it was Zsoronga had told him about the heretic, the Wizard named Achamian, and his claims against the Aspect-Emperor.

'Breeding and training for what?'

She looked at him with a wisp of a scowl, as if noting a regrettable sluggishness in his soul.

'To grasp the Absolute.'

'Absolute?' he asked, speaking the word, which he had never before heard, slowly so as to make it his own.

'Ho!' Moënghus called, yanking a small bass onto the riverbank. It thrashed silver and gold even as it blackened the bare stone with wetness.

'The God of Gods,' Serwa said, beaming at her brother.

———∞∞∞———

The Men of the Circumfix were born to proud War. Most all of them had been tested on a dozen battlefields and had not so much developed a contempt for numbers as an appreciation for skill and training. They had seen single companies of hard-bitten knights rout whole armies of Orthodox rabble. Numbers often meant nothing on the field of war. But there were numbers, and then there were *numbers*. A mob, when it became great enough, became a living thing, vast and amorphous, shrinking when pricked, engulfing when roused, always too numerous to possess a singular will. The Horde, the Believer-Kings were beginning to realize, was unconquerable simply because it was too enormous to ever *realize* that it was conquered.

'Ours is the station of glory,' King Umrapathur declared, 'for we have been given the yoke of victory. The fate of the Great Ordeal now turns upon us – the fate of the *very World* – and we shall not fail!'

'Ours is the station of death!' Carindûsû cried out in heretical contradiction.

And indeed, despite the lofty rhetoric of their lords, a presentiment of doom began shadowing the hearts of the common warriors. They were simple men, for the most part, hailing from Cironj,

Girgash, Nilnamesh, and beyond. They thirsted and they starved. They had marched to the ends of the earth, into lands where cities were overgrown graves, surrounded by an enemy they could not close with, whose numbers curtained the very sky with dust. They had witnessed the might of the Schoolmen. They knew well the indomitable strength of their mounted lords. And now they knew that power, for all its miraculous glory, was naught but a nuisance to their inscrutable foe.

What difference could their hungry ranks make?

No one dared speak this question, not so much for fear of the Judges as for fear of the answers. But it began filing down the sharp edge of their resolve nevertheless. The songs they raised became ever more listless and half-hearted, until many of their caste-nobles forbade singing altogether. Soon the Army of the South trudged in exhausted silence, fields of dusty men, shambling without spark or purpose, their faces blank with long-hanging apprehension. In the evenings, they swapped rumours of doom while gnawing on their meagre repast.

The attempts to clear their flanks were abandoned – the losses among the cavalry, in particular, had become prohibitive. Other tactics were explored, especially with regards to the Culling, but an air of ritual futility began subverting their efforts, arcane or otherwise. Daily the Interval tolled and the pickets rode out, the Schoolmen walked the low sky above them, and together they pricked the elephantine Horde with mere needles.

The true fanatics among the Zaudunyani, those who repelled for the violence of their belief, began haranguing the more skeptical souls, for their thoughts were so disordered as to see *redemption* in the horror looming about them. Of those they exhorted, some took heart, but many others took exception. Fights began breaking out among nobles and menials alike, many of them lethal. The Judges found themselves condemning ever more men to the lash and gibbet.

Meanwhile, the Horde grew ever greater, until its unearthly howl could be heard at all times. At night men held their breath listening . . . and despaired.

To his father's chagrin, Prince Charapatha told the council about the typhoon he once survived at sea. 'Sunlight fell,' he said, his eyes vacant with unwelcome recollection. 'You could drop a feather onto the deck, so calm was the wind. Yet thunderheads wreathed the whole world about us, a ring of dark that would span nations . . .' He looked across the assembled Lords of the Ordeal. 'I fear we march in just such an eye of false peace.'

Afterward in the privacy of his pavilion, Umrapathur struck his famed son full across the mouth, such was his outrage. 'Speak of *glory*, if you speak at all!' he roared. 'Speak of will and iron and enemies gagging beneath your heel! Are you such a fool, Chara? Can you not see that *fear* is our foe? By feeding it you feed *them* – even as you rob us of the stomach to fight!'

And Charapatha wept, such was his shame. He repented, vowed never to speak save in the name of hope and courage.

'*Belief*, my son,' Umrapathur said, wondering that a famed hero such as his son could still act a little boy in paternal eyes. 'Belief empowers men far more than knowledge.'

And so was their rift healed with respect and wisdom. What father does not correct his son? But several among their householders overheard their quarrel, and rumours of discord and indecision slipped from tongue to ear to tongue, until all the host feared their King-General desperate and weak. Umrapathur, it was said, had stopped his ears even to those he loved and would no longer countenance the Truth.

∓

The three hostages-to-be had come to what seemed a great forested basin, so vast its outer rim rose into hazed oblivion but proved to be a valley. A river wound through it, roping across the flood-plains in meandering loops, broad enough to enclose slender islands. The Holy Aumris, Serwa declared, awed and excited despite the toll of their leap. The very nursery of Mannish civilization.

'This was how *they* found it . . . the first Men who set foot in this vale so many thousands of years ago.'

While she slept, Sorweel found a seat overlooking the vista between the roots of a towering oak that stood poised over a slope so steep as to seem half of a gorge. He sat dozing, watching as the iron dark of the river transformed with the climbing sun, becoming green and brown and blue and, along certain sections, a miraculous silver. The River Aumris . . . where the High Norsirai had raised the first great cities of stone, where Men had knelt like children at the knee of their Nonmen foes and learned the ways of art and commerce and sorcery.

Some time passed before he saw the ruins.

At first he noticed only their sum, like a ghostly pictogram glimpsed through the trees, lines writ for the Heavens to read. Then he found himself picking out individual works, some actually breaching the forest canopy: the arcs of dead towers, the lines of once-imposing fortifications. Where before he had gazed across mere wilderness, now he peered across a monumental cemetery, a place humming with loss and history. It seemed absurd, even impossible, that he had failed to see it. But there it was, as clear as a Galeoth tattoo, only laid across the reach of the earth . . .

The remains of some mighty city.

Serwa began crying out in her sleep so violently as to send both Sorweel and Moënghus sprinting to her. The Prince-Imperial shrugged Sorweel aside when he hesitated over her thrashing form, then pulled her in his powerful embrace. She awoke sobbing.

For some reason, the sight of her clutching her brother with weeping *gratitude* unnerved him as much as anything he had witnessed since Sakarpus's fall. Everything but everything seemed to attest to the righteousness of the Aspect-Emperor's war against the World's second ending. The sheer might of the Great Ordeal. Eskeles and his unnerving lesson on the plain. The skin-spy so dramatically revealed in the Umbilicus. The terror of the Horde and the cunning of the Ten-Yoke Legion. Even the trust and charity the Anasûrimbor had extended to *him*, their enemy . . .

Not to mention the shining presence of the Aspect-Emperor himself.

She had dreamed of the nameless city below them, Sorweel knew. She had *relived* the horror of its destruction even as he had pondered its overgrown imprint. And it struck him breathless, stationary in a way he had never known. The sight of her weeping somehow resurrected the circumstances that had so reduced her, a woman who seemed impervious to grief. He could almost hear the horns clawing the wind, glimpse the dread Whirlwind that Eskeles had always described in hand-wringing tones . . .

Nothing is quite so easy as dismissing the folly of the dead – so long as they remain dead.

She brought them to the ruins, though she could have leapt much farther, across the valley if need be. The Cant taxed her as profoundly as any, but she insisted on wandering with them, through the ruins of ancient Trysë, the Holy Mother of Cities.

The trees towered, formed high-hanging canopies that made gloom of the forest floor. The walls and bastions still loomed where not pulled down by the ages, their foundations buried, their torsos stained black, the blocks spangled with moss and lichens. In some places the rising tide of earth had inundated all, leaving only mossed debris scattered across the forest floor, fragments that would be taken for mere rocks and boulders in a deeper gloom. In other places, the loam and life had not so accumulated, leaving random stretches of nude ruin: heaped bricks, canted steps, walls finning the ground, the drums of toppled pillars.

Serwa led them across the destruction, her face flushed with excitement, her voice fluting in the manner Sorweel had heard so many times from girls her age, only about matters far more profound and tragic. The Sakarpi King thought he recognized some of the things she spoke of, either directly or through the slanted similarity of names. But far and away most of what she told them he had never heard before – nor had he imagined that Men period, let alone those who had fathered his ancestors, had battled and strived and conquered in days that were thought ancient *by the ancients*.

He had never heard of Cûnwerishau, the first God-King to extend the might of his hand along the length of the River Aumris. And aside from Sauglish, he had never heard of any of the other cities that perpetually vied with Trysë for dominance: Etrithatta, Lokor, and Ûmerau, whose might would grow to exceed even that of Trysë, and whose language would remain the Sheyic of the Ancient North long after she was broken by a people called the Cond. '*Your people*, Horse-King,' she said, her eyes alight with connections Sorweel could not fathom. 'Or the cousins of your ancestors, to be exact, born to the lands just north of what you Sakarpi call the Pale. More than three thousand years ago, they cracked the walls of ancient Ûmerau and swept through this valley. Their ardour glutted, they spared all the great works they found and made slaves of those they would pillage.'

She spoke as if he should celebrate these facts, take heart in the far-flung incarnations of his people's blood. But again Sorweel was afflicted with doubt and wonder. To know a man among the Sakarpi was to know his father. And here was this woman, telling him the truth of his fathers' *fathers* . . . The truth of *himself*!

What did it mean to be better known by outlanders than by oneself? What kind of fools were the Sakarpi, to find heart and honour – let alone *self* – in flattering fables spun across the ages?

How wrong had they been? Even proud Harweel.

They came to rockier ground, and she quickened her stride so much that Sorweel found himself breathless for trying to match her pace up the slope. A mysterious clearing opened between the trees, and for the first time they found themselves wandering among truly monumental works: blocks of hewn granite, as tall as a man and as long as a four-wheeled wain, some spilled, others assembled into cyclopean walls. She rushed forward without hesitation, wending through slots of stone and inciting any number of curses from her brother. They raced after her.

Panting, Sorweel paused before the sight of open sky, the blue so much deeper than the plains. He squinted against the sudden collusion of light and openness. A broad rectangle extended before him, heaped with stone ruin, yet miraculously devoid of overgrowth. The encroaching forest loomed about its perimeter as if leaning against some unseen barricade – or restrained by some unknown horror. He stood upon a far corner so that he could see the aisle of gargantuan pillars that braced the concourse in its entirety, as well as the lesser columns that lined its outer precincts. Most of them had tumbled – the smaller, outer columns especially – but enough remained standing to conjure the sense

of the whole and to deliver the image of the long-lost ceilings
to the soul's eye.

Sorweel watched a bee spiral from the gloom, then reel away
to the edges of the clearing until it found a circumventing line.
Even the birds he saw batting between the crowns of the
surrounding elms and oaks seemed to avoid the open spaces, as
if loathe to dare the scrutiny of the stage . . .

The Sakarpi King caught his breath, knowing he stood before
an arena of lost glories – phantoms. A place that had lived too
fiercely to ever truly die.

Oblivious, Serwa raced ahead, darted across the heaped stone
and between the monstrous columns that remained. 'Behold!' she
cried with girlish disbelief. 'Behold the King-Temple!'

Sorweel and Moënghus shared a hesitant glance.

'Bah!' the Prince-Imperial spat, running after her.

Sorweel trailed walking, trying hard to smile.

'How many times?' she called. It seemed she jostled with long-
dead shades in his soul's eye.

'Stow your voice!' her brother commanded.

But she just frowned and continued, crying, 'Here! *Here!*'
looking about as though trying to orient her waking eyes with
her sleeping. 'On this *very* spot, Podi, I have supped and celebrated
with the High-King, Celmomas – our little brother's namesake!
– and his Knights-Chieftain.'

'Serwa, please!' Moënghus cried. 'Recall what Father told you!
The skinnies are drawn to places like this!'

'Stow your worries!' she said, mocking his tone. 'We leave
no trail for them to follow. No trail, no mobbing. Even if we
landed in the lap of an entire clan, they would be no match
for me. I have reaped legions in the Culling, Podi! You know
this . . .'

She climbed a small rise that had been chapped to gravel,

spun in a pirouette that made a wheel of her white flashing hair. 'I stand upon the axis of an ancient power,' she declared to the two wondering men. 'The hub of a wheel that once turned the World but now spins groundless in the smoky Outside.' She closed her eyes, raised her nostrils, as if breathing deep the uncanniness of the place – as if the occult were simply a more subtle perfume.

'Two thousand years ago,' she called, 'from this very dais, the *first* Ordeal was declared against Golgotterath.'

'Yes . . .' Moënghus replied scowling. 'The one that failed.'

—∞∞∞—

The rain began shortly after, spilling from a bank of woollen clouds that caught them entirely unawares. The sun just slipped into the sky's pocket, and endless waters followed chill upon the gloom. The two men ran to the shelter of Serwa's sorcerous parasol, and together they hastened to the river.

They could not see the far shore.

Moënghus had said nothing the entirety of the trek, and now, sitting side by side upon the puddled stone, his manner became even darker. While Sorweel gazed out into fogged shadows, he glowered at nothing, as if staring down hatreds only he could fathom.

'Father says this river is holy,' he finally said.

He stood and began stripping his clothes.

In disbelief, Sorweel watched him walk naked, following a shoal of sand and brush to where it dwindled to a finger prodding the water. He held his arms out for balance as he tiptoed to the very claw. He became shadowy as he passed through ever more veils of rain. He lingered for a moment, his powerful frame sculpted and gleaming. Then he leapt white and slicked out into waters. He vanished in a pale whoosh.

Sorweel and Serwa watched the rain fall, watched the white

spitting across the iron-grey waters, threshing away the rings of his submersion, until they could no longer say just where the river had swallowed him.

He did not surface.

At some point, Sorweel could feel individual heartbeats within his breast, such was the horror rising within him. He peered across the descending roar, waiting . . .

'Something's happened!' he finally cried.

He flew to his feet, but Serwa restrained him with a firm clasp upon his right hand.

'He does that,' she said in reply to his alarmed gaze. 'Pretends to be dead.'

'Why?'

Serwa frowned, once again far too canny and too wise for her youthful face.

'Surely Kayûtas told you he was mad.'

He gaped, and she laughed at his incomprehension, returned her gaze to the sparking waters.

Suddenly Moënghus burst from the Holy Aumris with an inhaling shout, his hair drawn like black paint about his face, neck, and corded shoulders.

'It tastes like dirt!' he laughed across the washing roar.

The Holy Aumris.

———

As the easternmost element of the Great Ordeal, the Army of the South was the last to pass from the endless plates of the High Istyuli into the more broken lands to the northwest. Ravines and defilades scored the once-simple distances. Monstrous stumps of stone breached the parch, formations that reared into saddle-backed summits. The Men of the Circumfix sighted ruins commanding bare rock heights, glimpsed the shadow of ancient and overgrown roads bisecting the horizon. Like their brethren to the west, they took heart in these signs, marvelled that places so far could have once been the centre of Mannish civilization. The sense of *trespass* fell from them, the aura of estrangement that makes wayfarers adopt the worried habits of the interloper. For the first time they understood that they were *returning* and not simply venturing – and their souls were fortified.

They would have thought themselves liberators . . . were it not for the curtains of dust drawn across the horizon about them.

They marched through the high heart of ancient Sheneor, the weakest and most ephemeral of the Three Kingdoms of Far Antique fame, the frontier sibling of stern Aörsi to the north and populous Kûniüri to the west. The Mandate Schoolmen, who every night dreamed of these lands in their nadir, looked upon the desolation and mourned. Where were the white-washed towers? The serpentine pennants of blue and gold? The companies of bronze-armoured Knights-Chieftain, cruel and proud? And they wondered that they had lived to see this earth with their waking eyes.

With the breaking of the land came the quickening of the rivers, and with this came the increasing complications of crossing them. Across the high plain, the drought had so reduced the flow as to make fording a mere trudge through mire. Now the Army crawled down into steeper valleys where they found denuded poplars, stripped to spears by the retreating Horde. The Men of the Circumfix took comfort in their campfires, the first in months, and feasted on what fish the Netters gleaned from the rivers. They sucked the grease from their fingers, spoke small prayers thanking War for their momentary reprieve. The Believer-Kings, meanwhile, argued logistics and debated the perils of crossing treacherous waters in the shadow of the Horde. The fords themselves were easy to find: the Sranc literally rewrote the landscape when funnelled into multiple crossings, such were their numbers. Banks worn into ramps, waters stamped into broad morasses. They imagined a writhing, shrieking world, the skies gauzed with dust, the worm-pale multitudes stamping and heaving, thousands flailing in the mudded waters, and they were troubled. The earth seemed to tingle with the memory of their raucous masses, like a sheet drawn from the body of a dead man. Everything reeked of pollution.

The fear was that the Horde would attack while the Army stood astride both banks – a fear that never materialized. At the first such river, Carindûsû actually remained behind with some hundred of his white-and-violet-gowned Vokalati, thinking they could use the fords to rid themselves of the Sranc massing on their rear flank. They slew many to be sure, thousands, sending plumes of foul steam into the already obscure air, but the Sranc discovered other crossings, or perhaps they abandoned their armour and simply swam; either way, the Nilnameshi Schoolmen found themselves withdrawing across seething grounds.

King Umrapathur continued taking precautions. But he became ever more confident that the rivering of the land was far more a boon to his host than a liability. He could not foresee the danger to come.

The three camped in the ruins of a fortress halved by the collapse of the scarps that had once motivated its construction. Dagmersor, Serwa called it. The remains of the citadel hung jagged and hollow above them, a tattered silhouette across the clouding stars. Unseen wolves howled.

Sorweel drew the first watch. He picked a position above the moribund fortifications, where the land mobbed out from beneath his hanging feet. Nocturnal forests. Solitary trees climbed apart from their brothers, propped on swells of earth and rock, their crowns silver beneath the Nail of Heaven, their branches a veining black. Noise pitted the black with a million unseen places, a creaking, creeping chorus that rose from the dark face of all, fading into the ever-expanding silence that was the emptiness of Heaven.

And it scooped the breath from Sorweel's lungs.

There was a beauty to this journey across the ruined landscapes of lost Kûniüri, one due as much to these moments of solitude as to the whorled terrain that framed them.

His thoughts wandered, as they often did, across the myriad spectacles he had witnessed since his father's death. And he wondered that someone so frail as him could participate in such legendary events, let alone *move* them. The things he had seen. He imagined what it would be like returning to Sakarpus, excavating whatever scraps of his old life that remained, and trying to explain what had happened – what was *happening* – beyond the Pale. Would his countrymen marvel? Would they scoff? Would they accept the epic magnitude of what he described, or would they dismiss it as mere conceit?

The questions dismayed him. Until now, his return had been a thoughtless assumption: he was a Son of the Lonely City – of course he would return. But the more he considered it, the more improbable it began to seem. Were he to work the Goddess's divine will, murder the *Aspect-Emperor* . . . Surely that would mean his doom as well. And were he to deny the Goddess, become a Believer-King at the risk of his immortal soul . . . Would that not mean a different doom?

And if he *were* to return, how could he describe, let alone explain, the things he had witnessed?

How could he *be Sakarpi*?

Moënghus loomed out of the dark long before his turn to take watch and took a seat beside him, his manner as wordless and sombre as the Sakarpi King's own. Sorweel's alarm quickly subsided. Even after so many months of duplicity, he was not a man who could comfortably think treachery in the presence of those he intended to betray. In the siblings' company he invariably gave reign to a certain amenity in his nature – one easily confused for cowardice.

He could only plot in solitude.

They sat in silence, staring out over the sunless tracts, soaking in the aura of companionship that often rises between speechless men. Since Sorweel did not look at the man, he remained a brooding shadow in his periphery, one laden with intimations of physical force and errant passion.

'Your father . . .' the young King ventured to ask. 'Do *you* think he has . . . grasped God?'

Sorweel would never know what motivated his honesty. A man, he was beginning to learn, could become as accustomed to contradiction and dilemma as to heartbreak.

'A strange question for a *Believer*-King,' the Prince-Imperial snorted. 'I could report you to the Judges!'

Sorweel merely scowled.

'Look about you,' Moënghus continued, shrugging and rubbing his shaven chin the way he always did when yielding to serious considerations. '*All the earth* rises to wage war against Father, *and yet he prevails*. Even the *Hundred* raise arms against him!'

Sorweel blinked. These last words pricked like a fistful of broken glass.

'What are you saying?'

'*Truth*, Horse-King. Nothing offends Men or Gods more . . .'

Sorweel could only stare at him, witless. Was it possible *for a god to be mistaken?*

But then that had been Eskeles's lesson those months past – had it not? The Gods were but *fragments* of the God, mere shards of a greater whole – like Men. Yatwer, the Schoolman would most certainly say, was just such a fragment . . . Just as blind to the whole.

Could the *Mother of Birth* be deceived?

If the Prince-Imperial noticed his bewildered horror, he betrayed no sign whatsoever. Moënghus was one of those men who cared not at all for the petty rules that measured verbal exchanges. He simply stared out to the constellations twinkling low on the western horizon, talking as if no listening in the world could matter.

'Of course Father has grasped God.'

The Army of the South had come to Hoilirsi, a province known in Far Antique days for the cultivation of flax. Hoilirsi found its northern boundary in a river called the Irshi, which ran fast and deep for some hundred miles before mellowing on its path to the Neleost Sea. Even in Far Antique times, the Irshi had been known for the rarity of its crossings, so much so that the ancient Bardic Priests often used it as a name for detour – and its crossing as a metaphor for death. *Iri Irshi ganpirlal*, they would say when speaking of fallen heroes, or of anyone who faltered in life: 'Cruel Irshi pulls them under.'

King Umrapathur and his planners knew of the Irshi, of course, but they had assumed, as was reasonable considering the hundred rivers they had crossed thus far, that it would also be droughted. They had even discussed the possibility of sending cohorts of Schoolmen out in advance of the Horde in the hope of catching it crossing fords. They did not realize they had come to the first of many rivers whose high sources threaded the peaks of the Great Yimaleti – that for vast stretches of its length, the Irshi had no fordable crossings.

The Horde found itself caught along its fanged banks. Multitudes were drowned, thrown into the gorges by the relentless press of their kin. Worm-white carcasses tumbled down the river's tempestuous lengths and formed macabre rafts along its idylls, stretches of bloat and filth that sheeted the Irshi from bank to bank. But as the clans retreated out of terror of the Shining Men, they soon began shrinking from the threshing waters as well. The raucous stormfront that was the Horde slowed, then halted altogether.

Prince Massar ab Kascamandri would be the first to bear the tidings to King Umrapathur: 'The Horde . . . It no longer withdraws before our lances.'

The council was thrown into an uproar. What were they to do? How could they assail such impossible numbers while masses more roiled about and behind their flanks?

Carindûsû was the first to upbraid them. 'Can't you see that this a *boon*?' he cried. 'All this time fretting, wringing our hands because the skinnies outrun us, because we cannot kill them quickly enough, and now, when Fate pins them in place, delivers them to our fury, we fret and wring our hands?' With the Horde trapped and with Mandate and the Vokalati combined, the Grandmaster argued, the Culling would become outright butchery. He and his arcane brethren would lay carrion across the horizon.

The Believer-Kings turned to Apperens Saccarees, who gazed at his rival with wary appreciation.

'Perhaps the Grandmaster speaks true,' he said.

And so the council fell to devising a new strategy. As men are prone, they took heart in what they thought was evidence of their own ingenuity. Prince Charapatha alone harboured misgivings, for among the Lords of the South, only he reasoned that the *Consult* would also know of the Irshi – and so know it would catch the Horde. He was not named the Prince of One Hundred Songs for nothing: he understood the advantage conveyed by the ability to *predict* a foe's actions. But he had taken his father's earlier admonishment to heart and was loathe to raise questions that might undermine the ardour of his Zaudunyani brothers.

And as much as he distrusted Carindûsû and his posturing pride, the Prince had come to regard Saccarees as a kindred intellect. The *School of Mandate* marched with them. How could they fail?

Sorweel dreamed of her bathing, trembled for the steam that rose from her gentle places. The waters were pure and translucent, sheathing and beading across her flushing skin. Wisps enveloped all. Then something crimson, something ragged and viscous, tentacled the waters, unlooped like spilled entrails, depositing scabrous filth across the clarity of her submerged form. But she knew it not, and so continued to cup offal in her hands, pour filth over her naked skin.

He called out . . .

Only to find himself splayed across forest turf, blinking at the midday sun broken through branches. He pawed an ant from his soft beard, saw Moënghus sitting nearby. The Prince-Imperial sat with his back against a tree, absently working his knife across his throat and chin, staring off toward the sound of his sister's singing, which rose with the noise of rushing water from behind tangled screens of foliage.

She bathed, Sorweel realized, blinking away memories of his dream.

She only sang when she bathed.

Moënghus turned to him for a moment, watched him with a preoccupied frown, then looked away when Sorweel hauled himself onto his rump.

'What you said earlier . . .' the young King said to the man, squinting against his grogginess. 'About the Hundred raising arms against your father . . .'

The Prince-Imperial regarded him with a long and canny look. There was a brutality to his face beyond the heaviness of his brow and jaw, one that made a snarl out of every glimpse of teeth.

'I was afraid you would ask me that,' he finally said. 'I wasn't supposed to mention it.'

'Why?'

A negligent shrug, as if he could trivialize catastrophic facts with mere manner. He was forever doing this, Sorweel realized, pitching his expression against the pious gravity of what he expressed.

'Some truths are too offensive.'

Sorweel instantly understood. The people, the common people, would be quick to turn against the Anasûrimbor were they to know that the Hundred actually sought – in their paradoxical, unfathomable way – to destroy them.

'But does it mean the Gods can be . . . can be *deceived*?'

And it struck Sorweel that there was something vicious in this, asking the son questions that could murder his father . . . or save him. Something more than simply devious.

Serwa's voice floated across the moss-soft earth, hooking and curling to exotic cadences, lilting in yet another incomprehensible tongue.

'*Entili matoi . . .*

'*Jesil irhaila mi . . .*'

'Just *believe*, Horse-King,' the Prince-Imperial said, holding his face at a partial angle to his sister's singing. Did she sing *to* him?

'Just believe, eh?'

A hard look. 'My father *wars against the end of the world*. Stop thinking about your thoughts or you'll go as crazy as my sister.'

'But you said your sister was *sane*.'

Moënghus shook his mane in shaggy negation.

'That's what you say to crazy people.'

———— ⚬⚬⚬ ————

Kites filled the low, iron-grey sky.

The Schoolmen assembled before the Interval's toll – even those who had patrolled the perimeter through the night. Their cadres took to the air moments before the breaking of dawn so that they strode ablaze in morning gold above a dimmer world. Innumerable companies of knights and lancers and horse-archers galloped out beneath them, scoring the immediate north and west with streamers of dust. The number-sticks cast, the footmen marched into their wake, tens of thousands watching in apprehension as the ochre smear of the Horde climbed the circuit of the horizon and made a burial chamber of the sky.

Never had so many felt so small.

The Schoolmen and the accompanying knights receded out of view. King Sasal Umrapathur called the main host to a halt several watches after at the ruins of Irsûlor, a city destroyed long before the First Apocalypse. Only mounds remained of the walls, a continuous series of embankments skirting the dead city's heights. Save for five decapitated pillars jutting from the summit – the Fingers, the men began calling them, for the way they resembled a hand thrusting from some enormous burial mound – no structure survived the tidal earth.

Staking his standard beneath the Fingers, Umrapathur watched the Army of the South assemble across the heaped remains of Irsûlor below him. The spearmen of Pradu and Invishi with their great shields of wicker. The Girgashi hillmen, whose axes would flash in unison when they raised them in ritual brandishing. The levies of Nilnameshi bowmen, arrayed in twinkling bars across the slopes. The famed Cironji Marines assembled in reserve, looking more like beetles than men with their round-shields upon their backs. On and on, the dusky glory of the Southron Kings come to lands of pale-skinned legend. The buried bastions of Irsûlor.

And it seemed a miracle, that out of all the indefensible lands they had crossed, they could find such a place – a *strong* place. How could he not think he had found more evidence of the Whore's favour?

He looked out across the desolate tracts to the shadow of the Horde, to the dust plumes rising high and tawny above ochre gloom. Others in his retinue swore they could see the distant flash of sorcery, but he saw nothing. He bided his time and waited for tidings. Periodically he craned his head back to study the chapped bulk of the Fingers looming about him, trying to guess at the figures worn into ambiguity across them. A man never knew where he might find portents and omens. He tried not to think of the souls who had raised the ancient pillars – or of their long-dead fate.

From the beginning the question had been what the Sranc would do when the Schoolmen cast their nets of light and destruction across them. Carindûsû had argued that they would crash into themselves, fleeing mobs running into mobs, until they formed a crush from which none could escape. 'I wager more will suffocate and drown than fall to our fury,' the Grandmaster declared to the others. Of course, he admitted, some would survive the Schoolmen and their fires, but they would provide little more than sport for the companies of cavalrymen riding the land behind the Schoolmen.

This did not happen.

As Saccarees had argued weeks earlier, the Sranc were not beasts. For all the base savagery of their instincts, they were not so stupid as to flee into corners.

Leading a great echelon of Nilnameshi knights, Prince Charapatha watched the Schoolmen wade into the boiling horizon, a thin line of glittering points stretched wider than his eyes could follow, and somehow he simply knew that Carindûsû had been beguiled by his arrogance – that they had raised a spiderweb about a dragon.

Seized by this premonition, he commanded, to the outrage and astonishment of his men, that everyone shed their iron-scaled hauberks. Many refused – an extraordinary mutiny, given the love and respect they bore their Prince. Scattered across rising and falling swales of gutted land, the companies milled in argument and indecision. Charapatha remained calm, simply repeated his order time and again. He understood the reluctance of his men.

One after another, the glowing Schoolmen vanished into the pluming sheets of dust.

Lights flashed from the brown and black.

The howling, which had keened as loud as always so close to the Horde, warbled with unfamiliar resonances, then almost faded altogether. The Invitic Knights watched astonished. Men famed for their bravery in the Unification Wars cried out in amazement and horror. More and more scaled hauberks clanked across the earth.

The warring lights, if anything, increased in frequency and fury until it seemed lightning itself walked the long rim of the world. The howling faded, and for several heartbeats, they heard arcane shouts in the crotches of the breeze – the Schoolmen. Then they heard a different sound, grim and slow-building, chorus heaped atop inhuman chorus, louder and louder, until horses reared and men shook their heads like fly-plagued dogs. Until the air itself pricked their ears . . .

Screams. Inhuman screams.

The proud and headstrong Knights of Invishi gazed out and instantly knew that their King-General had erred, that his plan had gone catastrophically awry. For months they had shadowed the Horde, watching the stormfront of dust change colour in accordance with the soil beneath their feet and change shape in accordance with the strength and direction of the wind. Many times they had seen streamers break from the base and spill toward them like tumbling smoke, and always they had rejoiced at the prospect of running down isolate clans. But now they saw a hundred such streamers racing toward them – a *thousand* – ribbons of dust blooming into high-drawn clouds of filth.

Far from retreating into the crush of their fellows before the advancing sorcerers, the Sranc were running *south* . . .

'Ride!' Prince Charapatha bellowed through the cacophony. '*Ride for your lives!*'

───────

For some reason Sorweel always took a deep breath beforehand, as if he were about to plunge into frigid waters. No matter how many leaps he suffered, a fraction of him always experienced it for the very first time. Her arm hooked fast about his armoured waist, her head a chalice brimming with singing light, and then the wrenching, at once violent enough to concuss the blood from his body, and as soft as wet tissue . . .

The step across the illusion of space . . . the Leap.

But something went wrong. Meanings grasped too numbly, utterances fumbled across a too weary tongue. Sorweel suffered the sense of not arriving *all at once*, as if his viscera trailed the shell of his body.

He fell to his knees on the crest that had been little more than a silhouette on the western horizon just moments before. He felt a sloshing barrel.

Both Moënghus and Serwa complained but did not seem quite

so unsettled as him. At least he spared himself the humiliation of vomiting while they watched.

They all agreed to sleep.

And so began the Horde's second assault upon the Great Ordeal. As the whip communicates the strength of the arm from the grip to the nail, so to did the rush of those trapped against the River Irshi spread across the entirety of the Horde, from those hooked about Umrapathur's flanks to those massed near the Neleost coast. In the stark light of day they ran, numberless, maddened with hungers both vicious and foul, a shrieking plague.

From his vantage at Irsûlor, Umrapathur was among the first to realize that something was amiss. For so long, the Horde's roar, wringed of its resonance by distance, had sounded like an endless death rattle. When the sound faltered, he and thousands of others had raised a ragged cheer, knowing that the Schoolmen had begun reaping their arcane harvest. But the sound that climbed into its place – more shrill, like the fluting of winter winds – did not stop climbing. Higher and higher it roared, until men began batting their ears. And Sasal Umrapathur III, the first Believer-King of Nilnamesh, looked out to the dust fencing the horizon and knew he had been deceived.

He cried out warnings and instructions. Horns brayed out against the building thunder.

Out on the broken plain, only the most foolhardy of the Grandees led their knights out against the Sranc as planned. Far and away most realized, like Charapatha, that something was amiss, but many tarried overlong in indecision and so were quickly overrun. The rest found themselves riding a great and desperate race.

Ensconced in their deep formations, the infantrymen watched

with breathless horror as more than fifteen thousand riders, fleet skirmishers and ponderous knights, rode scattered across the waste, throwing shields and cutting loose saddle-packs, slapping blood from the rumps of their screaming ponies. Mountains of billowing dust roiled behind them – as if the world's very limits came crashing in pursuit.

They watched company after company, strung out in panicked flight, engulfed in raving doom. They glimpsed shadows though the low ribbons of dust, skinny and vicious and innumerable. The skirmishers, like King Urmakthi and his fleet Girgashi, reached the ruined city in good order. Others, the heavily armoured knights of Nilnamesh especially, were pulled under en masse. The more quick-witted commanders abandoned the flight and arrayed their men in defensive formations that lingered battling, pockets of frantic order engulfed in gibbering chaos, knights shouting and hacking, quilled in arrows, their positions dissolving like bright salt in putrid waters. Massar ab Kascamandri, the youngest brother of the outlaw Fanayal and famed for severing his earlobe to demonstrate his determination to join the Ordeal rather than remain as a figurehead in Nenciphon, was felled by an iron-tipped javelin less than a hundred paces from Irsûlor's embankments. Prince Charapatha and his armourless knights, meanwhile, found themselves deflected westward time and again in his attempts to reach their besieged King. His Captains had to restrain the Prince, such was the violence of his grief.

King Umrapathur watched the world and sky vanish behind the Horde's veil. The air boomed with screeching until he could no longer hear his own plaintive commands.

The Horde closed upon Irsûlor, and they were naught but an isle in a shrieking sea.

During this time, the Schoolmen continued walking the skies to the north, raking and scorching the obscured earth. To a man they knew Carindûsû had erred, perhaps disastrously, but they had devised no means of communicating any alternative strategy – they could scarce see one another as it was. Eventually, the more decisive among them abandoned their northward course, and others followed, forming broken cohorts whose passage back was marked with fire and light. Some became lost in the dust and would never find their way to Irsûlor. Some, a few fools, continued northward oblivious and did not turn back until they passed beyond the northern rim of the dust clouds.

None would return in time to counter the Consult.

Sheets of ochre were drawn across the sun, and shadow fell across the formations crowded upon the dead city. The Sranc threw themselves up the embankments and against the bristling ranks of Men, who stood locked, shield to shield, shoulder to shoulder, as they had during the first battle. The Horde caught about Irsûlor as upon a jutting nail.

The Sons of Nilnamesh held the north and west, thrusting sword and spear between their cunning shields of wicker, nearly invulnerable in their gowns of plated iron. The vast bulk of them fought beneath the ancient standards of Eshdutta, Harataka, Midaru, Invoira, and Sombatti, the so-called Five Hosts of Nilnu, the tribal confederacies that had warred for the whole of Nilnamesh since time immemorial. Not since the days of Anzumarapata II had so many Sons of Nilnu marched beyond the paddied plains of their home. Gone were the antique rivalries, the mortal hatred that had so often set them against each other. Gone were the differences. And it seemed a thing of mad and tragic folly that Men might raise arms against Men, when creatures so vile so infested the world.

The Hetmen of Girgash held the east, fierce mountain warriors come from their high fastnesses in the Hinayati along with their softer cousins from Ajowai and the Vales. His horse abandoned,

King Urmakthi stood at the fore of his countrymen, his Standard raised in lieu of his voice. The Grandees of Kian held the south, the desert-vicious men of Chianadyni, as well as their taller brothers from Nenciphon and Mongilea, all of them decked in the chained splendour of their fathers' fallen empire. Such was the clamour that they knew nothing of Prince Massar's fall – and so honoured him with their courage.

Crying out with soundless fury the Men of the South thrust and hacked at the gibbering masses. Even on the slopes the inhuman ferocity of the assault forced those deep in the ranks to brace their shields against the backs of those before them, transforming phalanxes into singular structures of flesh, ligament, and bone. Missiles blackened the already shrouded sky, shafts that rattled without harm across the armoured men, save those unfortunate few. The Ketyai archers answered with great volleys of their own, laying low whole swathes of their foe. But with every draw they exposed themselves to the endless black rain, and their losses were grievous.

—∞—

Sorweel's eyes snapped open, the screeches of the Viturnal Nesting ringing in his ears. He actually swatted the empty air immediately before him, so vivid was the image of a sun-burnished stork standing upon his chest.

He sat up, blinking. They had leapt upon the treeless prow of a hill, so he could see immediately that he was alone. He could also see the surrounding sunlit miles, the creased terrain rendered as soft as ocean swells for the woollen canopies that clothed it. A land like an old woman.

He had fallen asleep on the shags of grass that edged the crude axe-blade of stone that capped the promontory. The shade had shifted while he slept so that he could feel the sun's burn upon his cheeks and hands. His hauberk, especially, radiated heat.

He peered into the adjacent gloom of the forest, blinking, searching for any sign of the Imperial siblings. A pang groped his breast when he realized their *gear* was missing as well.

Had they abandoned him?

He stood, shaking the fluff from his apparel and the grogginess from his limbs. Then he wandered into the wooded regions, following the uncertain line of the summit, hoping to find his keepers . . .

Hardened by the First Battle of the Horde, the Men of the South exacted a dreadful toll. When they looked out, they saw innumerable faces, white and cat-screaming, Sranc and more Sranc, wagging raucous arms, heaving across the basins below. When they looked back they saw the ranks of Men braced across the piled embankments, heights fenced in bright-painted shields and bristling with spears, standards torn ragged by javelins and freighted with snagged arrows. And they remembered the words of their Holy Prophet, that they would see sights awesome and horrific, that they would suffer unimaginable trials – that they would save the World.

And they *believed*.

The Sranc were speared and they were hammered. They were thrown from the bedlam slopes or pulled under by their howling kin. Soon the earth about the dead city was ramped with carcasses, to the point where many of the obscenities were simply trampled for want of footing, thrust stumbling and flailing into the spears and cudgels and swords above.

Their screeching resounded from the very ribs of Heaven.

High beneath the Fingers, King Umrapathur took heart, seeing that his host was too strongly situated to collapse, that it could only be ground to the nub. Soon, he reasoned, Saccarees and Carindûsû would return, and with so many Sranc snagged upon Irsûlor, mobbed to suffocation, the slaughter would be great.

Given his vantage, he was among the first to glimpse the great blemish on the Horde's seething skin, an almond of black, marching beneath umber skies, moving slowly through the ghoulish fields of Sranc, driving ever closer to the beleaguered Sons of Girgash. The height of the mass was the first detail he could discern: the creatures composing it towered over the Sranc. Then he realized the blackness of the thing was due to *hair*, great shaggy crowns upon heads like cauldrons. The fact of the creatures came to the King all at once, though his soul was long to comprehend their implication.

Bashrag.

Many saw their abominable approach, but like Umrapathur, all were powerless to communicate their horror and alarm. The Girgashi upon the embankment glimpsed them between frenzied assaults, hundreds of hideous frames rising above the Sranc tossing below, an iron-armoured formation, throwing and stamping the hordlings before them.

Bashrag. Three arms welded into one. Three ingrown chests. Three hands for fingers. They were an offence to the eyes, a sight that awed and sickened, such was their deformity. Idiot faces hanging from each grotesque cheek. Horse-tail moles springing from random skin.

Umrapathur saw the nature of the Consult trap instantly. Knowing the Horde would turn and strike at the Irshi, they needed only to wait in ambush and hope their foe would be so foolish as to send out their Schoolmen . . .

The Believer-King peered to the north, scanned the shrouded skies for sign of Saccarees or Carindûsû.

The abominations lurched ever closer. The surviving Girgashi bowmen found their range. They pelted the fell legion with arrows. And for a moment, Umrapathur dared hope . . .

But the Bashrag advanced unscathed, quilled like porcupines. They climbed the slopes until they towered before the Men of Girgash.

King Urmakthi was among the first to be struck down, for he had stood at the fore of his kinsmen, his banner held high as a beacon to hearten his men. The Bashrag waded into their midst, sweeping their great axes and hammers. Shields were splintered. Arms were shattered. Heads were pulped. Whole bodies cart-wheeled into the ranks behind. For all the courage of the Hetman and their tribal vassals, they were no match for the creatures clacking and bellowing above them. They crumpled as foil and were scattered.

Within a hundred heartbeats the Bashrag had seized the embankment's summit. Umrapathur's heart caught. Only the Cironji Marines and their burnished shields stood between the beasts and his army's doom.

Gilded in shining gold, King Eselos Mursidides led their rush, rammed his spear into the gullet of the foremost beast, only to be beaten to the quivered earth by the great hammer of another. But the famed Marines did not falter. They threw themselves at the monstrosities, and a battle was fought unlike any since the days of the Ancient North. Fearless, skilled, armed with the finest weapons of Seleukaran steel, the Cironji stemmed the lumbering rush. But for heartbeats only. For every Bashrag they felled, dozens of their brothers perished. They were thrown shattered, little more than sacks of human skin.

Men mobilized everywhere through the tight-packed encampment: priests, Judges, water-bearers, the sick and the wounded – it did not matter. All came rushing . . .

But the Bashrag swatted them dead. Men vanished beneath inhuman strokes. It was like witnessing a massacre of children.

What followed happened so fast that those beneath the Fingers could scarce believe.

Innumerable Sranc scrambled through the breach wrought by the Bashrag, and shrieking masses of them spilled into the narrow ways behind the Inrithi phalanxes. To a man, the Zaudunyani had been trained to fight encircled, to form shield-walls about them – and survive. And indeed, some did precisely this, but panic seized many others, and Men were felled in thousands. Umrapathur stood immobile, his gaze flinching from atrocity after atrocity. Men wailing in horror. Men pulled down, grimacing. The fallen convulsing beneath rutting shadows.

The pavilions and baggage trains vanished. Within heartbeats the entirety of the lower city was overrun, and those formations that did not fly apart or dissolve stood engulfed, dwindling lozenges of human form and colour in a threshing sea of monstrosities.

Death came swirling down.

The Nilnameshi Believer-King gaped and stumbled. A stray arrow caught his hand and pierced the gauntlet.

He raised his skewered palm in disbelief, saw the first of the Schoolmen come striding on sheets of murdering light. Some solitary. Some in ragged, impromptu formations. Motes pricked with brilliance, passing through clouds of missiles, dragging gowns of lightning-bright ruin across the Horde. First dozens, then hundreds, Schoolmen, hanging miraculous in the low sky, walking beneath mountainous scarps and troughs of dust.

The whole North, it seemed, flared with sorcerous destruction. But is was too late.

Men moaned in the dust. The World shrieked in inhuman triumph.

———❦———

Sorweel walked through what seemed a peculiar fog, one that whined in his ears and yanked short his breath. The forest floor wheezed beneath his boots. Oaks and maples climbed high and mocking about him, splicing the sunlight.

He heard them before he saw them. Nearby.

He stood breathless, listening through the creak and click of the surrounding woodland.

'Yessssss . . .'

A different kind of vigilance seized him, and he crept forward peering between screens of undergrowth. His ears stood poised between the sounds of his approach and the passion that gasped through the skein of leaves.

Like a thief, he crept . . .

———❦———

Seeing the devastation, the returning Mandati and Vokalati withdrew to the skies above the Fingers, formed a ring of floating, battle-maddened brothers. Their faces blackened for dust and tears, they sang out their hatred and spite, the Mandate Schoolmen wielding abstract architectures of light, the Vokalati shining phantoms. And they burned those who clawed and clambered the slopes. And they burned those fornicating with corpses of the fallen. And they burned those thronging through the multitudes.

The slopes became fields of thrashing silhouettes.

Saccarees turned to Carindûsû and feared for the vacancy he glimpsed in the man's eyes. He bid his former rival to stand by his side, mouthing, 'Let me show you what it is you shall win!' For nothing other than the Gnosis was the prize the Aspect-Emperor had offered the Anagogic Schools.

But a monstrous wrath overcame the Grandmaster of the Vokalati, the lunacy of one who cannot dwell apart from his pride. His was the name that would be immortalized for infamy. His was the name his kin would strike from their ancestor lists. He called out sorceries with savage abandon, lashed the ground with cruel fire, killing Men and Sranc alike. The survivors below cried out, stunned and appalled.

Saccarees closed with the madman. To the horror of those watching, the two Grandmasters battled above the inhuman multitudes, an exchange of wicked lights, Abstractions against Analogies. Overmatched, Carindûsû was struck from the skies, undone.

Not knowing what happened several Vokalati assailed Saccarees – then several more, until fairly half the Vokalati found themselves attacking for no reason save that their brothers had so turned in violence. And so did the Schools of Mandate and Vokalati consume each other in a final act of madness.

The surviving Men looked up from the looming Fingers. At first they could not credit their eyes. They gazed dismayed and incredulous, while all about them the Sranc surged up the smoking slopes. The frenzied creatures cast themselves upon the few hundred assembled against them, hacking and shrieking – a host that reached out to the obscured rim of the world.

And bloodied King Sasal Umrapathur saw that he was doomed. He fell to his knees and prayed that his Holy Prophet might prevail . . . that his beloved wife and many children might survive the horror to come.

He looked up and saw a sorcerer falling, his billows ablaze.

The Sranc seized him, raped him as he bled out his life remaining.

Sorweel could scarce breathe. His spit seemed gravel for swallowing.

Two pale forms against depths of grey and water-green, the one slight upon the one hard, locked in a clenching, quivering embrace.

Kissing as though the other possessed the sole breath.

Grinding, their groins famished, piercing and knowing.

Never had he witnessed such a thing, breath-stealing, filled with rage and horror and imperious lust. He was not who he was for seeing it. Not one of his concerns survived the trespass before him. Not his father. Not the Tear of God that would avenge him.

Nothing mattered save *this* . . .

The children of a god mating. The woman he loved *betraying* . . .

His little brother called out for him. He found him, grasped him, cold fingers opposite a burning palm.

And he coupled with the sinuous image writhing before him, arched in answer to the man's black-haired grunting, spilled his seed to the girl's high blonde cries.

—⚬⚬⚬—

The mounded heights of Irsûlor smoked and crawled.

The Schoolmen hung in the air above, raining death upon their wicked foe. They wept even as they spoke hacking lights, for when they looked out, all creation whorled and seethed with foul Sranc. And of the tens of thousands who had been their brothers, all were dead and desecrated . . .

Shields trampled. Corpses pierced, clotted with rutting forms, like ants upon apple peels.

The Schoolmen scourged the embankments, pummelled the slopes, until Irsûlor reared like a mountain burnt to the stub, sheeted in blasted, blackened dead. Man, Sranc, Bashrag . . .

And still the multitudes surged forward. The Horde reached out into obscurity, a cloak of twisting maggots thrown over the horizon, howling. Howling.

And the Schoolmen were so very alone.

His crimson billows black for filth and fire, Saccarees descended, set foot upon the charred summit in a heartbroken bid to recover Umrapathur's body. But he could scarce distinguish Sranc from Man, let alone man from man. He looked out, over the tiers of smoking carcasses, through the comb of brilliant sorceries, out across the tumult of the plains, and it seemed he gazed *upon the future*, what would become of the World should his Holy Prophet fail . . .

Raving. Vicious. Devoid of meaning or mercy.

The Schoolmen heard their Prophet before they saw him, shouting arcana in a voice like a thunderclap – the one voice that could shrug away the burden of the Horde's roar. He came from the west, the *Aspect-Emperor*, sparking a brilliant blue through miles of intervening filth. Where he walked the air, whole tracts of earth exploded beneath him, as though the God himself pummelled the powdered soil. Sranc were thrown in mangled thousands, flying hundreds of paces before raining across their inhuman brothers.

Anasûrimbor Kellhus came to them and bid them follow him home.

She lowered her head to his chest in carnal exhaustion and lay there, her breasts kissing the barrel of his chest, her back bent to the arc of an oyster shell. Sorweel stared, held motionless by the shock of his dwindling ardour. Shame. Elation. Terror.

Knowledge that he could not move without alerting them robbed him of the ability to breathe. He stood stupefied as she turned to him and smiled.

He ducked in abject panic and shame.

'Who are we,' she called out in a drowsy laugh, 'for you to abuse yourself so?'

He fumbled to fasten his breeches, then stood, knowing that the shadow of his lust could still be plainly seen. But it was almost as if their shamelessness demanded he be brazen in return. She climbed from her slack-limbed brother, stood in the dappled sunlight, entirely naked, and at one with the wilderness for it.

How? How could she do this to me?

Tears burned in his eyes. Did he *love* her? Was that it? Was the son of Harweel such an errant fool?

She stood utterly exposed before him, her limbs lithe, her hips narrow, her pale skin flushed for the violence of her passion. Sunlight drew the shadow of her breasts across her white ribs, made golden filaments of her sex.

'Well?' she asked, smiling.

Indifferent, Moënghus began dressing at his leisure behind her.

'But—!' Sorweel heard himself cry like a fool.

Her look was at once demure and arrogant. Moënghus glanced darkly over a muscled shoulder.

'You're *brother and sister*!' he blurted. 'What you . . . you *did* . . . is a . . . is a . . . '

He could only stand and stare at them incredulously.

'Who are *you* to judge us?' she cried laughing. 'We are the fruit of a far, far taller tree, Horse-King.'

For the first time he realized the derision and contempt they concealed in that name.

'And if you get pregnant?'

She frowned and smiled, and for the first time Sorweel realized that whatever warmth she had showed him was mere pantomime. That for all the human blood coursing through her veins, she was, and always would be, Dûnyain.

'Then I fear my Holy Father would have *you* killed,' she said.

'Me? But I have done nothing!'

'But you have *witnessed*, Sorweel – your thigh is sticky for it! And that is far from nothing.'

His breeches fastened, Moënghus strode behind his sister, reached about her to place a scarred paw upon her womb. He kissed the hot of her neck, twiddled the fine blonde strands of her sex between finger and thumb.

'She's right, Sorweel.' he said, grinning as if entirely oblivious to the madness between them. 'People have a habit of dying around us . . .'

The Sakarpi King stood squinting against his turmoil. His heart pumped outrage instead of blood.

'As do nations!' he spat before turning on his heel.

'A son!' the Grandmistress of the Swayali called out after him, her voice mellow and bewitching. 'A son. A daughter. And an *enemy*!'

He fairly convulsed, so violent was the shaking that overcame him. It wracked him all the way back to their camp on the promontory. He found himself fearing the drops beyond the edges. Never had he been so shamed . . . so humiliated.

Never had he hated with such dark intensity.

Though the Great Ordeal survived, though their inhuman enemy had been thrown back to the rim of the horizon, the Second Battle of the Horde was nothing less than a disaster. The Holy Aspect-Emperor declared the Breaking of the Ordeal undone and commanded the Armies of the West and the East to converge upon the Army of the Middle-North. None of the Believer-Kings doubted his decision, even though this most recent defeat of the Horde had increased the opportunities for forage. King Sasal Umrapathur, one of their number, was dead, as were his kinsmen and vassals. They felt his ruin keenly, for he had breathed as they breathed, ruled as they ruled, and, most importantly, *believed as they believed*. If they did not understand as much before, they appreciated the grim truth now: their faith was no surety.

'The righteous,' King Proyas would remind his fellows, 'bleed no less than the wicked.'

The Armies gathered without fanfare or celebration, for the Men of the Circumfix were too hungry and astonished, and there were far too many absences among them. A pall had been drawn across the hosts, a shadow immune to the arid sun. Old friends were reunited in grief and lamentation. They traded stories of Irsûlor between them, and the truth suffered little for the inevitable distortions. They had witnessed events so extreme as to outrun the possibility of exaggeration.

They had come to a land called Akirsuäl. In times of old it had been a frontier province of Kûniüri, sparsely populated, famed only for a hill called Swaranûl, which rose solitary and inexplicable above broken flood plains. Swaranûl was a place holy to the ancient High Norsirai, for it was here that the Gods had come to the chieftains of their many tribes and granted them tenure for all the lands within a thousand leagues.

The Holy Aspect-Emperor called on his Believer-Kings to assemble and to follow him. Climbing broken and overgrown steps, he brought them to the summit of Swaranûl, into the pillared ruins of the Hiolis, and stood so they could see the Great Ordeal spread across the alluvial plains below. And though their losses had been grievous, the tents and pavilions of the combined host still embroidered the land to the horizon. Arms and armour winked in the sunlight, so that it seemed diamonds had been scattered across the whole earth. And they took no little heart in this vision of their glory.

Prince Charapatha was there, and many were the condolences

extended to him. Saccarees, however, stood alone and brooding, shunned because of his rumoured fratricide.

The Holy Aspect-Emperor opened wide his haloed hands. The Lords of the Ordeal turned to him in reverence and sorrow.

'I have delivered you to the Waste,' he said, the resonances of his voice cupping heart and ear alike. 'And now even the stoutest hearts among you fear that I have brought you to your doom. For though I warned you of the Sranc, described for you the immensity of their number and the cunning of our Enemy's machinations, you find yourself dismayed.'

Several called out in contradiction, and a cacophony of warlike declarations reverberated through the temple ruins. The Aspect-Emperor silenced them with a glowing palm.

'They are the filings and we are the lodestone. Were we to concentrate, march ranks closed along the shores of the Neleost, they would come. Were we to scatter across the High Istyuli's desolate heart, they would come. It matters not what path we take. It matters not what we do. The Sranc will come and come, and we will be forced to destroy them.'

Like ethereal fingers, the intonations of his voice stretched wide then concentrated, to better seize the passions of his congregation, and to hold them . . .

'Irsûlor . . .' he said, breathing horror into the name. 'Irsûlor is the very proof of our greater peril. A dozen Ordeals could march as we have marched, slaughter as we have slaughtered, and still the Sranc would not be exhausted. Were the No-God to awaken, they would be seized by a single dark and malicious will, and for all its might and glory Mankind would be doomed. The very World,' he said, balancing existence upon an outstretched hand, 'would be given over to wretchedness and rutting darkness . . .'

Laments climbed into a ragged chorus.

'So what are we to do?' King Saubon called out. 'We thirst,

and are sickened for drinking. And we *hunger*, until our shoulders are naught but hooks, and our axes and cudgels grow heavy with our frailty. We have stumbled with Irsûlor. Now we stagger.'

These words provoked consternation among many of the Believer-Kings, for they thought such doubts an insult to Saubon's exalted station. 'Stay your impertinence!' the bellicose King Hogrim called out in reproach.

'No,' the Holy Aspect-Emperor said to the long-bearded King. 'We must speak plainly. Only honesty provides truth. Only truth delivers triumph.'

He stepped into their midst, placed his blessed hand first upon Hogrim's shoulder, then upon Saubon's forearm.

'As many of you have surmised,' he said, 'I have deceived you as to our stores, saying we had less when we had more. I have *starved* you so that our rations would carry us as far as possible.'

'So what are we to do?' King Saubon called out yet again.

More shouts climbed from the assembly, this time in discord, for as many called out in assent as against the Exalt-General's presumption.

The clamour wilted in the light of their Holy Prophet's sad smile.

'Scavenge what strength you will,' he said, striding from their midst to reclaim the ritual heights. 'Ponder your wives, your children – ponder your soul. Fear not the spectre of thirst, for soon the Neleost, the Misty Sea, will heave dark before us. And fear not starvation . . .'

He turned, taking two pillars as his frame and the enormity of the Great Ordeal as his beyond, the hundreds of thousands streaming and milling across all that could be seen. He burned as a beacon before it.

The breeze trilled through the plaited flax of his beard. The chutes of his gown swayed.

'To suffer is to bear evil,' he said, 'and we must suffer to see our World saved. No matter where it delivers us, what madness, what evil, *we must follow the Shortest Path . . .*'

The Holy Aspect-Emperor of the Three Seas walked, luminous among the doubtful and afraid. He acknowledged each of them with the simple, loving profundity of his gaze. He gave them heart even as he appalled them. For they understood what he was about to say, the truth they dared not whisper even in solitude.

'Henceforth, our very foe shall sustain us . . .'

The dread command had been given, at long last.

'Henceforth, we eat Sranc.'

CHAPTER FOURTEEN

Momemn

The truth of all polity lies in the ruins of previous ages, for there we see the ultimate sum of avarice and ambition. Seek ye to rule for but a day, because little more shall be afforded you. As the Siqû are fond of saying, Cû'jara Cinmoi is dead.

—GOTAGGA, PARAPOLIS

Any fool can see the limits of seeing, but not even the wisest know the limits of knowing. Thus is ignorance rendered invisible, and are all Men made fools.

—AJENCIS, THE THIRD ANALYTIC OF MEN

Late Summer, 20 New Imperial Year (4132 Year-of-the-Tusk), Momemn

Some journeys required immobility.

609

He took a room and waited weeks he had already endured. He did not prepare so much as tarry while the world grew ripe. He was the White-Luck Warrior . . .

His harvest would come as it came.

Every morning, he watched himself rise and leave the room for the final time. He chased his back about corners, between the intersecting crowds. An apple found him. A coin. A priest of Jukan, who gave him bread smudged with blue. He heard the people talking in the streets, voice piled upon voice, and he had difficulty sorting reasons from conclusions. He listened, and listened to his listening. Most people were oblivious, but some saw him with different eyes. A little girl shrieked and shrieked. A blind beggar clasped him about the knees, blubbering.

'You must give! Give!'

Sometimes he gazed out the lone window, where he could see the Cmiral Temple-complex in the near distance, the black monuments grey in the morning haze. Sometimes the stone reaches were empty, sometimes they were packed with rioting multitudes.

Sometimes he simply watched himself gaze out the window.

He saw the Andiamine Heights, the gleaming rooftops rising in a welter, the walls, sometimes white in the sun, sometimes smeared black for burning. He heard the horns call, realized what he had always known.

The woman he had murdered had been overthrown.

He saw a spider skitter across the floorboards, knew that the world was its web. He almost stepped upon it ten thousand times. Almost, again and again . . .

He awoke and saw himself dressing at the foot of his rack. He watched himself rise and leave the room for the final time. He did not prepare so much as tarry while the world grew ripe.

A prostitute accosted him, and the band of naked skin from her armpit to her thigh drew the eye of the Shrial Knight who had singled *him out for questioning. She caught something in his look and became instantly disinterested – called out to a gang of four young men instead. He passed into the Cmiral unnoticed. Looking about, he glimpsed his back climbing the monumental steps beneath the Temple Xothei. He saw the unwitting assembly, heard the howls of horror and disbelief. He wiped the blood already wiped from his blade, then stood gazing at the Empress, who was both dead and alive, triumphant and condemned.*

He heard the drums of the enemy, pounding from beyond the great curtain walls.

He saw the world roar and shake.

A prostitute accosted him . . .

If he were to pause and think about it, young Anasûrimbor Kelmomas would understand that his knowledge of the Palace was as intimate as imaginable. Only places that puzzled could be truly solved – which is to say, truly *understood*. Other places were merely known through the brute fact of their familiarity.

The Andiamine Heights had many ways . . . secret, sneaky ways.

Like the mirrors hidden throughout the Audience Hall, or the way he need only move his head the span of a hand to overhear conversations in different rooms of the Apparatory – such was the ingenuity of the passages that passed over and between them. Once he became adept at picking the locks that barred so much of the maze's extent, he truly came to appreciate the cunning that animated its design – his father's cunning. Many passages linked to others, allowing for rapid movements so that one could seem to be in two places at the same time. Some of the barred slots and chutes and tunnels allowed parts of the labyrinth *to be itself* observed, so that one could fool another into speaking confidences for the benefit of a third. And some allowed the same room to be observed from secondary vantages *unknown* to the first, so that one could pretend to be ignorant of a transaction and so test the veracity of another. Together the myriad ways combined and combined to create untold permutations. Were the Shrial Knights to discover him, flood the tunnels, they would require a hundred companies to flush him in a direction not of his choosing. And he would be able to prey upon them as a spider upon beetles.

He had become a creature of the darkness.

Even in the days of the Nansurium, the Andiamine Heights had been a piling of ascending powers, a place where blood and might became ever more concentrated as one neared the summit. From the temples and the campuses to the Apparatory, to the myriad chambers pertaining to the Congregate and the Remonstrata, to the Imperial Audience Hall and the adjacent apartments where he and his family dwelt. Since he could remember, Kelmomas had always prided himself on the *height* of his footing, the way he always looked *down* upon the teeming city. But that had been nothing more than a vain farce. Power, he now understood, turned more upon the penetration of places seen by places invisible. Inside and outside, rather than high and low.

The reconstruction, Mother once told him, had required a thousand slaves labouring for more than five years. She had never explained what had happened to the workmen, which suggested that she knew but was loathe to tell him. Kelmomas sometimes regaled himself with tales of their death, how they had been herded onto ships that were then scuttled on the high Meneanor, or how they had been dragged to the auction and sold to Father's confederates, who then had them strangled on their various plantation estates. Sometimes it was not enough to simply skulk in the shadows. Sometimes eyes had to be put out to remain hidden.

Father had managed to contain the secret of his labyrinth: the fact that no one so much as sounded the hidden halls after the Palace's fall proved that even Uncle Holy knew nothing of them (or that if he did, he wished to keep the secret of their existence as his own). Almost as soon as the assault was concluded, the boy began waiting for the inevitable charge into the tunnels, the raucous surge of torch-bearing men. A charge that never came . . .

No one so much as called for him.

The Shrial Knights returned the following day and began clearing the dead.

Then the slaves came, scrubbing blood from marble floors and walls. Sopped carpets were rolled into tree trunks and dragged away. Fire- and smoke-damaged furnishings were carried out in antlike trains. Censers were set throughout the halls, billowing violet-grey smoke: a haphazard collection of incenses that spoke more of availability than design. Soon the reek of offal – Kelmomas would have never guessed that *shit* would be the primary smell of battle – receded into his sensory background.

In a matter of days, it seemed the coup had never happened. And it began to seem a game, playing fugitive in the hollow bones of his own home. Everything was pretend. All he need do, he told himself, is cry out and his mother would come soothing and laughing . . .

'Let's just play,' he would tell the secret voice.

A little while longer . . .

The lower, administrative portions of the Palace resumed their previous functions. At first Kelmomas crept through the glare and boom of these precincts, his whole body prickling for fear of discovery. But soon he became so bold as to run through these passages, listening to the wax and wane of voices. A mere company of Shrial Knights had been assigned to guard and patrol the abandoned upper levels. He passed through their very midst, watching, hearing, even smelling. He saw them gamble, spit, or blow snot across the grand rugs. He watched one abuse himself in his mother's wardrobe. He silently cackled at their stupidity, poked their images in hate. When he retreated to safer depths, he would mimic their voices, then laugh at the echoes.

He scuttled and he scuttled, stealing glimpses through white slits, catching conversations on drafts. And after a time the *darkness* became what seemed real, and the illuminated world became naught but a congregation of impotent phantoms. He would exult, revel in the joy that is secrecy and deceit.

But no matter how hard-hard-hard he tried, he could only hold on to the fun for so long. Sometimes it would slip away drip by drip, boredom accumulating like knotted hair in a brush. He would bump around feeling hollow, doing his best to battle his stinging eyes and quivering lips. Other times it would drop from him entire, and he would find himself stranded where he stood, hands clenching air, throat cramping, face aching.

And he would cry like a little boy *for real* . . .

Mommeeee!

He had overheard enough to know that his mother had not been captured – and there was a time when he had wandered the labyrinth looking for some sign of her.

The realization that she was nowhere within the Palace was hard in coming.

How? How could she abandon him? After all his work, his *toil*, isolating her from distractions, infiltrating her, possessing her – *making her love* . . .

How could she leave without her little boy?

Some nights, he even dared creep into her bed. He would breath through her pillows and his head would spin for her scent . . . *Mommy*.

She was *missing* . . . He could not think this without gasping in terror, so he thought it rarely. He had always been able to sort his inner parts, to keep them one from the other. But within a week of the coup, the merest thought of her, or even a whiff of her favourite incense or perfume, would be enough to undo this sorting, to seize his face with grimaces, to draw his lip down trembling. He would curl into his own arms, imagine her cooing warmth, and fall asleep sobbing.

But he did not grow lonely – not for *real* real. Even though he was but one, isolate boy, he was not alone. Sammi was with him – the *secret* Samarmas – and they played as they always played.

You're filthy. Your skin and clothing are soiled.

'I am disguised.'

They stole food at will, baffled the slaves with their pilfering.

Uncle knows about us . . .

'He thinks I have fled, that someone shelters me.'

And they pondered the great game that had caught them, endlessly debated moves both possible and actual.

Uncle has her . . . He lies to deceive Father.

'She will be executed.'

And they cried together, the two brothers, shuddering within the cage of the same small boy.

But they knew, with a cunning not so different from that of mundane children, that he who covets his brother's power also covets his *things*. They knew that sooner or later Uncle Holy would take up residence in their Palace, thinking it his own. Sooner or later he would *sleep . . .*

And for all the alacrity of his senses, for all the profundity of his Strength, the Holy Shriah of the Thousand Temples would eventually err in his assumptions and fall to their childish knife.

They were as much Dûnyain as he. And they had time.

Food. Secrecy.

All they were missing was meat.

Fugitive days became fugitive weeks.

Imhailas would vanish for days at a time. When he returned it was usually with dismaying news carefully wrapped in false hopes or, even worse, the absence of tidings. Maithanet, the Imperial Custodian, continued to consolidate his position, exacting declarations of allegiance from this or that personage, concocting yet more evidence of her Imperial malfeasance.

No word on Theliopa. No word on Kelmomas.

And her children, she had come to realize, were really all that mattered. Despite the black moods, the endless anxious watches, the restlessness that seemed to perpetually threaten madness, she had found reprieve in her forced seclusion. When it came to titles and powers and privileges, she felt far more *liberated* than deprived. She had forgotten what it was like to live a life focused only upon the most basic needs and passions. She had forgotten the slow-beating heart that was simplicity.

Let the Empress die and the Whore live, she sometimes caught herself thinking. So long as her children could live free and safe, what did *she* care for the cloud of curses that was the Empire?

Only Naree prevented her from owning this sentiment outright. The girl continued taking custom, despite Imhailas and his violent prohibition, and despite the pricked eyes and ears of the Holy Empress.

'You do not know,' she once said to Esmenet in tearful explanation. 'You do not know the . . . the *insolence* of my neighbours. If I were to stop, they would think I had a patron, that someone great had taken me as a mistress . . . They would become jealous – you have no idea how jealous they would be!'

But Esmenet *did* know. In her previous life, one of her neighbours had actually pushed her down her tenement stairs out of jealousy for her custom. So she contented herself with being the ailing mother, laying in her cot behind the screen while Naree gasped and keened, pinioned beneath grunting men. A caste-noble woman, one born to the privileges Kellhus had delivered to her, would have died in some way, she imagined. A portion of her pride would have been stamped out. But she was not a caste-noble. She was what she had always been – an old whore. Unlike so many, she did not need Anasûrimbor Kellhus to show her around the barricades of vanity and conceit. Her pride had been stamped to mud long, long ago.

What troubled her was not her pride, it was her fear.

To listen to Naree pleasure strangers was to listen to herself as she once was, to once again be made a scabbard for edge after cutting edge. And she knew it all, remembered it with rank clarity. The liquid instant of insertion, the breath pent, then released, far too quick to be caught in a passion so clumsy as regret. The grinding tickle of the little, and the thrusting ache of the great. To be a flint struck, never knowing what fire would be stoked within her, be it disgust or tenderness or gasping pleasure. To make a tool of her turmoil, to make theatre of the wincing, flinching line that so inflamed men.

But what she had not known, not truly, was the *danger*.

She had respected her custom – to be sure. She had her rules, precautions. No drunks, unless she knew them well. No white-skinned teamsters or black-skinned mercenaries. No ulcers. But she had always – and she found this thought difficult to think – believed herself greater than the sum of the men who used her. She was at least as embittered as other whores and perhaps more inclined to self-pity. But she had never seen herself as a *victim* – not truly. Not the way Naree so obviously was . . .

She did not think herself a lonely child used and traded between lewd and dangerous men.

Sometimes, peering through the narrow slots between the screen's panels, she watched their faces as they toiled upon the girl,

618   THE WHITE-LUCK WARRIOR

and she balled her fists for terror, so certain was she that whoever
it was would break Naree's neck for simple domination's sake.
Sometimes, after the tall shadow had left, she would peer at
the girl lying naked across mussed and soiled blankets, raising
a hand as about to speak to someone, only to lower it in indecision.
And the deposed Empress of the Three Seas would lie riven with
thoughts of gods and animals, of heartbreak and pollution, and
the purity that hides in the bewildering in-betweens. The World
would seem a place of rutting hungers and Men no more than
Sranc tied into more complicated knots.

She would yearn for her Palace and her adoring slaves, for the
sunlight lancing through scented steam, and hidden choirs singing.
And she would cry, as silently as she could manage, for want of
her little son.

'I am . . . shamed,' the girl said to her once.

'Why should you be?'

'Because . . . You could have me damned to Hell.'

The Empress nodded in indulgence. 'So you're *afraid*, then . . .
not ashamed.'

'You are *his* vessel!' Naree cried. 'I've been to the Scuari – I've
seen *Him* at your side. The Holy Aspect-Emperor. He *is* a god – I
am certain of it!'

These words left a breach that only shallow breathing could fill.

Then Esmenet said, 'What if he were simply a *man*, Naree?'

She would never understand the dark whim that overcame her
in saying this, though she would come to regret it.

'I don't understand.'

'What if he were simply a man *pretending* to be more – a
prophet, or even as you say, a god – simply to manipulate you
and countless others?'

'But why would he do such a thing?' the girl cried, seeming
at once thrilled, confused, and appalled.

'To save your life.'

Naree, for all her beauty, looked plain in her moments of unguarded sorrow. Esmenet watched her blink two tears before trying to find shelter beneath the false roof that was her smile.

'Why would he do such a thing?'

———⊗⊗⊗———

They took their meals in silence, usually. At first Esmenet attributed the girl's silence to her childhood slavery – slaves were universally trained to remain quiet and unobtrusive in the presence of their betters. But the girl's boldness otherwise led her to reconsider. In her darker moods, Esmenet thought she might be protecting herself, doing all she could to ease the betrayal to come. When her humour was lighter, she thought the girl was simply oblivious to the meanings that forever soak silence and so was unnaturally content with it.

At first there had been a certain comfort to their cohabitation, one borne out of an alignment between Esmenet's bottomless exhaustion and Naree's subservient wilfulness. Indeed, it was the *neighbours*, the constellation of sordid lives about them, across the street, above and below them, that generated most of the conflict. Usually, Esmenet thought Naree was simply using something incidental, like a random catcall from the women across the way, as an excuse to vent unspoken passion. The girl was always careful to use her meek, slave voice to be sure. But otherwise she hectored Esmenet as though she really were an ailing grandmother.

'You need to walk slower in case they see your shadow through the shutters! You need to be more sick!'

The complaints were nothing short of ridiculous at times, and yet she played along. Nothing is so incendiary as anxious fright.

'You need to bend your back – hunch like an old woman!'

And so more and more terror came to own the air between them.

———∞∞∞———

The Shrial Knight watched with eyes that could only blink.

A young boy with shaggy blond hair played alone on the parapet before him. When he stepped out of the shadow, his mane flashed near-white in the sun. But he was filthy otherwise, as though he had only animal wilderness to rear him.

'So what happens with the Ordeal?' the boy said, speaking to someone the Knight could not see.

'War,' the boy replied as if answering his own question. 'But not just any war. *Skinny* War.'

He laughed at an unheard reply.

'Imagine there, at the top of *that* tree, there's a man standing, just standing, while below him, the skinnies run raging, a great mass of them, as big as the city, even bigger, unto the ends of what can be seen. Imagine the man singing in voices that shake through the bones of things, soaking the living ground below them with buckets of light – yes, *light!* – boiling the skinnies in their skin! Now imagine a necklace of such men, a hanging line of them, walking across the wastes, blasting the hordes shrieking about them.'

The boy did a whimsical cartwheel, his limbs arcing with acrobatic precision. He grinned at his unearned expertise.

'*Father* told me. In his own words, he said, "This is how it will happen, Kel."'

The Shrial Knight tried to scream.

'Well, mostly in his words. Some of my words too.'

He paused as if listening to an inaudible answer.

'Secret words – he even said so. Words that no one – *no* one – can hear.'

He walked like an acrobat following a rope, heel to toe, heel to toe. Despite his diminutive frame, he seemed to tower above the ink pool of his shadow.

'No. He never *told* me to kill anyone. But then, why would he have to? The words were *secret* . . .'

For the first time the boy turned to look at the watching Knight.

'Of *course* he would expect me to kill anyone listening.'

The boy skipped toward the paralyzed man, careful to avoid the pooling blood. He paused to peer down at him, hands on knees. His woolly head blotted out the sun's glare.

At last he addressed the Knight directly. 'You heard *everything*, didn't you?'

He leaned low before his face, reached into his eye – almost.

Again, the Shrial Knight tried to scream – but his eyes could only blink.

Somehow, impossibly, the boy pulled a silver skewer from beneath his left eye, as if the Knight's head were a sheath. He dandled the thing against his face, left bird-tracks of blood high on his cheek.

'That was supposed to be *secret* . . .'

And the little boy grinned, an angel with the face of a demon.

Naree had to stifle a scream when she saw him darkening her door – both women had fretted his latest absence.

Imhailas had become increasingly more furtive in his visits. Few women had as much reason to despise men as Esmenet, to think them vain, cruel, even ridiculous, and yet she found herself yearning, not simply for *him*, Imhailas, the man who had sacrificed all in her name, but for the simple aura of his strength. When it was just her and Naree, it somehow seemed as if *anything* might happen, and they would be helpless. They were refugees. But when he came to them, bearing the scent of public exertions, they almost seemed a small army.

As rude, as apish, as it could be, masculine strength promised as much as it threatened. Men, she reasoned, were a good tonic against Men.

He had dyed his hair and beard black, which probably explained Naree's almost scream. And he had changed his clothes: he now wore an iron-ringed leather jerkin over a blue-cotton tunic. His armpits were black, and his thighs were slicked in sweat. His height always surprised her, no matter how many times she saw him. She could not look at his arms without feeling the ghost of their embrace. His face looked stronger for the blackness of his beard. His blue eyes more wintry, and if it was possible, more moist with devotion. He had come to seem the very incarnation of refuge, the single soul she could trust, and she loved him deeply.

Esmenet froze where she stood. She need only see his expression to know that he had found some answer to her most desperate question.

Imhailas pressed a dismayed Naree aside. He strode forward and fell immediately to his knees at his Empress's feet. He knew her. He knew she would not forgive specious delays. So he spoke the very thing she had glimpsed in his eye.

'Everyone, Your Glory . . .' He paused to swallow. 'Everyone believes that Kelmomas is hiding with *you*. Maithanet does not have him.'

The words did not so much explode within her as explode *her*, as if Being could be palmed and tingling Absence slipped into its place. First Samarmas and now . . . now . . .

For so long Kelmomas had been her strongest, surest limb, and her heart had been its socket. Now that it had been wrenched from her frame, she could only fall back, bleeding.

Kelmomas . . . Her dear, sensitive, sweet . . .

'Your Glory!' Imhailas was calling. Somehow he had managed to catch her mid-swoon. 'Your Glory – Please! You must believe me! Maithanet genuinely *does not know* where Kelmomas is . . . He lives, Your Glory – *he lives!* The only question is who? Who could have smuggled him out of the Palace? Who has hidden him?'

And so, because Imhailas was a dutiful soul, one of those servants who truly placed the desires of his masters before his own, he began listing all those who might have taken her son into their protection: the Exalt-Ministers, the body-slaves, the officers of the Army and the Guard. He had known his news would dismay her, so he had rehearsed his encouragements, his arguments against abject despair.

She recovered some measure of herself in the strength of his ardour, in the beauty of his earnest declarations. But she did not truly listen. Instead she thought of the Palace, of the labyrinth hidden within the Andiamine Height's labyrinthine halls.

And it seemed a second mother to her . . . the subtleties of her Home.

Please keep him safe.

———

Dragging, huffing because grown-ups are so big. Mopping, scrubbing blood, because grown-ups become keen when one of them goes missing. Then dragging more, down into the dark where only memory could see.

Dropping, grinning as the dead knight plummeted down the well.

Then carving, cutting.

Biting, chewing – he must be quicker next time, so the meat does not grow so cool.

Chewing and chewing and crying . . .

Missing Mommy.

———

'So what are you saying?'

'We can trust this man, Your Glory. I am sure of it.'

Esmenet sat, as had become their custom, on the settee with Imhailas cross-legged at her feet. Naree lay curled on her bed, watching them with a kind of envious disinterest. An oil lantern set upon the floor provided illumination, deepening the yellow of the walls, inking the grooves between the tiles, and throwing their bloated shadows across the far regions of the apartment.

'You're saying I should flee Momemn! And on a *slave ship*, no less!'

Imhailas became cautious, the way he always did when speaking around her wilder hopes.

'I'm not saying you *should* flee, Your Glory. I'm saying you have *no choice*.'

'How can I hope to recover the Mantle if—?'

'You are imprisoned or dead?' the Exalt-Captain interrupted. She forgave him these small transgressions, not simply because she had no choice, but because she knew how sovereigns who censored their subordinates quickly became their own worst enemies. History had heaped their corpses high.

'Please . . .' Imhailas persisted. 'Few know the ways of Empire better than you, Your Glory. Here, Maithanet's rule is absolute – but not so elsewhere! Many of the Great Factions clamour – fairly *half* the Empire teeters on the edge of open rebellion . . . You need only *seize* that half!'

She understood the force of his argument – not a day passed where she failed to inventory all those she thought she could trust. House Nersei, in particular, in Aöknyssus. Surely she could depend on Queen Miramis – Saubon's niece and Proyas's wife – to at least give her sanctuary, if not prosecute the interests of her family. Sometimes, when she closed her eyes, it seemed she could hear the laughter of her children, Xinemus and Thaila, smell Conriya's saline winds . . .

'All you need do is find *some place safe*,' her Exalt-Captain pressed. 'Some place where you can plant your Standard and call on those who remain faithful. They *will* come to you, Your Glory. In their *thousands* they will come to you, lay their lives at your feet. Trust me, *please*, Your Glory! Maithanet fears this possibility more than all others!'

She stared at him, her eyes pinned open to avoid blinking tears.

'But . . .' she heard herself say in a small, pathetic voice.

Imhailas seemed to blink her tears for her. He looked down, and a part of her bubbled in panic. He knew that she had surrendered all want for power, that she had been truly defeated, not by Maithanet, but by the loss of her little boy . . .

To leave Momemn would be to leave Kelmomas – and that was something she could not do.

Yield another child.

—∞∞—

The girl did it, Esmenet knew, as much to spite her as to win him.

The coos in the dark. The creak of dowelled wood. The groan of dowelled loins. The breaths stolen, as though every thrust were a sudden fall.

He was a man, she told herself: you could no more ask a fox to resist a rabbit. But *Naree*, she was a woman – even more, she was a *whore* – and so commanded her desire the way carpenters commanded their hammers. If Esmenet had heard Imhailas cajole her, bully her with the cruel singularity of purpose that distinguished lust from love, then she might have understood. But instead, she heard Naree *seducing him* – in the very same tones she used to ply her daily custom, no less. The girlish pouting. The coy teasing. The restlessness of limbs impatient for carnal struggle.

She heard a woman, a *rival*, making love to the man between them for *her* sake.

Leave him to me, the girl was saying. *You are old. Your peach is bruised and rotten. Your passion is flabby and desperate . . . Leave him to me.*

Esmenet told herself it was nothing, merely the coupling of shadows in the dark, something that was scarcely real because it could scarcely be seen. She told herself it was his real motive, the primary reason why Imhailas wanted her to flee the city and abandon her son, so that he could plumb Naree with abandon. She told herself it was simply punishment, the way Fate chastised old whores so conceited as to think themselves queens.

She told herself many things as her ears roared for listening: the pluck of lips clasping about gasps, the cotton sweep of hot dry skin against hot dry skin . . . the pasty peal of wet from wet.

And when he began groaning, the Holy Empress of the Three Seas could feel him hard and beautiful upon *her*, as he was meant to be, the reverence in his flower-petal touch. And she began weeping, her sobs stifled, lost between the gusts of their passion. What had happened? What rite had she foreshortened? What deity had she offended? What had she done to be wronged so, again and again and again?

The bed cracked with pent tensions. What was languorous became rugged with pitched passion. Naree cried out, rose upon Esmenet's lover like the white on the forward curl of wave . . .

Leave him to me!

And the door exploded open on lances of torchlight. Armoured men burst upon its astonished wake. Naree gagged more than screamed. The screen was kicked aside even as Esmenet bolted from her blankets. Tear-spliced torchlight. Grinning faces, beards greasy in the uncertain light. Strapping figures, draped in impregnable chain. Gleaming blades. Golden *Tusks* stamped everywhere across the floating madness.

And Imhailas, nude and howling, his beautiful face cramped in wanton savagery.

A shadow clenched her hair, heaved her to the floor, yanked her to her knees.

'*Imagine!*' some leering voice cackled. 'A *whore hiding among whores!*'

And her Exalt-Captain battled, solitary, his broadsword whooping through the close air. An armoured man fell clutching his throat. '*Apostate!*' Imhailas bellowed, suddenly the pale-skinned barbarian he had always been. '*Trait—!*'

One of the Knights tackled him about the waist, carried him hard to the floor.

They fell upon him, hammering, stomping. One heaved him to his knees. Three others began striking his face with iron-girded fists. She watched his beauty disintegrate as if it were nothing more than leather wrapped about pottery. She felt something primal climb from her throat, heard it fly . . .

The Shrial Knight gripping his hair let him flop to the floor, where his skull drained. It seemed she could not look away from the socket that had been his face, so violent was its impossibility.

This could not be happening.

Naree's shrieking scarcely seemed human. It hung high, warbled with insanity.

And for the longest time it seemed the World's only noise.

The Knights of the Tusk looked to one another and laughed. One silenced Naree with a vicious backhand. The girl toppled from the far side of the bed.

Esmenet had forgotten the carelessness of men who kill – the danger of their dark and turbulent whims. But the old instincts were quick in returning: the sudden vigilance, the slack body, the numbness that passed for cold concentration . . .

The ability to see past the death of someone beloved.

The party consisted of some eight or nine Shrial Knights, but not from any company she could identify. Their breaths reeked for wine and liquor. A cloaked priest, whom she now recognized as a Collegian, walked to where Naree had retreated, curled naked beneath one of the shuttered windows. He bent above her, clutched her wrist with careless force, and as the girl wept and shook her head in negation, he counted out five gold kellics into her palm.

'And here's a silver,' he said, holding the coin to the light. He spun it between thumb and forefinger, and Esmenet glimpsed the grey of her outline in the white reflecting across it. 'To *remember* her by,' the Collegian said, nodding in Esmenet's direction, grinning. It fell with a crack to the floor between them.

Naree slumped at his feet. The Holy Empress of the Three Seas watched the girl's eyes follow the blood-tacked floors to where the Shrial Knights held Esmenet on her knees. Imhailas lay between them, grisly and unnatural.

'Please!' she cried to Esmenet, her expression a braid of anguish and vacancy. 'Please don't tell your husband! Don't-*doooon't* . . .' She wagged her head about a piteous grimace. 'Please . . . I didn't *meeeean* to!'

Even as they dragged Esmenet into the staring streets, she could still hear the girl wailing, a crazed immaturity to her voice, as if everything in her past the age of five had been murdered . . .

Instead of enslaved.

———— ∞ ————

She was not brought directly before Maithanet, as Esmenet had expected. Instead she was delivered to a commandeered watch garrison for the remainder of the night. She was beaten, almost raped, and generally suffered the leering absence of pathos that often belongs to servants who hold their master's enemy. She did not sleep, nor was she unchained. She was forced to make water in her own clothes.

Within a watch of dawn, a second company of Shrial Knights arrived, these belonging to the Inchausti, the Shriah's own elite bodyguard. A dispute broke out, and somehow shouts turned into a summary execution – as well as the hasty flight of three of the men watching her. Resplendent in their golden mail, the Inchausti took her back into the streets. They, at least, treated her with decorum and respect, even if they failed to remove the chains. She had not the heart to beseech them, let alone speak at all, and so found her way to the accidental dignity that belongs to shock and exhaustion.

She shuffled and stumbled in her ankle-chains, a woman dwarfed in a shining column of armoured men. It was still early morning, so that the sun touched naught but the sky, leaving the streets chill and grey. Despite this, more and more people gathered as they made their way toward Cmiral, craning and sometimes jumping for a glimpse of her. 'The Holy Empress!' she heard shouted in random, broken choruses – and periodically, 'The Whore!'

The cries obviously outran their small formation, for every turn revealed more people, crowding the stoops, jostling with the Inchausti in the streets, hanging their heads from windows and roofs, their eyes bleary with sleep and wonder. She saw all castes and callings, glimpsed faces that mourned, that celebrated, that exhorted her to be strong. They neither heartened nor repelled her. The Knights of the Tusk shoved their way forward, bellowing warnings, cuffing or punching the insolent. More and more frustration and alarm replaced their expressions of studied concentration. The Inchausti's Captain, a tall, silver-bearded man the Empress thought she recognized, finally commanded his company to unfasten their sheathed swords and use them as clubs.

She witnessed first-hand how violence begets violence – and found that she did not care.

Those behind them followed. Those before them called out, waking whole swathes of the city along their path, drawing more and more into the streets. The march had become a running battle by the time they turned on the Processional, just to the west of the Rat Canal. The Momemnites continued to accumulate, their gall growing in proportion to their numbers. She saw many of them raising clay tablets that they broke as she was hustled past, but whether they were curses or blessings, she did not know.

Freed of the slotted streets, the Inchausti formed a ring about her. The Cmiral opened before them, its expanses already hazy. It seemed all the world thronged within it, spread across the plazas, packed about the monumental bases. The black-basalt facade of the Temple Xothei loomed beyond the sea of faces and brandished fists, bathing in the morning heat. Pigeons took flight across the neighbouring tenements.

The Inchausti pressed forward without hesitation, perhaps buoyed by the sight of their fellows arrayed shining across the first landing beneath Xothei. Their progress was haphazard at best, despite the clubbing fury of the Knights. Esmenet found herself looking across the mobs to their right, the obelisks of their past rulers rising like spear-points from their seething midst. She glimpsed the face of Ikurei Xerius III raised to the climbing sun, suffered a bizarre, almost nightmarish pang of nostalgia.

She saw bands of men with Yatwer's Sickle inked across their cheeks. She saw innumerable Circumfixes, clutched in hands manicured, callused, even poxed. The shouts resounded to the Heavens, a kind of cackling roar borne of contradictory cries. Every other heartbeat, it seemed, she caught some fragment of 'Whore!' or 'Empress!' Every other blink she glimpsed some Momemnite howling in adulation or spitting hate. She saw men tangled in battling mobs, striking each other over shoulders, reaching out to grab hair or tear clothes. She glimpsed a man stab another in the throat.

The mobs surged against the company, and for several moments they were overcome, broken into battling clots. Esmenet even felt hands clawing at her. Her gown was ripped from her shoulder to her elbow. The nameless Captain bawled out, his battle-trained voice ringing through the din, commanding the Inchausti to draw their swords. Held fast in gauntleted hands, she saw the sunlight shimmer across the first raised blades, saw the blood rise in crimson-winking strings and beads . . .

Shouts became screams.

The beleaguered company resumed its advance, now skidding on blood. Xothei climbed black and immovable above them. And somehow she knew that her brother-in-law awaited her in the cool gloom beyond the gilded doors . . .

The Holy Shriah of the Thousand Temples . . . Her son's murderer.

The entire time, from Imhailas's unceremonious murder to the stairs of Xothei, she had existed in a kind trance. Somehow she had floated while her body had walked. Even the riotous tumult, which had torn her clothes and thrown her to her knees on several occasions, happened as if seen from afar.

None of it seemed real, somehow.

But now . . . Nothing could be more real than Maithanet.

She thought of her husband's treatment of the Orthodox Kings who fell into his power: Earl Osfringa of Nangael, whom he had blinded, then staked naked beneath Meigeiri's southernmost gate. Xinoyas of Anplei, whom he had disembowelled before his shrieking children. Mercy meant nothing to Kellhus apart from its convoluted uses. And given the rigours of Empire, cruelty was generally the more effective tool.

632   THE WHITE-LUCK WARRIOR

Her brother-in-law was also Dûnyain . . . What happened next depended entirely *on her uses*, and empresses, especially those who had to be discredited for power's sake, rarely found mercy.

Palpable horror. Her body clamoured as if seeking to shake free of itself.

She was about to die. After all she had witnessed and survived . . . She thought of her children, each in succession, but she could only conjure their faces as little children and not as they were.

Only Kelmomas stood fast in her soul's eye.

She struggled to climb the steps: her manacled feet were scarce able to clear each rise. She could feel as much as hear the rioting tracts behind her, the ardour of those who loved or hated, and the lechery of the curious. She stumbled, and her left arm slipped from the flanking Knight's grasp. She chipped free and fell face forward, her wrists chained to her waist. Her shins skidded along unbevelled edges. Stone bludgeoned her ear and temple. But she did not so much feel her misstep as *hear* it reflected in the mobs behind her: a thousand lungs gasping, a thousand throats chortling in glee – Momemn and all its roaring vagaries, passing judgment on her humiliation.

She tasted blood.

The two Inchausti who had let her fall pulled her back to her feet with dreadful ease. With gauntlets jammed into her armpits, they carried her the remaining way. Something slumped within her, something as profound as life.

And those watching could see that the Blessed Empress of the Three Seas was at last deposed.

Xothei's iron portals slowly ground shut behind her. She watched the oblong of light thrown across the floor shrink about her frail shadow, then the doors shuttered all in gloom.

Ringing ears. Airy darkness. A kind of perfume dank, like flowers hung in a cellar. Clamour hummed out from the immense stone-work hanging about her, an endless crashing. She knew the world dawned bright beyond the cyclopean walls, but she had the sense of standing in an ocean cavern, a place deeper than light.

She began shuffling from the antechamber out across the prayer floor, toward the great space beneath the central dome. The weight of her shackles bowed her, made burning effort out of mere walking. Pillars soared. Lantern wheels hung from chains throughout the interior, creating a false ceiling of circular lights. A fan of faint shadows followed her as she hobbled rattling with every step.

A dais the size of small barge dominated the floor beneath the high dome. She numbly gazed at the arc of idols arrayed upon it: wane Onkhis, fierce Gilgaöl, lewd Gierra, bulbous Yatwer, and others, a tenth of the Hundred, the eldest and the most powerful, cast in gold, shining and lifeless. She had learned their names with her mother's face, the souls that joined all souls. Her whole life she had known them, feared and adored them. And she had prayed to them. She had clutched her knees sobbing their names. . . .

The broad-shouldered man who knelt in prayer beneath them, she had known for less than half her life – if indeed she had known him at all. She knew him enough only to know that he *never* prayed. Not truly.

Anasûrimbor Maithanet, the Holy Shriah of the Thousand Temples. He turned the instant she came to a pause below, held her in his monolithic regard. He was dressed in full ceremonial splendour, with elaborate vestments hooding his shoulders, draping down in two long, gold-tasselled tongues. He had allowed his beard to grow, so that the plaits fanned across his ritual chest plate. They seemed to have stained the white felt of his vestments where they touched, as if he had used a cheaper dye than usual to conceal the blond that was his true colour. His hair gleamed with oils, making him seem of apiece with the idols framing him.

She flinched at the deep bass of his voice.

'The officers who beat you,' he said. 'They are being flayed even as we speak. Several others will be executed as well.'

He seemed genuinely apologetic, genuinely furious . . .

Which was how she knew he lied.

'Apparently,' he continued, 'they thought apprehending you without the knowledge of their betters would earn them more glory in this World.' His look was at once mild and merciless. 'I have invited them to try the next.'

She neither spoke nor breathed for several long blinking moments. She wanted to scream, *My husband! Don't you realize? Kellhus will see you gutted!* only to find her outrage robbed of voice by some perverse reflex.

'My-my chil . . .' she began instead, coughing and blinking tears. 'Where are my *children*?'

Her face crumpled about a sob. So long . . . So long she had toiled . . . feared . . .

The Shriah of the Thousand Temples loomed above her, his manner cold and absolute.

'The Empire is falling apart,' he said in a voice fairly bottomless for its wisdom. 'Why, Esmi? Why have you done this?'

'You killed my son!' she heard herself shriek.

'*You* killed your son, Esmi, not me. When you directed his attempt on my life.'

'I did not!' she cried, her limbs thrown to the impotent limit of her chains. 'I only needed to know if you were *hiding* anything! Nothing more. Nothing less! *You* killed my son. *You* made this into a war! *You!*'

Maithanet's face remained perfectly blank, though his eyes

glittered with what seemed a wary cunning. 'You believe what you're saying,' he finally said.

'*Of course!*'

Her voice peeled high and raw beneath the airy gloom of the domes, faded into the white hiss of the mob's roar.

He gazed at her, and she had this curious sense of throwing herself open, as though her face had been a shuttered window.

'Esmi . . .' he said far more softly. 'I was mistaken. Both in what I assumed to be your intentions and in your capacity.'

She almost coughed for shock. Was this some kind of game? She thought she laughed when in fact she wept.

'You thought me mad – is that it?'

'I feared . . .' he said.

The Shriah of the Thousand Temples descended the steps, then – impossibly – *knelt before her*, raised a hand to her bloodied cheek. He smelled of sandalwood and myrrh. He produced a small key from his girdle, crudely cast.

Esmenet reeled. She had assumed this audience would be nothing more than a pantomime, a ceremony required to stamp her inevitable execution with the semblance of legitimacy. She had hoped only to throw her defiance and her righteousness into the air between them, where memory could not deny it.

She had forgotten that pride and vanity meant nothing to him, that he would never merely covet power for its own sake . . .

That he was *Dûnyain*.

'Long nights, Esmi . . .' he said as he worked the lock on her manacles. And it seemed madness, the absence of embarrassment or contrition – or any other recognition of the *absurdity* between them. In a way, it seemed almost as terrifying as the doom she had originally expected.

'Long nights have I pondered the events of the past months. And the question is always the same . . .'

One by one he cracked open the locks, beginning with her wrists, then bending to free her ankles. She found herself flinching from his powerful proximity, not bodily, but in her soul, which had feared him for too long to so quickly relinquish its aversion.

'What?' he asked as he worked. 'What is my brother's plan?' The Holy Shriah looked up from the posture of a penitent. 'He must have known that the Gods would begin clamouring against him, that one by one their far-off whispers would take root in the Cults. He must have known his Empire would crumble in his absence . . . So then why? Why would he entrust it all to someone with *no Dûnyain blood*?'

'To me,' she said with more bitterness than she intended.

A roaring swell rose from the rioters beyond the walls, a reminder that for all the temple's immensity, it was but a small pocket of gloom in a world of sunlit war.

A reminder of the people they would command.

'Please, Esmi,' he said, standing to gaze down into her eyes. 'I beg you. Set aside your pride. Listen as your husband would listen, without—'

'Prejudice,' she interrupted, drawing her lips into a sour line. 'Continue.'

She gingerly rubbed her wrists, blinking in the manner of those with sand in their eyes. She could not see her way past her shock and incredulity. A simple misunderstanding? Was that it? How many people had died? How many men like . . . like Imhailas?

'Out of all his tools,' Maithanet said, 'I have long known that *ignorance* is the one he finds most useful. Even still, I succumbed to the vanity that bedevils all men: I thought *I* was the lone exception. Me, another son of Anasûrimbor Moënghus, one who knows the treacherous ways of conviction . . . the way certainty is simply an illusion born of ignorance. I convinced myself that my brother chose *your* hands, which were both weak and unwilling, because he had deemed me a *threat*. Because he did not trust where the Logos might lead me.'

For all the disorder of her soul, these words burned with peculiar clarity – probably because she had rehearsed them with such morbid frequency.

'The way he did not trust your father,' she said.

A grave nod, steeped in admission. 'Yes. Like my father . . . Perhaps even *because* of my father. I thought he might have suspected I possessed residual filial passions.'

'That you would betray him to *avenge* your father?'

'No. Nothing so crude as that. You would be dismayed, Esmi, to know the way caprice and vanity distort the intellect. Men ever cast themselves into labyrinths of thinking, not to lose themselves in the pursuit of truth, but to hide their self-interest in subtleties and so make noble their crassest desires. Thus does avarice become charity, and vengeance, justice.'

It was as if a drawstring had been yanked tight about her breast.

'You convinced yourself that Kellhus feared the same of you?'

'Yes . . .' he said. 'And why not, when Men so regularly yoke their intelligence to self-serving stupidity? I am half a man. But the Interdiction . . . The questions it raised plagued me, even as I acted in ways I thought my brother would demand of me. Why? Why would he forbid all communication between the Great Ordeal and the New Empire?'

She glanced at the shackles discarded at her feet, noticed a bead of blood welling from one of her toes.

'Because he feared that tidings of discord would weaken the Ordeal's resolve.'

This, at least, had been what she told herself . . . What she needed to believe.

'But then why would *he* cease communicating?' Maithanet asked.

'Why would he *personally* refuse to answer our pleas? From his brother. From his *wife* . . .'

She did not know. The Holy Empress of the Three Seas wiped at the tears burning in the creases of her eyes, but the filth on her fingers only made them sting more.

'Then it dawned on me,' Maithanet continued, looking out to the recesses of the shuttered Temple. 'What if he foresaw the *inevitability* of his empire's collapse? What if the Three Seas were doomed to unravel *no matter who ruled them?* You. Me. Thelli . . .'

His blue eyes fairly bored through her. He seemed apiece with the great weights soaring about him, so broad did he appear in his white-and-gold vestments, so impressive were the accoutrements of his exalted station. She felt a rag-bound whore standing in his Dûnyain shadow . . .

Another childish human.

'If the Empire was doomed to perish,' he said, 'what would his reasoning be then?'

The mob's roar heaved across the background the same as before, only marred with pitches that warbled across the limits of hearing.

'What are you saying?' she heard herself cry. 'That he *wanted* me to fail? That he wanted the world, his home, to come crashing down upon his wife? His *children?*'

'No. I'm saying he understood that such a crash would happen *regardless*, and so he chose *one* evil from among many.'

'I don't believe it. I . . . I cannot!'

What kind of man made *oil* of his children? What kind of Saviour?

'Ask yourself, Esmi. What is the *purpose* of the New Empire?'

She had the sense of retreating from his words as before a sword-point. 'To pre-prevent the Second Apocalypse,' she stammered.

'So if the Great Ordeal succeeds? What of the Empire then?'

'It has no . . . no . . .' She swallowed, so painful was the word. 'Purpose.'

'And if the Great Ordeal fails?' Maithanet asked, his woollen tone wrapped tight about the bruising iron of fact and reason.

She found herself looking down to her feet, to the charcoal grime between her toes. 'Then . . . then the No-God walks . . . and . . . and . . .'

'All eyes can feel him on the horizon. Every child is stillborn. Every man living *knows* that the Aspect-Emperor, Anasûrimbor Kellhus, spoke *true* . . .'

The world warred and rioted about them.

She looked up without breath or volition. 'And Men are . . . are . . . united regardless.'

The sense of what he said struck her numb, even as the greater part of her balked. The Great Ordeal. The New Empire. The Second Apocalypse. It all seemed some vast joke, a farce of monumental proportions. Mimara missing. Samarmas dead. Inrilatas dead. Kelmomas missing. *These* were the things that mattered. The enormities that preoccupied Maithanet possessed no rule that her heart could fathom. They were simply too immense, too distant to be thrown on the balance with something as utterly immediate as a child. They seemed little more than smoke before the fire of her children.

Smoke that choked, that blinded, that led astray. Inescapable smoke. Killing.

Maithanet stood clear and bright before her, at once her enemy and her champion. And her only hope, she suddenly realized, of understanding the ruthless madness of her husband.

He killed him . . . He killed my—

'I made the exact same mistake you yourself made, Esmi,' he said. 'I thought of the New Empire as an *end*, something to be saved for its own sake, when really it's nothing more than a *tool*.'

The boom of strife and discord. The Holy Shriah of the Thousand Temples graced her with a lingering look, as if satisfying himself that she had grasped the dire import of his ruminations. Then he turned his face to the high-hanging gloom, called out to invisible ears . . .

'We are finished!' he boomed. 'The Tusk and the Mantle are reconciled!'

'He has abandoned us,' Esmenet murmured into the ringing wake. When she blinked, it seemed she glimpsed the entire Three Seas burning: Nenciphon, Invishi, Seleukara, Carythusal . . .

Maithanet nodded. 'For now . . . Yes.'

She could hear a gathering of footfalls and hushed voices in the galleries.

'And after . . . after he destroys Golgotterath?'

The Holy Shriah glanced down at his palms. 'I don't know. Perhaps he will leave us to our own purposes.'

Her breath caught upon a pang. What would that be like?

The first sobs blew through her as a breeze, soft, soothing even as they tousled her thought and vision. But the tempest was not long in coming. She found herself weeping in his expansive embrace, wailing at all the losses she had endured, all the uncertainties . . .

How many revelations? she thought as the final gusts passed through her. *How many revelations can one soul bear?*

For she had suffered far too many.

She looked up into her Shriah's bearded face, breathed deep the sweet bitter of his Shigeki myrrh. It seemed impossible that she had once seen malice in the gentle blue of his eyes.

They kissed – not as lovers, but as a brother and a sister. She tasted tenderness on his lips. They gazed into each other's eyes, close enough to breath the other's exhalations.

'Forgive me,' the Shriah of the Thousand Temples said.

The Empire roared and rioted unseen.

She blinked, saw Imhailas's face unmade beneath pounding fists. 'Maitha . . .'

A glimpse was all he needed to fathom her question, so open was her face.

'Thelli is safe,' he said with a reassuring smile. 'Kelmomas hides yet in the palace.'

Terror hooked her throat – terror and crashing relief. 'What? *Alone?*'

His eyes seemed to lose focus, but even before she had registered it, he was *there*, before her, as immediate as her husband had ever been. 'He isn't what you think he is, Esmi.'

'What do you mean?'

He gestured to the floors behind her. 'In due time . . .'

She turned to the small crowd of Shrial and Imperial Apparati gathering about them, men she had known and trusted for many long years. Ngarau stood among them, Phinersa, and even ancient Vem-Mithriti. Some watched with expressions of hope – even joy – and some with apprehension.

She was not surprised to see so many loyalties overturned. Maithanet was her husband's brother. In some dark corner of her soul she had prepared for this encounter, but the curses, the cat-spitting declarations of outrage, were nowhere to be found. Instead, she felt only exhaustion and relief.

Few things are as inexplicable as the concatenation of souls. Kellhus had often told her how Men glimpsed but a sliver of the intercourse that passed between them, how passions and rivalries and understandings they could scarce fathom drove their intercourse like galleys before a storm. Perhaps they were all exhausted. Perhaps they simply yearned for the life they had known before Maithanet and his coup. Perhaps they were frightened by the battling multi-tudes surrounding the Temple. Perhaps they truly believed . . .

'He isn't what you think he is . . .'

Whatever the reason, something happened as she regarded them. Despite the embroidered fanfare of their robes, despite their cosmetics and jewelled rings, despite the pride and ambition belonging to their exalted stations, they became *mere* men, bewildered and embattled equals, standing together in the absence of judgment that was their Prophet's most beautiful gift. It did not matter who had erred, or who had betrayed or who had injured. It did not matter who had died . . .

They were simply disciples of Anasûrimbor Kellhus – and the world clamoured around them.

Maithanet resumed his position on the dais, and Esmenet found herself watching him with a worshipper's simple wonder, blinking tears that did not sting. He seemed luminous, not simply with the overlapping rings of light shed by the hanging lantern wheels, but with *renewal*.

And suddenly Esmenet realized that she could see her way past her losses and her hate. Somehow she knew they *would* find some way to hold the Empire together, whether her accursed husband believed in them or not.

'We will stage an official reconciliation,' Maithanet said in warm, informal tones, 'something for the masses. But for the nons, I want all of you to witness what we sa—'

Then there *he* was, clad only in a loincloth, stepping between the golden idols of War and Birth, stepping from where he had always been standing, in the one place that had escaped the notice of all – the one place *overlooked*, which exists in the world's every room.

Her assassin.

He stepped from the gloom. He looked hard, like something between brown flesh and grey stone. Three noiseless steps. Maithanet heard and turned. His face was emotionless, devoid of shock or surprise or any expression. Somehow Esmenet knew he turned with little more than curiosity, so certain was he of his security. He turned just as the man dropped the knife between his neck and clavicle. There was nothing remarkable about the assault, no display of inhuman speed or ability, only a step from the one place overlooked to the one place unguarded. A kind of discharging of the inevitable.

The figure instantly released the pommel . . .

The Holy Shriah of Thousand Temples gazed down at the knife as if it were a hornet or bee, teetered . . .

Esmenet could only blink as Maithanet sputtered and died before her.

'*Sister!*' he gasped. '*You must tell my broth—!*'

He slumped to his knees, his eyes rounding about an emblematic emptiness, then crumpled to his side. His chest-plate clattered against the polished tile. He died at her assassin's feet.

Out of reflex, Esmenet turned to the abject faces, held out her hands to still the cries of cracked disbelief and the charge of the more warlike among the Apparati. In the far pockets of gloom, she could see the Inchausti gathering into a golden rush . . .

She could feel the Narindar motionless behind her. Why didn't he run?

'Hold!' she cried out. 'I said, *Hold!*'

All those near fell silent and still. Some fairly flinched out of obedience.

'Vem-Mithriti! Does your fire still serve your Empress?'

The old man hobbled to her side without hesitation. Sorcerous words seemed to cough out of the surrounding air. White light spilled from his puckered mouth and perforated eyes, made him seem an ancient baby for the vanishing of the rutted lines. Wards flickered to life about them.

644 THE WHITE-LUCK WARRIOR

The nearest of the Inchausti began slowing to a wary trot, their broadswords still held on high.

'What you have witnessed is the work of our Holy Aspect-Emperor!' she cried out, her voice strong for the iron of her exhaustion. She had no nerves to suffer.

She knew what she must look like: beggared, wild and bloodied, wreathed in pale-glowing tongues of flame. Nevertheless, she posed before them as though gowned in full Imperial splendour, knowing the contradiction between bearing and appearance would smack of scripture.

'The name Maithanet shall be stricken from all scrolls and all stone!' she cried in righteous fury. 'For he is naught but a deceiver!'

She would do what her husband had bid her to do.

'The adoration you once felt, the dismay you now feel is the *very measure* of his deception!'

She would speak oil.

'*He!*' she shrieked, jerking her open hand to the bundle of fabric bleeding beneath the golden arc of idols. 'Anasûrimbor Maithanet! He has revolted against his sacred brother! He has murdered our . . .' Her voice broke about the truth of this last. 'Our Holy Prophet's son!'

The Shrial and Imperial Apparati stood aghast, some stupefied, others terrified, a crowd of wisemen and dandies trussed by mad circumstance. Beyond them, the Inchausti continued their clattering accumulation. Cries and moans and hissed conversations rose from them.

One of their captains stepped belligerently forward, began, 'Who sa—?'

'*Anasûrimbor Kellhus!*' she cried in scathing dismissal. 'Our Holy Aspect-Emperor!' She could see the man's example leaping like contagion, emboldening others throughout the assembly. 'To *whom* do you think he sends his holy dreams?' And though she could not sense them, she knew the Inchausti possessed Chorae . . .

She had to strike the will to fight from them. It was her only hope.

'*Think!*' she fairly screeched. '*Who else* could strike down the *Shriah of the Thousand Temples* with such ease? With! Such! *Ease!*'

This, she knew, would open a wedge . . .

'On your knees!' she cried, as if she had conjured as much as invoked her divine husband. '*On your knees!*'

Because acting and being were one and the same for Men.

She had no choice. She had to *own* the event. What chances did her assassin have of escape, even if he were Narindar? If captured, he would name her. She had to own the event and own it *as justice*, as the swift and brutal justice they had come to expect from Anasûrimbor Kellhus. The assassin would be spared, would be celebrated as a hero.

As he should, since he had only worked his Empress's will.

This was why he remained standing over his victim. This was why he had chosen this very moment to strike.

Many had fallen to their knees instantly, Phinersa among them, the ghost of a smile upon his nimble face. Some grovelled in abject shame, murmuring prayers to her where she stood beneath the golden idols. But a greater proportion of the Inchausti remained standing, held up by their outrage and the example of their indecisive brothers.

'Kneel! For those who stand now *stand with foul Golgotterath*!'

She would speak oil, heartbreaking oil. She would drive thousands to the executioner's sword, if need be. She would *burn Momemn to the ground* the way the minstrels accused her of burning Carythusal . . .

Anything to see her children safe!

'For *eternity itself* hangs in the balance about you!'

The last of the Inchausti relented, dropped to their knees, then to their faces. She watched it spread like a disease among them, the miraculous inversion that makes madness out of faith, the transformation of squalid catastrophe into divine revelation. And they could feel *Him*, she knew. All of them could feel *Him* emanating from her slight and bloodied figure. And in months and years hence, they would die thinking this the most significant, most glorious moment of their lives . . .

Grovelling before the Holy Empress.

A feeling of triumph unlike any she had ever experienced steeped her to the merest vein, an elation that transcended her body, a uproarious continuity of self and subjugated world. It seemed she need only yank high her arms and the very earth would be flapped like a blanket. And she looked down with imperious satisfaction, revelled in the fleeting intensity . . .

For even as she watched, the assembled penitents began looking about in wonder and anxious confusion.

The roaring that had been her pious chorus, her proof of Maithanet's discord, had dwindled, then trailed away altogether. The mobs had fallen miraculously silent . . .

And for the merest of instants, it seemed that the *whole Empire* had joined them on their knees.

But something . . . a kind of rhythmic pulse . . . had taken its place, rising from the deep temple hollows. She recognized it instantly, though her soul refused to credit the knowledge. For it was a sound that still thrummed through the darkest of her dreams.

Dreams of warring Shigek . . . of desert wastes and the abject misery that was Caraskand.

Dreams of Holy Shimeh, wrested from heathen hands.

The beating of war-drums. *Fanim* drums.

The Empress of the Three Seas turned to the idol of Anagkë,

who by some perversity of angles gleamed golden over the dead Shriah's inert form, the near-naked assassin passionless at her side.

She began laughing – clawing her hair and laughing . . .

Such a devious whore was Fate.

CHAPTER FIFTEEN

The Library of Sauglish

In life, your soul is but the extension of your body, which
reaches inward until it finds its centre in spirit. In death,
your body is but the extension of your soul, which reaches
outward until it finds it circumference in flesh. In both
instances, all things appear the same.
Thus are the dead and the living confused.

—MEMGOWA, THE BOOK OF DIVINE ACTS

Yet the soul lingers like a second smell.
A sailor wrecked at sea, it clings,
lest it sink and drown in Hell.

—GIRGALLA, EPIC OF SAUGLISH

**Late Summer, 20 New Imperial Year (4132 Year-of-the-Tusk),
The Ruins of Sauglish**

Suffocation. Blindness and bewilderment.

At first Achamian thought the gag choked him, but his mouth was clear. Had they put a sack over his head? He thrashed his limbs, realizing he was unbound – but he could not move more than the span of a hand.

Sarcophagus. Coffin. He was in some kind of . . .

Dream.

The old Wizard's panic dwindled, even as the panic of the ancient soul he had become flared into outrage. He was Anasûrimbor Nau-Cayûti, Scourge of the Consult, Prince of the High Norsirai – Dragonslayer! He beat at his stone prison with righteous fury, howled. He cursed the name of his miscreant wife.

But the enclosed chute grew hot with his exertions, and the air began failing him. Soon he was heaving, making a bellows out of his barrel chest, gasping. Soon he could do no more than scratch at his prison, and his thoughts unwound in shame and disorientation . . .

To think a man such as he would die scratching.

Then he was tipping and tumbling, as though his prison had been cast into a cataract. Stone cracked – a concussion that snapped his teeth. Air washed about him, so chill as to feel wet. He sucked cold, breathed against a ponderous fragment pinning him. He blinked at the night darkness, saw the moon low, glaring pale through rag-ripped clouds and thronging branches. He glimpsed broken forms strewn, sightless eyes shining in the twinkle of fallen torches. Dead Knights of Trysë. He saw his sword gleaming among rune-engraved fragments of stone, reached with nerveless fingers. But a shadow stilled him. Witless for lack of breath and confusion and horror, he gazed up at his monstrous assailant . . .

Phallus, greased and pendulous. Wings, scabrous and veined, folded into two horns rising high above the thing's shoulders. Window skin, revealing sheaths of raw muscle and a compound head: one skull a great oval, the second *human*, fused into the jaws of the former.

Aurang, the old Wizard realized with Nau-Cayûti's horror. The Horde-General. The Angel of Deceit.

The Inchoroi kicked away his blade, arched over him like a defecating dog. It wrapped fish-cold fingers about his throat. It raised him until he dangled helpless in its baleful gaze. Needles probed his breath-starved extremities.

The thing grinned – sheets of mucus pinned to its lesser skull. Laughter like pain blown through broken flutes.

'*None,*' the Inchoroi gasped through leprous throats. '*None escape Golgottera—*'

Shouting. Someone was shouting.

The Wizard bolted from the forest floor, blinking and peering in the stupefied manner of those just awoken. He coughed, convulsed as his throat warred against the gag. The world was predawn grey, the eastern sky a golding slate through skeins of branches.

The Captain. The Captain ranted at them to awaken.

'The *Coffers*, boys!' he cried in a macabre parody of Sarl's exclamation. The mad Sergeant chortled in delight, cried, 'The Slog of Slogs!' in answer, before a realization of some kind yanked his breath short. Afterward, he watched with the wariness of a dog long-beaten.

'Today is the day we *turn around*!'

Achamian glimpsed Mimara rising slight and slender from a depression in the ground, her lips hanging open as she beat at the leafy detritus pasted across her arm and shoulder. Suddenly Lord Kosoter was looming over him, the twin voids tingling as always beneath his splint hauberk. He grabbed the Wizard by the shoulders, heaved him to his feet as though he were a child.

'*Galian!*' he shouted to the former Columnary. 'Make ready.'

The Captain seized the rope about the Wizard's wrists and, accompanied by Cleric, led him like a votive lamb away from the others. He had a practised hand, shoving and catching so that it seemed the Wizard continually tripped forward. Eventually, he let him fall onto his face.

The Wizard writhed like a fish, kicked himself onto his back only to crush and scrape his fingers against a branch. Lord Kosoter towered over him, more shadow than man with the brightening east behind him. His two Chorae glowered with nothingness, like the empty sockets of a skull hanging about his heart. The Wizard watched him reach beneath his hauberk and tug one free.

'Our expedition has come to a head,' Lord Kosoter said, dandling the thing before him.

The old Wizard's thoughts raced. There was a path through this. There was a path through everything . . .

Yet one more lesson learned at Kellhus's punishing hand.

The Captain knelt beside him, leaned so low his beard brushed Achamian's own. His rough fingers worked the leather straps that held the gag in place. The Chorae was a coal that scorched the air with absence – burning oblivion . . .

'The time has come, Wizard. Xonghis says the solstice is several days away.'

The old Wizard shrank from the Trinket, writhed as if searching for a hatch through the forest floor. The Captain pulled the gag free.

'Speak with care.'

His tongue was cankered and swollen. Talking was onerous. 'Wha—?' He trailed in a coughing fit. 'Sol-solstice?'

The Captain's face betrayed no passion. His eyes gleamed dead within their rim of tattooed black. The ferocity of his suspicion lay compressed in the pause he took before replying.

'You claimed the Coffers were protected by powerful Wards,'

he fairly growled. 'Curses that could only be unlocked *during the solstice . . .*'

Achamian glared, blinking. It seemed a lifetime had passed since he had said as much. Lies. Where facts were like embroidery, each one stitched across the whole cloth of others, lies were like chips of ice in water, always slipping one past the other, always melting . . .

'*Our expedition has come to a head . . .*'

And it came upon the Wizard as a kind of falling horror, the profundity of his ignorance.

Were the Coffers still sealed after all this time? Were they buried? Were they gutted, long emptied of their riches?

For all he knew, the Map to Ishuäl might lie in Golgotterath . . .

Even still, he heard his voice rasp, spill even more ice into the water of expediency – and with more than enough hate to sound convincing. 'Th-the Wards . . . They yoke the movement of the planets – that is the source of their never-ending power. F-four sorcerous keys were given, one for each transition of the seasons. Summer to autumn is the only key I know.'

The Captain regarded him for a flint-hearted moment.

'You lie.'

'Yes,' Achamian replied in a cold voice. 'I lie.'

Lord Kosoter turned to Cleric, who stood looming behind. His Chorae drifted a fraction nearer as he did so, blistering the Wizard's cheek with salt. Seeing the Nonman, Achamian suddenly realized what it was he needed to do. He needed to convince Kosoter to send him *alone* with the Nonman King – with Seswatha's ancient friend and ally.

He needed to reach what remained of Nil'giccas . . . Or, failing that, kill him.

But how to convince him, a being gone mad for forgetfulness?

The Captain scooped the Chorae tight into his fist. Achamian watched, trying to squint the hope from his eyes, while the man drew his knife and began sawing at his restraints.

'I smell treachery,' Lord Kosoter said to his inhuman ward. 'You take him. Confirm his story or kill him.'

Cleric nodded. A band of dawn orange slipped across his cheek.

The old Wizard fairly shouted aloud for relief. How long had it been since the Whore had last favoured him? Seju knew he would need more of her capricious favours before this insanity was through.

His extremities prickled and stabbed at the sudden return of circulation. Groaning, he drew himself up, rubbing his hands and fingers against his forearms.

'You die no matter what,' the Captain spat, speaking as if the future were as irrevocable as the past. 'It's the *girl* who tips upon the balance.'

And suddenly Achamian understood why Kosoter had elected to remain behind. Logic – *scalper* logic. Who knew what sorcerous traps lay buried in a legendary place like the Library? Better to hang back, to direct events from safety, with a knife held to his hostage's throat.

'And the child within her.'

—∞—

The Great Library of Sauglish. Even beaten to its foundations, portions of the holy fortress reared above the trees. The merest rise or gap in the screening branches afforded him glimpses. His dreaded destination.

Even still, the old Wizard found an unexpected serenity walking with the Nonman through the wooded ruins. Ragged patches of sunshine waved across the forest floor. Birdsong chirped and chattered through the canopy, light and inexhaustible. Here and there sections of wall rose from mounds like teeth from earthen gums.

Layers of stonework ribbed the ravines they crossed. Blocks and fragments of every description stumped the ground. They passed a free-standing triumphal, the first thing Achamian clearly recognized from his Dreams: the Murussar, the symbolic bastion that marked the entrance to Sauglish's outlander quarter. Stripped of its inscriptions and engravings, it towered into the canopy, stone blackened, chapped with white lichens, shelved with moss. He need only blink to see the crowds bustling about its marble base: their garb ancient, their arms and armour bronze – men culled from all nations, from wild Aörsi to distant Kyraneas.

Prior to the First Apocalypse, the Holy Library had been famed throughout Eärwa, the destination of poets, sorcerers, and princely embassies. Entire literary traditions had grown about the long pilgrimage to the City of Robes, the famed *Caravaneeri*, of which only fragments now survived. Bards and prophets haunted the niches and alcoves of every street, crying out diversion and threatening damnation. Vendors lined the ways, hawking wares from as faraway as ancient Shir.

Sauglish had been infamous for its racket, the markets booming with commerce during the days, the streets clattering with teamsters during the night. There was something both tragic and beautiful, Achamian decided, in the contrast between that ancient clamour and the peaceful din he heard now – as if there were something *proper* in the passing of Men.

The Ganiural, the processional avenue that led to the Library, was still clearly visible beneath the mounding of centuries: a broad trough in the forest floor that followed a compass-straight bearing. The old Wizard had said nothing to Cleric in all this time: despite the wonder he felt, his outrage at his captivity remained too raw a thing to broach. But as they climbed toward the ruined Library, the scale of ages seemed to leach into his bones – generations stacked upon generations, innumerable lives snuffed after a mere handful of scratching years. The fact that the figure walking beside him had outlived *all of it*, long enough to break beneath the burden, loomed so large that his grudge began to seem preposterous.

'Incariol,' Achamian finally said, wincing at the way speaking pained his gag-cankered tongue. 'Why that name?'

The Nonman's stride did not falter. 'Because I wander.'

The Wizard breathed deep, knowing the time had come to plunge back into the fray. He squinted up at the figure. 'And *Cleric?*'

The Nonman's pace slowed a fraction. A scowl furrowed his hairless brow.

'It is a tradition . . . I think . . . A tradition among the Siqû to take a Mannish name.'

Siqû was the name given to Nonmen who walked among Men.

'But Incariol is *not* your name . . .'

The Nonman continued walking.

'You are Nil'giccas,' the Wizard pressed. 'The Last King of Mansions.'

Cleric abruptly halted and with an alien air slowly turned to face him. Because they had walked shoulder to shoulder or rather, shoulder to elbow, the Nonman loomed over him, broad and hale beneath his nimil armour.

The Wizard saw turmoil in his dark eyes.

'No,' the marmoreal lips said. 'He is dead.'

A sudden consciousness of what Seswatha had felt in the presence of the being before him descended upon Achamian. A sense of age-spanning majesty, grievous nobility, and *power*, angelic and unfathomable.

'No,' the old Wizard said. 'He is quite alive, gazing upon me.'

The *King of Ishterebinth* stood before him, storied and immortal. The legendary hero, whose triumphs and disasters had been stamped into the very foundation of history.

Drusas Achamian fell to his knees, bent with fingers interlocked behind his neck, the way the Grandmaster of the Sohonc had bowed so many times so very many years ago, even in this, the celebrated city he once called his own . . .

He knelt to accord honour to the great King before him.

She watches Cleric and the Wizard vanish over the burial rim that once was Sauglish's walls, swallows against the cry climbing her throat. The sight reeks of execution.

They have reached the Coffers. The Skin Eaters, she knows, will not suffer them long.

Mimara has never been a timid or fearful woman. Nor has she ever been like her mother, who continually swaddled her heart in doubt and misgivings. Their quest has doled out terrors aplenty, but almost always as calls to desperate action. There were always eyes she could claw. Always.

But the fear she feels now forbids all action. It gags her, as certainly as the Wizard had been gagged. Even her wailing is caught in the fist of her breast. It empties her limbs of blood.

The fear that taught prayer to Men.

She can feel Achamian walking alone, out *there*, a point of panic swamped in torpor. She can feel his doom close hoary about him.

The Captain and the others busy themselves with trivial labours. Pokwas whets his great blade. Koll seems to sleep. Xonghis fashions snares. Mimara simply sits hugging her knees, rapt, at times praying for Achamian, at times fending the images of disaster flashing through her soul's eye. She spends the early morning watches grappling with doom and futility.

But the focus of her anxiety is not long in changing.

Great Sauglish, the ancient City of Robes, extended about them, little more than a host of ruined grottos scattered through the forest. He would succeed in this, the old Wizard thought on his knees beneath the towering Nonman. He would wrest Cleric away from the Captain. He would recover Anasûrimbor Celmomas's ancient map from the Coffers. He would find Ishuäl and the truth of the man who had stolen his wife.

'You are confused, mortal,' Cleric said. 'Rise.'

And with these simple words, the old Wizard's sudden hope collapsed back into the morass of worry and embittered fear. Feeling foolish, Achamian climbed back to his feet. He gazed angrily up at the Nonman, then looked down in embarrassment and fury.

'Lord Kosoter . . .' he ventured as they resumed their climb. 'He's your elju? Your book?'

Cleric was reluctant to speak. The old Wizard knew he had to tread carefully. Famed King of Ishterebinth or not, the Nonman walking beside him was also an Erratic, one of the Wayward.

'Yes.'

'What if he lies? What if he *manipulates* you?'

Cleric turned to regard him, then looked to the glimpses of ruined walls in the distance before them. 'What if he's treacherous?' he asked.

'Yes!' the Wizard pressed. 'Surely you can see how . . . *diseased* his heart has become. Surely you can see his madness!'

'And you . . . you would be my book in his stead?'

Achamian paused to better choose his words.

'Seswatha,' he began with an imploring look, 'your old friend of yore – he dwells *within me*, my Lord. I cannot betray him. He cannot betray you. Let *me* bear the burden of your memory!'

Cleric continued in silence for several strides, his expression inscrutable.

'Seswatha . . .' he finally repeated. 'That *name* . . . I remember.

When the world burned . . . When Mog-Pharau shouldered the clouds . . . He . . . Seswatha fought at my side . . . for a time.'

'Yes!' Achamian exclaimed. '*Please*, my Lord. Take me as your book! Leave this scalper madness behind! Regain your honour! Reclaim your glory!'

Cleric lowered his face, clutched his chin and cheek. His shoulders hitched in what Achamian took for a sob . . .

But was in fact a laugh.

'So . . .' the Nonman King said, raising eyes savage for their mirth. 'You offer me oblivion?'

Too late, the old Wizard recognized his mistake.

'No . . . I—'

The Nonman whirled, grasped him with a strength that made the Wizard feel bone thin, bone frail. 'I will not die a husk!' he cried. He rolled his head from shoulder to shoulder in his curious, mad and explosive way. He flung out his hands to clutch the air.

'No! I will ruin and I will break!'

Few things unsettle more than the violation of hidden assumptions – or make us more wary. The old Wizard had appealed to his *own* logic – his own vanity – forgetting that the absence of common ends was the very thing that made the mad *mad*. He had offered himself as a *tool*, not realizing that he and Mimara were the *object* of the bargain struck: the shade of an ancient friend and the echo of long-lost love. *They* were the loves to be betrayed.

They were the souls to be remembered . . .

'Honour?' the Nonman cried, his sneer transforming him into a gigantic Sranc. 'Love? What are these but dross before oblivion? No! I will seize the world and I will shake from it what misery, what anguish, I can. I will *remember*!'

The old Wizard resumed walking, this time with a bearing more suited to a death march. *Let the victim lead the executioner,* he thought. Nil'giccas, the Last King of Mansions, was going to kill him in the Library of Sauglish.

Scenarios both disastrous and absurdly hopeful raced through Achamian's thoughts. He would ambush the Nonman with a Cant powerful enough to smash his incipient Wards – kill him before he himself was killed. He would plead and cajole, find the incantation of reason and passion that would throw Cleric from the mad track he followed. He would battle with howling fury, tear down what was left of the Sacred Library, only to be beaten down by the Quya Mage's greater might . . .

The impulse to survive is not easily denied, no matter how severe the calamities a man has suffered or how relentless the misfortunes.

'I mourn what Fate has made of me . . .' the Nonman said without warning.

The old Wizard watched his booted feet kick through forest debris.

'So what of Ishterebinth?' he asked. 'Has it fallen?'

The hulking Nonman made a gesture that possessed the character of a shrug. 'Fallen? No. Turned. In the absence of recollection my brothers have turned to tyranny . . . To Min-Uroikas.'

Min-Uroikas. That he spoke this with ease attested to the severity of his condition. Among the Intact, it was a name not so much mentioned as spat or cursed. Min-Uroikas. The Pit of Obscenities. The dread stronghold that had murdered all their wives and daughters, and so doomed their entire race.

'Golgotterath,' the Wizard managed to say without breath.

A heavy nod. Sickles of reflected sunlight bobbed across his scalp.

'I had forgotten that name.'

'And you?' the Wizard asked. 'Why have you not joined them?'

Long silence. Long enough to bring them to the base of the broken Library.

'Pride,' the Nonman finally said. 'I would bring about my own heartbreak. So I set out in search of those I might love . . .'

Achamian searched the dark glitter of his eyes. 'And destroy.'

A solemn nod, carrying thousands of years of inevitability. 'And destroy.'

Mimara does not know what alerts her to the sudden change in the air among the scalpers. Her mother once told her the bulk of discourse consisted of *hidden* exchanges, that most men blathered in utter ignorance of their meaning and intent. Mimara scoffed at the idea, not because it rang false, but because her *mother* argued it.

'Most find it difficult to stomach,' the Empress said with maternal exhaustion. *'They believe in a thousand things they cannot see, yet tell them the greater part of their own soul lies hidden, and they balk . . .'*

This proved to be one of those rare comments that would flank Mimara's anger and leave her simply troubled. She could not shake the sense that the object of the exchange, the *hidden* object, had been her stepfather, Kellhus. The nagging suspicion that her mother had been *warning* her.

A part of her awakened that day. It was one thing to realize that the men who wooed her spoke through their teeth, as the Ainoni would say. But it was quite another to think that motives *could hide themselves*, leaving the men they moved utterly convinced of their honourable intentions.

Now she can feel it. Something *hidden* has happened, here, among these idle men, on the ruined outskirts of Sauglish.

Something as ethereal and small as a soul committing to some resolution, yet as momentous as anything that has happened in her life.

She becomes quiet, watchful, knowing the only question is whether *they* realize as much . . .

The scalpers.

The Captain squats upon a toe of mossed stone that smacks of masonry, even though it looks natural. He stares out into random forest pockets with a kind of stationary hatred, like a man who never tires of counting his grievances. Galian and Pokwas recline against a hump in the matted humus, talking and joking in low tones. Koll sits like a cross-legged corpse, his hollow eyes sorting nothing. Sarl sits and stands, sits and stands, grinning his eyes into lines and gurgling about slogs and riches.

Xonghis alone remains both industrious and vigilant.

After a time, Galian bolts upright. With the air of settling some inaudible dispute between him and Pokwas, he asks, 'What will our shares be?'

A heartbeat of astonished silence follows, such is the general terror of addressing the Captain.

'As much as you can bear and still survive,' Lord Kosoter finally says. Absolutely nothing about his gaze or demeanour changes as he says this. He literally speaks as if not speaking.

'And what about the Qirri?'

Silence.

Despite the air of hard deliberation, Lord Kosoter has bred an atmosphere of volatility between him and his men, cleaving to thresholds so vague and so brittle that it seems anything beyond abject obedience might warrant execution. Galian risks his life simply asking questions for all to hear. But mentioning *Qirri* . . .

It seems nothing less than suicidal. The act of a fool.

The Captain shakes his head slowly. 'Only Cleric knows.'

'What if you were to *demand* he yield it?'

Turning his head on a hinge of granite, Lord Kosoter finally regards the former Columnary.

'The False Man is mad!' Pokwas calls out.

The Captain lowers his face, pinches his lower lip in contemplation. 'Yes,' he says in grim admission. 'But think. A year given. Our every greed slaked.' He seeks each of his men with his gaze, as if knowing he must cow them one by one. 'He's delivered us to these riches.'

Galian smiles like someone with arguments too devious to be refuted.

'Then why suffer him any longer?'

For the first time Mimara glimpses the fury sparking in the Captain's eyes.

'Who will deliver us back, fool?'

More silence.

A nightmarish intensity engulfs the two men.

Galian peers at the Ainoni caste-noble in mock reverence, his manner so feckless, so bold, that it raises an audible murmur from Mimara's lungs.

'I want a fire,' he says.

'We march on the dark.'

Galian looks to the forested deeps about them, then back to his Captain. 'Yes . . . Skinny country, is it?' There is nothing sly about his antagonism now. 'Where *are* the skinnies then?'

The Captain regards him for several heartbeats, his eye shadowed beneath heavy brows, his nose and cheeks like chipped flint above the brushed wire of his moustache and beard. There is something breathless, absolute about his composure. Grim deliberation glints from his eyes . . .

The look of a man, a murderous man, finding the shadowy centre of his enemy's web.

'Are you such a fool, Galian?' Mimara blurts aloud. The tension is too much.

But the former Columnary has eyes only for his Captain.

'You made your decision, *just then*,' he says with a lolling smile. 'Didn't you? You decided *to kill me*.'

Lord Kosoter glares, a hoary king leaning from his stone chair. A dark, tyrannical figure, passing judgment on the fool capering before him.

'Before the slit called out,' Galian presses. 'That moment of silence . . . You thought to yourself, *Kill the fool!*'

There is a sudden viciousness to his intonation, and enough mimicry of the Captain's growling voice to send Pokwas laughing. Even Xonghis, who is working on his bow, grins in his enigmatic Jekki manner.

Horror bolts through her. She has just glimpsed the savage shape of what is about to happen. Conspiracy and conspirators both.

'But then you thought it *before*, haven't you, Captain? Every time you glimpsed me leaning with the others, something cried, *"Kill him!"* in that cramp you call a soul.'

The Captain remains utterly motionless, watching the Columnary's approach from his impromptu throne.

'As it turns out,' Galian continues with bright humour, 'we *were* leaning together in sedition . . .'

The Columnary comes to stop immediately before Lord Kosoter, easily within reach of his broadsword. A kind of boredom seems to glint in the Captain's eyes – as if mutiny were an old and tedious friend.

'And you should know that every time *I glimpsed you* . . .' Galian throws out his arms and, as if daring him to strike, leans forward in vindictive contempt. 'I also heard something whisper, *"Kill him!"*'

The arrow catches the Captain in the mouth. He jerks to his side as if slapped, staggers back two steps. He hangs there for a moment, spitting cracked teeth.

A cloud occludes the sun.

The Captain of the Skin Eaters, the man called Ironsoul, raises his face, not to the bowman, Xonghis, but to the bowman's maker, Galian. The shaft is visible. It skewers the lower half of his face, draws bearded skin tight. Blood spills from the ream of his bottom lip. His laughter sputters through it.

A sardonic glee, malevolent for its intensity, shines like sorcery in his eyes.

The second arrow thumps into his neck. He whirls to the side and around, as if a rope about his waist holds him staked in place. He hangs for an instant, like a thing made of wax. Then he slumps face first across the humus. A convulsive moment passes. He begins shaking, his limbs tossing with bonfire violence. A crazed, bestial scramble follows, as if an elemental wildness or disordered spirit has lain dormant within him, hidden, and only now could thrash free of human constraints.

His expression loose with horror, Galian draws his sword.

The Captain claws the leafy humus at the Columnary's feet, seizes a branch no thicker than two thumbs. His spine arches against his blooded hauberk. His head pulls back. He grimaces about his tented mouth, blows rage and spittle and blood. His eyes gleam like pearl. Snorting with effort and fury, he begins twisting and wrenching at the branch, as if it were the world's own spine – the one thing to be broken.

He roars.

Then his head is gone, bouncing about the tail of its caste-noble braid.

Silence – this time of visible things.

Mimara watches, breathless. *Mortal,* something cold whispers within her.

Mortal after all.

———∞———

Strange, the way Qirri made hash of momentous things.

Omens of the world's end. The death of races . . . Standing in bare sunlight, it all seemed little more than beautiful paint, a kind of ornamentation.

The northern tower of the Muraw, the Library's forward gate, was scarce more than a mound. Wandering stretches of vertical blocks broke the slopes here and there, but otherwise it had ceased to exist. Inexplicably, the southern tower stood almost entirely intact, a cyclopean square that soared against the bald sky. Even the obsidian that had plated its base had survived. Turf and shrubs mounded its distant crown, and several tenacious trees hung rooted from its sides. Despite everything, a sudden, boyish urge to scale the tower struck the old Wizard, followed by a sense of exhausted longing.

There had been a time when he had spent days loafing among ruins far less significant than these. A time when his worries had been small enough to ignore.

Side by side, the old Wizard and the Nonman King strode into the Library's ruined precincts. The walls, or what remained of them, possessed the monumental feel of the Ziggurats in Shigek. In many cases trees, full grown yet bent and windswept, grew along their crests. Achamian could still recognize the Ursilaral, the central promenade where the One Thousand Gift-Shields had once hung, garish and beautiful, symbolizing the truce between the Sohonc and almost all the known tribes of White and High Norsirai. In Seswatha's day, the Library was often called the Citadel of Citadels because of its importance, certainly, but also because of its design: fortresses within fortresses, as if the outside were a kind of ocean, a flood to be fought chamber by grudging chamber. It possessed no fewer than nineteen courtyards, often call 'pits' because of the height of the surrounding walls, with the Ursilaral, its length jawed by numerous gates, connecting most of them.

The morning sun had climbed high enough only to bathe portions of their overgrown floors so that Achamian and Cleric found themselves walking through dry shadow. The growth was mostly restricted to thickets and clutches of shrubs, forcing Achamian to follow Cleric as he hacked his way forward with his sword. Plumes of fluff swirled in dry-wind eddies. Clouds drifted across the oblong squares of blue sky above them. Bees tracked spiral courses through the air, becoming white dots when they passed into sunlight. The Wizard even glimpsed a hare bolting through the grasses.

The experience became increasingly surreal. At times the Wizard found himself staring at Cleric's labouring back, broad beneath its sheath of shining mail, wondering whether he should just attack the Nonman and be done with the suspense. At other times he played a kind of game guessing what was the ruin of what. Mounds became fountains. Rectangular breaks in walls became windows onto barracks, apartments, and scriptoriums.

And twice he caught himself squinting across the northeastern heights, looking for thunderheads massing black and terrible . . .

For the Whirlwind.

It was like walking through *two* worlds beyond the actual: the one the issue of his reading, the other the product of his Dreams. He was Achamian, exile and pariah, wearer of rotted pelts. And he was Seswatha, hero, Grandmaster of this place, both during the time when its fall was preposterous, laughable, and during the days of encroaching destruction.

'I saw these towers burn,' he said in an old voice. 'I saw these walls tumble.'

The Nonman King paused, scanned his surroundings as if seeing the ruins about him for the very first time. Achamian wondered what it would be like, outliving great works of stone. When nations possessed the span of flowers, wouldn't everything seem but stages of ruin?

'All Ishterebinth lamented when word arrived,' Cleric eventually said. 'We knew then the World was doomed.'

Achamian gazed at the Nonman King, pinned by an immovable melancholy.

'Why?' he asked. 'Why would you lament our death when it was *Men*, not the Inchoroi, who destroyed all your great mansions?'

'Because we have always known we would not survive Men.'

The Wizard smiled in recollection.

'Yes . . . Because our dooms are one.'

———

At last, walking bent through a gate almost buried by the rising ground, they came to the Turret, the mighty citadel raised by Noshainrau the White. It was naught but an enormous ring of stone, broad enough to encase any of the great amphitheatres of Invishi or Carythusal. Pitted with bird-holes, the sloped walls rose some thirty or so cubits before cresting, a line of ragged ruin against blue sky. The shining bronze sheets were gone – the Skûtiri. In Seswatha's day they had ringed the Turret's base, nine thousand, nine-hundred and ninety-nine of them, each taller than a man, and each scored with innumerable lines of sorcerous script. The sun shone imperturbable, drawing shadows across hanging nubs of stone. Wind whisked through leaves and grasses. Never, it seemed to the old Wizard, had the world seemed so lonely.

'The sorcery here is very old, very weak,' the Nonman said.

Did he remember Lord Kosoter's earlier charge? Could he?

Was he accusing him of lying?

'The Coffers lie beneath these ruins,' Achamian replied. 'The

Wards protecting it are buried deep . . . and quite ageless, I assure you.'

Perhaps now was the time to strike.

No. Not until he knew for sure he wouldn't need the Nonman's strength.

The Turret's original gate was lost beneath ramped debris. They fought their way through a mass of scrub, then began climbing.

Of all his memories of the Holy Library, the final days lived most fiercely in Achamian's memory. Always the No-God was there . . . like a nagging sense, a direction steeped in dread, as if one point on the compass had been honed sharp enough to draw a gasp from his lungs. He would walk the walls and verandas and feel it . . . *there* . . . sometimes stationary for days on end, but always moving sooner or later – always coming *closer*.

And when the wind was right, he would hear the wailing of bereaved mothers from the city below.

Stillborn . . . Every infant stillborn.

The old Wizard stopped mid-ascent, leaned against pitted stone to recover his wind. Many years had passed since he last felt the horror that was Mog-Pharau while awake. The gaping sense of futility and loss, of things crashing, not here or there, but *every-where*. The immobility of heart as much as limb or will. The horizon itself had become a revelation, taking you out of yourself and binding you to a world of dying things.

It dogged the old Wizard as he continued climbing, a great shadow lurking in his periphery, a sky-staining malevolence that leapt into existence whenever he glanced away. And the convic-tion that *all Mankind* shared the very same premonition.

Cleric stood atop the summit. The ruined walls reached to either side of him, thick enough to house pockets of grasses and shrub along their summit, climbing and dropping according to the logic of things wrecked for the passage of years.

'Something is amiss,' he called down to the huffing Wizard.

He extended a hand in assistance as Achamian clambered near. There was a surprising reassurance in his grip, as if their bodies recognized a kinship too primitive not to be overlooked by their souls.

Leaning against his knees to catch his breath, the old Wizard surveyed the Turret's vacant interior. He suffered the same knee-wobbling sense of vertigo he always suffered when he found himself standing high upon fallen works. Swallows battled about the curve of the inner walls. The ages had entirely gutted the citadel, leaving only what resembled an absurdly immense granary. But he had expected as much.

What he had not expected was the great *pit* yawning below . . .

Rubble heaped about the inner foundations, making a funnel of the ground. The cracked rim of floors broken, exposing wasp-nest hollows, each a level of the Turret's cellars. Then obdurate blackness at the bottom.

'Do you smell that?' Achamian asked, frowning in disbelief.

'Yes,' the Nonman King replied. 'Sulphur.'

She is not sure when she resumes breathing. The remaining Skin Eaters – the sane ones, anyway – immediately fall to arguing.

Galian instructs Sarl to watch her, which he does with a kind of crazed reluctance. She and the mad Sergeant take turns gazing at the Captain in disbelief. At one point, Sarl grasps the very branch that Lord Kosoter had tried to snap in his final moment. Crouching a pace away, he uses it to poke at his dead Captain's face. He presses the tip against the waxen forehead, rolls the face skyward, then jumps when it slips and rocks back to face him.

He turns to Mimara and cackles.

'He's not dead,' he says like a drunk keen to slur some fact that others thought obvious. 'Not the Captain, no . . .'

Shouts climb from the near distance. Pokwas is jabbing Galian's shoulder with a long finger.

'He's too hard for Hell.'

It was like climbing down a monstrous rabbit hole.

A strange anxiousness dogged the old Wizard as the brightness climbed in stages above him. The pit fell at an angle instead of dropping vertically, opening about a ramp of packed debris and earth, like a burrow that was at once a road into the underworld. The Turret's cellars formed a kind of pitched roof above them, three distinct levels of corridors halved and chambers cracked open like eggs.

The depths opened before them, steeped in sulphurous mystery.

'Look . . .' Cleric said, motioning toward the side of the tunnel.

But Achamian had already glimpsed them in the grey light. Three gashes hooked like scythes: the centre one the longest, the innermost curving within its compass, while the outermost arced away at an angle.

Achamian immediately recognized the mark: any Man in the Three Seas would have. The Three Sickles had been a common heraldic device since Far Antiquity – the symbol adopted by Triamis the Great.

The scoring of long-curved claws . . .

The spoor of Dragons.

A profound ache climbs out from her back, roots itself in her knees and neck. But still she sits hugging her shins. She cannot move.

Galian returns, leading the others. Sarl scampers from his path, his Captain's head clutched tight to his chest.

'So what are you going to do?' she asks the Columnary.

'We're going to wait for Cleric to return. Then we're going to relieve him of that pretty pouch.'

Xonghis has already yanked the two Chorae from beneath Lord Kosoter's hauberk.

Galian smiles at her in the leering manner she knows all too well. 'In the meantime,' he says, 'we are going to feast on the banquet the gods have delivered to us.'

Her look is so sour, it seems a miracle that he can grin.

'Feast . . . On what?'

The day is dry and bright – beautiful. Wind falls through the lazy treetops, shushing the bestiary that is the world. Blood clots across the leaves.

'Peaches, my sweet. Peaches.'

Skidding on their rumps, the old Wizard and the Nonman King followed the burrow into airy darkness – the antechamber to the Coffers. The Upper Pausal had been reduced to balconies hanging amputated in the black. Debris choked the floors of the Pausal proper, heaped toward the sides by the passage of some monstrous bulk. Achamian shuddered, glimpsing what was left of the Nonman friezes that adorned its walls – memories of Cil-Aujas, he supposed. The Great Gate of Wheels had been obliterated; he could see its ensorcelled remains scattered through the ruin: the marmoreal white of broken incantation wheels, the chapped green of bronze cams and fittings.

Raw blackness gaped before him.

So, a dull and long-suffering portion of his soul murmured, *the Coffers have been looted.*

He stood motionless, gazing in abject dismay.

So much suffered . . . So many dead . . .

For nothing.

The great refrain of his miserable life.

The madness, when he pondered it, was that he had *believed* it could be otherwise, that he would trek all this distance – *survive this far* – and actually find the Coffers intact, the map to Ishuäl waiting for him like a low-hanging plum. He almost laughed aloud for thinking it, the thought that *Fate might be kind*.

This, he realized – this was what his fate had been all along. Snared in the machinations of his enemy, who had known his mission even before he had tripped across it. Confronted with the preposterous issue of his preposterous hopes. He had sought truth and had been delivered to madmen and a Dragon instead – a *Dragon!*

A Wracu of old.

He could almost hear the skies laugh.

Sparing neither word nor glance, the old Wizard and the Nonman King stepped across the cracked threshold and at long last passed into the Coffers.

The reek watered his eyes, mingled with his terror so that it seemed he wept for fear. Sulphur. The smoke of predatory life. And rot, profound and gangrenous. The putrefaction that ties a string to your stomach and pulls hard whenever breath is drawn too deep.

Achamian could *feel* as much as hear the thing breathing in the blackness, the whoosh of enormous furnace bellows. He could scarce see the debris beneath his feet, yet the sound grew into a kind of vision, such is the mischief of imagination. Great lungs betokened great limbs. The deep reptilian creak conjured images of scaled hides, of lipless jaws and grinning teeth . . .

A mighty horror awaited them, and a portion of the old Wizard did not *want* to see. A portion of him preferred the hysterics of his soul's eye.

They came to a slope of heaped ruin, picked their way to the summit. The blackness yawned out about them, a motionless vacuum. Cleric uttered a sorcerous phrase; his eyes and mouth flared with meaning. The pale brilliance of a Surillic Point appeared above them, and the blackness fled to far places, leaving a globe of empty, illuminated air . . .

Dragon. Wracu.

According to legend, the first Sohonc discovered a vast cavern when laying the Library's foundations. They dredged the depths, squared the walls, pillared the open spaces, creating a secret, subterranean citadel. It was Noshainrau, whose sorcerous research had cast such long shadows across the future, who would make it his School's treasury, a vault for the world's greatest glories and darkest terrors.

The famed Coffers.

Perhaps the ancient architects had feared the ceiling the earth had provided them. Perhaps the chaotic weave of natural lines offended their sense of beauty and proportion. Either way, they constructed a roof with the post and lintel principles they used to raise their temples. This second ceiling had long since collapsed in its centre, littering the floor with the ruin of giant stone beams and the cracked drums of toppled pillars. Peering between the remaining columns, the old Wizard had the impression of a black lake hanging above all that could be seen, as if the very world had been turned on its head.

Gone were the ponderous lantern wheels. Gone were the narrow aisles. Gone were the racks and shelves that had organized a thousand years of sorcerous hoarding. Treasure and debris matted the floors, a ragged landscape of contradictions that piled higher toward the chamber's heart. Coins gravelling the wrack of shattered frescoes. A tripod capsized in a swell of mounded powder. A crown staved beneath a jutting beam of granite. A chest of cracked bronze, spilling rivulets of jewels between horns of broken stone.

Because of age-old accumulations of dust and tarnish, nothing glittered, nothing gleamed.

Apart from the Dragon.

The shadows cast by intervening columns were absolute, so only fragments of the beast could be seen. Horned ridges. Wings folded into scarred curtains. Scales like overlapping shields, pale with filth and bronze. A single nostril weeping smoke.

The beast was *old*, Achamian realized. Exceedingly old. Wracu never stopped growing, so it stood to reason that any dragon he encountered in his waking life would dwarf the ancient monstrosities from his Dreams . . .

But this.

Wings that could have tarped the Shilla Amphitheatre in faraway Aöknyssus. A torso broad enough to hull the largest Cironji carrack, yet long enough to coil about the small mountain of treasure and ruin. Were it to rear onto its hind legs, the beast would stand as tall as any of the Mop's unnatural trees.

The bellow lungs continued to roar and croak in the deeps of Achamian's hearing. The sulphur pinched his own breath, quick and shallow and warm-blooded. Nausea rooted through his innards.

He turned to Cleric. Bleached in his own light, the Nonman King stood rapt, his left boot braced against a headless statue. The Surillic Point made polished marble of his skin, a diamond weave of his nimil hauberk. He looked more thoughtful than afraid or astounded.

'This . . .' Cleric murmured, his gaze fixed on the slumbering beast. 'This is where I am meant to die.'

'You and my loincloth,' Achamian replied.

The Nonman turned to him, his face blank and wondering. A vagrant pain seemed to seize his expression. Then Nil'giccas, King of the Last Mansion, *laughed*. The sound boomed through the hollows, a cackle that rolled like thunder, deep and earthen and utterly – insanely – unafraid.

Achamian grimaced more than smiled.

'Ah . . . Seswatha,' Cleric said, swallowing his mirth. 'How I cherish your wi—'

'OLD,' the very ground seemed to croak. 'SO VERY OLD . . .'

Rasping through roped mucus, sheathed in a bottomless wheeze. The voice was more than loud, more than deep; it was *great* in the sense of absurd disproportions, words cast across faraway orders of strength and immensity. Achamian suddenly felt like a fly in the presence of a Sempis crocodile.

The scrape and scuff of shifting debris. The tinkle of little things falling. The Dragon stirred upon its heap, raised its armoured chest on limbs crooked and knotted like hoary old treetrunks. Riven with horror, Achamian watched the head wag across a lane of pale light, the crest battered and majestic . . .

The saurian skull long-jawed and wicked . . .

'WE HAVE FLOWN AND FLOWN, SEEKING YOUR CITIES . . . BUT *RUIN* WAS ALL WE COULD FIND. RUIN AND VERMIN SRANC . . .'

Dust rained from the crotches of every hanging seam, every granite joist. The ancient Wracu hoisted its head, exposed its segmented throat in absolute confidence of its invulnerability. In an absurd instant, Achamian grasped the reason why the ancient Kûniüri called them *Sûthaugi* . . .

'TELL ME . . . HAS THE WORLD ENDED?'

Worms.

'The world yet lives,' Cleric called into the gloom. 'In the South, where snow falls as rain.'

Wisps of fire. Exhalations mighty enough to throw ships from their courses. The thing's head lowered in their direction, at last fully revealed in Cleric's light.

'THE WORLD LIVES . . .'

Achamian did not so much will himself to move as will himself to *will*. So much is forgotten in the flush of abject terror – from a man's bowel to his breathing.

'The beast is dead,' Cleric murmured. 'Dead and blind.'

The old Wizard struggled to peer through his terror, to study the great head beyond the jaws, to see more than the predatory malevolence in its lines. It differed from the ancient Dragons of his Dreams – no surprise given the florid diversity characteristic of the species. Its head was more aquiline, as if built to root out prey hidden in burrows. And a mane of black iron tusks flared from its brows, bloomed into chattering skirts along the back of the beast's skull. But where smaller horns serrated the line of the beast's left brow, only stumps and savaged tissue adorned the right. The eye beneath, he could see, had rotted away long, long ago . . .

'What do you mean?' the old Wizard muttered in reply. 'It *breathes* . . .'

But Men's eyes, once attuned to a possibility, scavenge evidence of their own volition: suddenly the old Wizard saw the bronze hide sagging like a hauberk, as if detached from the greased flesh beneath. The shrunken gums. The second eye socket, rotted as hollow as the first . . .

'I BREATHE . . .' the yawing, croaking voice boomed through the underworld spaces. 'IT IS MY CURSE TO BREATHE, SO LONG AS THE WORLD LIVES.'

The Dragon *was* dead – or almost so . . .

'TURN FROM THIS PLACE,' the bronze-shelled corpse said. 'FLEE TO YOUR HEARTHS, AND TELL THOSE WHO WOULD LISTEN HOW YOU SURVIVED FOR TELLING THE FIRST, THE *FATHER*, THE WORLD YET LIVED.'

Madness. Madness and more madness.

But there was always more world than explanation. To come so far . . . *so close* . . . There was no turning from this place.

'May I beg but one dispensation?' Achamian cried.

A hissing pause. 'GRASPING,' the dead beast said, shadowy and mountainous. 'MEN ARE FOREVER GRASPING.'

'I search for a *map*,' the old Wizard said.

Cleric regarded him.

'TURN FROM THIS PLACE, MORTAL. I WILL NOT PART WITH THE MEREST FRACTION OF MY HOARD.'

'But what use could you have of trinkets and baubles?'

'TO LURE FOOLS SUCH AS YOU! TURN FROM THIS PLACE – *TURN!* COME TO ME WHEN THE WORLD HAS TRULY ENDED.'

'I will not!' the old Wizard cried, casting his frail voice against the Dragon's booming echo. Thought and passion raced panicked through his soul. All at once, he found himself marvelling at his own stubborn courage, weighing the mad consequences of his baiting, and wondering – wondering most of all – that a Dragon could be dead, yet speak and breath still . . .

'I *cannot!*'

The Wracu laughed, a sound like a thousand hacking lungs.

'AVARICE AND NECESSITY ARE EVER CONFUSED IN THE SOULS OF MEN.'

'No . . . No! Necessity alone drives me!'

'SO DOES FANCY BECOME SCRIPTURE . . .'

The old Wizard grappled with his anger, the urge to retort. *The Coffers!* he reminded himself, hearing Sarl's crazed voice as he did so. *The Coffers!*

'SO DOES GREED BECOME GOD.'

In a blink, it seemed, he saw through the fog of the intervening weeks and the lies that accumulated in his veins. In a heartbeat, the confusion that was Qirri vanished, leaving windswept fact in its wake. He had murdered men with his fictions, imperilled the woman he loved – he had marched across the desolate bosom of Eärwa – *for this moment*, this very encounter.

It happens . . .

He breathed deep, held the foul air against his hammering heart.

'A bargain then!' he cried in sudden inspiration. 'I would strike a bargain with you!'

The grating of coiled limbs. The heaving of air through rotting windpipes.

'WHAT COULD YOU HAVE THAT I MIGHT DESIRE, MORTAL?'

The old Wizard clawed his scalp.

'Truth . . . Truth is all I have.'

The Wracu raised its bulk from the heap's summit, wagged its enormous crown in the air.

'YESSSS . . . YOU REEK OF SUFFERING . . .'

As deep as graves, the eyeless sockets fixed on the old Wizard.

'I SMELL DEEDS LONG DEAD, AND FEARS – *IMMORTAL* FEARS. PERHAPS YOU POSSESS RICHES AFTER ALL . . .'

It creaked forward, loosing tiny landslides of debris and treasure.

'TRUTH IT IS, MANLING.'

It descended its miserly summit, then more than two elephants tall at the shoulder stalked the blackness beyond the immediate pillars, dragging ruin in its wake.

'SHOW ME ONE TRUTH, AND YOU SHALL HAVE YOUR MEREST FRACTION.'

Achamian retreated, fairly stumbled doing so. 'I-I'm not sure how to begin.'

He glimpsed its dead-grinning maw between columns.

'WHAT IS THIS MAP YOU SEEK?'

The will to lie leaned hard against the old Wizard's thought, but he resisted, understanding that the beast before him was as much spirit as flesh . . . Who can say what the dead hear, when their ears are pricked to the voices of the living?

So he began describing his Dreams, the way Anasûrimbor

Celmomas had charged Seswatha with the map to Ishuäl, the final refuge of the ancient Kûniüric High-Kings. But he quickly became tangled in words. Every name he mentioned, required more names to be explained – names piled upon names, all begging explanation.

The eyeless creature yawned, revealing the furnace that smouldered within the dead hull of its frame. 'TRUTH IS OUR BARGAIN,' it rumbled, croaking out of the blackness. The head, cadaverous and crocodilian, leaned forward menacingly. 'WHAT IS THIS MAP YOU SEEK?'

The old Wizard blinked at the monstrous spectre, chewed his bottom lip . . .

'Vengeance,' he said.

'AND WHOM DO YOU SEEK TO MURDER?'

'Anasûrimbor Kellhus, the Aspect-Emperor.'

'AND HIS CRIME? WHAT INDIGNITY DID HE INFLICT UPON YOU?'

Instead of glimpsing Esmenet, the old Wizard saw *Mimara* in his soul's eye, pregnant and derelict, a prisoner of the *Captain*. If he failed here . . . If he stumbled . . .

'Enough!' he cried. 'You have your truth!'

'IS NOT TRUTH INFINITE?'

Mucus snapping like bowstrings.

'Yes, bu—'

'IS!'

The great bulk stamped forward one step, fissuring stone . . .

'NOT!'

The iron-horned chin dropped, as a wolf . . .

'TRUTH!'

Fire wicked from carcass nostrils . . .

'INFINITE?'

The pillared landscape hummed with reverberations. Sulphur

and rot settled as a mist through the black. The old Wizard fairly cried out for sudden weight of Cleric's hand on his shoulder.

'He plays you,' the Nonman said, his face white and serene. 'There is no separating him from his hoard. He is too wicked, and he has slumbered here too long . . .'

The Last Nonman King turned back toward the scaled abomination.

'He?' Achamian asked witless.

'Wutteät.'

Like some beast in nocturnal seas, the Wracu shrank into the darkness. Laughter like sloughing cliffsides crashed through the ancient hollows.

'He dies from the outside,' Cleric said, 'because Hell sustains him from within.'

'CUNNING . . .' the Wracu groaned out from the black. 'CUNNING-CUNNING ISHROI!'

'I have seen this before,' Nil'giccas said, peering after the thing. He turned to the old Wizard and smiled. 'I remember.'

Achamian gazed at the Nonman, found himself wondering who was more hoary, more impossible: the ancient, undead Dragon or the ancient, inhuman King.

'So what do we do?'

Something resembling dark humour flashed in the Nonman's eyes. Without explanation, he began picking his way toward the wheezing blackness.

'Run,' he called to the old Wizard behind him. 'Save them while you still can.'

'Them?'

A passing glance over his nimil-armoured shoulder.

'Your wife and child.'

Like most dwellings in the slums of Carythusal, the Worm, the brothel Mimara had lived in was walled against everything surrounding and open only within. Two mercenaries – little more than thugs, really – manned the entrance, festooned with ornamental menace. Every mouth needs fangs. But once past them, all was carpeted invitation. Gold paint. Garish tapestries representing battles that may or may not have happened. Incense and obscure liquors. Sunlight showered the courtyard gardens. Patrons reclined on embroidered settees in the reception hall, talking and laughing in low, shameless voices . . .

Their eyes flicking to and fro, as if counting the bare-chested children.

The bedding cells lined the eastward wall, as demanded by luck and tradition. Despite her price she would be chosen. She was always chosen. Leading him by a single, callus-horned finger, she would hear grunts and whimpers and moans, and sometimes shrieks and sobs. A kind of numbness would own her, and she would flatten against her motions as if against a wall in a slice of shadow. And she would be *hidden*, even as she scampered nude before the lecherous eyes of many.

Very similar to Qirri, when she thought about it, watching Galian's hanging grin.

Perhaps this would be easy . . . dying.

———⚫———

The old Wizard did not flee. He found himself chasing the Nonman King instead, muttering Wards as he tripped across the floors. With every step the Nonman King dragged his Surillic Point with him, illuminating the wasted interior of the Coffers.

Rather than retreat, the great Wracu watched eyeless.

'*Wutteät!*' Cleric bellowed.

Cold pricked the Wizard's skin, for Wutteät was a name drawn from the most ancient days of the War, when Men were little more than slaves or vermin. Wutteät the Terrible. The Black-and-Golden . . .

The Father of Dragons.

Revealed in all his decayed glory, the Wracu reared with chitinous grace, its neck hooking like a swan's, its mammoth head poised low. Blinding vomit cracked its lizard grin.

Fire.

Stone blasting. Gold melting. Unlike anything Achamian had ever dreamed. The world vanished, and all became white blindness, roaring, sparking. His outermost Wards simply blew away. His innermost buckled about cracks like incandescent veins.

'Cleric!' he cried, feeling a tongue of flame lap his arm and cheek.

There was no time. Blinking, he stepped into the air, into utter blackness – the Nonman's Surillic Point had winked into nonexistence.

Everyone was blind.

The wheezing grate of furnace bellows. Then a second geyser of fiery gold, this one roiling *beneath* his feet. Thunder and clacking stone. The light of it painted the ceiling and high pillars in pulsing tan and yellow. Crying out new Wards, Achamian climbed into the gap of a collapsed lintel, stepped through the grand chamber's false ceiling high into the dark.

'I am Quya!' the Nonman King cried from places unseen. 'I am Ishroi! Five of your sons and daughters have I slain!'

'YOU ARE BUT A SNAIL!' the impossible beast roared. 'A SNAIL TORN FROM ITS SHELL!'

'I am Nil'giccas – *I am Cleric!* And you will hear my sermon!'

Even high and hidden, Achamian could tell the Nonman ran as he called out, sprinted over ruin.

'FOOL. I AM THE *FIRST*. MY HIDE IS BRONZE. MY BONES ARE IRON!'

Above the ceiling, the old Wizard floated through a second, more barren world, one roofed with hanging precipices and floored with racks of masonry, ancient and enormous.

'You are blind!' Cleric shouted, the resonance of his voice thinned by the thunder that it followed. 'You are a beggar, a scavenger, a prisoner of your own spite! Your flesh is rotted. The stone of your strength cracked long ago!'

'AS THE AGES HAVE ROTTED YOUR SOUL, CÛNUROI!'

The beast spit another cataract of roaring fire, illuminating all the chinks and breaches in the ceiling. Achamian walked across emptiness, toward the central pit, which given the darkness of the cavernous attic, glowed like an afterlife of fire. Robbed of their supporting columns, the granite lintels had sheered according to the caprice of load and fracture. He alighted on the longest of these ribs, strode down the length of its powdered back. Fires small and large burned throughout the pillared spaces below. He saw Cleric – the briefest of glimpses – flit between distant pillars and vanish into far shadows. He was running circles . . .

'If I perish a fool!' the Nonman cried, 'then I perish my own fool! Not a slave like you, *Wracu'jaroi!*'

Achamian paused at the hanging precipice, gazed down upon the heaving beast. Coiled like a bloated serpent, the Father of Dragons turned and turned to the sound of Cleric's voice, like a leashed dog about its stake, only retching fire instead of barking, maelstroms that engulfed the scorched aisles.

'I EXCEED MY MAKERS,' the scale-shining beast thundered. 'NOT EVEN THE BLACK HEAVEN COMMANDS ME!'

The old Wizard swayed on his perch, squinted against the smoke and sparks that buffeted his Wards. Cleric distracted the creature, he knew. Using taunts to goad its pride, the Nonman King provoked it precisely so that Achamian could do what he was doing . . .

If only he knew what that was.

'Spinning in circles,' Cleric cried laughing, 'twisting hide against hide! So it has always been, *Wracu'jaroi*! Think! Think of the desolate ages!'

The blind beast stamped to and fro directly below. It swung its horn-crowned head in an attempt to anticipate the running Nonman, spewed torrents of braided fire. Achamian swayed, nearly retched for the reek of putrescence.

'DESOLATION IS MY BIRTHRIGHT!'

Think, old man! Think!

'SUCH *THINGS* THAT I REMEMBER, CÛNUROI! TWISTING IN THE VOID FOR SAILING AGES! WATCHING MY MAKERS DESCEND AS LOCUSTS UPON WORLD AFTER WORLD, REDUCING EACH TO ONE HUNDRED AND FORTY-FOUR THOUSAND – AND WAILING TO FIND THEMSELVES STILL DAMNED!'

Dragons! Monstrosities literally bred to battle and destroy the ancient Quya. So much of the Gnostic armoury was devoted to sorcerous duals or the mass killing of mundane Men . . .

What did Seswatha use?

'Only to arrive *here* broken and exhausted!' Cleric cried.

'YES – *YES!* AT LAST, THE *PROMISED* WORLD! I WAS THE FIRST – THE *FIRST!* WITH DREAD SIL UPON MY SHOULDERS, I WAS THE FIRST TO STEP FROM OUR HALLOWED ARK, TO SET EYES UPON THE LAND OF OUR REDEMPTION!'

The Nonman's laughter rose clear as sunlight from the booming echoes.

'And now look at you! Blind! Hidden in the dirt! Curled about the shit of dead ages!'

A cry like the blast of many waters. 'BECAUSE THIS WORLD YET LIVES!' the undead beast roared. 'BECAUSE THIS WORLD REFUSES TO DIE!'

Teetering above the monstrosity, Achamian shouted his Cant, a skinny old man hollering in a skinny old voice. The Noviratic Spike, a Gnostic War-Cant contrived to batter through great city gates.

'MURDER! MURDER IS OUR SALVATION!'

Light balled in Achamian's outstretched palms. The mighty Wracu lashed its head from side to panicked side, raised its smoking snout at the instant of the Cant's completion. Lines of light snapped in and out, deflecting and intersecting, forming a flying sheet of triangles, reproducing tip to tip, base to base, flashing down as swift as any bolt or arrow . . .

A noise that struck blood from the skin.

The Spike exploded against the creature's left shoulder, hammered it squealing down the side of its mound. Thrashing, Wutteät howled fire into the air. A brilliant geyser jetted up through the ceiling pit, a rooster's tail of brilliance washed across the cavern roof. Cascades of raw stone came crashing down.

Achamian crouched low on the lintel, muttered Ward after Ward.

A thunderclap from below.

And he heard it through the dragon's mewling shriek: the sound of a Nonman Quya singing his world-breaking song. The sound of a famed Ishroi, a hero of dead ages, closing with his ancient foe.

The old Wizard stood firm on his perch, cried out another Noviratic Cant. Below him, the Father of Dragons coiled in defence, spewed fire into looms of Quyan incandescence. Light flared from the Wizard's palms, made crimson glass of his hands . . .

But the dragon had coiled to *leap*, not to shield. The Wizard's Spike gouged slopes of treasure and rubble. Mouldered and wretched, the dragon vaulted into the underworld attic, stretched forth its diseased wings. For a crazed heartbeat, Achamian found himself standing frail and astonished beneath the plated monstrosity. Light from the conflagration below illuminated its undersides, gleamed across horns and scaled flanges. Wings scooped dark air . . .

It *knew*, Achamian realized. The beast drew back its battered skull, yanked open its maw in a feline hiss.

It knew precisely where he stood.

Fire.

Wards dissolving like egg whites in a stream. Concussions. Blistering skin. The triggering of incipient Wards . . .

The pier of stone collapsed beneath his feet.

'YEARS UNCOUNTED!' it boomed from the cavern attic. 'TEN THOUSAND SEASONS HAVE I LIVED WITHOUT EYES!'

The old Wizard fell, cartwheeled down the beast's heap of treasure and debris. Blinking. Coughing. He tried to claw his way upright, too stunned to orchestrate the counterpoise of voices, inner and outer, required for sorcery. He beat at his burning hair and beard. He felt an arm draw him up, saw Cleric peering down at him, the porcelain lines of worry and relief. He heard the whoosh of conflagration, the clack and thunder of enormous collapses. Ancient pillars toppled. Sheets of masonry dropped. The world itself seemed to shrug, then crash upon them.

Masses of stone pummelled the Nonman's Wards, a rain of godlike fists.

The last shreds of light were pinched to utter black.

Ringing ears. The taste of dust.

'It has buried us,' the Nonman King said in the clacking aftermath. 'Shut us in.'

She kicks off her boots.

She unties the laces of her jacket, pulls it back from her bare shoulders, lets it slide of its own weight down her arms. She shakes it from her wrists. It slumps across the humus.

She clasps her shift, winces at the reek of it as she draws it over her head. The swathes of down in her armpits tingle. Open air finds her breasts. Her nipples rise to the kissing breeze.

She unlaces her leather breeches. Wriggling, she pushes them below her knees. She steps from them. Open air finds her thighs . . . her sex.

She grabs the wire Circumfix – the one she found on the battlefield – hanging between her breasts. But she releases it, loathe to forsake the protection of symbols – even false ones.

Motionless, the scalpers gaze. Sarl gropes his crotch with his free hand. The Captain's head continues to glare from the crook of his arm. Even Koll, wasted to the very lip of death, watches with licentious hunger. They are but five, yet countless others seem to crowd them, making pews of the forested ruins, all gazing with lidless eyes, some in outrage, others with pity and hope, and still more with lust and crass desire.

She thought the Qirri would ease her passage, that it might have delivered her to the place where she had always hidden – for this was nothing new. But she was wrong. You have to be *more* than your motions to hide behind them, and she is not.

The Qirri has whittled her down to the bone of what happens.

She shudders with something deeper than shame, as if garments more profound than leather and fabric have been shed. The cloth of hope and flattery, perhaps – all the things she has called herself in the pursuit of her pain-numbing vanities. Sorceress. Princess. Warrior. All the lies she has conjured to hide the fact of her slavery.

For the first time, it seems, she is wholly what scripture has made of her – and nothing more. The quiver on the hip of the bowman. The pillow beneath the head of the king. She is chattel. She is sustenance. She is pleasure and progeny . . .

She is naked.

The two crouched for what seemed a hundred heartbeats after the clamour had settled, probing the cavernous black with pricked ears. They heard nothing, save the groan and clatter of settling debris.

Wielding ethereal geometries, the old Wizard and the Nonman King began heaving aside masses of rock and masonry. Throughout history, kings and princes had sought to bend the Few to menial tasks, to works that only the sweat and misery of thousands could otherwise accomplish. Roads. Fortifications. Temples. Wars had been fought to resist them. For men who could manipulate the very frame of existence, sorcerers, demanding such mean labour was nothing less than an outrage, akin to asking lords to wash the feet of beggars. As Tsotekara, the Grandmaster of the extinct Surartu, famously declared to Triamis the Great: to do as slaves was to *be* as slaves.

Even still, caprice demands all men, no matter how exalted their station, play the menial from time to time. Every sorcerer living knew some Cant adapted to the moving of earth.

The darkness clacked and roared with their excavations. The devastation of the Coffers stretched out behind them, easily outrunning their paltry light, a twilight world the old Wizard was loathe to consider, lest he recall the hopeless task of finding a single golden map-case amid such wrack and ruin. Only two columns stood that they could see; the others lay heaped and toppled like a felled forest. Shelves of rock continued to fall from the inverted cliffs and valleys hanging above, sporadically showering the blasted landscape with debris.

Huffing with effort, Achamian sank pinions into the mounded wreckage, raked it away with the flash of miracle lights. More debris would tumble into the gap he had cleared but never quite so much as he had removed. Braced on ever-uncertain footing – spilled gravel, canted lintels, or the curve of pillar drums – they thundered forward, dredging the entrance clear. When light at last rimmed the uppermost rocks before them, they paused to collect their breath and courage.

'The beast awaits us,' Cleric said.

Achamian nodded. He could see fell Wutteät in his soul's eye, poised to flush the waiting passage with coiling fire. Ambush was a notorious tactic of the Wracu. For all their savage might, they were exceedingly intelligent and devious creatures – far more so than Sranc. They had no choice but to rush the burrow, somehow survive the sum of its power . . .

'One of us must shield,' he said, 'while the other casts into the fire.'

The Nonman King began to nod, then whirled toward the darkness behind them.

Frowning, Achamian followed his gaze into the high void, peered squinting. He raised a thumb to scratch away a fleck of grit . . .

It breached the light – smoke that became a ghost that became shining, bestial reality – its claws outstretched, its wings hooked about emptiness, its horn-crowned head vanishing behind gaping jaws . . .

The ancient dragon dropped out of the blackness. Achamian threw up futile arms.

Conflagration.

The men stare at her, speechless.

'What do you see?' she asks.

Her voice seems to jar them. Galian's face darkens in unaccountable rage.

'See?' he cries, his face twitching about a compulsive blink. 'I see a world of plunder. You . . . The Coffers yonder . . . And when we return, every delicacy, every peach, and every silk pillow in the Three Seas! I see a *tasty* world, my little Whore-Imperial, and I intend to feast!'

Whore. The word stirs something within her, a habit long forgotten. She knows this, knows how to bridle and ride the crazed passions of men . . .

'And your soul?' she asks without passion. 'What of your soul?'

'Will be no worse for pillaging a witch, I assure you.'

'And pillaging,' Pokwas laughs from his side. There is something lecherous and angular in the Zeümi Sword-dancer's bearing, as if he leans over legs already prised open. She can even see the curve of his phallus through his breeches. 'And pillaging . . . and *pillaging* . . .'

Galian strides toward her.

She wracks her soul, searching for the hate that has always been the engine of her strength, but she can only summon moments of tenderness and love. She smiles, blinking tears. She draws the curve of her belly into warm palms. This is the first time, it seems, that she dares *clutch*, dares the making real that comes with grasping.

Hello, little one . . .

He grabs her throat, turns her head from side to side.

'Sweet Sejenus . . .' he murmurs with an almost tender breath. 'You *are* a true beauty . . . A pity about the maggot.'

'Maggot?' she gasps.

'The grub you carry in your womb.'

Tears spill from her eyes. 'What about it?' she asks about a sob.

The Columnary leans close enough to lick her face. 'I fear it will not survive me.'

'No! Plea—!'

'No indeed!' he cries with renewed cruelty. 'No *worms* in our peaches, eh, boys?'

Once again Pokwas and Xonghis laugh, this time like nervous adolescents. They have been led and they have been drawn. They have stumbled across obsessed-over boundaries, only to find themselves thinking unthinkable things.

Yatwer . . . Dear Goddess, please . . .

Her head caught in the vise of his hands, she stares down the curve of her cheeks, and somehow her gaze finds his manic glare, latches . . .

The Judging Eye opens.

She finds herself peering into something . . . inexplicable.

Contradictory passions roil through her, as if she were the scalper's lifelong mistress, the one most punished, the one who *understood*. For there is no sin without weakness, no transgression without want or suffering. She sees the cracks through which his infant nature bleeds. The father's cane, the brother's fists. The starving marches, and the *need*, to be admired, to be respected, to *steal* what he covets . . .

She loves him, and she despises. But she finds herself fearing *for* him most of all.

Often has she wondered how she could describe it, seeing the morality of things let alone lives. Sometimes it seems more a matter of memory than vision, like sighting a familiar treatise in the house of a friend. The object itself stews with significance, but all the passages – cherished and offending – are indistinct. Only the sum can be seen, inchoate and confounding. This is what she most often sees: the abbreviated mash that is judgment passed, the balance of a soul, good and evil, writ in a stick-figure scrawl.

But sometimes, if she concentrates, the tome of a lived life flutters open beneath the Eye, and the *crimes themselves* become visible, the way carnal images flicker about the glimpse of a long-absent lover.

And sometimes, more rarely still, she sees the particulars of their coming damnation.

The Columnary stares, his eyes wide with panicked fury. She clutches his wrist.

'Galian . . .' she hears herself gasp. 'It's not too late. You *can* save yourself from . . . from . . .'

Something in her words or manner jars him from his intent – the trill of frantic sincerity, perhaps.

'Hell?' he laughs. 'There's *too many* of them.'

Such torment. Clenched and cringing, huddled in ways outside worldly dimensions. Prised and flayed, the innumerable petals of his soul peeled back in shrieks and sulphurous flame. Screams braided into screams, pains heaped upon agonies.

She sees it, his *future*, a gleam across his eyes, a fiery halo about his crown. His suffering disgorged like paint, smeared and stroked into obscene works of art. His soul passed from Ciphrang to feasting Ciphrang, dispensing anguish like milk through the endless ages.

She sees the truth of the Excruciata, the One Hundred-and-Eleven Hells depicted on the walls of the Junriüma in Sumna.

'Galian. *Galian*. You m-must listen. Please . . . You have no idea what awaits you!'

He tries to grin away his horror. He's strangling her as much as holding her now. 'Witch!' he spits. '*Witch!*'

'Shhhhh . . .' she manages to whisper. 'It will b—'

He slams her to the raw earth. She cries out. He thrusts apart her knees, pins her while fumbling with his breeches. Belts pinch her inner thighs. Twigs bite at her shoulders, her buttocks. Dead leaves press cold against her back, like reptilian scales. His breathing is ragged, his look unfocused. He smells of shit and rotted teeth.

The world spins and roars about the fact of his damnation.
She cries into his ear, murmurs, *'I forgive you . . .'*
Frees him of this final sin.

The beast had lain hidden, waiting for them to dig their way into the entrance antechamber, a dead end where they could not use the greater debris field to either flee or flank him. But it proved a treacherous trap. Had they not stood side by side, where the combined strength of their incipient defences purchased them the heartbeats they needed to reinforce their Wards, they would be dead.

Apparently Wutteät could not hear the distance between them . . .

Fire boiled over and around them, blinding them, ripping away the gossamer meanings they shouted against it. An inferno like no other, scorching some hard stone surfaces into liquid while exploding others.

Then the beast itself was on them, a crocodile falling upon sparrows. It clawed with feline savagery, tearing and rending, while the Gnostic sorcerer and the Quyan Mage sang in desperate tandem, slowing accumulating the glowing shells that preserved them.

The boom and crack of mountains breaking, and underneath, the rot of sorcery's unearthly murmur.

Roaring. Raging. Scales burnished, flashing as crimson as infant blood. Claws the size of wains swatting. The great saurian head ramming, snapping horns as thick as young trees.

Planes of spectral glass cracked and shattered, collapsed into aether. Rock rained down. Stone congealed like blood.

'It lives by its ears!' the old Wizard cried between thunders.

His eyes blazing, Nil'giccas nodded in immediate understanding.

The beast reared above them. Another incendiary eruption.

The world beyond their defences became an amorphous glare. Wards cracked and burned . . .

But the Nonman King was attacking, howling in tongues as old as his race. Achamian could scarce see the light of his conjuring, just the faint blue of lines like parabolic wires, arcing into the heights . . .

The inferno lifted, streamed exploding across the scorched heaps to their right. The fire sputtered into a ground-strumming shriek, and they saw Wutteät, the dread Father of Dragons, flailing backward, smoke pluming from its eye socket.

'The *head!*' Achamian screamed. '*Attack the head!*'

They assailed the beast, Man and Nonman, as in days of old. They threaded the air with arrays of wicked, dazzling illumination. And it screamed, squealed even, like a pig doused in burning oil.

They stepped into the cavernous air and pursued him. Wutteät's wings kicked the ground with gusts, swept up sheets of ash and dust. Yet they could see him.

Geometries of incandescence. Geometries of destruction.

Like a moth in a jar, Wutteät smashed its shoulders into the cragged ceiling, tried to bring stone down upon them. Deaf and blind, it spat fire across hanging cliffs . . .

The Gnostic sorcerer hung above one of the two remaining pillars, striking the thing with scissions and concussions. The Quyan Mage sailed an arc about the beast, uttering Cants that burned. They struck and struck until the iron of its bone glowed, until Wutteät's head was smashed ruin, a charred stump possessing jaws.

The beast dropped, and Achamian rushed to jubilation, thinking they had felled it. But it crashed into a lurch that became a run, its claws kicking up stone middens. It raised its blasted snout, snuffing against a piteous growl. Unerringly it charged toward the remnants of the entrance.

'No!' the Nonman King cried.

Coursing like a snake, it bolted through the punishing gauntlet of their sorcery, smashed through the entrance into the pale-glowing hollows beyond.

They pursued it into the breach, climbed as if up the throat of a toppled tower. But the dragon was too quick: they could already hear its shriek score the faraway sky. Climbing. Coughing. Breathless, they found themselves within the ring of the Turret, squinting up at the jagged circle of afternoon brilliance. His heart hammering with mortal violence, the old Wizard finally gained the summit.

Wutteät thrashed in the light of day, throwing up trees and gouts of dirt. It caromed against the Library walls, crashed like a thing thrown into the forest beyond. Trunks and limbs cracked. Over the wall's dusty halo, the crowns of a dozen trees convulsed and vanished. The beast spat wild gouts of fire, uttered shrieks that drove nails into their ears.

And then, suddenly, the dread beast was *flying*, white and black and golden, its ravaged wings buffeting the forest as though it were wheat. Scales shining, the Father of Dragons soared heavenward, spiralling and smoking like a bird afire. Astounded, the man and the Nonman watched, until finally, moth-small with distance, it vanished into the slow-tumbling flanks of a cloud.

Cleric stood atop the heights of a shattered inner wall, gazing high after the thing. Brush fires raged beyond him, throwing lines of orange across his jaw and cheek. His nimil chain glistened in the dry sunlight, and for the first time the old Wizard saw the faint lines of filigree worked across its innumerable links.

Herons. Herons and lions.

'Triumph!' Achamian cried out in relief and exaltation. 'A victory worthy *The Sagas*!'

He hesitated in sudden realization. What did glory mean, when none could remember it?

And what was life, without glory to illuminate it?

The Nonman turned his profile to him, said nothing.

'You won't remember, will you?'

'Shadow,' Nil'giccas replied, resuming his study of the distant sky. 'I will remember the shadow it casts . . .' He turned to regard the Wizard. 'Across the grief that follows.'

The grief that follows.

The old Wizard matched the Nonman King's gaze for what seemed a hundred heartbeats. Finally, he nodded in slow resignation, scratched his chin beneath what remained of his beard.

'Yes,' Achamian said. 'Seswatha loved you as well.'

<hr/>

Galian makes a noise, a grunt or a sob – she is not sure.

One moment he's an iron shadow grinding flaccid against her. Then he is gone.

She bolts upright, sees him arched across the forest floor, kicking his left foot, desperately clutching at his back. Koll stands above him, hunched and famine-frail, his hands clenching and unclenching. Galian flops onto his stomach, gags and screams. She sees a pommel jutting from below his left shoulder blade, a flower of crimson and black blooming through the links of his hauberk.

A breathless heartbeat passes. Xonghis rushes to assist Galian while Pokwas draws his great tulwar from his waist, sweeps it through the air before falling into his Sword-dancer stance.

'Fucking Stone Hag!' he cries. 'I knew I should have cut your throat!'

Still clutching Lord Kosoter's head, Sarl sits rocking on the Captain's inert back, begins cackling. Light sparkles through the screens of foliage beyond him – from the direction of the Holy Library. A roaring whoosh follows . . .

Pokwas falls upon Koll in sweeping fury. His blade seems like silver ink, sketching sigils through open air. Koll effortlessly threads the gauntlet, ducking, leaping . . .

The Zeümi Sword-dancer pauses, eyes round in disbelief.

Koll dives to his right, cartwheels across the ground like a crab, toward Sarl and his Captain's draining corpse. The Sergeant scrambles backward.

Koll flits past him, rolls past the Captain's forgotten pack, then comes to his feet brandishing Squirrel. His stance low, his look darts from Pokwas to Xonghis, who has taken up a flanking position, his bow drawn.

More explosions rock the near distance. A titanic roar shivers the sky.

The starved Stone Hag begins laughing, a sound that begins human but ends like screaming wolves. Xonghis releases his shaft. Koll swats with Squirrel but misses. The arrow thuds into his neck.

Koll falls backward but somehow rolls back onto his feet. With his free hand he clutches the shaft. Pulls.

Screams.

The fingers of his face break apart, then fly open.

Mimara lurches to her feet, stumbles to Galian, who lies dying.

Crying out in Zeümi, Pokwas rushes the thing called Koll, his tulwar cutting poetry into the air. Steel rings against steel. Squirrel is nicked but does not shatter. Xonghis lets fly two more arrows. The thing lunges clear the first, but the second catches it high in the thigh. It barely survives the black giant's hollering assault.

Mimara stands breathless. Qirri pulses through her, makes a war-drum of her heart.

Xonghis whirls at the sound of her approach, releases. His arrow whistles past her left ear – a sound like a rip. She plunges Galian's sword into the Imperial Tracker's exposed armpit. She feels his death, the *inside of him*, communicated through blade and grip.

Beyond their clearing, the forest burns about the silhouette of stumped ruins. Sarl has resumed his phlegmatic howl, his expression crushed into a thousand laughing lines.

The whooshing tulwar catches the thing called Koll mid-leap. It careens through the air, tries to land on its remaining leg, tumbles backward. Closing for the kill, the Zeümi howls in triumph . . .

Fails to hear her naked approach.

Smoke piled over the derelict fortifications, drawn twisting into the high blue sky. Within the ruined Library, several smaller fires fanned bright in the gusting wind, sending showers of sparks and ash over the old Wizard and the Nonman King.

'You don't have to do this!' Achamian cried.

Still standing upon the wall he had climbed to peer after the dragon, Cleric tore his runed purse from its leather cord. He stared at it meditatively, hefted it in his palm. Achamian felt his heart clutch at his breast, seeing it dandled so near open flame. He realized he has worshipped this thing. The shrivelled folds pinched into creases about its drawstring. The faint impression of weight bulging within, as though it contained a mouse. It seemed absurd that such a low object could become the talisman, the fetish from which the whole expedition had come to hang. A pouch filled with soot.

'No!' Achamian cried.

But it was too late. Cleric bent his head sideways, as if to itch his ear against his shoulder, then swung the pouch upside down. The ashes of Cû'jara Cinmoi poured out in a dun stream. The wind fanned it into ghostly nothingness.

'You don't have to do this!' the old Wizard cried.

The dark eyes fixed him.

'I do . . .'

'Why? Why?'

'Because I remember no triumph . . .' He flinched, seemed to lose the thread of his voice. Sudden fury claimed the heights of his expression. 'Only *betrayal!*' he roared. 'Heartbreak and ruin!'

A kind of indignation welled through the Wizard, the outrage that overcomes Men whenever absurdities are stacked too high. 'No!' he bellowed. 'I *will* name you! I will be your book, and *you will* read me! You are *Nil'giccas!* The Last King of Mansions – the greatest of the Siqû!'

The fires seemed to wax at the sound of Cleric's warbling laughter.

'Seswatha!' the Nonman called. 'Old dead friend . . . Will you hear my sermon?'

Achamian could only gaze in disgust and disbelief.

The Nonman muttered blasphemies that filled his eyes and mouth with light. He stepped from the summit and was aloft, climbing a floating arc that took him high above the fires surging through the courtyard.

'"Nil'giccas!" you call – *beseech!* as if trying to awaken some *truth* slumbering within me.'

Flames roiled about the silhouettes of trees. Smoke wreathed him. Heat rippled across his hanging form. And the Wizard realized that he was actually *going to attack.*

A Quya Master of old, a hero of wars older than the Tusk, made ready his murder.

'You think Nil'giccas is something *I* have lost!' the Nonman King called down. 'And therefore something that I can *recover!*'

Achamian was weary. He was bruised and he was burned – even well rested and whole, he would not dare a contest such as this. At least he was practised, thanks to the dragon. He could feel the Cants and Wards within him, tingling weaves of arcane meaning, hanging like possibilities . . .

Yet he did not strike.

'You forget,' Cleric shouted, 'that before the Nonman King's passing, *I did not exist!*'

The figure continued floating on a rising arc, one that took Achamian as its compass point. Sheets of stone toppled into the inferno below, kicking constellations of sparks in the wind.

'I can no more recover him than you can recover your mother's virgin womb.'

Achamian stood rooted and frail before the rising conflagration. *Strike!* something howled within him. *Strike now!*

'I am Incariol!' the Nonman screamed. '*Cleric!* And you shall not survive my lesson!'

But instead of attacking, the old Wizard arrayed himself with Wards, cloaked himself with shining panes of light. He had flattered himself after the underworld debacle of Cil-Aujas, told himself that perhaps Cleric was not so mighty, that the rot that had devoured so much of his soul had blunted his meanings as well . . .

Now he was not so sure.

Strike, you fool!

'You think *me* the cripple!' Nil'giccas cried. 'You think Cleric the *ruin* of someone whole! But you are wrong, Seswatha! I am the *Truth!*'

The Nonman King had climbed a half-spiral above burning bark and foliage, over headless towers and blunted walls. Now he hung motionless before the monumental frame of the Turret.

'We *are* Many!' the Erratic roared. '*We are legion!* What you call your soul is nothing but a confusion, an inability! A plurality that cannot count the moments that divide it and so calls itself One.'

His eyes flared white. Words boomed out, words that made a crimson globe of his head and face. The sound of vacant space ripping, a growl in the deepest pocket of the ear. Abstractions lashed the open air between them, wracked Achamian's Wards. The old Wizard raised arms against the glittering violence.

'Only when memory is stripped away!' Cleric cried out, the glow fading from his eyes. 'Only then is Being revealed as pure Becoming! Only *when the past dies* can we shrug aside the burden that is our Soul!'

Fractal lights tangled the figure's outstretched arms. More arcane words, reverberating across ethereal surfaces. More flashing Abstractions, cracking and hissing across the glowing shells that shielded the Wizard. Fire consumed the thronging scrub and trees. Fire garnished the truncated walls. About them, the famed court-yards of the Holy Library had become burning pits.

'Only then does the Darkness sing untrammelled!' Cleric cried. 'Only then!'

'And yet you seek memories!' the Wizard cried, at last delivered to tears.

'To *be*! Being is not a choice!'

'But you claim Being is deception!'

'Yes!'

'But that is nonsense! Madness!'

Again the Nonman King laughed.

'That is Becoming.'

The forests are burning.

Pokwas jerks around so quickly that the pommel is torn from her hands. *You!* his glaring eyes shout. Blood spills from his strange smile.

'The Slog of Slogs!' the mad Sergeant howls in their periphery. 'I told *you*, boys! I told you we would stack them!'

She retreats before the Sword-dancer's groping lurch. He skids to his knees, sways over sheeted leaves. His eyes find Galian, then Xonghis. He looks to her with childlike curiosity. Blood bubbles to his lips.

'I em-embrace . . .' he gasps. 'I-I . . .'

He slumps to his side, flops across the ground.

She steps around him, stumbles to stand over the thing called Koll.

'Why?' she cries, and a cold part of her is surprised by the salt and heat of her tears. 'Why would you save me? *Sacrifice* yourself! I am the daughter of your enemy! Your enemy!'

'Kill . . . me . . .' it coughs.

'Tell me! Soma!'

'Mim . . . Mim . . .'

'Who? Who is your handler?'

Something hooks her stomach. The madness of what just happened, the debasement, the transcendence, has blinded her to the obscenity. This thing before her has been cut from the meat of the World. Were it sorcerous, it would have possessed the numb glaze of unreality. It is raw and abhorrent instead. Suddenly she cannot look away from the mastications of its mouth, the way the lipless gums climb unbroken to the lidless eyes, to the air-clawing digits, which are furred and skinned and ridged with apparently random fragments of face.

Revulsion does not so much course as slam through her.

'I beg . . .' it gasps. '*Beg you* . . .'

Bile rises to the back of her throat. She draws away from the thing, lurches backward, falls to her rump, catches herself on a single thrown arm . . .

Smoke twines through the air between them, a translucent veil. Through it, she watches spasms rock the skin-spy.

Sarl rushes from nowhere, bent and bandied. He lands on the creature, drives his sword square through its chest. The thing clutches at him, but the mad Sergeant wrenches his blade with vicious strength, back and forth, as if testing a hated wagon's brake.

'Yeeesss!' he screams up to the broken canopy. *'Yeeessss!'*

The mad Sergeant turns to her with canines bared. His eyes are crimson slits. Blood sops his beard.

'A real *chopper!*'

The thrashing weakens beneath him. The facial digits fall slack at the same instant. Sarl lowers his cheek against the fist he holds atop his pommel. Gasping, he wipes a filthy cuff across his face, manages only to smear the blood. He releases his sword, then with a chuckle like a dog's growl, he draws his knife. He crawls over the creature, sways above it with a knee on either of its shoulders.

She watches dumbstruck.

'*Spider-face,*' he grunts, hacking and sawing with his knife. A manic grin squeezes his eyes into two more creases. 'A *thousand* gold Kellics at least!'

Madness, is all she can think.

She runs, heedless of her bearings or her nakedness.

Away. She must get away from all the madness.

The whole World burns.

And so they battled, the Gnostic Wizard uttering no Cants, the Quyan Mage speaking no Wards. Broken walls encircled them, surrounded in turn by the oily tumble of smoke and trees wrapped in shining flame.

Hanging high before the Turret, the inhuman Mage blazed with arcane meaning, unleashed a logic raised to killing light.

His feet braced against the earth, the human Wizard sang his unholy counterargument, wrapping himself in glowing spheres, long-winded pyramidal forms, planes arrayed to deflect dread energies outward.

The First Quyan Fold. The Ribs of Gotagga.

Burning cables. Sparks so brilliant they blinded. Concussions so immense they blew sheets of debris from the crests of the surrounding walls. Blisters of warding light cracked, slumped before sheering into nothingness.

And the dread voices droned on, unravelling into echoes too cavernous to be called sound, ringing from Heaven's vault as if it loomed as low as a cellar ceiling.

Achamian shouted between gasps of fiery air. He raised Ward after Ward, only to see them smashed, swept away.

The Third Concentric. The ever-risky Cross of Arches.

But the Quya Master was like a sun above him, glaring with destruction, cracking his defences with wicked and relentless incandescence. Beating. Hammering. Scissoring. A rain of cataclysms. Until Achamian was breathless and stammering, able to cough out only the lowest and quickest Wards.

For the briefest of instants, the underworld angel above him paused.

'Madness!' the Wizard cried out in sobbing frustration. 'This is not you!'

Fire crackled and hissed, filling the heartbeat of silence between them.

'Can't you see!' the Nonman King cried. 'Your appeals *only incite me*! You will die and I will remember! Because all you do is reach for the love I bear you!'

'No! I will not strike you!'

The face of Nil'giccas resolved from the dwindling glare. The setting sun rimmed his scalp with sickles of gold. 'I remember . . . I remember your name . . .'

Light filled his howling mouth – blasphemous meaning . . .

At long last the Wizard struck.

An Odaini Concussion Cant. Simple and low, meant only to stun – to knock back into reason perhaps. But Nil'giccas had floated above sharp ruin . . .

He plummeted from on high, broke about a low spine of stone. The ground fires caught and consumed him.

The old Wizard puffed out the flames with a sorcerous cry. He hobbled around blocks and between flanged foundations, swallowing at the sobs that wracked him. Streamers of smoke twisted and dissolved about his passage.

He found the Nonman King prostrate across a shoulder-high segment of wall, bent as though he had half fallen from bed. Black scored his milk-white skin. Blisters puckered his cheek and scalp. Blood sopped the heron and lion links of his nimil harness. He seemed that much more broken, given the perfection of his form.

'What just happened?' Nil'giccas gasped, hacking gouts of blood with the words. His lips worked about the glistening arc of his fused teeth. 'Wh-what just . . .'

'You found glory,' the old Wizard croaked. He coughed as if at some fact too acrid to be breathed. He reached out to clutch the Nonman's cheek, saw Death swirl up in the eyes of his ancient friend. He watched the spark of sight dull into sightlessness. Cleric's body heaved, then settled, as if finally coming to peace with its own anguished corporeality.

Blood pooled in the mortises.

Burned, battered, the old Wizard looked about, from the wreckage of the Library out to the blazing forests of Sauglish. This was how it would end, he realized . . . The was how all of it would end.

Heartbreak and fire.

She runs.

Twigs and branches pinch and cut her feet, but it seems proper that she should suffer. The breeze brushes like silk across her body, but it seems proper that she should find succour for her grievances. Leaves lash her arms and outer thighs.

Horror animates her. Horror that runs with her legs. Horror that tingles throughout her body, heat rimmed with cold, as if she bleeds from a thousand internal wounds.

She clutches her belly. She assumed she would feel it hang from her as she ran, the life she carried. But it is at one with her, the centring counterweight, the ligament that binds her to future and fate.

She climbs a low rise, a place away from the eye-stabbing smoke. She turns, glimpses the flicker of sorcery. She climbs higher, searching for a break in the canopy. She sees it once again, luminescent white lines twisting like language from the Library. She sees a form hanging, a dark figure silvered about the waist and shoulders, suspended over the walled depths adjacent to a destroyed citadel – what looks like a broken amphorae jutting from the ground.

Cleric, she thinks. *Ishroi* . . .

She turns, and begins walking back the way she came.

The Skin Eaters lay strewn like castaway clothes. The Wizard stumbled to his knees at the sight of the carnage.

'Where is she?' he cried at the last man living – Sarl, looking like something out of a child's nightmare.

'The Coffers!' the mad scalper croaked. He raised his hands in crazed gesticulation. Something bloody flapped in the right. 'Make ready, boys! Plunder them like a whore! Shake them like your purple pommel!'

'What happened here?' Achamian cried. He looked from dead man to dead man. Galian. Pokwas. Xonghis.

The Captain . . .

The very World pitched beneath his feet.

Suddenly the thing swinging in Sarl's hand became clear, the digits knuckled with fragments of expression. . .

A skin-spy's face.

'Speak up, fool! *What happened?*'

'Ahhh,' Sarl crooned to him. 'The World will be our wicked little peach! We'll be princes! *Princes!*'

The old Wizard seized him about the shoulders. 'Where's Mimara . . . Where's *my daughter?*'

The madman nodded and gazed the way he had that second night in the Cocked Leg's common room, after smashing his wine bowl. A *knowing* gaze, the Wizard suddenly realized, one brimming with the intuition of the insane . . .

That Fate is madder still.

Achamian turned to the demand of some instinct, peered . . . glimpsed something slight passing through screens of smoke. He fairly doubled over for relief when she stepped naked from a fire-curtained world.

She ran to him, clutched his shoulders as he grinned and keened.

'You live!' he cried like a fool.

'As do you.'

'You're naked!'

Her look of reproach made him want to cry out for joy.

'And they're dead,' she said. '*All* of them,' she added, with a glance at Sarl. 'Come . . . We must flee this fire.'

They moved with the quickness of looters racing dawn. She retrieved Squirrel, then paused at Xonghis to relieve him of the stolen Chorae, the one loose, the other affixed to a fletched shaft. Achamian gathered her clothing, threw a rotted cloak about her shoulders. Then together they stumbled and ran through the smoking galleries.

The mad Sergeant stayed, cradling the Captain's hoary head, rocking on his rump with laughter and congratulating his dead fellows.

'Kiampas! Eh? *Kiampas!*'

Night swallows the earth. Only the light of stubborn fires twinkles through the courtyards of the ruined Library.

Sitting on scorched earth, knee pressed against knee, they take Cleric's pouch and slowly press the inside out. They wet their fingers, run them along the residue. The black gathers into a thin crescent against the pad of their fingers. Out of some communal understanding, they reach across the meagre space between them, place their fingers upon the other's tongue.

Relief crashes through them as a tingling wave, leaving dizziness and nausea in its wake.

Qirri. Blessed Qirri.

They build a bier of charred wood and scrub, pile it as high as their shoulders. The corpse of the Nonman King they place upon it. They set it alight, watch the flame climb in shingles, until the illustrious form is engulfed in rushing fire. Then they climb into the starlit ruin of the Turret and descend into the absolute blackness of the Coffers. Achamian utters a Bar of Heaven, and the door of creation cracks open, revealing subterranean wrack and ruin.

'Should have used this earlier,' he mutters as the light fades from his eyes and mouth.

Mimara looks to him, clutching her shoulders against memories of Cil-Aujas.

'I could have saved more of my beard!' he explains with a rueful smile.

They labour by sorcerous light, wracked by a thirst and a hunger they do not feel. Deep into the night.

They find a shirt of ensorcelled mail, golden, as light as silk and as hard as nimil. Sheära, the Wizard calls it, 'Sun-skin,' a far antique gift from the School of Mihtrûl. Mimara sheds her rags and dons it against her naked skin. Cinched about the waist it falls to her thighs, humming with a warmth all its own. She stows her Chorae in her boot to avoid killing the ancient magic. They find a bronze knife engraved with runes that glower in certain angles of light. This too Mimara takes, as a complement to poor Squirrel.

At last they find *it*, the golden map-case from Achamian's Dreams.

'It's broken,' he murmurs with something resembling horror.

She watches the Wizard pry apart the tubing, then gingerly draw out the vellum sheet curled within.

They emerge from the Turret looking like wraiths for the dust and filth that powders them. Dawn has broken. The walls loom dark and chill against the gold of the eastern sky. Tailings of smoke rise from random clutches of ash and charcoal. Silence rings through the waking chorus of birdsong.

The bier has burned down to a smoking heap. All that remains of Nil'giccas is his nimil hauberk, which lies unscathed save for black scorching. With wary fingers, the Wizard pulls it open, revealing the chalk of a different ash. Mimara gathers it along the edge of her new knife, spoons it with breathless care into the Nonman King's rune-stamped pouch . . .

'Look,' the Wizard says in a cracked voice.

She turns, sees a figure watching them from a cleft in the great outer wall. Sarl, she realizes after a heartbeat of ocular confusion, for hanging below the Sergeant's scrambled grin *another face smiles*. The Captain, she realizes with more numbness than horror. Sarl has braided the severed head's hair into his beard, so that the face swings about his groin, lips tented about an arrow shaft. A maniacal grimace.

'*Sometimes the dead* bounce!' she remembers the mad Sergeant crying on the ashen plains. '*Sometimes old men awaken behind the eyes of babes! Sometimes wolves . . .*'

Sarl. The last surviving Skin Eater.

She finishes gathering the ash, and the Wizard pulls the nimil shirt from the heap. It smokes as he shakes it. He drapes it over the singed pelts that clad him. Too large, and without hooks or clasps, it hangs as a kind of cloak from his shoulders, black belied by a low, silvery glimmer.

Still propped between stone jaws, Sarl watches them from a distance. Sunlight warms the world beyond him.

Once again they sit knee to knee, as father and daughter. Once again they taste the other's finger. But this time the ash is more white than black, and the strength that shivers through them has a more melancholy tenor. The Captain and the mad Sergeant are still watching them when they turn.

Mimara gazes at him, thinking she should at least call out. But even from a distance she can see the blood painting the creases of his face. And the Captain's mood looks exceedingly foul.

'*A real chopper!*'

By some miracle an oak leaf falls before her, swinging to and fro through the air. She picks it out of emptiness. Purple lines vein the lobes of waxy green. Yielding to an unaccountable impulse, she takes Cleric's pouch and taps a small pile of ash into the bowl of the leaf, which she then folds around it. Gazing at Sarl, she sets the small packet upon a low marble stump jutting from the earth before her – an armless shoulder.

'What are you doing?' Achamian asks.

'I don't know.'

The scalper watches them, as taut and intent as any other starving animal. They hear a low-clucking gurgle . . .

Then horns, Sranc horns, pitch doom across the horizon. Mimara clutches her belly through her armour.

'Come,' she says to the old Wizard. 'I tire of Sauglish.'

Interlude: Ishuäl

The heroes among us, they are the true slaves. Thrust against the limits of mortality, they alone feel the bite of their shackles. So they rage. So they fight.

We only have as much freedom as we have slack in our chains. Only those who dare nothing are truly free.

—Suörtagal, *Epimeditations*

Late Summer, 20 New Imperial Year (4132 Year-of-the-Tusk), Kûniüri

They flee through the forests and valleys of what was once Kûniüri, more exposed, more fugitive, than at any time in their tumultuous lives. A week passes before the skinnies find them.

Nights of madness follow.

She finds it strange the way they simply appear out of otherwise idyllic forests. Sranc. Famished mobs of them. They are like a nocturnal cancer, poisonous for not belonging. The Wizard explains their manufacture, how in ages lost the Inchoroi used the Tekne to pervert the *Bios* of the Nonmen. 'They coveted the world,' he says, 'so they fashioned a race that would spare it, creatures that would hunt their foes only, consuming the low things of the earth otherwise.'

The fugitive couple cleaves to the sun as much as possible during the days, but they are often attacked regardless. The old Wizard wants to walk above the mayhem, but she refuses to abandon her two Chorae. So each night they search for high places where they can huddle behind his Wards.

It is always the same. The old Wizard bids her to crouch at his side, to take care that she not let her Chorae stray too close to the circuit of his sorcerous defences. And he sings his mad-muttering song, assails their howling rush with wicked lights. They do not stop. They never stop, not even when the smoke of their burning bodies pillars the sky. They throw themselves at the glowing curves, shrieking and wheezing and hacking. Crude axes, hammers, and swords. Loose strips of iron for armour. Gibbering chieftains decked in what totems and heirlooms the brutes recognize. And their deranged faces, indistinguishable from the porcelain perfection of Nil'giccas when expressionless, crazed with seams and wrinkles otherwise, enough to make Sarl seem a smooth-cheeked youth in comparison.

The Wizard lets the abominations gather, until all is threshing madness about them – until it seems the two of them occupy a glowing bubble in Hell. Then, while Mimara hugs the earth, he cuts them down with glittering Compasses of Noshainrau. The slaughter is magnificent and appalling. And yet still they come, night after night, their dog phalluses prodding their dog bellies.

The rare nights when they fail to appear, she dreams of them, night terrors that give voice to the screams she denies herself while awake.

Food is scarce, so much so they sometimes sob for the rare deer the Wizard is able to take down. Once, on the reeded verge of a marsh, he fells a massive, hoary old creature he calls a musk-ox. The smell alone would have made her gag were she still a child of the brothel, let alone the Andiamine Heights. Yet they fall upon the carcass like starving dogs. The mosquitoes are so bad the Wizard raises Wards against them.

Sleep is the rarest of luxuries. They double their ration of Qirri, then double it yet again. She comes to appreciate the subtlety of tyranny, the way it lurches into stark prominence in times of scarcity and withdraws into invisibility in times of plenty. She manages to forget her old misgivings. For all the Wizard's power, they would be dead a hundred times were it not for the Qirri and the illicit strength that is its gift . . .

Were it not for Nil'giccas.

She whispers prayers for him sometimes, Cleric, even though she knows his soul is irrevocably lost to Hell. There is no harm in prayers.

He screams somewhere, she thinks. His shade.

The attacks begin to abate when the Demua Mountains first serrate the curtains of mist across the horizon. The Wizard's ancient Map makes no sense whatsoever to her eyes. Scrollwork frames the interior, the pale residue of paints that had once illuminated the thing but had long since moulted. Achamian tells her how the ancient Kûniüri, like all peoples, observed customs of representation peculiar to them and them alone. The Map, he says, counts mountains, uses them as markers to find Ishuäl.

'What do you expect to find?'

'Honeycakes and beer!' he snaps.

The testiness of his old manner is quick to return whenever she raises questions that recall the mad proportions of his gambit. After all the death and toil, the possibility that they will find *nothing* remains – a fact the old Wizard is loathe to consider.

But she has learned how to weather his moods, just as he has learned how to master hers. They no longer fall into spirals of senseless retribution – at least not as frequently.

'Akka . . . Come now.'

'The *truth* of Kellhus! I've told you this a hundred times, Mimara – more!'

She glares at him.

Achamian collects himself with a long-drawn breath. 'One cannot raise walls against what has been forgotten,' he says, reciting a proverb she has heard before. 'And nothing is so forgotten as Ishuäl. For two thousand years it has survived – in the very shadow of Golgotterath, no less!'

She watches him the way she always watches him when he annoys her with the vehemence of his claims. Never, it seems to her, has she known a man more desperate to be believed. She looks down to her belly, which she holds in two palms, murmurs, 'Your father can be a fool sometimes . . .'

'*Think*, Mimara,' he says, balling his fists about his exasperation. As much as he hates discussing Ishuäl, he despises recalling his paternity more. 'The Dûnyain sent one son into the wild. *One son*, and within twenty years he commands all the Three Seas! We are here to *remember* – nothing more, nothing less. Remember and if need be, raise walls.'

'Against the Aspect-Emperor.'

'Against the Truth.'

Days of peace follow. The mountains pile into prominence on the horizon. They remind her, curiously enough, of the Meneanor Sea in winter, with dark waves arrayed in chaotic ranks, white-capped and cloven. After spending several watches examining the Map and staring across the range, the Wizard decides they have come too far south, so they strike north across the Demua's gullied foundations.

She wonders at her burgeoning pregnancy. In the brothel pregnancy was nothing less than a horrific affliction – suffering for those forced to abort, heartbreak for those who carried to term, since invariably the infant would be taken. What little she knows she has gleaned from her mother when she carried the twins. But where the Empress had continually huffed and complained, Mimara's swollen womb seems little more than a flimsy satchel, she carries it so easily.

The Qirri again, she realizes. She avoids all thought of what the ash might be doing to her child.

She weeps the night she feels the first series of kicks, such is her relief. The old Wizard refuses to place his palm on her belly, and she flies into a fury, a madness unlike any she has suffered. She shouts and throws stones until he finally accedes. Of course the babe has ceased moving.

They happen upon a clutch of deer, and Achamian fells four of them before they can sprint into wooded obscurity. They feast. Then, in preparation for their eventual trek into the mountains, she skins the animals using the ensorcelled knife she found in the Coffers. 'Chipmunk,' she calls it. The work horrifies her, more for its *ease* than its bloodiness. She thought she would need to sharpen the blade, its edge felt so rounded, but the Wizard bade her to use it regardless. 'Mihtrûlic knives possess otherworldly edges,' he tells her. 'And they cut only according to your desire.' He is right about the knife, but it disturbs her, peeling deer like rotted pears.

Draped in furs, they work their way into the mountainous footings. Since they know nothing of treating pelts, the skins rot even as they warm them. After two days of the Wizard gingerly rolling and unrolling the parchment and peering this way and that – including, alarmingly, behind them – he finally becomes excited, begins muttering, 'Yes! Yes!' He raises two fingers to the south, gripes at her until she spies two peaks to the immediate south. 'There!' he says. 'That mighty ramp of snow climbing between them . . .'

A glacier. The first she has ever seen.

'The Gate of Ishuäl.'

The horns return that nightfall – a *chorus* of them, communicating from different points across the forests below. 'Mobbing . . .' Mimara gasps, remembering the madness of the Mop.

They continue fleeing through the dark, relying on the Qirri to carry them. They follow high ridges, running at a ramshackle trot. The stars astound her for their strewn brilliance. The Wizard tries to show her a constellation of ancient fame – 'the Flail,' he calls it – but she cannot pick out its principals. 'Only in my Dreams have I seen it so high in the sky,' he says. 'Only as Seswatha.' They skid down ravines and trip across gorges. They scramble until their fingers bleed. At last they find themselves staggering across sloping moraine, the glacier rearing enormous blue beneath a flaring Nail of Heaven.

They come across a river, which they follow until it breaks into a braid of white blasting streams. The glacier looms ever higher. The Sranc horns, when they blare, always sound incrementally closer.

Their breaths begin piling before them.

They gain the ice just as the sun broaches the low eastern horizon. The ice fields flash into kaleidoscopic life, blues sheeted with white and gold. For all the beauty, the crossing is arduous. Mimara quickly loses count of her falls. But at last they gain the glacier proper. Twice, they cross chasms with inner faces that gleam like mantlets of knives before plunging into blackness. They skirt blue-rimmed pits that rumble with hidden waters. They need only glance over their shoulder to see the Sranc – hundreds upon hundreds, thousands – filtering like some kind of plague across the icefields. The two climb and climb, race across fields of powdered snow, until the their legs cease burning and simply become numb, until their hearts hammer like trinkets of tin.

The skinnies gain more icy ground, a horde numerous enough to darken the glacier's midriff. The Wizard and the woman can hear their shrieks, the raw edges of malice cawing through hooping delight. 'Just run!' Achamian barks. 'Let their howls be your goad!' But she finds herself turning whenever her flight affords her an opportunity and involuntarily clutching her belly through her golden hauberk.

Finally the two of them clamber onto slopes of drifted snow – ground they can trust beneath them – and the Wizard finally turns to face the surging masses. The Gnosis flashes pale in the high snow glare, cutting into the disordered rush immediately below them. The Sranc scatter, spread themselves too wide for the Wizard to strike en masse. War-parties dash out to either side, climbing so as to descend on them from above. Again and again, the Wizard sends light scything into the ring closing upon them, but the skinnies are too many, and they come from too many directions. For the first time, she senses the pin-prick absences of Chorae among them. She cries out a warning to the Wizard, but he already seems to know. Echoes carom across high and hanging places . . .

A cohort of hundreds closes upon them from the east. But just as the Wizard turns to them, they fall in a slumping sheet, all of them in unison, vanishing into tumbling explosions of snow and ice. The two fugitives watch slack-jawed. The shrieks and howls of the others climb to pitch, then dissolve into a world-engulfing roar.

Avalanche.

Thunder. Rags of blue darkness blowing across the sun. Blackness.

They are buried, but somehow able to move. The Wizard mutters, and the light of his eyes and mouth reveal a sphere of blue and white about his Wards: untold sums of snow, melting about the glowing curves, forming runnels of water. He raises his hands and a line strikes out, eerie for its geometrical perfection. It pierces the snow like tissue. Water flushes down. Steam blasts and sputters without release. A hole opens about the line, which the former Schoolman begins waving in wider and wider circles. Soon sunlight shines through the upward rush of steam.

Water rises about their boots, climbs to their shins.

The Wizard abandons the line, begins throwing Odaini Concussion Cants into the breach above them. Snow booms outward, sparkles as it heaves beneath high sunlight. They are uncovered, thanks to the Wizard's damnation.

Wet and numb and shivering, they climb back to the surface.

White light and the absolute absence of smell. There is no sign whatsoever of the Sranc.

She is crazed for exhaustion – she knows this – but never has she felt quite so sane. Other mountains loom about them, isolate heights rendered fellows for the gaping emptiness that surrounds them. She can even see the white smoke of the wind blowing across them, as if they were nothing more than winter drifts heaped to the stature of clouds. At last she understands why men *look up* when they call out to the Heavens, even though the Outside lies nowhere and everywhere relative to the World.

The human heart possesses its own direction.

They continue their arduous trek, labouring across plains stepped in blank desolation. Two specks beneath peaks that spiral in the sunlight.

The final, wind-sickled crest draws down with every laborious step, revealing the world beyond in creeping stages. The white-cloaked heights of the far mountains give way to snowless pitches, then to monstrous slopes mossed in pine forests. At last the two of them stand side by side on the glacial summit, sucking air that never seems to nourish, gazing out across the basin of an enormous green-and-black valley.

And they see it clutching the roots of the nearest peak to their left . . .

Ishuäl. The home of the Dûnyain. The birthplace of Anasûrimbor Kellhus.

At long last, *Ishuäl* . . . The sum of so much toil and suffering.

Its once grand bastions overturned. Its curtain walls struck to their foundations.

Another dead place.

Character and Faction Glossary

House Anasûrimbor

Kellhus, the Aspect-Emperor.

Maithanet, Shriah of the Thousand Temples, half-brother to Kellhus.

Esmenet, Empress of the Three Seas.

Mimara, Esmenet's estranged daughter from her days as a prostitute.

Moënghus, son of Kellhus and his first wife, Serwë, eldest of the Prince-Imperials.

Kayûtas, eldest son of Kellhus and Esmenet, General of the Kidruhil.

Theliopa, eldest daughter of Kellhus and Esmenet.

Serwa, second daughter of Kellhus and Esmenet, Grandmistress of the Swayal Sisterhood.

Inrilatas, second son of Kellhus and Esmenet, insane and imprisoned on the Andiamine Heights.

Kelmomas, third son of Kellhus and Esmenet, twin of Samarmas.

Samarmas, fourth son of Kellhus and Esmenet, the idiot twin of Kelmomas.

The Cult of Yatwer

The traditional Cult of the slave and menial castes, taking as its primary scriptures, *The Chronicle of the Tusk*, the *Higarata*, and the *Sinyatwa*. Yatwer is the Goddess of the earth and fertility.

Psatma Nannaferi, Mother-Supreme of the Cult, a position long outlawed by the Thousand Temples.

Hanamem Sharacinth, Matriarch of the Cult.

Sharhild, High-Priestess of the Cult.

Vethenestra, Chalfantic Oracle.

Eleva, High-Priestess of the Cult.

Maharta, High-Priestess of the Cult.

Phoracia, High-Priestess of the Cult.

Aethiola, High-Priestess of the Cult.

The Imperial Precincts

Biaxi Sankas, Patridomos of House Biaxi and an important member of the New Congregate.

Imhailas, Exalt-Captain of the Eothic Guard.

Naree, a Nilnameshi prostitute.

Ngarau, eunuch Grand Seneschal from the days of the Ikurei Dynasty.

Phinersa, Holy Master of Spies.

Thopsis, eunuch Master of Imperial Protocol.

Vem-Mithriti, Grandmaster of the Imperial Saik and Vizier-in-Proxy.

Werjau, Prime-Nascenti and Judge-Absolute of the Ministrate.

The Great Ordeal

Varalt Sorweel, only son of Harweel.

Varalt Harweel, King of Sakarpus.

Captain Harnilas, commanding officer of the Scions.

Zsoronga ut Nganka'kull, Successor-Prince of Zeüm and hostage of the Aspect-Emperor.

Obotegwa, Senior Obligate of Zsoronga.

Porsparian, Shigeki slave given to Sorweel.

Thanteus Eskeles, Mandate Schoolman and tutor to Varalt Sorweel.

Nersei Proyas, King of Conriya and Exalt-General of the Great Ordeal.

Coithus Saubon, King of Caraskand and Exalt-General of the Great Ordeal.

The Scalpoi

Drusus Achamian, former Mandate Schoolman, lover of the Empress, teacher of the Aspect-Emperor, now the only Wizard in the Three Seas.

Lord Kosoter, Captain of the Skin Eaters, Ainoni caste-noble, Veteran of the First Holy War.

Incariol, mysterious Nonman Erratic.

Sarl, Sergeant of the Skin Eaters, long-time companion of Lord Kosoter.

Kiampas, Sergeant of the Skin Eaters, former Nansur officer.

Galian, Skin Eater, former Nansur Columnary.

Pokwas ('Pox'), Skin Eater, disgraced Zeümi Sword-dancer.

Somandutta ('Soma'), Skin Eater, Nilnameshi caste-noble adventurer.

Sutadra ('Soot'), Skin Eater, rumoured to be a Fanim heretic.

Xonghis, Skin Eater, former Imperial Tracker.

Koll, one of the surviving Stone Hags.

Ancient Kûniüri

Anasûrimbor Celmomas II (2089–2146), High-King of Kûniüri, and tragic principal of the First Apocalypse.

Anasûrimbor Nau-Cayûti (2119–2140), youngest son of Celmomas, and tragic hero of the First Apocalypse.

Anasûrimbor Iëva (2125–2146), treacherous wife of Nau-Cayûti.

Seswatha (2089–2168), Grandmaster of the Sohonc, lifelong friend of Celmomas, founder of the Mandate, and determined foe of the No-God.

The Fanim

Fanayal ab Kascamandri, the Bandit Padirajah, and sworn foe of the New Empire.

Meppa, the Last of the Cishaurim.

Malowebi, Mbimayu Schoolman, and the emissary sent by the Satakhan of Zeum to assess Fanayal and his insurrection.

The Dûnyain

A monastic sect whose members have repudiated history and animal appetite in the hope of finding absolute enlightenment through the control of all desire and circumstance. For two thousand years they have hidden in the ancient fortress of Ishuäl, breeding their members for motor reflexes and intellectual acuity.

The Consult

The cabal of magi and generals that survived the death of the No-God in 2155 and has laboured ever since to bring about his return in the so-called Second Apocalypse.

The Thousand Temples

The institution that provides the ecclesiastical framework of Zaudunyani Inrithism.

The Ministrate

The institution that oversees the Judges, the New Imperium's religious secret police.

The Schools

The collective name given to the various academies of sorcerers. The first Schools, both in the Ancient North and the Three Seas, arose as a response to the Tusk's condemnation of sorcery. The so-called Major Schools are the Swayal Sisterhood, the Scarlet Spires, the Mysunsai, the Imperial Saik, the Vokalati, and the Mandate (see below).

The Mandate

Gnostic School founded by Seswatha in 2156 to continue the war against the Consult and to protect the Three Seas from the return of the No-God, Mog-Pharau. Incorporated into the New Imperium in 4112. All Mandate Schoolmen relive Seswatha's experience of the First Apocalypse in their dreams.

The Kellian Empire in 4132 Year-of-the-Tusk

Anasûrimbor Kellhus was proclaimed Aspect-Emperor after the defeat of Fanayal ab Kascamandri at Shimeh in 4112. Both the Kianene and the Nansur empires collapsed shortly thereafter, leaving him the undisputed master of the Western Three Seas. Thirteen years of internecine and expansionist war followed. Many factors were instrumental to his success, including his martial brilliance and the fanaticism of his Zaudunyani Inrithi. But it would be his control of the Thousand Temples (which allowed him to so quickly consolidate his gains) and his alliance with the School of Mandate (which gave him the sorcerous advantage on every field of battle) that would prove decisive. The so-called Unification Wars ended with the final capitulation of Nilnamesh in 4126, rendering Anasûrimbor Kellhus the greatest conqueror since Far Antiquity. Not even the legendary Triamis the Great (2456–2577) achieved so much in so short a time.

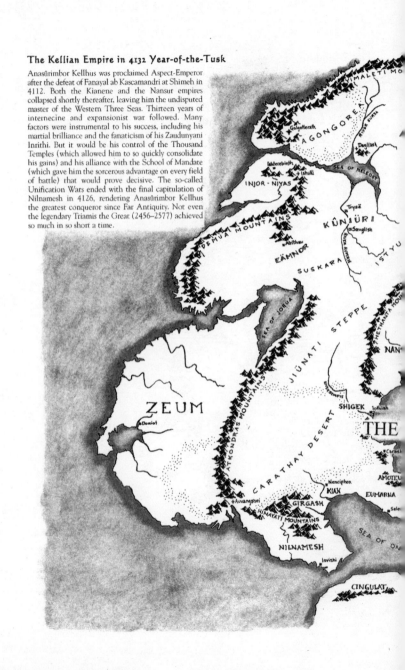

NTAINS

ÖRSI

PLAINS

Sakarpus

ÇPALOR

Summa

mema

MENANOR

NEW EMPIRE

SEA

inch

AKKSERSIA

Myclai

OSTHWAI MOUNTAINS

GALEOTH

Oswenta

Marrow
Ol-Aujas

THUNYERUS

Meigeivi

CE TYDONN
CENGEMIS

FAMIRI

CONRIYA

t'Atyerus

CIRONJ

MEORN WILDERNESS

THE LONG SIDE

SILVER WITNESS

SEA OF CERISH

GREAT KAYARSUS

EAZZA

DEMUA MOUNTAINS

Aöknyasus

Carythusal

JEKHIA

RIVER SAYUT

AINON

SANSOR

SEA OF NYRNYSIAS

KUTNARMU

GREAT KAYARSUS

R. Scott Bakker 2008

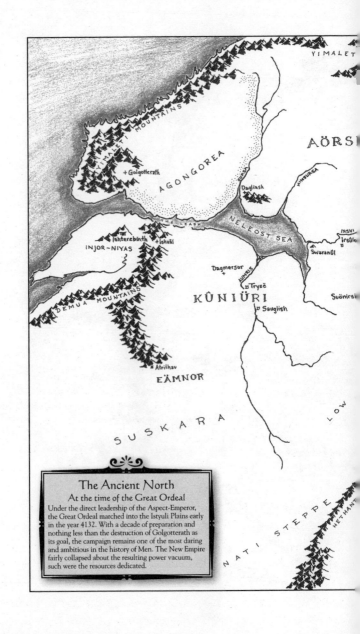

YIMALET

AÖRSI

YIMALET MOUNTAINS

+ Golgotterath

AGONGOREA

Dagliask

HINBURGA

THE LASH

NELEOST SEA

IRSHI

Irsûlor

Ishterebinth + Ishuäl

INJOR~NIYAS

Swaranûl

Dagmersor
+

UMIRIS

Trysë

Suönirsi

KÛNIÜRI

DEMUA MOUNTAINS

Sauglish

Atrithau

EÄMNOR

SUSKARA

LOW

The Ancient North

At the time of the Great Ordeal

Under the direct leadership of the Aspect-Emperor,
the Great Ordeal marched into the Istyuli Plains early
in the year 4132. With a decade of preparation and
nothing less than the destruction of Golgotterath as
its goal, the campaign remains one of the most daring
and ambitious in the history of Men. The New Empire
fairly collapsed about the resulting power vacuum,
such were the resources dedicated.

NATI STEPPE

HETHANT

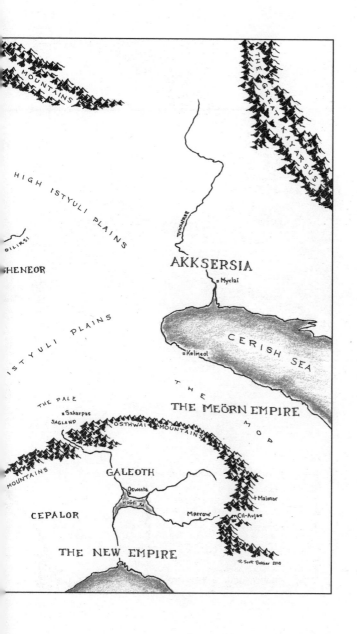

Acknowledgments

The Second Apocalypse has grown to such an extent that I'm beginning to feel the need to thank *everybody* who helped along the way. The myriad agents, editors, illustrators, and translators across the globe. The web reviewers and moderators. Most of all, I want to thank *you*, the reader, for placing your trust in what must have seemed a mad experiment back when it was all new. Things are starting to get *big* . . .

Otherwise, I need to thank all the habitual offenders: Darren Nash at Orbit UK (I already miss you, Dude!) Adrienne Kerr and David Ross at Penguin Canada. Aaron Schlechter at Overlook. And last but not least, my agent, Chris Lotts.

I also need to thank my brother, Bryan Bakker, and Todd Kuhn. My deepest debt of gratitude I owe to my wife, Sharron, and to our breathtaking little girl, Ruby.

extras

www.orbitbooks.net

about the author

R. Scott Bakker is a student of literature, history, philosophy and ancient languages. He divides his time between writing philosophy and fantasy, though he often has difficulty distinguishing between them. He lives in London, Ontario.

Find out more about R. Scott Bakker and other Orbit authors by registering for the free monthly newsletter at www.orbit-books.net

if you enjoyed
THE WHITE-LUCK WARRIOR

look out for

ECHO CITY

by

Tim Lebbon

Chapter 1

'This is not my home,' Peer Nadawa whispered as she came awake. They were the words with which she had comforted herself on the afternoon she arrived in Skulk Canton, and now their recitation was a natural part of welcoming a new day. They had started as defiance but quickly became a mantra necessary for her survival. And they were never spoken lightly.

She opened her eyes to see what sort of day it would be. The ghourt lizard that lived in a crack between her bedroom wall and ceiling was scampering across the wall in a series of short sprints. It was gathering flies and spiders early today, and that meant it would likely rain before noon. Great. Another day spent harvesting stoneshrooms in the wet.

Peer watched the lizard for a while, preparing herself for the morning ritual of rising through the discomfort of old tortures. The lizard shifted so quickly that it seemed to slip from point to point without actually moving, and there were those who believed that ghourts really belonged in the Echoes below the city. Peer was not one of them. It was a foolish idea to believe that such simple creatures could become phantoms. And, besides, her parents had taught her stillness. Relaxed from sleep, she calmed her mind and watched each tiny movement of the lizard – its fluttering heartbeat, lifting toes, and the darting streak as it ran from one place to the next. She pitied the people who did not have the time to see such things, because she had long ago stopped pitying herself. She had all the time in the world.

She sighed and scratched an itch in her left armpit. The little lizard flitted back into its hole, startled at her sudden movement. Propping herself on her left elbow, she grimaced as she started to sit up.

They'd used air shards to penetrate her right arm to the bone. Sharper than any blade made of stone or metal, the shards could never be removed, and they were a constant reminder of her crime. They were set in her bone and cast in her flesh, and it took a while each morning to warm them until they became bearable. That's all they ever were – bearable. Some nights, and on the very worst of days, she could picture the torturer's grin as he slid them in and see the virtuous expression on the Hanharan priest's face as he stood beyond the torture table, praying for salvation for her errant soul. Of the two, it was always that fucking priest she wanted to kill.

Grimacing, Peer sat up and started to gently massage her right arm. The pain from her left hip was flaring now, past the numbness of sleep. They hadn't been so creative with that: the torturer had smashed it with a hammer when she refused to acknowledge Hanharan as the city's firstborn. It was only thanks to Penler's skill with medicines and the knife that she was able to walk at all.

She closed her eyes and went through the pain, as she had every morning for the past three years. Each morning was the same, and yet she had never grown to accept it. She fought against what they had done even though the evidence was here, in pain and broken bones. Penler had asked her many times why she still fought when there was no hope of return, and she had never been able to provide an answer. Truthfully, she did not know.

Gorham's face flashed unbidden across her mind. Perhaps he was haunting her, though for all she knew, he was dead.

Gradually the pain lessened and she sat there for a while, as always, looking around the small room in the house she had been lucky enough to find. It had two floors, and she always slept on the top one. There was a ledge beyond the window that led to other rooftops if she needed to escape, a system of alarms and traps built into the single staircase – that had been Penler's doing as well – and if she stretched and stood just right, she could see the desert from her window. Some nights, if she could not sleep, she spent a long time simply looking.

One of the downstairs rooms still contained several paintings of the family that had lived there before the salt plague a hundred years before. Peer had no idea what had happened to them other than they had died. *Everyone* in Skulk Canton had died, either from the plague or from the brutal purging that quickly followed, ordered by the Marcellans. But she liked keeping their images in the house. It had something to do with respect.

'Time to leave,' she muttered. 'Important places to go, powerful people to see. Stoneshrooms to pick.' She often spoke to herself when there was no one else to listen. In Skulk there were many who would understand, and probably many more who would consider her mad. There were also those who viewed her as fair game; Echo City's criminals were a varied breed.

After washing in a bowl of cold water and eating a quick breakfast, she set about arming herself. A knife in her belt, three soft widowgas balls in her pocket, and the wide, short sword on view. She had never grown used to the sword, but Penler assured her that it would scare off any casual aggressors. Up to now, it had seemed to work.

He often chided her for living on her own. *A woman on her own here in Skulk* . . . he'd say, shaking his head, then pursing his lips because he knew exactly what she thought of such attitudes. Still, she knew that he had only her safety at heart. After berating him with a playful punch, she'd argue that most criminals here weren't really criminals at all. *They execute the really bad ones*, she would say. *Some always slip through*, he'd counter. And so their little play went on.

Today. she and Penler were meeting for lunch down by the city wall. He said that he had something to tell her. As always for Penler, the mystery was the thrill.

When the sun was up and birdsong filled the air, and Peer was feeling sharper and brighter than usual, she often considered Skulk Canton as evidence of the basic goodness in people.

Since the devastating plague, it had become the place to which criminals and undesirables were banished by the ruling Marcellans. Murderers, rapists, and pedophiles were still crucified on the vast walls of the central Marcellan Canton, but lesser criminals – pickpockets, violent drunks, and political dissidents – now had a new place to be sent. The vast underground prisons in the Echoes below the city had been closed, because the abandoned Skulk was far easier and less dangerous to police. It was a city unto itself, and the criminals were left to make it their own.

Over the past few decades, they had done just that. It could hardly be called thriving – they still relied on regular food deliveries from Crescent Canton, and a new canal had been built from the Southern Reservoir in Course Canton to ration their water – but the majority of people in Skulk lived a reasonable life, and most contributed to making their community a bearable place to live.

Naturally, there were those who viewed it as their own private playground. Thieves ran rampant in certain areas; gangs formed, fought, and dispersed; and there were a dozen men and women that Peer could name who considered themselves rulers of Skulk. But as with elsewhere in Echo City, these gangs and gang leaders ruled only those who were at their own level. Violence was frequent but usually confined to rival factions.

Those who kept to themselves were mostly left alone.

Upon her arrival, Peer had been convinced that she would be raped and killed within days. Terribly injured, traumatized from the tortures she had endured and the fact that she was no longer considered an inhabitant of Echo City, she had scampered into a building close to the razed area of ground that marked Skulk's northern boundary with the rest of the city, and there she had waited to die. She drifted in and out of consciousness. Time lost itself. Day and night seemed to juggle randomly with her senses. And one day after passing out, she woke up in Penler's rooms.

He told her that three men had brought her to him and then left. He did not even know their names.

Walking along the street toward the stoneshroom fields where she spent most of her mornings, Peer tried to deny the sense of contentment that threatened. She'd been feeling it for a while, as it sought to put down roots in a place that she had never believed she could call home. There was so much she missed – her friends, her small canal-side home in Mino Mont Canton, and Gorham most of all – that it felt wrong to be happy here. She had been banished from the world she knew, escaping execution only because the Marcellans knew it would be dangerous should she become a martyr. In Skulk she could fade away. She was a prisoner who was growing to like her prison, an exiled victim of an insidious dicta-torship who was forgetting the fire and rage that had fueled her past. Often she would strive to reignite that fire, but it never felt the same. *Just let it come*, Penler would say to her, referring to the gentle contentment and not the righteous passion she had once felt. She hated him and loved him for that, the infuriating old man. He was trying to save her, and she was determined to convince herself that she did not want to be saved.

This is not my home, she thought again as she walked through the narrow streets, but this morning Skulk Canton felt just fine.

She passed through a small square and saw familiar figures setting up stalls for breakfast. She bought a lemon pancake and had her mug filled with rich five-bean, and she dallied for a while, enjoying the sights and smells of cooking, the sound of bartering, and the good-natured air of the place.

'You'll be late!' a big man called as he stirred soup in a huge pot.

'The 'shrooms will wait, Maff,' she said. 'What's cooking?'

He motioned her over, and Peer smiled as she negotiated her way through a throng of hungry people. Maff always enjoyed revealing the recipes to his top-secret brews.

'Tell no one,' he whispered as she drew close, his breath smelling of beer and pipe smoke, his big hand closing around her long, tied hair. 'I had a consignment of dart root delivered yesterday. I'm mixing it with rockzard legs, some sweet potatoes from Course, and my own special ingredient.' He tapped the side of her nose and glanced around, as if they were discussing a coup against the Marcellans themselves.

Peer raised an eyebrow, waiting for the great revelation.

'Electric-eel hearts,' he whispered into her ear, 'Fresh. Still charged.' She felt his bead-bedecked beard tickling her neck and pulled away, laughing softly. When she looked at him, Maff was nodding seriously, pearls of sweat standing out on his suntanned skin. He touched her nose again. 'Tell no one.'

'Your secret's safe with me, Maff.'

'So . . . ?' he asked, lifting a deep spoon of the soup toward a bowl.

Peer held up both hands. 'I'd like to wake up in the morning.'

Maff shrugged and continued stirring the soup, and even as she bade him farewell, he called over a short, ratlike man. He whispered in the man's ear, nodded down at the soup, and his secret was told again.

In her early days here, Peer would have wondered what crimes Maff had committed to deserve banishment. Such thoughts rarely crossed her mind anymore. She left the square and weaved her way through narrow streets, the buildings overhead seeming to lean in and almost touch. The sun shone, though she still thought it would likely rain that afternoon, and Skulk Canton was buzzing with life.

She passed a group of men and women lounging on the front steps of a large building. They wore knives and swords on show, and all bore identical scars on their left cheeks – the unmistakable arc of a rathawk's wing. They observed her with lazy eyes and full purple lips, displaying the signs of subtle slash addiction, and one of them called to her softly. Laughter followed. She ignored the call and walked on, maintaining the same pace. She didn't want them to think she was running because of them, but slowing could have been seen as a reaction to the voice. They were part of the Rage gang – slash dealers and sex vendors – and she had no wish to be involved with them in any way.

She soon reached the first of the stoneshroom fields. There were already dozens of people at work, scrambling across the spread of ruined buildings in their search for the prized fungi. Much of the wild plant growth had been cleared from the rubble, making the stoneshrooms easier to spot and giving them space in which to grow, and the ruins were stark and depressing in the morning sun. Some areas still bore the dark evidence of fire, even after so long, and to Peer the ruin seemed recent, not a hundred years old. She breathed in deeply, closed her eyes, smiled as she tried to drive down the dark thoughts that always haunted her, then went to work.

She knew most of the stoneshroom gatherers, and they were a friendly group to work with. They were all out for themselves – picking the 'shrooms was only the first part of the process, the next being their cleaning, preparation, and sale – but often, if a good spread was found, word would filter quietly to the several other harvesters in the vicinity. They were a prized plant because of their heavy meatiness, and they were one of the few foodstuffs harvested within Skulk Canton. *If ever we claim independence*, Penler had once quipped, *we'll all turn into stoneshrooms.*

Peer worked hard, delving down into the spaces between collapsed walls, shifting small blocks aside where she could, and spending long moments of stillness sniffing for the fungi. Some hunters sang, and the song was taken up by others, but Peer remained silent today. She was looking forward to seeing Penler for lunch, and she hoped to have several 'shrooms prepared for him by then.

As noon approached, storm clouds drifted in over the city to the north. Peer derived some small satisfaction from knowing that it rained on the rest of Echo City before it rained on Skulk Canton. She made the most of the final touch of sunlight, then set off for the city walls.

Penler was sitting on a wooden bench looking out over the Markoshi Desert. Peer saw something symbolic in that. The bench must have been placed atop the wall by Watchers long ago, because the Marcellans and their Hanharan religion looked only inward, and Penler knew her Watcher history.

'Penler,' Peer said as she approached. The old man glanced up and smiled, wiping his lips. He nursed a bottle of Crescent wine in his lap, a good ruby red, and she smiled at his flagrant display of resourcefulness. Close though they had become, he had never told her how he still procured such produce from outside.

'Peer, my dear,' he said, shuffling along the bench. 'Been keeping it warm for you.'

The first drops of rain spattered the stone paving around them as she sat down. Penler was wearing a heavy coat with a wide hood, and she pulled up her own hood. The sound of rain striking it made her feel isolated, even though she sat there with her friend.

'I brought some stoneshrooms,' she said, taking the folded cloth from her pocket. 'Not the best of the crop today, but I arrived at the fields late.'

Penler nodded and ran his fingers across the proffered fungi. He moved his hand back and forth, then paused above one of the smaller, darker slices. He leaned in and sniffed, then grunted in satisfaction. He could always hone in on the best of everything.

'I have some fresh bread,' he said as he chewed, 'and the wine is good.'

'They'll execute me for drinking it,' Peer said, laughing and taking a swig from his bottle. He was right; it was excellent.

'Even the Marcellans themselves won't be drinking better wine today,' Penler said, and beneath the humor lay the familiar seriousness. He'd been sent here many years before when he published a book exploring the Dragarians' beliefs. The prosecuting Hanharan priests had claimed it was not the publication that marked him as a heretic but his sympathy for the Dragarians and their dead prophet – murdered by the Marcellans' own Scarlet Blades, after all – that shone through his writing. Proud, stubborn, Penler had confirmed or denied nothing, and his future was set.

'Fuck the Marcellans,' she said, 'and get that bread out.'

They ate in silence for a while, comfortable in each other's company without feeling the need to fill it with noise. Peer looked out over the flat, featureless desert, watching the line of rain progressing outward as the clouds drifted overhead. Sands darkened, and before long the rain front had moved too far for her to see.

'The weather knows no boundaries,' she said, but Penler only laughed. 'What?'

'You,' he said. 'Still watching.'

'I was born a Watcher,' she said. 'It was in my heart, such belief. I can't bear ignorance. I can't understand people who *don't* think such a thing.'

'You don't understand me?' he asked, a tricksy question. She glanced sidelong at him, and he was staring at her with raised eyebrows and a curious smile on his lips. For an old man, his mind was agile. That's why she liked his company so much.

'You're an explorer,' she said. She'd told him that before, and it seemed to please him immensely. In Echo City – a place mostly known – true explorers had only their minds in which to travel. That, or down into the Echoes.

Penler smiled, but it did not quite touch his startling blue eyes.

'Penler?'

'My exploring days are long behind me,' he said. 'I'm getting old, and sometimes I wish I could . . .' He trailed off and looked at the stoneshroom in the palm of his hand.

'Wish you could what?'

But he shrugged and stared back out at the desert.

The rain fell around them, light but drenching, and soon they were huddled together, sharing warmth and closing in so they could hear each other speak. It was strange, sitting side by side talking, because their raised hoods meant that they could not see each other unless they turned. Peer spoke and, when Penler responded, it sounded like a disembodied voice. The Marcellans claimed that Hanharan spoke to them in their sleep. *We're ruled by ghosts*, Peer thought, but that could not make her angry. She believed in a larger world beyond the deadly desert – never seen, never known – and what was that if not a ghost of possibility?

'You said you have something to tell me,' she said at last. She heard Penler sigh and take another drink of wine. The rain fell. The desert sands were dark and wet. She loved sitting here at the southern tip of Echo City with the whole world behind her.

'Whispers,' he said at last. 'Peer, you know I have . . . ways and means.'

She turned to him, took the wine bottle, and lifted it in a casual salute. '*Something about you*, is how they say it. Dark arts. Bollocks, I say.'

'Getting things is easy,' he continued, 'and the border is not solid. There's money, and people will do a lot for that, whatever their declared allegiances. But I've never dealt in money.'

'No. You deal in information.' Peer sipped at the wine. It was almost gone, and she wanted them to relish the final drop.

'Yes. Information. It comes, and it goes. Much of what comes is of no consequence or is likely false. Some of what I hear, I store.' He tapped his head, gave her that lopsided grin once again. 'And some of what I hear, on occasion . . . sometimes I try to forget.'

'Now you're worrying me.'

Penler pressed his lips together and turned away, and as he did so the rain caught his face and spilled like tears.

'What is it?' Peer asked, suddenly afraid.

'Murmurs from the Garthans,' he said.

'The Garthans?' Peer had never even seen one. They lived way down below the city, in some of the earliest Echoes that were supposedly tens of thousands of years old. Some said they were pale and blind and so far removed from surface dwellers that they were another species. Others claimed that they were cannibals, fondly feasting on offerings of human meat presented by those eager for their strange subterranean drugs. The only certainty was that they were no friends of top dwellers.

'Rumors of something wrong,' Penler said.

'You've heard such things before. You've told me, there are *always* stories from the Garthans.'

'Yes, that's true. But this time they're afraid.'

'Afraid of what?'

'I don't know. But the Garthans are never afraid of *anything*.'

Peer waited. Penler felt the pressure of her stare and turned so that she could see his face, hidden within his coat's wide hood. She was concerned for him, because his voice had sounded . . . different.

'Why tell me?' she asked.

'Because you're a Watcher.'

'And what does that make you?'

Penler smiled then, but once again it did not touch his eyes. Raindrops struck his face again as he tilted his head back to laugh, but his effort to lighten the heavy mood felt strangely false.

'I think that sometimes people need to build falsehoods for their own ends.'

Peer bristled. For such an intelligent man, Penler often displayed an ignorance that she found shocking. She'd tried to see through it many times, but his opinion was a solid front, and whatever lay behind wallowed in shadows that perhaps even he could not breach. Once, perhaps . . . years ago. But now he was growing old. Maybe the fire had gone from him.

'That's what the Marcellans call any beliefs they don't agree with,' she said coldly. 'Falsehoods. They told me to deny my own false beliefs as they slid the air shards into my arm.' She held her right biceps with her left hand, squeezing to feel a rush of warm pain. It always fueled her anger.

'Peer,' Penler said, and his voice carried such wisdom and age.

'I know very well what they did to you. And you know me better than that.'

Do I? she thought. It had been only three years, though in truth it felt like more. In all that time, Penler had yet to betray his true beliefs, even to her. Sometimes she thought he was a secularist, sitting apart and observing while his friends expended time and effort on their own diverse philosophies. And other times, like now, she suspected that he might be a devout believer in something he craved to disbelieve. There were contradictions in Penler that scared her and an intelligence that she sometimes suspected would be the death of him. Even while he told her to be calm and accepting, he fought.

'So the Garthans are afraid,' she said, 'and the rain still falls where no one can walk.' She stared out across the desert from atop the city wall. A hundred years ago this would have been a place for market stalls and street entertainers, but now the wall's wide top was simply another place to sit and wonder.

'I have to go,' Penler said. 'Will you eat with me this evening?'

'Are you cooking?' Peer asked.

'Of course.'

'Hmm.' She did not turn, even when she sensed him standing beside her. And she could not contain her smile. 'Last time, you cooked that pie and I had the shits for a week.'

'Bad pigeon,' Penler said. He was already walking away. 'I'll see you before dusk. You can stay, if you like.'

'I will,' Peer said. It was not wise to walk Skulk's streets after dark. She watched Penler leave. and as he reached the head of the stone staircase. he waved. She waved back. Through the heavy rain, she could not see his expression.

Chilled, she stood and walked to the parapet, chewing on the last of the stoneshroom as she went. She liked looking over the edge and down at the desert. Where she stood was civilization, order, comparative safety, and the whole world and history of Echo City. Down there, where the desert began, was the symbolic boundary of their world. People often walked the sands close to the city wall, of course. In places the wall had degraded and crumbled, and it was easy enough to work your way down to the desert, because where the wall was solid there were no doors or gates. There was no need. But those brave explorers never remained there for long; soon they were scampering back up the stone pile again, waving away the respectful cheers of their peers or the admiring glances of those they had set out to impress. The city drew them back.

The desert was death, and those who had ventured far out and returned had all died horribly. Some had time to reveal what they had seen – the Bonelands, the dead, those who had gone before them shriveling in the sun – but most died without saying anything, diseased flesh falling from their brittle bones and their insides turned to bloody paste, rotted by the desert's toxicity. Gorham had once told Peer that he'd seen two people die this way, and he would never forget the terror in their eyes.

The desert had always been this way, and such a terrible place attracted its myths and legends. There were the Dragarians, shut away and isolated in their canton for more than five hundred years now, who believed that their savior, Dragar, would emerge from the desert at the city's final hour to lead them into their mysterious Honored Darkness. There was the Temple of the Seventy-seven Custodians, who claimed that the desert was home to six-legged gods that watched over Echo City. But the Markoshi Desert – commonly known as the Bonelands – was the end of the world. And there were the Watchers, her people. They believed that there was something beyond and that their future lay in countering the desert's terrible effects.

She never grew bored of this. As the rain came down heavier, Peer leaned on the wall and watched.

* * *

At first, she thought it was a breeze blowing through the rain. The shadow shifted far out in the desert – a slightly more solid shape amid the unremitting downpour. She frowned and shielded her eyes, blinking away moisture. The day had grown dim, and the cold was making her hip ache.

The top of the wall remained deserted. Most people were sheltering from the rain or doing whatever it was they did to make their lives easier. Penler had probably reached the place he was happy enough to call home. Peer was alone . . . and the chill that hit her when she next saw the shifting shape made that loneliness even more intense.

There's something out there, she thought, and the idea was shocking. *Nothing* lived in the desert, because it was a place of death. She strained to see farther, leaning on the parapet in a vain attempt to take her closer. Curtains of rain blew from east to west, wiping the movement from view, but between gusts the shape was always there. *Something out there, and it's coming this way.*

She glanced frantically left and right. To her left, a tower protruded above the wall, but she knew that the staircase in there led only up, not down. She knew of a small breach to her right, maybe half a mile away, that had collapsed a hundred years before, during the purging of Skulk Canton. Many fires had been set back then, and it was said that a pile of thousands of bodies had been thrown from the wall and burned. The intensity of the flames had made the stonework brittle, bringing down a section of wall.

Peer ran. She paused every few heartbeats to glance out over the desert; the shape was definitely there, closing, resolving, and her heart started to pummel from more than exertion, because *it looked like a person*. The way it moved, the way it shifted behind the veils of rain, seeming to hunch over as if trying to protect its face from the unrelenting storm, gave it all the characteristics of a human being.

And then she saw something strange. The figure stopped, and perhaps it was the first time it had looked up in a long while, because it paused where it was and leaned back, looking at the great wall before it and the city beyond.

Even though it was impossible through the rain and over this distance, Peer felt that she met the person's eyes.

She ran on, finding it difficult to tear her gaze away, and tripped and went down. *Right arm*, she thought, *left hip*, and she fell awkwardly so that she jarred both. She cried out, then looked around to see if anyone had heard her. In the street below, a couple of people dashed from one building to another, but they seemed unaware of her presence, and she was happy to leave them to themselves. Biting her lip, standing, she concentrated on the cool rain instead of the heat of her old injuries.

When she looked again, the figure had started running.

It was a man in a yellow robe.

And past the hushing rain, past her thundering heartbeat, she heard his scream.

Peer reached the breach in the wall and worked her way down the precarious slope. The rain made the tumbled blocks slippery, but that shouting still reverberated in her ears, driving her. She stumbled once or twice, jarring her right arm again, but then she reached the bottom.

She paused on the final block, feet a handbreadth above the ground. *The desert is death.* This was drummed into everyone in Echo City, from birth to the moment they died, and though she was exiled for sedition and still in possession of her own inquiring mind, it was difficult to deny such teaching. She stared at her heavy boots, then past them at the sodden ground. It was muddy. Sand flowed in rivulets, shallow puddles were forming, and for the thousandth time she wondered where the death dwelled. In the sand? In the air she was breathing even now? Many had written and spoken of the Bonelands, but none had derived a definitive answer.

And then she heard a shout, and, looking to her left, she saw a man kneeling in the mud at the base of the city wall.

She stepped down on to the sand and ran. She slowed only when she neared him, then paused a dozen steps away. He looked up, his eyes wide and fearful, his face gaunt, and he seemed as terrified as she was.

Who? she wanted to ask, but she could not form words. His clothes were of a style she had never seen before, his robe a dirty yellow. Over one shoulder he carried a bag, and strange things protruded from it. The rain ran from his white hair and down across his face. And then he opened his mouth.

'Who . . . ?' Peer managed, because she felt it was important to say something first.

'You're not her,' the man said. Then he fell onto his face and, somewhere over the city, lightning thrashed